The Mississippi Run

Books by Paul Darcy Boles

*The Streak*
*The Beggars in the Sun*
*Glenport, Illinois*
*Deadline*
*Parton's Island*
*A Million Guitars*
*I Thought You Were a Unicorn*
*The Limner*
*The Mississippi Run*

# THE MISSISSIPPI RUN

Paul Darcy Boles

THOMAS Y. CROWELL COMPANY   NEW YORK
Established 1834 CB

Manufactured in the United States of America

*Library of Congress Cataloging in Publication Data*

Boles, Paul Darcy,
  The Mississippi Run

  I.  Title.
PZ4,B688Mis      [PS3552.0584]      813'.5'4      76-27875
ISBN 0-690-01158-X


1  2  3  4  5  6  7  8  9  10

For
Dorothy,
for many fairs

# 1

It sure wasn't Grayboy's fault. A horse like that, a Standardbred with a smartness in his eyes, he'll take the right road every time if you give him his head—which I hadn't. Long about nine o'clock by my father's old turnip, which I could barely see then in the night's half light, I'd swerved him into the bypath, thinking I could make this a shortcut and get to Yadkin faster that way.

I'd been on the road three days and was tired of all of it. So was Grayboy. He was going well, with the saddlebags and the boxwood fiddle in its case—also boxwood—and carrying me too, of course. But a horse like that, like anything splendid, needs to do his best. I'd not let him out once, all the way from Dango Falls, in Alabama, and he resented that too. He needed letting out from time to time, just like a woman needs loving and quick-minded talk now and again if she's going to go right on being a real woman on the earth.

So now it was the close side of midnight—maybe a few minutes till —and here the rain was coming down. And we were bordering this swamp where everything smelled as fatal and old as the first of the earth getting itself born, and the reeds were so close to the path—no bigger than a towpath—they brushed over Grayboy's fetlocks and hoofs on his near side. Ahead was a kind of hole in the dark, made of a place where the cypress-tangles came apart and let just a meek spring of light through. All I could hear was the rain on my hat and pattering on Grayboy's quarters, and there was a rill of rain dripped off the peak of my hat and went down right before my nose in a young waterfall. We came to the lighter place where the cypresses spread; I pulled in on the reins. I'd not have needed to; he stopped here anyhow, and gave a quiver all over his hide as if the rain was flies and he was shaking off every last one. Now I could see the bayou on our left; rain pocked into it with a kind of steady noise like arrows being shot from the banks, and a couple of old logs snouted downstream in the shape of alligators waiting for some business.

Holding still in the rain-touched deep of the night, for maybe a sign or a promise, I thought about Grayboy's first race in Dango Falls two years before. It was a harness race that first showed just what kind of pacing he could do. He could trot, canter, gallop and all the rest, but pacing was his hearth and home; it was what he'd been placed in the nation to do.

Some horses never venture more than one gait. Some are born with the wisdom of just about any gait already fixed in their muscles. You find them like nuggets amid a heap of fool's gold. When you find them, if you're like my daddy and me, you shine them up and bring them out in decent time to show mankind. You help them discover their brightest, most sure talent.

As we'd done with Grayboy.

It'd been a kindly well-featured day in the deep of summer with about a hundred people clustered around the Foggy Meadow which ran for two miles around my daddy's horse-barns. I'd sat edgy with my feet in the sulky-racks and the lines cool to my palms and waited while Sugar Man, the opposition horse and the lone contender for the fifty dollars Daddy had bet on Grayboy, snorted and blew and tossed his head and eyed us as if we were bounden enemies. Grayboy was a fledgling animal then—we'd run him secret and clocked him careful, but he'd never raced against anything but watch-hands. We had a rope slung for a wire above our heads and its shadow looked to me like the difference between being a child and a man. As if that tight clean shadow marked the whole change. Old Man Renfrew, the Dango Falls banker and my daddy's best friend, called the start, making us circle back of the stretched wire rope and then come up under it and get an even-Steven, head-to-head start—Sugar Man, a bay with black points, surged ahead at the first two false starts, then on the third we were level and Old Man Renfrew called in his scratchy voice, "Go, gentlemen!"

That was the first time I felt the true thunder in Grayboy's bones. He got his rhythm without breaking it once or even wavering. His head slugged out as if he could stretch himself to be twice his length and his forearms and knees and cannons and pasterns were working with his driving hocks the way a great sledgehammer might have been marking time for all mankind. From behind me I could hear the yammer and yelling from the start-line, and as we flashed along I felt something open up in my chest as if I was a flower starting to break open from its bud and bloom in space and sun. I could see Sugar Man from my eye-corners, the bulk of him striving there with Clement Ainslee, his owner and breeder, leaning forward and hollering; then we were pulling up farther, and beside Sugar Man with his smell floating to us tart-sweet and heavy, then we were past him and smelling only the field-daisies whipping by us and I was only seeing the line of fence stretch in a ripple and the rosy light flicker along Grayboy's loins. It was like loving a woman for the first time and knowing what your bone-marrows could do, as if they were savaged with lightning and freedom. When we came in and they told us we'd done the two miles in four minutes, three seconds, I was still hearing the noise of Grayboy's plates rocking in my eardrums. Old Man Renfrew and Daddy were standing together, and Daddy was smiling, and Old Man Renfrew said, "Son, he was thunderin' so hard they put up umbrellas all around the country." He'd been with Daddy in the Alabama cavalry and they'd been wounded just about the same time.

That was the first time, the first real race. And now we were lost here in Mississippi on an October Sunday night—a night wet-assed as an old creditor.

I swiveled my head around—rain was in my eyelashes too—and then I could see what could have been either a true light or a will-o'-the-wisp over to the east. Will-o'-the-wisps don't shine much in the rain; it takes a foggy fall night for them to dance around swampland and show at their eeriest. Some call them foxfire, but they're not. A real fireball will-o'-the-wisp moves and darts and skims and leads you on; foxfire on the flank of a rotten log just stays where it is and shines like a thousand glowworms asking questions. Must be a human-made light, I thought.

I leaned down and patted Grayboy along the neck; his hide there felt like slick, new glass with a little cold water streeling along it. I said, "Let's head for there, friend. Sorry I misled you. Too late to go back to the true road."

I'm not saying he understood me; maybe not the whole sense of the words, but he was a swift horse to get the gist of anything. I clucked to him and hardly had to knee him around or twitch the reins the right way before he headed east toward the light. Sometimes as we went along through these fern and spraddled moss and heavy-flowering swamp weeds—now and then a wild orchid, you could catch it like a pale torch out of the edges of your eyes—I thought: We'll come belly-deep in a slough and founder, or we'll hit quicksand. But hell, it was the only light in what looked like the dismalest prospect in a hundred miles. And when we came close to the foot of a little hill, where the ground was firmer, and started up the hill, we could both see the light rising above the ridge, stronger now and more beautiful. It was misty but it was solid and there; something had to make it. When we breasted the rise, the saddlebags shifting and making a gurgling, sopping noise, I loosed the reins a whit and let Grayboy out just for the run across the near meadow. He leaped out like a big cat jumping. The meadow had old tares and stalks of spindling cotton in it—hadn't been cultivated for years, I judged—and they switched under us like lean whips. Then we went through the ruins of a back-fence gate and there ahead was a monstrous house. Could just make it out under the drumming rain. Spreading here to yonder and back. Kept my eyes on that light twinkling from what I judged to be the rear; we headed like one creature, straight for it.

All it was was a lantern swinging in the rain-wind from a post hung over the mouth of a stable back there. I said, "Glad to see you!" I slid down. My boots landed in a skift of old hay spread around in front of the stable-mouth under the lantern's light. Grayboy was splashed high on the hocks with the muck we'd gone through. I hitched at my belt and walked toward the stable. It was a fair size and it had old blue green alfalfa piled in one corner, could just make it out under the lantern's beam, and back farther were stalls—eight of them—and a tack room with leathers so dry and cracked I could see even from here they hadn't been used for a parlous time.

The stable was sure part of that great house. Reckoned it was also part of what'd once been a plantation; the summer cookhouse and the cabins would be between here and the plantation house, in a kind of generous compound; the stable would have been built back here because not far from it ran a main road.

Behind me, Grayboy whiffled his nostrils—not the way he did when he was just wet and mad, or scenting a mare in heat, but as if he'd winded some strange animal or man approaching. I stayed right where I was, out of the churchly light of the lantern with its little halo playing around it, and waited for whoever it was to show up out there in the rain.

Didn't know if it'd be a haunt or a night-scavenger, maybe a swamp-cat come up from the river bottoms in the dark, padding hungry. I had my knife in its sheath but I don't carry any weapon outside that. The knife works all right for skinning anything needs skinning—or working on harness—and you can eat with it if you want to. One of the things I got when Daddy died was the knife, along with the boxwood fiddle and bow, and the saddlebags and such gear, and his watch and of course Grayboy. All the rest went for back payments on what he'd borrowed from the Dango Falls bank; if he hadn't been friends with Old Man Renfrew, he'd have starved from betting on everything and anything long before. There'd been enough left over to pay for his coffin. If he'd been at his own funeral, he'd have bet whether it was pine or oak or hickory, giving good odds and probably losing.

I thought of all that fondly now, light and quick as spring blossoms going through my brain. Stepped just a shade farther back in the stable's shadow and kept myself quiet.

Then, through the steady rain out there, someone comes around the stable-side and stops and sees Grayboy and just stands there looking at him for a breath. This someone was wearing a cloak with a dark sheen to it, looked like a crow's wing in the uneasy light, and the cloak had a hood on it. I thought, well, maybe it's the Black Monk of the Swamp, come to trouble me for my sins and point the way to my death. But that was mere fancy; this was a living person, real enough, for just then I caught a glimpse of a hand at one of the cloak's seams. It was a pale hand, not very large, and nicely shaped. Then the person turned around and was clearer in this light—I stepped back a whisper more—and started peering in here; she couldn't see anything of me yet, but I could see her face. A strong bright face, with a sure quickness about it, and eyes the size of a doe's, silver and gray and amber in the soft wet light; and the hood canting down over dark red hair, which was knotted in wisps and trails of rain-slickness around the forehead.

Seemed a good time to show myself. I stirred out of the shadow and into the stable-mouth so she could see me, moving gradual and not like any attacking raider. She stayed just where she was, except for stiffening up a trifle under that soaked cloak and hood. Just a smidge of steam on the night from her breath when she said, level and even, "Who are you, mister?"

"My name's Thomas Broome," I said. I was maybe even wetter than she was, but the way she'd talked made me at ease right off. She spoke with a low, soft voice in words shaped and rounded like she'd gone to school. I reckoned maybe a young ladies' academy—my mother'd gone to one, why she married a horse-trainer and gambler I'll never know, saving that she loved him body and brain till the day of her death. Anyhow, one of these tender-minded schools where the girls learn china-painting and a smattering of history and a nodding acquaintance with the works of Sir Walter Scott. It's always a marvel to me that such women took over the running of plantations and made them hum, and, when the war came, ran them like steel and fire until the last of that life was gone, and then stood up to the Yankee weevil-heads who ripped apart the South and defied them with their final breath, and couldn't be broken any more than you can break an outlaw mare. And there was something else, besides all that, under this voice—warm and leaning, wishing and looking. In the handful of seconds leaping between us, I felt her look me over like my daddy looking over a fresh deck.

I said again, "Tom Broome. Traveling from Dango Falls, Alabama, up to the Yadkin Fair. Took a wrong sidepath off the road about three hours back, and I've been seeking habitation and a dry room ever since. So would you mind, ma'am, if I pull my horse back in here and rub him down, and maybe spend the rest of the night in this stable?"

Rain speckled and bounded on the black shine of her cloak, over her shoulders and down the crest of her peaked hood. Her chin was forthright enough, the cheekbones well wrought and handsome in bone; but the eyes were still the finest articles, tipped up a trifle at the corners as if she had conjur-blood somewhere in her. Tell as much from a woman's eyes—or a man's—as you can from a horse's, any coper with sense can tell you that. And I liked the way she stood too, a tree growing and not to be uprooted. About four inches shorter than I am.

She kept inspecting me, then nodded. "The stable hasn't been used for a long time, Mister Broome. I heard you coming across the old meadow. I was on my way back here to the chicken-house—it's been plagued by foxes lately. It's right around there at the end of the stable. I'm French Chantry, Mister Broome . . . well, Francia. Friends call me French."

Liked the name, liked the voice, liked the woman. Didn't think I looked exactly the soul of sociability and ease, having been on the hoof this long, and wetter than a garfish in the bargain. But it didn't seem to faze her. She raises a hand and waves it to Grayboy. He still had his head up—he wasn't a horse put his head down much, save when you offered him an apple or some other likely comfit. His eyes caught the small light and gleamed, and he looked down and back at her as if she was a curious but appealing bait of oats. "That's a noble stallion, Mister Broome. I've hardly ever seen a more likely. My father raised horses, in the old days. I was quite young then—" It tickled me, somewhat, to hear her saying it so, prissy and pursed, as though she was a hundred and ten right now.

"—but I do recall his first settling me in the saddle and leading me around. He was a wonderful horseman, a perfect centaur."

"He's gone?" I asked.

"Yes sir. He died in action in Virginia. Colonel Robert Chantry. This"—she looked all around her, as if she was building all the spread of the place in her mind, making castles of it that grew up out of the rain and her yearning—"this is Chantry Hall. Welcome, Mister Broome. I regret that I can't offer you the hospitality of the house. It wouldn't be moral, or even practical. I hope you'll be comfortable here, Mister Broome."

"Christ, yes—" I almost bit my tongue. "Lord, yes, ma'am. And I do promise I'll be gone by dawnlight. Reckon I can pick up the road to Yadkin again near here."

"Yes sir. It's not a furlong from where we're standing."

"Ah, that's fine, Miss Chantry," I said. Wanted to call her Miss French, but we hadn't been acquainted long enough for that. And I didn't want to put her out a stitch, not for the earth. A place like this, this long after the war, would have more trouble just staying alive than a blind man in a faro game. The land I'd seen even under the rain was lorn and gone to bush grass and chickweed, unplowed and open to any marauder, beast or man. The house itself in the glimpse I'd had of its shadowed, lengthy stretch hadn't had but a fleck of light in it; coal oil is cheap but not for strugglers. I says now, kind of fast, "And I've got all the food I need for me and Grayboy. I carry it with me. I promise I shan't build a fire of any kind. Even tonight, this place would be a tinderbox."

I stopped.

And, "I'm sure you seem to be a gentleman bred," she said. Murmuring it nice as if offering me a tea-cake. "Now, Mister Broome, if it's not presuming, please allow me to help you settle your horse for the night. I'd enjoy it, I haven't had the pleasure of acquaintance with an animal of his mettle for a long, long while. By the by, I'll ask you to leave the lantern lighted, if you please. If I do find the fox I intend to kill it."

Well, I was going to tell her she didn't have to help me out in the least; but I couldn't turn her down when she was sighting at Grayboy as she was. And I liked her being here; the two of us meeting in the huge sobbing night, under this pinpoint of a lantern. I said, "I would appreciate your assistance, Miss Chantry." And watched while she turned and took Grayboy a good hold by a bridle strap; watched her having to reach considerably to do it, so I could all at once see her bare legs under the length of the cloak. Legs fashioned the way you'd do it if you could fashion them yourself and call this, Woman. She was crooning to Grayboy as if she was a hostler born, then, and he was wheeling a little and starting toward the stable. I stepped out and took him from the other flank. Right then was when I caught a glimpse of the hand she'd been keeping out of sight under the dripping cloak. Had a derringer in it. Could just see the barrel and part of the lean butt she was clutching. Then under Grayboy's downswinging head as we led him in, his hoofs booming some on the dusty gray old boards of the sill, I went on watching her and reckoned her to be even more than at first sight I'd bargained for. And I'd liked her well enough at first sight.

You move around as I'd moved since I was about five, following the races and the cards, harness racing and flat racing and any kind of cards you can think of—you move so, you see a lot of women. You can't recall much save in bits and flashes of your own mother; but your father tells you about her, a good bit, especially when he's easy with drink. And you rub shoulders with all manner of female. The starveling women in the towns near the mountains, the hill towns where their men are hunters and trappers and there're ten to fourteen kids and it's a good Christmas when they get blackstrap on their johnnycake. The fancy women in the towns— you're in Memphis where your daddy visits a whorehouse, and the women downstairs pour champagne in your hair and fuss over you and call you Beauty, which makes you squirm. The farm women and the city-bred, mingling together at the fairs where the races go regular as clockwork and the noise fills your ears when you're riding well or driving a sulky with the pacing going perfect, on a clear blue day. Once and again, you stay with a woman—one of the fair-working women, as a rule—and it's pleasing, but next day it's gone from you.

But a woman like Miss Francia—French—Chantry wasn't any road-traveler; yet there was that freshness, ease, about her now as she peeled back her cloak and hung it on a manger's rim, and stood there in a gray blue, dove-colored dress that was as old as the hinges of the stable door, and no doubt came out of a trunk of her mother's, but still had a loving tightness at the tits, with the sweet line of the belly pinched in just enough to make you see the rest without stretching your imagination more than a tad. Her hair reminded me of a waterfall with late sun on it, burning in the light that crept in from the lantern. She laid the derringer down in a heap of straw beside the cloak. Saw me seeing her do it, while I took the saddle off Grayboy and humped it over a saddle-rack that hadn't had anything put on it for a generation.

And when she noted I'd seen the derringer, she said, quiet-voiced still, unruffled, "I'm a good shot. If the fox does show up, he won't have a chance."

"You shoot many?"

"A fox now and then, and a skunk this spring. The fields and woods are overrun with them. I raise Dorkings, and Buff Orpingtons—and I do detest having them vanish down the throats of night-creatures."

She'd picked up a hearty handful of straw now, and I had one too; and we were rubbing down Grayboy. He stood still enough—he happened to be a tolerating horse, save for when he felt his oats too much and hadn't been exercised a while and might wish to show his playfulness by kicking down part of a stall. And Miss Chantry had to reach again, to rub him along the withers and then later along the croup. She worked her way along that distance on his hide, whistling soft to herself, and after a while she was back working down the croup to the stifle. I kept up with her, rubbing on Grayboy's off-side. There was a smell about her, just woman, not a whiff of perfume—a smell mingling with Grayboy's own cleanly animal scent, and twining into my nostrils. Then when we'd finished, with Grayboy grunting and glad to be cosseted, I came on around his head and said, "I do thank you kindly, Miss Chantry. For your goodness in letting us stay."

"You are most welcome, and it's little enough, Mister Broome. And now I reckon you'd better turn in, sir. You have a long pull up to Yadkin as yet."

"Yes ma'am. I'll stop on my way back through and let you know how the harness racing went."

"That would be good of you, and welcome. I hope you win it all. He looks as though he'd have magnificent action. Trotter or pacer?"

"Pacer, Miss Chantry. Though he goes straight back to the Hambletonian strain, and the Hambletonian was a trotter. Pacing's just what he does the best."

"You have your own harness, Mister Broome?"

I nodded to the stall where I'd put the bridle and saddlebags. "In one of the bags. At the fair, I'll dicker for a sulky."

She was sweeping the cloak back over her shoulders. Just letting it drape like wings around her. The hair-knot over her forehead was drying out, and the whole of her hair was silky and thick as a rich pelt, falling to her shoulders. The eyes with lights of silver and gray and amber flickered to me, thoughtful, while she picked up the derringer and swept it back under her cloak. With her free hand she patted Grayboy. "Ah, Mister Broome. How you must enjoy traveling with him. It would make any road shorter."

"It does, and next time I'll try not to wrong him by pulling him from the main road. Though it's had its rewards, Miss Chantry."

I bowed slightly at that, and she gave the ghost of a smile—moving over her lips like wind over still and loving waters—then lifted the cloak's hood, quenching her hair as if a door had been shut over a warming fire. Goes to the doorway, says, "Good night, Mister Broome." Just as staid now as though recalling that a well-brought-up lady makes her obligances and leaves quiet.

"Good night to you, Miss Chantry."

Next instant she was gone into the raining dark.

Couldn't even hear her going, with the rain still falling and brushing around the stableyard. But I stayed there looking after where she'd vanished, for a breath or six. Felt sad about it; I'd have admired talking to her for the rest of the night, even though sleep was knocking at me as if it just had to get in somehow. Goddamn it, I thought, if I'd had the time and didn't need to get on first crack of light.

I led Grayboy into one of the stalls by the hackamore I'd put on him after unsaddling. And tied the hackamore rope to the joist of a manger, leaving plenty of room for him to swing around in the rest of the night if he so desired. I went into the next stall where I'd put the bags and the bridle. Lay down with the back of my head on the dry underside of one of the bags, looking up to where a family tree of spiders had spun webs over one beam of this roof to another. In the haymow above me something rustled; didn't bother me, there was little enough in here for even a woods-rat to nose out and enjoy. The straw around me felt old and stiff, but not unsoft in general. Out against the dark the lantern moved on its post where the lantern-bail was hooked, just swaying away, and changing the light in here as though some haunt was blowing on a candle flame.

Through the whisper of the rain, lisping like a lost child trying to tell of its peril, I thought I heard, on the edge of drifting off, a flat sound—a stick busting maybe, far away. Could have been a shot, too. Grayboy shifted in his stall, and I was too drowsed to tell him good night.

When I woke up it was just new light. The lantern out in the doorway had burned out in the dark. The rain had stopped; all I could see was primrose-washed and going to be a bright Monday. Could just make out the green blue shadowy meadow down on this side of that hill from which I'd come, and past that, the sky like a pearl covering the world, no rain falling from it. I raised on an elbow—had the stiffness in the thighs and back and arms, the riding stiffness—and lay there, still looking around. Then it came to me it was much too quiet. Aside from the throating of some hens not far off, and a few drops of rain stringing down from the eaves, it was quiet as a peaceable cemetery where all the mourners had gone homeward.

Couldn't believe such quiet. I stood up, knocking a boot against the wall of this stall. Looked over the wall; I couldn't see Grayboy. Sort of holding my breath, I walked on around to the stall-entry next to the one I'd slept in; and he was gone. Was some fairly fresh evidence he'd been there, but that was all. I couldn't believe this either, but then all at once I could. I turned and ran out into the nearly sunup side of the morning. I reckon I'd been madder in my life but I couldn't right now recall just when.

When I'd got outside—air felt like it was about to whelp a cool day—I looked back; caught a glint of Grayboy's saddle still on that ancient rack. My God, I thought, he walked out quiet as a sheep, and bareback. Only one other person to my knowledge had known he was there. I started running for the great house, seeing it rise up from the last of the night as I ran, and thinking, Miss Chantry—whose friends call you French—you and I and this Chantry Hall have got a bone to pick now. My boots which I'd slept in because when they're wet they're hard to stomp into the next morning, creaked and squashed underfoot, and I wished they were my feet's fierce wings.

# 2

---

I'd been right about there being slave cabins and a summer cookhouse in this compound. All the cabins were bedraggled and dark and overgrown; some of their logs had sagged in and along the ridgepole of the cookhouse grew a furze of moss. There were about a dozen cabins; this had been a powerful plantation in its time. Reflecting on this didn't slow me up. I went tearing along through magnolia leaves that dragged and skittered; I charged past the stones of a big old well-head that also looked clotted with leaves, and then I was at the back steps of the plantation house itself. Five steps mounting to a shut door. I stopped and listened.

The only sounds on the morning were water-drops falling from the eaves and a light motion of wind through the magnolias and through the pines and the oaks farther back. I went on up the steps and twisted the knob of the door at the top. The door was locked. I cupped my hands around my mouth and called, "Miss Chantry!" Then, louder, "Francia! French!"

Then on a hope, I whistled short and sharp for Grayboy.

And stood still, listening again.

My whistle got swallowed up even before it had left this back gallery. Just drowned among the magnolias and the tall pines flanking them and the oaks with their tattered end-of-the-year leaves swaying a trace in the swelling daylight. I could see better now. Stooped down and looked in through the pane of this rear door. A red curtain shut out most sight, but through its crack I could see the back entrance to the kitchen. The kitchen looked shadowy and still, I could make out the curve of a huge black washpot or hog-cooking pot, and nothing much beyond. Had the notion for a second of crashing through the pane—it was traced with a scrolled frost of a design in its glass—but didn't do it. I bounded back down the stairs and started to the left, the north, around the house. Old vines and dead azalea plantings hooked so low over the flagged walk here, the flags all sunk in the ground and skewing galley-west and unsmooth, I could hardly crash my way past them. Windows of the house, arched and mullioned and blank, floated above me as I made my way. Then I came around under the porte cochere, which was floored with dark red brick, and up and onto the front gallery leading to the vestibule. Chinaberry trees grew up around the gallery; its boards felt solid enough under my heels as I crossed it. Past the gallery the columns went up, eight of them, each about seventy feet high with scrolls leafing around them up in the shadows. The door I faced had a beveled fanlight over it, the new light starting to pinken its glass.

Was so mad I wasn't even breathing hard, just saving all the angered part of me for action. I didn't lift the knocker. Its brass might've been polished some years before; now it was cloudy and dull. A first spear of sun struck it as I stood there. I reached for the latch and pressed down the thumb-spring and the door—about twice as tall as I am—swung back quiet enough on its hinges.

And I was looking along a hall. Red carpet on the floor. To my left, a row of mirrors—their glass-shining secret, some of the glass spotted with age. To my right, a line of doors leading to the side rooms. Straight back, a staircase sweeping up into more shadows. And something was huddled at the foot of the staircase, bulking there against its lower treads.

My boots made the only real noise in the whole place. Outside a late-awake owl talked a couple of times. In here it was quiet as spring-water in a cup. Smelled of age and old wood with a little overlay of polish, as though somebody still oiled the floors and dabbed into what corners could be reached. But I wasn't studying about those things. I came to the foot of the staircase.

The newel post on the right was carved in the shape of a lion's head. A thick-maned lion with his eyes picked out in gold and his mane also gold-leafed in its curls. I wasn't studying about that very much, either.

For against a couple of the lowest stair-treads lay a man. In life he'd have been considerably taller on the hoof, and weightier, than I'd ever reach.

But the point was he wasn't in life anymore, and hadn't been for a spell.

He wore a black broadcloth coat and trousers, along with a vest that was pale gray with white edging; and coat, vest, and pants were smudged with his blood here and there. He'd been shot in the forehead—low and just above the right eyebrow. Both his arms were flung out as if he'd tried to break his fall when he went down. Long gray black hair tumbled over his collar. When I knelt in front of him and touched him near the jawline, I could feel how cold he was. Cool as channel-cat laid away in an icehouse.

But I reckoned I'd have known something was wrong here even if it'd been too dark to see him or I hadn't touched him. Killing's got a smell about it. I'd sensed and sniffed it before—once, for instance, when Daddy and I'd walked into a tavern near Mobile where there'd just been a shooting scrape. The scent was heavy yet sharp, as if Old Scratch was standing by and grinning. I'm not religious, but it was a hell of a lot like that. Made your own skin go rough and something in you flinch away. Daddy and I'd got out fast, that time; I wanted to get out of here with the same speed now, but didn't.

Instead I stood up slow, staring up past the dead man along the staircase. It made a long curve. At the peak was a balustrade, also picked out in faint, old gold in walnut dark as pitch. But nothing human was in sight or sound up there. I stepped back, wishing my boots were quieter and knowing they needed some tallow, and stood there listening mainly to my own heart and breath.

I turned around, also slow as sorghum. Light was falling gentle through the doorway whose big door I'd left open. It was reaching, rosy, into the hall and touching up points of blaze in the tarnished mirrors. In the mirrors I could make out small but true reflections of myself and of the man behind me at the foot of the stairs.

I walked back then along the hall past the mirrors, and stopped in the front vestibule. Here a couple of chairs bottomed with tapestry, a dark old design of crowns and roses worked into them, stood side by side along the wall. I glanced back; nothing had changed; and all around me I could feel the emptiness of the great lonesome house. Feel room blossoming out of room, like curves of a shell spiraling one into another. I'd have bet one of these hall doors led to a ballroom, which would be just as hushed and tomblike as all the rest. I could feel the full weight of the house, secret and biding, with maybe every mouse and rat and chewing insect in it holding its peace till I was gone.

Sun struck my eyes when I turned to the doorway again.

I wanted to sing out into the light, call out for anybody at all.

Other hand, I didn't think it would do a touch of good.

Then from the day outside—as you sense more than hear a steamboat on the river long before it comes in sight, not sure at first and then surer as its engine moves closer—I could make out hoofbeats off in the deep distance. They were sounding from the west. Just a soft thudding, but getting plainer. I got myself out there and down the front gallery steps so fast I hardly touched the wet treads. Thinking: Grayboy. Then I was all the way at the end of the front walk—which was more of that stout red brick—and through a sagging front-walk gate. Here a strip of road curved before the gate and ran on around below the stable, a long distance behind the house. Red clay in the road was waiting to dry off in this sharp quiet day. Oak shadows were starting to show along the clay, striping it in long lattices. Oak leaves, those left on the trees, shook a trifle in the now blue-edged morning.

But I knew from the hoofbeats by now it wasn't Grayboy.

Not unless he'd been magicked into another and slower beast entirely.

Around the curve from the west came a horse and buggy. A black cob, stepping out—its shadow grew under it as the sun sprang stronger. The man driving it hunched forward, a campaign hat low over his eyes. He reined in like he didn't give a damn for the cob's mouth, sawing to a stop. Came out of the buggy so fast he was all flapping, coat ballooning and the bag in his hand making an arc in the air with its old buckles and straps shining. A little man with rooty hands and humped shoulders, a wide-spread moustache and a limber, all-peering set of brown eyes. He took a spit of the chew in his cheek and the ambeer jumped off into the shadows and splashed in some azalea leaves. Strode straight to me and said in a sawtooth rasp, "Well, sir! Got here as quick as I could. And Miss French's on her way. Reckon you're Broome?"

"Thomas Broome," I said. "And you're—?"

"Doctor Mattison. Roy Mattison. So—you're the byrider stayed in the stable last night. Whose nag she borrowed to get to town. Well, folla me, Broome. Seems there's been a shooting and the party got shot's bad-injured. Miss French doesn't know for certain, but there might be life in him yet. Wants me to save him if I can. I'm of two minds about savin' the scannel, but I'll do anything for Miss French."

I said fast, "It's a favor you can't do this time. The patient's cold. I reckon you mean the man in yonder at the foot of the steps. I went in and touched him."

"That ain't a profound medical opinion, Broome. Unless you're a doctor besides bein' a racing man. She told me a little about you—much as she had time to tell."

"She tell you she lifted my horse while I was asleep?"

"Yeah, she was in a tearin' hurry and there wasn't no time to beg your kind permission. Goddamn it, Broome, come on . . . folla me."

I did better than follow; kept up with him, at his side, even though he was going like a streak of saber-light. We went back up the walk and then up the steps in long strides. Above us the columns were taking the light brighter now, saintly and white, if peeling a whit in the still sharp air. I took a look behind at the road; felt a chunk of lead in my belly that the horse hadn't been Grayboy. Mattison kept moving and was ahead of me now. But the second he'd lunged in through the open doorway to the hall, he stopped, squinting toward the base of the staircase. More light was flooding in there now. He said, "Ah, God, Broome. Happens you were right, she was wrong. She needn't have bothered till full daylight. Can tell from here he'll never make trouble again. Miss French won't be bothered again in all her days. Not by this blackguard."

I said, "She shoot him?"

"No sir! She'd have told me if she had! She found him!"

I said, "That's interesting." Didn't say anything about the derringer she possessed. I whirled around and inspected the road again. It was quiet out there, no slate gray Standardbred boiling along it with his hocks driving and his shoulder-muscles laid back. The black cob was nibbling at some grasses. I turned back again. Mattison champed down deep on his mouthful, then looked around for a place to spit in here, and then took the chew out and thrust it in a side pocket. Then he went on toward the staircase, with me at his back. He bent over the body. "Already goin' stiff." He picked up the dead man's right wrist, holding it as if it was so much whang-leather, light but firm. He waited a few seconds. Cast his crow sharp eyes around to me. "Yeah, this son of a bitch has been gathered to his fathers. Standin' at the knee of Jesus. Who'll cast him out fast without even botherin' to say hello. Well, aside from the ruckus it'll cause in this part of the county, it ain't no loss at all."

He straightened himself, creakily. "Been dead quite a few hours, the bastard. And don't tell me different, Broome."

I hadn't been about to.

Maybe it was just that from what he saw on my face, he thought I might argue.

Reckoned I was looking dark as the backside of a chimney.

"Hell," Mattison said. "I've brought 'em back to life at Gettysburg and the Plank Road. Could always do it long as they had a limb or two left and enough spark in 'em. But isn't a perishing thing I can do with a corpse, save to agree it's gone. Or maybe cry over it, when it's worth the crying, which this one never could be." He cocked his head. His jaws were like a nutcracker's, with just the glint of teeth showing. "I'd say the one shot did it. Needn't have been more. Why didn't Miss French see it? She must've taken no look at all—and just requisitioned your nag without thought, and gone a-bumping . . . she was flustered, though I've known her since I brought her into the world, and never seen her flustered before. That's it. Miss French was flustered."

I had my hands on my hips. Breathing slow, trying to stay quiet and patient. Besides keeping my ears open for Grayboy—no more sound of hoofs wafted in through this hall—I was thinking of that sound I'd heard, that might-have-been limb-crack—just as I'd shunted off to sleep last night. Was thinking this man could just as well have been shot then.

I said, "Doc, the horse she took's not a nag. He just may be the best Standardbred in the South."

His bronze gray compaign hat waggled, his eyes flashed.

"Broome, this ain't no time to offer me his pedigrees. I saw your stallion. Damned handsome critter. And he's in safe hands. Miss French's been riding all her days—up to the time when she couldn't afford no more mounts. Her daddy, Colonel Bob, was maybe the best man we ever had with horseflesh, outside Beauty Stuart himself. She rode for me without even botherin' to saddle, woke me from a sound sleep, just on the hope I might be able to keep this hog alive. Which was wonderful of her, considerin' most people in her place would've let him expire. Still don't know why she didn't note he was nothin' but dead, but I reckon it was good dark on the stairs here when she found him, and, as I say, she was flustered. She'll tell us all about that soon as she gets here."

Then he got a mite less testy and glanced at the dead man again. "Lot of pother ahead. I'll have to make out a death certificate. But he can't be moved yet. Sheriff Planteu'll have to be notified. Have to come out and study the remains and look around and draw his judgments. Have to scour around for the scallywag done this. Though by all honest rights—" He put down his bag; it balanced on the lion-headed newel post as if the carved lion was wearing a wide cracked-leather hat. "—by rights whoever done it, even if he was a Yankee, ought to reap a reward."

I said, "And just who is this body you've been praising up so much?"

He glared at me. His eyebrows tangled all they could, since there was only skimpy hair in them. Then he shook his head, let out a whiffling sigh, and says, "I forgot, Broome. You don't have the pleasure of livin' around here. Why"—he jerked a gnarled thumb downward—"his name's Gary Willis." He spoke the name as if he was talking about Beast Butler in the midst of Reconstruction. "He's Miss French's cousin. Blight and bane of her days, and not only hers. Battened on us all, includin' the nigras."

His coat rucked up around his shoulders as he gave a massy shrug. "Oh, not close cousin—twice removed. But her only livin' kin. After the war, with her daddy and mamma both gone durin' it, he took her servants first. All the nigras who'd been freed here but who'd wanted to stay on, but who couldn't because she couldn't feed them ary thing but wind. Took 'em over to his place, Fountainwood. Gave 'em short rations there, but they stayed because there wasn't no other place to go. The nigras say he messed about with odd things over there—Satan-worshiper. I wouldn't doubt it. Willis prospered fast after the war, dealin' with every carpetbagger came swarmin' from Washington after Abe was killed.

Miss French sold off most of the good belongin's to him—all the things Colonel Bob and M'linda—that was Miss French's mama—had amassed over the years here in the hall. Miss French didn't have a choice. Had to live, and the eggs from her fowl—she sells the eggs—wouldn't keep her alive. Willis kept her in penury, like he kept the Chantry nigras . . . I'd say there'll be rejoicin' goin' on among them now, when they find he's gone . . ."

He was looking past my shoulder now, into the sun pouring in from the vestibule. "That door's never locked—reckon Willis just walked straight in last night . . . he'd talked a lot about how he was goin' to marry her—Christ, she'd no more look at him in that light than she'd bed down with a cottonmouth. But if she says she didn't kill him, she damned well didn't."

I had my head half turned. Still listening for more hoofs.

He knew it. "Don't know what in hell's holding her up. She was ridin' behind me. Till we got to the Lanceton Pike. I didn't look around after that, just came hell-for-leather for here. Well"—he picked up his bag from the newel post—"we'll wait for her; she can go back to town with us and tell her side to Sheriff Will Planteu. Reckon you're all of an itch to be on your way, Broome, but the law's got to be honored. My throat's parched. Gets that way every autumn; it's the river-bottom mists. Let's see if we can find some coffee—if Miss French's got some . . ."

I watched while he swung along from here to a side-hall. Heard him opening a door at its end; I reckoned it to be for the kitchen. Then I followed him back there. The only sounds in the whole new day came from birds warming up in the trees, and from far back at the stable, a few fluttering squawks of hens. I stepped into the kitchen. A jay squalled outside, and a redbird flashed past the dark kitchen door curtains. Sun came creeping into this monstrous kitchen in bits and slashes, angling onto a great washpot and gilding its lip. Fingering the bricks of the chimney-throat and warming its hearth. No noise of hoofbeats from near or far.

Mattison found the coffee; he seemed to know just where everything lived in this place. Measured it out careful, saying that Miss French had known such meaching times that even this pinch of coffee was a trespass upon her, and that he'd offer to pay her for it later, but that she was so proud-born it would only make her mad, and that she had a strong temper when crossed. While the coffee was brewing in a good old high-spouted pot, he took another chew—using a side window which he yanked open, for a spittoon—and muttered some more about Gary Willis.

Said, "Any vagabond could've strolled in and struck him down. Or maybe it was a passer-through, a robber, trailed him from Fountainwood—over northwest side of the bayou. Waited to throw down on him till he was here in this house . . ."

I looked out of the window he'd opened. Past withered morning glory vines I saw a flock of teal flying over from the swamp I'd come from last night. Shaping their flight like the head of a broad arrow.

I said, "Seems strange to me. That this Gary Willis's horse—he'd have had to ride over here from his place, wouldn't he?—isn't anywhere in sight."

Doc Mattison rolled that around his mind. Coffee-scent was beginning to stir. I was right hungry; but the coffee would have to stay me till I could get to my saddlebags for some jerky and pone. And I thought of the oats I had in one of the bags. Hoped Miss French Chantry might be delayed only because she'd thought to stop and water Grayboy and breathe him before she got back here.

Hoped to God that was all that was making her so tardy.

Mattison cleared his throat. "Well, now, this killer, Broome—he could've made off with *both* horses when he left. Leadin' Willis's, maybe, and ridin' his. That's likely, ain't it?"

He sounded puzzled about it, though, as if he hadn't thought of this till now. He stopped, and scratched his nose, halfway to the big round table, the coffee pot in his hand. "Just as likely as anything in the whole foofooraw. A murderer and a horsethief. Maybe it's good he couldn't've known about your stallion, or he might've made off with him too."

He slapped the coffee onto the table. Went back for some cups. Says as he dipped into a cabinet, "We do get some rare creatures travelin' through here. Times still hard, and not much to pick over since the Yanks left. But they still try. I've often worried about Miss French off here by herself—as if Willis wasn't enough to contend with . . ." He was coming back to the table. "You from close by, Broome? Don't recollect Miss French mentioning it . . ."

"Dango Falls. It's in Alabama."

"She did say you were on your way to Yadkin. To the fair up there."

"To the harness racing. I'm entering Grayboy, driving him myself. Fact is, nobody's ever been on his back but me. Not till now."

"Told you you needn't have any fears about that."

"I'm taking your word for it," I said. "My father and I raised him. He's out of Nickajack by Galleon. Best dam and sire in my part of the country. Daddy couldn't drive any longer after he got back, after Appomattox. Got a ball through his hand, twisted it up." I knew I was talking just to keep from listening for hoofbeats that didn't fall on the air. "When he died a couple of months ago, Grayboy was the chief thing he willed me." He'd poured the coffee; I lifted my cup. Cup so fragile you could see light through it. Like it was frail as one of the leaves dangling at the window. "He was a horse-coper, trainer, breeder, and gambler." I took a sip. "If he knew I'd let Grayboy out of my sight now, he'd have taken after me with a whipstock. Wound or no wound, and even though he was smaller than I am."

Mattison was listening as if the white nests of hair in his ears filtered each word.

Didn't answer me now, but took a sip of his own cup. And put the cup down and touched his moustache. The moustache was a shade darker than his frizzled hair.

Then all at once he flounced back, shoved the cup away, and said, "Shee-ut! Damn my soul, Mister Broome, she's dawdling!"

"Uh huh," I said. "I was just about to remark on that."

In my shirt, where I carry Daddy's turnip, I could hear it ticking. I took it out. The watch is old gold with considerable engraving on the case. When you plunge down a couple of spring-butts it chimes the nearest hour. I pressed, and it chimed eight times. The pretty bells filling the sun between us, then dying away. I had laid my hat down on the table between us. It gave a jump as Mattison hit the table with the edge of his fist. He says, "Pardon me, Broome. Just goin' to take a gander out along the road. To see what I can see."

He got up, scooping up his bag from the table, and walked out into the side-hall. Then I heard him going into the main hall. And then out to the vestibule and the gallery, and down the front steps. His footfalls were out of earshot. I put away the watch, picked up my hat, went to the kitchen door and unlocked it. It had an old brass key in its lock. Opened the door and looked down across the compound and the cabins, the summer cookhouse and the trees. All the sky was a rare clean blue with the day full of promise for horseman and horse. But not for a horseman without his horse.

I hauled off and planted a good kick on one of the back gallery posts.

It was strong; I didn't do anything but dent my boot.

I slapped my hat on again and went down to look for some feed for the chickens. Could hear them complaining away in their house next to the stable. When I'd found the feed in a nearby shed, and taken my time about strowing it—they were Dorkings and Buff Orpingtons, as she'd said—I left them pecking and made my way around toward the front of Chantry Hall again. Taking it slow; giving Miss French Chantry all the benefit of the doubt I had left in me. The house was so long, so multiroomed, it took me about three minutes to get clear of it and back on the brick front walk again. Leaning on the canted iron gatepost, I saw Doc Mattison next to the road, sitting back against one of the giant oaks. I could hear his cob over farther along, breathing and breaking wind in the buggy shafts.

I went up next to him; I joined him in letting the tree hold us both up.

After a time I said, "I fed the hens. How's it come she locks the back door but leaves the front unlocked?"

"Reckon because she's set in her ways like anybody with a lot of lonesomeness around them. And a thief's more likely to try the back. And Colonel Bob and M'linda never locked the front door of the hall; anyone was welcome who needed welcoming."

"Know her well, don't you?"

He grunts. "She's my godchild."

After another and even more thoughtful and longer time, I said, "Quiet around here, on the whole. You could hear a dog bark a mile away . . . well, maybe she got lost."

"Hah! Miss French lost!"

"How far is it to town?"

"Eight miles." He just barely let the words out past his moustache. His crabbed right hand, tight around the handle of the bag in his lap, gripped tighter. His knuckles shone like the chine of a hambone. "I told you she was right behind me up to the time I came out on Lanceton Pike. The rain was just quitting then, but it was still dark." He got up, hoisting his bag and said hard and straight, "Come along, Broome. Seems to be a hell of a lot more in this than meets the eye."

"Or the ear, or the flesh. Still," I said, "it's horseflesh I'm most interested in." I brushed dead grasses off my trousers and caught up with him as he made off toward his buggy. I'd say for him that he moved fast when he wanted to; it must have come from being a medical man in wartime. His jaws were working like seasoned leather bellows. I swung up beside him in the buggy. Shooting more ambeer out into the grasses, taking up the reins, he said, "I'll cut around back near the stable. The road borders it. You can gather up your saddle and other truck. Then you'll be set to go straight on to Yadkin from Lanceton. After all this is settled and you've got your mount again.''

We started out at a sharp trot, surprising the cob.

"Sure," I said quite soft. "After I've got my mount again."

# 3

He drew in the cob down near the stable yard and I went back to the stable and hauled up my saddlebags, the saddle and Grayboy's bridle, and the boxwood fiddle in its case. Heaped them high in my arms and trudged down across the corner of the yard, and dumped them in his buggy. He set the cob going again, and we spanked around the next curve and past a couple of locust trees, then the road straightened out for a time.

All the day was staying clear. Copper-edged, brushed with all autumn.

I was locked in my thought. Though still scanning all the countryside like a spy.

I thought about how after that first race Daddy and I'd started entering Grayboy in more serious races. Mostly those near Dango Falls. Bringing him along easy. How we'd found he paced best with light plates, though sometimes we used toe-calks. Remembered how I'd inspected his plates the evening before, just before wheeling him into that sorry bypath; mulled over the point that his traveling plates were light too; I didn't use the toe-calks except sometimes for the track.

Wasn't much room now in this buggy, what with my gear. I leaned far out to look at the drying clay of the road.

And it didn't take me long to make out Grayboy's hoofprints. His plates left signs clear as a man's signature. They gouged along the right-hand side for the most part, though some were stiffening toward the middle of the roadway. And they were a good distance apart where I was looking; she'd had him in a gallop.

The buggy wheels clacked and spun under us.

I noted there weren't any Grayboy prints heading back toward Chantry Hall.

I sat back, watching the land spin by. A few farms came in sight. Touch and go places where you might make a crop or just hope for it. A young boy was herding cattle down a path from a barn lot. He called out to Doc, and Doc touched his hat to him. We were past that farm.

Over the noise of wheels, I said, "Doc, is Miss French Chantry a good shot?"

He nodded, wattles creasing under his chin. "Better'n most."

He wasn't looking at me, just gripping the reins and bouncing with his buggy. "Why? You think, 'spite of what I said, she shot Willis? Advise you to swallow that thought, Broome. Keep it tucked away from sight or sound. If she'd shot him, she'd have said so. She'd have known not a jury in Lanceton would convict her. And let me tell you, Lanceton's a close-coupled place. Nobody there'd favor anybody from outside comin' in and makin' an accusation. This girl's word's her bond, just as it was with Colonel Bob's."

This time he cut an eye at me. And back to the cob's bobbing haunches. "God knows I know how you feel—with your livin' revolvin' around your horse. And I can't yet see for the life of me why she should take so much time gettin' back a mere eight miles; it's unnatural. See you castin' an eye at the road. You see your stallion's prints?"

"All pointed away, nothin' coming this way."

"Means she never really got back on the pike, then. I'm gettin' a notion. Or a hope. She could have turned around even before she got back on the pike, and rode for Will Planteu. He's the sheriff. She could have done it without tellin' me, knowin' I'd go right on out to Chantry Hall. She could be waitin' there now, or Will and her could both be ridin' back to meet us. Keep your eyes skinned."

I kept them so. There wasn't a soul in sight now. Only the land, rich as could be but hardly touched by man along here. The road snaking in front of us. The cob laboring and puffing some, as if thinking about getting the thumps.

Says, "Doc, might I know what Miss French told you when she hauled you out of bed?"

"Don't see no harm in telling you. Unless you shot him yourself and want to know if she happened to be aware of it."

"I don't favor gunpowder weapons," I told him. "Daddy didn't either, after the surrender. He cleaned the house of them. Said they were in the main made by fools to indulge idiots."

He nods. "I've known a good many men to feel so, after long battles.

Puts things in perspective. Like to've known your daddy. But I don't recall a Broome in my part of the cavalry . . . well, let's see. Miss French told me she'd got up in the early dark and gone downstairs. And nearly stumbled over Willis there at the staircase bottom. As I pointed out to you a while back, it was mighty dark then. So she mightn't have got a real close look at him—though it's not like her not to've made sure. And she told me she went down to the stable, where you were sleepin' like a child, and reckoned she couldn't waste time wakin' you and doin' any explainin', so just took your stallion bareback, and flew. All which speaks well for her—as her whole life has, Broome. Faced with the same decision, not knowin' if that rotted limb of Satan was dead or not, I'd have just sat down and waited for him to expire. I give her some kind of high marks and stars in her crown for tryin'."

Sun was warming my eyelids. Pulled my hat-brim down. Said gentle as I could over the wheels' racket, "All right, Doc. But two things bother me. One, when I was about to go to sleep last night—maybe twenty minutes after midnight, around there—I heard a tree-limb crack; or a shot. Could have been either, and maybe it's got nothin' to do with any of this. But maybe it does. Other is, Miss French Chantry had a derringer with her when she came out to the stable. She told me what it was for. Foxes."

This time he didn't change expression. The road was turning to dust, and it blew up around us.

He gives a stiff jerk of his head. "Derringer Colonel Bob left her. I've seen it often. Hard piece to be accurate with, except at close range. Hell of a piece to get a fox with. But all she had. Listen, Broome." He'd slowed the cob now; the reins were almost slack. There still wasn't another human—or animal either—in sight on this road. He rolled his quid to my side. Made a tight cheek-bulge. "You tell the same thing you just told me to Will Planteu; he'll not believe she done it. It's your duty to tell it. But it won't make a particle of difference. And let's leave it right there till we get to Will Planteu's office, where I've got the hope she'll be waitin' for us, since we ain't seen her or Will on the road. With your horse intact and sound and just as ready for Yadkin Fair as he ever will be."

"I purely have that hope too," I said.

Didn't seem profitable to say another word right at the moment. I kept my gaze on the pike-road. Grayboy's marks were still there for a time, then I couldn't see them any more because we'd come to where the road-surface changed to pebbles mixed with sand, which couldn't have taken an elephant's tracks. A gray signpost with a board on it said Lanceton, and I reckoned this other surface went through town. I wondered if it dropped away to clay again on the other side.

Lanceton was a town I'd have ridden through in the night and the rain, if I hadn't been so burr-headed as to try the shortcut. Nice place this time of morning, with the houses along its center street basking in the sun through crepe myrtles and elms and oaks, and the town square lying ahead, and children moving along to a school whose bell was clanging. I counted three churches, and saw a firehouse with its high-wheeled water-pumper, and the white horses in the firehouse stable, one of them tossing its head over the half-door. Mane was fuller than Grayboy's, but it didn't have the mettlesome arch of his crest. We rolled on past more houses—Doc jerked his head, grunted, "There's where I live," and I looked back at his place, with bushy oaks leading to it beside the drive. Then we were down to a walk, the cob sweating, and past a grain-and-feed store, and in front of a building with a sign, Sheriff's Office, in gold framed with black alongside its door. There wasn't a horse tied to the hitching post in front I'd have given more than a first look. All up and down the rest of the street, the same. Kept staring around, though. Doc pulled up the cob and clutched my arm as we got out.

"Let me do the talkin', at the first anyhow. Doesn't look like she's here; don't see your stallion. And if she ain't, this is goin' to bother Will a lot. He thinks as much of her as I do, and we don't cotton to mysteries when they deal with our own friends, in Lanceton."

"He her godfather too?"

"He might as well be. We all kind of keep an eye on her. And Will won't want this to disturb the mayor—the mayor's mighty old, heart's not too strong; he's pulled this town through times of grief and darkness. Don't fear, though—we'll look for Miss French, and find her. And your prize property 's well."

I wondered how French Chantry felt about having an eye kept on her all her life. Something in her own eyes had been too dancing and seeking to put up with that forever. I kept my mouth shut. We went up the path to some shallow steps, and Doc swung open the door without knocking. Reckoned I must look half like a tramp and half like the rider and harness driver I was, but didn't know which side showed foremost. Also wondered what the long-eyed man in the office—man with high sloping shoulders, good spare body—was thinking about me as he raked me once with his tea-colored eyes, got up from behind the battered rolltop and strolled over to us through a swinging gate. "Good morning, Roy," he says to Doc. "You're too late for breakfast. Sorry."

The star hung on his vest winked in the greenish light through these smudged windows.

His eyes slid to me, back to Doc.

Doc said, "Didn't come for a bite, Will. Trouble brings me . . . this here's Mister Thomas Broome, traveling through from Alabama on his way to Yadkin Fair. He's a harness-racing man. Stayed last night out at Chantry Hall in the stable. Mister Broome, Sheriff Will Planteu."

The sheriff gave a head-nod, and thrust out his hand. I shook it. A hand hard as a chinkapin. His vest was scuffed leather, with gilt buttons, much worn, from what I supposed had been a cavalry uniform, sewed onto it. Frayed moleskin pants were stuffed in his boot-tops. A pistol enholstered in more scarred leather at his flank.

No quick-stabber in the dark, he waited while Doc slumped into a chair. Doc said, "Miss French been in to see you this mornin', Will?" Planteu shook his head. "Well, you seen her anywhere this mornin'?"

Planteu fingered his chin. He was shaved better than Doc Mattison, and I'd not shaved since the morning before.

"Nope. Saw her last on—Friday, it was. She'd caught the stage on the pike and brought her eggs to market." His voice was just about sleepy, but he wasn't. "Saw her catch the stage back to the hall that evenin', too. If that does you any good." He rolled a short cigar out of his vest pocket, and wetted its end between his lips.

"It don't," said Mattison. "Not a thread of good. Damn it! Well, Will, she's come up missin'. On Broome's stallion—big gray, rangy devil. With no saddle, and just a hackamore."

"Breed?" said Planteu.

"Standardbred," I said.

"A sight I'd have marked well in my mind," said Planteu.

I had the feeling he talked soft and slow just to put up a simpleton's wall. His eyes didn't look as though they'd ever missed much.

They widened just a hair when Doc said, "And Gary Willis is dead. Shot through the skull. Over at the hall on the staircase."

Then they narrowed again, like a biding panther's.

"Suppose you just tell it all, Roy. Not the curlicues, just the meat of it."

Doc's tobacco-stained lower lip went in and out, then he put his head back and sighted the ceiling. And he told the story. Told it well, I thought; quick and all to the point. He even mentioned what I'd passed along to him—the limb-crack or shot, and Miss French's derringer. All the while he was spilling it, Will Planteu kept silence. He made me think of a fisherman whose bobber was dandling up and down, watching the line. Doc finished up, with no flourishes but with everything out. He looked around, found a spittoon, and hit it square. "That's all," he said, wiping his mouth.

A couple of flies buzzed around over Planteu's desk.

Planteu said quiet, "Damn those flies. This late in the year, and you still can't get shut of them. Roy, you say Miss French was kind of upset."

"Real bothered, for her."

"Never seen her so. Not even when she was no taller than that desk. Might be a kind of shock. It can happen to the coolest heads. You observed it yourself many a time when the shot was flyin'. But it just comes to me"—he shrugged, dropped his lean, wide shoulders—"maybe she did know Willis was dead. Maybe she was stirred up about somethin' else, somethin' we don't know about yet."

"Why'd she ride eight hard miles for me, then? Why couldn't she wait till good light?"

"I'm only speculatin', Roy. Not drawin' conclusions."

"Why'd she toll me out there in the Goddamned rain?"

Planteu gazed solid and quiet at Doc. And Doc said, "Sorry. Got any more speculations?"

"A few at this stage. Maybe by gettin' you to the hall, she knew you'd start the law workin'. And with that done—she's not a young woman does things light, or without purpose—she'd have done her duty for the time bein'. And would be free to do whatever else it was she had to do, that needed a horse for the doing. Had to be an errand with high meaning for her." He gave another shrug. "Or I'm just a fool reachin' in the dark, and all was as she told it to you. She thought Willis was still alive, and summoned you. And then when she got to the pike, somethin' or somebody interrupted her."

Planteu and Doc looked at each other. The flies went on sounding. Planteu's forehead wrinkled. "Jesus," he said soft. "If she was trailed in the dark—maybe by the same party did away with Willis—"

I cleared my throat. Sounded harsh and abrupt, even scaring the flies for the nonce.

Both of them swung their heads to me. With full attention.

I said, "I'm a stranger, passing through. Not the man you'd trust for an opinion, Sheriff. All the same, it's kind of amazing to me you mightn't just once have had the idea Miss French herself shot her cousin—"

"Distant cousin," murmurs Planteu.

"—her distant cousin. And then rode away on my horse because she was rattled about it, or wanted to go think things over before she came back and confessed it, or—"

Planteu's voice was smooth and flat as a river-stone.

"Nope. Not Miss French. She might have rode for Roy all right, even if she'd killed Willis. Just to be with a friend. And then I think she'd have come along and told me. But she'd have done it right then. Told us both. So either she had this somethin' else in mind—a plan, an expedition only she could carry out—or she was waylaid."

My throat was dry. A pot-bellied stove was going near the desk.

My voice didn't even sound like me; it husked too much.

"Either way, my horse is gone."

"We'll find her, and your horse," Planteu said. "I'd like to inform you of somethin', Tom Broome. You're within your rights to say what you've said, think what you're thinkin'. But Miss French doesn't go around liftin' valuable property from someone she likes—or even someone she may not like. And she likes you, or she wouldn't have let you stay on Chantry land last night, not for a minute. So it was a sudden emergency that came up. An action, as I say, only she thought she could carry out. Otherwise she wouldn't have caused you this tribulation. Or, also like I said, she's met with foul play."

I said, too loud for the room, "I think I've got a right to go with you lookin' for her. I think that's my right, and I know it's my need."

Sheriff Planteu looked me up and down, taking his time. A pair of mules plodded by in the street, pulling a wagon.

Then he inclined his lean, tough-corded neck. "You can go along, Tom Broome. I'll call in my deputies now."

"Thanks," I said. "And I'm hungry—that coffee at the hall didn't cut my hunger. I'd like to step out to Doc's buggy yonder, and get some pone and jerky from my saddlebags—unless I'm under some kind of suspicion."

Planteu fingered his unlit cigar. "Can't say you are. You've got a lot at stake." His voice went lower. "We're horsemen too, Doc and me. Haven't had much wonderful to ride for years, but we did once, in the

Army of Northern Virginia. Go along, get your grub, but don't go far, we'll be movin' before long.''

I told him thanks again, and went out. It was still coolish after the warm office, and a spangled day. I pushed my hat back—it was dried out now, and so was the rest of me, but I was going to need the services of a body of water before long. I went to Doc's buggy. Got out the small saddlebag, with the food in it, and rooted around among oats and such till I found some pone, off which I blew oat-chaff and munched, leaning against the buggy. Looking back toward the office, I saw Sheriff Planteu go to a side door and yell something down the street, and heard a man answer, but I couldn't make out the words. Reckoned he was rounding up his deputies.

I'd noted no sorrow expressed by Planteu about the passing of Gary Willis. Had the feeling there'd be few flowers at his funeral, and maybe a general rejoicing afterward. Thought how Francia French Chantry'd appear to have every reason in the earth for slaying him. I gazed around at the horses gracing this street, but there was still no talent to speak of.

Children were mainly off the street and in school by now. But down near the statue of the soldier, in the town square—the square, a wedge of dusty green, with the statue rising from it in grayed marble, rifle canted and blanket roll slung smart and cap-a-pie—I could see men sitting around on the benches. Some were wearing parts of old uniforms, a coat here, a cap there, a pair of worn Confederate dusty pants. Sun was spilling into the grasses where a couple of the men were aiming horseshoes. From here I heard the clink of a shoe plate hitting a spike. Chewing pone, I sauntered on down that way, it wasn't far from Planteu's office.

When I got near them, a couple of the men looked around, but paying me no more than casual attention. Sat down on the end of a bench—a weathered oak plank with gnarled legs. Laced my fingers, and inspected the horseshoe players, and then gazed over past them to the town pump, the tin cup slung to its spout by a wire bail. A man sitting two places down from me leaned forward, spitting between his knees. Said, "See you over at the sher'f's. Any ruckus?"

"Stolen horse," I says. "Mine."

He snickered. I judged him to be in his fifties, but already old, first from the war, then from the tight living after. He had the hands of a hardscrabble farmer. A farmer who spent a good deal of his time in town, where he could talk about battles gone and shore up his past with remembering.

"Ain't at all a rare thing. If the horse was any good."

"Pretty fair horse," I said. "About the best I'd say in three or four states."

He'd been about to show sympathy, but now he soured his mouth as if I'd been talking too high for any stranger. In every town I'd ever passed through, strangers were thought to be bereft of plain sense, till proved otherwise.

"Oh, I wouldn't go crowing, son. There's some sweet horse hereabout—even if there ain't none in sight. I see a gray, this morn. Stallion—stones wasn't cut, had too much piss and vinegar in his going, for that. Went out the yon end of town." He tipped his head to the west. "Small light to see by, but it wasn't no dream. Rainin', and, thinks I, that horse'll slip on the cobbles—patch of 'em right over where the courthouse is—and bust a leg. But not so. Sailed right over the cobbles, and then if I'd had a clock on him I'd of been called a liar. Or the clock would, one. And my eyes are just as good as they were when I's with the militia."

I was sitting forward. Like a bow about to loose an arrow. Holding tight to the bench. Hoped he didn't note it.

Says quiet as I could, "Went west? Could you see the rider at all?"

"Hell no, I couldn't. All went by fast . . . shouldn't of been out myself, in the wet. But there's a ball still in my left shin, and it aches. They didn't take the leg off; sometimes I wish they'd done it. Aches, starts along three in the morn, then there's nothin' for it but to get up and walk the pain out. Which is why—anybody should ask you—I know every stone and bush in town, and every dog, too. And what folks are doin' that time and till first light—" He snickered again. "Hell. Studhorse was movin' at such a clip I couldn't of told if Old Horny was up."

The man sitting between us says, grinning, "Don't pay no mind to Ed Travers, friend. He likes to fill up a mollikin here and a mollikin there with tales. Got some tall rare ones too—but they're tales."

Ed Travers hunched his left leg back under the bench. Face turning turkey-wattle pink under the gray, whiskery growth. He said, "God rot you, I'm tellin' the truth about that there stud-horse!"

I got up, nodded to him, nodded to his friend and some of the rest and walked back west. Didn't take long to get to where the wooden sidewalks left off; the road here was just fawn-colored dust now, touched with red streaks of clay. I didn't bend over, but kept on looking into the road as I went on. I stepped under the shade of a flowering jasmine—no flowers on it now, buds like shining small beetles gone quiet for the winter. I was coming to the last of the houses in Lanceton. Back of me the sand and pebble street lay in a blaze of morning. Then, there was a hoofprint. Grayboy's, I'd have known it from a thousand. And ahead were more prints, ridged in the clay. All led straight west. And he'd been going not like he had Old Horny on him, but at a long gait, and I hoped he'd enjoyed it. He was sure getting let out now.

My throat was dry as beached driftwood.

Over beside this end of the street was a fair claybank horse, loose-tethered to the black trunk of a persimmon. No fruit on the persimmon, I reckoned it had been picked soon as the first frost sweetened it. Near me a couple of women were sitting on the upper step of a front stoop, talking hard. So far they hadn't looked up. I untied the claybank horse as fast as I could. It was saddled, with a crokersack serving for blanket. I got up on the horse, a gelding, and had him moving away from there and into a full gait before I heard the first noise from the women. Clapped the claybank across a shoulder and leaned down to keep the drying hoofprints in sight, and fled.

# 4

Or maybe I should say I sped, not fled. Hadn't any idea of escaping and going off on my own. I just wanted to follow these prints as far as I could for the time being.

The claybank had a nice action even if he was astounded at being urged along at such a pace. He was the kind gets to be a piece of furniture in a family like a rocking chair—or a rocking horse. I chirruped in his warm ear. Was riding low over his neck like an Indian sighting for buffalo trail. The trees of the town swept behind me. Giving way to wilder trees. The road widened out and made a bend to the south. The hoofprints were still plain in the road for a space, then they went veering off-road into high moist grasses. I reined in the claybank; he was breathing hard now and slobbering a little around the bit just to prove he'd been working.

I sat up and looked over and down the hill where the grasses waved. They looked like the dark silver fur of an uneasy beast. Then below the hill I could see the river winking—tawny and bright—the Lanceton River, down whose bayou I'd slugged along with Grayboy the night before. I patted the claybank and let him blow. I'd have liked taking him down to the river's brink to see if Miss French Chantry had put Grayboy into the water at about this point. Had the good notion she must've; she wouldn't have had any trouble, he liked water. I'd have liked to search around for his marks by the riverbank too. But I didn't put the claybank down; just marked the place well in my head.

Rising in the banged-up stirrup-irons, I sighted across toward the opposite bank. Thick woods grew there as far as the eye could reach. The kind you don't just call big woods but know is a forest. From here some of it looked like first-growth oak, mingled into with pines and some clutches of gum and cottonwood. A light wind was blowing along the river as it crawled to the south. But hardly troubling its water which was smooth as a baby's fawn bottom at this point and had a shallow look.

The claybank was all through being stupified by the first spurt of genuine riding he'd maybe had in all his years. He was trying to reach the grass-tussocks beside the road. I pulled his head up and swung him and started him back. Went slower now, jogging along at a pace fit to please him. Came to me I'd come a little farther from town than I'd thought. Then the town started showing again. And just about fifty yards from where the pebble and sand street started, out from under the tame trees arching over it, here came a high-backed roan put to a racking gait, and on the roan, elbows tight and head up, was Sheriff Will Planteu. Behind him streamed a couple of other horsemen. They all sighted me and slackened their pace. Doc Mattison wasn't with them. Then the sheriff was riding up to me, and pulling up, staring at me with his sleepy catamount eyes nearly shut. Says, soft enough, "What the holy knobs of hell you think you're doin', Thomas Broome?"

The other horsemen behind him drew in closer. They were able-looking men, rough-edged and ready, and I reckoned them for Planteu's deputies. One was thickset with small eyes and a wide jaw, and was edging his horse close to the claybank. I pulled the claybank farther from him, didn't want him to collide with my borrowed mount and give him a shoulder-bruise. He had a rifle canted over his saddle in a leather scab-bard. The other man with the sheriff was thinner and more wizened and a mite smaller in heft than I am, but capable-handed with his mount.

I said, "Sorry, Sheriff Planteu. I thought I'd be back before you knew

I'd come up missing. I ask you to look down there—before all these horses foul them—and note the hoofprints leadin' out from town.''

He bent over and gazed down and in his hat-brim's shadow his eyes narrowed even more. I said, "Those are Grayboy's. I saw 'em leading into the other side of town—till the town-street started—all the way from Chantry Hall. I found 'em coming away from town on this road again toward the river. They sheer off and go down right to the river. I apologize for using the claybank. But I needed to follow my urge.''

He straightened up. "Thomas Broome, kindly don't go getting any more urges in a county under my jurisdiction. Not another one, hear? The claybank belongs to Mort Tyler. His old woman's just now havin' a booger-fit because you borrowed him. I'm well aware of your need to find your stallion—but if you go on like this, could be you'll end up with a ball in your back. I don't want two corpses on my hands; it would mortify me and in your case might even make me a little sad.'' He was sitting back in his saddle. "Thomas, this man over here is Grody Flieshacker. He's my deputy. And this small one who don't ever say much is Phil Adams, my other deputy. They've heard your tale and Roy Mattison's backed it up. We're going to try to make a meed of sense out of all this. We'll be workin' together now—pray heaven it ain't long, I want to see Miss French safe and your horse between your own legs worse almost than I ever wanted to throw down on William Tecumseh Sherman. So you go right along with me, and these boys, and keep any more urges to yourself, or at the least share 'em with us.''

Then Grody Flieshacker stretched a hand and I shook it. He didn't seem eager and enthusiastic to make my acquaintance, it wasn't much of a hand-shaking. I shook the hand of Phil Adams. It'd been a fairly long speech for Sheriff Planteu, and he'd clammed up again now, his unfired cigar riding a corner of his lips. Both Flieshacker and Adams were peering at me as if they didn't mean to trust me farther than I might hoist Mort Tyler's claybank with one hand. Didn't blame them—it had been a spur-of-the-moment thing to do, maybe just foolish. Except I knew more now than I had before, and so did they.

Planteu gave me the eye. His own eyes showed just slits of eyeball among wrinkles. "Show me where the prints move down riverward. Reckon I could find them myself but it'll save time later.''

He raised a hand palm-out for Flieshacker and Adams to stay where they were. I turned the claybank and rode along with Planteu to the point

where the road widened. Then I reined in and he followed suit, and I
pointed to where the grasses shelved down to the river. Planteu leaned
over his pommel and nodded. "Jesus, if we're not lucky in some respects,
we're lucky for the soakin' rain last night. You're a fair tracker for a racin'
man." He brooded, gazing across the river.

I said, "I didn't track out here without a hint. Man back in town,
believe his name's Ed Travers, happened to remark he'd caught a glimpse
of a gray stallion going full-tilt through Lanceton this mornin' before
light. Said he was heading west, couldn't make out the rider."

"Sometimes Ed tells the truth, as a novelty. This seems one of the
times . . . I've got an idea what Miss French must have done was this.
She rode from Chantry Hall to Roy's house, trailed him back as far as the
Lanceton Pike. Then gave him the shake and circled back straight through
town to the river. She knows both river and woods—Colonel Bob used to
take her along when he was huntin' the woods, from the time she was a
tyke. She'd surely know this is the simplest point to ford. Well, we ain't
got time on our side—she's got the hell of a start, whatever her purpose.
Ain't any other following prints close by. So we can surmise she wasn't
followed. Which to me is a pure relief—in the back of my mind I had
notions of her bein' slain, maybe for your prize horse."

The slight wind was rustling the tips of the grasses. Wind smelled of
falltime and rotting leaves and river water. All brisk in the sunlight.

Planteu said, "She's well ahead of us. We'll have to put at least one
good tracker on the trail. I do wish I had me a solid band of brothers—had
'em all through the war, for all the good it done—but all I got workin' for
me is two good men. And unofficially, I got Roy Mattison, and Howard
Markley—he's the schoolmaster, I don't want to bring him into this yet. I
don't want Marcus—he's our mayor—to hear a whisper about this Goddamned trouble. Marcus has served his stint, through the war and God
knows, after it—he's the wisest man I know, he deserves to rest."

He batted at a green-bottle fly between the ears of his roan. "Wonder
why the Lord made flies? To improve our patience? —Thomas, we'll go
back to town now, and there I'll get you a mount. One you don't have to
*borrow* from an innocent bystander. And you and Grody can come back
here and start the trailin'. Grody's a good cuss, if set in his ways, he can
find sign where you or I wouldn't see it. You may find him a mite
prickle-edged; he thinks the very planets whirl around Miss French. He
used to propose to her, regular, along with a good many other town
swains. Till he found it wasn't gettin' him doodly-squat. Didn't take

kindly to your sleepin' in her stable, or in a hundred miles of her. You got to admit she's a fetchin' girl, Thomas.''

"I admit it freely," I said. "Plus havin' a bait of protective friends."

"And some enemies . . . some who think she's too high and mighty and proud-blooded. So you see another reason why I don't favor any of this comin' out." He was turning the roan; I turned the claybank with him. "Let's go. I'll deputize you before you and Grody set out. Damned if I've ever deputized an out-of-towner. First time for everything, and I'm just real glad you ain't Yankee to boot."

We rode back and joined Flieshacker and Adams. Then we all went at a smart clip back into town.

But we'd hardly come under the spraddling town trees when here toward us came a strong wash of human tide. Both the women who'd been on that front stoop when I'd purloined the claybank were in the crowd—I never did find out which one was Mort Tyler's wife, they were both carrying on so free—and a couple of men from the town square were in the small mob too, one of them even carrying a rope with him.

Before we got up to them, Planteu checked his roan and stood up in the irons. Hadn't known that behind the soft purring voice he had such thunder. "All right!" he shouted. "Mister Broome, here, was just carryin' out my orders! Needed a horse fast and used Mort's! It ain't wind-broke or saddle-galled, he didn't beat it, he didn't render it into glue!" He had his head back, eyes a-glitter. "I'd think in a town this quiet you could find smarter ways of amusin' yourselves . . . maybe makin' cats' cradles out of string or just catchin' up on your sleep. You men get on back to the square and take that rope back to Jackson's store. You ladies go back to your bakin', your men'll thank you for it."

We rode through between the men and women, who'd not only simmered down but were gazing around hangdog-style by now. In front of the house where he'd been tied, I slipped off the claybank and tied him again to the persimmon trunk, gave him a pat on the flank, and walked the rest of the way to Planteu's office while the sheriff and his deputies rode there. I was feeling a pinch tight in the neck—it had been a new yellow rope. Doc Mattison was standing in the office doorway; he'd heard the commotion and stepped out here. Planteu and the deputies talked to him a minute, filling him in on events, and then I joined them. We all went in the office, Planteu shutting the front door with a crisp slam. He laid out his orders then. Grody Flieshacker and I to make off riverward; Planteu

himself and Doc and Phil Adams to ride back to Chantry Hall. Then he
turned to me, and said, "That noise you heard when you were about to fall
to sleep last night, Thomas. Think back. Can you say any more'n that it
just *might*'ve been a firearm?"

I understood that in his quiet listening to Doc Mattison's telling of the
story, he'd taken it all in. Now he was sifting parts of it. Getting a line on
what might have happened at Chantry Hall, before he went out there to
scout around.

Taking my time, I thought back. Could feel Grody Flieshacker glower-
ing at me. I said, "No, I can't say more. Not with the way it was raining,
and sound being what it is through rainfall. I do remember Miss Chantry'd left the stable about ten minutes before I heard whatever it was."

I didn't say what I was thinking; that if it was a shot, the one that killed
Gary Willis, she'd most certainly have been in the house by that time, and
must have heard it. But she hadn't ridden to town for Doc Mattison till
toward morning. But I could see from Planteu's eyes that he was mulling
over just what I was.

He glanced toward Mattison. And Mattison answered the question
without it being voiced. His skimpy eyebrows were trying to draw
together again. "From the condition of the body, Will, Gary Willis could
have been shot about that time, yes. I'll be able to tell you better later,
after the autopsy. Hate to soil good medical steel on him, but I'll place it
close as I can." He was frowning heavy. "Gimme a cigar, Will. I'm out
of plug."

Sheriff Planteu handed him a cigar, passed them my way too—I didn't
favor one—put them back in his vest, and slapped his hands together.
"Hand me that extra badge outa your hip pocket," he says to Grody
Flieshacker. Grody did, and then Planteu deputized me. I'd never had it
happen before.

While he was saying the words it made me feel a little too stern about
myself. As if I was going against something that flamed and brightened in
Miss French Chantry's eyes. As if even though she had Grayboy and I
ought to be feeling mean and righteous, this ceremony would have
brought out that quick loving smile I'd seen just once blow across her lips
like peach blossom.

Then Planteu had pinned the badge on my shirt and we were all fanning
out of the office again. I caught glimpses of Lanceton citizens eyeing us
considerably, but they were doing it mostly across the street and at a

comfortable distance. While I went to Mattison's buggy and got out the saddlebags and Grayboy's saddle and gear and the boxwood fiddle in its case, Planteu led up a small white mare, about six years old, with black stockings. "Gentle and sturdy," he says. "Her name's Alice. Don't try any racin' skills with her, or she'll balk on you. Belongs to the county, the only other good animal I've got besides the roan. So treat her nice."

I told him I would. She stood still and meek as a foundation stone while I got Grayboy's saddle on her. Then I had to cinch up his saddle girth a good many notches before the saddle would sit well. I slung the bags across her, and hung the boxwood fiddle case from its thongs, then got up. She felt a lot lower to the earth than any mount I'd enjoy riding for more than a day or two.

Grody Flieshacker was on his black gelding. It had rusty stripes and wanted currying. I wheeled Alice's head toward the end of town, west. Grody went along with me. I caught little murmurations from the people watching us. Just the tag-ends of whatever rumors they were discussing among themselves. Couldn't make out the real words, and it didn't make any difference, I reckoned. It made a sound that went on under the noise of Grody's mount's hoofs, and Alice's, as we rode onward. Then the other sound was gone, and we were where the town trees gave way to the open country. I gave a look back, then remarked to Grody, "If I had to lose a horse, I'm glad it's Sheriff Planteu helping me look for him."

Grody only grunted. His wide jaw fitted down into his neck like the bottom of a squat jar. "Yeah, you're lucky. He can handle about anything. Only he wants to keep the crowd out of it, and the mayor . . . mayor's still home restin'. Best thing for him to do, he's an old, old man." He was quiet for a while, just the gelding's hoofs sounding, then he said sudden, "Around this town and county we don't like anybody who has even a little bit to do with disturbin' our peace, Broome. 'Bout all we've got left, since sixty-five."

"You think I made a point of disturbin' your peace?" I said. "You think I just naturally willed Miss Chantry to take my horse and go off into the wild unknown with him, when I'm all on fire to get to Yadkin and haven't got too long to do it in before the races start?"

We were coming to the point where the road widened out and swept around above the river.

He said, "If you had the sense of a dog, you'd have kept to the pike and gone right through town. Sense of a yellow dog."

"And then I wouldn't have brought about any trouble, is that it, Flieshacker? And wouldn't even have clapped an eye on Miss Chantry, or had a whisperin' thing to do with her."

Now we were reining in beside the tall grasses above the river. Grody Flieshacker's skin was a dull red flannel color. But warmer than most flannel. I said, "It's a lovely wonder to me how the people who run this town—Sheriff Planteu and Doc Mattison and a couple of others Planteu mentioned to me this morning—how they think Miss Chantry can do no evil. And how by the way you're acting around me, you believe the same thing. She looked to me, in the time I saw her—and I wish it could have been longer, because she's beautiful—like a natural human being. One who's lived a hard life, but has all the native instincts of any woman worth pasturing. I get the feeling you've all put her in a bell jar like a dried lily, and wouldn't give her credit for even havin' legs, but would call them mere limbs."

I could feel him steaming even before he burst out. "Goddamn you, Broome. Goddamn your stallion. I hope she breaks his leg. Don't think the badge makes you a citizen of this county, able to speak your mind. Mine does. I've worn it a long time. You're speakin' of a lady who's— who's an angel. When we find her—and I intend to find her, even if I have to leave you in some hollow tree—if you got even a thought of touchin' her instep, or lookin' at her crosswise, I'll tear your fuckin' head off and tie it to your saddle. Or just shoot you, shoot you with this here carbine." He patted the rifle-scabbard.

I just looked at him. About the only motion I could make. A fine, fresh note for a couple of deputies to start out on, I thought.

Then he was looking away from me, and after that, clucking to the black gelding, and riding down through the rough-tipped grasses toward the water. I let him go first. In these grasses insects were humming and darting, clouding around our mounts. Came the squashing of the gelding's hoofs as it went through dark reeds in the wet bank. Then Grody was checking, and I checked behind him. The river was about forty feet wide at this point, no more. Still appeared shallow to me, with small riffles on mud-bars farther downriver. Across the river the sky was the same blue it had started out today, not a cloud staining it. Grody's tone was quieter in front of me, and he wasn't moving his head around. The back of his neck was a nest fit for small owls. "There's a mark. Right next to the toad-frog settin' still."

Hell, I couldn't even see the frog. I blinked, and leaned a little. Then I finally made it out, about the size of a silver bit, breathing low in the muck and making like we weren't alive, and it wasn't either. I shifted my gaze, and there next to the frog was a Grayboy hoofprint, deep here, and shadowed by a burdock leaf so I wouldn't have made it out for another hour.

"Right here," Grody said, speaking mainly to himself. "We'll put ourselves to the water in the same place."

He didn't say, "Come on." He just rode. His gelding went into the water like a hoe cake settling into molasses. I put Alice in behind him.

It was shallow enough so the mounts wouldn't have to swim. And the current was slow, in this lazy bend. The water didn't even rise to our saddle skirts. Under me Alice was wading polite and steady, as if she did this every day for the joy of it. The breath of the water's surface was cool and the mosquitoes and flies and midges fell away behind us. When we were in the middle of the river—which got a lot wider downstream— Grody stopped the gelding, and kept sighting forward into the woods. There they were, rising dark and high over the bank.

Air was full of sun and wet horse smell and river mud smell.

Reckoned he was getting a line on where Grayboy had come out.

Then he got it, and went on. He rode out on a bank that had a more gradual climb to the woods than the bank we'd left. Far to the north before the trees started I made out a white fence gleaming sharp in the sun.

Grody was leaning forward again. I said, "Whose place is that? Before the woods starts?"

I didn't know if he'd answer or not. I didn't care a whole lot.

Without moving, he said, "Gary Willis's. Fountainwood."

I looked harder, but all I could see from here was just that corner of the fence. It didn't look like a sinful place, or one whose owner had kept his cousin twice removed in pain and poverty. Or the place of somebody who kept men and women who'd been slaves still in a kind of bondage. Or for that matter the plantation of a man who might have practiced devil-worship witchcraft, which I'd always thought had to be done with black cocks and conjur-rags and goofer powder in shacks.

Grody had started the gelding again. This time he swept his head around, eyes flat balls of black even darker than Doc Mattison's. "We're goin' up in where them little ash and elm start. Into the big trees beyond. When we get there, I'll dismount. You get off too. If you don't you'll tear up Sher'f Will's Alice. Lead her and I'll show the way."

Up the slope we went. The gelding's hocks knotted, and Grody hit him across the shoulder. Alice dug her back hoofs into the marks the gelding had left in the slope. A few blue bog flowers drooped on the slope. Then we were in among the ash and elm. Grody got off. I watched him as he stooped over, then I got off Alice and pulled the reins over her head. Grody was looking at the ground like a wildcat disturbed at kitting time. Scouring the ground with his gaze. He turned over a fern-frond, hardly touching it with fat-tipped fingers which were as delicate on it as if only a butterfly had sat there for one instant. Then he moved on, leading the gelding with one hand hooked into his reins. Looked like a bull calf trying to walk tiptoe, but with something else light and quick and still about him. As I led Alice after him, I felt the forest coolth shadowing around us, rising up into our nostrils. The ground with its layer of leaves burned ahead like French Chantry's dark red hair.

# 5

Being in these woods with Grody was a lonesome feeling. Lonesome and urgent, by spells. There wasn't anything for me to do but follow along for the time being. He was the appointed chief tracker—and so much better than I was at it, that it was best for me only to lead Alice along and trudge at his heels, and not bother him from his work. Other hand, I couldn't keep from wanting him to move faster. Which he didn't. Right off the mark you could tell he would be slow and thorough and dedicated to it, like a plow-horse with its eyes down as it trudges, shearing a single furrow. And around us the woods folded in, so we might have been the first men ever to come in them. Everything would be quiet for a time—the only noise, the sloughing of our mounts' hoofs in the leaf-mast, and the light crunching of our own boots. Then there'd be a clatter from jays ahead of us. And the whir of their wings as they rose and flew ahead to warn the rest of the secret woods of our coming. And sometimes the snort of the mare, or Grody's black gelding. And smaller sounds you could hear as we got farther into the woods. Twigs crackling soft, and a leaf landing with the light touch of an elegant small ship coming to dock. Grody was finding more hoofprints, and working his way inward.

This went on until about noon. I didn't get out the watch, but the sun was straight above us—a long way up past the soaring crowns of these trees. They were dark and magical and dignified trees, looking down on us a long distance from their lofty heights, their topmost boughs where some of the bright-painted leaves still hung, stirring only a trifle in the slow air up there. You couldn't smell the river now. Just the thick, rich, teeming scent of forest itself. And sometimes as we went along there was the high scent of crushed mint underfoot, and the dark raw smell of the humus under all these layers of leaves, which had fallen here for generations. In some places the great oaks grew so close together there was only a kind of lane where Grody could go ahead of me, stooping over with his swagging belly close to the ground, and leading the black gelding so the gelding's reins almost brushed the ground-leaves.

We moved on like that for another couple of hours. I was getting hungry again, sharp-set. Both horses were sweating quiet, even though they were hardly doing anything but inching along. Grody had just straightened up to ease his back and was leaning against the trunk of a stunted gumwood. I looked at him past the black gelding's flank and said, "You like something to eat? I've got some extra if you want it."

First time I'd talked to him since we'd come into the woods. Which seemed a powerful time ago now. My voice sounded faraway and puny here under these massy oaks.

He looked at me as though he'd forgotten all about my being with him. And wasn't too overjoyed about finding I was still there. Little eyes squinching, and sweat bunching on his forehead and down his nose. "I got my own grub, Broome." He glanced up where the sun was a ball of light you could just see through the skeins of topmost branches. "It's a mite past two o'clock. Reckon I might have a bite." He had a small, fat saddlebag hung on the black gelding's pommel. He went to it and opened the flap. And pulled out half a rhubarb pie, a flask of fresh water wrapped in fern—the fern looking crushed and cool around the flask—and four thick chunks of bread, and a slab of side-meat wrapped in butcher-cloth. And then an ironware plate and a knife and fork and spoon. He took all these things over between the roots of an oak with jewel green moss shining along the root-knuckles, settled himself down and started in eating. I turned to the mare and opened up one of my bags and got out some of my pone and a few strings of jerky. The pone was dry and the jerky was even dryer. I tried not to watch Grody, but couldn't help hearing him take a good long swig of his water from time to time. So after a time I turned my head to him. "Think we're catching up on her any?"

He mulled that over, while he tucked food away and washed it down. Didn't think he was going to answer, then he did.

"Hard telling. May take a day and a half. She could be clear down over the Alabama line by now. Unless she's put your horse in a deadfall and busted his leg or lamed him bad."

You fat son of a bitch, I thought. It's what you'd like to have happened.

I swallowed the last of my jerky-portion. Said, "I would appreciate it if you'd let me have enough water just to wet my whistle."

"Christ. You didn't bring any water of your own?"

"There's always water here and there on the road. Didn't see the need for it."

"Man can go a long while without water, Broome. Longer than you think. And lick the dew from the ground-leaves come nightfall. We'll hit the creek later on. It meanders through here in a good many places."

I swallowed, and kept my voice level. "You going to give me a drink?"

He took his time about it. Capped the flask very slow. And then lifted it and threw it over to me. I caught it. As I uncapped it, he said, "Don't go swilling much of it. It's mine. You can get yours with the horses when we come to the creek."

The water tasted like cedar. I reckoned it came from a cedar bucket let down in a stone well. When I was finished, I plugged the flask again and tossed it back to him. He caught it with a slap in one heavy, meaty hand. Then he finished up the rest of his meal and wiped crumbs from his mouth and heaved himself up and went back to his bag and stuffed the plate and the utensils away, and shut the bag-flap. And then he took up the black gelding's reins again and bent over, examining sumac leaves, moving away from me. The water-flask now bulging one of his pockets. I reckoned he thought I might get at it in his bag when his back was turned. I told myself right then that I wouldn't ask him for another drink even if I fell on my face and expired before we reached the creek.

The shadows of night came in here much faster than they would have come out in the open. They made blue and gray swamps of darkness around us between the trees. The moss changed color from bright to soft green and the trunks of the oaks stood showing in just dapples of the long light searching down from above. Now and then one of the heavy webs of Spanish moss drooped so low it would shroud the heads of the horses as they went through it, and they would twitch their ears back and then cant them forward when they were past the dragging, dry, feathery clutch of it. I was sick unto the gut of looking mainly at Grody's ass in his stained pants as he strained their seams and went crouching and finding more sign. So for a long time now I had kept looking all around us—to north and south and east and west as far as I could see through the aisles of trees. I kept telling myself that with one of these looks I would see Grayboy with his hide shining in the secret light and Miss French Chantry up on him and gazing along at me with her gray and silver and amber eyes wide. But I didn't. I did see a herd of what might have been a dozen deer, once—a buck and his does and the fawns all floating along as silent as the hushed light itself, all those little hoofs making much less noise than the breath in my body, all the deer-hides catching streaks of light in gold and ginger-root red, and then all of them gone as if they'd been a thought instead of a plain fact. Later there was a drumming on a log off to what I thought would be the north, and I nearly drew Grody's attention to it before I caught myself up and reasoned it was probably a woodcock and that he knew well enough what it was. As sundown went on deepening the shadows in here, there was a whirring from just above the treetops and, looking up, head back, I could see a flock of pigeons making a giant fan up there—passenger pigeons, all thrusting themselves along and darkening the sky for a time. Grody must have heard their thunder, but he didn't even look up. When they were gone I kept looking where they'd been. Their wing-thunder reminded me of the thunder of hoofs on a trotting track and made me sick and mad and almost lonesomer than I'd yet been.

The sun had gone under and the ghost of moonrise was showing in here by the time Grody quit for the night. I could just see a ball of sweat drip from his nose as he raised himself and stretched. A squirrel chirruped from a bough just above him as if daring him to get out his carbine and aim. Shadowy in the coming dark around us—you do feel boxed-in in a woods at night; you can hear motion all around you but you can't tell just what's making it—the horses tossed their heads, and Alice gave a little nicker.

Grody sounded as if he was talking to himself, not for my benefit at all. "We're maybe three miles in, not much farther. Far as I can make out, she's aiming for the creek. Or was when she rode this far, anyhow. Seems to've sort of zigzagged back and forth on this side of it. Why, the great God above knows." Then he was talking to me plain enough. "You can make yourself useful, Broome. Unsaddle these horses and take their gear off and lead 'em about sixty feet straight past that silver birch with the lightning-mark on it. The creek's over there. Don't try to steal 'em because I'll find you if you do, if a bear don't get you first. Here." He threw his flask over to me. "Fill that up too, after you've watered the horses. We'll bed down here and be started again in first-light. You got more of your grub?"

"Sure," I said.

"That's good, it saves the county money. I got more of mine. You got grub for your Goddamned Standardbred in them saddlebags?"

"I have," I said.

"Good. Saves the county more money. You can feed Alice when you get back." He stumped over closer to me. His jaw spread like the side of a double-bitted ax. "I'll feed my own horse. Get movin', Broome."

I unsaddled Alice, and then the black gelding, and put the saddlebags, my own and Grody's, alongside the saddles. Then I unbitted both horses, leaving their bridles loose, and took their reins and started away. Grody was already scraping together twigs and brush for a small fire. I could see the silver birch with the lightning-mark on it and when I'd led the horses past it a few yards I could smell the water ahead in the leafy dark. Alice nickered again and the black gelding came up faster. I patted their noses and told them it wouldn't be long now. Owls were starting to make hunting noises in the boughs. Then I could see the creek, starshine and a moonglint showing in it. It wasn't more than a few yards wide here. The grasses on its brink were long and arching and the water was clear and about two feet deep over the sand. The sand with clear bright-washed stones in it. I let go of the reins and Alice and the black gelding thrust their heads down and started drinking. Their drinking made deep satisfying sounds. When they'd had enough I pulled their heads up, and, reins bunched in my hand, led them a little way off and tied them to an oak-sucker. Then I went back to the creek and sank Grody's flask in it, the stopper out and the water filling the flask in small bubbling gurgles. I took off my hat and leaned far over, sticking my head deep into the water and feeling as if I was letting it wash away all sight and sound of Grody. Then I sat back and cupped my hands and drank. It was even better than the cedar-tinged water that had been in Grody's flask.

When I was through drinking and straightening up again I saw the raccoon. It was crouched on a flat stone on the other side of the creek. Face smart as a mountebank peddler, eyes not scared at all. Black hands as small as a baby's as it dabbled them in the creek. I stood up higher and it took its time turning around and moving off. With one look back at me over its shoulder. I wondered if it might have given Grayboy and Miss French Chantry the same sort of wide-open look. I was thinking of what Grody had said about her heading for the creek but zigzagging back and forth this side of it.

Then I saw something on the other side of the creek waving gentle in the first of the night breeze. Could have been low-hanging Spanish moss, but somehow even from here it didn't seem to have the same texture. At first I thought I'd let it go, then I thought I wouldn't. I jumped the creek.

I knew it was her cloak even before I'd lifted it off the snag it was hanging by. It had been hanging fairly high—about the height it might have been if she'd been wearing it while riding here. The old cloth was easy to the fingers as butter. I wondered if she'd lost it, or had hung it here on purpose. Maybe being close by and even hearing Grody tell me to water the horses and knowing I might find the cloak here and know she was nearby. I had the sense of her being near. But when I gazed around there was nothing like her in sight. Told myself I was only fancying things. But here was her cloak, in my hand.

I said out loud, "Miss Chantry?"

Not a human sound answered. Down the creek a couple of frogs were beginning to sound off from their bellies.

Could feel something watching, waiting.

I said, quiet but plain, "Miss Chantry. If you're round about here, you'll have to give me another sign. If you want me to help you and don't want Grody to know, you'll have to wait till he's asleep. But let me know then."

Felt foolish, making that speech to the empty air. But I'd have felt worse not making it.

I folded the cloak and stuffed it under my shirt. Then I stepped back across the creek and pulled the flask out of the water and capped it again, and went over to Alice and the black gelding. Untied them, and started leading them back where I'd come. Looking back over my shoulder I could see nothing out of the way. The creek-side melted behind me into the night. I reckoned I should be thinking about telling Grody about the cloak. If she'd just naturally lost it, it would help him go on trailing her faster in the morning. But if it was a signal of some kind just meant for me I wanted to know that too.

So I kept the cloak out of sight. Grody's little fire was going fine now. He'd already eaten some more of his sumptuous and no doubt fine-tasting food—he was stuffing the ironware plate and the utensils back in his bag. I tied Alice and the gelding a little way off to a low oak-branch and came back to the firelight and out of my own saddlebag got some more jerky and chewed on it. I put the flask with Grody's gear. He belched and walked away from the fire. Came back in about three minutes, buckling his belt up. He got a sack of oats out of his bag, and went over to the black gelding. I got one of Grayboy's oat-sacks from one of my bags, and walked over and sprinkled it down for Alice. When we'd come back inside the wavering circle of light and put the sacks away, Grody had his knife out. He stooped and stropped it a little on the flank of a boot. Knife about the size of the one Daddy had left me, with a deerhorn haft. He balanced the knife on his palm, drew back his arm. The knife sailed out of firelight and glanced off the silver birch trunk and fell into the leaves. He went to get it. When he got back I had my knife out. I balanced it on my hand, then drew back and let it go. I had a little luck. Or maybe I was just so tired of him and so quiet-mad I had to make the knife obey me. It stuck well into the silver birch. I went to get it.

I didn't even look at him to see how he'd taken it. Neither of us had said a word.

By the time I'd come back to the fireside with the knife, he was wrapped in a ground-spotted green blanket, head turned away, liplets of fire shining on the butt of his carbine where it lay near him in its scabbard. Didn't say so much as good night.

I lay down on the other side of the fire and folded my arms against the night coolth. I looked straight up through the lofty crowns of the huge trees at the beginning stars.

The horses had finished their feed and were chewing on what grasses there were near them.

The noises of the night were sounding all around here.

I touched the bulk of the cloak under my shirt.

Sleep was the farthest thing from me.

# 6

Grody started snoring. It was a rolling absolute snore, not restless. The kind that tells you a body is in full sleep.

I sat up. I took the turnip-watch out, opened its case and in a slant of light read the time, which was about nine-thirty. I'd thought it to be much later; being in a woods does that to you too; it transfigures time.

I put the watch back, and stood up. Walked, soft enough, over around beside Grody. In the same slants of light drifting down through oak-boughs, his face looked silver-soft as an old grandmother's. Eyebrows weren't even beetling now. I reckoned he might be having good dreams—possibly of throttling me and finding his lady love, Miss French. Maybe in his dreams she was being kind to him and consenting to be courted and even married to him. At least, I thought, he sure stayed loyal to her even after being turned down as Sheriff Planteu had told me he'd been. You could hardly find anybody more loyal than Grody Flieshacker unless you bought a watchdog and trained it to bite all outlanders.

I made my way to my saddle and my bags, lifted them and walked over to Alice. I saddled her again and tightened the bridle straps and got the bit in firm. Then I slung the bags up, saw that the boxwood case was riding well, and came around and led her off into the slow-dancing shadows. In the little firelight that reached here, Grody's black gelding, still tied to the oak-bough in a loose rein, looked around at us and walled his eyes as if he'd like to come along.

I headed past the lightning-touched silver birch, Alice following with her hoofs not making much noise through fern, and led her across the creek.

When we got on the other side, I mounted. I was almost under the oak where I'd found Miss French's cloak. I looked around, and said clear enough—knowing Grody couldn't hear me back at the dying fireside—"All right, Miss Chantry. Now Grody's asleep. And if you were trying to tell me somethin'—if you hung your cloak here for me to find—I'm all at your service and available."

Again it seemed a foolish speech, made to the gathering air. But not foolish along the lines of what I was feeling. Sheriff Planteu had said Miss French Chantry might well be about some special errand of her own. He'd said she knew these woods well. I reckoned it was possible that not all the watching and waiting I'd felt during the whole day and part of this night had come from beasts and birds of the wild. I said, also clear, "And if you're listening, I'm not mad. I've gone through being mad and now all I am is hoping. If you hear me, please understand I'm yearning to get my horse back and will forgive you, gentleman's honor, if you'll just hand him over and let me go on my way. Whatever you may be about that needs a horse for the doing, you can accomplish with Alice, here."

There wasn't any answer but the creek purling along with a quick low voice. And more owls hooting not far away.

Then I saw her. One second, she was there off to what I judged to be north—the North Star shone far up there above us through the crowded treetops—and next second, she was gone. But not before letting me see her, and on purpose. She stood alongside a tree in the bright-beating moonlight. Not a ghost or a flicker of my imagination. The dove-gray dress gleaming, her head back, the soft dark red hair burning in its free glory. Her eyes on me. In the same wonderful second I saw she had a willow basket over her arm.

And in the tail end of the selfsame second, I was urging Alice after her. I couldn't hear anything but more of the night-noises above the thump and flurry of Alice's hoofs. I was having to guide her in and among the oaks and up a small slope. Then around a stand of sycamore and over a fallen oak that leaned here on the ground as if it had been toppled by a giant in his careless passage. And it wasn't till Alice and I came out in a strong flood of moonlight onto a ride between oaks—a kind of natural, wide aisle where the ground was flecked with light and shadow—that I caught sight of Miss French Chantry again.

And of Grayboy.

He was going easy, not even into a gait, just a steady walk under dribbles of light in the center of the ride. She was handling him well even if all she had was a hackamore. It came to me that if somebody else had to ride him it was good that it was her. She was so small on him that she might have been a jockey on a kind of mountain. I slapped Alice on the neck and leaned to her. She wasn't bred for racing and I didn't intend to make her balk as Sheriff Planteu had warned she might. But she was tired of trailing through leaves all day and glad to be let out a little. She picked up into a kind of amiable canter, and I called, "Miss Chantry! Damn it, ma'am!"

This time I saw her better as she turned without checking Grayboy. She wasn't sidesaddle; I doubt that she'd ever ridden that strange ladylike way in her life. The willow basket hung from the crook of her left arm. She gave me that same touch of a loving smile that had drifted over her face back in the stable the night before. And with her right hand, motioned for me to keep following. Same instant, she clucked to Grayboy and he gathered himself and started to stride out. He wasn't yet driving, but he would drive for her. I knew the feeling as well as I knew the power in his laid-back shoulders and long-muscled hocks.

Then Grayboy and Miss Chantry, he in that creamy gait that could cover miles when you were on his back, or change to a ground-eating pace when you were behind him in a sulky, were out of sight under a wedge of tree-shadow laid over this avenue of leaves. I rode into it, and out of it, and there they were again—well ahead of me. Nothing to do but grit my teeth, bide my time, and go along with her pleasure. I thought of chirruping to Grayboy, or giving the whistle that was just between us, man to horse, and that nobody else knew. Didn't seem much sense in doing that, either. He was well under her command, I didn't want him confused and skittish because of me.

The avenue or ride or aisle was widening out now. The oaks and sycamores and gum trees and cottonwoods farther back from it. I could tell now it had been made here, this long thoroughfare of good riding ground in the deep of the forest, some time in days of yore when a forest fire had ravaged here. Maybe even before the Indians came, when the forest had never felt the touch of man. The fire had gone in a belt north to south, and no heavy growth had ever come up in the place of what had first been here. The ground had a pulpy sound under Alice's hoofbeats, as if it was all burned out and mushroomlike beneath the skift of leaves. Rich growth came right up to it, then ceased. It was a witching ground, swallowing Grayboy's hoofs that would ring on most roads.

After a while I began catching glimpses of Miss Chantry and Grayboy again. This wide secret pathway curved farther south; a scarflike mist floated across it in patches, and I could smell the creek. Then later, it wasn't only the creek nearby; it was the Lanceton River with its heavier, smoky late fall and nighttime smell; and I could see it where the trees thinned out to the westward. Just a black bronze glimpse of it now and again, flowing unruffled to the south past those trees. I reckoned we were on the same side of the woods where Grody and I had come across. But a good bait farther along.

Ahead the witch-track where the fire had cut through in those bygone times ended. Just a wall of first-growth oaks in front of me. Looked as heavy as the canebrake of the Natchez Trace, where many a traveler had been sunk without a sign. Vines that had been poison green but were going sere with the falltime hung down the trunks of the oaks. I reined in Alice, sat staring into the vines, then heard Miss French Chantry's voice.

Wasn't far ahead of me. And just as pleasing as I'd remembered.

"Ride straight ahead, Mister Broome. You'll come out in a moment."

I stroked Alice's neck, a skin of sweat on it. And put her into the vines.

We crashed into that limbo—she was a willing mare, Planteu had been right to call her a good one—and for a tangle of time, the vines were brushing around us, leaves rough-edged on my face and nearly sweeping my hat off. Then in another trice we were out of that. Blinking, man and mare.

For we'd come out into moonlight blazing on a hillside. The hill swept down from us in short grasses to a long line of white well-painted fencing. On our right the river rolled along, much wider here than it had been at the fording place near Lanceton. Straight ahead past the beautiful fencing was the yard of a plantation house. The house on a little knoll beyond it, overlooking the river. The house looked as still as if it had been made of white marble, instead of white boarding. Its windows held no touch of light. Behind it stretched stables—not the broken-down stable of Chantry Hall, but a line of stables facing inward to a dark compound where tulip trees grew around the slave cabins. All as furbished and shined as though it was a gift carved for pleasurable sight from the darkness.

I drew my eyes back from that.

Miss French Chantry had turned Grayboy; she and he were facing me. He had his head up, nostrils working, neck stretched in its high, long arch. I slid off Alice. Went over to Grayboy. In the pouring, plain light I could see he had no marks to show he'd been lifted and ridden hard. He was sweating lightly but his breathing was steady. I didn't look up to Miss Chantry, who stayed on him. I went to his off fore, lifted the hoof, looked at the plate. Then to his near fore. Then to his off rear, then the near rear. I came around and looked at his knees.

Not till then did I stare up.

Miss Chantry was looking down at me—reflective, it seemed, even comfortable. She patted him, and said, "He's a glad horse, Mister

Broome. The most joyous I ever rode. If he was a man he might die of being valiant."

"I'm a man," I said after a few seconds. "And I thought I might die of him bein' missing."

"I'm well aware of that, Mister Broome. May I call you Tom? For I think you're my friend." And as I nodded, "Well, Tom, you'll have to take my apologies for granted. I needed Grayboy sorely, and I took him without asking you first." Her voice so light and round, and purposeful beneath its quiet. "I had a great shock last night. Finding Gary Willis stone-dead at the foot of my staircase."

"Yes, ma'am," I said. Then, "Yes, Miss French." First time I'd called her by that. I reckoned I had the right now, and she didn't say I didn't. I had a hand on Grayboy's hackamore rope. He was curving around toward Alice now, and snorting. Alice stood where she was. "But if you knew he was dead—yes, I know he was your cousin twice removed, I know he was blind mean to you, I've heard a good deal of that—if you knew he was dead, why did you ride for Doc Mattison and tell Mattison there might be life in him yet? And you say 'last night.' Didn't you find him pretty shortly after midnight? That's when I heard what could have been a shot fired, just as I was falling to sleep. Why didn't you ride for Mattison *then*?"

That was two questions. French Chantry didn't look to me as though she'd have any trouble handling more than two.

She swung the willow basket, light on her arm. It had creek-cress in it, nesting on something else. Fresh cress, delicate green and toothsome.

"I found him at about the time you mentioned. It wasn't until toward morning that I rode to get Doctor Mattison. By then I'd had the chance to make up my mind about what I had to do." I was looking up right into her eyes. Their amber was strongest now, mixed into the silver gray in sparks, as if she was a cat. "I told Roy—Doctor Mattison—I hadn't shot Gary. Which is the truth, Tom. I did not shoot him. I also told him to hurry on out there because Gary might still be alive. That was a lie, Tom. I told it because I knew Doctor Mattison would summon Will Planteu, and that they would move the body, and even in death, I loathe Gary Willis so much I wanted him out of Chantry Hall as swiftly as could be." There was a small pause then. Grayboy was used to Alice now; he wasn't snorting at her anymore. "Can you understand that, Tom?"

"Sure," I said. And I could. I said, "Sheriff Planteu said something— when we were talkin' in town, after Doc Mattison and I'd stopped in to see him and tell him about Willis, and about you being missing with my horse. He said you might've taken Grayboy because you had some kind of high mission to accomplish. Do you? And—do you know who shot Willis?''

That was two more questions.

"Well, Tom. I do have a mission."

I waited.

"And I'm not certain who shot Gary. I'll tell you what I know."

She got off Grayboy, the willow basket still on her arm. Got off him so fast and neat there wasn't time for me to give her a hand-step down. I wouldn't have minded it; the small, ancient ballroom slippers—looked as if they'd been danced in, last, maybe on the eve of Chancellorsville—would have been kindly to my hands.

She took a step or two, and stretched. From the plantation house below us came no sound, even though it still wasn't as late as it felt. Her nipped-in waist and the fine tits looked marvelous against the thread-worn dress as she stretched.

"Gary was in Chantry Hall, alive, when I went back to the stable to look at my poultry, and heard you riding in across the meadow. He was drunk. He could never hold wine, or any spirits. He had ridden over from Fountainwood to pay me this uncalled-for visit. I must admit he made some uncommonly foul suggestions. Which I did not favor. I also admit that I threatened him with my weapon—that little old derringer. When I returned from assisting you with Grayboy, he was still there, however. I hoped devoutly he would go back to Fountainwood, sleep off his drunkenness and meditate on his sins. By this time he was sitting on one of those chairs in the vestibule . . . did you go into Chantry Hall this morning, Tom?''

I nodded.

"Then you know where he was. He didn't see me put the derringer away. Nor did he know where it was kept. I keep it in the lion's head—there's a sort of little cache there in the newel post. You press the lion's eyes and the head swings out. Daddy loved such things. And then—'' She was gazing away from me, down the hill to where the clean-painted fence ran back from the white, hushed plantation house. "Then I went on up the stairs, and to my room. Very shortly after I had reached my room, I heard a shot. From downstairs. I returned to the upstairs hall, and went down. I saw Gary, dead. And I saw Jupiter—

Gary's bodyservant, who I reckon had followed Gary over from Fountainwood—duck back inside the ballroom door, and heard him go out of a window, and then heard the hoofs going away. Only—it's puzzling—I would swear I heard *two* sets of hoofbeats instead of one. As if there were two horses."

She shook her head, making her hair shimmer like many dark torches in one.

"Jupiter was once our servant. As were all the others now at Fountainwood, who used to work at Chantry Hall. I called out to him, but he didn't stop. When I ran out of the front door—it was open, and it has never been locked in my lifetime—there was no one in sight. I went back in, and I was remembering what Jupiter had told me not long before. That if ever anything happened to Gary, he and the rest of our old nigra friends would burn Fountainwood." She shrugged a little. "They consider it the house of the Devil, you see. They say Gary has—had—evil powers. It may be superstition, but I don't know. No man who wasn't in league with some sort of darkness could have spread ruin around the countryside as he did. Or could have ground the spirits of his own kind so into the dust, ever since Reconstruction." Again her shoulders went up and down. "That's as may be. When Jupiter says he'll do something, he does it. And as I looked down at the body of Gary, all this went through my head. I formed a plan, quite slowly."

A hound howled sharp at the moon, from the other side of the river. It was miles off.

"That's the Morgan's hound. I stopped there early this morning just after I'd ridden through Lanceton. I borrowed a sack of oats for Grayboy, and some biscuits to sustain me. Mister Toddy Morgan is bedridden—he was Daddy's aide-de-camp; he doesn't ask questions . . . but I'm getting ahead, Tom. I was telling you about my plan. It was to rescue my merry-go-round."

She was talking straight to me again, and the slow smile drifted across her mouth, especially at the lip-corners.

"You'll think I'm moon-touched—I'm not, though living by one's self does put peculiar ideas into one's mind from time to time. The merry-go-round—carousel, or flying jenny—is hundreds of years old. Daddy and Mama gave it to me for my seventh birthday. It was one of the last things I'd been forced to sell Gary—a few months ago. I reckon you'd love it; it's a gladsome thing. It has just eight horses, and it's small and I think quite valuable. It came from Florence, Italy, where Mama and Daddy were visiting before the war. It has wheels on it; you can draw it along like a cart.''

"A horse could draw it, then," I said.

"Yes, Tom. And that came into my plan, too. I knew if I took Grayboy from you for a time—borrowing him, in what I consider a good cause, even though you think I'm a fanatic about my merry-go-round—I'd have to hide up in the woods during the day, because of the hue and cry about him being gone, and the hue and cry about Gary's death. But I knew, too, I could visit Fountainwood tonight.''

"Before the nigras burn it," I said.

"Yes. I was afraid they might burn it before now. But I've been watching it from back in the woods, on and off, all day. And they've loaded a lot of wagons up, and a lot of them have gone off—I reckon they'll have to go north to find work, there isn't anything more for them around this part of the country in these times. But Jupiter's still in there.''

I said, slower than she had, ''And you had an eye on Grody Flieshacker and me. Even when we were fording the river. And you've kept watch on us ever since. And you tolled me along tonight by hanging the cloak where I'd see it. Maybe if I hadn't seen it—''

''—I'd have made myself known to you some other way, Tom. I need your help. Just a short time ago, I heard you call out to me that you weren't angry any longer. That if you could have Grayboy back you were at my service and available. I might have gone to Sheriff Will for help—but I don't know if I'd get it, for something he might regard as a whim. I love him and Roy Mattison and Howard Markley—he's the teacher in Lanceton—and Marcus Westerfield, the mayor. And even Grody, in a way. But they do keep watch on me as though they were so many hawks. Thinking I can do no wrong. This—plan of mine—which I took so long thinking up, and which didn't solidify till early this morning—it might've horrified them.''

Her lower lip was out. "I've got to have my merry-go-round back, Tom. Whole and unburned. It's the last fetching joy out of all the old days.''

"Besides," I said, "if you'd gone straight to Planteu, you'd have had to tell him Jupiter probably killed Gary Willis. And you didn't want to do that, did you? Did you check in this hidin' place in the newel-post lion to see if the derringer'd been fired, by the way? Or have you still got it with you under that basket of cress?''

I was asking three questions this time.

She lifted the cress. Under it was what was left of a short sack of oats. Nothing else. She snipped off a piece of cress and held it to me. "It's very good, Tom. A person might live in the woods a long time without starving. I love the woods; I have since Daddy took me there when I was little."

I ate the cress. It still tasted as fresh as the creek water itself.

She said, "It was still there in its cache. The derringer. But it had been fired . . . I don't know if Jupiter did it or not, but if he didn't, he might have seen who did the killing. He's had enough trouble in his life, I don't want to give him any more. He'll help me get the merry-go-round hitched up, but that's enough for him to do. Then I have to transport it across the bridge and back to Chantry Hall. No one has to know it's back. I'll lock it in the ballroom at Chantry. I have to do all this tonight, Tom, and then, I suppose, spin some tale for my friends—though I detest doing it—while you go off to the Yadkin races."

"Yes," I said low. "I can see all this is a matter of time. And has been from the time your plan started spinnin'."

She didn't say, "Will you help me." She was only half gazing at me, the rest of her attention was on the plantation house. Which of course was Fountainwood. Still didn't appear to me a place for devil-worship or dark monkeyshines, all brilliant there and cool in the light.

I squared my shoulders. Said, "Well, I've already lost a day of going along to Yadkin Fair."

I unpinned the badge Sheriff Planteu had fixed to my shirt after swearing me in as a deputy. I thrust it in a side pocket. I hoped Grody Flieshacker was sleeping most sweetly. And would for the rest of the night, and maybe oversleep to boot.

Then—I couldn't help it—I took her by the shoulders, skin like warm velvet and smooth beside the neckline of that decrepit but nice old dress. I drew her to me. Her lips didn't answer much, they were just there. Her hair clouded around and brushed my face. She felt wiry and solid and yearning and dedicated, all of her. I stepped back, and took my hands away.

Caught just a touch of the lights shining in her eyes.

"We have hardly time for that, Tom."

She sounded cool as the cress whose taste was still on my tongue.

I said, "No ma'am. No, French. Maybe you've never had time for that. Living poor and being proud."

"I think we'll save this discussion for another time."

I gave a nod. "I'm a gentleman born, as you said last night. You stay on Grayboy—you've done right well with him so far. I'll take Alice. Reckon we should ride right up to the front door and knock?"

"I don't want to frighten Jupiter. We'll go around the back. I've never been inside. But I think I could find my way."

It fell in my brain to tell her I thought she could find her way through Hades, and get her way as well. But I didn't say it. I gave her a hand up on Grayboy, and the little ballroom slipper felt just as kindly to my hand as I'd thought it would. I hoped my daddy wasn't looking at me from somewhere in horseman's heaven. He'd have been cussing like the guns roaring in the Wilderness. I went around and got on Alice again and took up her reins and nodded toward French. She was off down the slope for the fence ahead of me by twenty feet.

# 7

She aimed for the fence dead ahead. I knew Grayboy could take it. I reckoned she'd put him over a few fallen logs that day. She was at the fence. He lifted like a powerful gray wave. Clearing the top rail by a clean two feet. She rode him tight and pleasing, bringing him down again without stopping the motion at all, as if he'd been water and had flowed over the fence-rail in one clear arch and was now flowing straight on.

I wasn't so sure of Alice. And she was carrying all my gear. But it was too late to check her now. For the bite of a second I thought she'd balk and could hear Sheriff Planteu's voice in my ears. Then we were over, maybe leaving a scurf of horsehair on the rail we'd brushed, but whole and without real fault. I put Alice back alongside the fence toward where I could hear Grayboy still going, though I couldn't see him. He was in shadow now.

On our right was the bulk of the house. A house even bigger than Chantry Hall. Much newer as well. With not a board out of place or a shake-shingle loose. With its paint as scrubbed as if it was all white swan-feathers. All the windows on this side still blank and dark.

Reflecting the scudding pictures of Alice and me in their black panes as we whipped by against the moonlight. Eight columns in the front as there were at Chantry.

Ahead, I heard Grayboy stop and stamp once on the brick flooring of the stable and cabin compound. His plate rang like a bell and sparked in the shadows. Then I heard him snort. I checked Alice and went on through the shadows under tulip trees leaking light through their boughs. Drew her up alongside Grayboy. French was off Grayboy and had tied the hackamore rope to one of the tulips' boughs. It was all freckled with swimming light under here. I got off Alice and tied her. Said, soft, "No coffee coolers or bummers came through here in the war. Nobody's ever raided this place."

"No, Tom." Her voice at my shoulder. "Even before the war was over, I believe Gary had an understanding with the North. Of course his understanding flowered and bore fruit after Mister Lincoln died and that Johnson came in. And sent that unspeakable damned Thaddeus Stephens to throttle us."

I'd never heard her swear before. Came out smooth and yet with fire backing it. Could see just a portion of her face now, eyes and mouth and the sweep of hair glinting.

Came to me how much she must resemble her father. Her mother of course on the wonderful well-coupled body side, but her father in the shine of her eyes. As if she was somehow fighting a war that'd been over a good while. Helping send the South straight through to the front steps of the White House in Washington. Which after all was where they'd just about gone, and would have if it hadn't been for Jefferson Davis's holding back that time.

I brushed back tulip twigs. Peered out. This summer cookhouse was brick, like the stables and the cabins and the rest of the compound. A gallery wound around the back of the house. Nearby were the stables. I could smell well-cared-for horse cut over by the scent of old honeysuckle with that earthy lingering scent it keeps even after it's dead. A lantern burned low in one of the stables. Its door hung open. I peered harder. Could see the black shining rump of a horse seemed to be tethered in a loose-box. The door of the box was open too.

I was working the cloak out from under my shirt. I handed it to French, finding her hands in the shadow. "You need this more than I do, Miss French. Much as I might like to keep it as a memento when I'm away from here and on my way to Yadkin. Reckon it's a keepsake."

"It was Mama's. She's been gone a long while."

"Doc Mattison told me."

"I wear her clothes sometimes. She had trunkfuls. And they become me more than the few common dresses I can afford. Are you feeling compunctions, Tom? Or second thoughts? I assure you I have no recourse but to reclaim my merry-go-round. He paid me very little for it."

"Oh, Lord," I breathed. "Miss French, if I wanted to back out I'd have done it before this. Stop that, you fool!"

I was talking to Grayboy with this last. He'd edged near me and brought his head down and taken my hat off with his teeth. He didn't do it every day, but always thought it was a very comical trick. I groped for my hat and he edged back. I brushed past French, feeling the softness of her tits and the smooth line of her belly along my arm as I reached, as if I'd touched fire in the earth. Got my hat and brushed it off and put it on. Battered but friendly, only hat I had.

She'd laughed a little at this. Not a nervous laugh. Just the way you'd laugh in the field of war if you were set to attack and somebody fell over his own boot-tips.

But now she was quiet. Peering along with me. There were more tulip trees and some ailanthus growing around the back gallery.

She'd put the cloak on but left its hood down. She beckoned as she stepped out into the stronger light ahead of me. I followed. We went past the stables and cabins. There wasn't a fallen leaf on the bricks. Behind us Grayboy and Alice shifted a little. The back gallery steps were at one end of the gallery. Not square in the middle as at Chantry Hall. Along the gallery were rocking chairs taking night-mist on their seats. Frosted and dead wistaria vines climbed some of the gallery uprights. Wasn't the squeak of sound from any of the cabins or from that one horse I'd seen in the stables.

French climbed the gallery steps. I'd caught up with her now. She walked along to the door. My boot soles and arches were making ungodly noise, I still hadn't had time to tallow them. Tried walking on the balls of my feet but it didn't help greatly. But I thought maybe it didn't matter because French already had her thumb on the back door latch. The door opened and swallowed her up in blackness. Then it gulped me. I shut it soft behind us.

After a few blinks I could see her outline against a window. We were in a mammoth kitchen. Could make out the black shine of a range and the upper curves of plates along a sideboard rail. Could smell herbs and the ghosts of cooking. A chimney with benches set either side of it showed on my right. The chimney stones had a cool flinty scent as I went close to them. French was past the chimney, opening a door. Soon as she had it ajar, light sluiced in.

It fell over her slippers and part of her dress around the knees and touched the black cloak hems. Then she was opening it wider, with me beside her. The light fell over her face. Her eyes were wide and waiting. Had those cat sparks in them again as if they drew all the light. "There's our dining set," she said soft. "It came from France."

This was a very lengthy room. You could just about have held a flat race in it. The kitchen had been floored with wide-sawed pegged oak. This room had carpets with patterns mingling in pale gold green and ivory and in peacock-feather swirls under our feet. The table stretched a considerable way. The chairbacks were pretty and fluid as the bosoms of women wearing pinched-in corsets. Crystal glasses glittered on another sideboard. Behind us from the little serving pantry we'd come through near the kitchen I thought I heard a sigh. But when I gazed back there was nothing. In the shine of the moon through the dining room windows you could have heard a leaf crisp off from a tree and come rocking down easy.

She went ahead of me again now. On the waxen silky floors between the carpets my boots sounded louder than ever to me. But French was moving like a fish in tranquil waters. Opening another door—this time into a hall. And at the end of the hall—I noted a portrait on the wall of the hall as I passed; in the modest light it appeared to be of a naked woman being butted, or I hoped nothing worse than butted, by a black goat—at the end of this hall, she was opening yet another door. She said just under my chin as I stopped behind her, "Despicable!"

I didn't know if she meant the picture of the woman or something else. The woman had appeared to be enjoying the goat's attentions. But then I saw French meant this room we were now going into. Even more capacious than the dining room and with the floors slicked with light cross-hatched where it fell past the divisions of the panes along the west wall. It was nearly day-bright in here and would have been if it hadn't been for the shadowed staircase to the right and now behind us, as we went in. And for the puddles of shadow at the unwindowed end of the room out of which flickered the shine of piano keys and arched the breast of a gilded harp.

Off to the flank of those instruments, on their raised but low platform, was another chimney. This one in marble done in soft gray and blue slabs with the mantel one stark white pure slab. The mouth of the chimney gaped like a track-tout's jaws. Above the white mantel slab over the throat of the chimney was a carving in marble, glaring down at the whole room and taking what light reached it there to lick its blank eyeballs. It was of Satan, no two doubts about that. He had the regulation horns and ears as long as a Sumpter mule's and pointed. His mouth was laughing as if he'd gone sick with laughing ten thousand years before and still couldn't stop.

The cool boards of the floor stretched away and away under us as if we were standing on the deck of a steamboat five times bigger than the *Robert E. Lee.* I didn't think the ballroom at Chantry Hall where French was going to lock up her merry-go-round—once she got it back—could be half the size of this one. I hoped it wasn't anything like this. For it wasn't a ballroom where, even when there's no dancing in it, you shut your eyes and nearly hear the music gyrating and see the dancers whirl and smell the perfume of the ladies and smile to yourself. It was a place where something knocked at the back of your mind, saying, Get out. As if all the dancing here had been done by creatures grinning deep and aiming to pluck out more than your gizzard. And there was a smell about the place, not strong, just wafting from second to second. Pass a sulphur well and sometimes you get the same thing—though they do say sulphur water is good for the blood.

French's cloak gave a slight rustle. She said, "Desecration!" I could tell now what she was talking about. She was aiming for the merry-go-round. It stood between the chimney and the orchestra platform. I could catch a gleam of its roof—a little roof like a fancy generous umbrella. With a soft gold brilliance. I started along after her. Then halted.

Because I'd heard that sighing behind me again. As I'd heard it from the serving pantry. Goose-flesh started up on my arms. It does that sometimes before a race too, even on warm days. I thought quick about how there were no doubt stairs leading down to the serving pantry from the upper rooms, so Gary Willis—and his guests, but from the feel of this ballroom I didn't want to speculate much about what guests he'd had—could have hot biscuits and tisane in bed on fast notice. And how whoever'd been behind us in the serving pantry might now be on the upper floor. For the sigh had seemed to come from there this time.

The ballroom was a good fifteen feet high. Small swashes of light from the windows touched the ceiling, even so. Showing a lot of ebony heads of imps looking down and sticking out their scarlet-tipped tongues. They were imps, no pickaninny ever looked like that. But the outside light didn't reach back over the balustrade at the top of the stairs.

I studied the blackness up there. Then there came just a flicker of red light.

As if from a lantern carried low and maybe with a hand curved around it so not much of its flame showed.

I kept on gazing up there.

Then a lot of things happened all together. The way they happen in a harness racing tangle when there's a wheel-hook and the horses are plunging and even though it goes like greased fury, you can sort it out as if it was happening slow as hourglass sand.

First thing was that French said, loud, "Keeping it in here, where he entertained his low friends! Where they could laugh at it, and he could exult in his bargain! Despicable!" Same time, the lantern shone strong from the upper landing, swung up high in the hand that held it. And I felt sweat race down from armpits to ribs, and brought my right hand over my knife-haft, and pulled the knife out. And there was a rush and tumble of feet on the stairs, the lantern coming down with it, making a bobbing lake of light on the treads. And French had turned from the merry-go-round and come running back beside me. She saw my knife and held onto my shoulder—fingers tight—and kept my knife-arm down with her other hand. And then the lantern was shining above us, and in moon-and-lantern-light here was a man six feet eight or so—if an inch—with plates of muscle shining in his bare chest. Like suns in a black river. He hoisted the lantern even higher. Stared down at me behind its flame, saying in a low furry voice, about three tones deeper than the bass drum in a silver cornet band, "Greetings, Miss French. Hardly anticipated no visit from you tonight. And bringing along a gentleman friend too. My, my."

His voice was polite as lint falling from a cotton gin. I was blinking. He says, seeing it, "Sorry, young gentleman. Any friend of Miss French's, I wouldn't wish to go blinding."

He set the lantern down with a click and a wash of its coal oil on the smooth floor.

French said, "Jupiter—are you all by yourself here?"

"Yes ma'am. Only old Jupe left." He'd straightened now, looming over us. He was barefoot. His chest hadn't a hair on it. Maybe he wasn't the tallest man I'd ever see, but I reckoned he'd be the strongest. Weighed maybe three hundred without saddle-gear. In the light reaching up from the lantern and from the windows his eyes were dark as old fire-pits. With deep hollows around them. He swung around in the direction of the chimney. Muscles moving in cables along his shoulders and arms. His pants were chopped off just below the knees, and hard-frayed. "I'll just shed some light on us, begging your pardon."

Over at the chimney he was striking a lucifer, bringing up a fork of flame and then higher flame from a big lamp on the mantel. He settled its bowl back and examined its wick, then came walking back to us. Over his shoulder I watched the carved marble face of the Devil grow extra shadows under its bearded chin. The horns appeared to be moving in the lamplight, the mouth opening and shutting a bit. Jupiter said to me, "Ugly, ain't it, sir? Mist' Willis, he admired it a gre't deal. I do beg your pardon for frightin' you, if I done so. I was takin' a few cat winks on the upper balcony, ain't had no sleep since last night when Mist' Willis was took. I heard some soul comin' in by the back, the kitchen way. Crope down the stairs to the pantry, heard people movin' on thu' the house, and went back up the stairs and come out up there. Recognized Miss French's voice just when I'd got down the staircase."

I'd put the knife back in its sheath.

In the cross-light of the lamp and the lantern on the floor and the shining from the windows, French's hair was a dark red lamp all on its own.

She said, "Jupiter, this is Mister Broome. Tom Broome."

He ducked his chin to me. Hadn't a trace of flab under it, all of him glossed as teak oiled a hundred years. There was a light smell of drink around him. "Very pleased, Mist' Broome."

"He's here to help me take my merry-go-round back to Chantry. He knows you're going to burn Fountainwood. It's all right, he wouldn't tell a soul. Unless you've thought different of burning it, and maybe could go on residing in it—*in* it, not back in your cabin—"

Jupiter smiled. "Miss French, bless you—I wouldn't go on livin' here if they made me king of Judah, with trappings of jasper and gold. This house is cursed and damned. Now, I never give thought to your little flyin' jenny—or I'd have got it over to you at the hall at Chantry some time last night. I thought there might be somethin' you'd like, from the old days, among all them dadoes you had to sell to Mist' Willis. But the flyin' jenny didn't cross my mind. See, I been right pressed for time. Mingo and Dabney and all the rest, they've already cleared out. Goin' north, to see what they can see. Gone on their ways grievin' to leave the South land but rejoicin' about the oppressor bein' smote. And I had to help 'em get the wagons ready, and carry off what goods they pleasured to take. Ain't but one horse left in the stables, and I'll take him with me. After the Lord's work is done and the house is scoured to the ground.''

He looked around. ''No, Miss French, not me nor one of them would live in here. Bad enough livin' back in the cabins and workin' here. For me bein' bodyservant to a devil's minion it might be even worse. Had to spend more time in here than they done—they got out in the fields more. Had to serve the tipple while Mist' Willis and his friends put on them dark robes with the signs on them and said the Lord's prayer backward. And killed good hens there on the chimney-hearth, and drank their blood. And then what they done—'' He shook his head. ''I can't tell you 'bout that, Miss French. Can't even tell your gentleman friend, Mist' Broome.'' All at once he raised both arms toward the ceiling. ''Halleloo! Pharaoh's dead and the children delivered from his grindin' heel! We all come out from the fiery furnace!''

French said very quiet, ''Jupiter.''

''Ma'am?'' His arms came down.

''You walked over to Chantry Hall last night. Following Gary. Did you shoot him? I saw you there—I know you went out the ballroom window.''

Jupiter's eyes slid to me.

''Mister Broome won't say a word. I've told you that.''

''No'm, it ain't that, Miss French. I trusts you—with my life, always done so—so I'd trust him likewise. Since you speak for him. It's only—I couldn't have killed him. I was feared to. Mingo and Dabney and Reba and Luther and Nappy and all the rest, they was the same.'' He was looking around again, at the chimney. Turned back to us, then. ''See—it's hard to say—man my size, used to could wrestle any buck in the county, they'd bet on me up and down the Delta—it shames me to say it. But Mist' Willis, he had a spell on us. All of us. We couldn't cross him. He put the spell on us when we first come here, Miss French, time you couldn't keep us no more—time Mist' Willis was first dabblin' in devil-try. Else, you think I wouldn't't've beat him to the ground, placed my foot on his neck and cried, Aha? But—we was *under* him. Couldn't run away, couldn't so much as mumble when he was around to hear. There's spells that *work*, Miss French—Mist' Broome. But the spell is bust', the speller is no more!''

He'd have raised his arms again, and his face, but French stopped him. ''Did you see who shot Gary, then?''

His face changed. It wasn't secret but it went quiet.

"I might've, Miss French. But I can't say it. It's between me and the Lord who brought about my deliverance through this party. Mist' Willis left here last night in the downpour and rode his Arab horse Robin over to Chantry Hall. I followed along over the bridge, far enough behind so he couldn't see. I can still run fast as a colt in spring, and Mist' Willis' wasn't seein' too well, or ridin' too straight. Thought he might do harm to you, Miss French. He'd been talkin' like it."

"And you risked his spell—his hex—for me?"

"Yes'm." He said it simple as grass. "If he'd have laid hand on you, wantin' you to marry him as he done, I'd have done away with him and been consigned to the place of the eternal worm and the flame that undieth. But I didn't have to. It was done for me. And when it was done, I cut out thu' the ballroom and raised the window there and jumped out, and ran around and got on Robin and rode back here. And called thanks to the Lord every foot of the way. And roused up all the people, and told 'em. And we rejoiced, the rest of the night and half today. I was elected to set the fire that'll remove the curse of Azriel and Beelzebub and Ashtaroth from these acres evermore. Reckon I done told you just a little of how we planned that to come about, when we was talkin' not long ago in town, Miss French."

"I heard you on Robin, riding away. I heard another horse too . . ."

"Please, Miss French. I can't never say it. I'm too grateful and fullhearted to cast blame or name a name. Please don't ask me no more, or even ask me with your eyes."

Which she was doing. The back of her left hand touched mine and then she was holding the hand. So I held hers. I could feel what was going on in her. Wanting to know who'd killed Willis. But not being able to ask any more of a man who loved her enough to have risked his soul for her. At least he'd thought he was doing that. And when you think you're laying your whole self on the line right to the finish-wire, I reckon it's just the same as really doing it.

Instead of asking him any more, she took her hand from mine and put her arms around Jupiter. As if all the good times and bad behind them were summed up in the one second. He stood still as an angel—I reckon there can be black angels as well as devils and the ones in between—looking down at the top of her head. "I mind the day Colonel Bob and Mistis' M'linda brought you that little flyin' jenny," he said. "Just back from the land of Europe, they was. My, my. We thought the good times was everlastin' then. And I recall the day two months back when me and

Nappy and Dabney took a wagon over to Chantry Hall to get it and bring it back to this house of perdition. Thought bad times would last evermore then. But though the good's gone, the real bad's partly goin'."

He stepped back, and picked up the lantern. "You got horses?"

French said, "A great horse. Mister Broome's. And that mare of Will Planteu's."

"Alice? She ain't bad. You hadn't had horses, I could have give you Robin. I could get away by shanks' mare, I'm still kind of nimble. With just one horse you could pull the jenny. But since you got the two, we'll rangle up some kind of harness and take your little jenny right out thu' the windows where they give onto the yard. Now let me take a squint at the jenny and see what we'll need in the way of harness."

He walked, fast for his size—thought of a tiger I'd once seen in a traveling circus; it had been a little moth-chewed, but it still had spring in its hocks—across to the merry-go-round alongside the orchestra platform. He held up the lantern. From a corner of my eye I saw the carved face of Old Scratch gazing at us from over the mantel. It looked crazy and evil and hating. And as if it knew what I didn't. Again in this house I felt a goose tread on my grave. That strange roughened skin on the arms and the nape. For the same split second I could feel what power the place, and the life in it, and Gary Willis, had had on Jupiter. And what power had sprung back with Willis's shooting.

He looked fondly down on the merry-go-round. There in the lantern-light it shone.

# 8

I looked fondly enough on it too, though I was wondering if Grayboy would take kindly to pulling it. Or even hauling it in tandem with Alice. All he'd ever pulled was a lightweight sulky, never running over twenty-five pounds; my point is, he wasn't any plowhorse, for all his size. And he knew it.

The merry-go-round was bigger than any sulky. With the eight hand-carved horses circling it, as French had said. There was room for full-sized people on them, if the grown person scrunched a little. But mainly, the apparatus had been made for children. The handwork had been done with pleasure and whittling joy. If you set out to make something that might last a thousand years—in spite of rot and mildew and people—you couldn't have done better. No horse was meant to look real. But they had zest in their eyes, and were ramping. Forelegs as pretty as willow-boughs in their fine curves. Ears laid back, nostrils flaring scarlet. One horse was in gold and just a tad bigger than the rest. A sort of dusty gold like bullion bars. The others were purple with sunset pink spots, and cream with gilt around the curling mane, and dark green, and deep bronze, and light early-day blue, and coal black, and forsythia yellow. The canopy had a frill of wood under it, in curtain shape.

I bent over to see the wheels. They were under the round platform, attached to a couple of crossbars leading to their axles. I could see the bottom of a stove too, and reckoned it was run by a little boiler over the stove. And there were little reed pipes coming up in the middle of the platform.

French said, "It's a steampipe sound, like a calliope. But it's far prettier to the ear. The horses go around and up and down in time to it."

I said, "They don't have far to go. It's a short track."

"When I think of him running it here for his unspeakable friends. As a gewgaw, a play-pretty."

"You don't have to fret about that anymore," I said.

I wanted to be out of here. Not to talk. I straightened.

Jupiter was spanning the wheels with his hands, figuring.

He nodded and stood up too.

"Reckon we'll just knock the lines straight into the crossbars," he said. "Then you can fan out the lines for a team or for one horse. Which you favor, Mist' Broome?"

"A one-horse harness," I said. "We'll use Alice. Miss French can ride alongside to keep her calm."

He nodded.

"And I'll ride her while she's pulling," I said.

He ducked his head again. Then still carrying the lantern, he stepped across to one of a set of double windows. Opened it by snicking a latch, and it swung out all the way from the sillboard on the floor. You could get a whiff of river-water now from the yard. He opened another window— both windows stretched all the way to the floor—and the night-breeze came in more fully. It bothered the air in here, touching the long drawn-back curtains. Swung a hem of French's cloak where she stood. Jupiter said, "I'll lash up the harness. Got plenty of spare in the stables. You won't need drivin' lines if you're going to ride Alice."

"That's right," I said. "But Miss French is on my horse bareback. And with a hackamore. Would there be spare saddles and bridles around?"

"Mist' Willis had him plenty of them too. You favor light saddle or the heavier Spanish, Miss French?"

"Spanish please," she said.

"Yes'm. Now you two young people, you can bring the horses around. Back 'em right into this window-way here. Right from the grasses. I'll bring the lines and harness and the rest."

He went out of the windows. Looked so big between them, against the moonlight, he almost blotted out the yard and the river down past it. I walked after him. There were a few clouds to the west but nothing packed with more rain. I stood with a hand on a window-latch. French was still looking at her merry-go-round though it was mainly in shadow again.

Around us the great ballroom made whispering noises and creaks. One of the wires of the harp on the platform hummed.

I said to French, "This place gives me the fantods. I know how Jupiter feels. I even know a little why he wants to burn it."

She said, "Oh, I believe Gary made a pact with the Devil. If there was time I'd like to take along everything he ever touched of mine. Everything he had his hands on. The next thing he'd have taken was Chantry itself, and for a pittance."

God knows, I thought, she had plentiful reason for killing Willis herself. And knowing Jupiter had seen her do it, and putting on this show for me with Jupiter, knowing also he'd never tell she'd done it. And depending on her do-no-evil reputation with Sheriff Planteu and Doc Mattison and her other friends to carry her through. She had a kind of queenly look now as she joined me at the windows, as though she was daring the Devil herself, single-handed.

We went along through the moistening grasses back beside Fountain-wood's plantation house to the tulip trees. Along the way there I looked close in at a side window. This was the library, I reckoned, with moon-flashes lighting its rows of dark calfbound books. I could make out the gold-lettered title on the back of one of the books where the light touched it. A history of magic. By somebody named Cagliostro. I reckoned I'd stick to stud books and breeding records and volumes on horse-diseases, when they came my way.

Grayboy had been nibbling some defunct tulip-tree leaves and Alice seemed half asleep, but she woke up and whinnied when I got her in motion. Back near the loose-box with the Arab horse Robin in it, Jupiter was gathering up lines and harness and the rest. He joined us when we'd backed Grayboy and Alice near the ballroom windows. Ran his hands down Grayboy for a second or two, and his eyes went brighter inside their red rims.

"You got a man horse here, Mist' Broome. Archeth his neck and stampeth and sayeth, Ha, Ha, among the hills. Three years?"

"And a few months."

"My, my. That line of bone."

"Alabama long grass put it there. All he ever had for a staple while the bone was growing."

"Had I my hopes, I'd have helped raise horses after leavin' Chantry. But there wasn't no place to go like that. Mist' Willis didn't raise 'em. Just bought what his eye fancied."

French slid down from Grayboy. Went around to his head and talked to him along with Jupiter while he backed farther. The grasses were on a level with the windowsills. I got off Alice and picked up the blanket and the Spanish saddle and the dark red bridle to match that Jupiter'd brought with the harness. I saddled Grayboy while French held him and kept on murmuring and cosseting and crooning to him. Then I took my saddlebags and the boxwood case off and slung them on the fresh saddle. Jupiter had gone back into the ballroom and was lashing the harness to the merry-go-round. He was nailing it and roping it there. The sound of his hammer came in hard, deep strokes echoing through the ballroom and coming out of the windows like trumps of doom. I stood back and noted how the dark red of the saddle was almost the color of French's hair. But with fewer and duller lights in it.

Wanted to put my hands through her hair. And had to keep my hands quiet. Again I was swinging between thinking she might have killed Willis and thinking she couldn't have. In the house and ballroom earlier I'd thought she couldn't. Later the doubts had come easing back again. So I busied myself with the Spanish leather girth, and stole side-glances at her.

I wouldn't have blamed her if she had. No more than if she'd removed a whitlow on the thumb of the world's health.

But, if she had, I'd have hoped she'd tell me so. As she'd told me straight about the merry-go-round.

She was holding both sets of reins now, Alice's and Grayboy's. She said, "What's in the case, Tom?"

"A fiddle. My daddy made it years ago. But the bow came from a side-road peddler."

"Do you play it?"

"I play at it, often. It passes time on the road."

"I'd like to hear it some time."

"I'll give you a tune when I get back from Yadkin Fair. Cheery if I win something, dismal if I've lost."

Then she said, like a soft arrow-shot, "Do you have doubts about me, Tom? Do you think I killed Gary and Jupiter saw me and I was simply putting on a little old show for you a while ago? Because I was aware that Jupiter loves me so much he would remain silent in front of you? Do you think I would trade on that?"

"I don't know, Miss French." I'd have liked denying what I thought, but I couldn't. "You enlisted me in your service on my gentleman's honor tonight. That seems to be as far as it goes. Uppermost in me's the belief you told me the truth. Little side-doubts keep peering in all the same. And I have a wonder that you didn't just ride right over here tonight, by yourself. Not needing me. You could've returned Grayboy in the morning and spun your story to Sheriff Planteu and the rest and I'd have gone straight out of your life . . ."

"I had planned on doing just that. Earlier. Then when I was watching you plod along through the woods after Grody—I watched you now and then, for quite a time—I thought what a help you could be. And—" She was looking square-on at Alice. Who was simply shaking her head a little. French breathed deep. "—and if you truly must know, I like you. I like you, and I felt sorry and remorseful I was causing you such pain and delay, and decided the very least I could do was to bring you in on my plan. I'm not a woman who likes anyone lightly, Tom." She'd faced me now. Grayboy made a half-hearted grab for my hat, but this time I ducked him. I put a hand up to his nose and let him lip my fingers.

"—once I was engaged, Tom. To Lieutenant Algy Marsden; they ran a plantation downriver. He fussed around me a lot, as much as he could. He'd sustained a wound in my father's troop. So he couldn't dance as much as other men, and had to rest a lot. One afternoon I brought him some calf's foot jelly—his mama was out, I went over there on the stage. It was during one of his invalid times. I went upstairs to his room. I had hardly offered him the jelly, when he was on me, and—well, he attacked me, Tom. And yet it seemed so pitiful. I did not have a baby from it. I felt sorry for him afterward. And angry. And sorry for myself of course. After that, I believe I gleaned a reputation in Lanceton County for being overproud and haughty. Among a number of men, at any rate."

"Well . . ." I couldn't keep from smiling somewhat, though I tried to do most of it inside. "Don't worry about Grody Flieshacker. He'd defend you to any man, even if you took his food away from him."

"And that's tiresome as well. Having him and Will Planteu and Doctor Mattison and all the rest—defend me. I have always thought I had something in me—inherited or just *myself*—that might do its own defending. I don't feel I'm too good for, or too far above, anyone at all. It's just that not everyone, man or woman, interests me. But—I was saying— Algy Marsden died, shortly after our . . . encounter, and after I broke the engagement."

I wondered for a second if the effort might've killed this Marsden. If it had, I hoped he'd thought it was worth it, and died happy. Many men would have.

"Sometimes I visit his grave. It's right there in the old cemetery up from the west field behind Chantry. Not far from Mama's and Daddy's. I can't shed an honest tear for him, but I still feel sorry—and cheated. And not as angry at him as I've always naturally been at Gary, whom I didn't kill, a fact I'm not going to bring out again since I've already told it to Roy Mattison. Now."

Inside the ballroom, Jupiter was calling. "Mist' Broome." His voice booming louder than the hammer-strokes had, yet with that softness around it.

I was still looking at French, staying where I was.

"Now, Tom. When you accused me of living poor and being proud, it was part of the truth, but not all, you see. And when I said we'd save the discussion for another time, I had some notion I might tell you all this when you'd come back from Yadkin Fair. Yet I find myself wishing to tell you now, so you shan't go back on the road with . . . doubts, or bad memories of me."

"Mist' Broome. Come and give me a hand, if you please?"

She didn't drop either handful of reins when I stepped to her.

She didn't keep her lips firm either, when I drew her up to me and kissed her. It was the fire in the earth all right, for sure. And under the earth and in the tumultuous waters of the sea. The whole length of her against me through the elderly cloak and the thin-threaded dress, and her slippers nearly coming off the ground. The yearning, seeking, and wishing coming out in the one instant thrust of it.

She kept looking after me, still holding the mounts, when I went back into the ballroom.

I'd lost more than a day to Yadkin now, but it all felt worth it.

I knew what Lieutenant Algy Marsden must have felt, the scannel, and even felt pitying toward him in his lonesome grave.

# 9

Then Jupiter and I had pushed and maneuvered the merry-go-round over to the windows. And we backed Alice and hung her with the collar and lashed up the harness. She was a hell of a lot more tractable about it than Grayboy would have been. He walled his near eye down at these ructions and appeared to disapprove of them highly. French had got up on him again. With the saddle and the bags and the fiddle case and the willow basket over her arm, Grayboy didn't appear weighted down at all, but he looked more like a charger of old in one of those picture books about knights than he had before. I had the bare memory of my mama reading from a book like that in the days before she'd died and before the war. While I was smoothing out this harness on Alice and helping Jupiter square away I could still feel the print of French's mouth on mine.

When everything was set, I mounted Alice. After I'd swung up and was gentling her—she didn't exactly trust this machine at her heels—Jupiter says, "You ain't got no victuals to speak of. 'Cept that bunch of cress. And there's still horse-food galore in the stable bins. You wait right here one more little minute, young folks."

He was gone, padding back through the house this time.

Grayboy tossed his head. One hand on the high Spanish pommel, French smoothed him with the other. I looked behind me. The merry-go-round wouldn't take up much more room on any road than a sizable cart. Jupiter had lashed an old canvas over it to protect it from the night dew. Far at the end of the ballroom I could still see the marble face of the Devil in the upspraying light from the big lamp. Now he seemed to be looking at us. Bidding us a baleful farewell.

French watched while I got out my turnip-watch and pressed the chime-bosses. The chime to the nearest hour rang three times. I slid the watch back, and she said, "I've told you more about myself than I've ever told anyone else since I grew to be a woman, Tom."

"I appreciate the confidence, Miss French," I said.

"I wish I had something of value to give you—as a keepsake for this night. And something you could hold with you in your Yadkin racing. But I have nothing but my good will and my blessing."

"They're sufficient," I told her.

Alice slugged her head against the bit and the merry-go-round made a light tin-dinkling noise. There was a bar under the platform which locked the wheels. Jupiter and I had loosed the bar before getting the merry-go-round in place. I pulled Alice's head up firm.

"You need not come all the way to Chantry with me, Tom. Just as far as the Morgan's—where I borrowed the food for Grayboy and me yesterday morning. It's beside a knoll where you come out on the pike from Lanceton. We can exchange saddles there, and then I'll take Alice. And we'll say good-bye."

"Can you get the merry-go-round back in your ballroom at the hall? By yourself, without help?"

"There's a big door on one side. It came in that way, those years ago. And went out by the same door, when Gary bought it. When it's in place, I'll unsaddle Alice and take her back to the road. She'll find her way back to Lanceton."

I was thinking that by that time I'd do well to have made a lot of tracks to Yadkin. I could see Sheriff Planteau's face when Alice showed up without me. Didn't say anything of that, but looked over at French. Feeling the thing she felt, and I felt. Running along like a silent river between us.

Jupiter was back, with food wrapped in cloth and with three full oat-sacks. French handed him down her basket and he put some of the food in it. There was some guinea hen and a dressed-out and cooked woodcock and a ham and three pones of bread and a bottle of wine. He put the food and the oat-sacks under the merry-go-round canvas. "Gentry food," he said, straightening. " 'Cept it never got fed to gentry. Only to riffraff and evil. Pleased to have made your acquaintance, Mist' Broome.''

"Glad to've met you, Jupiter."

French had swung in the saddle. "Are you going north with the others, Jupiter? When people find out Fountainwood's been burnt—"

"I got my plans, Miss French, thank you. I know they'll be plenty of hooraw roundabout. I ain't feared of it. I'll lay low and keep my old head down. If I'd wanted to get away—in the old days when we was all at Chantry—I'd have give the patterollers a good run. But I never wanted to get away. And when the colonel manumitted us all, towards the war's end and before he got kilt, I still didn't favor Jordan freedom. None of us who'd been at Chantry wanted to leave till we'd come over here and found what the yoke of the tyrant could be. My obleegances to you, Miss French. Fair days and fine ones be yours.''

He stood tall beside us. I clucked to Alice and we moved on out, Grayboy's bulk shadowing Alice on her off-side. The merry-go-round made its light bell-like traveling noise, the wheels moving well over the yard turf. We came out on the drive leading to the road above the river. When we were near the road with the gate-posts shining white and the gate open, I checked Alice and French and I looked back. Jupiter was still standing in front of the open windows. He'd raised a hand in farewell. Against the whole beautiful but sorry house he somehow seemed bigger than all of it. He was still standing there when French loosed Grayboy's bit a touch and rode to the right. I wheeled Alice. We went along under oaks and leaning pines, sometimes gazing back to Fountainwood where Jupiter still stood with his hand raised.

There's a company-feeling in riding along with anybody, even though you don't talk much because the noise of the horses interferes. This was a special company-feeling, as though we might be reading each other's thoughts. French raised her cloak-hood against the cool morning air. Now and then we came out from under the trees in a patch of light. When this happened I looked as close at her as I could without staring. Now and then her eyes shut but she was still handling Grayboy well. I felt a kind of sleep mixed with excitement yeasting in my own body. Along with the regret that was piling up at knowing I'd soon leave her. I didn't get out the turnip again but I could tell from the sky when we'd gone along about an hour. Sometimes the road veered away from the riverbank and then came back to it so you could see the water moving between brush and canebrake. Then all at once I realized I'd dropped into a catnap because Grayboy was halted beside me and I'd let Alice pull a shade ahead, and French's voice had wakened me saying, "Tom, we cross here."

I pulled my head all the way up, straightened my hat.

I'd been cock-dreaming about being deep in a woman, I reckoned Miss French but didn't know for sure. You can't always rein in those urges. I felt warm in spite of the cooling air, and happy for some reason. French was looking straight at me, I hoped I didn't show what I felt. Gray and silver eyes with the amber flecks bright in the light peering down through oak-boughs.

She was wide-awake enough. Nodding toward the bridge on our right. It was a long bridge with a slight hump to it like a cat stretching. Spread out before us with its planks gray and mystery-shadowed and railings high above the brown water. Here the Lanceton River ran faster, boiling along around the uprights which were thirty feet down. The noise of the river sounded as cold as its breath around us.

"The pike starts on the other side, Tom. But we'll take the side-road to Morgan's. It's not much more than a lane but it will accommodate the merry-go-round."

There was a skein of mist and dew on the canvas over the merry-go-round. "Toddy Morgan—I told you he was Daddy's aide-de-camp—runs a sugar mill in the hollow behind his place. Or his nigra runs it for him; Mister Morgan's bedridden. There's a spring above the hollow, we can water the horses there and change the saddles and—"

"—and say good-bye," I said. My voice sounded as if I hadn't used it a while. Dry in spite of the wet air here.

Grayboy snorted, breath pluming a trifle. His head looked giant against the stars which were lower in the sky.

"And say good-bye, and go our ways."

Wasn't anything to do but agree. I nodded, and we started across the bridge. The planks so sudden-loud under us I had the notion they might rouse the whole countryside. I was better awake now. Grayboy snorted again and pulled at the bit. She kept him back and level with me. He always liked to take bridges such as this as though the hollow noise of the planks gave him joy. If I'd been on him and we'd been by ourselves we'd have been in a full gallop by the time the bridge ended. We were rising a tad now, climbing toward the center of the hump. The merry-go-round wheels clacked and the planks rattled. The water foamed around the uprights under us. A nighthawk came downriver in the middle of the current and swooped under the bridge and then flew up on the other side. Alice was pulling well, the harness holding strong and the collar bulging.

From here I couldn't see a farm in sight, even a sleeping farm. Just brush along both river-flanks.

Then all at once on the high point of the bridge Grayboy shied. He wasn't playing. His head swung around, eyeballs fleering. Same time, there was a strange flush of color all around us, painting the whole upper curve of the bridge. In the split second I saw French's black cloak go sudden rosy gold in this light, and was yelling sharp at Grayboy to hold up, and reaching for his bridle which was a good deal higher than I was with me on Alice. I missed the leather with my fingertips, and then French was bringing him down, he was rearing and stretching high above the rail for another breath, but she was bringing him down with all her strength. And Alice was standing and neighing, and then Grayboy trumpeted. Standing with her. Their heads curved around, eyes wild. The light was like a pine knot filling the sky.

I got a hand on Grayboy this time, near the pommel. But she had him in check.

Then both Alice and Grayboy were shivering. Ripples of fright going through them. And the light behind us was brushing the underbellies of clouds.

French and I were gazing back along with Alice and Grayboy. Couldn't have kept from it.

The light spread over the crowns of oaks and down the green of pines and spilled over the brush so the shoreline was painted in tones of hell. The shadow of the bridge fanned out under us.

I thought how fire is a terror to the eye and the spirit, burning something in the beholder as well as whatever else it burns. I thought of those long high rooms at Fountainwood, the dining table and the crystal on the sideboards. And mainly of the snarl-smiling face of Old Horny staring into the flames. Reckoned the fire had just shot up to its peak, the ridgepole going before it all crashed inward. Could smell the horse-sweat—scared horse doesn't smell like anything else on earth—and under it just the merest taint of smoke. While we watched, the reflection of the flames went even higher, then burned away and then the sky was almost as it had been.

"Jesus," I said, and didn't apologize to French for it, and this time it wasn't exactly cussing.

Then I wasn't saying anything. Because out of the road we'd just left and lunging onto the bridge, here came Jupiter. He was on the black horse, the Arab, Robin. The horse was lathered to cream, and thundering. I swung to French and hit Grayboy with my hat, urging him over. But he wouldn't have had to stir. When Jupiter reached us, bent over the Arab's neck and looking almost as big as his horse, he pulled the Arab to the right and for less than a second he was on the berm beside the bridge-planks, then gone with the Arab's tail streaming and the sound rolling back to us. And just before Jupiter got to the bridge-head in front of us, he stood in the stirrups, seemed to stretch the iron-leathers, and turned around. A great smile on his face, his hand lifted. Then he'd shot the Arab into the shadows. You don't find so many black Arabs, I reckoned Willis had paid a mint for him. I didn't reckon Willis could ride him like that, though.

"Come up," I said to Alice, and we went on, the shivering dying out of her, and out of Grayboy. Then we were off the bridge and pulling right again. And then into a narrow track, French going ahead, feathery cool leaves dipping around us. The track turning from time to time, with ridges of land above it. I thought how she knew this land as well as a man would, better than most men. The flaring light that had shone in the sky seemed to be still on my eyeballs. But after that the feeling of wishing to sleep rolled back, and even though I kept my eyes open by main force, they shut. I could feel Alice going along under me, hear the merry-go-round sounding. If I had any dream it was of being in a sulky behind Grayboy then, neck to neck with two other horses, and feeling him beginning to bore as he always did when he felt others beside him and was racing. He was boring and I had him off the bit. And the merry-go-round wheels had turned into sulky wheels and they were singing.

When I opened my eyes the singing was going right on. But it wasn't sulky wheels, it was birds starting to limber up all around us. And ahead I could see Grayboy's haunches plain, and French on him with the black cloak streaming over the Spanish saddle, and the air all around was still gray but lightening up fast. The branches and leaves netted over this track were plain against the air.

"Christ," I said, but all to myself this time.

We were caught by daylight.

# 10

By the time we got to the top of the next draw I could hear roosters crowing for the new day. Then we were stopping on the lip of a hollow at the edge of the draw. Around the hollow were pecan trees with their leathery boughs seining the fresh light and their fruitage fallen on the ground and rotting in the high grass. All the sun was moving over the land around here and bringing out shapes of trees and the line of the Lanceton Pike far below us, and the grasses were like moist bright fur. On the other side of this hollow and away from the pike was a farmhouse tucked into the flank of a knoll, and in the cup of land below the farmhouse was a sugar mill, the skimming-hole next to it a round splotch of dark moist green. Even this early the nigra French had mentioned who worked for Toddy Morgan—whose farmhouse I reckoned that was—was feeding stalks of cut cane in through the sweep-burrs. And an old mule was moving in a circle, pulling the sweep.

Down in the hollow near us ran a creek, flowing into a pond. The pond-water looked fresh and clear enough to drink. Grayboy had already scented the water, Alice a few seconds behind him in lifting her nose and wrinkling back her lips. French put Grayboy down the draw into the hollow. The grasses were lofty enough to reach nearly to his belly. Shadows of the pecan trees fell across his hide and her cloak in soft ripples. I followed down slower with Alice, hoping the merry-go-round wouldn't catch us up and hit her heels. But the angle was easy enough to keep the merry-go-round from running away. Then I was pulling Alice up alongside Grayboy. French eased on his reins and he thrust his head down and drank. I let Alice do the same.

French lifted a hand and pushed back the cloak-hood.

Turned her face to me. "It simply took too long," she said. "We'll have to wait here till nightfall, Tom. I don't want anyone to see us on the pike. And you'll have to take the pike toward Yadkin—and circle around Lanceton on your way—and I'll have to take it in the other direction to get back to Chantry Hall. So we'll have to stay here till good dark."

"True enough," I said. "But you don't have to feel sorry on my account. I pledged myself to assist you, taking rough with smooth. Not that anything's been smooth so far. But I don't see it as your fault, Miss French."

"Don't you?" She pulled Grayboy's head up. He'd had enough long gulps of the pond-water. It dripped from his nose. I pulled Alice's head up. Through the water-smell I could smell the deep grasses and a touch of cane sweetness from the sugar mill. Nobody could see us from down there or from the farm. It was a good place to lay up for the day if we had to. "I think I've just been willful," French went on. "I wanted my merry-go-round so strongly I wouldn't let anything stand in my way to get it. Now I have it, and I've pulled you deeply into trouble because of it. Not to mention costing you yet another day's delay to the fair."

"I don't see it that way," I said. "When a good horseman loses a race he just cuts his losses, and looks to the next one. We lost a race with the sun. With some luck I'll still get to Yadkin Fair in time to enter Grayboy and take my chances. Anyhow—" I stretched in the first warm of the sun "—Grayboy's had a long time of traveling back and forth in the woods; he could use a day's rest before we set out again. So could I. So could you."

She looked around, then she was swinging down off Grayboy. She lifted her arms and stretched as I'd done. The cloak fell back and she unhooked its throat-clasp and took it off and put it over an arm. She picked up Grayboy's reins and lifted them over his head. I could see a reflection of her in the pond-water which was still trembling from the horses drinking. I got off Alice. And stretched some more, easing my thigh-muscles. Then I pulled Alice's reins over her head and let her stand and started unharnessing her. The harness Jupiter'd rigged hadn't galled her; I lifted off the collar and put it under the canvas he'd lashed over the merry-go-round. Then put the rest of the harness there. When I looked over my shoulder, French was unsaddling Grayboy. He gave wriggles along his back, glad to be saddle-free. When she had his bridle off he raised his head and shot his lips out as if he was drinking the sun now, instead of water, then he ambled up a little way to the growing shade of the pecans, and rolled in the grasses under them. He rolled like a kitten in catnip. Hoofs in the air, then he was scrambling up and standing aglow under the pecans, then trying out the grasses for juiciness. I put his saddle which had been on Alice under the canvas, and his blanket and bridle the same, and by that time French had carried the Spanish gear to the canvas and stowed it away. I got out the feed-sacks Jupiter'd bestowed upon us, along with the willow basket and what he'd called the gentry food. Both Alice and Grayboy appeared as though they might sleep for a time. Alice was wandering a little way up the incline to join Grayboy. I took the oat-sacks up to them and strowed oats in mounds under the pecan shade. They started eating, and I came back down again, to where French was laying out the cloth that had been around the bottle of wine and the woodcock and ham and pones of bread. I got out my knife and started prizing the cork from the bottle. French had laid her cloak out on the ground to sit on. I sat next to her. I thought how we might've been a lady and a man, possibly a gentleman, out for an early picnic in a restful spot far from prying eyes. And not a lady bound on a curious errand of stealing back a flying jenny before it got burned, and a man doubtless now wanted for stealing a sheriff's mare.

A dragonfly floated over the grasses and hovered on the pond. Around this part of the countryside down along the pike the roosters had stopped crowing now, and day-noises came distant and muffled; the creak of the sugar mill sweep and the calling of crows as they passed from one field to another. And closer, the sound of Alice and Grayboy finishing the oats and then tearing at the grasses.

I wondered if French was feeling as I was, that even if we were penned in here for the day, we didn't have to say our good-byes as yet. I had the notion she felt so.

When I had the cork out of the bottle—its label said *Montrachet*, I didn't think it came from Mississippi or even Alabama—I took my knife again and cut some of the woodcock and ham and bread into strips. I passed the wine bottle along to French. Said, "Sorry we don't have glasses."

"It's really just as good this way." She tilted the bottle back and drank. The dark wine sparkling in its reflection over her eyes. "That is quite a favorable wine, Tom." She handed the bottle to me, and picked up some woodcock and bread.

She was right; the wine was a good bit tastier than the last strong drink I'd had, which had been out of a corn-jug belonging to a peddler who told me he'd been a sutler serving the army. He'd charged three silver bits for the drink, and I'd told him I bet it hurt him to sell turpentine that cheap.

When we'd finished the bottle—it went down quite fast—and some of the viands, she folded everything up in the cloth again and put it away under the merry-go-round canvas. I was lying back now, hands behind my nape, sometimes angling a glance toward the shade where Grayboy and Alice grazed and slept, and sometimes just half-shutting my eyes and feeling the heat of the day touch around me. French went up a little way above the horses, and spread her cloak again, and when I next looked, she was stretching out there, on her side, her hands under her cheek, like a lady cat in a patch of sun and shade. I made myself comfortable in the warming grasses. Put my hat over my eyes, and shut out all thought of peril or puzzlement. Shut out even most thought of French, though that was difficult.

When I woke up the sun was tilted to midmorning, and far down from the pike, hoofs were sounding on the road. Along with the creak of a wagon, but all of it wrapped in cotton wool from here. After the sound was gone there was, again, only the creak of the sugar sweep from the other side of the hollow. I scrooched around and sat up. Up under the pecans, French lay in full shade, now. Unstirring. Both Grayboy and Alice were lying down in the long grasses on the yonder side of the ring of trees. I stood up and walked around the pond, to its furthest side. Here cane grew fairly tall and a few frogs rested in the cane-shadow. In the shadow I pissed, and then when I was about to button up, noted how clear the pond was all around, with sand sloping down to marl and with the creek feeding it in a light tinkling flow. I went back around the pond, and worked my razor and some potash soap out of one of my saddlebags. Then a stick of tallow. I went back around the other flank of the pond, and wrested off my boots. Tallowed them well, then stripped the rest of the way and carrying the soap and razor, went into the pond. It was already warmed on the surface, and not too cold as I strode deeper. Up to my belly there, I lathered good with the potash soap, all over, then bent to peer at my face as the water stopped shaking, and shaved. I waded back shoreward, and put the razor and soap with the tallow and my clothes, and turned around and went back toward the pond's center. It wasn't deep enough for real diving, but you could stretch yourself out all the way and skim along in it like a grebe about to take to the air. I'd done this a couple of times when I heard something from the bank. I raised all the way up, the water here only coming about to my knees.

The noise of the water swirling in the pond died down, and a few small waves lapped against my kneecaps.

Francia French Chantry was sitting on the bank, where the high grass led down to the water. She had her knees drawn up and her hands around them, and how long she'd been there I didn't know. From where I was she looked brooding and thought-filled, but she wasn't gazing away from me either. And hadn't been for quite a time, I could tell that. I could just see the sparking of her eyes. A meditating cat's.

She said, "Don't turn around, Tom. Don't be abashed. I have never seen the body of a man before. I did notice Algy Marsden briefly, during his attack on me. But that was quite flurried, and I fought considerably. I've seen statues, of course. But it's not the same thing. It's quite beautiful."

I said, "Thanks. Never thought of it that way."

"The way your shoulders go, those bulges at the upper part of your arms, and your stomach. Very different, and wonderful. And then your hair there—it's the same color as the hair on your head. And your—I don't even know what it's called."

"Many things," I said. "Sometimes a root. Sometimes a cock. But many other things, French. And under it, the balls, or eggs, or stones, or whatever. And the doctors have other words for those too." I stayed where I was. "I reckon I don't mind you looking at me," I said, "but if it's just curiosity alone, and you don't have any other intentions, I'll excuse myself now. I just don't think a lady as well brought up as you are ought to be amusing herself, if she isn't serious about these things."

"I'm not amusing myself. I assure you, I am most serious."

"And I wasn't put on earth just to be looked at. Like a show horse that never runs. I'm feeling a need for you. Your father ever breed a mare among those horses he used to keep?"

"Yes, of course. But no lady would come around the paddock at such times."

"Well, I'm like that. Like a stallion, if you want to put it that way. I'm different from that as well—I'm a man, and it's more curious even than bein' a stallion. I've lived a free life and had women when the women were willing, and even quicker when they were eager. What I think I'm sayin'—you're playin' with more fire now than just a fire that might burn up your merry-go-round. I want to remain a gentleman in your sight, because I reckon I value your opinion of me more than I ever did any other woman's on the face of this earth, far as I've seen the world. Maybe it's just the wine speaking in you now. Think about that, and think what it could mean.''

All of a quickness she was smiling. That same loving look that had first drifted across her face, gentle as all the sun itself, when we'd stood in Chantry stable.

"Tom, ah Tom. You sound a trifle like the Reverend Holcomb. He's a preacher in Lanceton. And you don't *wish* to sound like any man of the cloth at all. It's not the wine, there wasn't that much of it. It's something in me that loves you. I wouldn't care if you were rakehell and devil, even if you were worse than Gary Willis, though you never could be. I'm twenty years old, Tom, and I'm sick in my marrow of being an old maid and perhaps a little fetching, and proud. I'd hold you a gentleman no matter what you did to me, or with me.''

She was talking like the sun itself on my spine.

"You kissed me twice, Tom. The first time I hardly had time to know what was happening. The second time I knew. If I wrote poetry like Mister Whitman or Lord Byron or Sir Walter, I'd have the words for it—stars and fire.''

I'd never heard of this Whitman. Or much about Byron. Scott I'd looked into, but Young Lochinvar sure didn't sum up much of what I was feeling. It didn't wrap around what she was feeling either.

"Tom,'' she said low. "Come stand beside me.''

I shut my eyes a little, then I let everything—all the knotted-up way I was feeling inside—drop away like iron melting. I waded on toward her. As I got closer she stood up, the dove-gray old silk flashing. When I'd stepped up to the grasses of the bank she was taking off her decrepit but gay ballroom slippers. Then she was turning, and unsnapping something. And when I was beside her she was in a shift, with white old lace at its straps. Then she was turning again, and I could smell her over the warm grasses, her flesh cleanly and noble and all of her standing there.

She said up to me, "Don't look so pained, Tom.''

"I've never been made love to before,'' I said. "I always made it.''

She touched me. Just reached, slow enough, and marveling, and took me in her hand. I put a hand on one of the shift straps, peeled it back and down, and took hold of the other, and pulled it down. She was looking down where she had hold of me. "They call it a cock,'' she said, with the same marveling in her. "Because it's so fiery and proud and strutting? But it's not like that—or a root, either, Tom."

She stooped and kissed it. And straightened and stepped out of the shift all the way.

Her tits swung up against me. Their nipples hard but warm, and then her belly curving in against mine, and her arms going around me, and her hair shaking to her shoulders. Her woman-smell ripe around me as if the whole morning had handed me a gift of magical bread. Through me ran the thought that she was a single-minded woman, the most so I'd ever known, and that I didn't ever wish her to believe she owned me. Not as her daddy'd once owned Jupiter and those other slaves, even if he'd manumitted them. I didn't wish to own her either, have a bill of sale for her, keep her to race for my profit.

There wouldn't be time to say those things now. Even time, much, to think them. They'd have to be said later; and understood.

I put one arm under her shoulders—silky as a magnolia in full bloom— and her hair swept back and hung like a dark flag and her eyes were upturned to me and rolling back, and I put the other arm under her, and lifted her, and had my fingers under the cleft of her haunches, opening her even as she sank to the grasses. Her nest-hairs were warm and curling like a rich pelt, she was so ready she was waiting with the sweet clean juice as I was. When I went into her, slow at first and feeling dark fire and bone-spirit climb my spine as though I was sweating outside but had the sun's heat itself gathered in the head of my rod, she lay back further, arms out and back as if she clutched at the sun herself. Then when I went deeper and she moved up around me, tight and rising, breasts swaying back and rib cage shadowy and taut, I felt in my soul—but much quicker than it could be told—that we might never have to say anything about owning or not owning each other. That we were already saying it. Each giving more than either'd known was there to give.

Then it was after the first time, and everything around us swam back into being. But looking brighter than it had, clear-outlined. As if each grass-blade had its own humming secret life and was sharing all the secret with us. As if our nakedness was part of the grasses and the water and the sleeping horses and the pecan trees and the air going noonward.

I lifted her hair, fingered a strand of it. Could just see a corner of her eye, looking at me. And the smile blooming on her lips and the sleepy love simmering around her.

Said, "French."

"It's nice to be called that. Not Miss French. Something happened inside me. I'd known it would, Tom. I never want you to call me Miss French again. If you do, I'll know you're bothered with me. I'd had dreams about something occurring inside me."

I said, "French, I came first. Shot into you first. Sometimes it happens together. Whores usually pretend it's happening to them while it's happening to the man—they earn their money that way, by doing some pretending. Once in a while it happens together though. Not this time. It doesn't matter all that much though; it's no race where people have to come out neck and neck."

She was playing with me. Running her fingers down my shoulder blade and then deeper along my belly, and in the line of furze there, and into my bush. Then taking up my cock—which you might as well call it as anything, even though it's a foolish word—and letting it stiffen in her hand. I pulled her around over me, and brought her down on me and looked at the world through her hair.

Some time still later, I picked her up and took her up into the pecan-shade. And went down and got her dress and shift and those dainty elderly ballroom shoes, and brought them back handy. It went through my mind how you'll be talking with somebody, card game or around stables, and the somebody will say, "I fucked that little filly over towards Gadsden," or words of the kind. But the truth is, I was reckoning, nobody fucks anybody else. Two people do it, not one. And man for all his wit and wisdom—which for some reason he keeps thinking are mightier than horses, dogs, and squirrels—hasn't yet got around to admitting that.

She started dressing, and then turned to me when she was dressed, and though I meant only to kiss her once more for luck that time, we ended up doing it all again, shift and dove-gray dress and the whole kaboodle. Then she was lying back on the cloak, on an elbow, and combing her hair with a tortoiseshell comb she'd taken from a pocket of the dress, the sound hissing and sleep-drowned, her eyes veiled and only watching me quiet. I felt light and sky-clean and as if I weighed five pounds less, and reckoned she did too. When she was through combing her hair and lay back and shut her eyes, I went on down in the sun on the slope again, and around the pond and got my potash soap and tallow and razor, and my boots and hat and clothes, and brought them around and dressed and sat on a saddlebag slicking my hair back in the sun. Then pulled my hat down, gazing up under it at her under the trees. She was asleep again, but not as she'd been before. A deeper and fully loving sleep. Could have slept some myself. I hunkered there with my boot-heels in the air for a moment, watching her asleep. She was a jewel, a prize men might murder for. I wondered if somebody had murdered Gary Willis for her. Or just for their own pleasure. I touched one of her eyelids with a fingertip, soft as though a gnat had lighted there. She didn't stir. Tits, or breasts, or whatever your word is for those, rising and falling with her even breath.

I stood and gazed at Alice and Grayboy. They were flicking a few flies away with skin-shrugs, but they were asleep too. It was noon by the sun, or after. The screel of the sugar sweep had stopped, folks for miles around would be getting their fatback or pone or whatever stayed them till nightfall. Though I wanted to sleep, other things were knocking at my mind. French had said the derringer was still in its cache after she found Willis dead, but that it had been shot. She thought a lot of her poultry, too. I was curious to look around Chantry Hall more than I'd had the chance to yet. And I could feed the chickens again.

If there was any obstacle in my path between here and Chantry Hall, I'd bypass it somehow.

Getting right down to the base of it, I was feeling that ample and free way you do sometimes when you've been with a woman and feel that you might never die of dire causes, but live to be ninety and a trouble to your friends and relatives.

And since the woman was French, the feeling was doubled.

After a time I moved up the hill slope, keeping my eyes open for anything untoward. I followed the side road a short distance back, the way we'd come here; then I grabbed a tussock of bush-grass and raised myself up to the ridge, and looked down again. There was the Lanceton Pike, red gray now in the tree-shadows printed across it. Over yonder was the knoll where the Morgan farmhouse stood, and past it the valley with the sugar mill, and on past that the pond-hollow. I had my bearings straight enough in all this showering sun. Chantry Hall had to be to the southwest.

I dropped down to the road-ditch and made my way along it. Nothing bothered me or hailed me but a chicken-hawk eyeing me from high above, and grasshoppers flailing around my legs from the ditch-dust. When I'd gone on bordering this pike a while, I raised my head. Sneezing from the peppery scent of the grasses at the ditch-rim, and reaching up and parting the grasses to see better. After a spell of squinting I could make out the chimneys of Chantry Hall, rising out of a sea of oaks and pines and magnolia and gumwood in front of the compound and stable. I'd walked too far and was around behind the hall-grounds, where Doc Mattison had waited while I picked up my gear the morning before. I gazed both ways along the pike. Then I raised myself up and went fast across the pike-road, and angled across a corner of the desolated cotton field and pasture, and walked in through the tumble-down back gate to the compound.

# 11

After you've had a woman you wear her around you for a time, a garment nobody can see. But a garment you can feel. And when it's a woman such as French, meaning more than anything you've known before, the garment stays on you a good while. So I was thinking as I went through the compound—and around the stable and past the chickens in their house—noting with a part of my mind that the chickens had been fed a short time ago, and were clucking drowsy-like.

If I'd had my mother-wit about me I'd have come up short and understood what that might mean. But no use lying, I hadn't. I walked free and bold past the summer kitchen, and around beside the cabins and the well-head. Even stopped for a second to clear away some leaves from the stones of the well-head and stare down into the quiet circle of black water. Smelled the breath of the cold stones and glimpsed my face very small down there against the quicksilver light of the sun on black water. I was thinking of all the passion and gold and thunder French had in her, how when she gave of herself it was like being locked in a lightning-bolt. Elbowing myself from the stones, I sauntered on. And came to the five steps going up to the back door of the back gallery. Mounted them, and tried the knob. It moved well enough—the door was unlocked as I'd left it the morning before; I opened it and went into the shadowy huge kitchen. Shut the door behind me. The brass key was still in its keyhole.

I passed through the kitchen, boots quiet now, and came to the hall down which Mattison had led me, and around its corner, to the main hall.

With the staircase now on my right and the mirrors twinkling and gleaming in shy lights as they reflected sun from the door open at the end of the vestibule. I came to the staircase and rounded its newel-post. There was nothing lying on the stair-treads here; even the flecks of dark blood that had touched the risers around Gary Willis had been scrubbed away. I could see the lighter spots where somebody had used dabs of lye soap. A little morning breeze came all the way from the door and along the hall to make motes dance in the spill of sunlight on these risers. I went along the hall, over its thin red carpet which had once been gracious to the boot-soles; passed a mirror, and came to one of the side doors. I opened it. It was a dining room with a coffered ceiling; glints of sun were peering in past window vines and it had a hollow, empty feeling of disuse. Not a stick of furniture in it. I shut its door soft, thinking of the dining room at Fountainwood.

But the next door past the next mirror gave onto the ballroom. It wasn't a tinker's patch on Fountainwood's, but it was ample enough, and even now with its high arched windows smoky with age and crowded with vines had a touch of old-time brightness that, for me, put Fountainwood's to shame. People had done true dancing here, maybe with the big door between the windows open to the night full of fireflies, and the fiddlers in their balcony up on one side—a balcony with its uprights now sagging out from the wall—playing the reels and waltzes with a will. I hummed a snatch of Roger de Coverly under my breath, and pulled the door shut.

I went back along the hall to the newel-post and regarded it. The lion's gilded eyes and mane—the gilding gone dim with time—shone easy. After a time I pressed the lion's eyeballs, spanning finger and thumb to do so. There was a spring-click inside and the lion's head swung out. I peered down into the dark space beneath. It was just a little box-shaped space about the size of a blacksmith's box where he keeps spare nails and hoof hooks and pliers and salve. Sun slanted into it but I couldn't see a derringer. I felt inside it, on the cool well-joined cedar. There wasn't anything in it. I pushed the lion's head back. It fell to with another low click.

I'd taken one step into the hall again and toward the vestibule past the mirrors and the side doors when I heard the voices. Somebody was out on the front gallery. Then past the open door with its beveled fanlight above it splashing soft sun to the vestibule chairs, I saw a shadow move over the gallery flooring. Next second, Doc Mattison came in sight. Campaign hat drawn down close over his eyes, his jaws working as he chewed, hands clasped knotty behind his coatttails as he strode along crabwise. Like a man in deep doubt relieving himself by strolling. All he had to do to see me was turn his head. I hit the floor with a thump, stretched full length and wishing I was lower than the height of the stair-riser which my right fingertips were almost touching. Out on the gallery the voices and footfalls came again. This time from where I was I could hear the voices well.

First, Doc's: ". . . forty-one caliber rimfire. Lodged in the bastard's cerebellum. I ain't sayin' it came from Colonel Bob's old derringer, and I ain't sayin' it didn't."

Then Sheriff Planteu's, much slower, and with a frazzled edge to it: "Since the derringer ain't in sight anywhere, whatever you speculate's still goin' to be pure guesswork. And whatever I speculate, the same. Reckon French took it with her when she rode for you yestermorn." He cleared his throat, and came in sight. Another unlit cigar—or maybe the same, I thought, maybe he kept them from one day to the next—cocked in his teeth. He sauntered across in front of the doorway, legs in his moleskin pants looking very long from where I sprawled. Face with the splotches of chinaberry-leaking light on it drawn and worn as thumb-rubbed copper.

"I recall Bob's derringer. Longer-barreled than most. Stud trigger, pops out when you cock it. But God knows I've looked high and low, Roy. Still think maybe Bob had some special secret place for it. He was like a little chap that way. Loved hidey-holes and dinguses. You mind the code he used to drill into our scouts? Had so many passwords and signs and countersigns the scouts'd forget it and worry about endin' up shot when they came back to report." He walked out of sight, but I could still hear him. "A hidey-hole only the fam'ly knew. Meaning in this case, only French."

Doc's shadow came back, then he was standing right in front of the door. But with his back to me. Planteu's voice went on. "Yet I've looked in all the hidey-holes I can find. Found the door under the back staircase; nothin' in there but a rat's nest. And the hollow back of the baseboard in the gun-room. Two dusty duellin' irons couldn't't've been shot without blowin' your own head off. And the hole in under the lion's head, empty as a bluebelly's heart. Only one I'd ever known about was the lion's head. Reckon you did too."

Doc's shoulders hunched in the black coat. From where he stood he spat out over the gallery's front rail. His shoulders settled and one hand went up to wipe his mouth. "Bob never confided in me about his other little devices, Will. Just that one. Though you're right; he took pleasure in 'em. But we don't even know it *was* the derringer in this case. Whatever weapon it was, I can't say I ever explored a corpse with more enjoyment. I'd've thought Willis might be stuffed with copperheads, but he had the same blood and muscle and bone and brain-pan a good human mortal shows under the knife. When you planning his rites?" He took a step away from the door. "I mean, I ain't hustling things, but of all the bodies've laid on the coolin' slab in my office, that's the one I'd most like to get shut of."

"Oh, Christ, Roy. I don't know. Soon as Grody and Broome get back to town. With French . . ."

"Town's startin' to buzz with talk, Will," said Doc. "They know Willis's body's there. They know Grody's gone into the woods with an out-of-towner. They know you and me and Phil've been piroguin' around the hall here. I bet they even know you sent Phil and Howard Markley out to Fountainwood to quiz the nigras this mornin'."

"Nest of buzzards," grunted Planteu. Then he showed up again, leaning against the front door's jamb. "I just thought Howard might help Phil considerably. Howard's got the dignity for it—Phil's a little too wimble-wamble, all the Adams's never weighed much to the bale. If the nigras know anything, Howard might likely get it out of 'em. *I* didn't want to go; it'd have scared the tripes out of the blacks havin' a sheriff show up." I could see him shake his head, the creases in his long sunbaked neck moving. "He didn't favor bein' deputized. He's new-married—second wife; his Emma got took in the cholera epidemic in sixty-nine—"

"I know, I tried to save her," said Doc Mattison.

"—and he kept saying how his job's to stay in town and teach school—how he'd taught French in his school before she went off to Miss Wentworth's academy. And how he knew she didn't have it in her to kill anyone, man or woman. Schoolteachers! I'll be deputizing young boys and girls and little dogs next. But Howard's safe . . . I don't want any more of this to get out than's already leaked."

Both of them were quiet.

Then Mattison said, spitting again—this time I saw the ambeer fly past the railing—"Town can turn nasty against Miss French, Will. Some of the young bucks—those about her age, who've pestered her to ride out with 'em in the moon's shine, puttin' on their best bibs and tuckers and ridin' all the way out here and bein' turned away as if they'd come up against an icehouse. Some of the town biddies, who've given up askin' French to attend their socials and quiltin' bees and sewing circles and church meetings.''

"Well," said Planteu, very slow now. "There's a shabbier breed of people than we had around here in sixty-one. Flower of the earth, then. Now they sit around too much, talk too much, hate too much—the Yankees are too far off to vent their spleens on, so they get turned in on themselves. Even on French, I agree. They hated Willis, but in a different way, the way you and I did. They don't like Miss French because of her quality. Even though she don't live better than they do—worse than most, to be sure—she lives *here*." He turned around and sighted along the hall and if he'd lowered his eyes he would have seen me for sure. "Goddamn it, I just don't want this fuss to reach the mayor. He's done enough for Lanceton, he don't deserve bein' dragged into a mystery at his age . . ."

Doc Mattison walked off, heels hard on the gallery boards. He stood looking down the drive from the edge of the steps. "I still can't place the time of death from the condition of the body, Will. Not to within four, five hours. I'd do better if I could. Between us and just while we're talkin' here and waitin' for Phil and Howard to rendezvous, you know damned well French didn't fire any weapon at Willis. You do know that, don't you?"

"I've never had a doubt."

"Fine." Doc turned; he was staring straight at Planteu. "Just so we keep that, always straight, uppermost in our thoughts, we'll bring French through all right, and the town'll simmer down again, even if we never find Willis's slayer."

He wheeled back, hands clasped behind him again, teetering on the edge of the steps. Then he was leaning forward, looking at the end of the drive. "Horse comin'. Maybe it's Phil and Howard with news of Fountainwood."

I couldn't hear hoofs from where I waited. I couldn't yet try to get up again and move backward, either. Sheriff Planteu was still too close to the door out there, for that. He said, soft-toned and almost to himself, "Speakin' of horses, I'd still give a mess of greens to know what happened to Willis's. He *had* to come here horseback from Fountainwood. He was a man it hurt to walk."

"Wore a corset to keep his belly in, too," murmured Doc. "Bet you hadn't known that. Found it when I undressed him to do my probin'." He was leaning farther. "Hell, it ain't Phil and Howard. It's just one of 'em. One horse." Then he said, "Hell, it ain't even one of 'em." After that he said, "Good God, Will, it's Grody!"

# 12

You might be thinking I'd ought to have made my way back along the hall and through the side-hall and kitchen and out the back door, then, while the going was good. Because Doc and Planteu were tumbling down the front gallery stairs and striding out to meet Grody. But I reckoned, even though I'd been here too long and was crowding my luck at not being discovered, and was a trifle worried in the back of my mind that French would have waked up by now and be wondering where I'd got to—reckoned I had to stay. For there were tall puzzles building up around me. French had said the derringer was right back in the cache under the lion's head which Planteu called a hidey-hole. And she'd said the derringer had been shot. Now it was gone, and Planteu and Doc hadn't found it in their searching. I had a second or two, lying there and gazing out along the hall past the mirrors to the front drive, of wondering if Gary Willis's ghost—it would be a mean ghost, bent on some kind of revenge—lingered here in Chantry Hall. And was dogging every move anybody made around here. And maybe putting that curse Jupiter had mentioned on French, and even on me. I lay still while an ant walked over the knuckles of my left hand, and didn't even disturb it.

Out on the drive, here came Flieshacker. On his rusty black gelding. I'd seen horses with more mane-tangles and muck around their hoofs and up their hocks, but only in flood-time. Down around the Tombigbee in Alabama. All the mud had dried on the horse, and Grody hadn't bothered to scrape it off himself. He was slumping in the saddle, that fat saddlebag which he kept all his tasty food in open and flapping with each tired step of the gelding. Gelding was so tuckered it might've been put through some massive horse-wringer.

Doc took the gelding's bridle and halted it. Grody just sat there. Planteu was standing on the gelding's off side.

He said, "How'd you know we was out here, Grody?" Said it soft but searching. "And where in the holy knobs of hell is Thomas Broome, and my Alice mare?"

Grody shifted his head around, staring down. Flat-jawed and slow as Moses about to deliver the whole roster of commandments.

Then he says, "I came in through town and stopped at the office, Sheriff. Nobody was there. So I went along to Doc Mattison's place. Looked in his office, and see Willis's body under a sheet. And Doc's housekeeper told me you both come out here and was meeting Howard Markley and Phil here when they get through scouting around Fountain-wood."

He took a gulping breath.

"As to Broome, he's made off with Alice. And I think he's made off with Miss French."

Sheriff Planteu didn't speak word one to that. For which I kind of admired him. Takes a good man to hold his steam at a time such as that.

Grody was getting down from the gelding. Did it very gradually, with a lot of groaning. Got his left boot caught in the iron, he was so tired, and Doc helped him remove it. Then he pulled the reins over the gelding's head, and, walking between Doc and Planteu, came up the steps. Planteu vanished from my sight, then came back in sight lugging a rocking chair. He put it down not far from the door and bade Grody, "Sit down here." Grody lowered himself. Like Noah beached after that parlous time in the ark.

Planteu said, "Doc, go back in the kitchen and pump Grody a cup of water."

I thought, Here we go, I'm caught like a rabbit in a snare. Stiffened myself.

But Doc said, "Hell, Will, water won't do him a whit of good." He was beside the rocking chair now, and reaching deep in the pockets of his black coat. He brought up a buckram-covered flask. He twisted off its cap and gave it to Grody. "Take a heavy dose, Grody. Specific for snake-bite and general megrims. Or if you're havin' a child, which it does appear you might."

Grody lifted the flask and drank for a time. Then he gave a small gasp and handed the flask back to Doc. I could see his meaty hands curving over the ends of the rocker-arms. "Broome is a depraved bastard. I knew it from the start, Sheriff, even when you were bein' nice to him and coddlin' him after he'd made off with Mort Tyler's claybank. He's a knife-fighter too."

Planteu leaned over him, voice gentle. "He knife-fight you?"

"Not exactly, but he throwed his knife in a tree seventy feet off and hit it square."

It had been about half that far off. And I'd been luckier than I usually am.

"He's a dangerous cuss and a menace to all who cross his pathway. Wouldn't be surprised but what that Standardbred of his is stole. And I got so much grief in me for lettin' him get away, there ain't no speech for it. Oh, the widdling bastard . . . I want to resign my job, Sheriff. I'll get me a little stone-farm and raise grass and pebbles. I ain't no good. A kitty with no tail is a better deputy. When I think how Broome's maybe on his way out of the county right now, no doubt havin' raped and throttled Miss French—"

"Grody," says the sheriff, still gentle. "Get a firm hold on yourself. Your resignation ain't accepted. What gives you the notion Broome even caught sight of French?"

"My eyesight, Sheriff. We'd trailed—or I'd trailed, Broome didn't do nothin' but folla me and eat his damned head off and keep up a runnin' line of chatter disturbed me from my trackin'—trailed Miss French on that stallion about three miles into the woods and borderin' the creek. Night caught us and I made camp. I slept light, watchin' him for a long while. But then I dozed off, and when I woke up—I had to go move my bowels—he was gone. That was about two in the mornin'."

Sheriff Planteu just waited. Something about his waiting told me he knew Grody wasn't exactly a light sleeper.

"Gone on your Alice mare, Sheriff. Gone carryin' all his own be-longings—saddle and bags and that fancy case—"

"That's a boxwood case for a fiddle," said the sheriff.

"—off into the dark. I waited till first-light. Then I was after him. Alice's tracks led me to that ride where Colonel Bob used to set up blinds for ducks about this time of year. And there was other tracks. The stallion's. So I knew then he was close-trailin' Miss French."

Sheriff Planteu took his cigar out and gave it a long, almost cross-eyed, look. Said, "Trailin' her? By night with the help of what moon there'd be through those trees along the ride, and a few stars? You're makin' Thomas Broome sound purely supernatural, Grody. Unless he had her in sight somehow."

He gave a glance at Doc. Doc shrugged, and said plain and quiet, "Unless she wanted him to see her."

I could see that was a thought that hadn't come near Grody's mind. He blinked, and even under the mud on his face, went pale.

"Oh, my Lord, Sheriff. How can you and Doc stand there and even think such things? Miss French wouldn't have no more to do with such an out-and-out, fly-by-night flim-flam horse turd as him than she'd desecrate her own daddy's tombstone."

"She'd already had somethin' to do with him," said the sheriff. "She'd borrowed his horse. Go right on, Grody."

"Well—" Grody shook his head, strong. "I follaed where he was close-trailin' her, and came up short where the stallion and Alice, both, had gone into the brake. Wasn't no way to get through there. Or trail 'em if I'd been able to go through."

Yes there was, I thought. If you knew where to go into the brake, as French did.

"So, Goddamn it, I went back the way I'd come. Forded the river, finally, at the shallow bend, and then came out on one of them lanes leadin' to the pike, the short way. You know them back lanes circle around the town?"

"No, Grody," the sheriff said. "I've only lived here sixty-five years, through before the war and all the times gettin' back on our feet after it, and hunted rabbit and squirrel and even courted in them lanes, and killed a man in them once—he was tryin' to rob me, it was kill or be killed—and been sheriff for the past ten years. So tell me about them lanes."

Then he got a grip on himself, taking out another cigar to replace the one he'd snapped in his fingers. "Sorry, Grody. Reckon I'm a shade restless."

"Yes sir," said Grody. "I was goin' along there, headin' for the pike and your office. And all at once here came Robin, that Arab horse Gary Willis bought last spring and has been sportin' around ever since, though Willis never learned to ride like a man. The Arab was comin' right at me, and comin' so fast and throwin' up mud from the lane—it don't dry out quick under there, Sheriff"—the sheriff didn't answer him, and Grody went on a trifle faster—"which of course you know . . . comin' so fast, anyhow, I hardly had time to see him, or see who was on his back. But I caught me enough of a glimpse . . .''

Sheriff Planteu had full control of himself again. He purred, ''Don't tell me Gary Willis was on his back, Grody. With raw head and bloody bones, cryin' for vengeance.''

''No sir, nothin' like that. It was Jupiter, that big nigra used to be kind of head man of 'em here at the hall, who went over to Fountainwood with the rest after Miss French couldn't keep 'em any longer. He hardly gave me a look. Just spurred on. He scared my horse and my horse threw me in the ditch, and then rolled down after me. Last I heard before I hit was the Arab's hoofs makin' for the river.''

I could see Grody straighten up, and he picked out a lump of mud that had hardened in the hair-nest at the back of his neck.

''I was—you might say—riled. I was goin' to ride after him and teach him manners. But then I reckoned my duty was to report to you, even if I've made a hominy hash of the whole job, and would still like to take off my badge and quit for all the good I've been. I'd still like to stand under a pump for a time, and go home and get some sleep, too. But my conscience won't let me do it while Miss French is missing . . .''

Planteu laid a hand on his shoulder. ''You did your very utmost, Grody. I appreciate it. Grab yourself a little nap now. Reckon I'm goin' to need you and Howard Markley and Doc here, and Phil. We'll have to fan out and scour the woods, and the roads too.'' He straightened, and said to Doc Mattison, ''Now we know about Willis's horse. I'm grateful for one piece of evidence in a haystack of conjecture.''

''Yes indeed,'' said Doc, walking away. I could still hear him. ''You think it was Jupiter, then?''

''Roy, how in the nation can I tell? If Jupiter followed Gary over here—and there's no other way he could have got the Arab, unless he found it wanderin' later—he sure might have shot Willis. We've got to look for him *and* French and Broome, *and* Alice and Broome's stallion. Once over near Jackson I saw a travelin' band of players. *East Lynne* was what they were acting. It started out with just a handful, and pretty soon the stage was so full there wasn't hardly room for the leadin' lady. I'm still of the opinion that behind this was a mission of French's—but till I can figure out what it was, and why she went on it, I'm just stumbling.''

He walked out and sat on the edge of the gallery where it let down to the top step. Sat hunched there, high shoulders and lean back like a jackknife blade not quite shut.

Closer to me, in the rocking chair, Grody had slumped again. He was breathing deep. Doc Mattison walked out and down the steps past Planteu, and then I saw him again when he'd moved out a distance from the foot of the steps. He went around on the off side of Grody's mud-caked gelding, where I could just see him in that distance. Then he was coming back again, carrying the scabbard with Grody's carbine in it. He climbed the steps, and leaned the scabbard and carbine against one of the rail-posts. Between the lofty columns past the gallery, the light fell in heavy warm veils, one of them lighting up the mud-clogged barrel of the carbine where it leaned.

Far at the end of the drive beside the pike-road I saw Doc Mattison's horse and buggy, and near them, Planteu's roan tied to the sagging gateway and grazing. I looked back to Planteu when he glanced back at Doc. "Yeah, thanks, Roy. I'll make sure he cleans it before we start out." He looked on back at Grody's face, which I couldn't see now; but I could tell from the sound that Grody was asleep.

I was about to start inching backward as fast as I could without making any noise, when Planteu stood up. I stayed where I was as he let out his breath and said, "Ah."

Two more horses were coming up the drive. One was the horse Phil Adams had been on when I'd first seen him, a mouse-colored gelding with forelegs too straight for much hard running; Adams sat him well, and was coming at a fair, fast walk. The horse behind him, moving slower, was a hard-mouthed big dapple gray that could have been taken straight from plow-hames, and on him, a man older than even Doc or Planteu, a man with a capacious gray white beard and a gray cavalry uniform coat flapping as he rode; he had seams around his mouth as deep as scars, and a face that generally put me in mind of the engravings of Stonewall Jackson. I put him down for Howard Markley, the Lanceton school-teacher both French and some others had already mentioned a good deal.

Adams swung off his horse, said, "Evening, Sheriff,"—the sun had gone well past noon—and came up the steps. He stopped on the gallery. "I see Grody's back."

"Let him sleep," said Planteu. Much as he wanted to ask questions—I could see him holding them in—he kept his council until the other man had dismounted and come up the steps. Then he said, "Howard. I know you don't like bein' deputized, but I thank you for bearing it. And I think you'll have to bear it a time longer, out of friendship and for the general good of the county and the town. Grody didn't find Miss French, and

Broome's come up missing too—with my other best mount—and it seems Jupiter, from Fountainwood, is runnin' wild on the horse Gary Willis must've ridden over here on before he was shot. And Doc's been remindin' me, the town will get stirred up over all this mighty fast; you've got to help me find out the truth and put an end to it. Will you?''

Howard Markley, taller even than the sheriff, gazed down at him with warm blue sorrowful eyes.

Then he nodded. And as Planteu kept gazing at him, asking questions now without saying them, Markley said, "Will, you'd better prepare yourself for another development.''

"Oh, Jesus in the mountains," said Planteu. Then he nodded in turn. "Say on.''

"Will, Fountainwood's a ruin. It is smoke and char and little else. It resembles what I believe Troy might have been after it was burned. I do not think there are any bodies. Philip and I searched—we found none. The ruins are still smoking, we couldn't look closely. The servants are gone. So are the horses.'' Markley had a voice in tune with Jupiter's, the same depth and strength. "I've seen nothing like it since the war. Since you and I and Roy and Marcus—''

Planteu flapped a hand. "Damn it, damn it, damn it. The war's long gone. We're here now. In what's meant to be a peaceable countryside, just now startin' to lift itself out of the slough of despond, as the fella says. With just the average number of scrapes and killin's, and time to breathe and start existin' again. Burned *down*?''

"Yes, Will.''

Doc Mattison had his eyes narrowed under his slight skift of eyebrows. "Fountainwood ain't far from the brake Grody mentioned. Where he ran out of horse-tracks.''

Planteu said, "French wouldn't have burned it, save by accident. And I can't see Broome doing it either. Oh, God.'' He pounded a fist in his other palm. "Why would they go out there? What's the motive in it? A crazy man don't have a motive, he just spreads slaughter and maybe fire with it. But French ain't crazy, and Broome didn't show a sign of it. All I'd have ever said he wanted was his stallion. A mission, what mission could she have?''

And maybe I should have stood up right then. And walked out along the hall and out of the front door and said, "Evening, gentlemen.'' It would have cost me more time in Lanceton County, to be sure. And maybe if I hadn't been that close—as close as you can get in the body, and with some of the spirit already there too—to French, I'd have done it anyhow. Maybe if I hadn't sympathized with her in what she'd told me about wanting that merry-go-round back so bad she was willing to go through what she'd already gone through for it. And maybe if I hadn't sympathized even more with what she'd said less about, which was her feeling of being put on a pedestal and treated as an angel-creature with no guts, no legs, no arms, only air and old piousness.

As it was, I wavered.

And wavered too long. Because Grody stirred, and stumbled to his muddy feet. And said, "He's killed her. And he's took his stallion back, and all the horses from Fountainwood, and when we find him I ain't waitin' for a trial, I'll strangle him on sight, and—"

"Shut up, sit down, and clean your carbine," said Planteu. "I'm not feeling too good about Broome myself. When we find him—with or without Miss French—I'm goin' to keep him in jail a time, just to cool him off. He won't get to Yadkin Fair this year, whatever circumstances might seem to absolve him. But I don't see why he'd have killed Willis, and I don't think he did. And I still know Miss French didn't, if only because she gave Roy her word on that."

He gazed at Doc, who gave a solemn nod. Then Howard Markley was nodding, and Grody was nodding hard, and Phil Adams was nodding, and it was a true love feast among them of faith in French's word.

If I'd ever had people who believed that much in me, as though I wasn't human at all, I'd have done something evil—like knocking the head off the town's Confederate statue with a paving stone—just to prove I was still able to breathe.

And yet, I thought, it wasn't even so much faith in her as it was in what she'd sprung from. Colonel Robert Chantry and his wife M'linda, and all of Chantry Hall and the bygone war itself, and the past as it had been before Harpers Ferry and Fort Sumter. And French knew damned well, in her soul, she couldn't just represent this all her life, but had to be herself all the distance. Knowing it had made her go after her merry-go-round, which though it was part of yesterday was part of her days to come. Knowing it had made her look upon me in the pond, say what she'd said, do what she'd done.

I kept myself where I was. And Planteu turned around to Phil Adams. "Phil, we'll start the search. Goin' to be pretty widespread. And so far, just among ourselves—still don't want the town or, God knows, Marcus in on this. You'll stay here tonight and keep watch. In case she comes back, or Broome brings her back, or something on that order. I don't think the way Grody does. I'm not love-blinded in that kind of sense. I got a notion he's helping her in something or other. If anybody shows up here, detain 'em. At gunpoint if you have to.''

Phil nodded, very thoughtful.

Then he was looking out past Sheriff Planteu's eyes, along the drive.

Planteu turned around to see what Phil was watching. And so did the others, one at a time.

I heard Planteu make a little noise under his breath. Not cussing. But just as if he'd kept hoping for the best all through this, and now the worst had put the cap on his desires.

A pony trap the shape of a large coal-scuttle was coming up the drive. It creaked and wobbled. The pony pulling it had a mane as rich as a great chrysanthemum's petals, and snarls of curls all down its legs and fetlocks. When it got close the little man driving it pulled up. He was so short he'd have had to be boosted on even a moderate-sized mule. His face was like a frail gray leaf with a strong clear light behind it. He had the oldest voice I've heard before or since. But with much sweetness in it, like a buried winter apple keeping all its savor.

"Good evening—all." He took time between words too. Spacing them as if each was a journey. "Doctor Mattison—Roy. I had dropped into your—office. To renew my supply of—medicine. Your housekeeper— told me—you were—out here." He was smiling, softly; I thought of a gnarled apple tree, still with blossom. "I saw—the slain—and dissected —body of—Gary Willis. He was—such—a stupid man. I know—the opinion is—that he was born—evil. But none of us—is born evil. I feel I must—look into this—myself. Was he—slain—by unnatural—causes?"

Sheriff Planteu had his eyes shut, his face turned partly my way toward the hall. He said quiet-toned, "No, Mayor. The cause was natural enough. Somebody put a ball in his head."

The mayor smiled even more. "But—you know very well—what I meant, Will."

Planteu opened his eyes and went down the steps. "I know, Marcus. But I didn't want you into this. You've had enough to do in your life, and most of it's been done for us, for the town. Nobody but you could have kept the peace when the 'baggers were down here. How you did it's still a mystery to me. You're too damned good for us. That's why I didn't, and don't, want you fretting about all this. You should be home, reading. Just living.''

"Oh, tushery and nonsense, Will. Thank you for your arm—I will accept it—I'll just sit here on the lower step. Thank you. Now, overcome your foolish—worries about me—I recall you worrying at Second Manassas—and later, when I asked you to run for sheriff—but I have not reached—the nineties without—learning a few things—that may be—of assistance. Patience—is one of them."

From where I lay I could hear him now, but not see him—or Planteu either. But I could still see him in the eye of my mind, looking around like a joyous new-fledged bird. "See here, Will. I picked this up—just out there—in the drive. A derringer, is it not? It resembles—one I remember —Bob Chantry carrying—in the field. Such a—silly—little—weapon. Not at all accurate—I believe—over six or seven feet. This one—is very clean. I can—smell no evidence—of its having been—fired, recently. And it is loaded. Rim-fire, is it—not? Yes, take it—I don't—want it."

I thought, French said it was back under the lion's head. And had been fired. Sheriff Planteu looked up and down and sideways for it. Didn't find it, even under the lion's head. And now here it was.

Somebody—here or round about—was protecting French. And, naturally, themselves.

Marcus Westerfield's voice—I recalled French and Grody had both talked about him with fondness—went floating on.

"Tell me—everything—Will. Not stinting. Taking—your time. Start at the beginning. A splendid—place. And take the opportunity—to look well upon—this day. It is—miraculous. I woke up—with this running through my head—'Hark hark, the lark—at Heav'n's gate sings—and Phoebus 'gin arise—' "

Then Planteu's voice went low in response. I could hear the tone only. He was telling it all. The voice was level and held-in, with angriness under it, and hating to have to tell it.

I started crawling back. Then I was behind the staircase and could stand up in shadow. I was stiff from my long stint there. I trusted it had been worth it. I went along the side-hall then, through the watchful stillness of the great kitchen, opened the kitchen door, and went quiet down the back gallery stairs. A minute later I was through the compound and across the field-corner, and then across the pike-road. And hastening along the ditch, even breaking into a run when I thought of French awake and waiting.

# 13

The plashing of the little waterfall into the spring-fed pond was the only noise I heard as I rounded the last curve of the lane to the Morgan farm and then peered down into the hollow. Then I caught the shine of Grayboy's eye under the thick shadow of the pecan trees, and then I could see all of him as he came out into the full light, being led by French. Behind them, Alice was hitched to the merry-go-round again, but I saw French had swapped saddles; Grayboy wore his own and had my saddlebags and the fiddle on him, and Alice was bedecked with the burnished Spanish saddle, which appeared far too rich for her plain blood.

French stopped, and I came in under the pecan-shade. She said, "You made me fret, Tom. If you were going to leave, I'd have appreciated your waking me and telling me so. I thought you might not come back—or if you did, that you might have dire news. Have you such news?"

"Sort of," I said. I sat down and motioned her to do the same. She did. Looking at her, I thought what a cool and collected woman she was; we might not have been as close as two people can be, only a few hours before. But then she reached and took my right hand and I could feel the pumping of her heart through her fingertips. "One point," I said. "Phil Adams is going to stand watch at Chantry Hall all night. So you can't take your flying jenny back there tonight. Not unless you want to run into an awful lot of questioning, which won't suit your purpose. Seems to me you've got two choices, and two only. One is to go down there right now and meet Sheriff Planteu and Doc Mattison and Grody Flieshacker—yes, he's back from the woods—and Phil Adams and Howard Markley and even Mayor Westerfield—they're all at Chantry Hall right now. You can ride in, your merry-go-round with you, and tell the whole truth, while I take advantage of them all being in one place and make myself scarce toward Yadkin. But with that choice, there are a few other things you ought to know about."

"Tell on, Tom," she said, her hand tightening on mine.

I told her about everything I'd heard and seen. A frown flitted across her brow when I mentioned the point that the derringer hadn't been in the lion's head cache. I told her about what Doc and Sheriff Planteu had mentioned, about the town feeling resentful toward her and on edge because of this general mystery. I told her about Grody coming back, and having seen Jupiter and having been run off the lane into the ditch by Jupiter on Gary Willis's Arab. I told her about Phil Adams and Howard Markley having visited Fountainwood and finding it burned to the ground. Then I told her about Mayor Marcus Westerfield showing up, and about his finding the derringer in the drive leading to Chantry Hall. "Seemed it hadn't been shot, or somebody had cleaned it," I said.

She stirred her shoulders. "Tom, somebody cleaned it—it had been shot when I found it there, after I discovered Gary's body on the stairs. To me, Tom—" She was gazing off at the rim of the hollow where the grasses took the lazy sun, "—this means no roving thief and murderer killed Gary. It was someone who wants to avert suspicion from me— someone who hadn't dreamed I'd go running around the countryside on a mission of my own, someone who's worried that suspicion would point to me because it was *my* derringer, and because it *had* been fired, and because I've vanished from sight as if I was guilty."

"Yes, I reckoned that," I said. "And it's also someone who knew the derringer was in the cache. Who'd know that but you, and the person who put it back there?"

She had the battered ballroom slippers placed close together, their tips touching. She frowned down at them. "They do watch over me and watch over me, Tom. I'm so eternally tired of it. Well—" She plucked a grass blade with her free hand, and put it in her lips. "I know in my soul Jupiter was telling the truth. From what you say you heard Grody say, it sounds as if he's going to hole up in the woods. So it'll take some maneuvering to get word to him, in the woods, that I want him to come out and back up my story of the burning of Fountainwood, and to tell people—even though he doesn't want to—that he knows who shot Gary. And to name the name. But I think that's what'll have to be done. And," she sucked in a good breath around the grass blade, and it whistled, "I'll ride back there. I'll do it now. We've come to a parting of the ways, Tom. I have to do this, even though it doesn't suit my purposes and even though as I said before, it'll shock and horrify and amaze them all, my whim about retrieving my merry-go-round. And you'll have to go straight on to Yadkin. Come, Tom. Now's the time."

We stood up. Then I clasped her to me. Seemed to me I was letting something go that had already altered my life as much as if I'd shed my old skin and found a grand new one beneath. I held her as if we were the one human being and not divisible by any air or time or space. I wanted her again, but under that deep urge there was so much more that we'd started to make between us. You sleep with a whore or a road-going woman or a fair-worker, and afterward it's just a quiet parting of the ways, no regrets and maybe see you again if our paths cross, and thanks for the enjoyment. It doesn't reach down and pain you, and burn your liver and lights. I took the grass blade out of her mouth with a finger, and put my mouth over hers and then when we'd stepped back a little, I said, "The other choice is to go on to Yadkin with me. For that we'll have to wait till dark, of course; and chances are good we won't make it without bein' caught, because they're all going to be mighty orry-eyed and on the prod around this part of the county. It'd be a lot worse for you—and sure worse for me—if we got caught together now. Sheriff Planteu's going to keep me locked up a while if that happens—he said so, and I believe him. And when it came out that you were escapin', even your dear protective friends would look at you with different eyes—and those who think you're too proud for your own good, in Lanceton, would truly have somethin' to wag tongues over."

She was nodding. Eyes silver and gray, grave and sorrowful, the amber sparks in them hidden like rays of light behind clouds.

"I'll have to take the first course, Tom." She was whispering it. I was holding her shoulders. Past her I saw Grayboy, in the striping shadows under here, lift his head and his nostrils go wide. He gave a slight snort; near him, harnessed to the merry-go-round, Alice lifted her head as well, testing the air that moved up over the rim of the hollow.

Same time, I heard the noise. It came from where the Lanceton Pike lay below us, off to one side of the lane-road we'd followed when we came up here. At first I thought it was a shivaree crowd visiting someone's farmhouse and celebrating by pestering the newly married couple. But then I remembered there weren't any farmhouses nearby but the Morgan's over on the opposite flank of the hollow with the sugar mill going easy in the evening. Yet it had that rangle-jangle sound of a shivaree, of people beating on pots and pans, and mixed into it was a noise that might have been a banjo but just a little more wailing and long-noted. The whole sound came here on the bright almost windless day, coming closer as it ranged down along the pike-road. I'd stepped back farther and turned to face the sound, as Grayboy and Alice were doing. French looked at me, her fine-shaped eyebrows rising a trifle. A rotted pecan crunched under my bootheel as I moved again. I was stepping over to Grayboy; I swung myself up; she'd saddled him well, just as well as I could.

He jerked his head, tasted the bit, raring to go. I held him. "I'm going down to the pike and take a look," I said. "I'll keep out of sight."

She nodded, and when I looked back she was almost out of sight again under the trees, a hand on Alice's borrowed Spanish bridle. The noise was louder through the sun as I rode down toward it. I took the lane for a short way, the clifflike walls beside it leaning in and Grayboy fighting the bit for a time, then we got lower and I cut to the west where long grass and heavy oaks would screen sight of me from the pike below. Grayboy still acted like he was full of three days' mash and idleness and wanted to run away, and I talked to him and told him he should be ashamed of such churlishness just because he'd had a fair rest. Then I pulled him up short and gazed down through the furzy but fall-bitten trees.

Around the bend of the pike under me came the procession; and it was a procession, not less. First the lead-cart, painted purple and gold and delicate blue, but all of it faded from years of wind and weather, yet with a strong feeling of brightness about it still. This cart was pulled by a double team, the horses stout and slow-going, with some strain of Suffolk Punch or Clydesdale in them, good horses and well kept even through their dust. Behind the lead-cart were seven others, all a lot like the first, with the pots and pans and copper flagons and kettles and bowls flashing and making their din upon the air as they swung from hooks along the carts' sides, and all these carts were pulled by single teams, their horses kin to the double team at the head of the line. Behind the tail-cart was a huge van, a horse-box I judged, but triple the size of any I'd ever seen, with a lofty arched bracing roof on it, its flanks covered with oak wood-strips like a house. It was hauled by yet another double team, the four horses knotting their muscles and their hocks and legs dappled with road-dust that fell from the big box's wheels in long trailing streams. And behind the great box-cart was a string of more horses, these lighter and slim-headed and moving along a rope leading to their hackamores, nine horses with the clean look of racing blood under their sweat and grime. Behind the last of the string of horses a boy padded barefoot in the dust, keeping them from straying on the rope. The whole caravan was in clear sight now. I could hear above the jangling of the cookware the sound I'd thought was banjolike, and I saw the man playing it—it was a mandolin-shaped affair like half a watermelon with strings attached, and a long neck that came up past the player's throat; he was leaning a bit from the second cart in line, and making his fingers go like the legs of a spider. I switched my eyes back to the first cart. It was approaching nearly under me. On the box and driving sat a man twice my size in girth if not in height, a full moustache, India-black, draping from his jaw. He wore a headcloth of dark green silk, shining like emeralds to the jogging of the cart. Gold or brass earrings dangled from his ears. He handled the double team as if he'd been born handling it—at no great speed, but at a pace ready to eat up miles through all day and night. Through the scent of riled dust and horse-sweat and people, I caught the scent of herbs—marigold flowers and coltsfoot and yarrow, foxglove and nettles and elder.

I'd known Gypsies before, though I'd never come upon a band with horses this fine, or with this many tight carts and traveling gear. They were always good people to talk with, though seldom to buy a horse from. The horse might be splendid, but if it was, you'd find yourself paying too much, and if it wasn't, you'd still find yourself listening to their gab and convincing yourself you could make a flat-racer out of a decent plug. And overpaying. But they'd come out of Persia long before—more years than this country'd had white men in it—and India still longer before that, and what I liked about them was their keeping to themselves and guarding their people as a she-bear guards her cubs. If Daddy'd been alive he wouldn't have missed the chance to drop down on them and talk at leisure; but I didn't have that sort of time.

I thought of Sheriff Planteu and the rest, even now probably starting out from Chantry Hall—Grody no doubt with his carbine cleaned and oiled again.

Took a ripe, full breath—then tossed myself on the mercy of God and horseman's luck. And put Grayboy down the bank, which he took in about ten long plunges, ending up with us both in the road and wheeled around in the direction of the oncoming caravan. The lead-cart driver squinted at me through rolling dust, then hauled up on his double team, and all down the line the carts stopped, the tall traveling loose-box the last to come to a halt, with the string of horses whinnying and milling slightly back there, and a dog barking at me from under a cart. The big man on the lead-cart was smiling at me, eyes so black it was like looking into wells by midnight. He wasn't looking only at me, but at Grayboy. The mandolin-instrument hushed down to a thoughtful little whisper, and out of all the carts came heads—men and women and children, faces dark, eyes jet, all silent, only watching.

The lead-cart driver squatted there in fleshy comfort.

And said, "Greetings. You spi the kalo jib?"

I shook my head, and put Grayboy closer. The horses in the double team stretched their heads toward him. "No sir," I said. "I know a little black language, but not enough to make a difference. But if you don't mind talking American, I've got a little business proposition you might like."

He settled back, his eyes hard put to stay off Grayboy, but moving back to me all the same. Said comfortably, "We will speak your tongue. The Romany Chai is not the only tongue we have, it is only the easiest. You seem in haste."

"I am," I said, and rode in closer.

# 14

He wasn't a man who was going to give anything away till I'd told him my proposition. Gypsies aren't. Every time I'd had dealings with them, I'd noticed that they had the power of listening a lot better than most people have. As if they soaked in what you said but actually read your meaning behind it. He sat back, broad and affable, as if he had all the day to hear what I would tell him. Back in one of the carts, the mandolinlike instrument started sounding just a tad louder, as if the man who played it was mocking me with his fingers on the strings.

I said, "My name's Tom Broome, and I'm in trouble." No point in saying less; or more, right now. "I've got to get out of Lanceton County; I'm on my way up to Yadkin Fair. Haven't got a whole lot of money, but I'll pay you to let me travel with you—it'd be safer in your midst. If you haven't got anything in that big loose-box cart right now, maybe I could put Grayboy in it, and me along with him. Just till we're out of the county."

Grayboy was side-curvetting and trying to nip the neck of one of the horses pulling this lead-cart. I reined him back, solid.

The lead-cart driver had his bundle of reins bunched in one of his fat dark hands. With the other he slicked his massy moustache. And just kept on regarding me, as if I tickled him a good deal.

I surmised he weighed in at about two hundred, without saddle.

He rumbled in his chest, as if coughing or laughing—I couldn't tell which.

Then he said, "Broome. That might be a Gypsy name. But I can see you are no Gypsy. A Gypsy would have talked about the weather, and wished me and my tribe well, and asked about other tribes along the road. Very well, you are pressed for time. Did you reiver that beautiful man-horse?"

"No sir," I said. "I didn't steal him. I'm just in trouble, that's all I want to say."

"That is your right, not to say. It was a foolish question. I do not know if you have enough money to allow me to risk your company. Is the trouble to do with the white man's law?"

"In a manner of speaking. But I didn't harm anybody, or steal anything. It's a misunderstanding."

"So many of those come about, do they not, Mister Broome? They come from suspicion. It is a most suspicious countryside. But you are in haste . . . I will tell you." He had his head canted back, and was giving Grayboy a good raking with his eyes now. Some men can drink in every point of a horse with their eyes, and he was one. "Hola! I have seen one other Standardbred with that line. That was long ago, in England, I was a boy. I never thought to see another. I will tell you . . . the horse-box is empty. We, my people and I, are on our way to Tennessee. There is a stallion in a town up there—not like yours, but a great sire; I have desired him for several years. This year we will buy him—we will make much money with his children. The horse-box is his traveling home. So that part of it is possible. But—"

He was stroking his chin. "But I do not know if you will agree to another idea. You are on your way to Yadkin Fair; so you are a harness-racing man."

I ducked my chin, yes.

The mandolin-affair made a little icy sound, like cold amusement.

One of the dogs had poked a nose out from under the lead-cart and was sniffing at Grayboy's forelegs. The lead-cart driver picked a whip out of its socket and snapped it—a lazy snap—an inch in front of the dog's muzzle, and the dog ducked back under the cart.

"So," this man said, "I do not know if you will flat-race him. You see,

I am thinking of more money than I believe you have. Between here and the road where we will leave you—near Yadkin—are some flourishing towns. Each has its fair horses. There is pride in those towns. Every year we come through, and we have these flat-races. Mostly we win—you see my string back there"

I gazed back through settling dust along the cart-line to the horses bringing up the rear.

"—but sometimes, in a matter of luck, we lose. I think if your beautiful man-horse can flat-race—he has the bone, and most of the courses are a mile, which would allow him to reach stride—we would win every time, this year. I think we would clean up. But maybe he is single-gaited—a trotter or a pacer, and that only . . . ?"

"A pacer," I said. "But he's not single-gaited. He can do whatever I ask him to. I'd have to ride him—nobody else."

"Understood, Mister Broome."

"And in no more than one mile-race a day. I don't want him tuckered out by the time we get to Yadkin. And even if we weren't goin' to Yadkin, I wouldn't force him."

A spark came in his eyes. "If I owned him—or only had him—I would feel the same. Such horses are jewels, not for easy spending. But—" He gave a huge shrug. "Maybe we are merely talking. Maybe my idea is not good. You say he can flat-race, but I would have to see it proved. I would have to know that with his bone and height—he is very tall, I would say a shade over seventeen and a half hands—"

He'd hit it right on the hairline.

"—he can get a swift start, and can run against the little quick horses and not be pocketed or lose heart."

"I'm willing to show you what he can do. But not here."

"Very well, Mister Broome. Along this road, not half a mile from here, on the left, you will come to a trace. There are willows along it, you will not see the opening—just ride in between the willows. We are going to camp there and have our evening meal, and then go on by night toward the Chickasawhay River. The trace runs beside a bayou, and there is room for a little trial heat. You can follow us now, if you wish—"

I said, "How long will you be at the trace?"

"Until we have made our evening meal, and tended to the horses and fed them. We will not start again until the moon is high."

"And say you like what Grayboy does. How much will I get out of these flat-races on the way to Yadkin?"

"Mister Broome—I am taking a chance. You are in trouble—which means men are seeking you. I am running the risk of having them find you with me. I avoid unnecessary violence. Our people have never engaged in wars. For the risk, I must be compensated."

"There's not that much risk," I said. "Only while we're in the county. After we've crossed into the next county, I doubt they'll still be following."

"So you say, but I cannot be certain. Well, I can see you have dealt much in horse-chaffering. My offer is—a quarter of what your man-horse wins on the way to Yadkin. And when you consider that I will be putting up the money for the bets, that is generous. All of this, of course, provided I am happy with him when he has been tested."

He was running his eyes over Grayboy again. Grayboy's ears had been laid back for a time, but now they were coming forward; he was getting used to the caravan.

"All right," I said. "I'll be along at the trace come nightfall. I don't want to stand out here in the road any longer. I'm obliged to you for your offer; it sounds better than the one I made you. And—what's your name, sir?"

He switched his sharp eyes back to me. Drew himself up fully—as full as he could while sitting there on the box.

"Shangro," he said soft-toned. "I am the king of this tribe."

"Shangro," I said after him. "Pleased to meet you, Shangro. I'll be there right after sundown."

"I will be waiting. And, Mister Broome, let me add that you can travel with your man-horse in the horse-box—there is plenty of room in it. And you can eat with us. Provided, naturally, that your man-horse stands up to this little trial."

I pulled my hat-brim to him—he gave a laugh this time, it wasn't a cough—and put Grayboy back along the line of carts. While I passed them, children and women and young men and old men looked out at me, their eyes steady, following me as I went along; when I passed the towering horse-box I could see it must have room in it for a lot besides a stallion; then I was riding beside the string of horses, and wondering which one Shangro would pit against Grayboy for his trial-heat. The caravan was starting up again now, Shangro's cart moving and his whip sounding, and then all the rest wheeling along, and the small boy handling the horse-string on their line looked back after me as if his eyes couldn't get enough of Grayboy.

I thought how this was the first time I'd ever met a king—or at least anybody who said he was one.

It had been a good, lucky meeting so far; outside meeting French, it had been the first real piece of luck I'd run into in Lanceton County.

On the way back and up the lane and then coming into the hollow—where the pond-water lay as if it was just a single sheet of glass now, all of a piece, reflecting the quiet evening sky—I didn't encounter anything more threatening than a turkey-buzzard pivoting in the middle of the day. I got off and led Grayboy back under the pecans. French had laid out what was left of the pone of bread and the woodcock and ham; she sat beside this collation as if she was waiting for me in a drawing room. I could see she'd been in the pond; her hair was still wet with it, and her woman-scent was blithe under the old gray dress. She turned her face up to me—as I came into this freckling shade, she'd been looking over at her merry-go-round, which was still shrouded under that canvas Jupiter had lashed over it.

In a low voice she said, "I fed Alice again, then I put her bridle back on. You were gone longer than I'd thought you might be." She reached up, and I took her hand and raised her to her feet. "I've just been sitting here for the past minutes thinking, Tom. It breaks my heart to know I shan't see you again after tonight. No, no—" She shook her head as if I was about to say something about that. "You can talk about riding back to Chantry Hall after Yadkin—but you won't be able to do it. I've been thinking about my own wilfullness and selfishness—they've made you a hunted man and this is, truly, the last we'll ever see of each other."

I said, "No, French. After Yadkin I'm coming back anyhow. I don't mind sitting in jail a few days till all this is cleared up. I've been in jails before. Can't say I like the food, but by that time maybe Sheriff Planteu'll have a better idea of who killed Willis, and all the rest."

Her drying hair was a darker red than usual; almost black, but with puffs of sunlight forming in it like rubies.

I pulled her to me—she felt damp under the dress, and smelled as good as all the bread of life.

She kissed me, but not with her whole self. And looked off toward the flying jenny again. "I've been wondering why I made such a to-do about the merry-go-round. I've always felt that way about it—since it came to Chantry Hall—but there's even more reason. Did I tell you Daddy wrote in his last letter from Virginia—the last before he was killed and brought back by Sheriff Will—only he wasn't sheriff then, he was Captain

Planteu—wrote that whatever happened after the war, Mama and I were to keep the merry-go-round?''

"No, you hadn't told me that," I said.

"I think Daddy knew he was going to be killed the next day. He wrote the letter the night before. I have it at home—it's a short letter, as if he was in a hurry to get it all down—as if he knew in his deep self that the war was going to be lost—and the one thing he makes a point of, he says it twice, is that we must keep the merry-go-round as a reminder and a joyful truth to remember the old days by. I remember Mama crying when she received it. And of course she was right to cry, though we didn't hear of Daddy's death till weeks later.''

She shook her head. "And yet, by getting it back now, I think I've just put you deep in a slough of woes, and I haven't helped myself much. Oh, I have not, Tom. I love you—have I said that?''

"Seem to remember you murmuring it and making 'mirations a few hours ago," I said.

She blushed just a little; a lovely touch on her good cheekbones.

"You were most gentle with me. You didn't fall on me as if you were—well," she smiled a bit, "I reckon I'm recalling Algy Marsden, now. Tom, I wish we could live in Chantry Hall—the rest of our lives, in amity and fullness. I want you to be beside me every night.''

"I'd like the same," I said. I was thinking pretty hard myself. "But you've got to remember, I'm a horseman, not a farmer or a man who runs a plantation. I don't know much about seed-corn, only the kind you feed horses. I've never made a cotton crop in my life. I'd shrivel and die in such an occupation. All the same—" My thinking was all through now; I was just saying this with my guts, and it came out of the center of my own self. "All the same I'm asking you, right this split second, to marry me. If you'll have me after all this is over and done. And I'm not makin' you an honest woman, as they say—it's not for that reason, or any reason other than that I admire you more than anybody I'll ever know, and I'm sure of it. I won't make a stay-at-home husband, and you won't be able to make me into one, even if that's what you favor. I'm not quality or gentry, for all you seem to believe I'm a gentleman bred. I've got itches in both feet, and I can't keep from a race-meet even if it's two spavined mules in a back pasture. There's the warning, and here's my mark on it.''

I gathered her to me, and when our faces moved apart she said into my ear, "I'll be proud to marry you. Whatever you say you are, and however hard it may be to bear—though I don't think it will be hard at all. It might not please Daddy—or poor Mama, for that matter; they had other notions."

We were looking at each other a couple of inches apart.

I said, "I know what other notions. Somebody like your Lieutenant Algy Marsden. Or somebody of equal upbringing."

She tipped her head to one side, the amber sparks brisk in her eyes now.

"But you see, Tom, Daddy's gone, and Mama with him—and even if Will Planteu and Roy Mattison and those people might not approve, I have my own existence to think about. I might well have gone on being an old maid till I blew away on an evening breeze, if you hadn't happened by."

She'd turned around. Had her arms folded around her, as if there was new coolth in the shade under here. "I don't want to go back to Chantry Hall yet. I purely detest going now. It's not just because I'll have to face a lot of questioning . . . it's being away from you, knowing you're on your way and may be trapped and caught and brought back. Knowing anything in the earth can happen while we're apart, to keep us apart, Tom." She'd whirled around. The dove-gray dress-hem lifting, whirling with her. "I've often thought what with Gary and his goings on through these past years, I labored under a curse. Maybe Jupiter was right; maybe Gary did put spells on people. Maybe we're somehow under the spell of his death now, brute and fool that he was. But—" She was stepping light toward me again, didn't even disturb the pecans underfoot. "Maybe we could lift it. By just going back and being married now, in the sight of all—all the Lanceton people, the well-wishers and those who don't wish me so well—"

Grayboy was putting his head down to what was left of the pone of bread spread on the cloth which lay on her cloak. I walked over and lifted him by the bridle strap to keep him from destroying it. Then I gave him a cheek-pat and came back to French.

"We can do better," I said. "You can come with me to Yadkin and we can get married while we're on the road. I've just made some arrangements for traveling. Wait'll I feed Grayboy and then let's sit down and have our evening meal and wait for the moon to come up, and I'll tell you all about it."

Her eyes went wide as if she was a fox suddenly coming face to face with a man on a forest path.

Then that dreaming look of delight, that drifting smile started moving around the corners of her lips.

"Tom, you wretch. Tell me!"

"You wait till I've done my feeding chore, French. And then we'll sit like a lady and gentleman and I'll put it forth for your examination, while we have supper. I'll just say for now that even after we're married, and have gone to Yadkin Fair—however the races there come out—we'll head back here, as man and wife, or gentleman and his lady if you want to think of it so, and face up square to your friends and neighbors. Which isn't telling you I'll farm at Chantry Hall."

The creak of the mill sweep was rising on the air beside the grasses of the hollow. I couldn't hear anything from down on the pike, though I had the notion Planteu and his men might well have spread out from Chantry Hall some time before.

I went to get the oat-sack from the willow basket and to unbridle Grayboy. I felt French watching me for a time—once, I looked around, and that happy, delighted, joying expression was still in her eyes and on her mouth—and I thought, You're in for it now, Broome. Pledged and plighted. But I was feeling wonderful about it too. At least part of my luck had started to turn, and now it was her luck as well. I didn't know if she favored Gypsies—didn't feel she might—but she could take that in stride too. For a middle-sized and even small-boned woman, she had enough stride to take anything.

# 15

It was going to be a clear night; good for traveling. Though I'd have appreciated it if there'd been no moon at all while we aimed down the Morgan farm-path and across through the grasses, and then came to the lip of the hill leading down to the Lanceton Pike. As it was, the moon rode high and bright, bringing out russet gleams in French's hair, and polishing the studding on the Spanish saddle which Alice wore; she was riding Alice now, and the merry-go-round made a soft bell-like sound as it moved behind her. I rode just a shade in front of her, gentling Grayboy and keeping him to a sedate walk. Which he didn't like.

French hadn't balked at the idea of traveling with Gypsies; she hadn't

exactly been overjoyed by it either. In her I could feel the same excitement I felt; it's always good to move again after you've had a long delay
on a journey. And there was a touch of stealth in the very moonlight, the
sight of a rabbit-scut as the rabbit dived into the bushes; the snort and
pluming of Grayboy's and Alice's breath on the cooling air. I could feel in
French the underrunning excitement of the idea of us being married. All
new to me, it was; I'd never even given a thought to being married before.
Just as new to her, I thought; a parting with her hemmed-in past, a saying
good-bye to old ways and gone times.

I scoured the pike with my eyes. There wasn't a touch of dust moving
on it. The red clay and the fawn earth lay as if waiting for a rider to disturb
their quiet—everything was as if cut out of black and white and bronze by
the silver hands of the man in the moon. I had the feeling I've often had
when moving at night along country roads or through little towns from
one horse-deal to another; as if you move along in a sleeping land through
a dream world, as if night changes the face of the land utterly, brings it
right back to what it was before any man touched it at all. A lonesome
feeling, it had always been then; now I had a woman, and a friend, and
knowing that made me warm in my belly, and made me wish good fortune
to all the hunting animals of the night. And to the humans in it. Even to
Grody Flieshacker, who'd be waiting for me somewhere not far off, with
his eyes peeled.

Grayboy's saddle creaked as I leaned forward. I'd soaped and tallowed
it before we set out.

Behind me, French said, "It's all so lonely . . ."

I reckoned she was thinking of all the time she'd spent by herself, these
past years at Chantry Hall.

"That's over," I said. "It's behind you. You won't be lonely on the
road. There's always somethin' coming up around the next bend." I
started Grayboy down the slope. "Sometimes just something pleasing,"
I said over the scrunch of his hoofs in the grasses. "Sometimes not so
pleasing." I was thinking then of the time I'd come around a curve past
midnight on a Louisiana road and there dangling on a rope from a live oak
that arched over the dirt, had been hanging the body of a black man. An
old man, his head canted as if he was looking up at the sky to ask why he'd
been put on earth in the first place. I'd stopped Grayboy, who didn't like
the smell of death, and tied him under the live oak and shinnied up and cut
down the body, and dragged it off into the bushes and covered it with
grass and fern. Daddy'd still been alive then, that had been a year ago;

when I'd got back from trading with the Louisiana man I'd gone down to see, I'd told Daddy about it. He'd said I'd done right. He'd said if he had it to do over again he wouldn't have fought for either side, South or North. His wound had been paining him that day.

At the pike-road I held up a hand. Behind me, French reined in Alice.

From the direction where Chantry land lay, silence. From the other direction, just the howling of the same hound I'd heard the night before while French and I waited beside the canebrake and Fountainwood's plantation house rose white below us. Only the hound voice—it was the Morgan's—was closer now than it had been then.

I said, "Come along now. And pretty sharp."

And I urged Grayboy to a quicker gait. French came along behind. Ahead I could see cart-tracks drawn in the dust, and the marks of a buckboard's wheel on top of them, and when we came to the first bend and the locust trees I recalled from riding back this way with Doc Mattison, I wanted to veer off to the side just in case we met somebody spang in the middle of the road. But I kept to the course; it was dare all and be damned right now. Alice's light clopping and Grayboy's deeper plunging of hoofs and the trembling and glide of the flying jenny's wheels all seemed to me to be loud as sin and fit to rouse the countryside. But then we were at the stand of willows. They draped over the trace fully; I wouldn't have known there was a trace there if Shangro hadn't told me.

I pulled Grayboy to the left, and put him straight at the drooping willow boughs. From here I could smell bayou-water. When we'd gone in halfway onto the trace—it was covered with leaf-mast, but firm enough for good footing—I stood in the saddle irons and looked around and back. French was ready; she nodded and rode Alice onward. Then we were on the trace where it was so dark you could only make out driblets of light sweeping over your hands and arms and the necks of the horses, and ahead were pools of blackness and at our side bayou-sounds, and the stench of brackish water growing stronger.

We rode on so for what I judged to be five or six minutes; I'd wound the turnip-watch before starting out for here. But I couldn't have seen it clear now if it had been pressing my nose.

Then the brake and trees to our left fell away, and there was the Gypsy camp. I couldn't help heaving a small sigh; I hadn't thought Shangro was fooling me, but it was good to see the camp there all the same.

The moonlight fell strong on the clearing. Coloring the purple and gold and pale blue of the carts, which were drawn up at one side; showing strings of smoke from fires and touching the hides of the horses, which were tethered and clumped over near where the bayou made a curve. Beside one of the fires, over which a huge pot hung on a cant-hook, I saw the emerald green of Shangro's headcloth; nearer to us, Gypsies were turning around to look. I rode right in past them, and next to Shangro. He had his hands on his wide hips, his yellow faded shirt reflecting the firelight, his eyes quick and merry and calm as he gazed up at me and Grayboy. In back of me French reined in Alice, and sat there as if she happened to be Empress of the Night, and I saw Shangro's eyes flick to her—it looked as if he had appreciation for the sight—then they moved back to me.

"Well, Mister Broome. We are ready. Would you join us in a bite before our little contest? You—and your lady?"

He didn't say he hadn't been expecting two of us.

I said, "I'll just drop these bags and the fiddle-case—I'm all set any time you are. And thank you, but we've already supped. French, this is Shangro." He moved over nearer her, looking up. French nodded down to him, and said soft and cool, "Mister Broome and I are delighted to be traveling with you, Mister Shangro."

"That is not yet wholly arranged, dear lady. But if it works itself out, I assure you we will be just as delighted to have you along. You are very beautiful. Mister Broome has excellent taste in horses, in ladies." His eyes had narrowed, just a trifle. At his side stood a taller man, who seemed to have just formed himself on the air there, walking so quietly I hadn't heard him come up. He had a headcloth like Shangro's, but pale blue, and pants of rusty silk that ballooned a little where they were tucked into his boots. His face didn't show any more than Shangro's; his cheekbones were high, and he made me think in the one look of a sleepy panther. "This is my son, Pella," Shangro said. Other men, and women among them, were showing up now around us. They ringed us, and the flying jenny, the way you see water flowing into the basin of a spring; one second it's not there, then it simply is filled up. With no special sound to speak of. Shangro said, "Have I not seen you before, Miss French? I have been coming through this part of the country for many years now. Are you not Miss Chantry, of Chantry Hall? Many years ago your father allowed us to camp on his land—just below the cemetery. You were younger, then, but you have not lost your great beauty—you had it then as a child, you keep it now."

"I remember, Mister Shangro," French said slow. "It was in high summer. You wanted to buy the flyaway filly—Daddy wouldn't sell her, but you talked a great deal, and I was sad when you left. There was an elderly woman with you—she told my fortune. I've forgotten her name, I am sorry.''

"Malana," said Shangro. "She was my mother. She has left us, I regret to say. She would have enjoyed seeing you again, as I do." He had laced his plump fingers around his belly; I thought how Chinese he looked, as if he could wait forever for anything, but also as if he was summing up everything while he waited. "I trust she gave you good fortune when she read your hand?''

"She said—I think she said we would meet again. By that she meant your people, I believe. And of course she was right, wasn't she?''

"My mother was never wrong. Even when those whose fortunes she told might laugh at her, she told them well and gave true value. Come, sit over here with me and be comfortable." He walked to Alice and held up a hand. He did look like a king, handing French down from Alice. "What a fine saddle," he murmured as French got down. She looked as if she was used to being handed down by any kind of royalty. The firelight caught her eyes in tiny sparks. "Over here," said Shangro, nodding to where at the base of an oak were several benches covered with bearskin rugs. Some of the women stepped back to let French walk between them. A handful of the children were staring at the flying jenny where it stood under its canvas, and I admired them for not lifting a corner of the canvas and peering closer. French was looking up at me, and sitting on one of the benches. She arranged her cloak around her and held it at the throat with one hand, the hood falling down her back, her hair from here in the fireshine like a dark copper river.

"And now," said Shangro. He nodded to the tall man he'd said was his son Pella. Pella reached up for my saddlebags, and the fiddle-case; he took them over beside French, and laid them down carefully. While he was doing this, Shangro put two fingers in his mouth and whistled. It was a low whistle, like a quail calling another. And into this firelight—again as if he'd grown from the ground, with no bustle but the sound of hoofs on the firm grass-beaten ground—rode a boy with sharp cheekbones, a jib of a nose, and eyes that looked me over once—and Grayboy in the same sweep—and then turned back to Shangro. "My son, Aldan," said Shangro. "Mister Broome."

Aldan barely nodded to me. He was lighter than I am; he had a light saddle, no horn, the English kind. It was the horse I was looking at, mainly. I'd seen him in the string earlier, but only had a glimpse. Now he'd been curried and shined to a fare-ye-well; he was a close-coupled quarterhorse, or with mostly that blood; his forelegs slanted back to packs of muscle, and his eye was good; he was staring at me, and at Grayboy, and standing with not much tightness in his mouth, even though Aldan was holding him in. Grayboy blew a soft greeting at him.

"I think," said Shangro, "to be sure of a fine, even start, we will back your horses in against that pine—" He gestured over to it. Already a lot of the men had moved over to the pine, and were standing lined up in front of it, in a double row, their arms folded. So they would form a kind of fence or corral into which we'd back our mounts. One of the men was the musician; he had the banjo-sounding half-melon-shaped instrument slung from his belt. All of the men had their eyes on us.

"I shall give the start," went on Shangro. Out of a pocket he brought a bright-colored handkerchief—silk, with suns and moons and zodiac signs on it. "When I drop this, you see. And the race will be as on a track—to your right, around the clearing, as close to the stand of birch beside the water as you can come, following the bayou on around, and back to the pine. It is not quite a mile, but nearly. Agreed?"

I said, "I'm agreed."

"Good. Let us back the horses, then."

Aldan wheeled his horse—coal black except for a ragged star just below the forelock—and was already riding over to the double fence made of men. He kept the horse tight, and the horse stepped with his neck high and curving, hard on the bit but not tense, with the titupping motion you see in an animal that loves to go, and wants to badly. I went along not far from him, noticing French out of my eye-corners as her eyes followed us, and Shangro giving an amused look at the shape of the flying jenny under its canvas, and the men at the pine and Pella beside Shangro staring at Grayboy, watching his motion. Then Aldan was backing the horse in. He went as smoothly as though he'd done it many times. Aldan's knees gave most of the direction; I couldn't hear what he was saying to his horse, but it was understood.

I ranged Grayboy in front of the double line of men, wheeled him and told him to back. It wasn't something he was used to doing. For a breath he hung up, standing and swinging his head around to me; I crooned to him, in no words, but gently, as though he was a good child. Then he was backing, coming into the pine's shadow alongside Aldan's mount, and snorting a little as he came into place. I could have reached and touched

Aldan, we were that close. On Grayboy's off side the eyes of Aldan's horse were looking straight ahead, Grayboy might not have been there.

Aldan was gathering the reins closer. I pulled just a mite on Grayboy, enough to bring his head up all the way.

Aldan and I were watching Shangro, who stood foursquare, as though rooted to the firelit ground.

Then the bright-colored handkerchief fluttered and shone as Shangro raised it, and then it was floating and fluttering to the floor of the clearing.

Aldan's horse was out between the rows of men as if he'd been shot out; I was a full length behind, and I knew, as I'd already known deep in my bones, but this was all out in the open now, that I was in for a real race.

You can always tell; sometimes it doesn't come till later, but sometimes the challenge comes right off the mark, as this one did. The Gypsy horse was a fast starter, maybe the quickest I'd ever ridden against. Every part of him worked right, and Aldan was a rider who knew just what the horse could do. From the *ugh* of sound both horses made in their bellies—a kind of sound like letting everything loose, which I always like hearing—to the slug of Aldan's horse's hoofs ahead of me across the clearing to the birch trees, and the noise of Grayboy starting to make stride and move under me, everything was wrapped in both of us. As if it wasn't even night, or a big clearing, or any time at all, but just a space of being we'd carved out ourselves, with nobody else in it. Maybe that's what racing is all about, flat-racing or any kind, I don't know.

I knew by the time we were midway to the bayou and those birches that I'd have to catch up now or lose the race. You can tell that at the start too, sometimes. I leaned over Grayboy's neck, smelling the ammonia-scent and seeing the sweat start out on his neck and watching the earth-clumps fly back like bats flinging out of a cave, and talked to him strong and deep. He had stride now, not the pacing stride, which is different and locked into the harness and the sulky. If he could hold it we'd overtake Aldan, and if he could turn, sharp as light, at the birches, we'd be ahead from then on. It was the turn I was worried about. Aldan's mount was as wiry as a weasel, and damned near as fast to maneuver. Turning Grayboy in that place near the trees would be like turning a ship, and if it wasn't done in time we'd go straight through the birches into the water.

Just as we drew level with Aldan, I could tell that was what Aldan was going to try for. Because as we moved ahead, he swerved his horse—the horse's ears were tight along its head as a panther's in the crouch—and hit

Grayboy's off shoulder. Wasn't a jolt heavy enough to throw Grayboy off stride, but the next one would be. He was going to try it again. He was coming up now, giving every ounce he had, and aiming for the off side as he came. If I'd let Grayboy all the way off the bit as Aldan wished, I'd have crashed right through the birches. Which were swimming near in their falltime paper-thin bark against my vision, with the smell of bayou water like a dark wall around us.

I checked. Did it so fast Grayboy reared back, back-haunching and towerlike, so I seemed a mile off the ground and the stars high above the birches rolling around me, then I brought him down and for one pant of a second he just stood, and in the same second Aldan and the little marvelous horse rode straight in through the birch-tangles and then there was a deep splash, and a yell from back at the pine, and I was wheeling Grayboy left, and following the curve of the bayou, but not looking back. I brought Grayboy back around, and cut him to the pine, as if Aldan was still a hot breath from our heels. Then I rode Grayboy in between the lines of men—they weren't standing with arms folded now, but yelling and laughing and slapping Grayboy on the ribs as he came in. At the pine I stopped him, turned him, and rode back to Shangro.

Across the clearing, Aldan was walking back across the moonlit and firelit ground, leading his mount.

French was at my side. She took Grayboy's bridle as I swung down. She led him a little distance off, stroking him. When I followed her with my eyes, she gave me that smile again, as if a golden joy had flitted just for an instant across her mouth. A couple of the men had flung blankets around Grayboy, and were walking with him as French walked him out.

Shangro's gaze followed Grayboy, and came back to me.

I said, "Your son Aldan's quite a rider, Mister Shangro."

"Yes." His moustache shone like a bird's wing as he lifted it, preening it. "He is very capable, Mister Broome. I hope you do not think that was a—what do they say?—a dirty Gypsy trick."

"No," I said, consideringly. "I'd have done the same, if I'd been up on his horse."

"But if he had been on yours, I do not think he would have had the wit to check. He is a very good boy, but he would not have thought of that in time. I think you will be friends . . . Aldan," he said. Aldan was beside us now; the little horse was covered with strings of weeds from the bayou, and shaking its head and eyeing us askance. The English saddle was soaked. "Aldan, you may now congratulate Mister Broome. You rode Flambeaux well; do not despair."

Aldan stared at me. Then he grinned. It was a grin like the grin of a happy wolf. "I congratulate you, Mister Broome. And it will be a pleasure having you with us."

Pella, the tall son, was coming over to us. He put an arm around Aldan's wet shoulder. "You have a certain stink," he said. "Take your clothing off, and wrap yourself up. I will rub you with balsam." Under one arm Pella carried a box of herbs. "I will tend to Flambeaux." He took the little horse's bridle. And shook his head. "A trifle too eager," he said. "He will outgrow that. Meantime, it was a bump, and no more. If I could buy your horse, Mister Broome, I would give you a thousand English sovereigns for him. Or the same in American money. But you won't sell him."

"That's right," I said.

"Where would you find a thousand English sovereigns?" said Aldan to Pella.

"I would make it my work to find them," said Pella. "But the horse is not for sale. Off with you."

# 16

I went to the saddlebags and got a currycomb and after I'd helped French walk out Grayboy and rub him down, I gave him a shining. Shangro was striding among the carts now, giving orders in a low, quiet voice; I noticed he never shouted. I examined Grayboy's shoe-plates well; the near fore was just a shade loose. I'd noticed a small forge over beside the string of horses where Pella had taken Aldan's Flambeaux, and where the cart-horses were being cut out now, their drivers doing it neat and easy, without the bumping around and yelling you'd hear in most big stables. French stayed with Grayboy as I walked off. A couple of the Gypsy women were sidling up to her, about to speak to her in a shy way; she was talking with them when I looked back. I found Shangro with his son Pella helping him as they harnessed the double team. The big draught horses backed in as tidy as mice going into holes. I said, "I notice you've got a forge. I'd like to use it, and your smith. I'll pay him if you think I should."

Shangro left off buckling harness and smiled. "I told you, Mister Broome, if you passed the little test, you would ride in the horse-box. I said you would eat with us. You have also the other privileges. Cando is our smith; he will give you whatever your man-horse needs. We have a mare coming in heat, by the way; I am not asking you to breed her with your man-horse. But it would be wise to keep him in the horse-box tonight, and as soon as possible. I will help you get him in there, and yourselves settled, in just a few minutes." Pella was finishing the harnessing. Shangro stood back, eyeing the canvas-covered flying jenny. "Is that what I believe it to be, Mister Broome? A carousel?"

"Yes sir. It's French's."

"May I?" He lifted a flap of the canvas. "Ah!" He peered in at one of the horses—the cream one with gilt around the mane. "Magnificent work. From Firenze, I would say—beautifully turned. Yet—I have seen it recently—" He dropped the flap; a couple of children had been standing close by, peering with him; they looked at each other, large-eyed as otters, and muttered to themselves. "Get along to your mothers, Rico, Jal," Shangro told them. They scuttered away. Light broke on Shangro's dark copper face. "I know where now. Maybe a month since—I was passing the plantation called Fountainwood, the other side of the Lanceton River—the master there, a man named Willis, sent a man to summon me to see him. I had, of course, known of him; I had heard he dabbled in, let us say, the black arts." Shangro's lips went out in disgust. "It is not a good thing for a white man—or for any man not versed in lore he has inherited with his blood. Such a man may summon up more than he can handle . . . at any rate, Mister Broome, I was not impressed with him. As soon as I saw him I knew the stories to be true. A weak man, in general—and a vulture, preying upon the countryside after it had been ravaged by the fools who came from the north following the war . . . he told me he and his friends who visited him from the north—carpetbaggers is your word for them, we have other words in the Rom—had conducted certain rites. And he was attempting to pump me about those same—rites. He offered me money to tell him what I knew . . . ptah!" Shangro spat lightly. "Had I told him what I know . . . what my mother knew, and my father, and their mothers and fathers before them, back into time so far only the heart's blood can see—it would have shattered him. I refused his money, he called me a name and told me to leave. But that is where I saw the carousel—in that ballroom, which was stained with his presence, and the presences of his magic-dabbling friends. It looked out of place there. Something innocent and fresh and with grace, set down in a den."

"A desecration," I said, remembering what French had said there.

"Exactly. I am wondering—but you may keep silent if you wish, I shall always respect your right to—I am wondering how the carousel came to Miss Chantry."

I pressed my lips together. Then because I didn't feel bad about telling it to Shangro—and knew as I decided to, that he wasn't about to betray me, and knew as well that I needed somebody outside, so to speak, to tell all this, and had needed such a body for some time—I said, "It was hers to begin with. She got it for her seventh birthday. And as for Gary Willis, he's dead—shot through the head, the ball went right back into his cerebellum, as I heard a doctor say today. And Fountainwood's burned down. The flying jenny—the carousel—is most of the reason French and I are here right now."

He'd been leaning back against a cart wheel. The great draught horses were in place now. Over at the tall, lofty horse-box I saw men harnessing the other double team. And somebody had let down the back of that horse-box, and it looked ample enough inside to hold the whole yield of cotton bales from a sizable plantation.

"That is interesting news indeed," murmured Shangro. "Come, let us get your man-horse and visit Cando." He gestured over to the forge. "If you wish to tell me more—you have whetted my curiosity—I would appreciate it. But at your discretion, Mister Broome."

"I trust you," I said. "Since we're going to be racin' partners, I reckon I have to anyway. But the trust is there."

"Thank you."

We walked over to where French stood with Grayboy, a clump of women around her now. One was touching her hair, fondling it easy and with admiration. Grayboy glistened like a horse made of dark shiny marble, and ducked at my hat, but I foiled him and took his hackamore rope. Shangro bowed to French and said, "Your home is being prepared, Miss Chantry. If you need anything in it while we are on the road, let me know. I repeat, it is good having you with us." Then in Rom he said something soft to the woman who was fondling French's hair. She took her hand away. And French said, "Please don't chide her for that, Mister Shangro. I'm glad to be admired."

"It is the color," said Shangro. "Rare and unusual, for us who are so dark. Her name is Garsina—she has little English, but a large soul." He said something in Rom, again, and Garsina nodded and put her hand back on French's hair, wonderingly.

While we went over to the forge I started telling Shangro about what had happened. I put in everything, except naturally about the making love beside the pond, but I reckoned he'd gather the gist of that without it being embroidered on a sampler. His eyes got very thoughtful when I came to the taking of the flying jenny, and I said, "Maybe it's a sin to reclaim your own property when you've already sold it—or had to sell it—to a man you detest, but I don't see it that way in French's case. And too, it was practically the dyin' wish of her father." I told him about that, too.

We were at the forge by then, with Cando, a man so old I thought he wouldn't have beef in his fingers, but a man who handled the tongs and the hammer on the anvil as if they were a child's toys—and Grayboy was skittering a little, as he always does around a smith. Cando didn't speak American at all, but he told Shangro in Rom that he'd prefer making a whole new plate rather than renailing the old one, and Shangro passed it along to me, and I said all right if he could make one as light as the others. Cando sniffed and glared at me, and set to work making it after he'd taken a close look at the loose plate. I held Grayboy and gentled him—he was getting a little randy too; he could smell the mare Shangro had mentioned, here somewhere in the night. Shangro said, "I do not consider what Miss Chantry did at all evil. Or the least wrong. Strong-minded, yes." Sparks blew past his shirt as Cando blew the fire up. "Her father I recall as gifted with the same spirit. I pity the man—Jupiter, very tall, massive?—he is the manservant who summoned me to the pitiable presence of Mister Willis—I pity him for his belief that Mister Willis might have placed a spell on him. Mister Willis could not have put a spell on a grasshopper. I can see that he would wish to cleanse Fountainwood with fire. But he must be found and disabused of the idea that he cannot tell who murdered Willis. No doubt it was someone he thinks highly of . . ."

"Not French," I said. "Hold up, you lovely bastard—" That last was said to Grayboy. Shangro gave me a hand with him, stroking his cannon-bones.

"No, I think not, Mister Broome." He was talking loud over the hammer, which had started now. "Maybe your friend Sheriff Planteu will find him. I gather he and the other friends of Miss Chantry are fretting a great deal?"

"Yes sir, and I regret it!"

"They are good men—even your Mister Flieshacker, who means well. I have known them only casually, for many years. But the best among them is their mayor, Mister Marcus Westerfield. Maybe you have not met him. He seems absent—touched with moonlight—yet he has greatness of character, of comprehension. It was he who kept the town alive during Reconstruction—who turned away the carpetbaggers, and who did it without bloodshed. It was he who—"

"I've met him!" I said. Then, pretty loud because I had to talk over Cando's hammer, and keep Grayboy calmed at the same time, I told Shangro the rest of it—about going back to Chantry Hall this same day, and hearing what I'd heard, and especially about Mayor Westerfield finding the derringer after the sheriff and Doc and I reckon Phil Adams who'd have been there then with them, had sought for it in the very place French had seen it last. I told Shangro about the point that the derringer had been cleaned, and didn't appear to have been fired when it was found in the Chantry Hall drive. "—so you see I've met the mayor," I finished up. "It's just he hasn't met me."

Then Cando had the plate ready, and Grayboy's near forehoof pared a little; he did it as right as I've ever seen it done, shaving so fast and true it was over before Grayboy could snort twice, and he was crouched with the hoof nuzzled in the crook of his left arm against his apron, and had the nails in quick and tight and Grayboy was tossing his head but quieting down. Cando gave me another stern look. Said something in their language to Shangro. Shangro laughed. "Mister Broome, he wishes you to know he can make plates even lighter than this. That if you wish a mule shod, you may go to a smith whose skill deals with mules. But for true horses, he is your man."

What Cando'd said had sounded more salty than that. I reckoned Shangro had toned it down for me.

I reached and shook Cando's hand. It was still warm from the shoe and hard as sole-leather. He didn't grin at me, only gave a tiny jerk of a satisfied nod, and turned away.

Shangro and I walked Grayboy along to the high horse-box. A couple of men—Pella and Aldan among them—were waiting there. Most of the fires were out now. The moonlight showed highlights of the horse-string, which was in its place behind this huge horse-box. The mare going in heat was with them, I knew it from the way Grayboy's nostrils tasted the air and his crest started to swell higher. Shangro turned and called to the small boy back there among the horse-string, "Tomas—hold Farella now. If she is hurt, I will be very sorry."

I could just see Tomas's eyes among the horses as he clung to a brown mare. She was shying, she wanted to run off and be a coy maiden, the way mares get when they come to season. She wanted Grayboy to follow after her, too. She could scent him as he could her.

While two older men, and Pella and Aldan and Shangro steadied the horse-box ramp, I got up on Grayboy and brought him up to the base of the ramp. Then I fanned him hard with my hat, and said, "Up!" He'd never been in a box before, except a box stall, and his nostrils went even wider and his ears came back with those veins—soft as velvet to the touch—around the ears swelling. Then he gave a jump as if he'd go clear through the end-wall and out the other side, and in the box—he hadn't touched many of the ramp-cleats coming up—I had to pull on the hackamore till I brought his head back, to keep him from putting a forehoof through the wood. The box—so high shadows got lost in its roof—was divided in two parts, with a door in the dividing wall; I'd ridden him through the door. There was a capacious manger in here and water and racks for the tack. I slid off and patted him, and tied him by the hackamore rope to an iron loop. There was corn in the manger. Horse-blankets hung on the walls.

At the end of the box, back of the manger, was a peephole with a lath over it that you could slide back and get air from, or talk to the horse-box driver if you felt like it. It wouldn't have been a bad place to travel in, all by itself. But when I stepped back into the other part of the place, and shut the door, I could see this was even more favorable, at least for human traveling. There were two lamps burning, wicks trimmed, the lamps hanging on chains from the ceiling. And a bed built into the wall like a bunk, and cabinets for gear and staples. A couple of thundermugs—sort of splendid ones, done in china and scrolled flowers—under the bunk. Shangro was looking in at me. "It is not a terrible home. And there are many sights to see. The curtains draw back when you wish them to. Do you want your saddle and bags—and I see you play the fiddle—with your man-horse, or here? And here is the splendid saddle for Miss Chantry's mare . . ."

Aldan and Pella were carrying them. "The mare can go with the string," Shangro said.

I shook my head. "No, she can't. She belongs to Sheriff Planteu."

"Oh!" His eyebrows cocked. "The same one you went into the woods with. I have it straight now. I had thought Miss Chantry perhaps owned her . . ."

"No sir," I said. "All she owns outside Chantry Hall and the grounds is what she's got on her back and in her willow basket. And a half-interest in Grayboy, since he's mine and she has an interest in me."

"That is not so little, I believe," he said. He said it in a grave manner. And frowned. "I have been thinking of the discovery of that derringer you mentioned. Someone is protecting Miss Chantry. But it must be the same person who either committed the murder or saw it done. The black man, Jupiter? There are mysteries inside mysteries, here." He sighed. "Sometimes—I will tell you this because we are friends now—I have the second sight. It is nothing, no rich gift. It bothers me at times. But it does me no good at deciphering the actions of mankind. If it did, I would be able to tell exactly which opponent would ride best, and how he would ride, and I would be wealthy, but it would take the joy out of life. Well—back to the disposal of this mare. She is, we must face it, reivered."

"Borrowed," I said.

"In a good cause, Mister Broome." He had plumped himself on the end-flooring, legs swinging down beside the ramp. Aldan and Pella brought Grayboy's saddle and bridle and the bags and the fiddle-case inside, and stowed them on the floor, and with them, the Spanish saddle and bridle. Aldan gave me a grin as he swung down again. "And her saddle, surely that is not Sheriff Planteu's?" went on Shangro.

I filled him in on what I'd left out about Jupiter giving us the saddle from the Fountainwood stables. I could hear Grayboy moving in his new home, his plates troubling the straw and hitting the floorboards. I filled in some other cracks of information, telling Shangro all about how French had *had* to use Grayboy because he was the only locomotion around Chantry Hall after she'd found the body, and making it all as clear as I could this time. He nodded. "Yes, she has her father's fire. I can see she would not have tolerated the corpse of a man who had treated her as Willis had, in her home. I can understand her riding for Doctor Mattison, before she set out for the carousel. The town of Lanceton would not, on the whole, understand that. Or comprehend her wishing to have the carousel before it burned. Or understood her allowing Jupiter to burn Fountain-wood. They are logical, practical people. With the great exception of Mayor Westerfield . . .'' He stood up. "Mister Broome, the disposition of the white mare is in your hands. Contrary to legend, Gypsies never steal horses. They may make a fine-drawn bargain from time to time, it's a matter of pride and skill as you yourself know, but it would go against my judgment to take the sheriff's mare with us. But I leave it to you. Pointing out, as I do, that if the mare joins my string, she is so obvious she will have to be dyed—and the coloring will take time.''

"I think we'd best turn her loose," I said.

"I agree. It is a distance from here to Lanceton. She is of an age to have good sense. She will find her way back, and while she is finding it, we will be going the other way, to northward. Tomas!" he called.

The small boy with the horse-string came running, feet as dusty as the earth itself.

"Tomas, take Miss Chantry's mare—the white with black stockings. Take her all the way to the pike-road, and head her toward Lanceton. Ride her.''

"Her name's Alice," I told Tomas.

"Give Alice a slap on the rump, Tomas, and tell her to go home. Then come directly back here. And when you have done this, tell Rico to walk with the string the first part of the night, and Jal to walk with it when the morning star rises.''

"Aye, sir," said Tomas.

From the side of his moustache, Shangro said to me, "He speaks English very well. Better every day. He is my grandson, Pella's boy. His mother—Garsina—clings to the old ways, the people's language. But he will grow to be skilled in other manners, without losing what he was born with.'' He clapped his hands softly. "Repeat after me, tell me my orders.''

Tomas nodded. He looked like a small post with hair all over the top.

"Ride the white mare, whose name is Alice, to the pike-road. Give her a slap on the ass in the direction of Lanceton. Come back here and tell Rico to take the string till the morning star shows, and Jal to do it after that.''

"Rump, Tomas. Not ass. Horses do not have asses. Nor do asses. They have haunches, rumps, hindquarters. Otherwise, very good. And when you have done all that, go to sleep."

"Aye, sir."

Tomas ran off. I said, "He'll learn a lot about men being horses' asses, soon enough, though."

"Indeed, and I wish him to. But for now we must be correct in our terminology." He cast a glance around at the Spanish saddle, shining in the lamplight beside Grayboy's.

"You think I ought to've sent that back with Alice too?" I asked.

"Certainly not, Mister Broome. A gift is just that—a gift. I would accept it as such. We too, Mister Broome—" He put a hand on the flooring, and dropped down to the ground—light for all his weight, as Grayboy could move when he wanted to. "We too can be practical, and logical, we Gypsies, within the rules of our existence. It is only that we do not let it blind us to more important matters. Ah." He had turned around. "Here comes your lady, with Garsina." French was walking toward the horse-box. She carried a couple of boxes of herbs; I could scent elder and dockroot and violet plant. My mama had collected herbs; I could hardly recall her, but when I did it was with that soothing fragrance. Garsina, dark and tall, carried more boxes. Shangro bowed. "Miss Chantry, your home is in readiness. I wish you a good night. Mister Broome has told me of your plight. I sympathize with it—with all of it. I hope you rest most pleasantly."

He looked at her for a moment longer, then took the fingertips of her right hand and kissed them.

There wasn't anything fancy, or funny about it.

It was like wishing us both an extra dab of luck, and wishing it for himself in the bargain.

Garsina put her boxes on the floor here, and French put hers down, and French said, "And the same to you I'm sure, Mister Shangro," and made a quick curtsy. Then Shangro and Garsina melted off into the moon-glinting dark. I reached a hand down to French, and pulled her the rest of the way up the ramp. Looking around the horse-box side, I could see carts coming into line, the caravan forming. After a second or so while French was looking around this cave of a room with its lamplight-washed walls, I pulled up the ramp by the rope handle and that really shut us in for the time being.

The merry-go-round, still with its coat of canvas lashed around it, was over on the left wall as you faced the dividing wall of the box. I reckoned it was the first thing Aldan and Pella and the others had put in here for us. I hoped to win Shangro, and them, some races. I hooked up the side-latches of the ramp, which made a tight rear door over this establishment.

I said, "Good evening, ma'am," to French.

"Good evening, Tom."

I had a feeling about her stronger than I'd ever yet had, though I hadn't known that could be. Looking at her bright face, the handsome nose, the elegant cheekbones, the spill of rivering hair, I had the pure notion she'd look like this when she was eighty-two, or even more. Still with that brilliance about her, still reaching and yearning. And finding, I reckoned.

"You think I was wrong to tell him?" I said.

"No, I would have if you hadn't, Tom. I declare, I like these people. I hadn't anticipated—"

"No, not like this, I hadn't either. They're supposed to be thievish and mean. The way black people are supposed to have some kind of special smell. Well." I crossed to the window over the bunk and pulled aside the curtain. There was a bustle of doing out there, and the jingle of harness and the smell of the whole night moving in past the herb-scent from the boxes.

"I can't even talk to Garsina," French said. "But she's a dear woman, and she likes me."

"Well," I said, "you don't have to talk to people with words to know them, any more than you do to horses. There's a great deal people can learn just by learning it. We'll get married tomorrow, if we can, if there's a town handy we can do it in, and we're out of this county."

"Maybe it doesn't matter that much, Tom. Getting married."

She'd said it at my back. I was still staring out. The window had little diamond panes in it, you could leave the whole sash open to the air, or pull it in on its hinges. I left it open and dropped the curtain.

"It matters to me. Unless you've had other thoughts."

"I mean, Tom, as a matter of—sanctification. What other people think."

"My, my," I said. "You're going to be astonishing me, one way or another, all your existence long. We'll get married anyway, first chance we get. I couldn't take you back through Lanceton and to Chantry as other than a bride."

"Tom, I wish you would come here and love me."

"Yes," I said. I was next to her now, and taking off the old cloak.

Which pooled on the floor behind her. Grayboy knocked a plate on the floor again, on his side, and made a rustling in the manger of corn. "If we win anything up at Yadkin," I said in her ear, "I'm going to buy you another gown. And better slippers. Right now you don't need gown or slippers or shift, though. Do you?"

"I reckon I do not, Tom."

I carried her to the bunk. It was smooth enough, a most redoubtable bed.

# 17

Whippoorwills woke me.

They were chanting that song they make just before morning. All around us along this road, sounding above even the noise of wheels and the rattle of the horse-box and the sound of many hoofs moving.

As if they sang their souls out just because they welcomed the fresh day.

I lay close to French, nestled into and around her as though the two of us were good silver spoons fitting into each other.

I could feel the long, lovely moist line of her spinal column; I ran my fingers along it, in those tiny hairs there, so lightly my fingers could have been the tips of leaves.

She was sleeping deep, the breaths moving soft through her; when I sat up and looked down at her I could see she was smiling, just catch the curve of her mouth-corners under that spread of darkling hair.

I pulled the blanket up around her, and ran the curtain back. Stared out of the diamond-shaped panes, feeling the coursing of the breeze through the partly open sash.

Back of us, the horse-string, with the boy, Jal, walking with it and keeping the string from straying, came along with the eyes of the horses and the shine of their nostrils showing just faint in the coming day. I noted the brown mare who was in heat, and Flambeaux, the well-coupled horse of Aldan's. I turned my eyes the other way. I could see the cart at the head of the caravan; it was just making a swinging curve to the right, the rest of the carts following in neat procession. The man driving must have been Pella, he was wearing a blue headcloth, though I couldn't see him clear.

I got up and used one of the thundermugs, drawing it to a corner so the sound wouldn't wake French. Sitting there and swaying to the motion of the high-sided cart, I thought how I'd lost two days to Yadkin.

But what days they'd been. Didn't think I'd have given them back and started over, not for gold.

I got up and dressed, then took the thundermug and went in through the dividing door to the box where Grayboy was. He rolled a crystal eye around at me, corn-grains hanging from his lips. I shut the dividing door, and opened the little swamping door at the end of his stall, and threw out the thundermug's contents into the side-road bushes. Then I took a pitchfork and swamped out Grayboy's stall through the swamping door.

I said to Grayboy, quiet, "Don't look so fat and satisfied. You've got work ahead."

I patted him along the crupper, and he switched his dark-haired tail.

The singing of the whippoorwills was tailing off. I slid open the communicating slit to the driver's seat.

Aldan was driving the four-in-hand horses, sitting back easy and gazing up ahead where the caravan was finishing this curve. He looked fresh enough, his high-bridged nose like a curved knife in the soft light. I reckoned he'd slept enough; these people seemed to take turn and turn about, in shifts, at their driving. I said, "Morning, Aldan."

"Good morning, Mister Broome." His teeth were whiter than dogwood in spring. "A good enough day for the track."

"We'll run on a track? I was thinking a meadow or some such."

"They have a track in Pharis. It is ahead, about two miles. They are people very—" He sought for a word. "Very jealous about their racing. They have some fair stock. I think we have better. And with your horse—" He clucked to the double team; the backs of the draught horses were moving like ocean waves; we were coming up a draw, and the outlines of a field were on our right. A cotton field with the end-row bins empty and looking like the gray backs of turtles as the first sun struck them. "With your horse, we will prosper. My uncle, Jantil, has gone ahead. He will set up the racing for us. Each year about this time they expect us in Pharis. We will camp just outside Pharis."

"How do the stakes run?"

"They are good. The pride—envy? jealousy?—it makes these people seek out their last plugged copper cent. And then, we lost a little last year. I did not have Flambeaux then.''

"So it's a ripe town.''

"Like a bunch of muscadines in their best flush.''

Grayboy was lipping the air, then smelling it strong.

He let out a low nicker.

"Get that mare off your mind,'' I told him over my shoulder. "She'll keep.''

Aldan said, "Here ahead is the county line, Mister Broome. Where the roads cross.''

I could see it now; we were still swinging right. The roads made just a dusty "X" at the crossing.

I mulled over, quick, how I didn't believe Sheriff Planteu's authority would reach into the next county. Unless he sent a kind of posse out scouting all the distance to Yadkin, and he didn't have enough help to do that. Especially since he wished to keep all of this quiet in Lanceton.

The dividing door came open. French stepped in and shut it behind her. She was dressed, and her hair had been combed and she'd drawn it up in a bun at the back of her head and tied it with a little ribbon. She came to me and kissed me, just a greeting brush, and nodded to Grayboy, who looked at her gravely; she had the fragrance of herbs around her, I could drink in some of the nettle-salve I reckoned had been in one of those boxes.

"Good morning,'' she said low to Aldan.

He didn't quite turn his head this time. Through the slit I could see he'd tensed up. He looked as he'd looked the night before when we were about to start the race. "Good morning, Miss Chantry . . .''

I leaned close to the slit. "What's wrong?''

He shrugged, but didn't loosen up. "I think we are stopping. Though it is too soon. The camp is along a distance yet.'' I could barely see through the slit and around his right shoulder the road ahead. Brighter now with the first sun painting both it and the road that crossed it. Then, tiny in the distance, I made out a high-backed roan. Even from here she looked beat to the marrow. And alongside her was a buggy, a dust-covered buggy with a cob in the shafts, and then beside that, a work-horse that might've just left the plow, and beyond that, the rusty black gelding of Grody Flieshacker's, and still past that, a wickerwork pony trap with a shaggy pony harnessed to it.

"Jesus,'' I said.

Aldan was pulling up his bunched reins. The cart ahead had almost stopped.

I shut the slit-door.

Said to French, "It's your friends."

Her eyes got that large fox-bright look. But she said, cool enough, "They can't see us. I'll go close the curtain."

"All right," I said. "They can't see us yet. But they can look in this horse-box. And Grayboy's acting up a little; come back in here, when you've shut the curtain."

She went out through the dividing door.

I opened the slit again. Slow.

Aldan heard the slight sound it made. He said, without turning at all, "My little nephew, Tomas—you know him?"

"Yes."

"Last night when he took the white mare back to the Lanceton Pike. He said there were men along the pike, moving this way, not back to Lanceton. They did not see the mare when he turned her loose, he said. She was going the other way, toward Lanceton. But I think these are the men. We did not waken you; my father was going to tell you this morning. Ayee!" he said then.

I couldn't see past his back now.

"What is it?"

"They are speaking to my father. The sheriff—Sheriff Planteu—and the doctor—what is his name, I forget, I have only seen him a few times when we passed through Lanceton . . ."

"Mattison," I said.

"Yes, the chewing man. And with them is a fleshy man on a dirty gelding, and a powerful man on a field-horse, and the mayor—him I know, my father has praised him—Mayor Westerfield, with his pony and cart. The powerful man—he is of Lanceton, I have seen him before—"

"Howard Markley," I said. "He's the schoolmaster."

"He is speaking now. My father is getting down; he is coming back with them. They are coming alongside the carts."

Great, I thought.

All of them but that little Phil Adams, and he's still back at Chantry Hall, waiting for somebody to show up so he can take them in custody.

French came back in through the dividing door and shut it behind her again.

She'd heard the last of what Aldan said.

At my shoulder, she said, "I shan't go back with them, Tom. I'll simply refuse."

"Oh no," I said. "If they get us, we're both going back. Even the way they feel about you wouldn't keep them from insisting you go back with them now. And if that happens, I'll be along."

"And Yadkin?" she said.

All the whippoorwills had ceased now. As if all the promise they'd made for the daylight had been taken back.

"What do you want me to do, French?" I said. "Saddle Grayboy and drop the ramp and take him into the woods? There's no time. And even if there was, I'm sick of dodging. If we get over the line, it's just ahead, then our luck's in. If we don't, I'll go back. All or nothing—plain odds, and I've got gambler's blood."

I shut the slit up.

Then I moved around to Grayboy's head. "If they take us, I'll still marry you. Even if I'm in jail; you can come to the jail and we'll have it done."

"I'll insist on going to jail with you."

"I wouldn't have you in a place like that. I doubt it's better than any other town jail I've been in."

I had hold of the hackamore rope, one hand on Grayboy's nose. She came around through the straw and touched his neck.

Back in the horse-string, the Goddamned brown mare whinnied.

Grayboy's teeth showed, and he shifted his muscles and tightened. I stroked his nose.

Then neither French nor I was saying even a whisper. Every sound outside this horse-box seemed to grow to masterful size. I could hear the light racket of roosters far off. And closer, the sound of hoofs, and a buggy and a pony cart with them, drawing alongside the carts. And then Shangro's voice, sounding cheerful and wide open, without a care in creation. "Sheriff Planteu, I am sorry you have had all this disturbance. You have known me many years—there has never been any trouble with my people."

French had shut her eyes. She leaned around to me. Mouth a little open.

I kept my hands on Grayboy, and kissed her deep. Might be the last one we'd enjoy for a spell of days. And nights.

Grayboy waggled his neck, and I drew back.

Planteu's voice said, "What's in here?"

"A stallion," said Shangro. "A very mean man-horse, I am afraid. A killer, Sheriff Planteu. And we have a mare in season, so he is more on edge than he might be otherwise."

"What color?"

"Black. Do you wish to see him? I warn you, he may break his tether. But I am proud of him. His name is Ajax, there was a warrior named Ajax, they tell me, though I am ill read."

The mayor's light, round, joyful voice came floating.

"Ah, Mister Shangro—Ajax or Achilles—either would be a fitting name—for a proud stallion. You must drop in—some day—when you are going through—Lanceton. Together, we will read—the story of Troy. To think of Homer—blind—yet summing up all passions of man—in words still so strong—they depict all of the faults and follies—all of the dark, willful courage—of this dust we call mankind."

Shangro said, "And I, Mayor Westerfield, I will tell you stories—only made in the head, never written down—of how my forebears came from Persia, and much later of England—of England as she was when I was a boy, of the moors and the cities. Of the boxing champions the Rom had who fought the Borely Boy, and Mad Taggart. Of the making of the patteran, which we can read in a few sticks laid so, and so, and which tell us more than the stars tell seamen."

Sheriff Planteu said, "How old is he, Shangro?"

"Five years. With a bad scar across his haunch, where he was caught in wire when he was a colt. Maybe that gave him his temper, or began it. Come, I will show you and you will leave satisfied."

Doc Mattison's voice came. Scratchy and tireder than I'd heard it yet. "You didn't see Broome's horse, Will. I did, but Grody didn't either."

"I'd recognize Broome, though, in the midst of a troop of Yankees and covered with shit," said Grody Flieshacker. If Mattison sounded tired as a wilted brown fern-frond, Flieshacker sounded worse. Then he said, "Sorry, Your Honor. Didn't mean to say what I said."

Mayor Westerfield said, "It is—a perfectly useful—Anglo-Saxon—word—perhaps—more honest—than many euphemisms—but its usage—often precludes—the flow of language—itself—making conversation—a little on the barren side."

The weary rumble of Howard Markley cut in. "Gentlemen, I must return to town soon. There are children waiting for me in the schoolhouse. And my wife will be frantic. I don't believe young Broome and Miss French are anywhere around. I think they are both comfortably, if perhaps guiltily, on the road to Yadkin. I am bitterly disappointed in Francia, if this is the case. And I cannot but keep from thinking that young Broome is an immoral influence upon her, and that she will come to her senses with a great deal of grief. Colonel Bob—and M'linda, bless her—would be plunged in desolation."

"They're together, I'll say at this point," said Grody. Grating it, as if he hated even to say it. "But he's got her gagged and bound and is wreakin' his will upon her. Oh, hell! Go ahead and open up the box, Sheriff. And let's get back to town."

"We all need sleep," said Doc Mattison. "After that, we can go into the woods. Jupiter's some kind of key to all this piroguin' around. And we got to bury Gary Willis yet; why, I don't know, I'd as soon hang him in a tree and let him rot, the way the Chickasaws used to do with their braves. Till the buzzards've done their work. Except a brave's burial's too good for him."

I was watching French. When Howard Markley had said that about her mother and father and the desolation she might be bringing them, she'd firmed her lips tight. And shaken her head as if gnats bothered her bountiful hair. Now she'd drawn herself up and had laid a hand on the back of the hand I was holding Grayboy's hackamore with.

Small and lithe, and a little work-worn as her hand was—and beautiful—it was also powerful. Felt like a touch of the sun falling there on mine.

The brown mare called again. A sound pleading and wild, shaking the morning behind this horse-cart.

And I wasn't quick enough. Grayboy jerked loose and swung his head, then his crest was arching and his lips open and then he was trumpeting. The noise seemed to almost split the stall boards, ringing and with echoes after he'd lowered his head again. He tried a lash at the back boards of the stall, but didn't quite make it. I had his nostrils then, covering them, almost swinging from his head. His eyes looked down at mine as if he'd never known me.

And outside, over the clatter here, I heard Sheriff Planteu say, "He sounds horny as a buck rabbit in Maytime . . . we'll let it go, Shangro. You've always been a good cuss, and if we took a look at him he'd aim for the daylight and the mare, and I'm too tuckered to enjoy a raree-show at my time of life. Come on, let's make tracks."

I was still holding Grayboy's head. I didn't believe they were going, I wasn't even thinking of it. Just standing here as if I hadn't the power to hope or trust. But French's hand came back atop mine, and that was better.

I heard bits jingle, and the scurry of the buggy's wheels and the slower lighter noise of the pony trap turning, and Mayor Westerfield saying, "Before you go on, Mister Shangro—I wish to purchase—a few boxes—of your herbs, and some salve—for with no offense—to the medical profession—and particularly—to the representative of it—in our midst—I find that they do me—nearly as much good—as the medicines which my friend Roy—prescribes. I think you agree with me—sir—that in this life—the man who scorns no palliative—to make life more livable—is great in—discernment . . ."

His tones faded out like blithe flags waving back at us, and then I could hear Shangro answering.

And then they were all gone from true sound.

I lifted my hands down from Grayboy. And held French so close for a few seconds it felt as if we were pressing through each other's backbones. I said quiet, "All or nothing. And it's all."

"I would have stayed in jail with you, Tom. I would have made them let me do it."

"Yes, I reckon you would. But I'd have fought against it all the same. We've both got minds of our own, French."

The slit-door was shaking; Aldan was rapping on it, easy.

I went over and opened it. Aldan rolled his eyes high, then down. Past his jawline this time I could see the head cart moving. The four horses pulling on and up the slope. The day was full of a thousand flashes of new light. Shangro was getting back up into that first cart. Pella's blue headcloth shone from the driver's box. And farther along, vanishing down the crossroad, Grody's gelding with Grody on it so head-low in the saddle I reckoned he'd gone to sleep, and behind him the pony cart of Mayor Westerfield, which went out of sight behind some sugar-bushes as I watched.

Aldan said, shaking the reins as this horse-box cart started up under us, "We will make camp very soon now. My uncle Jantil will meet us there when he has made the racing plans with the people of Pharis. Is not my father wonderful? If he had said there was nothing in the box, they would have been certain to look. And then they would have had you, and no doubt us."

He shook his head. "He only had to lie a little."

"I'll do my best to make it up to him," I said.

I shut the slit. French had gone back into the rear of the box where we lived. I saw to it Grayboy hadn't strained or twisted the hackamore rope, and went back with French, shutting the dividing door. She was kneeling on the bunk; she'd opened the curtain again. She turned around as I said, "My daddy used to play a tune on the fiddle. A tune or two, when his fortune had changed for a time, and he was happy. It wasn't too often, because cards or horses were usually running against him, for some reason. He played when he was very sad, too, but that was a different sound. Anyhow, now I'll play the fiddle for you. I'm in the mood, even though it may not sound like much."

She was smiling her all-over smile, which wasn't just the face, as I've maybe said, but used the whole body. Her long well-coupled legs giving something to it, and her breasts and belly in it as well, and her eyes full of it along with her mouth, and even her hair in that drawn-up bun brought in to swell the effect. Sun all around her as she turned all the way around and sat with her legs drawn up and hands around her ankles.

I picked up the boxwood case and opened it, and took out the fiddle and started plucking its strings to tune by ear.

I was remembering the way those whippoorwills had sounded.

# 18

First I played "Bundle and Go," which is about as old a tune as you can find, coming out of Ireland and Scotland—so my father had said—in the days when famine was on the land and bundling and going was all you could do unless you wanted to sit in one place and starve.

I put a speck of the way I was feeling—relieved, and free, at least for the time ahead at Yadkin Fair—into it. I'm not an all night fiddler, or a fiddler who can crochet a tune into doilies. But it's a glad tune for all its desperation, and maybe the gladness got into it. Out past the cart-window I could see gum-trees flowing by, bobbling to the jolt of this horse-cart. And closer, the same sun streaming over French's hair and so strong in swashes I couldn't even make out her eyes as she listened.

Then I played "If You Want a Good Time, Join the Cavalry."

Everybody knows that. Jeb Beauty Stuart used to have his banjo-player, Sweeney, play it for him when he was seated in his pure silk tent of a night. I reckon it's as powerful a song as "Dixie," and it means the same. And so does "The Bonny Blue Flag," which I sailed into next. My fiddling elbow was still greased with my own feeling of ease.

So I went on into "Lorena," which is about as ravishing a dark-minded tune as you could find if you haunted graveyards and hobknobbed with ravens all your days. It'd been a song much enjoyed by soldiers both of North and South persuasion in the war, and though to me it was always a little too quavering, I managed to get some fun in it this trip. Then I tailed off with "Camptown Races," which poor Mister Foster had made as jouncing a duty for the fiddle-bow and the strings as ever made a barn-raising party warm up.

I found I had my eyes shut during those last ones. I opened them.

The skirling notes still seemed to dance around us in here. Going right along with the motion of the cart. We were pulling up in a clearing, which wasn't as ample as the bayou-trace clearing we'd left the night before, but which had a limestone spring falling between blue green rocks in its center, and was surrounded by more gumwood and oak and maple and sycamore and loblolly pine. We stopped while I sat blinking. And just outside our horse-cart came a sound of somebody else playing—it was the mandolin-shaped but somewhat banjo-sounding instrument I'd first noted when I first met Shangro. Then the player hove in sight. He was sitting on one of the horses from the string, a just-past-the-filly-stage mare with a black swatch over its rump and belly, the belly-swatch like a surcingle the Lord had put there. He looked related to Shangro, Aldan, Garsina, Tomas, Rico, Jal, Pella, and all the rest. Same high head and blazing steady expression. He was gentling the mare with one hand and had the instrument slung around his neck by a cord and was strumming it with the other. Fingers spidery and quick. Just chording with one hand, which is a beautiful trick and takes practice; his thumb was doing the fretwork stops. He was playing "Camptown," but not as I'd played it—a hell of a lot better. French was watching him now.

He said, "Good morning, Mister Broome." Over his music.

I was at the window with French, and was casing the fiddle.

I nodded to him and thrust the sash higher.

"If you are ready for Pharis, Pharis is prepared for you," he said. "Pardon. I am Jantil—the brother of Shangro, father of Jal and Rico."

He had a scarlet headcloth. I reckoned having a special headcloth was handy—you could even from a distance tell Shangro by his green one, Pella by his blue one, and this man by the tanager-flash of his. "My brother congratulates you on shaking Lanceton County from your feet. He also wishes to tell you food will be ready very soon. And I am also to tell you there will be three heats in Pharis—of which you will ride in the third. I will ride the first, Aldan the second. The betting is to be even, no odds at all."

I nodded. "Thanks, Jantil. This is Miss Chantry, I don't think you've—"

"I have only admired." He made his fingers do something to the strings I didn't think one set of fingers could do. The notes slid icy and brisk, like you see newts do on a riverbank. It was a decent compliment all by itself. "Dear lady, good morning."

"Delighted," murmured French.

"When you bring out your man-horse, Mister Broome, we will move Farella—she is a mare much in love—" He gestured with his head to the horse-string behind us, where the brown mare was quiet now. "So you and he will not be bothered. But I have something to ask of you, later, in that respect."

"Ask it any time," I said. "And back to Pharis—what are we running against?"

"First, a Morgan about five years old. That is my problem. Second—lift your ears, nephew!"—he was calling this to Aldan, who was leaning from the driving-box—"a rough-coated quarter-bred, almost a Pinto in size."

"Ha," said Aldan over the music.

"Attend me, Aldan! This horse is half wild, never truly broken, but it has a fine stride and its rider is a man who will kill it for the single win. I think you must break very quickly and stay ahead all the way. If you win, the man I have mentioned will turn surly. You have seen him before; his name is Teague. Pella and I will watch out for that. If you win, and when you win, do not bring Flambeaux back to the starting line. Ride on to the first turn near the backstretch and stay there, and we will be there."

He finished what he'd been doing to "Camptown," with another special flourish—if I could have done it with a fiddle I'd have showed off most of my life—and slung the instrument from his neck to his belt. He was younger than Shangro but there were deep seams in his cheeks. "Now, Mister Broome. You will be riding against an excellent horse. A mare, named Amber—a little overbred, but I would not be ashamed to run her against the best in this country. Her rider is her owner, Major Jack Deveraux. He is extremely skilled—a mile is not long, and inside it he will give you as much flame as you might have on any three-mile race.''

Aldan said, ''He whipped me last year. He rides in a line—he has trouble moving from outside to inside, or inside to out. I was not on Flambeaux, then, though.''

''It is the mare Amber who has the trouble, not him,'' said Jantil. ''And you are not running against him this year, Mister Broome is. Mister Broome, we will have groom-starters—the constable from Pharis, a man called Ballard, and one of our men, I think Cando from the forge.''

''How do the stakes run?'' I asked.

''Very high. They matched all my father wagered, and wanted more. They are greatly confident.''

''Which way does Amber break?''

''She does not break left or right.''

''A bung-starter,'' I said.

''Yes indeed. She would not move from the shadow of a jute-string if you ran it all around the track from her nose to her tail. I will go along now. Jal!'' he called to the boy, his son, who had taken over the horse-string with the morning star. ''Cut out Farella. Do not bring her past this cart, but lead her down to the spinney behind the spring, and tie her tightly to a tree, feed her, and blanket her against flies for the day. Then have Tomas stay with her; it is time for your sleep.''

The boy called something in Rom.

Jantil answered him in the same.

And Jantil ducked his chin to me. ''He wishes to attend the racing today. I told him it is impossible. We want no children there. None of our children . . . there will be plenty from Pharis. The selling of herbs must be done before the racing, too. And the women safe back in the cart and here at camp again.''

I said, ''Mean people?''

''It could go either way. As I said, they are confident. Constable Ballard is honest, he will hold the stakes. We will take the horse-cart here, and one other cart. I will ride my Malden—'' He stroked his black-patched mare, long fingers arching down her neck. ''She is named after an old English battle. Aldan will ride Flambeaux into Pharis as well. The starting time is one o'clock. We will leave here at half-past noon.''

He lifted a hand and rode off.

Behind him the camp was getting made. Draught horses being unhitched, men carrying wood and water, the main pot slung from its crane, other pots settling over fires.

I turned to French. "I think—somethin' he said—about he wanted to speak to me later—he wants me to breed Grayboy to Farella."

She said, "If you don't mind, Tom, it would be a nice sort of payment. For all they've done for us up to now. Look—"

She was still at the window. At the limestone spring children were naked and sliding down the blue green rocks into the water-pool. As though they were brown fish covered with the silvering water. They were throwing up their hands and sliding with pluming splashes. Then while we watched, Garsina, French's new friend, came around the bulking rocks and stood there for a breath. Naked as a fish herself. Her dark hair flashed in the light through the pines and gum-trees, she lifted her arms over her head while she climbed to the highest rock, then made a shallow dive. I'd hardly ever seen anything prettier. Now a boy of about fifteen, just about a year younger than Aldan—Aldan was unhitching the horse-cart horses—appeared, and followed her in a dive. I saw Jal lead the brown mare Farella off to one side and disappear into the copse behind the spring. When I looked back to the pool, Cando, the old smith, knotted as a pine covered with burrs and scars, but with a dark bronze heavy chest and arms that bulged at the shoulder biceps even from here, jumped from the rock to the pool. His elderly prick lifted on the air like a loose flap of harness leather, then he was splashing in. Three younger women came next, unconscious of anybody watching as so many brown-dappled natives in one of those foreign islands over the sea, where palm trees wave and trading in copra thrives. Or so I'd heard. Knew an old jockey once who said he'd shipped on a whaler before the war, and had known such a life. But he said they didn't know spit about horses. And then Pella came climbing up there, and sailed down in beside his wife Garsina. They rammed water at each other with the heels of their hands. Shangro was last to show up, a monumental frame covered with hard fat. His dive was stately and widespread. Some of the children were already out, sitting on the bank and being rubbed down with mixed herbs by their mothers.

French had her hand at her throat, a finger curved into the throat's hollow. I said, "I reckon it works up an appetite for breakfast. I'll see Grayboy's got enough feed left, then let's take our buckets down and fill them up. And maybe get some appetites ourselves." I was gazing back at the rainbows dancing on the water there from all the motion and splashing.

I wondered if she was thinking about what Colonel Robert Chantry and his lady would have thought, even in their graves, of their only cherished daughter watching such a sight. Or what they'd have thought of what I believed she was making up her mind to.

She said, soft, "They look—the way you play the boxwood fiddle, Tom."

"I think that's a thoughtful thing to say," I told her. "If I could play as well as Jantil, I'd long ago have got a job entertaining on a river-packet, though, and not had to fret sometimes about feed for my mount. You go ahead on down there, but wait for me before you make up your mind about any nymph-diving."

She said, "The Reverend Holcomb—I've mentioned him, he has the Episcopal church in Lanceton—always preached that we were made the same in the sight of God."

"Did he preach it to your servants in those days?" I said.

"Surely he did. They sat in the slave gallery."

"Well," I said, "you make up your own mind. I'm not speaking a word about this, it's your own skin to show or not to, as you please."

"Will it be my own after we're married?"

"Just as mine is mine."

"You mean you wouldn't call out some sneaking rascal who peeped at me?"

"That is wholly different," I said. "These people think no more of it than they think of breathing. And it's a good use for fresh water. I'm sayin' no more at the given moment, French."

. I busied myself with putting the fiddle away, and getting out the track-harness from the big saddlebag, and giving it a few dollops of oil, and going back into Grayboy's side of this traveling abode and getting a couple of buckets. All the while I could hear the watery noise from the spring-pool. Some of the men were cleansed and brushed now, and they came sauntering back to the horse-string and started cutting out more of the racing pack. They led them away to the shade on the yonder side of the clearing. I brought out the china painted thundermug from Grayboy's section with me, and this time when I shut the dividing door French was gone. Then I picked up sight of her through the window. She was walking fast like a smart ship in full sail toward the spring. Seemed to me the way her tits lifted that the nipples had that hard, risen and brave expression they got when we were kissing or otherwise playing with each other. I could see it through the gray dress and the shift beneath.

She went out of sight in the trees around back of the spring.

She'd lowered the ramp; I walked down it and followed her.

Aldan had the draught animals unharnessed and they were feeding; their coats were as glozed as beaver-pelts.

He came up alongside me.

"I forgot to ask your uncle," I said. "Is there a place in Pharis Miss Chantry and I can get married?"

"I do not know—I think there are churches—"

"I meant churches where they don't ask you a lot of questions first."

He grinned. "I do not know any of that kind, Mister Broome. And I think in Pharis—"

"Yes, I know. It sounds touch and go, unless we lose good and plenty. Are the other towns you race in like that?"

"There are only the other two towns before we will part with you outside Yadkin. One tomorrow, and one the next day. The first is Quincyville, the other is Appleton. They are not as big as Pharis, and not as—" His shoulders went up and down.

"Meaching?"

"Yes. They think we are filthy Gypsies, but they will not take vengeance on us if we whip them."

I looked up from where our shadows were skimming over the ground as we walked to the pool. Shangro was still in the pool, up to his chin. He hadn't lost a shred of dignity. He waved at me. I stopped on the bank— Aldan, already taking off his shirt, ducked into the gum-trees. I scrubbed out the thundermug with sand from the pool's edge, then set it to dry and took the buckets over to where the spring skittered down in its slipping stream. Shangro was floating on his back now, his weighty firm belly rising like the dome of some palace. I dabbled my hands in the falling springwater, which was cool to my fingers. When the buckets were full and I'd set them down, Shangro said, dark hands laced behind his neck as he floated, "I have been considering what you told me last night, Mister Broome. Seeing those gentlemen this morning has brought it even more firmly into my consideration."

"Thank you for handling it the way you did."

"There is no need for thanks, Mister Broome. It was my own soup I was pulling from the fire, as well as yours." He dabbled his hands in the glinting water, brought them back clasped above his navel. "I am thinking that, after we have parted—there are many ways of gleaning information, among my people—it comes to us like rain, through seepage here, a crevice there—I will make some inquiries. Maybe it will come to nothing, maybe it will not." His shoulders moving in the water were like round shields. A child, a girl with eyes as quick and bright as a golden weasel's, jumped up near him and laughed at him. He held her out of the water and swung her over to his other side, and she scuttered away. "It is the man, Jupiter, you must find, and convince to tell you what he saw."

"I'll appreciate what you can do along those lines. It seemed wrong for me or Miss Chantry to ask him any more while we were at Fountainwood. He was nerved up."

"He felt he had the spell—which was false—of Mister Willis still around him. He had brought himself to the point of burning the house. I think if you spoke to him, quietly, either you or Miss Chantry, and impressed upon him what deep water you are in, his loyalty to Miss Chantry and all she stands for of his past, would bring him to speak of whoever he is protecting. I will do what I can about finding him—or discovering where he is—and let you know."

Other rim of the pool, Pella and Garsina were climbing out. Garsina's hair hung down the center of her spine like a mare's tail, sparkling; her hips were almost as loving to the eye as French's, but longer and deeper-muscled. They went into the trees. Shangro flopped over toward me, hauled himself up and flipped water back from his hair, then squeezed his moustache dry with big drops falling out of it, and picked up a forked twig. "Here," he said. "This is not our full patteran, it is only a tiny part of it. You know patterans? They are for our eyes only; this one will tell you, when you see it, that we are near. I turn the fork of the twig, so, you see. Then I lay it a little above the earth, on a bush, in the hanging bough of a tree, beside the road. So it juts out a little—so if you know what you are seeking, you will see that special shape. For you, I would make it larger than this—you were not born with the eyes for it, which is certainly no fault of yours. The downturned end will point to us. A quarter of a mile along, there will be another—and so on, until you find us. I will bind it with grass—" He snipped up a grass-withe—"like this, to the bush or tree or even stone, so rain and wind will not take it. You can read a fresh patteran by the freshness of the twig, you can test the freshness by biting it. A stale one may be no good. After Yadkin, watch for them. We will be in Tennessee, trading for the brood-stallion—I want him very much—only a few days. After that we start down across this state again, and we will winter under the vines of the trace."

"The big one? Natchez?"

"Yes. You have been there?"

"With my daddy, younger. It's a daresome journey."

"We have spent winters there for some years now. It is not evil if one knows how to skirt the danger of cutpurse and throat-slitter. But you will find us before then—if I have news, and if I leave the patteran." He nodded to Jantil, who had appeared on top of the tallest rock. Jantil nodded back and stepped off into the water. Shangro crumbled the twig he had bent, and tossed it away. "My brother has told you of the racing—everything?"

I said, "All I need to know, I'd say."

"He is a strong rider himself, Jantil. You will see. He handles all that part of it." He patted his belly. "Once, before my father died and I became king, I did that part myself. Before my years and hunger caught up with me. Miss Chantry came by a moment ago. I think maybe you want to bathe with her."

He gave me an upward quirk of a look. "She may be shy. Our customs are not hers."

"Reckon ours are strange to you all."

"No, it is only that a long time ago we decided that yours are useless to us." He smiled just lightly.

I was turning away, but I turned back. "Do you marry people, Shangro?"

His eyes were serious now, snapping but considering hard.

"In the Romany way. It is not a marriage ceremony recognized by most of the world's people."

"It doesn't matter if it wouldn't stand in court."

He ducked his chin slow. "It might matter to your children, if you have children. But if you desired the ceremony it could be done. You could then have it made solid in the eyes of others by standing in a church, or before a registry office. So the barbaric rite would be sweetened. But think about it a time yet, Mister Broome. Let me know—both you and Miss Chantry—tomorrow some time. I am at your bidding, we are, as I said last night, friends."

Under all we'd said I could feel him thinking of what Jantil had half told, half hinted to me about the temper of the people in Pharis. I could see Shangro wanted this first race over and done, wrapped up and behind us. I walked off; I hadn't asked him how much he'd bet. But you never ask that of a gambler, and he was one, among a lot of other interesting things.

I went into the trees, where light was falling in long gold pencils. A few people were dressing nearby—Cando the smith among them—and a few latecomers were just shucking their clothes. French came up to me from where she'd been leaning against a sycamore trunk. She was still fully clad. She had one of the herb-boxes under an arm. She still had that both calm and excited appearance, as if she was in reality a small girl about to put on a ball gown for the first time and mingle with the grown-ups.

She said, "Garsina told me last night, Tom, if you take this elder mix and make a fomentation of it while you're bathing, it keeps off a lot of things such as phthisic and wrinkles."

I sat on a beech-log and took off my boots and socks, and then stood up to get the pants.

I said, "Those herbs work; you heard what Mayor Westerfield said this morning."

I kicked out of the pants and started on the shirt. Laying the clothes in a mound, hat on top. Said, "But you thought Garsina meant bathing by yourself. In a tin tub in the horse-cart."

French nodded. I was stripped; I shrugged.

Soft-speaking, I said, "If you sagged in front, or drooped down behind, or had the spavins or the foreleg-bows, it might be different. All I can see wrong with you is about half a hundred years of a kind of pride. There are all kinds of pride, and some of it I'm pretty partial to myself. But I told you I'm not speaking any more on this score, I've already gone too far."

The light laced her bundled-up hair in a kind of rosy dark helmet.

"You asked me to stand still while you studied me, yesterday," I said. "I'm glad you did. Love itself—as I see it—ought to be a secret thing. Joyous and part of the night, or day if you feel like it, but between just two. But this isn't anything like that. It's only something—as your Preacher Holcomb said—in God's sight."

"*Reverend* Holcomb," she said in an absent way.

"You've already made me say too much," I said. "And I don't want to just stay here facing you, or I'll start wanting you and show it too much for general public study. Come on if you want to, French."

I walked out toward the rocks above the pool. Felt wonderful there, with the main pot on its crane sending up good odors of game and stew, and somebody nearby the pot across the clearing with fresh-baked bread, the savory stew treated with all sorts of herbs I wouldn't even have a name for, the bread mingling with the clean woodsmoke and water smell. I filled my ribs for a dive, and was just about to take it, when French stood alongside. Just in her loving skin. I felt then as I'd felt about the whippoorwills, and then as I'd felt playing the fiddle. I turned and looked at her. She shone like cream, all of her brightening the day that much more than the light did.

I gave her a short nip on the nose with my teeth, as a friendly horse will do, and then went off the rock. She came down right after me, a falling like a sweet arrow, and then we were splashing each other, and she was rubbing me with a palm full of herbs she'd brought with her, and through the spray Shangro looked over at us and grinned, then turned his head away to watch a redbird skimming. The brown mare, Farella, gave a pleading whinny farther back among the trees where Jal had taken her, and there was the muffled noise from the horse-box of Grayboy in the distance, answering her.

# 19

After breakfast, with our clothes feeling lighter on us because of the swimming, and French letting her hair dry before she put it up again, we sat on the ramp in the sun, while I shortened Grayboy's stirrup leathers a little; they'd felt a bit stretched in the ride against Aldan the night before.

Breakfast had been that savory stew, squirrel and side-meat and bay leaves and marjoram and a touch of chicken, and camp-bread made in small loaves. It was all fairly quiet now, just the noise of the camp going on around us like a sturdy, well-oiled machine and sometimes one of the horses sounding off from the other side of the clearing, and the water flashing and falling into its spring-pool. I thought to myself how Shangro and his brother and his sons and all the rest of the men and women had this whole traveling idea down to a clean science, the way the cavalry did during the war. So they could live from the land and leave it quiet and unsullied behind them, and wherever they were would be their homeland. Except that the cavalry had had to move even faster, and strike quick and out-think the Yankees to stay alive themselves; the Gypsies could take it a shade slower.

I said, "Shangro can marry us."

Her back was to me. Thought I saw her shoulders stiffen just a trace. But I couldn't really tell because her hair was spreading its great flag over most of her shoulders. I didn't think I'd done any insisting on her swimming bare; she'd made up her own mind to that. But I was starting to understand that with a woman I cared for, there were more responsibilities than I'd ever dreamed there would be. With one I didn't care for it would have been simple enough.

"He said we could have it done again later," I said now. "He told me to think it over a little. I'd like to have it done. Maybe tomorrow."

She turned around, her face coming forward in rosiness and brightness from the cloud of skinned-back hair.

"I declare, Tom. I like this life more than I'd anticipated doing. But I need a little time before I have a Gypsy wedding. I don't see why we couldn't just wait till Yadkin itself—it won't make any difference to *us.*"

"I reckon I've got some guilt in me," I said, pondering as I moved Grayboy's saddle around and studied a notch in the off stirrup leather. "I feel kind of like I've talked you into comin' with me. I know you started it all, but somewhere along the line I took on a load of family-man troubles myself. I've never had them before. It would make me feel better if we were hitched in double-team no matter if it isn't a regular church ceremony." I looked down at the leather. "Then if I got killed or something —you never know when you might take a last tumble, in this game—and you had a child, it'd be a legitimate kind of human being."

She had her head lifted. Looked as if she was staring at the fall of Vicksburg, and defying the North to do worse.

"I went into all this with my eyes wide open, purely and simply, Tom Broome. I looked upon you naked because I love you—it wasn't just curiosity and giggling foolishness. I like doing what we do together, and I walked out naked just now and went in the water with you in front of everybody because I wanted to, as well—you left the decision to me, and I took it all on my own. I've hardly ever been a weak-willed mollycoddle, and if I should have your child without you to be close by to father it through the years, it wouldn't kill me. I don't think you're going to come to harm. And I don't think I'm going to have a child—not immediately, at any rate. If you think you feel guilty, well, consider me and how I feel! All those people who plague me by thinking so much of me—Howard Markley, and Doctor Mattison, Sheriff Planteu, the mayor, all of them—I'm betraying them by going against principles that built their whole world. I—"

"Is that why you don't want a Gypsy wedding?" I was standing up now. "Seems to me a woman who is plighted to a man ought to fit in with his life—however rough or smooth—and put all the rest behind her. And seems to me she'd welcome a ceremony even if it didn't stand up in the sight of most religions. It's a little more of a decision than just getting back a flying jenny you've set your mind on—"

She was standing too. Comb in one hand, hair cascading in the fire of the latening morning.

Made me, more than ever, think of one of those women in the old-time stories, the princess who waited while the knight went forth to slay. The princess worth slaying ogres for.

"You're asking a great deal—more than you know, I reckon—and too soon, Tom. But since you ask it, I'll go through the Gypsy wedding, whatever it is. And in Yadkin we'll have the true ceremony. Maybe I'm just still holding back part of myself—part of my old self. I can't leave it all behind! You say you won't live at Chantry Hall, but it's been part of me too long to leave or ever forget. Ruth, in the Bible, said she'd go 'whither thou goest.' I'm not Ruth, I'm Francia Chantry—who wasn't born to be a Nomad! I can't answer all your wishes right quick and calm. I've protected too much, most of my life, to do that. But we'll swear in blood, or whatever they do . . ."

I said, "*I* don't know what they do. But I know being together's not—not takin' back a toy, like your merry-go-round. Not just having a man who'll wear varnished boots and stick them up on the rail of the front gallery at Chantry, and living a life that's gone—or pretendin' the life that's gone is still there around us. Not even making love—which is a good deal, but a long way from all. It's me growing into you, and you into me. And I'm a road-goer and a rider and a harness-driver. Think it over longer before you say any yes to this."

Slow, she nodded.

"And," I said, stepping into the cart, "maybe we'd both best think it over longer. Just cool off a little and not touch each other till we're sure, for a time." It hurt me to say that. I wanted her so much I could have grabbed her hand and drawn her into the cart after me and put up the ramp and undressed her again and said it with all my body, right then.

Her color was high and her eyes with those jewel flecks were touched with extra brightness. Maybe tears, I didn't know—I knew it was the first fight we'd had, and that it had been building a while. I was feeling edged-up about the race to come, too. Yet I felt I'd spoken the deep truth about something in us that set us apart no matter how much we might desire each other.

She had stepped into the cart behind me now. She lifted a tuck of the canvas and looked upon the merry-go-round horses there. Didn't look toward me. She said, very soft, back of her throat—which was pulsing with that tiny heartbeat you can sometimes see in a woman's throat, which is one of the most beautiful things about her—"I should have let it burn up, I shouldn't have taken Grayboy and then attached myself to you. It's the past, and the past is a ruin."

I said, "What was good back then is good now. At least so I believe. But you've got to get it all straight inside yourself to make the two run together. Damn," I said, mostly to myself, "I sound like some kind of preacher myself again. All the same it's the bulk of how I feel."

I opened the dividing door and went in with Grayboy, lifting the saddle onto him. He shifted and wangled his head around, and I kicked the dividing door shut and started saddling. It wasn't too long till half past noon; he'd been idle all the night and this morning, and I wanted him to know he was going to run again soon.

At half past midday by my father's turnip-watch, which I looked at just as we started, we left this clearing and moved up a side-path, the ramp door shut now, and the old smith, Cando, driving the four cart horses that pulled this high cart; Jantil on his black-splashed Malden rode ahead of us, in the lead; then Shangro on one of the horse-string horses, even though he wasn't going to race; then Aldan on Flambeaux. Pella, his jaybird blue headcloth flashing, drove the cart behind us, which held nine or ten of the women of the tribe with their herb-boxes and herb ointments ready for sale. All the rest of the carts and horses, and all the children, were left behind; I noted that Shangro had given orders to have the other carts back there hitched up again, and the breakfast fires were out and those we were leaving had the general expression of being ready to move as soon as we got back.

Shangro, on a dark bay, had the look of having once been an able rider;

he rolled a little too much in the saddle now, but he had a good knee-grip. French and I were watching out of the side window of the horse-cart, above the bunk. Neither of us had spoken much to the other since we'd had our words—when either one of us would catch the other looking at him or her, we'd stare aside and away. As if we hadn't even met yet for the first time. We were mighty polite, too, begging each other's pardon for bumping with an elbow or stepping in one another's way. It was a kind of game, but under it I felt mortally sad, and I knew damned well French did too. All the same it seemed necessary.

The side-path ended, and then we were right on the rim of Pharis. A line of stores and a livery stable or two, and beyond them the houses tailing up to the horizon. It was, I judged, about twice the size of Lanceton, with streets raying off from this main one; Jantil had checked Malden, and was looking along down the street. You could fairly feel the eyes of the Pharis citizens roving around and suddenly coming face to face with the Gypsy riders, and the cart we were in, and the cart with the women—which was Shangro's own gold and purple and faded blue cart, hauled by his draught-horse double team. As if some sort of lightning had dropped from the sky and painted the ordinarily sleepy street and burned their eyes. Jantil rode on now, crossing the street, Shangro behind him, then Aldan tucked close behind. Then our lofty cart, and the cart with the women. I saw men dressed in what would be their Sunday clothes, laid away all week and with the creases of the clothes-press on them, following along with their eyes close on Aldan and Jantil, and women converging on the women-cart and following along, and children coming along behind them, small boys racing alongside our own cart and staring up and in. One boy who had milky eyes and a pinched face stared up at French and hollered, "They's white people with 'em! They's a white woman in there!"

French gave him back quiet stare for stare. He peeled away and other children raced where he had been. We had crossed the main street's dust and were angling down a slope toward a track, which stretched east and west, the short arcs of the oval to north and south, a track with elder trees and oaks and smaller pin oaks around it, and no grandstands except the wagons and buggies and buckboards and farm-carts drawn up around it, where people, sometimes whole families, were already sitting. It was a good mile-track, the fences in fair repair, the earth of it well beaten to a gray-squirrel-colored darkness; there was a shed near the starting end where some of the rails had been lifted to let horses through.

We went around the north of the track, then stopped in the shade of some pin oaks near the shed. Shangro and Jantil and Aldan were swinging themselves off their mounts, approaching the standing men and the riders who waited there. Cando pulled up the double team and our cart rolled to a stop, and behind us Pella stopped the women-cart. French, whose hair was now put up again, high, with that ribbon binding it, helped me unloose the ramp latches and I lowered the ramp, holding onto the rope handle. Light fell in like a burning wall; heat and light and all the sound of the track and the track-watchers with it. And the smells of the town and the people, smells I'd forgotten from just being with the Gypsies for a night and morning; the frying scents of the houses above this slope, their shingles baking in the warmth of an unseasonable hot fall day, the sweat of the people and the sweat of the horses gathered here along the shed's flank. Behind the dividing door Grayboy was moving, not alert to a mare in heat now, but feeling and sensing the crowd. He'd been in like situations before.

I stood there for a second, looking over the field we'd be running against. The rough-coated half-wild Pinto-sized horse, a quarter-breed. That was Aldan's challenge. Beside him stood a man wearing gumboots, hand on the bridle; he had a red face and a large nose as if it had been stepped on young, and thick, stubby hands, and the look of a fellow set to dare or die, who might have to dispose of a lot of people around him before he did either one, but who was willing to. I watched the motion of the quarter-breed, tossing its head and then having its head jerked down as if the man wanted to take the mouth out of it; it had a bad eye, I noted, with a frost of blindness over it, on its near side. So the owner-rider would have to mount from the off side. Aldan had already noticed this. Flambeaux stood fairly quiet, with that tension in his hocks and his short-coupled forelegs drawn close and his hoofs as neat as a cat's forepaws. I raised my eyes to the Morgan Jantil had talked of. It was a clean-lined horse, though a little too straight in the forelegs and with a saddle-gall on its near side, showing even under the saddle it now wore, which was smaller than the one that had rubbed the gall there. The man holding it was middle-aged, with pale blue eyes and a shock of white hair, and he gentled the Morgan as he stood, being closer to it than he was to the people standing around him, and I thought he'd give Jantil a decent run. I switched my attention to where a good many of these other observers were looking, over at the shed-corner. And I drew in a breath.

There was Arab blood, and hackney, and maybe a few more, in Amber, but they'd all come into her in a tight, beautiful blend. She wasn't a mare I'd ever have expected to see in any town this size. Her eyes were so black they were almost green, picking up the grass-light from the track's center oval, and her line was as light but joyous as Grayboy's, for her smaller size. Her owner-rider was up. Jantil had said she was good, but I hadn't dreamed this. I stopped staring at her, and studied her rider. He was about as old as, say, Sheriff Will Planteu, but he'd weathered the years more finely. He sat as if he held himself about half a mile above the rest of the crowd around him, like a lark in the sky, but brooding more than a lark. His face was dark and steeped in sun, his neck-cloth white and ruffed above his clean-cut Tattersall vest—no sign of belly on him—and his boots shone reflecting all the stir and bustle around him, as bright as Amber's wheat-gold flanks. He wore a top hat, just as shining. Major Jack Deveraux, I thought.

Out of the women-cart the women were coming, now, Garsina first and then the rest with their boxes of herbs in their arms, and the scent of the herbs cutting above the other smells out yonder; they walked with a wider motion than the town-and-countryside women who came to examine their wares and ask them to lift the box-lids so they could pry deeper; they stood quiet while they answered what questions they could, and those who couldn't speak English, like Garsina, let those who could speak the prices and simply smiled and waited for buyers. But they might have been off as high in the blue day as Major Deveraux. Not part of the town in the slightest.

Cando was climbing down from the driver's box; he joined Pella behind Jantil and Aldan and Shangro. A wide-shouldered man with a hump to his spine, wearing a swallow-tail coat which was going gray in its seams, and work-pants stuffed into boot tops, was talking with them now; he wore a badge of office, and I put him down as Constable Ballard. Beside him their clothes made them gay-plumaged birds of passage, Jantil's scarlet headcloth and Pella's blue one and Shangro's green one drawing the light as the hide of Amber did, and as the sky blue riding coat of Deveraux did over his Tattersall vest.

French was standing with me. Her right hand touched mine.

This time she didn't say, Beg your pardon—I turned and looked full at her. Across at the shed-corner Major Deveraux was gazing our way now, as if something about us had riveted him. I could feel his blue eyes on us.

French said, "I'm sorry, Tom."

"So am I," I said. "I'm sorry we ever have to say the way we feel. But maybe it's better we do."

"Tom." Her hand was close around mine now, not covering it by a long shot, it wouldn't ever grow to that size. "I'll wed you, Romany style, and *live* with the Rom ever after, if you want me to."

"No you won't," I said. "You'd have big second thoughts about that, right away. So would I. We're a little like a cat and a dog courting each other. I'm not the cat." She smiled, faint. "But I won't give up my own customs for others either. We're only about two days out of Yadkin now, and we're going to have a little money when we get there. In some ways you're right; we got wedded when we stayed beside the pond back along the Lanceton Pike. So we can skip any Romany rites, and just wait till Yadkin."

"No. Don't fight about this now. Not this, along with everything else. I want what you want, and I want us married in the Romany style as well as the other."

"Are you going to insist on it?"

"Yes."

"Then I'll be glad to. Tomorrow. . .

"Let go my hand," I told her then. She did, and I scooped her in and kissed her. Set and sealed again. She kissed me just as deep. When I looked around again, and started back to Grayboy, who was shifting considerably now as if he might be going to break down the door and step out all by himself, I saw Major Jack Deveraux was still gazing upon us. He hadn't once looked away. He had a little brush moustache, neatly trimmed, and under it his lips were set straight as though graven of iron. The splendid mare, Amber, stood under him as though they were a single body.

# 20

All the time I was untying Grayboy, and mounting him and turning him and facing him out into the sun past the dividing door, I could hear the noise of the crowd outside. A murmur that seemed to swell and then subside like a huge beehive busy as the devil, all up and down this mile-track and even on into the clean blue day. I'd have bet the people who lived in Pharis, and in half the county around it, had waited for this day in which they could prove themselves better horse-people than Gypsies, for at least half the year. I clucked to Grayboy and he came out of his half of the cart and into our half, high-necked, raring to go; then he faced the ramp, but it wasn't going to be any trouble to get him down it. It was only trouble to keep him from trying to jump the whole thing without touching its slat-boards. His hoofs hit it three times, no more, then we were on the ground. With French behind us, standing beside the canvas-covered merry-go-round and with one hand on the ramp-door's jamb; and I was hauling in Grayboy as if I was battling an ironclad, single-handed.

In another two, three seconds, he stood still. And I could hear the buzz and murmur near us stop as though a knife had cut through it. For a full second there was just a silence you could have dropped a stone through. Major Jack Deveraux had pulled his eyes from French—it was her he'd been looking at mainly, I realized, not me. And he and the swallow-tail coated Constable Ballard and the splay-nosed man with the rough-coated quarter-breed and the white-haired man with the Morgan and all the men and women close by this starting point were staring upon us with a kind of stuporous blinking.

Then the noise cut loose again, and I could feel it, even from here in Grayboy's saddle, swell again and travel down the line of fencing, from wagon to buckboard to jitney-rig to farm-cart, on the lips of everybody who was gazing this way, and then reaching those who couldn't see us but who would be getting the news fast and complete.

Constable Ballard whirled around, coat-tails lifting—I saw he possessed a handsome old side-arm—and walked over under Grayboy's muzzle. "Evening, sir."

"Good evening," I said down to him. "I'm Tom Broome; maybe Mister Jantil—he set up this race of three heats with your people—mentioned me. I'm the third-heat man; I believe we're runnin' against Major Deveraux over there."

"That was the idea," he said, eyeing me strange. "But the Gypsy sets up these things—" He jerked a thumb to Jantil, who was standing by, a hand on Malden's bridle, and who appeared as calm as Shangro and Aldan and Cando did, "—didn't mention they had a ringer."

"You mean I'm a ringer, Constable? Or my horse is?"

"You, I'd say. How long you been travelin' with this pack, son?"

"Just a short while," I said. "And bein' a different color than they are doesn't make me a ringer. A man riding is a man riding, even if he's the color of those pin-oak sprouts yonder. Wouldn't you let me run even if I was an ape who'd learned to sit saddle?''

"Dare say I would." He sounded kindly enough, just puzzled; I didn't fix him as a man who could ever keep this crowd in a quiet state once it had broken loose, but I liked him enough. "But it's up to the major, Mister Broome. If he says scratch, we'll have to scratch you. Lord, that's a handsome stallion you got. A little slow-starting for a mile track, wouldn't you say?''

"He's got his own virtues," I said. "He's edgy, but you can touch him if you wish. He doesn't mind people, he just wants to run."

Ballard reached up and fondled Grayboy's lower cheek on the nigh side. Then he stepped back and touched his hat-brim up to French, who bobbed her head back at him from where she stood in the rear of the horse-cart. "Your wife, Mister Broome?''

I'd known this might come up, at this race in Pharis. It was one of the reasons I wanted to have us man and wife, even if the wedding was a Gypsy-done rite. Then we wouldn't have to lie, at least about this. I said, "Yes sir."

"A true lady," he said, and turned and started striding to Major Deveraux. But he didn't have to go far, for Deveraux had ridden his Amber mare closer. She had a motion like steady water in a stream. Grayboy swung his nose to her, and she stood prim and tidy, only acknowledging him with her eyes, which weren't one jot frightened. The major was studying Grayboy a little, with just a few raking glances. Close up, he was just as powerfully knit and preserved as he'd looked at a slight distance. He said, not straight to me, but out to the air, sort of, "The best I've seen since General Lee's Traveller. You're not wasting him on events such as this one, I hope."

"I don't know as he's wasted," I said. "There's a lot of money bet here, I understand. I need it to get on to Yadkin Fair."

"I see. The harness racing."

He wasn't a man I'd have wanted to lie to. I hoped I didn't have to.

But he wasn't even studying Grayboy anymore now. His eyes, that fierce burning blue some men never lose when they're blue-eyed and steady of sight, even when they get to be very old, were back upon French. He took off his polished top hat. He had all his hair, grizzled and combed close to his scalp.

The mare Amber took another few steps, at the bidding of his hand, toward the horse-cart.

I saw that where French had plucked part of the canvas back from her merry-go-round earlier, part of one of its horses could be seen. The forsythia yellow one, the arch of its canted neck. A beam of sunlight struck its brilliant staring eye.

Major Deveraux looked from it, to French, and back again, and then to her face once more.

"Major Jack Deveraux, ma'am, of Deveraux Farm," he said.

"Mrs. Thomas Broome," I said from where I sat.

He didn't look at me.

French said, "Glad to make your acquaintance, I'm sure, Major."

And he sucked in a short breath, as if he'd been waiting for her voice. I'd freely admit it was like no other voice I'd ever heard, always with that schooled roundness about it.

"Ma'am. Did I not make your acquaintance, years ago, in the summer of sixty-two, when you were quite young, and your father and I and a handful of brother officers made rendezvous at Chantry Hall? We held a small soiree there—your charming mother, Melinda, did me the honor of dancing with me, and you yourself joined with me in a waltz, though you were so little your feet could not tread the measure with ease—yet it was a high point in my existence, I do assure you."

It wasn't as flowery as the words sound. There was something else under it, hard as the bit in Amber's mouth.

There wasn't any lull in the noise from the crowd around the track fences, but right here there was a gap in time and hearing. As if French wouldn't ever answer.

I looked at her close; that vein was beating in her throat. She had her head lifted, smiling, pretty as a laurel bough, and she might have been chatting with any new acquaintance, but I knew she wasn't.

"Why, Major—I have never been near Chantry Hall, though I have heard of it. I'm a Roundtree, from down on the Delta. India Roundtree was my maiden name. My aunt is Delilah Roundtree, and my sister is Everbe Phillips, who married among the Cartonsburg Phillipses." The names tripped so nice off her tongue, I knew she must have known them well. "My father was Barbour Roundtree, he served under General Van Dorn, and was wounded near Corinth. I am so sorry you've mistaken me for another. I regret it exceedingly."

She lifted a hand and pushed her hair-bun, which was glorious, back a touch. "That is a magnificent mare you have, Major Deveraux. I look forward to your heat against my husband."

The lines at the sides of Deveraux's mouth were cut deep, as if put in with a graver. I reckoned the graver had been the war, and he'd lived heavy ever since.

Before he could speak again, French said, "Is your lady here today, Major Deveraux? I should enjoy making her acquaintance . . ."

Hat still in his right hand, brim curled in his fingers, he gave a short head-shake. "I have never married—Mrs. Broome." His throat didn't even want to say Broome. Or Mrs., for that matter. He was staring at the bright yellow neck of the flying jenny horse. Slow as if he was creating the words from his own flesh, and being wounded with each one, he said now, "The little girl's name was Francia. I believe—nay, ma'am, I know—they called her French. That carousel, or one so like it I cannot believe it is not the same, stood in the ballroom of Chantry Hall, near the orchestra. As a pleasant intermission, your father started it—he had a manservant fill it with pine chips and ash wood, light them, and it turned around and around, and you and several other little girls—I beg your pardon, Miss Francia Chantry and several other small ladies—rode upon it, and its music filled the ballroom."

"A lovely experience, sir," said French. "But you are confused. It was not my father, or his manservant. And I must insist, I was not present. I do assure you I remember my own past, Major. And this carousel comes from Afton, where I grew up on the Delta. If you are ever down there, Afton will welcome you. I am transporting the carousel to Yadkin, where I've heard there is a man who can repair it. And of course my husband is racing there, in the harness-events."

If the first pause in time had been long, this was nearly forever. In truth it was only a few seconds, but it had a massy tone to it.

Then the major was shaking his head again, lips more hard-bitten than before. He had Amber's reins gathered in his left hand, and with them, a pair of white gloves. I could see the gloves trembling; yet he didn't seem to me a man who ever trembled much. His face under the dark bronze of weathers—I'd have bet he rode every day, rain and cold or warm—was just a touch white. He said so quiet, and harsh, you could hardly hear it, "Beg pardon, and my thanks," and wheeled Amber, and she moved at his feathery bidding. As he faced away from the horse-cart he clapped his hat on again, firm, and cut an eye sideward at me. I met the eye, cool, but

I didn't wish to. He took Amber back near the fence. The voices of the Gypsy women came liquid-toned as dark doves to us on the slight breeze as they sold their wares.

Constable Ballard called over to the major, "You'll take the ringer, Major?"

He was facing us again. Shadow cut over his eyes. "Oh, most assuredly, Constable. I shall take any ringers they care to offer. The bets stand."

Ballard said, "Thank you, Major."

From his voice-quality I could tell something of the way the major was thought of around here. I didn't get the notion Deveraux mingled much with people in and around Pharis. But they'd listen when he spoke. Up inside the horse-cart, French had stepped back a little into shadow now. Just a fold of the skirt of her gray gown showing in a light-streak.

I pulled Grayboy around, and joined the men at the gate where Jantil was edging Malden out through the gap. Following him went the Morgan with the white-haired man up. Constable Ballard and a couple of the other men were lifting the fence-rails back into place. A wire glistened, stretched across the track, above the heads of Jantil and the shock-haired man. Ballard ducked under the fence and went over to the white-haired man and with his hands on the Morgan's shoulders—I still thought its legs were too straight, though it was obedient as a hunting hound—braced back, pushing it close under the wire. Cando, for all his years, vaulted the fence and joined Jantil and braced himself against the black-splashed Malden mare. Both mounts moved into place without extra fuss. Jantil wasn't wearing his instrument; I hadn't reckoned he'd want to play a tune while riding. He had long hands, like Pella's; the fingers were light on Malden's reins.

I glanced at Shangro. Nobody could have read anything from his quiet face. It might have been wrapped in the sleep of a lot of centuries. His earrings moved as he looked over at me. Pella sat on the rail beside him, his panther-look as sleepy-seeming as Shangro's own. Aldan sat Flambeaux near me. He wasn't staring anywhere but at the track. But the crush-nosed man with the quarter-breed was sizing him up, and grinning around. I recalled what Jantil had told Aldan about that man.

Then Ballard was saying, "One last time, gents. Look to your tack." But nobody had to look; they were ready.

And Ballard said, sighting at Cando who was holding Malden, "Go!"

He jumped back, not quite as quick as Cando; the Morgan knocked him off-balance, and he staggered and caught himself in time to keep from sprawling. But nobody was noticing now, because they were off. Jantil took the lead in the first half second.

Malden's tail was lifted and she was streaming; she got gait as fast as Jantil wanted her to, and I leaned from Grayboy, watching her dig in. The Morgan was a length back. They were already nearing the first turn. All the people were lining the rail, leaning in so close they stood to get themselves crushed if there was any slamming done, and those in their carts and wagons and such were standing and whooping, and even holding up babies to stare.

At the first turn the Morgan made his play, the white-haired man with the mild face rising in the irons and rocking, the Morgan, on the outside—Jantil had won the coin-toss for the start-position—coming ahead and crowding Malden as he came; then they were neck and neck into the backstretch. I looked back to the horse-cart. French had come forward again—you can't help it, when there's a good race going—and was looking around at the backstretch. Over at the shed-side, Major Deveraux was watching her; I had the feeling he hadn't taken his eyes from her or the cart or the carousel. Grayboy tried to dance in the dust here outside the fence, and I stroked him and told him under the roaring, "Shut up, you damned noble affair!"

I switched attention to the backstretch. Jantil was riding low now, almost crouched over Malden's flashing shoulders, so low he could have reached and touched the earth with the fingertips of one lean spidery hand. The hoofs of both mounts were starting to make that thunder which you can't hear at the first turn but which starts to rise, through the crowd, at the far turn and into homestretch. Dust rolled back from the whole track in pluming waves, you could taste it over the other smells, it lay covering the first turn's arc and clear along the backstretch and was just starting to settle past the wire. I thought how much better I liked it in harness-going, in the sulky, where the tires would sing above both hoofbeats and crowd-eruption, and where you felt hooked to your competition as if you were bound by cords nobody could see. But this was making me happy, too, and it was still only God and the last few feet that'd tell who had won it.

Then they were around the far turn, crowding close, you couldn't see air between them, and the mild-faced man was still high in the irons, standing, Jantil still so low and leaning to the near side you couldn't see anything but his hip and one leg in his boot from here, the mounts surging, the Morgan showing all it had, Malden's hide shooting through dust and spurning ground as she curved into the turn, deep, the Morgan's ribs plastered with the dust on its dark sweat, and they were swooping toward the wire like hawks. The lips of the white-haired man were drawn back as if he was in agony. Malden came up so fast now I knew Jantil had held her, even riding as he was, all this time, and then by a head Malden was first under the wire and they were slowing down at the first turn again. Aldan said, "Ayee!," but there was gladness in it. The crowd-sound came down fast, like a groan fitting into what had been a steady great cheering, and somebody gave a little Reb yell but it sounded thin down there at the first turn.

They rode back. Jantil straight now, easy-sitting. The man on the Morgan leaned from it and touched Jantil's arm. Jantil grinned at him. I reckoned what the man on his Morgan—you couldn't even see the Morgan had been galled, now, under the dust-caking—had said to Jantil had been good. I didn't think the man on the rough-haired quarter-breed would do as much if he got trounced. For he was riding forward now, the frosted blind eye of his horse walling, his own eyes wet and already mad, and his gumboots which he hadn't bothered to clean since swamping out some time previous, flapping in the irons.

And he didn't halt while Constable Ballard and his helpers took out the outside fence rails, but rode right up, the quarter-breed chesting them. Aldan was moving on Flambeaux just a trace behind him. Ballard motioned the man on the quarter-breed back. "Damn it, Wesley," he said sharp. "You'll have time to get through!" Cando was assisting Ballard and the other men in lifting the rails off. Wesley turned and leaned down from the quarter-breed, and, his crushed nose wrinkling, flapped his hat down slashing at Cando. Across Cando's shoulders. "Git away, nigra! I can't stand that smell!"

Cando gazed up at him; then down at the quarter-breed's plates, as if he was only mulling over what thick, battered plates the breed had, and how he might better them. No expression on his mouth, in his eyes. Then he gave a short bow, and moved back. He would be the groom-starter for Aldan on Flambeaux; he had to stay nearby. I rode Grayboy closer to them. Ballard and the others had the rails off now. Wesley was about to ride onto the track. I said, "That's a damned fool way to speak to a man a lot older than you are, Cuz."

Beside me, I could feel Aldan tighten up; I could even see Flambeaux respond to his tightening, his shining black head with its rough star moving high.

Wesley's hat was back on; he had about an inch of brow under it. I could smell the corn whiskey and the dirt. Nothing wrong with good corn, but it sits bad on some people. I wanted to take the quarter-breed out from under him and curry it, and give it something for its gaunted flesh.

He was looking up at Grayboy. And at me.

"I ain't your cousin, nigger-loving boy. I ain't ever going to be. I wouldn't piss on the best part of ary'body rode with this trash."

He said it loud.

I felt my hands clench the reins. I couldn't help it. In back of Wesley I saw Shangro, only watching me, and Pella, sitting forward on the fence along there, and then the horse-box and French's bright hair flaming, and Constable Ballard, angling his face up at both of us, his brow seamed and his mouth open, and then another voice cut through all this. Not as loud as Wesley's, but with a bite to it that augured through the whole crowd sound and bit a tunnel in this warm air.

"Mister Teague. Wesley Teague. You will do us the comfort of keeping your mouth shut for the duration of these heats. Your task is only to try to beat the black horse. Do you comprehend, mister?" The major stopped talking, then.

Teague's lips shook; he wanted to say more, but he didn't. He rode onto the track. I swallowed what I'd been about to say, and held back what I'd been about to do. I sat back while Aldan put Flambeaux to the track. The rails clapped back into place. Cando went over one, and circled behind the quarter-breed, and took position at Flambeaux's chest. Constable Ballard stooped beneath a rail and came up on the other side. He pulled a silver dollar out of his pocket near the side-arm, and laid it on his right thumb and forefinger. Teague said in a thick, slurring tone, "I call heads."

The quarter-breed shook off a fly. The silver dollar sparkled.

Ballard said, "Tails."

Aldan said, soft enough, "Inside." Could just see his lips.

Teague's neck-muscles were working. Then he said, keeping it down, stubby hands holding the quarter-breed as if it was on a check-rein, "Damn it, no. He'll shy. Can't you see he's blind there? Goddamn it, can't even a stinkin' Gypsy see that?" But he still wasn't speaking to be heard past the track. I hadn't seen him mount the quarter-breed, but I knew he'd done it from the off-side.

Aldan gave a shrug. "There is small difference." He clucked to Flambeaux, kneed him back; he backed as well as he'd done the night before when I'd run against him, and then Aldan angled him to the outside rail slot. In place again, Cando moving to Flambeaux's chest, Aldan stared straight forward. He was like the others in the tribe, like the women softly selling their bundles of herbs and salves, like Major Deveraux had been at the start of all this. He wasn't connected with this place, this time; he was by himself except for Flambeaux. Both of them carved in a place where no others could come, a place older than the ground they stood on.

Cando had his wide-muscled hands on Flambeaux, holding him under the wire. Faces like the brown petals on a peach-bough in late summer gazed at us all along this stretch, and from the first turn. Ballard shouldered against the chest-muscles of the quarter-breed. The breed backed too far, had to be nudged forward again. The wire's shadow fell across both mounts' forehoofs. Ballard grunted, "Go," and got out of the way faster this time, and the crowd yelled and a hat sailed in the air, and along the track the dust that had settled rose again as the breed and Flambeaux charged into it. I watched them, and not Deveraux or the horse-box. I thought I knew where the major would be gazing again.

# 21

Aldan did what Jantil had told him to when Jantil had talked to us early that morning. He got the lead early right next to the outside rail, and for a time he kept it. By the time Flambeaux was at the first turn and they were sweeping around and coming to the backstretch, Flambeaux was two lengths ahead of the quarter-breed and stretching the lead.

Wesley Teague rode like a madman. He didn't have a good seat, but it didn't appear to matter to him; with the butt of a short whip he was beating the quarter-breed over the head and yelling. You could almost hear him over the crowd. I caught a glimpse in the distance there, through the dust both horses had left—like looking through a yellow red curtain—of Flambeaux moving into the backstretch, and then the quarter-breed coming along, well back. There were gouts of the track-clay under the dust flying back from Flambeaux's heels around the breed's muzzle and over Teague's head. When you watch a friend or even somebody you just favor a little, riding a race, it's as if you were riding it yourself. I found I was mumbling, "Keep to the rail!" to Aldan, even though he didn't stand a chance in hell of hearing me. Grayboy cocked his ears back at me and I gritted my teeth. Because Flambeaux was pulling away from the outside rail, toward the center of the track. I knew the little black horse was doing it on his own; Aldan didn't have anything to do with it. Some horses will do that, when they're young and you're driving them all out—they can't seem to respond to anything but going as fast as they can. Nobody ever said a horse is the smartest animal in the universe. But it's about the only one I can think of will kill itself for you. Outside a 'coon dog maybe.

I slid a glance at Jantil. His eyes were very slitted and he was sitting a fence-rail beside Shangro—he had the mare Malden reined and blanketed behind him, he'd been cooling her out but he'd stopped because he had to see Aldan run.

Out on the backstretch the breed was starting to come up. But it was coming with its near blind side aimed next to Flambeaux, between Flambeaux and the rail. "Goddamn it, Aldan, pull over!" I yelled. Knowing it wouldn't do any good. I looked at Jantil again; he was getting down from the fence and vaulting on Malden and riding her quick, outside the fence, down to the first turn, and Pella, on foot, was trotting along with him. I stayed where I was; I had to ride next. The white-haired man who'd raced Jantil on the Morgan had paused, walking the Morgan on a lead, and was gazing with me over at the backstretch. He said above the noise, "Teague'll go through the fence!" I thought so too. He meant the outside rail—the one on the breed's good side. The breed was nearly up to Flambeaux, nose level with Flambeaux's streaming tail. Aldan could still have yanked Flambeaux over but if he'd done it he would probably have had to check and have lost the heat. It was too late to turn Flambeaux and just let him drift without losing the full stride. Aldan wasn't looking back, just riding with his eyes straight on the track ahead, and rather low as his uncle Jantil rode but not quite so far down over Flambeaux's neck, and I thought maybe he didn't see the breed and Teague come up between him and the outside rail till the last bare second. Then the breed, Teague beating him and flopping on him and crowding him on both flanks with his swaying seat, was moving farther up. He was a wonderful horse under all that grime and rib-gaunted condition and even with his blind near eye. It wasn't till the blind eye was level with Aldan's light English saddle that the breed must have felt and sensed and known the shape on its blind side, and shied to the right so fast it was like watching a fish turn and jump in a net. Just like that, the arch of the breed's back like a fish as it leaped, and as it curved with the leap and went clean over the outside fence coming into homestretch, and landed scattering fence-rail watchers as if they were chaff before a wind; and then it went clattering up toward a stand of pin oaks behind the track to the west, with Teague still on and then, as the breed stopped all on its own, with Teague going over its head and landing and rolling and then getting up and walking to it, where it stood dappled by the pin-oak shade, and beating it and getting hold of it and wrying its head around by one ear and still beating it. So over the sound of the crowd shouting you could even hear the hollow noise of the short whipstock hitting the breed's skull. Constable Ballard was running up there, and so were some of the fence-rail watchers who'd been bowled over, not stopping to dust themselves off. When I looked back at the shed near the horse-cart I could see Major Jack Deveraux standing in his stirrup-irons, watching the ruckus; then he eased down again and turned his attention to the cart and French again. As if even if the earth cracked and dropped us all into it, he couldn't keep from staring at her.

Down at the first turn Jantil and Pella, Jantil on Malden, were waiting for Aldan to come in, and he was already well under the wire and slowing. Pella lifted off a rail down there, and Aldan rode Flambeaux out through the gap. Jantil leaned from his saddle on Malden and took hold of Flambeaux's bridle, I could imagine what he was saying to Aldan about not drifting Flambeaux back to the rail when he strayed. But I still didn't think Aldan could have helped it. Pella was putting the rail back in its posts. The wedge of crowd around them stood by without helping Pella, as they hadn't helped him when he lifted the rail off, and I could see they were mad and full of mean spit at having lost to Aldan and Flambeaux. Just as they'd started to get mad when Jantil won the first race, though that had been perfectly clean and well run with both mounts. As Aldan rode Flambeaux back with Jantil on Malden—Malden still blanketed—at his side, Pella walked close to them with his panther-eyed head up, not speaking no matter what the people in the crowd were calling after them.

Shangro was moving, quick for all his weight as always, rounding up the women and ushering them back into the women's cart. They all folded into it and the door of the cart was shut, and Shangro was standing there looking at me, and then canting his quiet eyes at Major Deveraux, who was riding Amber out of the shed-corner shadow and over toward the starting point. Up at the stand of pin-oaks, Teague had left off beating his breed and had tied it to a branch up there—or somebody had tied it for him—and with a good many well-wishers and sympathizers around him, was coming back down to the track. Constable Ballard came with them. As they got closer I could hear Teague—you could have heard him two counties over, I was thinking—shouting as he rolled along, "Disqualify the nigger! He bumped me!"

Constable Ballard said, "He wasn't within two feet of you! You rode that horse with the blind side right up to him! You could have come up on the inside! It's a fair win and I'll call it such!"

Teague's face was flaked with spittle, a lot of it his own.

The blunt stock of the whip in his brick red fingers had horsehair on it and caked sweat and blood.

He sighted at me as if he was blind himself—but in both eyes—and never even saw me, and then his head went around and he was sighting at Aldan who had just slid down off Flambeaux, and at Pella who was taking off Flambeaux's saddle. He made a lunge over there, and Constable Ballard reached to grab the shoulder of his sweated shirt, and got shaken off, and then Teague was making for Aldan, the whip raised with its bird-shot-filled end up, and then Major Deveraux from beside me where he'd reined in Amber said, cold as death, "Wesley. Wesley Teague." Deveraux even sounded bored, through the ice. And not talking loud, as he'd not before. "I believe I asked you to keep your slack mouth shut. I'll ask you again. And put away that whip. And get yourself out of my sight. I refuse to let your presence taint this handsome day any longer. Now go, and I warn you, don't answer me."

Teague swung and blinked at the major. Mouth opening and shutting and his dark teeth showing yellower than his breed's at each opening. The major said, still soft but clear and true, "You were fairly beaten. If you'd been in my regiment—but of course you weren't; you merely sat out the war, didn't you?—I'd have shot you for what you just did to your animal, and enjoyed my supper afterward. As it is, I cannot abide you in this vicinity. Keep well away from me should you see me in town."

He gave just the mildest twitch of his knee and his left rein, and Amber wheeled around, facing the track again. Behind him Teague stood with his lips still working, then turned and trailed by seven or eight of those who'd gone to commiserate with him, went back up toward the clump of pin-oaks. Up there in one of the nearest oaks I saw a bough shake and a black face peer out from fall-spangled leaves. It was the face of a child about twelve years old, I judged, a black child with old eyes and a serious, thoughtful mouth. Then the brown eyes went my way, and the mouth curved up in a pleasing smile. Next second, the child was down out of the tree, a rag and a bucket of water in his hands, and was laving down the flanks of the breed, which stood there tied to the branch, wheezing and coughing as if it had the rales and thumps together. I hoped Teague hadn't knocked out its remaining eye. I reckoned the child was Teague's farm-help, and found myself wondering what it would be like to depend for your joy in life on Wesley Teague. I'd seen a lot of his kind all my days, but they were still outnumbered, I thought, by their betters. At least I judged that was so this side of the Mason-Dixon line. This child handled the beaten horse well, working delicate as though the hide was made of flowers.

I went on looking back there, and said no word to the major at my flank. Didn't feel I had much to say to him; I admired him and felt deeply sorry about his having recognized French, but the less we talked, the easier I'd feel. So it was the major who talked first. First thing he'd said to me for quite a time on this day.

"When were you married, Broome? You and Miss—India Round-tree?" He spoke it with a certain slant to it. As though he tasted the lie on his tongue's tip.

I was thinking he didn't care anymore for me than he did for Teague. Couldn't rightly blame him.

"Back at her father's place on the Delta, a year ago," I said. I flicked a fly off Grayboy's forelock. "I don't know what you're after, Major Deveraux, but whatever it is, I'd say it's a mistake. Mrs.—Mrs. Broome is with me of her own free will. Nobody kidnapped her and dragged her here. With all respect, we've our own lives to live."

I turned my head just a trifle, looking over at the horse-cart. French was watching us, and she looked as if she was about to leap, that quiet tightness in her golden face.

"Oh, no," said Deveraux. "I can't swallow that, Broome. You have your lives—to live, as you say. But I will not be fobbed off with a fairy tale about the past. I do not mind legends, fairy tales. I rather favor them, as a rule. But when they touch on my own remembrance of a gallant friend—Colonel Robert Chantry saved my life twice, I shall not give you the details—and his lady, and their daughter, then I refuse to let them clog my throat. I give you this warning, Broome.''

I said, "Sir, maybe I can understand that. How something from the past got mingled in your mind with what's going on now—''

He was gazing at me straight-on, the blue eyes filled with fury.

"Are you suggesting I am senile, in my dotage? An old man dreaming dreams and fashioning what might have been from what is? Go to hell, Broome. I would have recognized Francia Chantry in rags, or on her deathbed. I would recognize her if I were twenty years older than I am, and if she were going gray. I tell you I will not have it. I have no idea why she is lying, why you are. But I shall find out. I don't believe in coincidence, or *Doppelgängers*—if you don't know what a *Doppelgänger* is, it's a double, alike in face, carriage, voice—and I particularly do not believe in duplicate carousels. I'll see you again, Broome—''

I said, "That's as may be, sir. But when you do, my name's Tom Broome. And if you're in love with my wife because she looks like a little girl you once took a fancy to, ask for Mrs. Tom Broome. I'm certain sure she'll be glad to see you, and you can both speak of your respective families and experiences.''

Thought for one flash, he'd hit me with his gloves. He'd just started to pull them on. He didn't carry a whip.

Then he wheeled away—one smooth motion—and paced a few paces along the fence-side, and turned Amber—she moved with the grace of a sea-wave—and was facing the rail again. We were about ten feet apart. I studied him for a second, the jaw squared and set, the powerful face with its grizzled but neat-shaped eyebrows, the dark flush of his skin and the elegance he sat with, and I was both mad and sorry. I'd have liked meeting him in a square race when he didn't even know me aside from my riding. I couldn't see his eyes now under the shadow of the perfect top hat.

I noted Teague was out of sight.

Which was one worry gone for now.

Most of the crowd had come back to swarm at the fences, all around most of the track. Shangro had mounted the bay he'd come here with us on, and was sitting her back beside the wagon that held the women and their wares. Pella was still cooling out Flambeaux, Aldan walking at his side. Jantil had Malden cooled, and had pulled her under the shed, where his scarlet headcloth showed like a red mirror when it caught touches of the sun. Cando and Constable Ballard were taking out an entry-rail again.

The crowd sounded all quieter now, but I'd liked it better when it was yelling. There was something about it now, lower-toned, that reminded me of how I'd felt in the half dark of the Fountainwood ballroom. From the window of the cart with the women in it, which Shangro had drawn up even with the horse-cart—the draught horses never had been unhitched, and their horse-brasses gave back the sun as hot as if the brasses were little suns all by themselves—Garsina was leaning and talking, or anyhow sign-languaging, to French. They seemed to get along well without a common language.

I found my palms were sweaty. Made me a little disgusted with myself. I reckoned it came from feeling how much the crowd wanted me to lose. They'd wanted it for Jantil, and for Aldan, but now you could roll their will against me on the back of your tongue. A white man riding with Gypsies, against his own kind.

Ballard's mild eye, but with some fret in it, caught mine, and he nodded. The rail was down. I rode in onto the track.

Grayboy stepped to his near and then his off, and then I brought him back to where I wanted him. He was so ready to go he was bursting with it, like a great gray bird.

Major Deveraux brought Amber through the breach and on the track. Ballard and Cando had the rail back in place. Ballard got his silver dollar out.

I said, "The major can have choice. I'll take either side."

"I don't accept favors," said the major, very soft. Staring straight ahead. "Toss the coin, Constable."

I was sorry I'd said anything. I should have known.

The coin went up high, caught the light, came down, was scooped in by Ballard's knuckly hand.

As it came down the major said, "Heads," and as Ballard showed it the head-side was up.

The major said, "Then I'll stay here."

I would have too. If a horse runs in a given path and is hard to swerve the outside rail is a good place to stay. If it moves cross-track at your bidding that's another story. I was recalling all Jantil had told me of Amber. I didn't think he'd in the least overestimated her running style. I knew the outside rail itself would keep Amber running close to it, and not fret her about moving to nigh and off. And give her more confidence. Deveraux was a man who'd no doubt always given her all she wanted.

The track-dust was hot in the waning evening. Down at the first turn there were waves of heat rising from the ground. And the people elbowing the railing didn't make it cooler. A baby was crying as if its gums hurt. Thin and keen above the crowd's murmuration. Grayboy's hide felt cool to my hand as I touched him on the neck. He was bobbing his head against the bit, and I held him middling tight. Cando came up under us, putting his hands and his shoulders' weight into Grayboy's chest-muscle, moving us back two inches. The wire's shadow had changed since Aldan's heat with Teague; it was spreading narrower now. Ballard was moving Amber into place. It seemed to me we were level. Ballard squinted over at Cando, and Cando nodded and jumped away just as Ballard said with the part of his breath he wasn't using to pant with, "Go!"

Ballard yawed to one side, and Amber as she moved out just missed him. Cando was already out of the way. Amber wasn't only a bung-starter, she was the whole barrel flowing out in one long ripple. I reckoned that during the war Major Deveraux had been a rider to make your hair curl, and the years between hadn't dulled him. It was as if he didn't even have a saddle or reins, or needed them. And if he'd had a mare like Amber in wartime he must have set the fields and streams on fire. All I could see was Amber's clean rump, the tail rising, and the heels moving the dust and dirt away as if they weren't even there, but she rode six inches above them. The major's top hat tight to his skull, the brim hardly moving more than Amber's head moved, only his sky blue coat flailing out a little as the wind caught it.

I leaned down over Grayboy's neck. Could smell his sweat strong there, the sweat starting to flow and stand out in its sweet-bitter rising, a good scent like the bark of a quinine tree. We were almost down this stretch to the first turn and he hadn't yet reached stride. I shouted toward his ear, and felt him reach out and start to bore. He was boring, driving, then; with one more horse on the track he'd have done it even sooner. The inside rail was swimming by with its green grasses lush in the infield, the outside rail was all clear with Amber still ahead and the faces of the crowd whipping by like beads snapped on a string. We were around the first turn. In my belly, deep where it twangs like a fiddle-string when you're making love, I felt the news that we could lose and all the reason for us being with Shangro would drop out of sight like the light out of the sky. All the way around the arc of this first turn I felt the same thing, a pain and a biting in my belly and lower ribs. And we were in the back-stretch.

Win or lose, I'd never felt like this before.

I knew Deveraux was riding as even he seldom could have, before or since. And Amber in such trim this might be the peak of her career.

Ten yards past the head of the backstretch I pulled on Grayboy to move to the outside rail. He swerved without losing a beat. Then we were spang behind Amber, and yet coming up on her, and when I felt the coming-up, saw the distance shorten, I kept Grayboy almost on the rail, kept him boring and moving up until his nose, higher by what seemed three feet than Amber's tail, was nearly shooting over her haunches, and he was breathing down the major's back, and the major was trying to give Amber more speed, but couldn't, and then knowing he couldn't swerve her to let me by—and wouldn't—and that we'd both go down if she stumbled—which I didn't think she would, she had feet like a fox's—I pulled to the nigh side, and Grayboy was moving around her. Having her there dead in front of him had made him give more of himself than he would if she'd only been on his off-side and in the lead. I'd recalled how he couldn't bear a sulky before him, and how even sometimes when I wanted to save him in a two-miler, for the second mile, he'd keep on until his forehoofs were almost clipping the sulky-wheels of the driver before us. Now I knew he was the same way with a horse, any horse. But it had to be dead ahead, not just in sight.

I knew if I was ever again in a two-man flat race with him, I'd have to give him the same challenge. It was always there in him, and this was what brought it out.

We had the track ahead by ourselves now, nearing the far turn, and then we were into it—Amber's hoofbeats still so close I couldn't pull back a hair, but had to just let him off the bit all the way around—then the homestretch was swimming up, the Gypsy horse-cart and the women-cart cut dark against the sky, the trees up the slope catching glints of sun like spear-flashes.

And the wire spun over us, and was swallowed behind, and then I was pulling him up, slow and easy, and he wound down like a good child after a romp, tossing his head and blowing, then I was turning him, and riding him back; Ballard and Cando had the rail down. When we got next the rail, the major was coming back on Amber. Sunlight stood low behind him, reddening, and he held his head up as if a rod rammed down his spine, and rode past me as I said, "Fine race, sir," and didn't look back but rode right on out of the track. I went behind him. Pella and Cando were throwing a blanket over Grayboy even as I got off. Pella said, "Walk him a little, Mister Broome, but do not linger. You can rub him down once he is in the cart."

I saw that Aldan and Shangro, mounted, were over beside the horse-cart.

French was standing in it above the ramp. She lifted a hand. She looked gorgeous and with the same elegance the major had, but as if hers could never sour or go old in a million years of time. Just in the one look. Jantil on Malden was sitting beside the cart with the Gypsy women in it.

I heard the plod of Grayboy's hoofs and plates now in the sunned earth here outside the track, and it sounded louder than it should. So did the noise, ever so slight, of Pella's boots, and my boots, and Cando's. Cando was walking back to the horse-box then. And I looked around and understood—the crowd was leaving, not lingering to talk as a crowd does nearly always, but moving away from the track, and from us, and up the side-slope to the town, already wagons were creaking up there, and buckboards swaying; some of the men stared back at us, their eyes something you couldn't read at this distance. But you didn't have to. A goose walked on my grave, sending the touch of its web-feet down my spine. Ballard had run up alongside Shangro, who leaned from the bay to listen to him.

Then Ballard was counting out money in Shangro's hand. And Shangro was still listening to the constable.

I marched Grayboy along under his wraps past the shed.

Near it, Major Deveraux was standing, while a young Irish-looking white man with a carrot head of hair walked out Amber. The major had his back to me. As he'd had for too much of our heat, to make me comfortable. He kept it that way as I went past.

Without turning, he said then, "You ride well, Broome." He wouldn't call me by my full name to save him. "And your horse is a marvel. Don't expect anything more in the nature of a compliment from me."

Well, I hadn't. I hadn't expected even that.

I went on, and turned Grayboy and started him back past the shed, but this time Deveraux had gone back behind it and was staring up the hill away from town. Toward that oak where Wesley Teague had tethered his breed and started beating it. The breed was gone with Teague, and the black child who'd eased the breed's wounds was nowhere in sight.

All the grass around the fencing was mashed flat where the crowd had stepped it down. It smelled used and tired. I turned Grayboy and brought him back again, this time almost to the horse-box. From the saddle of his bay, Shangro said, "I think we will go now, Mister Broome." I brought Grayboy up to the ramp. "You and your man-horse did admirably, as I had thought you would. Here is your quarter of our winnings." I took the money, but didn't count it. It felt like a good-sized wad. "Pella will drive the cart with the women, and Cando will drive yours, as we did coming here. But this time we will not go through town, we will move up westward, and then cut across to the side-road when we are beyond the town." Shangro looked down at me, his eyes shining but not with any gladness. "It is very satisfactory to have won. But there are sometimes consequences. We must avoid these if we can."

His faded yellow shirt ballooned as he sighed. He jerked a thumb toward the hillside leading to town. The last of the people who'd been down here in mobs were straggling up there now. I thought Pharis would have saloons, and they might soon be doing a tidy trade. I said, "It was a decent three heats, Shangro. There hadn't ought to be any hard feeling."

"No, there had not. However, Mister Broome, when we reach camp, we will go straight on tonight. Maybe we can stop for supper some time toward morning. We follow the Chickasawhay for a time before we travel northeastward."

He wheeled the bay.

Cando was already on the driver's box of the horse-box cart.

Aldan and Jantil and Shangro were lining up their mounts in front of the horse-cart draught horses.

Pella was on the driver's box of the cart behind us.

Garsina called to French and me from the window of that cart, in Rom.

Aldan turned from where he sat Flambeaux and said, "She wishes to tell Mr. Broome he rode masterfully, and he should give me lessons. I agree, but I did not know that fool would bring his horse up on the outside. But I should have stayed to the rail, so he could not; I know."

I looked over at Garsina where her black hair caught the last of this light like a forest pool. "Thank you!" I called. She smiled but it appeared to me she looked as on-edge as everybody else. Even as French did as I got on Grayboy and urged him up the ramp. This time he took it like a lamb, he'd done it before and knew it. I got him back to his part of the cart, got off, tied him, peeled off his blanket, and started rubbing him down. Then I heard the ramp being pushed up from outside; I reckoned Pella was doing it. I felt easy and uncoiled as I always do after any heat, and I didn't yet feel the need for any rushing or sneaking off, in spite of the way the crowd might feel. Somebody had already brought Grayboy's saddle and the rest of his tack into the cart. I heard French latching the ramp door in place.

She came back into this shadowy cavelike room. She carried one of the lamps which she'd unhooked from its chains. She held it while I finished Grayboy. By this time the cart had started to move. I laid down the rags and comb I'd been using, turned around to French, steered her and the lamp into the abode-section of the cart, took the lamp from her, rehung it, and said, "Well, Mrs. India Broome. And how are affairs down on the Delta?"

"I hated telling him that. He's right, you know. I mean, Tom, he's right in everything he said—I even recalled him as he was speaking. He was at Chantry Hall, that night long ago. Tom, I was so proud of you and Grayboy."

"So was he, the major, I'd say. At least enough to tell me I rode well and he's a good horse. But aside from that he hates my liver and lights."

"And he thinks I'm despicable."

That was a favorite word with her, I'd learned, for anything really bad. As she'd used it on Gary Willis when we were at Fountainwood.

"And I am," she said, "and I don't enjoy it, even though it has seemed needful."

I looked at her careful. Both lamps were swaying as we went along. The light and dark they cast moved over her face in dark bars and beams of warm yellow. I said, "I'd like to just hold you a time, if you don't mind. Not anything else. We've got some real money now, to use at Yadkin. I do think we ought to cheer up just a mite."

She came to me, put her arms around me. Felt she fitted there as if we'd been joined in any kind of matrimony, Gypsy or Baptist, Lutheran, Methodist or Episcopalian, for a tide of years. I noted she was peering over my shoulder at the merry-go-round. She said, very soft, "It's caused all this trouble. When we get to Yadkin Fair I'll make it earn its keep. I'll run it for children there."

# 22

While we were on our way back to the camp I took a bucket of water and took off my shirt and splashed myself, getting off the dust of the Pharis track. Evening light was easing in through the window above the bunk, rippling a little as it fell through bosky trees; French busied herself slicing and laying out some of the last of the gentry food Jupiter had endowed us with when we left Fountainwood. This was the guinea hen. Then I put my shirt on and while we rolled along, we supped; if we weren't going to stop for supper till morning, it seemed like a sound idea.

I felt the motion of the down-slope as we rolled into the clearing; then I heard Shangro, talking low but urgent, outside this cart. I unsnicked the hasps of the ramp-door and lowered it by its hempen handle, and looked out to where, in the glow of this clearing before dusk, Shangro and his grandson Tomas and Jantil and Pella were cutting the horse-string loose from its line, and leading the horses and mares back toward the front of the caravan. All but two of the mares, including the brown one named Farella that had given Grayboy such a teasing, were spayed; the other race-horses were gelded. Already the caravan was lined up; the fires were out long ago and the limestone spring and pond were catching the last of the green light through the trees around them. Shangro saw me, French at my shoulder, and said, "I have not sufficiently congratulated you, Mister Broome. I do not know why you took the man-horse so close behind Major Deveraux, but that is your business."

I explained about challenging Grayboy with a horse square in front of him.

"Ah! And I think you, like him, respond to any challenge. We are moving the running herd, as you see . . . for one thing, it will remove Farella from scent of your man-horse. For another, it will be better for them to stay up near my cart, in case—" He shrugged. "In case anything should happen."

I could see that if there was any fuss made by somebody trying to overtake us, it would be best to have the string up where the Gypsy men could keep an eye on them. Shangro swung young Tomas up in his arms, and placed the boy on his back. Frogs were starting to sound off around the pond and spring. Tomas said, "Next time I will watch you run, Mister Broome. At Quincyville. My grandfather has told me it is all right."

I said, "That damned fool, Teague. Did you run against him last year?"

"Pella ran against him," Shangro said. "We won the heat, then, but Pella's mare, a little piebald, was badly hurt. He followed her down past the finish-wire and ran her through the rail at the first turn. Teague was riding a hammer-headed chestnut, which I do not think was long for this world. The piebald broke her off foreleg. I had to cut her throat. Major Deveraux made Teague pay for what he had done."

Tomas said chirpily, "I will watch everybody run at Quincyville. When I am older I will run myself."

"And I hope you win everything," I told Tomas. I said to Shangro, "This Major Deveraux. Struck me he didn't have much to do with the general run of people in Pharis."

"He is—" Shangro smiled. "He is like Miss Chantry. He is an aristocrat. He does not soil his splendid boots with most of the folk in Pharis."

Beside me, French said thoughtfully, "Mister Shangro, this is one aristocrat who would like you to marry her; according to your custom, tomorrow. To Thomas Broome."

Shangro touched his moustache, and settled Tomas more comfortably on his shoulders. "I have already told Mister Broome I will be glad to perform the ceremony. I think you have both made wise choices. I noted Major Deveraux expressed great interest in you, Miss Chantry."

There wasn't much Shangro didn't note, I thought.

"He knew me," French said. "I pretended he couldn't have known me, but he'd served with Daddy—and he'd been to Chantry, in the old days." She was frowning a little. "I had to tell him some lies . . . I felt bad doing it, and I still do. He's too good a man to fool."

"An excellent man, yes. But maybe a little inclined to keep to one line of track, like his wonderful mare . . ." Shangro stroked Tomas's fingers, which clutched his plump neck. "There are those who are sunk in the past, steeped in it. To the extent that they sometimes shut out the present, and cannot see the future, and approve of neither. It is like old silver, which tarnishes if it is kept too long in a cabinet, away from the light of the sun . . . he is a man still in battle, but the battlefields are empty . . . but a patrician, and a man to trust.''

He was gazing full-faced at French. ''But enough—Mister Broome, my son Pella will ride behind your cart as we proceed. He will be there if he should be needed.''

It came to me I hadn't seen a firearm among any of this tribe. Some knives, handsomer than my own; but not a weapon that shot.

I said, ''If he's needed—Shangro, you're using your men for outriders on all the carts, aren't you?'' I'd seen a couple of men saddled up near the other carts, ready to go.

''That is true. It may be a useless precaution.''

I said, ''And it may not.'' Much as I wanted to just keep on relaxing and taking it calm for the rest of this night—as I've said, after a heat, even of only a mile, I always feel easy and free—I was also feeling the edge of watchfulness in this coming dark. Above the pond, bullbats were starting to swoop and whirl. ''Shangro, if anything does come of this rangle-tangle in Pharis, I wouldn't want to be shut in here, doing nothing. Wouldn't want Grayboy where he is, if they—set the cart afire, or something. I'll ride him outside.''

French said, ''And I'll ride on the driver's box.''

Shangro wriggled Tomas around on his shoulders, and the boy squealed as if he was up on a fretful mount.

''I would appreciate that, Mister Broome. Unless you feel strongly about saving the man-horse for Quincyville—''

''Hell, you don't save your string. And at the pace you travel, it doesn't hurt a horse. Just keeps them from goin' to sleep. I'll be with you.''

''Excellent—I can use every man. Pella will ride further forward, then.''

It struck me what a good officer he'd have made in the Confederate armies. But then I didn't believe they'd used Gypsies, and even if they had I didn't believe Shangro or the rest interested themselves in any wars. They were like outlyers on the rim of life, who made their own judgments and lived their own way, with pride and grace in it, and it wasn't any wrong way to exist.

Shangro spoke to French now. ''Miss Chantry, I do not wish to disappoint you, but it would be best for you to remain in the cart. Not that Cando—he has the first task at driving your cart tonight—would not welcome your company. But with all friendship, you draw the eye as the summer draws fireflies—and they would make this cart a magnet for their"—he shrugged—"attentions." His teeth showed. "That is a strange compliment, but you will take it in the proper spirit."

He wheeled around, and started moving off, making little hops as he went like a horse going over rough ground, Tomas squealing at every hop.

Jantil, with his sons Rico and Jal running at his side, came alongside the cart leading Farella. She reflected the water from the pond on her brown withers like little forks of lightning running, and she was balking as Jantil pulled her.

I called to Jantil, "Good race!"

He said, "But I had a good man to run against. The Morgan could have passed me, if it had been saved for the first half-mile. It was a matter of judgment." He was wearing his instrument slung around his neck again. "Mister Broome, something I mentioned this morning—I wished to wait to ask you till the Pharis heats were over—"

I said, "You want to breed Farella with Grayboy. I don't mind, and it'll clear his mind for what I want him to do at Yadkin."

"I will pay you—"

"Balderdash," I said. "I've already got more than I've ever made for a single heat in my life. Your people salted the ground at Pharis—in fact, you did a lot of the ground-laying yourself." I'd counted the money Grayboy had won, while French and I were supping. It was enough to put up at a fancy hotel in Yadkin—if Yadkin had any of that kind, though even if it did I wasn't going to favor anything like the Gayoso in Memphis—and to have enough left over for the entry-fees and the betting. And some besides. I'd never been to Yadkin before, I hadn't thought Grayboy was ready till this year. "Listen to him," I said.

Grayboy was whickering, soft, then louder. Farella answered with a mild nicker, and danced back. One of Grayboy's plates hit the stall in the cart a solid crack. Farella's eyes moved as if she'd just seen the Devil and was pleased by the sight.

Jantil said, "That is splendid, Mr. Broome. There is a good fenced lot beside an old cotton barn outside Quincyville. In the morning, then."

He and Rico and Jal coaxed Farella past our cart. Grayboy bugled after them. The whisper of the strings of Jantil's instrument went along with the clopping of Farella's light, quick hoofs.

I tasted the night—it was almost dark now—a second more, the float of mint in it, the falltime brilliance that seems to come right straight from the edged stars. French touched me on the shoulder, ran her fingers down my spine. I gave her a solid look of loving, wanting her all right but keeping it down because there was other work to do. When she straightened and went back under the lamplight, fluffing her hair with that lovely motion a beautiful woman has as she lifts her arms, I felt how lucky it was just to be living and breathing; no matter if some people didn't like this style of life, and called it alien; I wouldn't have changed it to be in the White House, wearing a gilt high hat.

I went back and examined Grayboy's plates, which I hadn't done when I rubbed him down and curried him; I'd intended to do it when we stopped in the morning. The plate Cando had made was firm as stone, and the others had held, though they were just a bit worn; French held a lamp again while I worked. I saddled him, he was cooling down some now that Farella was out of scent-range, and rubbed the dust of the Pharis track off the pommel and seat and cantle, and wheeled him while French went to the door. I rode him out and through the side we lived in, and down the ramp, again in about three long strides. Outside, I could see the whole caravan, the carts showing lamplight in their windows, gentle light that spilled to the clearing's frost-touched grasses and made every blade glisten. Up ahead, Shangro was on his driver's box; Cando was on ours; I saw Pella midway of the caravan, his blue headcloth a shade brighter than the rising moon. As I watched, Aldan on Flambeaux drew the black horse up beside another cart. There was an outrider for each cart now. I threw down Grayboy's reins, got off and went to lift the ramp-door. From the horse-string which was just behind Shangro's cart now, Farella was calling, but not as loud as she had. Grayboy answered but stood fairly still. French was framed in the ramp-way.

Lamplight touched all the strands of her hair, played behind her as she stood there. "Well, I declare, Tom, I'd rather ride outside than be cooped up on such a night. Since you cannot be in here with me." She was lifting her eyes to the sky. Her eyes looked like the sparkle you see on grapes in this light, but deeper and more back-shining. The amber-quick flecks sparked. She brought her gaze back to me. "I think I'll just improve the shining hour by cleaning up my carousel. So it will be ready for Yadkin. I'll show you how to start it, in the morning."

"You don't have to run it there," I said. "I'll do the running for us."

"Oh, but I wish to." She swung the lamp she'd brought from Grayboy's stall. "I may never have another chance. Not for a lot of people—children-people—to see it and enjoy it. And besides, at a ten-cent piece per ride, it will help out.''

She was like a little girl, creating mighty plans.

She was also like a magical woman with the whole earth at her neat fingertips.

I reached and kissed her; she straightened again. "I love you, Tom. There's a poem by Mrs. Browning, we learned it at the academy—'Let me count the ways'—I'll say it to you some time. I won a little cup for elocution saying it, one time. Good night—my love.''

I said, "Good night, and don't stay up all night fussing with that flying jenny.''

I wanted to say a deal more, but it wasn't a time for it and besides I'm not quick with fond speeches. She knew just how I felt, I thought, the way I said it. The tone of it.

I pushed the ramp-door up, and heard her setting down the lamp on the inside, and then latching the door on both sides. She said again, inside there, "I can look out and see you now and then beside the window.''

"I'll wait for it," I told her.

I went back and mounted Grayboy. I gazed over at the pond-pool where the water from the spring fell slipping down over those blue green rocks. Recalled how she'd appeared beside me, naked and noble in her small-ness as a bright fish in the air, waist nipped in naturally, that delicate line of waist and belly and thighs burning in this morning's sun. Her breasts and their lift, her fleece as dark red as her hair, but tight-curled and springing. Since I didn't have the fiddle with me, I just whistled a few bars of "Join the Cavalry," and Grayboy moved his legs, impatient to be off to wherever we were going.

Then up ahead Shangro's cart was moving, and then the next behind his. Finally after the other carts had started, Cando—a dark humped shape on our driving-box—chirruped to the double team, and clacked the reins, and the team dug into it, brasses tinkling, the pots and pans and bowls in all the carts making their low singing, and we pulled on up and out of the clearing. I looked back just before the sycamores shut it from sight. It was as empty and clean of refuse as if no man had ever touched it, no horse-plate or bootsole had ever stepped into it at all.

# 23

We were going northwest, away from Pharis. Quincyville lay somewhere out in the rolling dark. The moon came up slow and grand after we were out of sight of the clearing and on this road, its light just flicking drops of shine onto the road and over the carts under the thick elm and cottonwood and gum and brake-brush. Sometimes as I walked Grayboy—or as he walked, it was the quickest we could go along here in the slipping earth—I'd see the moon poised just above the furze of the treetops, then again the boughs would shadow it almost all from sight. It wasn't long, not more than a quarter of a mile, before the river swam in sight on the west. The Chickasawhay, I thought. Its water-scent charged the air with that teasing touch it has, of rotted leaf and mist and secret deeps and easy shallows. We were moving above it. Down through the foliage, already winter-touched and lonely, the lamplight from the carts reached and spilled dabs and jabs of light over the boughs, and sometimes you could see the shine of small animals' eyes, and maybe animals not so small. Owls coasted low down the slope and near the river, and somewhere a heron sounded. The noise of the caravan was a steady surging, made of many sounds—hoofbeats and cart wheels and people—together, warning anyone ahead that we were coming. It bothered me to think the sound could just as well be heard from our rear. No way to disguise it.

I wasn't in the least ready for sleep. From the great horse-cart ahead of me—or sometimes beside me, when I rode Grayboy up next to it—I could see chinks of light, and once when I was under the window above the bunk, French looked out, waving to me. I lifted a hand back to her, and stayed where I was for a little time, and then she showed me the polishing rag in her hand, and went out of sight again, back to working on her flying jenny. I dropped back to the rear, centering in the road to keep the moss-beards on the river-side from brushing off my hat.

The North Star showed in the sky fierce as a burning diamond. I watched it and the stars scattered around it until I felt dizzy and pulled my eyes back to the cart wheels turning ahead of me. In this light the road-dirt sluicing off the rear wheels turned a silver blue that kept dropping like earth and ore coming out of a flume, down a couple of ever-filling channels. I slowed Grayboy a little and let the huge cart pull twenty or so yards ahead, because watching that motion of the back wheels was just as dizzying as keeping my eyes on the stars. It was better back here, and quieter, and I could make out Grayboy's own steady hoofbeats above the other sounds. We'd gone maybe another quarter-mile, passing a river-man's shack above the water in a cleared space where the stumps of the trees still showed the marks of long-gone ax-men, and then, on our left, a farm-road leading back past cottonwoods, when I heard other hoof sounds.

I pulled in Grayboy while the horse-cart got slightly smaller ahead. I had to make sure. It could have been any traveler coming along here, riding faster than the caravan could travel. Grayboy was tossing his head around; he sensed it too. A pulse was going strong in my wrists. I listened.

It was more than one set of hoofs. It still could have been a party of night-riders about their own business which wasn't ours. All the same, I rode Grayboy across this road and into a stand of dark long grasses above the trees thrusting up from the river's bank. I turned him so we were facing the rear of the caravan again. The caravan's noise was lessening as it pulled away. I ran a hand down the bridle and patted Grayboy's cheek. The hoofbeats came louder. I thought, A lot of riders. They made that streaming sound of a whole bunch galloping, a sound that always shakes a road and is magnified in the dark as if the dark itself sharpens every plunge of the plates. I leaned forward and said, "Hah!" and Grayboy was up and out of the grasses like a black gray cannonball, then his shadow was scudding alongside as we whipped toward the caravan. Behind me I heard somebody yell, "There they are!"

The voice was like a claw ripping black cloth.

Same time, the first shot came.

It slugged past me and hit the back of the giant horse-cart, chipping the wood at the off-corner, then spanging off toward the river.

Up till then I could have been just spooked by a party of innocent riders.

Our horse-cart was picking up pace. I could hear Cando yelling at the draught horses in Romany. I pulled Grayboy to the off-side of the cart, rode under the window, and shouted up at the gentle light of the lamp as I rode through it, "Keep down, get to the front!" I couldn't see French but hoped she'd heard me. I heard another shot and this time saw the flaring red reflection of the pistol going off, and smelled the powder, the reflection shining in the side-window of the horse-cart, the powder slicing above the natural smells of horses and river-smell and making me think for this flash of that brimstone-scent I'd thought I inhaled back at Fountainwood.

I didn't know where that shot had gone. I stood in the irons, riding sharp-close to the horse-cart just ahead of its window-shine now, and I could see Jantil on Malden, standing in his own stirrups, calling ahead to Shangro in the lead cart. Then on the other side of our horse-cart a rider came into sight, going with all he and his horse had, the rough-haired quarter-breed's good right eye shining and the bumpy, flannel red, sweat-streaming face of Wesley Teague, bent over his withers, showing plain as his hat-brim fanned up from his eyes, the eyes crazy as a betsy bug's and then Teague and the breed gone on the nigh side of the horse-cart. I wheeled Grayboy, cut around in back of the horse-cart, whose wheels were churning now, with the draught horses galloping, and brought up Grayboy on the near side of the cart, just ahead of a man riding on the withers as Teague had been, a man on a tall mount that looked like an Irish hunter gone down in the world, and he flashed an eye at me and roared, "Pull up, here's the bastard!" But I was in front of him, I'd just had that one glimpse of him from the tail of my eye, and it was enough— they didn't want French, they wanted me. Me first, and then maybe all the Gypsies. I was between Teague and the rest of the riders now. Cando was pulling in the draught horses, their heel-plates were digging earth as he sawed the reins, the horse-cart was bumping and shuddering as it stopped, and just ahead, the next cart was pulling up. And then Aldan, on the near side but off the road, was riding Flambeaux back, galloping Flambeaux through the brake under the road on this flank opposite the river, the twigs and brush seeming to explode as he bored through; he brought Flambeaux up from the brush and checked him, the black little horse blowing and jerking its head so the star on the forehead looked like a shooting star, and I had checked Grayboy. Teague had gone all the way up near the lead-cart, but now he was riding back, I could see his firearm as he came in sight, and smell more of that rancid corn-breath. The gun was a Walker Colt, I knew that because Daddy'd had one before he'd cast all weapons away for good. Behind the man on the hunter were at least ten others, ranged up there and leaning to look over the shoulder of the man astride the hunter. He was a thin-cheekboned man with birdshot blue specks over the bridge of his nose and under his eyes. He was breathing hard. One of the riders behind him carried a pine-knot torch, waving it off his saddle, so the dripping from it whirled in the air like a crazy comet.

Wesley Teague rode up alongside me and Aldan. Aldan had his right hand around the haft of his knife. Teague said, slow and strained as if he was talking through mush, "Git his knife, Fenton."

The man on the hunter slid off, and went over to Flambeaux. Teague had the Colt on both Aldan and me, moving it from one to the other. Fenton reached for the scabbard on Aldan's hip, then he had the knife and it was bright in his horny palm. He said, "Always wanted one of these Gypsy toad-stabbers." Teague's breed-horse with its coat sopped and its breath heavy stood with its head half-down and the blind eye staring at the cart-side in the chancy light. Behind Fenton the saddles of the riders with Teague's party were creaking and their horses were breathing moist clouds in the cool air.

Teague's time-fouled shirt billowed in and out with his breath, his gumboots hung from his shins in folds, and he said still slow and blurred, "Stevens, bring up the ropes. We got all we want right here. Reckon there's a pine down in the bottoms can hold both of 'em—" He waved the Colt, which even though it hadn't been polished for a time, caught the burning pine-knot's shine and sparkled.

Aldan said to me in a low clear voice, "I am sorry I could not help you, Mister Broome."

I signed to him to keep quiet. He'd tried. He'd tried to get back here and ward off the party from going into the horse-cart. I wondered where the other Gypsy men were. The whole train of carts seemed very quiet.

Fenton, balancing Aldan's knife in his palm, looking up at me, said, "Reckon you'd best pick out an oak for this here carcass." He meant mine. "Pine might snap, and we don't want no halfway stretchin'. The little 'un—" He meant Aldan. "You could hang him like a tomtit from a sugar-bush, he wouldn't strain it. Almighty, look at that horse!" This time he meant Grayboy. "When I see him run, I didn't take in half of him. Reckon he's worth a thousand?"

Teague shifted in his saddle, which was stained and older than his breed. "We'll settle all that later. Stevens, where in hell are them ropes?"

A man called back from the pack behind us, "Bringin' 'em right up, Wesley." The riders in back of us swerved their mounts to let Stevens through. He was on foot. The ropes he carried looked like hay-baling ropes, right out of a loft. He was a short, bow-legged man with a slanted mouth like a cracked pitcher-lip. "Ready any time, Wes."

"Git down," Teague said to me and to Aldan.

Aldan sat steady. So did I. I could feel from the spread of bile in my belly nobody was bluffing. But once off our mounts we wouldn't have any chance. There wasn't much chance as affairs stood.

"Better take his knife too, Fenton," Teague said, his voice as if coming from a sleepy mile off. But plain enough. He sounded as if he was about to give a woman his seed, almost a panting tone. "Come on, git down!" This was to Aldan again.

Aldan sat still. Flambeaux stood as if made out of black glossy rock, only the flank muscles twitching.

I thought of the children in the carts. Young Tomas, and Rico and Jal, and all the rest. Mostly I thought of French and hoped to God she'd stay silent. There wasn't a pinch of noise from the river or this other side of the road, only a horse whinnying softly where the string was up near Shangro's cart, and the shuffle and stir of the horses behind Fenton and Stevens, and one of the night-riders coughing. Fenton walked over to me and reached and took the knife that had been Daddy's out of its sheath.

"This 'un ain't even a Bowie," he said.

Grayboy flicked his head away from Fenton, and stamped.

"Jesus to Jenny, we can run him over a'rything the state's got to put up against him," Fenton said. "I'll cut his balls off though. I ain't handlin' anything with that hellfire in it."

Teague said with that distant cotton-wool soaking his voice, "We'll do a little more ball-cuttin' than that b'fore the night's out."

Somebody laughed, if you could call it a laugh.

"And mebbe with them same knives," Teague said. "Alroy, you and Flacker climb up on that travelin' ark they got there, the one this white man and his stallion rides in—git in through the window or the roof if you can't see no other way. Bring out that red-haired pretty woman this Gypsy-asslickin' son of a blue bitch rides with, and bring her nice—I could see she had nice manners, today. You." He was pointing the Colt at Aldan again. "I'll give you three counts, I note you can speak the Lord's English, so you know what I'm sayin'. If you ain't off your horse at three, I'll blow your head off. Codsway—you back there?"

There was a "Hey, here, Wes," from the rear.

"You and Tutwiler and a couple other boys go up front and git the money the old fart's got. We'll take whatever this other fancified stallion-rider's got b'fore we stretch him. We got to burn the carts too—I can't stand nigger scent, just as I done told this chap once today. Burnin' 'em 'll purify the air." He hadn't looked away from Aldan. Breath sucked in through his snuff-colored teeth. "One," he said.

The halfblind breed had its head even lower. It had weals all down its forelegs, and a cut still open under its right ear.

Two of the men in the shadows behind us had dismounted and come forward and they were climbing up the sides of the horse-cart. One on this side, reaching to grab the roof-eave and then dangling, the other around the river-side where I could hear him trying the window. Four other men were riding around behind the cart and then on to the front of the caravan. From here on Grayboy I could see the legs of their horses moving past the wheels. The moonlight mixed with the pine-torch sputter and its dripping, making shadows leap high around Teague's head. "Two," he said.

Just a breath after he'd said it, the snake came looping out of the bush and branches behind him.

Save it wasn't a snake, it was a whip. Its lean-tapering tip went around Teague's shoulders twice, lacing him in so fast with the heavier thong of the whip his arms were pinned to his sides, the Walker Colt slanting groundward. The whip drew tight and back, and he yelled. The breed backed with the whip-cage pulling Teague, backed with its haunches almost in the leaves. And Shangro, on the bay, keeping a distance from Teague and the breed and the whiplash drawn as tight between his hand and arm and Teague as if it'd been a line with a dozen channel-cat on it, brought the bay out of the leaves and brush and sat there in the moonlight. He said quiet, "Let the gun go, Mister Teague. And the rest of you—" He'd lifted his dark head, his arm back and the muscles cording through the fat. "If you have other weapons, do not use them. With one more turn, I can have Mister Teague's neck. Aldan, go back and help your uncle Jantil against those at my cart. Pella and Sendar are already there. Mister Broome, if you will do me the favor of taking his gun—he seems strangely attached to it—we can handle those who are trying to enter the horse-cart. At least we can try, you agree?"

I looked back and up. One of the men was on top of the horse-cart. He didn't have a weapon I could see, but it wasn't clear light. The other came scrambling up as I watched, from the window side, and I could hear him plain over the noise of the man behind Fenton who stood there with the two knives still in his hand as though he'd been handed them as prizes at a knife-throwing match and didn't know what to do with them. This man on the roof of the cart was groaning, "She throwed down on me through the winda, the Goddamned bitch! Throwed a chamber-pot over me!"

From the front of the caravan I could hear yells and somebody cussing, but no shooting. Aldan was already riding Flambeaux back along the row of carts to the head of the train.

All of this was happening in about four seconds. I slid off Grayboy and let him stand, and as I went over to Teague on the breed—his knuckles around the grip of the Walker Colt were as knobbed as china eggs—I heard the inside latches of the ramp-door coming loose, and then the whole door come down with a heavy rushing thud in the dirt. I couldn't help looking around again. French was in the lamplighted doorway, outlined against the yellow wash behind her. She jumped down, not even taking the ramp, then she was hasting over here to me, her dress flying, her hair quick and alive as a flag in the pine-knot's splashing brightness. I turned back to Teague. The whip-coils were still tight as barbed-wire around his shoulders and high on his chest. But he was trying to work his forefinger away from the grip of the Colt, where his whole hand had fallen back when the whip pinioned him, and forward around the guard to the trigger. His hand was a piece of soiled leather and the fingers of it like crawling centipedes. Another inch and he'd have the trigger. I didn't think he was sane enough to stop even if Shangro took a loop around his neck.

I had the barrel of the Colt, then, and was pulling it up and to the side—and I could hear French behind me, hear her breath at my shoulder, she was saying, "Damn them, damn them!"—when Stevens threw the ropes. He threw them clear around Teague's breed and at Shangro and the bay, they wallowed in the air and against Shangro's eyes, and he lifted his free hand—leaving the bay without a hand on him—to ward them off, and at the same time Teague wrenched around, squirming, and loosened the whip's tautness enough to get his forefinger on the trigger. He shot straight at me, but even with the explosion in my face and the singeing bark of it around my eyebrows I knew he'd missed, because in the selfsame blink of time I could hear the ball cut leaves above us.

At the same time, while the smell of powder was still crowding my nostrils and the flash was hanging before me as if I'd stared into a bloody sun, there was a crashing and a scattering of men both horsed and afoot from Teague's night-riders behind us, and as I kept on opening and shutting my eyes, through those Teague men and up to us, past Stevens and Fenton, who dropped both knives in the road, came a gloss-coated mare and behind her a shag-maned hack with bony hocks. And the voice of the man on the mare was just as it had been when he'd last dismissed me at the Pharis track.

Only Major Deveraux wasn't speaking to me right now. I rubbed my eyes and could see him clearer. Damned if he didn't still have his top hat on, the brim smart and level, the Tattersall vest showing its genteel check, but this time his coat was a dark red, and his boots showed all the scene before him in little snapping mirrors in their curves. Before him on the neck of the mare Amber rode the young black child I recalled seeing tend Teague's breed after Teague had taken out his wrath on it. The child didn't even look very surprised. He had deep eyelids as if he was an old wise man in child's flesh.

Shangro had ridded himself of the ropes, and had a hand on his bay's rein again; behind him along the rim of the road next to the brush Jantil was drawing up on his Malden mare, and behind him in turn, Pella, on one of the Gypsy horse-string, was pulling in toward us. In front of them were the four Teague night-riders Teague had sent up to the head cart, but they were walking now, and one had a knife-slash on his brow. Up on the roof of the horse-cart the two Teague men stood with their mouths open, staring down; the one who'd been baptized, so to speak, by French, was a discouraging sight.

Major Deveraux was still speaking, though. Not loud, just sure. "—you may release him, Mister Shangro. I shall keep him covered." Just at Amber's off-side, Constable Ballard, large-eyed and with pain on his forehead and seaming his cheekbones as well—I was sure he didn't like any fuss at all—was holding his sidearm on the night-riders in back of Deveraux. Deveraux had a dueling pistol, couldn't have been anything else with that silver chasing on it and the long barrel, pointed steadily at Teague. Shangro rode his bay up around Teague on the breed, the whip uncoiling and falling away as he did so, and then he reeled the whip back to him and sat solid, waiting. Aldan and one of the other Gypsy men, Sendar, came riding from the front, and checked beside him.

There was a stir from the carts now, old Cando climbing down from his box, other drivers climbing down and streaming back to us, the calls of women, soft as doves in a cote, the chatter of wakened children. Constable Ballard's bony hack snorted heavily, and Grayboy eyed it as if it was no kin to him at all. Aldan got off Flambeaux and took the Walker

Colt out of Teague's hand. French said alongside me, "Are you hurt?" and I said, "Not in the least, you?" and she shook her head.

Deveraux's voice clipped on. "—I have never believed there is any remedy for mad dogs but to treat them as just that—ravening dogs. Teague, Fenton, Stevens, Codsway, Alroy, John Flacker—all of you. You are under arrest. Constable Ballard will see you are tried for attempted murder."

Teague had his eyes screwed up toward Deveraux. "Willie done scampered and told you, hey?" he said, fur-soft. "Willie done left his own bed and board and skallyhooted right over to the great Major Deveraux, and told what we was up to. Well, little Willie, we'll see about that. Ain't no jail holding Wesley Teague, and when I git out I'll visit you, Willie. I treated you as well as any nigger I ever helped out—"

"I know how you treated him," said Deveraux. Teague had been speaking just to the black child. "I think everyone knows that. Do you know why he stayed with you? Because he loves that poor benighted animal of yours—his ministrations are all that keep him alive. But I am speaking to a clod, and I don't relish it. You, Flacker and Alroy—come down off that cart." The men on the horse-cart roof started letting themselves down. "Mister Shangro, have you sustained any injuries?"

"No, Major Deveraux," said Shangro. He'd recoiled the whip, the same one he used for driving, that I'd first seen the evening before. "A slight delay, but no more."

"Mister Broome?" His words snapped at me, still cold, still scorning.

"None at all, Major."

"Mrs.—Broome?"

French stared back at him, raising her chin, her arms folded now. "Major Deveraux, I thank you, and Tom does as well, for what you have done tonight. But I need no sharp rebuke from your lips." They were two of a kind, I thought sudden; they had the same queenly-kingly expressions, they used the same sort of speech. "You were brave, of course, to ride after these—these renegades. But bravery to my mind does not excuse your imperious attitude toward my husband and myself. If you believe we have falsified ourselves to you, I regret it. I trust we shall some day meet again under kinder circumstances, and perhaps when we do, and if we do, you will make your apologies."

The major's mouth turned up, just a trifle, under his smooth small moustache, which had the same neat grizzle his hair had.

"Oh, bravo. Bravo, Francia. But I assure you you *shall* see me again, both you and your Lochinvar rider. And I beg you to remember, as well, that you spring from the best stock in the South—I would not have stood by and seen you ravaged by these idiots, not if you had betrayed your heritage a thousand times over. And,'' he was leaning over his pommel in front of the black child, Willie, and his eyes were frost blue upon her, ''I will have the reason for that betrayal, I will find it out, and I will tax you with it. It is the least I could do for the memory of your gallant father, and the trust of your mother.'' He sat back slightly. He'd never taken the dueling pistol off Teague. ''As for your so-called 'husband,' had it been only he who was in danger, I should have remained at Deveraux Farm, and enjoyed sound sleep.''

I didn't think he'd have let Shangro and the rest of the tribe suffer. I knew he meant that if it had been just me, he'd have let it go.

But I said, anyhow, ''Whatever your reasons, I thank you, Major Deveraux.''

He didn't even acknowledge that.

He'd turned Amber a little, keeping the dueling pistol on Teague, but not sighting down it now. The man named Fenton had picked up the knives he'd dropped, and he took Aldan's to him, then brought me mine. This brought him close to Teague, who was slumped in his ruinous saddle, the breed reaching down to get some grass-tussocks beside the road. All at once the child, Willie, made a motion and said, ''Look out there—'' and Deveraux brought his full gaze back to Teague—he'd been saying something in an undertone to Constable Ballard. But it was too late. Fenton was blocking Teague from Major Deveraux, and Teague had seen it and he was moving. He had the breed's head yanked back and was aiming it down into the bushes, all so quick it was just one oiling motion, and Ballard fired his piece over Deveraux's left shoulder, but it missed as Teague had missed me, then the major was aiming at nothing but bush-darkness and trees. He spilled Willie from Amber's neck in one more motion, but by that time I'd whirled and was over at Grayboy, and on him. I wanted Teague myself. Without Teague's Walker Colt. Out in back of us the Teague rider with the pine-knot had dropped it in the road where it made a resinous burning and rolled smoke against the sky. Ahead I saw Teague and the breed go between carts and then toward the river. Then I could hear them crashing down there, and going on to the north. In a flip of a glance behind I could see Ballard, covering the rest of Teague's men, and the major, leaning hard into Amber now as she got into a gallop. I was well ahead of him.

I swerved Grayboy into the brush, we cracked and plunged down a short slope, then were on a river path with Teague ahead. It was so dark under here, the over-boughs holding off most moonlight and allowing no groundlight, I could hear Teague and the breed better than I could see him. But the hearing was good. Teague was making more noise than a steamboat gone aground. Dry leaves whipped over Grayboy, over me, and I was riding low, in a crouch; then in a slash of the moon's cool pouring light ahead I saw Teague just at the second I stopped hearing him. I couldn't check Grayboy here. I was alongside and getting my boots out of the irons, all at the same time, and also at the same time I could see, very sudden, very sharp, the second Walker Colt Teague was pointing at me. He was holding it next to his ribs; I should have known a man like him would have had a pair. His breed moved as he shot, then the breed was screaming and falling, and Teague, still in the irons, was falling with him, and all I could feel was the pain like a branding iron or the plate of a horse just before the smith dips it, in my left thigh. I was off Grayboy, in the dank cool-smelling leaves, boots free of the irons, Grayboy rearing. And the stars all rearing with him.

# 24

I opened my eyes. I'd been off in a warm place where the hair of the planets was brushing my eyes and nostrils. Whipping through space with the stars, and as light and free as a wild goose stretching his wings above all earth and the tiny lights of earth.

But I came back down now, and my left leg was cold as if it'd been dipped in an iced stream in January, and I couldn't pull it out of that numbing water.

French's eyes were an inch from mine. Her hair was shadowing me, brushing my nose and eyes. Her eyes were soft silver and gray with the cat-sparks of amber gleaming through.

She smelled like a welcoming tent to which I'd come back cold and hungry after hunting for five days and nights.

I said, "Where's Grayboy?"

"Shhh . . . Aldan has him. He is back in the horse-box, love."

I grunted, but didn't move. I didn't want to move my left leg at all. I thought, It's busted. And the bone is showing through. Gangrene will set in, it will mortify. Daddy lost the true use of his left hand and couldn't harness-drive any more. Can you harness-drive with one leg?

I said, "Did he act all right for Aldan?"

"Perfectly. And he is not hurt, my love." She touched my forehead. "Shangro wishes to speak with you, dear. Can you talk without pain?"

"Yes," I said. I tried to sit up a little, and she pushed me back down with firm enough hands. I was lying on my back on a litter of pine boughs. I could scent them past French's natural glorious scent. I said, "Stop treating me like I was a wounded hero and you were some kind of soft-talking nurse, French." I said it quiet. "I'm not Lieutenant Algy Marsden, I don't intend to die." But I wished I could see my left leg. She was between me and sight of it. I was just about where I'd spilled off Grayboy when Teague shot. I could see the same overarching trees and smell the same river and the leaves stretched around under my pine-bough litter to left and right. Past French's shoulder Shangro was standing, and there was hot water steaming somewhere, I could see a waft of the steam, and there was woodsmoke on the air drifting down from the roadside above the river.

Off at one side and out of my sight I could hear somebody crying. It was a very light voice.

This time I made a real shove against French's hands and did sit up. Shangro had a bowl of steaming water and some rags. Behind him stood Pella, and then Jantil. There were four or five horses down here, their eyes reflecting the light of a lantern carried by Cando. As I watched he set the lantern down careful in the leaves near my head, his forge-toughened fingers treating it as if it was a precious egg, so it wouldn't tip and set the leaves afire. I wasn't sitting very high, just balanced on the tips of my elbows. My left boot was off and the trouser leg rolled almost to my crotch.

I cast my eyes over to where the crying came from. It was the black child Major Deveraux had called Willie. He was squatting beside something bulking rough-haired on the ground, half covered by leaves where it had skidded when it fell and dug into the leaf-mast. I narrowed my eyes past the lantern's light. Then I could see it was the breed-horse, and it wouldn't ever have to fret anymore about being beaten, or about something coming up on its blind side and scaring it. The ribs looked like stark ladders in the rough-matted hide.

I said, "My God, French."

Shangro was leaning over me. His moustache hung down oddly from this angle of sight, like a dark rick hanging over the edge of a wagon in harvest time. "Mister Teague is dead, Mister Broome. He broke his neck when his unfortunate horse was shot and fell."

"But who shot the horse?"

The crying was going on. Not loud, just persistent.

"It appears Mister Teague did. His horse moved as he shot. The ball went through its brain and came out and struck you."

I could see how it would have happened. The breed plunging and tossing its head as Teague fired.

I thought, Anyhow and no matter how strangely it happened, the poor breed got even with Teague.

I said slow, "And just where's Teague now?"

"Major Deveraux and Constable Ballard have taken the body back along with their prisoners to Pharis." Shangro's eyes shifted to French. "Miss Chantry, if you will hold the knee, so, and Pella, if you will hold his foot—not hard, just enough to keep him from moving."

I could barely feel French's hands on my knee, and Pella's fingers on my left ankle and around the arch of the foot. I trusted both of them all right. French as a matter of course and Pella because he was Shangro's son.

Cando was holding a copper bowl full of more steaming fluid. But not water. He brought it close under my chin. With the hand not holding my left knee, French cupped the nape of my neck and brought my head up. I said, "What's this?"

"Cayenne and goldenseal, heated in a little wine," Shangro said.

It was a hell of a distance from the calomel and whiskey and bone-saws my father had told me about when he'd been on the battlefields with Barksdale's Brigade.

I drank it. Tasted like a gulp of a summer noon, as if a warmer season lived in my mouth and went down my tongue and rambled through the belly.

Cando spoke the black language in a little spurt of it to Shangro. Shangro smiled, faint.

"What did he say?" I said.

"He said Mister Teague will never again have to smell Gypsy-Negro smell. How lucky for Mister Teague."

I looked up at Cando. "You're a wicked old man," I said.

He didn't wink at me, but his eyelid trembled and he nodded, fierce and short. I could see that Jantil had his musical instrument slung from its belt-cord again. Its strings made a muted jangle as he walked over to where the black child, Willie, hunkered beside the dead breed-horse.

He stooped down there and put a hand on the child's shoulders.

I said, "What's wrong with the boy?"

French said, close to my ear, "He refused to go back with Major Deveraux and the constable, Tom. He wants to stay with the horse."

"It could have been a great horse if it'd been given the chance of a boll weevil in winter," I said. "Maybe it was great anyhow." Then I drew in breath and said, "You going to take my leg off?"

Shangro said, "The ball passed through the flesh of your thigh on the outside, Mister Broome. A clean wound, all the way through. But we must make it even cleaner." He was spreading the rags on the pine-boughs. The steaming water sent wisps up past his arching nostrils. He dipped a rag in the water, and then the rag steamed. "Salt and hot water, only," he said. "Now lie on your right side, not far over, just so—" His hand guided me. "Keep hold of the knee and the foot," he told French and Pella.

I rolled over as he bade. I said, "Quincyville and Appleton. How can I—?"

"You cannot," said Shangro. "I think your time of flat-racing is over, with us, Mister Broome. I am sorry. But you will be able to ride on to Yadkin, and I think surely you can drive from a sulky. The wound did not go through a muscle. And it is at the flank, you see, so it can heal well without strain on the flesh." All the time he was talking he was moving the rag. He had it at the back of my thigh, about seven inches above the back of the knee, it felt, and then, sudden, fire hit me there and I gritted my teeth, and knew what he was doing. He was pushing the rag all the way through, using a finger, and the salt and water were biting about the way the ball had felt just after it tore through. I felt sweat roll out of my skin and down my ribs and stand out and stream on my cheekbones. Then the rag was through, and he was pulling it out the other side. All of it. He said, quick, "Hold him so," and Cando handed him a fistful of leaves. "Marigold," he said. The leaves were dry and he crushed them almost to powder around the wound, back and then fore. Then he was lacing them down with white soft thread, packing the leaves on, and the binding felt as if a spiderweb wrapped my thigh.

He stood up, and French and Pella let go of me, and I stretched the leg.

French was rolling the trouser down, doing it easy.

The boughs rustled as I sat up, all the way now.

Anyhow it's not my ass, I told myself. Wouldn't need a pillow.

I was a little stiff where I'd fallen, along the shoulders, but that was nothing. It was the first time Grayboy'd ever thrown me, though God He knew I'd been thrown plenty from the time I was five.

Willie, the black child, had come over here and was standing right alongside me. His eyes had those hooded lids like a turtle's. It was a calm face and the tear-stains were drying like marks in a levee when the water goes down.

I said, "Hello, Willie."

"Hello." He didn't say Mister.

"I'm sorry the horse got killed."

Jantil was standing behind him. Jantil said, "He will not go back to town, Mister Broome. I have offered to take him. He says he has no place to go."

The other Gypsies down here on the river-path were watching and the horses were shifting just a little, nerved-up as they always get around a dead horse, or when passing a knacker's yard.

I said, "Willie, you better go along with this man. Teague wasn't married? His wife can't use you?"

"No, he wasn't hitched," the black child said. "I'll stay while they bury him." He didn't mean Teague, he meant the quarter-breed. "Then I'll move on."

"You could go see Major Deveraux," I said. "He'd find work for you. Enough for three squares a day, I'd reckon."

"Major lives too high for me. He don't need me. He got all the grooms and other boys he needs. I don't want nobody doing good for me without I do it back."

He hadn't said sir once, either. I didn't know why, but I liked that.

"And my name ain't Willie. It's William Makepeace Ritter. Nobody called me that in Pharis."

"All right—William," I said.

He didn't even swallow hard, or brave himself up to it. He just said, "I'm a ring-dizzler with horses. I kept Bombo alive when there wasn't nothing between him and dyin' but a little nerve. He won a mort of races roundabout. You're going to Yadkin Fair, you need a groom. A real groom, not nobody you pay by the day while you're there and don't speak to your horse and treat him like he should be treated. I talk horse and I know horse, and when the horse is worth it I get secret with him and he tells me what he needs. Your horse is worth it.''

"I *know*, William," I said. "But—" French was kneeling near us, and patting sweat from my forehead and around my ears with one of the little kerchiefs she'd brought along in her willow basket from that first day.

"You can call me W. M.," he said. "It don't have to be the whole name."

"I *know*, W. M.," I said. "But *I'm* Grayboy's groom and hostler and stable-boy and rider and driver. I was there when he was foaled."

He cast a side-glance back to where the quarter-breed lay stretched half under leaves. And his eyes came on me again.

"Mister Grayboy got some of the Hambletonian in him."

"That's right."

"I would die to make him win. Not just to win but to make him happy with winning. I know Yadkin. Last year I ran off up there—Wesley Teague, he was drunk for a week, he hardly noted I was gone that time—and I helped out in the Charlemagne stables. He's a good horse too, they are running him again this year, I'd bet anything. I know about the trial heats for the entry and where to go for the best smithin' and who'll cheat on the sulky-rent and who won't. I know how the betting goes. I would have stole Bombo and took him up there this year but he wasn't no trotter or pacer and he never learned harness good. Goddamn it," he said then, "why did that no account locust have to shoot him dead?"

He'd turned a little away from French and me, from the quarter-breed too, and was just looking off in the dark. The river-breeze came sharp here, and he took a good lungful of it. And said soft, "I won't bother you no more, then. Reckon you think I'm a little boy too big for his linsey britches. Ain't a word I say going to convince you I could do you good and more'n earn my keep. And it ain't I eat much."

He took a crackling step off into the leaf-mast, up the slope from this road. Could hardly see him now in the shadows. Shangro and Cando and Pella and Jantil and French and all the other Gypsies back a distance, and even the horses, were watching him. Something about him that made him bigger than just the frail bundle of stick-bones he was. He turned around, eyes showing faint, and spoke from the shadow. "I'll just make myself scarce till you all ready to put Bombo in the ground. I'd like to cast some earth from my hand in with him. Way they do for people."

He was walking off there again, couldn't even see him now.

The pistol-ball wound was throbbing, but I felt all right.

I thought how, by ordinary, the quarter-breed would just have been left here till the flies and the turkey buzzards and the ants had done their work and the bones themselves would have fallen away into the mulch of leaves. But Shangro's people would put it in the earth, like a man. Shangro wasn't giving me any advice, and neither was French.

I said under my breath, "Oh, hell." Then out loud I said, "W. M., you come back here and join us. When we've got Bombo laid away you come on back to the horse-cart with us. We'll talk about things."

He came walking back, bare feet not much bigger than a large dog's in the slashes of light. And not walking any faster than he'd walked, going away. He had his hands behind his back like an old man, maybe a judge. I looked at him, full, and told myself, without speaking it, W. M., what am I going to do with you?

# 25

Two of the Gypsy men dug the grave for that poor old breed W. M. called Bombo—I'd have wagered Wesley Teague had never given it a name at all, just used it—and when their short mattocks had the hole ready in the dark receiving earth, they tumbled the breed in and W. M., standing by—still looking bigger than this whole night, to me, as Jupiter had seemed larger than all of Fountainwood when I'd last seen him standing in that doorway to the ballroom—scattered a few handfuls of river-path loam into the grave. Then the Gypsies covered it. I watched from the pine-bough litter, where Shangro and Pella had now spread a bearskin over me. It was a peculiar scene, this burying a horse. It looked like something done by night by the old-time Louisiana pirates, Lafitte and Dominique You. The headcloths and shirts and pants of the Gypsies made them look more than ever like pirates. But Bombo wasn't treasure, he was just an animal that had never had a chance outside what W. M. Ritter gave him.

After that, Pella and Jantil and Cando took a hand to the pine-bough litter and carried me up the slope to the road, while the others came along on foot and horseback. At the horse-cart as they were loading me in—I felt foolish being treated like I was made of crystal and could break— Shangro said, "I think, Mister Broome, we will go on to Quincyville now. We will make plans there for you to leave us and travel on. There is a short way to Yadkin, by the back roads, from Quincyville. We will discuss all that in the morning. I think you will sleep without pain."

I said, "Well, I'm still getting married in the morning, and we're breeding Grayboy with that brown mare of yours."

"Jantil informed me of your generosity. I wish you pleasant sleep."

He was gone toward the front of the caravan. Somebody had cleaned the whole inside of this horse-cart again—I reckoned it had been slightly awry by the time French had got through dousing that night-raider with the contents of the thundermug through the window—and the merry-go-round, with all the canvas off of it now, shone like a glittering great bauble over against one wall. W. M. walked over to it and gave it a head-cocked inspection, and said, "This here jenny yours?"

From the bunk where they'd laid me, I said, "Belongs to Miss Chantry."

He wheeled around to French. "If you plan to run it in Yadkin, I could give you a hand. Besides grooming and swamping and helping your man with his horse." He took a quick breath. "There's plenty of chirren in Yadkin; you'd ought to run it, you could make good cash."

French said, "I was thinking about a ten-cent piece for every ride, W. M. The rides to last about two minutes each."

W. M. shook his head. It had a nap like a young lamb's wool. His eyes were as old as time itself. "No, I don't think so. A one-minute ride and fifteen cents each. I can help you get the chirren on and off and see there ain't no strays or twice-riders for one admission. How you start the contraption?" He was bending to see the stove and the boiler. French showed him how the stove could be stoked, and how the boiler made the whole platform turn and go up and down, and the music come out of the reed pipes sticking up through the center.

I watched them through a sort of veil. The posset of wine and cayenne and goldenseal was taking hold of me more. But I didn't want to drift off yet.

W. M., hands no bigger than a Tom turkey's feet locked behind his back, walked to the dividing door and opened it. His eyes under the lamps were praising and a little larger as he looked in. "His name's Grayboy, you say," he said, his back to us. In there, Grayboy was staring down at W. M. "It's a good name, it ain't too curly." He was squatting down. "I see he wears thin plates. He got bones he ain't even used yet. Look at the length in them cannons. I could sleep right in here with him and wouldn't bother you no more tonight. The Gypsy chief, he said he would make arrangements for you to travel on to Yadkin come the morn. I could go right with you then, takin' up no more space than I need to breathe in."

I said, "Shangro's a king, not a chief. And I've got one horse, and no cart. How you suggest the three of us and the one horse and the flying jenny are going to get to Yadkin, as things stand?"

W. M.'s bird-slim shoulders raised and fell. "I'd be willing to walk while you and Miss Chantry went two to the saddle and Mister Grayboy pulled the jenny."

I said, "That wouldn't work. You'd be worn to a nubbin by the time we got there, and anyhow, I don't want Grayboy hauling the jenny. And even if I did work out some other arrangements—hell, W. M., I'm a poor man. I can't pay you what you might be worth. And not only that"—I'd lifted myself on an elbow—"Miss Chantry and I are running away from justice. We didn't kill anybody, but we're wanted back in Lanceton for questioning about a killing. Wanted very sorely."

"That don't make a whistle to me, now or tomorrow. I'm set on winning at Yadkin. That's the purest thing in my mind."

Aldan appeared down at the ramp-door. I said to Aldan, "Thanks for taking Grayboy."

Aldan said, "He gave me no trouble, Mister Broome. He was scared after the shot but he came back here without shying. Do you need anything more now? There is fresh food in the leaf-packs in the cabinets. Some Gypsy bread and some venison. My father told me to caution you not to take the dressing off your wound even if it should bother you. We must hurry on now, to be in Quincyville by morning." He nodded to W. M., and said, "I will shut the ramp-door now, if you are ready."

I looked over at W. M. And beyond him to French, who was just waiting for me, still not giving a half cup of advice.

I said, "Damn it. All right, W. M., you can come with us to this next town. Which isn't saying you'll come with us to Yadkin. If you're hungry, Miss Chantry will give you whatever you need. There's fresh straw on Grayboy's side. And water there and a spare pot beside the swamping door. I might as well tell you, Grayboy's tolerant around people as long as they know horses and treat him gentle.''

W. M. looked at me as if I was teaching his grandmother how to suck eggs. "Mister Grayboy and I'll have our own 'mirations,'' he said. He went on inside Grayboy's part of the horse-cart and shut the door behind him.

Aldan had stepped back, and was shutting the ramp-door. When it was up, French latched it on both flanks. In Grayboy's stall I could hear him snorting a little, quietly, as if he was glad to have some company in there.

Up ahead I could hear the other carts starting. Then this one gave a lurch. "Who's driving?" I asked French.

"Aldan."

"Then Shangro doesn't think he needs any more outriders tonight," I said. "For which I'm fairly grateful—I reckon I could sit a saddle but it wouldn't yet be joyful. I did think I was a dead man when Teague threw on me with that spare Walker. That was a fiery mouthful you gave Major Deveraux, French. You mean it?"

"I admire Major Deveraux," she said. She had come over and was sitting on the bunk. "But I feel he has overreached himself in his attitude toward us. I realize what makes him feel as he does. I respect him, Tom, but I won't have him consigning you to the part of a Yahoo who has led me into evil and corruption. Or treating me as if I was still ten or eleven years old."

"I never quite knew what a Yahoo was," I said. "I'm just a horse-man."

"A Yahoo was what Dean Swift—he wrote *Gulliver's Travels*, we studied it at the academy, though some of the parts were clipped out—called people like Wesley Teague. It is wrong of Major Deveraux to lump them all together like that. To classify you with Yahoos."

I said, "You're just alike, though. You and Deveraux. As if you came out of the same egg."

She shut her eyes. The lids beautiful, delicate as twilight air before the first star shows.

The horse-cart was rolling now, and the night wind slipped along under the window over the bunk.

"I am *myself*," she said low-toned. "I began being myself when I first saw you, when we talked at Chantry. I became more myself when you tried to kiss me the first time, and when you did kiss me at Fountainwood.

And at Toddy Morgan's pond I became completely myself. We may fight about this and that, Tom, for a long while. But whatever happens, remember you have made me myself, without detracting from yourself to do so, and without robbing me, but, instead, *giving* me myself.''

She got up and went to one of the chain-swinging lamps, and lifted its shade and puffed it out. Dropped the shade, and went to the other. The wine-and-herb posset was roiling around in me, making me slumberous, but there was something more important under the slumber. The other lamp winked out. The smell of the coal oil mingled with the leather scent of the Spanish saddle and the herb-boxes. The moonlight touched and rippled over the bunk. I'd thrown the bearskin back. I watched French undress. The gray dress, then the shift, then the scarred but jaunty ballroom slippers. Her cloak hung across the foot of the bunk. She stood naked, lifting her breasts for a second with her fingers, their nipples catching points of light and rising in dark pink buttons. Her legs were more shapely than any filly's. The knees beautiful, the calves sweet and clean-lined, the thighs catching spots of light as if the light fell into magnolia white rivers. She took the ribbon out of her bound-up hair, letting the hair tumble and rush and touch her shoulders and her spine. Then she came back to the bunk and lay out beside me, stretching full length, turning all the way to me. She touched my shirt, her fingers careful on the buttons. She murmured, ''You must not agitate your wound. But I believe there are other ways.''

She had my shirt open, and was opening my belt. The belt fell back. She moved her fingers down along my belly, as if she was enjoying with their tips each hair curling there. I moved my head into her breasts. There was a touch of moisture like dew in between them, and my lips fitted that for a breath, then I was putting my lips around her right nipple, and reaching down to cup her cunt, which eased up and into my hand as though it had been born and created to fit so.

It didn't hurt where Teague had shot me and where Shangro had salted it out. Nothing at all hurt in the slightest.

We lay facing each other and fitted so, with the next town ahead and the caravan wheeling under the cool-touching starlight.

Both of us had our eyes open, river-light washing hers from time to time and, once, showing her wide and full-moving smile. An abundant smile like all the rest of her, and all the rest of her was a bountiful field in high summer, when the land all shimmers and arches and seems to open to greet the full light, and to get even more of it if it can.

# 26

I woke up with the sun bothering my eyes and knew I'd overslept and that we were in camp near Quincyville. French had drawn the bearskin almost up to my nose. I threw it off and elbowed up, looking around. The ramp was down, the dividing door was open, Grayboy was in his stall but French wasn't anywhere in sight and I couldn't see hide nor hair of W. M. Ritter. The sun was beating in on the floor of the horse-cart and filling the flying jenny with brilliance, so all the small carved horses seemed to quiver as if they were underwater and swimming. The Spanish saddle leather caught more sun and its studs glowed. Grayboy's saddle was beside it, along with my boots and hat. I was still wearing my shirt though my trousers were pooled around my ankles. I dragged them up, fastened my belt, saw the knife in its sheath was at my side, got up, and sat on the edge of the bunk feeling the day whirl around me. I was hungry, but aside from that whole and complete. I wasn't dead down on a river-path and Grayboy wasn't shot or marred. The shot-wound itched but outside that and a mere tingling, wasn't going to disturb me much. I counted in my mind. This was the fourth morning since I'd left the Chantry stable. My God, it seemed like four months. Sometimes when you've run a race and then later re-run it in your head you can remember every furlong of it as if it had lasted for a time of stretching years.

I used a chamber pot and then went into Grayboy's side of the cart. Past the open window—the curtains back now—over the bunk, I could see that this camp was on a bluff overlooking the river. Across the river, half obscured by trees as if it had begun to be drowned in fall-bright leaves, was the town I took for Quincyville. Just below this camp which was in a natural pocket of the uppermost lip of the bluff were a couple of log cabins with the chinks between the logs showing dry and a curl of smoke coming from one of the cabins' chimneys. Behind the cabins was a cotton barn that was half falling down. Near it was a fenced lot with the brown red earth shining and past the gray fencing the beginning of what had been cotton rows. Down on the river a fisherman was sitting in a motionless scow, tiny from here. I could hear horses moving and the clank of cooking utensils and as I took another glimpse through the side window and stood with a hand on the dividing door's jamb, Aldan, followed by his uncle Jantil's children, Rico and Jal, came running along with an armful of firewood. Each of the small boys, his cousins, carried a smaller heap of wood.

I looked in at Grayboy. He'd just been brushed and curried and shined. It was as good a job as I'd ever do on him. Fiddle-strings of light bounced from his coat. He turned his head around to me and thrust his neck down and I patted his warm muzzle. He'd just been fed. There was fresh water in the buckets. His bridle-tack had been oiled and hung on a peg. He looked full of sap as a maple in the prime of its growth.

I went out and shut the door, and from a cabinet got some of the Gypsy bread and some cold venison and ate it. I was wiping my mouth when W. M. Ritter came bounding up the ramp. He stopped when he saw me. "How you feeling?"

"Good as grits," I said. "Where's Miss Chantry?"

"She's down the line, preparing for her weddin'. I'm supposed to get you and bring you along. You like the way I done Mister Grayboy?"

"He looks fine," I said. "Have some breakfast."

"I ate a hour ago. So'd she. They're still eatin' at the main cook-fire if you want some."

"I've had some. How'd you get up around Grayboy's quarters and withers and around his head? I mean, you're not that tall."

"Stood on a box. It ain't difficult. He got a little tiny gall on his left fore-elbow."

"He was born with it."

"I'll take it off, the way you take off warts. Just use stump water."

"I never heard that about galls. Some burn them off."

"Anybody ever laid fire to him, I'd knock his head off."

I reckoned he'd try. Weighing about fifty to sixty pounds, even with his pockets full of iron.

I sat on the bunk and dragged on my right boot and had a little trouble with the left. Having to lean on the wound a little. W. M. came over and braced himself and gave the left boot a shove. I stood and put on my hat. W. M. stared up at me.

"Reckon you'd best shave."

"A man ought to, on his wedding day. You're right."

"Here's a bucket. Cold water, but you ain't got much time. Your razor in the saddlebags?'' I showed him which bag. He got it out, and some ash soap. "You play that fiddle in the box?" he asked as I started to lather.

"Some. Not wonderful."

"Gypsy man named Aldan, he says you play nice. That rider with the black-splash mare, look like an Appaloosa—"

"Jantil."

"Yeah. He plays that thing of his like angels comin' out of a brush-fire. He tunin' up for your weddin' now. You ain't gettin' that place nigh your jaw. I like a clean-shaved man."

I shaved close, doing some places twice according to his wishes. Then we were walking down the ramp. He said, "That flying jenny got wheels. I could ride it nice as you please, going up to Yadkin. It wouldn't maybe pull so well, all that distance, with the lashing is on it now. But there's the harness for it and if that old smith—"

"Cando."

"Yeah. If he brought up a wedge of iron for the crossbar, it'd stiffen the whole thing and make it fit for longer rollin'. Wouldn't hurt the jenny none. Make it like a tough little cart."

He was taking about two steps to every one of mine. Scudding along here.

"And maybe you got some notion of what would pull it?" I said.

"You'd have to get another horse. Not one of these draught animals. Somethin' small and light and wiry but that could pull too. I talked to the Gypsy chief."

"Shangro. He's a king."

"Yeah. You know that deep bay he was on yesterday in Pharis."

"Gelding, five or six years, worth about two hundred or a shade over, depending on the dickering strength," I said. I could see the bay over with the horse-string, in among some of the others of the racing-pack, where they were feeding in an old log corral. The draught horses were with them. There wasn't any limestone spring here but a creek ran in a small valley not far from the corral and some of the Gypsy men and women were carrying buckets to the corral. I couldn't pick out the brown mare, Farella, and decided she must be out of sight in the old cotton barn. "I don't have that kind of money to spend."

"You're just like every gamblin' man I ever saw. Play poor-mouth and save it all for the one big splurge."

"That's probably true," I said.

"The chief'll let us have the bay for fifty dollars. Throw in the services of that old smith for free, to fix up the jenny for better drawin'. He says he wouldn't do it for no one else, but you fattened his pocket richly at Pharis, and you tried to save his folks last night, and he's your good friend always. That Spanish saddle you got would go right on the bay. Miss Chantry could ride him while he pulled. Me on the jenny."

I stopped walking. So did he.

"Got it all figured out, haven't you. Right down to the tee."

"That's right. I ain't no leech-bug just lazes along living on the fat and not pulling my share. But we ain't settled it yet neither. You ain't said yea, or nay. I don't need nothing but my food and I already told you, I eat light. I can stay with Mister Grayboy most of the time in Yadkin when he ain't running, and help out with the jenny like I told Miss Chantry last night."

"Where's your folks?" I said. "Didn't you ever have any?"

"Not so far as I remember. I just got raised up in and around Pharis. When I was about maybe five Wesley Teague, he bought me for a shoat. Wasn't a very likely shoat. He traded the shoat to Cassius Mingle, he was an old man and a nigger like me who'd let me sleep in his mule-shed and hoe his strip of corn and cotton and tend the mule. I'd of left Wesley Teague this year if it hadn't been for Bombo. He won Bombo in a card-game last spring. Reckon he cheated to win him. Now's the time for you to cinch all this or go about your way, and let me to go about mine."

Over under some spraddled cottonwoods stood a clump of Gypsy women, wearing their best—the silks gleamed and flashed through the shadows. I could hear Jantil's mandolin-affair going, soft now. Then I saw Shangro, standing on a stump at the end of the avenue of trees. He wore another yellow shirt newer than any I'd seen yet and he looked powerful and dignified as I thought a bishop might—though I couldn't recollect ever clapping eye on a bishop—and he had two wreaths in his hands. Made of leaves twined tight, like crowns. He saw me and raised the wreaths above his head to show me. Behind him stood Jantil and Pella; Aldan joined them there. Cando and another bunch of the men were on his other flank; the men were facing the women across the leafy space between trees.

I looked back to W. M. He was gazing off in the distance seeming as unconcerned about what I'd say as if he hadn't a care in the nation about it. His thick eyelids nearly shut.

I said, "If you ever want to sell gold bricks or lightning-rod umbrellas, W. M., I'll stake you. All right. You're with us—for Yadkin and I reckon even after it. But I want you to know you won't have Grayboy all to yourself, with me goin' off and leaving him time out of mind. His dam, Nickajack, was a favorite of my daddy's. Had to sell her and a passel of other good mares and horses when Daddy died. I never favored leaving him in anybody else's hands for long."

"You won't have to. He'll just be both of ours. You better step along and get married. They're waiting."

He didn't even say thanks. As he'd never said sir or mister. Some way I liked that too.

We walked along slower now over to where Shangro and the rest were gathered. I still couldn't see French.

But she came out of the leaf-shadows when I'd walked down the aisle flanked by men and women; she was walking quiet and dressed in a silk dress spangled with blues and scarlets and deep orange and light, clear green, as if she was almost all the colors of the steeds on the merry-go-round. A Gypsy dress; and behind her came Garsina, who I thought must have loaned or given her the dress for the wedding. French's hair was up even higher, only falling a little along her neckline; her eyes when they met mine were wide and she wasn't smiling—as she smiled when we made love—but near it. Garsina's deeper darkness behind French's red-haired darkling beauty set it off as if both went moving through some old picture from a time not even known in the South or the North. Shangro held the wreaths high. Jantil's fingers danced quick on the strings of his mandolin-dingus; what leaves remained on the trees above us shook in the reaching sun.

Shangro said a string of words in the black language, except it didn't sound black, only old. I'd taken my hat off and spun it away on the ground. One of the women—a little old one, without many teeth, I'd seen Cando with her around camp and thought she was probably his wife—bent down and took my hat and started to plait small tidy vines around its rim. She did this all through the ceremony. The children of the camp stood by large-eyed, maybe at what Shangro was saying, young Tomas closest to his grandfather, Rico and Jal and the rest of the boys and girls farther back. Not nitting around and grinning as you'd see white children do at such a time, but as quiet as W. M. himself. Jantil was playing low again now, you could hardly hear it. Shangro's voice was heavy as a drum, I thought of Jupiter's. In myself I wished Jupiter well and found it in me to wish everybody well back at Lanceton, even Flieshacker. I even spared a good thought for Major Deveraux. I didn't have any extra good thoughts about the Teague riders, though.

Shangro had stopped talking. He reached down from the stump and put one of the leaf-crowns on French's head. Looked as though it had grown there. Then he put one on mine. It sat gently. Garsina came around and took my right hand, and crossed it over in front of my chest and then took French's right hand and placed it in mine. Shangro talked again, and I thought, Here come the knives, the mingling of blood, but it wasn't so. Shangro was lifting his wide arms, sunlight rippling over him—he said something up to the sky. And nodded down, it was over. He stepped down from the stump, and Jantil's instrument went singing high and fast, as if he played it not just in a country or countries but all over the earth at once, with even Persia and Egypt listening just for the trice of this time.

I gathered French to me. We'd get it done again in Yadkin, I thought, but I doubted it would mean more. Around us the people were walking off, not fast, just going away about their business. Garsina lingered and kissed French when I was through with her. Then she walked off with the rest, in a swinging motion like a proud mare, and that left just Shangro and French and W. M., standing a little way off, and me. The children had broken their stillness and sprayed off like birds from a bough.

I felt like shaking somebody's hand, so I stuck mine out to Shangro. We'd never shaken hands. I didn't think it was something that meant much to him, he'd never done it to seal a deal. He took my hand now, brief, then he said, "Farella is in the barn. Jantil has gone to get her ready." I missed the music around us. "You should have no difficulty with your man-horse, Mister Broome. Has your friend told you of my offer?"

I said, "Fifty's a scrap of cash for the bay. Not enough."

"I will not take *less*." He smiled. "He would never make a flat-racer. Too thick in the barrel. Mrs. Broome—" It was the first time I'd heard that from him. Gave me a slight jolt. He was turning to French. "If you will go along with Cando, he and some of my men are waiting at the horse-cart. They will take out your carousel, and Cando will devise an iron bar so the carousel becomes safer on the road . . . I think too he should make your man-horse a full set of plates, Mister Broome. Your friend—" He gestured to W. M. "—says all but the new near-fore plate are going thin. Do not shake your head, you will not pay us for these either. You have rendered us service, both in wealth and in protection. I think it would be best to breed Farella first, while Cando and the others are at work on the carousel."

French touched my hand. Then she was gone off toward the horse-box. Still wearing her wedding wreath, as I was mine. She walked lighter than Garsina, not such a swinging stride, but if you'd never seen her before you'd have watched her out of sight.

W. M. said from where he was listening a few feet away, "I'll go bring Mister Grayboy."

"Wait a minute," I said. "Can you handle him out of the stall?"

He only stared at me.

Then he picked up my hat, which the old lady had plaited with small leaves, and walked off toward the horse-box without a word.

"Go along to the barn, Mister Broome," Shangro said. "Do not worry about your friend and the man-horse. I told you I sometimes have second-sight—though it is not constant, and does not bring me riches. There are those who have it with horses, as well. He is one. How do you imagine he kept that poor beaten breed alive and running with all its heart? You must learn, I think, to trust luck when it is thrust upon you. We have a Gypsy saying . . . we have many sayings, but this one I like very much. 'Behind bad luck comes good luck.' You must accept it when it is there."

He was walking down across the stubbled clearing in the direction of the log cabins and the cotton barn. Down on the river the scow hadn't stirred a jot, the pole of the man fishing, small there, seemed dipped at the same angle. The town of Quincyville on the other side of the river showed just a hint of houses through its fiery leaves. I walked with Shangro toward the barn, a dog slipping under the corral fence and nosing one of the Gypsy dogs that had run down there, then both dogs wagging their tails, and the Gypsy men sitting on the fence watching the dogs and waiting for us. There was a warm quick whinny from the depths of the half-ruined cotton barn. An old man who belonged to one of the clay-chinked cabins had come out to sit on his stoop—two half-logs leaning against the cabin's gallery which was held up by peeled, faded sycamore poles—and he was smoking a pipe and watching us. Most of me wanted to go back to the horse-cart and help W. M. bring out Grayboy and bring him to the barn lot. But I kept that feeling down. He'd only covered a mare once, back in Dango Falls. He'd not been any rabbit to handle then. I hoped second-sight with horses could make up for W. M.'s pipestem arms and legs. I wasn't fretting about W. M.'s will to do what he wished to do. He had damned near as much of that as French Broome, who wasn't any longer French Chantry, and that was God's plenty. I fished out money from my pocket and handed fifty dollars to Shangro, and he took it while we moved along barnward, and said, "With what we shall win in a few years with Farella's offspring, I feel sad even taking this from you. But you will like the bay. Look there—" He put the money away in a sack hung from his neck and slipped the sack back under his bright shirt. He was pointing. "Where the road—you can just see it through trees—goes below Quincyville. When you leave us, follow that road north. It is not well traveled but it is good. It skirts Appleton and several other towns and brings you to Yadkin. If you are on your way by noon and do not stop tonight you can be in Yadkin by tomorrow. All of us will miss you."

I was looking across the river to the road. It hadn't until this second come home to me that we'd be leaving Shangro's people so quick. But I felt all of me yearning toward Yadkin too.

I turned back to Shangro. His eyes were level on mine. Dark, quick, thoughtful, wise in their depths.

"This is a Thursday—by your calendar. You will be there Friday. The races begin on Saturday and continue through Monday, as I remember—we were there last year. I think your wound has started to heal. It will leave a scar, but it will never hamper you." He gave the coughing laugh I remembered from when I'd first met him and we'd talked on the Lanceton Pike. It was a shy laugh, I thought; I hadn't recognized that before. "Mister Broome, I will not have time to say this again. We must prepare for the Quincyville racing at once, when we have done with your man-horse and Farella. So I will say it now. I told you when we first met that you were no Gypsy. But I could wish you were. I could wish to have another son much like you. And—" He was walking on, scissoring over the ground fast for his bulk, as always, and he hadn't given me time to answer. Not that I'd have known what to answer to that. "And remember what I told you about the patteran. In case I should have something important to tell you, later on, and you might wish to find me. Ah!" We were coming to the fence. In the mouth of the cotton barn I caught sight of Jantil and Pella holding the brown mare by a double hitch around her neck, one on each rope. The mare danced forward, sun on her hide as it shot in glances off the river below, and they held her and talked to her; Shangro vaulted the fence; I went over it behind him. Shangro put a hand on the mare's wet cheek as she came into the full light. His hand was a lot quieter than it had been on the whipstock when he'd snared Teague with the lash. "Ah, Farella, you are ready, now. A horse-colt or a filly, whatever you wish. But conceive, my beauty, conceive." Then he was murmuring to her in the Romany, which she just about seemed to understand, for all her fret.

# 27

Up at the horse-cart Cando and some of the Gypsy men, and a lot of the children who weren't really assisting but were taking close looks at the merry-go-round which was now flashing free of its canvas and plain to see for the first time in the light of day, were rolling it down the ramp. I sat on the barn lot fence with these other Gypsies and watched them. The merry-go-round looked like a gaudy huge toy that had dropped down from the sky to make the clearing shine. French supervised their moving it, still wearing her Gypsy gown and her marriage crown. I was still wearing my crown; I didn't know if it was customary to keep it on or not, but it felt friendly. The flying jenny came off the ramp all right, and then they were rolling it over to Cando's forge, which smoked beside his cart. I kept watching the ramp, hoping to God W. M. could handle Grayboy as his own confidence said he could. All at once, then, here came Grayboy into the light, W. M. perched on his back like something that had just casually dropped there, something small that didn't even seem to be part of Grayboy's muscles and height and rolling smoothness. Riding him bareback, with just the hackamore. I could hardly see W. M.'s head because he was wearing my hat. He had more gall and brass than people four times his size, but I still liked him—maybe liked him more than ever, though I certainly wasn't going to tell him so; it would have puffed his brain.

As before, Grayboy didn't touch many of the ramp-cleats going down, he just jumped. But W. M. stayed on him, high on the neck. Then he was turning him and aiming him for the cotton barn and the fence. I had to bite my lip to keep from yelling to W. M. to pull him up. But W. M. wasn't even pulling on the hackamore rope, just leaning far forward and speaking into one of Grayboy's sharp-slanting ears. They came on, down across the clearing toward the fence, and behind me, Farella stood quivering with Jantil and Pella holding her, and Shangro at her head. When he got within wind of Farella, Grayboy stopped dead—I thought W. M. would go over his head—and W. M. kept crooning to him, as if telling him secrets of horsehood only W. M. knew. Then Grayboy was coming on again, shadow big on the stubbled ground, W. M. with my hat hiding his eyes and Grayboy with his nostrils opening and shutting like the bellows of Cando at the forge.

Aldan, who'd been perched on the fence not far from me, whipped down and opened the creaking gate. Grayboy swept in and through. Aldan slammed the gate shut and dropped a wire around the posts to keep it shut. W. M. slid down from Grayboy, still holding the hackamore's rope, and handed the rope to Shangro. Then W. M. walked over, full of dignity and offhandedness, and handed me my hat. I took it and stuck it in my belt. W. M. said, "He ain't going to raise much sand. I told him to be nice."

"Maybe you could predict what the mare's going to throw," I said. "A horse-colt or a filly."

"I ain't got that down to a fine point yet. But he'll act like sweet folks."

W. M. got up on the fence and sat there with his eyes brooding and his stick-legs and arms small and spidery. I got off the fence and helped Aldan and Pella throw a few ropes around Grayboy's head and down along his neck while Jantil held Farella. Then while we held Grayboy— save for the fact that if he hadn't wanted to be held he'd have jumped half as high as the eave of the cotton barn—Jantil and some of the other Gypsies tied Farella to the fence. She was giving Grayboy over-the-shoulder looks now, and her own nostrils were wide and shaking, and her eyes were white-showing, flaring. She had that hot, sweet, musty smell of her heat and need, and a lot of scare in her too, her flanks running sweat and nearly lathering. Jantil stepped back and raised his hands to us, signaling that she was tied tight. I turned to Aldan and Pella and the others, and said, "Let him go," and they dropped their rope-ends as I dropped mine.

We made for the fence.

Grayboy stood absolutely quiet for about two breaths. His crest was swelling, it looked like a mountain's curve against the sky. Over at the nearby cabin the old man with the pipe had got up and was leaning forward to see better. Grayboy shook his head, the ropes dropping away from it, and snorted low. Then as quick as chain-lightning on a sultry night he was moving, you couldn't even see him start the move; it was as if everything in him burst at once; as if a mountain had started to pour itself down into a valley and had been thinking about doing it for a long time so the motion was just a completion of all the thought that had gone into it and that had been stirring itself, beforehand. He went in a long circle, his head back and his lips peeled and his teeth bright as huge rice-grains, his mane lifting and spreading like flying dark glossy hemp, his tail stretching, his hocks spurning the ground, the breeze of him passing us on the fence hot and wet and fanning, the thunder of his hoof-plates rolling and sending old ground-chaff and dust in a sneeze-making trail behind him. He circled twice, each time a tighter circle, then he was at Farella's neck, and nipping her—it was a hard nip but with no blood—and she nickered loud and heavy, half calling for help and half responding to him with a kind of fearful joy. She stretched her ropes, the fence was shaking, but the ropes held. He came around again, not so near us where we sat the fence now, his own eyes mostly white, and when he got to Farella again he reared, shadow brusque black as a huge bird with its wings spread, against the rotted gray boards of the cotton barn, and he pawed the air, plates flashing like knives, then he was trumpeting, bugling. The sound sending a bunch of pigeons streaming above us out of the cotton barn loft, their wings fairly creaking with their urge to leave, and the sound also falling down toward the river in a huge blast you might have heard in Quincyville. And shaking us where we perched on the fence. Then he was going around again, slower now, with longer strides though, so you could see him stiff and ready, his sleek man-horse muscle wet and long and hard as forge-iron, his balls deep beneath it, the rest of him like a cataclysm ready to strike an army. And this time when he reached Farella he reared high and granite gray streaked with the black lacing of his sweat. And was down on her, as she crowded the fence with her chest and her crupper rose and her haunches spread, the brown sleek barrel of the mare seeming to squeeze forward and back like a living accordion, Grayboy's head and shoulders stretching and canting as he gave her love-bites and swung in her, the seed moving and racing, planting.

Then he was off, Farella turning her head, nickering soft and warm to him, not coy now or with fright in her; he was moving back around the lot, throwing his head back and forth, enjoying the sun and stepping high. I heard Shangro sigh as he dropped from the fence. "A good mating, Mister Broome. She is unhurt—a few scratches." He and Aldan and Pella were going to Farella. I dropped off the fence. I said to W. M., "You brought him on pretty good."

"Yeah. He'll run the better for it at Yadkin. He don't want nothing sitting on his mind but the harness-racing there. If somebody'll open the gate I'll take him back."

The old man had slouched to the fence by now. He wore his pipe in a corner of his jaw as if it grew so. He blinked bleary at W. M. as Jantil swung the fence-gate open with a long screak. "You all let that nigger boy handle that stud? I never see such a stud. You let him fetch up the stud and put him back?"

I said, "He's a part owner. I'm just the rider."

I said it quiet so W. M. couldn't hear. Didn't want him to get drunk with power. The old man gave me a look, spat without taking his pipe out, said, "Goddamn Gypsies," and hobbled on back toward his cabin. I went over to Grayboy, and after a couple of grabs—he was most interested in my wedding crown; he tried to eat it as he sometimes tried to eat my hat—I got hold of the hackamore rope and brought him to the fence-side. Farella gazed back at him with a melting look in her eye as if she'd met the Devil and taken all he had and somehow bested him. W. M. stood up on the fence and made a little leap, which put him on Grayboy's neck, not exactly like a flea on an elephant, but not much different either. He picked up the hackamore rope, bringing it up like a boatman hauling in the lead-line from a river packet, pulled on it slightly to face Grayboy around, and they went out through the gateway.

I watched W. M. take Grayboy across the clearing, to the creek. I reckoned he'd let him drink a bit, wash him off, and probably shine him up again till he glistered like high-cost satin. I didn't feel the chancy way I'd felt as he brought him on. I felt just a touch jealous, still, but maybe that would go away and I could do what Shangro'd suggested I do, accept some luck. I was going to need all of it I could scrape up at Yadkin; he wouldn't be running against even a fine mare there; he would be up against the cream of five or six states. And if he got scratched the first day at least he'd have tried.

All the Gypsies were moving around the clearing now, getting the women-cart—Shangro's, but used to go into town with as it had been used at Pharis—ready with their herb-wares; at the forge Cando was working on the flying jenny, fitting an iron piece onto the crossbar that would strengthen it while we pulled it to Yadkin. A small crowd of children watched him. As I came up I noted the dark bay had been cut out of the horse-string and was tied to the back of the horse-cart near the ramp. Cando and a helper—a boy about Aldan's age—were lifting the iron piece into place; it was still warm and they handled it gingerly; then they bolted it down with their arm-muscles straining. Cando gazed up at me, rubbing his hands. He said something I couldn't understand, and turned, impatient, to young Tomas to translate to me. Tomas said, "He says if you will move the carousel away now—he must shoe your horse, as he has promised. All but the near fore, which he did the other evening. They will be his best plates, light like the other. But he is in a hurry, for he must drive the woman-cart in a short while; we race in an hour."

I took hold of the pulling bar—still warm as I'd thought—and pulled the jenny down and away from the forge. French came running from the women-cart where she'd been saying good-bye to Garsina and the rest. Aldan and Pella and Jantil—I reckoned Jantil had ridden in, early, to Quincyville to tell them they were coming and set up times and bets for that town, as he'd done in Pharis—were up on their horses; Aldan's Flambeaux was circling near the women-cart, as if he couldn't wait; Pella was sitting on a lean spayed mare with a quicksilver and buckskin hide; Jantil sat Malden as if the black-splotched mare was already coming up to the start-wire. I felt a pang at knowing I wouldn't be riding with them today. Shangro, this time on a lean sorrel gelding, was riding around slow, giving last orders in his soft tone, seeing that all but the forge-fires were out, gentle as if he'd never cracked a whip and wound it around a man named Teague, now defunct.

French was still wearing her crown too. I thought she probably felt about it as I did mine. It was a special day even if the wedding wouldn't have stood up in a white man's court.

Tomas and Rico and Jal and a few of the other Gypsy children stood alongside us, still looking at the jenny. One of the little girls touched the shoulder of the dark green jenny-horse. Tomas said, "I would like to ride it. I am going to ride the real horses very soon, when I am only a little older, but all the same I would like to ride this. My grandfather is letting me go along today to see the real heats, but all the same I would like to ride this fine carousel."

French said, "It doesn't take a lot of wood to start it, Tom. We have time."

"Might as well see if it works—if Gary Willis didn't harm it," I said.

"Him." She gave a little stretch in the sun. "He and his doings had purely dropped out of my head." She gave me a pat on the cheek, drawing her fingertips down my jawline. "You are shaved so neatly, Tom."

"That's right. Seems I've got—what do they call them?—this valet, now. This horse-handling, horse-breeding know-it-all valet. He made me shave clean."

"I'm glad you took him on. I was hoping you'd see your way to. He's like a little ghost, removed from this earth. In the old days we'd have brought him into Chantry Hall; he could have helped in the kitchens, and helped serve."

"He's got ambitions past that," I said. "I doubt he'd serve anybody at table. Got as much pride as you have, when it comes right down to it. Times change and he's changing with them—for all he's a bite-sized child."

I said to Tomas then, "Get some wood—ash, I think—little twigs first, and then some good-size chunks that'll still fit this stove. Go on, we'll try out this great, wonderful jenny."

He spoke to the other children, then they were scattering off toward the brush. From the creek W. M. was riding—or anyhow neck-sitting—Grayboy up here, both of them coming at a slow, sedate pace. Grayboy was washed and he bulked like a moving island made of smooth rocks and shining with sea-water.

Cando's helper took his rope from W. M. as W. M. slid down. Cando had the fire hot again, the barrel of water set for plate-dipping, and W. M. crowded close to them as if Cando might do something he didn't approve of and have to be chastised. When Grayboy shifted a little away from the fire, W. M. said something to him, not even touching him, and Grayboy stood easy.

French plucked up a fold of the Gypsy dress. "Garsina gave it to me. She said I must wear it in Yadkin."

"You could wear nothing at all in Yadkin—even the ribbon in your hair—and I'd be just as pleased."

The color of the forge-fire was touching her face. She looked as she had the night before when she'd been about to blow out one of the lanterns in the horse-cart, face in that warm flush over the lip of the lamp-chimney. Lips spread and pursed the same way.

"Did you hear Grayboy and the mare?" I said.

"Yes. And I am a little mortified to say, Tom, not only did I hear, I watched. I couldn't see it all from here, but it was most thrilling. Garsina was watching too, and some of the other women were. They appeared to be—enjoying it. I must say I was not raised to be near the stable or the stable-lot when something like that was going on. It still astonishes me that I—enjoyed it, too.''

"Maybe it's just becoming more yourself, the way you said last night," I said.

"I reckon so, Tom. I couldn't keep from thinking of—of what Major Deveraux would have thought of me, drinking in that sight."

"Oh, him," I said the same way she'd said "Him" when talking about Gary Willis.

Then the children were coming back with ash-wood, and I was stoking the stove. While the noise at the forge went on, and sun fell steeper into this clearing, I filled the stove and put some wood beside its firebox for later use, and shut its door most of the distance but leaving room for a draught, and borrowed a coal on tongs from Cando's helper, and started the flames going. After a short time, as the children watched and were as quiet as they'd been at the wedding, the boiler, in which French had poured a bucket of water from the forge-barrel, started to simmer and hiss. And French, standing near the jenny's platform, threw a short lever there—and the platform started to wheel around. It moved slow at first, with just an "ah!" slipping out of one of the children's mouths, then they were all exclaiming as it whirled faster. It wouldn't ever get up any great pace, but it was a kind of jubilant speed at that. And the horses, the bullion-bar gold one, the purple one with its strawberry spots, the cream with its gilt-tinged mane, the forest green one, the bronze one, the first-daylight blue one, the jet black and the brilliant yellow, all started going up and down, as stately as if they were so many old-time ladies in a lovely dance. And the music began.

It pushed out of those little reed pipes in the center of the platform, a music that in its form sounded as old yet as young as the strings of Jantil's instrument. All the people in this clearing, on foot or on horseback, and even Cando at the forge, stopped what they were doing for an instant, and watched. Then Cando went back to hammering, the sound clinking clear above this piping and reedlike and marvelous music, and others went back to their work, but the children drew even closer. Tomas was the first onto the platform, swinging onto the gold-bar-colored carved animal, his black hair gleaming in patches of sunlight that brushed it as he rode, his face looking more like Shangro's than it did like his mother's, Garsina's, or his father's, Pella's; then a small girl jumped onto the platform, then Rico, and then another little girl, then Jal, and finally all of them were on the platform, more than eight, but those who weren't riding the jenny-horses were holding on to its upright bars. They swung their hands out, cupping air, as they rode, and they made me think of flowers motioning in the morning.

French got on too, stepping light—as she went around with her wedding crown shining in its leaves, her hair's deep gloss warm in the stroking sun, the Gypsy dress blowing against her body, I thought how I'd like to recall all this a long time, even when I was an old man. If I got to be old, which most horsemen don't. A shadow fell on me; it was Shangro who'd ridden his sorrel gelding close, and was looking down, and smiling all across his face, even his rich moustache smiling.

"It is beautiful, Mister Broome. And the children, and Mrs. Broome."

After a time then French had stepped off, and pushed the lever back. And the jenny came to a slow halt, and the children got off. The pagoda of the jenny stopped sending its dull gold, coinlike shine back to the leaves of the trees here, and I noted that at the forge W. M. had shinnied back on Grayboy, and all but one of Grayboy's plates was fresh now. W. M. gave the whole jenny and the children who were walking away, a strict cool glance. "Next time the chirren will pay," he said. "Fifteen cents a ride, any chirren in Yadkin'll pay that. I'll go saddle up that bay and Mister Grayboy for the road. That Gypsy smith makes decent enough plates, for an old man. There's plenty of room for me to travel on that jenny, just like I said." He grasshoppered forward more on Grayboy's neck. "You all best be making tracks now, we got a good haul to go." He turned Grayboy with the mildest twitch, and they went walking back to the horse-cart. I doubted he'd ever wanted to ride a merry-go-round in his life. His mind had been on harder matters; it still was. He'd given me that smile when I first saw him in the pin-oak at Pharis, but now he was set on proving himself, all the way, and I just hoped he didn't bust a leg doing it.

Cando and his helper and some of the Gypsies who'd helped move the jenny from the horse-cart were gathering here now, and I lent a hand in pushing and pulling it. It would seem odd not to be riding in the horse-cart tonight. I could still hear the echo of the jenny's music far back in my ears. The sun was nearly at noon. We got the jenny down in the flat center of the clearing where the bay could be hitched to it without much maneuvering; and French and I went to the horse-cart to clear our gear out of it and prepare for the road to Yadkin.

# 28

It was warm when we started out; a waft of fox grapes and sassafras came on the nooning autumn air. French rode the bay, which she said she wanted to call Bellreve, because that had been the name of one of her daddy's horses in the gone days back at Chantry; it sounded like a frilled-up name to me, but it could be shortened to Bell. The animal was thick in the middle, as Shangro had pointed out; but it had a lot of years in it yet, and a willing neighborly eye. With the Spanish saddle and bridle on it, French's cloak draped over the pommel, it became her nicely—went with her dark sunset hair which was an autumn all by itself. All the extra gear, saddlebags and so forth, we tucked onto the flying jenny, which had its canvas over it again now, shrouding its brilliance. And that left enough room for W. M. to ride in comfort; he sat among the herb-boxes and the spare viands Shangro's people had put in the horse-cart for us to take along when we left, his head poking up through a swathe of canvas as if he was a badger looking around from a cave. Bellreve—or Bell—took to the harness Jupiter had gifted us with, and didn't shy or fight it as French clucked to him and we started out. Grayboy was pawing and prancing some, as if he hadn't just enjoyed a mare but wanted to get on to the next track as soon as possible, and I took his steamed-up attitude for a good sign. French and I had stowed our wedding crowns back with the gear; I didn't think they'd keep well, but neither of us wanted to cast them away just yet. I was wearing my own hat again; didn't want W.M. to think he had a lien on it.

We drew away from the horse-cart at just ten minutes past midday; I'd taken a listen to the turnip-watch, the small chimes near the hour sounding a dozen times, sweet on the ear under the noise of the women-cart's rolling wheels and the shuffle and plod of the three racing horses' hoofs as Shangro and his party set off up around this clearing for the road to Quincyville.

We followed the women-cart at a distance of about twenty yards, the women gazing at us as we trailed them, looking out of the cart's side-windows, and Garsina's lissome arm waving at French. Then we were on the road to Quincyville, and below it snaked the lower-bluff road Shangro had pointed out to me; up ahead, the three race riders, Aldan and Jantil and Pella, on their racers, stopped and Shangro on his sorrel rode back a brief way beside the women-cart. He looked like something you imagine from old-time patriarchal days, but Chinese too in his quiet and his massiveness. His yellow shirt took all the light as he stood up in the stirrups and lifted a hand. He didn't call out "Good luck," or anything common; he knew we knew how he felt about us. There was only the lifted hand. I raised mine, and French hers, and when I glanced back, W. M. was raising his as well, like a little dark clump of twigs. Then French and I cut Grayboy and Bell down toward the road under the bluff, and in a few seconds more, the Gypsies were gone from sight.

I knew how I'd miss their company, and how French would. I'd never been with people just that short spell of time who'd shed their power of liking on me so much. We couldn't see the camp-clearing near the cotton barn anymore now either; there was just foliage crowding on both sides of this road. But the footing was good and it was blithe going for the start of what I dearly trusted would be the last leg of our Yadkinward journey.

At about three o'clock, when we'd been into the rhythm of the stint for quite a while, we rode under the back galleries of houses perched above this road—looking tiny as birds' nests up there in their higgledy-piggledy roofs and chimneys—and I figured that this would be Appleton, where Shangro and his brother and sons would be racing next day. I pulled off into a grove of trees of heaven, in the shade, French moving Bell with me and the flying jenny bumping soft along behind. W. M. crawled out of his nest in the canvas and French and I dismounted and threw down the reins, and we all stood stretching and getting the kinks and lumps out of our bodies from the riding. Then we got out some of the food stowed on the jenny, and ate it and watched redbirds and waxwings fight and sport and jitter among the boughs of the leaf-shedding trees; we fed our mounts and after we'd moved off, one at a time, into the woods and relieved ourselves and then come back, we lingered for just another minute while I quizzed W. M., somewhat, about the best place to stay in Yadkin.

He wrinkled his forehead, slitted his eyes like a meditative lizard, and said, "Mama Gatchin's."

"Boardinghouse?" I said. "It's got that ring."

"She runs a boardinghouse all right, but it's the cooking she does draws them in, not the surroundings. She got a bunch of sheds out back too—reckon she'd let us use a big one for Mister Grayboy and this here Bell nag." He jerked a thumb toward French's horse. I'd already got the strong idea W. M. didn't care much for or waste much breath on anything that couldn't run fast. "They're watertight, and they got stalls. She's cheaper than anybody else in the town, on rent. She might make a fuss about Miss Chantry not wearin' a wedding ring, if you pass her off as Mrs. Broome—"

I said, "She *is* Mrs. Broome, W. M."

"Not in the sight of church-people."

"You were there, you saw us get hitched."

"That was a Gypsy wedding, it don't count outside Gypsy-dom. Plenty of folks free and easy in Yadkin—they got a row of whorehouses on Center Street, the cook works for the madam in one she kept me supplied with scraps when I was there last year. But Mama Gatchin is strict I-Will-Arise-Second-Coming-Split-Off Baptist; she won't stand for snatch-and-go stuff in her house. You asked me, and I'm telling you."

French was looking at her ring-finger. Handsome finger, it was.

"I got just the thing," said W. M. He was hitching at a pocket of his ragged pants. I thought I'd like to get him a new outfit soon after we touched Yadkin, and I hoped he'd take it. He dredged around in the pocket and brought up a blue green madstone, which had come from a deer-liver at one time or another and was supposed to bring luck—I'd seen them before around stable boys—and then five or six trot-line hooks wound in moss, a hoof-frog hook in fair shape, a Barlow knife with a cracked handle but the blade in one piece, and then a small ring that shone gold but was no doubt brass. It was one of those little adornments you could attach to a bridle-ring if you felt like dressing up your steed. They usually came in pairs.

He handed it to me. "I found it back at the Pharis track yesterday when Bombo was running. Was going to put it on his bridle—you seen his bridle, the rings were about rusted out—but of course I didn't get no chance to. It would serve to fool Mama Gatchin. Look like gold if you don't bite it."

I looked at French, she at me, then she was lifting her left hand and had the ring-finger extended. The ring fitted her finger fairly well. She clenched that left hand and brought the ring up close to her eyes when it was on, and said, "It's a lovely ring, I'm most pleased with it."

I said, "We'll use it when we have the other wedding."

"You can do that over on the Church Block in Yadkin, that's how come they named that block," W. M. said. He squinted at the sun, lines like an old man's raying out from the corners of his eyes. "But you got an awful lot else to do tomorrow—get your entry-fee in, that's ten dollars, hard cash, and it don't mean you'll race, it just means you can get onto the trying track where they clock you. Then if you make time anything like Charlemagne or Bedford Forrest—and only then—you'll qualify for the champion heats. Besides Charlemagne and Gen'rl Bedford I'd guess there's going to be some other Standardbred to keep an eye on this year. And even before that you got to rent you the sulky, which the best place for is down on Sutton Road, third harness-and-sulky place from the east. If we don't move on we'll be right here speaking tomorrow morning." He jumped up onto the jenny, and burrowed his way into the canvas, and then his head came out. "You favoring your flank any where that flash-wound got you?"

"Smarts a speck," I told him.

"We got some more of that marigold dust and some thread, you put them on right now," he said sharp. "Wind the leaves around and crush 'em the way the Gypsy chief done. Here's the thread, and here—" He was digging in our stores, "—'re the leaves. And we all got to get going or you won't get no rest at all, in the morning. Which you'll need—the rest—for the trying track."

He was treating me just like I was a part of Grayboy. Which in a lot of ways I was. I swallowed, wanting to laugh and at the same time wanting to be a shade mad, but took the marigold leaves from him along with the thread. He watched while I sat down at the roots of a tree and rolled my trouser leg up and while French, her fingers cool and her new brass ring—the only one I'd bet she'd ever won from her merry-go-round—flashing, wound the soft thread around after the leaves were crushed. The wound was red and puckering at the edges but it wasn't flaming.

W. M. gave the whole fresh bandage a critical eye. "That's fair enough, Miss Chantry. Don't fret, I'll call you Mrs. Broome in Yadkin, especially after you get married again. Let's all mount up now."

I rolled the trouser leg down above my boot and we got up again. W. M. had seen to it that Grayboy had just enough oats and bran and water, no more; he hadn't paid any attention to the bay horse, Bell. I'd fed Bell myself. I said, "Come up," to Grayboy and we hit the road again, the jenny bumping quiet over the hard-packed ground, the air getting cooler now toward evening under here, with the pine-scent and the fox grapes mingling with the smell of the road itself as day moved to dusk.

But it was true dusk long before we got off this road, and we were moving along in shadow as if we were swimming in dark water, and I was wondering if Shangro'd given me the right directions—but knowing he had—when the peddler's cart came along from the other way. It showed up as if it had always been part of this road and you'd all the while been aware of it, its screaking and axle-shouting heralding it a long distance off, so you were used to it and rather glad when it did finally heave in sight. It was a slabby cart with a horse almost as racked as Bombo had been—but without his speaking single eye, and with no touch of his running fire and heart—slumping in the thills, and the man with reins slack in his fingers was nearly as slabby, a wool hat on the back of his head, his cheeks silver with beard and his eyes big. He whoa-ed the nag-horse, not that he'd have had to; it wanted to stop anyhow.

"Now, here, what's this? Damned if it ain't a stallion—and that there pretty rosy lady on that bay, and ain't her cheeks just as rosy as her hair, damn it, and back there's a jimmy-hickle if ever I see one. Well, I got pots and pans and calico and serge and broadcloth and silk to sell, and you people look rich as Jay Gould in his palace in the North—cartin' a jimmy-hickle machine along for your own pleasure—and I ain't budgin' off this here crown of this here road till you buy at least a ribbon. I got the Holy Book too, good size for family readin', bound in genuine mule-hide with copper rivets so it'll last you longer'n your mortal bodies will. And I got tonics for the bile and the epizootic and the chilblains and"—his eyes were like an old crow's, and one of them winked like a buzzard moving its eye-membrane— "some that put the dander in a man, young or old, till he can't hardly stand it for the enjoyment he brings his lady or spouse or whatever."

"We're in a hurry," I said. "And bound for Yadkin. Kindly move aside."

"And we don't require your goods," said French. She had her head far back and was blazing at him with all she had in her own eyes. Colonel Chantry's daughter, I thought quick, meeting some stupid troops.

"Not many knows of this road, Missus, or goes to Yadkin by it. It's a road the peddlers and the thieves b'longin' to the Gypsy tribes know."

"And what are you doin' on it?" I asked, riding a little closer. "Just keeping it warm?"

He was reaching under the cart-seat. "Don't rile me, boy, I ain't made a sale for a lean time, I reckon to git me one now."

I saw the old buffalo rifle start to come up, and had his arm before he could pull it out. I was leaning from Grayboy, and Grayboy stood quiet but whuffled at the flank of the nag, which had sores up and down its hocks.

From the jenny W. M. said, his head only showing above the canvas, "Give him a couple of silver bits, and let him go. They throw him out of Yadkin regular—they done so last year, and I heard it goes on every year. He ain't right in the head. If he was right in the head, you could kill him."

"That's the ticket, I'm addled," said the peddler. "They call me Sammy Spelvin; I'm knowed all through here and down to the Delta, but Spelvin nor Sammy ain't my real names. I lost my names at Sharpsburg, and I ain't never got 'em back. The shot and shell was coming at me so quick they blowed my brains out through one earhole, I seen them fly off. I ain't been whole or hale since. I'll just set here kindly, not touchin' my rifle, and let that draw-mouthed little nigger boy tell you who I am and why I am. I'm a namby-pamby lamb and they's no meanness in me. I made my circuit up from the Delta through Lanceton, two days ago, and the sher'f halted me and asked me if I'd seen a stallion gray like this 'un—" His eyes were even bigger, like a crow's seen through a field-glass. "And asked me if I'd seen a lady like this proud-nosed 'un, and I said I hat'n't—but if I see him again I'll say yes, with all my heart. And they throwed me out of Yadkin and they'll haul me out o' Pharis, whither I'm bound next. I'll tell 'em in Pharis what I seen, too, though, for I'm a very truthful man in spite of my gone brains. And sher'f acted like he wished to bring you in, ma'am," he pulled at his wool hat-brim, "and you, sir, and now leave go my arm and gi' me them bits the boy spoke about."

I could see the rifle clearer now, it was half in sight. It was choked with rust, the barrel falling off. The stock was loose.

I let go of him. Pulled my hand down Grayboy's hide to get rid of the feeling of soured cloth and withering flesh.

I reached in my pocket and got out a bill, not a big one, and handed it to him, and he took it as though he was gulping down rain after drought.

W. M. said, shock-voiced for him, "That's too much. Now he'll remember you. He wouldn't remember you for just the silver bits."

"Never mind, W. M.," I said. "I feel sorry enough for what I said to him."

"So do I," said French. "I apologize to you, Mister Spelvin. Maybe you were at Sharpsburg, and if you were, I am truly sorry."

"Still too much," said W. M.

The peddler stared at us, slack-jawed now, and then down at the bill in his hand, then he rustled the reins and the old nag shunted to the roadside, and as we all drew past I could feel him looking after us. I thought of him babbling about us to Sheriff Planteu down in Lanceton, when he got there again. I didn't think it would matter much, Planteu knew we were on our way to Yadkin. Or anyhow knew that I'd been bound there, and had a smart notion French was with me. I still didn't think Planteu—or Flieshacker, or Howard Markley, or Doctor Mattison, or Mayor Westerfield, or even Phil Adams—would bother us over the state line. But I didn't like thinking about the peddler talking around Pharis, talking to Major Jack Deveraux.

I felt that French was thinking much along my lines, as we all went on. But neither of us spoke of it, and the only conversation between us was made of bit jingling and saddle leather, and the humming sound from the merry-go-round as its reed pipes spoke under the canvas to the motion of the wheels.

After a time when the full dark came a wind came up with it, blowing right for us out of the north, straight from Tennessee.

# 29

French saw it first.

I'd been taking quick naps for the last couple of hours, head down on my chest and Grayboy just keeping up his steady motion—he could have been asleep too, and walking in his slumber. And French, now in her cloak against the cold, had been cat-napping as well, and W. M. back in his canvas cave in the jenny hadn't made a squeak. We'd stopped a couple of times, but just quick stops, only to stretch and then get up and go on again, and for the past two hours toward dawning, we hadn't checked at all.

I heard French say, "There it is, Tom, below us," and snapped my eyes open, sitting up straight.

Light was tingeing the crowns of the pines below us, and painting stripes of first yellow down their millions of green spears. The pine-tops were like the weapons of an army standing high under us, like something out of old times made manifest and shouting without sound. The only sound was the day-wind humming through those pines. Beneath, this road ended as it swooped down through those trees and came to the main street of Yadkin. And the steeples and roofs and harness-tracks and sheds and barns and stores and raying streets of Yadkin already looked like the most bustling and tumultuous place I'd ever wished to be in. Not like New Orleans or Memphis or Jackson or Baton Rouge or even Atlanta; not a city, but a place dedicated to fine horses and the best of the men who could run them. A place you might say drawn to a point in time and being, with banners flying like flags over nearly all its streets, and with the sun striking it as if it had special meaning even for the sunlight.

I don't know if Yadkin is still a town. I mean if it is today, in these times. It could have just fallen away to nothing with the years, as so many of those little places have. And even now, I knew it came alive only this time of the year, these few October days; aside from that it was just a sleepy crossroads trying to get along and worrying about how to eke out enough trade till the racing came around again.

But it was like Camelot in this dayshine, and you could nearly smell the excitement and bustle of it.

The same fresh wind was blowing down from the north, lifting French's hair on the light as she dropped her cloak-hood back and raised herself in the irons from Bell's capacious Spanish saddle.

She laughed, like a small girl; she looked back at her merry-go-round and said, "Tom, do you know what carousel means?"

I eyed her quiet. "I ought to, by this time," I said. "You going to give me some more of the benefit of your academy learning?"

"No, don't be touchy, Tom. It means not simply a merry-go-round—it has come to mean that through the years. But, early on, it meant a tournament. With men riding for favors, and jousting, and even having chariot races."

"Chariot racing, like harness racing," I said.

"Like that, indeed. That's how carousels came into being—they were devised for those who couldn't afford horses and armor—and chariots— to compete in the other contests. That was back in France, long ago. And then carousel came to mean the merry-go-round itself. And merry-go- rounds became popular not only in France but all through Europe, and then whites brought them to this country . . ."

"Your father told you that, you didn't just get it at the academy," I said.

"Daddy was very interested in the antecedents of my merry-go-round, to be sure." She was leaning forward as if drinking in all the bright sun-wind. "You're entering a carousel, a tournament, Tom."

I couldn't help it; I felt gooseflesh form on my shoulders, along my spine.

"And you'll win for me, for both of us! For the honor of Chantry!"

"For both of us," I said, keeping a grip on myself—Grayboy whin- nied, he wanted to get on, he could already smell the town. "I don't know about Chantry's honor. I reckon I represent yours and mine and maybe W. M.'s and surely Grayboy's, at this stage of the game. And as for the flying jenny, you'll be running it in its meaning as a merry-go-round—a carousel that just goes around and around, for fifteen cents a crack."

"Ah, Tom. You have more romance in you than you let on. Don't bring me down to earth. On, then! The town is ours, my love."

"Now I know why you brought your jenny along in the first place," I said. "I've had a speck of wonder about it. I've thought, once in a while, you could have left it back say at your friend Toddy Morgan's, near his sugar-mill—and just come ahead with me. But I believe all the time in the back of your mind you've had the notion of running it in Yadkin, because it fits in with your idea of what things should be—a carousel run in a town where a carousel-tournament is being operated—and maybe from the time you tolled me away from Flieshacker back in the Lanceton woods, that's been your purpose. Even if you wouldn't admit it to yourself, all the distance."

She nodded. "Maybe it has; but I didn't know it until now." Her hair was a banner all by itself, easing out from under its ribbon and lifting around her. "But isn't it marvelous to think of. As if we lived five hundred years ago. You, my knight—and Chantry the castle from which we rode forth—"

I felt the goose bumps again. As if Jantil was playing his old-time instrument near my ears.

I said, wry, "Chantry with its fields gone to fallow, and for all I know with Phil Adams in his job as one of Will Planteu's deputies still guarding the front gallery to see if we don't come back so he can nab us as fugitives."

"That has nothing to do with it. It's merely the surface!" The brass horse-ornament W. M. had dowered her with gleamed as she flung her left arm out, pointing down to Yadkin. "It is a town to be conquered. You have made me myself—and now we're coming into our kingdom." She smiled, wide and golden. "Don't worry, Tom, I'm not *all* flitter-minded. I'll behave myself in Yadkin—at Mama Gatchin's, if that's where we're going first."

"Yes, I think it's a sound idea to behave yourself," I said. "If you spread this kind of talk around in a boardinghouse, they'd likely bore us for the simples. But I have to admit, I kind of like the other idea—not the surfaces of things, but the old-time power of it." If Bell hadn't been pulling the jenny I'd have challenged her to a race to see which of us could get to the main street first. Looking at me, the tail of her witching right eye regarding me, she knew that too, and she laughed again. "You even have a squire," she said quieter. She flicked a glance back at the jenny; W. M. was still out of sight, sleeping under the canvas.

"Sure," I said. "As bull-headed a one as you are a lady, too. All right then—" I chirruped to Grayboy to come up again, and set him down this last tail of the Gypsy-peddler road. "Here we go—to conquer."

I rode ahead, down under the pines. This last of the road had a gentle slant to it, soaking in the first warmth of the day, the coolth of the pines like water over the face and hands and the pine-smell winey in the nostrils and on the lips. Grayboy was eagering for a stable; tossing his head, snorting as if he talked big to the gray squirrels and the birds in under here. I heard the bump and shift of the jenny-wheels behind me, Bell's hoofs bracing on the slope.

Then I was out at the head of the main street, and down the street I could already hear horses whinnying in the line of stables set back there from the dust, and the elms and oaks of the street had that town-feeling they give, a sea of blowing boughs with leaves skimming off over the lawns, and as French brought Bell to a stop and W. M.'s lamb-pate showed above the jenny canvas, here came a horse-van moving into town along the regular road. It was drawn by a handsome double team of matched Belgians, but it was the van I was most taken by—smaller than Shangro's horse-cart, but painted in broad bold scarlet and blue, with *Charlemagne* lettered in gold on that backing, and through the slits of the van I caught a glimpse of a horse almost as tall as Grayboy, a little lighter in the hide—like moonlight on swamp water—and as the sunrays licked over his length through the padded van, he lifted his head as far as he could on the short tie-rope and blared a little at Grayboy. Grayboy gave a hide-shiver and lifted his head even higher.

I knew damned well Charlemagne had won here the year before. News of that had traveled to every decent horse-barn in five states, even to people who didn't read newspapers. Behind his van trotted a fat small man, a cap on the back of his head, his eyes shrewd as a badger's; he gave me a nod which made his red tight cheeks firm up as he smiled toward me, and turned around to look back at Grayboy—and maybe at French on Bell and at the jenny as well—as he rode on. He sat a Welsh pony, a good deal bigger than Mayor Westerfield's pony back in Lanceton County.

"That's Charley, no other," said W. M., breathing it soft. "They always bring him in the last day of the entries, though I reckon folks would hold the entries for him. And he ain't the only one; like I said. I bet they got Bedford Forrest here already. That round man, he's Buck Torbert. Drives Charlemagne, owns most of him. We're on Center Street now." He'd got out of the canvas and was sitting just under the pagoda of the jenny, cross-legged. "We'll go on down to Mama Gatchin's first, get settled and set. I found your harness in the big bag, looks to me in fair shape though I'd like to bind the lines at the tips, they could frazzle there. Go on now."

He pointed west, the direction the Charlemagne van had gone. I set Grayboy there, and French drew alongside as she brought Bell up.

Then we were riding past a lot of houses—I decided some of them must have been the houses of ill-repute W. M. had mentioned earlier; they had a beat-down expression about their paint and the windows were heavy-curtained, and on the gallery of one a woman was sitting in a shift and not much more, maybe she was taking a breath of fresh air after working all night—she leaned to the gallery-rail as we passed, and waved, and I waved back at her, and so did French, though W. M. didn't deign to—and then past other houses which though they abutted these first, had a primmer cast to them, as if they regretted having come down in the world so they needed to consort with bad houses; and on down the street were the stables, or the first of a long row of them. Grayboy stretched toward them, I held him in. Even from here you could smell horse in the new daylight, and the straw and the warm stalls and the runways between them; and you could hear the grooms cussing soft as they led the horses around the yards, and a long sharp whinny of an animal greeting the day with all its juices. Looking down there I saw the Charlemagne van pulling in to a stable drive, Torbert on his Welsh pony in the rear; W. M. said, "We ain't going there. We going right here, like I said. Pull up."

I pulled up on front of a tall-gabled place, rising from the foggy ground and the houses around it like a monument; lights showed in most of its downstairs windows. It was three stories at the least, and curlicued with fretwork like a lady's ivory fan, and painted a flat solid brown. There was a line of hitching posts out here; I got down and tied Grayboy, and gave French a hand down from Bell. Then tied Bell. The bay looked settled and sleepy and not fazed by the long haul from near Quincyville. Best fifty-dollar gelding I'd ever invested in, and I had the hope Shangro and the rest had cleaned up fine at Quincyville. French pulled her cloak smartly around the bright Gypsy dress and took my arm as we went up the walk past dew-dripping chinaberry trees whose boughs sifted the sun.

The gallery had a passel of rockers leaned back against its house-wall beside the windows, and I had the idea Mama Gatchin's boarders mainly occupied those during the day; this would be a good spot to sit and watch the color of the crowd swarm by on path and street during this fair and harness-meet. French had her head up, proud; I was rapping on the thick brown-painted door. French had a fresh brightness about the mouth and eyes, for all the ride behind us; again I felt a kind of vision of what she'd be like when age overtook her. Always much the same, straight back and lovely head, eyes with the same silveriness and amber, and the tilt at the corners; and all of her as if made out of the best, most resistant china, with a touch of rapier steel mixed right into it.

The door opened. A thin little woman with hair spiring out around her pink scalp, hair nibbed around with leather curlers, and eyes snapping like a terrier's, stood there. She had a frying spider in one hand, and a live chicken by the neck in the other. The chicken was scrawking and wriggling somewhat; over its noise she said, "Well? Do for you?"

I said, "I'm Tom Broome, this is my wife Francia, and out yonder's my horse and hers. I'm entering mine in the races. We need to put up here for four days—today, Friday, through Monday, if you've got the room. And my stable-help—that's that child out there sitting on our gear—says you've got sheds around in back for stabling, so I'll need to rent a big one of those, if that's free as well."

I saw her blackberry eyes squint, first at French—who had the brass ring on her finger kind of uppermost with her arm laced through mine—then at French's face, and then back to my face, and then out to where the horses stood. "Goshen, he's a big 'un," she said of Grayboy. "If there ain't somethin' wrong with him, he's the best Standardbred I've seen since they brung Charley on. 'Course you can never tell, maybe he ain't got the wind. My husband, bless his mem'ry, was a driver for thirty years—he expired of a cough and no doubt the drink which he dosed hisself with against the cough, nine years agone. He never had a horse that was worth red beans. Well—Goshen, what's that under the canvas, a roundabout? With that peaked roof, I'd say it's a roundabout."

"A carousel, a merry-go-round," I said.

"A roundabout! Well—you circus folk?"

"Not a whit of it, though my wife may run the merry-go-round while we're here in Ydkin," I told her. "And how about the room and the shed? A sizable shed," I went on. "And the child can sleep in it."

"He'll have to eat there too, or at the back door; some of my boarders would frown at a nigra any closer in the house," she says. "Not that I always do what they say—did I gather your name, Broome, and this is Missus Broome?—not that I always knuckle under to what my boarders wish, I run things to suit my own style, and it's a style suits me. I'm Emma Gatchin, Mister Broome." She thrust out the knobbed hand that wasn't holding the hen, and I shook it and French took it. "And people call me Mama, which I'd want you to feel free to. You don't look used to boardin'houses," she said to French. "Not with that style and git-up. That dress is pure silk, or I miss my guess. Becomes you. And the cloak's velvet mixed with wool, though it's seen better days. You've got the look of quality stamped all over you, Missus Broome. Be a welcome addition to the horse-men and women I take in as a rule. I'm tellin' you all this now so you won't get drawn into somethin' you'll want to back out of later. I don't suffer complaints gladly, or fools neither, as the Good Book tells us we're meant to. I set a good table, maybe you've heard that or you wouldn't be here. Lord! This town dies all the rest of the year, then there's these handful of days and they wring me out so I'm good for nothin' till the next autumn. I can give you a room for yourselves and a shed for your horses and the child, and board thrown in, for three dollars a day and night. That's twelve dollars, take it or leave it, no time to bandy words more. There's straw in the shed, and a lock for it, I'll give you the key, but you got to get your own horse-feed."

"Done," I said.

I was holding my hat under one arm, and with the same arm reaching for money.

"You don't have to pay now, you look to be good for it, and you pay up when you leave, makes bookkeeping easier for me," she said. "Manny!" She calls this last over her shoulder; her shoulder has the same scrawniness the hen's has, but of course lacking the feathers. "Git out here and take this fryer out of my hand! Go kill it on the chop-log and then start the cornbread!"

She whirled around to us again. "When I say you pay when you leave I mean pay," she said fast. "If you try to skip out, I got a mort of friends around the whole county. Step in and I'll show you the room and you can wash up or whatever before you go over to Sutton Road—it's three blocks north, you can't miss it, it's right across from the trying track—you'll want to rent you a sulky, and then you'll want to sign up, the signin' stops at ten o'clock so you ain't got all the whole day to lollygag around."

She opened the door farther. We went in. French said, "Mama Gatchin, I'm sure I shan't complain about your home, and neither will my husband."

"I told you I hope not. How long you been married?"

"Since yesterday," French said.

"Yes, I reckoned as much—no longer. You look bedewed, the bloom hardly off you. And you speak as if you came out of high-handed people, for all your niceness. You'll set a tone for my boarders, I tell you that once more." From a board in the hall she took down a couple of keys. "This 'un's for your room, this is for the shed-lock. Manny!"

A girl had just come running. She wore a slipshod apron—too big for her—over a dress of cornflower blue stained with cooking and serving spots. She had a pretty face, which would have been prettier if it hadn't given the idea she'd been chased for most of her existence and hadn't ever stopped to sit down. "My daughter," said Mama Gatchin. "This here's Mister and Missus Broome." She held the squirming hen out to Manny. Manny took the hen by its long-stretched neck and ran off toward the kitchen, the heels of her slippers making a fast shuffle on the bare hardwood floor. I could smell bacon frying, and coffee in the making, and grits and side-meat. Manny had just ducked her dark eyebrows and nervous face to us, she hadn't even had time to say hello. Mama Gatchin balanced the frying spider on a bottom step and we followed her up the stairs. We went up three flights, the flights narrowing in farther the higher we climbed, and some of the stair-lights made of old stained glass which showed you whoever had built the house in the first place had been fanciful, maybe cotton dealers before the war. From a table at the head of this last landing Mama Gatchin snatched up a lamp, burning low, and led us along the hall and opened the door to a room under the roof eaves. She hoisted the lamp high. It wasn't a room much bigger than the horse-cart of Shangro's, and not as big if you considered Grayboy's part of the Shangro-cart, but it was ample as to bed size. The bed could have held four cavalrymen side by side with room for their sabers and saddles at the foot. It had a canopy top, of rich old sagging silk in dark mauve patterning, and the silk tassels depending from its four high dark posts—like curled masts—had faded out to a light pink through the years. There was a table with washbasins on it, and a chair in one corner, and under the chair a couple of plain crockery thundermugs.

In the light washing up from the lamp, which Mama Gatchin set on the bureau beside the chair, French's face looked slightly astonished and amused at the same time. I could see her face in the bureau's crinkly mirror. "Breakfast for them who want it starts in a quarter of an hour," Mama Gatchin reported. "Eat all you want but don't start no fights you can't finish. I'm good friends with the town constables. I run a God-fearing house. No bringing horse-tack into the rooms, or even the hall. But you can have a toddy if you do it without smashin' anything up."

Up here past the sash of the partly opened window beside the bed I could hear sparrows murmuring and see the leaves of the trees growing close and hear the tide of the day full of outside voices and horse-hoofs filter up. Mama Gatchin said, "That Manny—if there's anything you want, extra coal oil or candles or such, ask her; I'm run off my feet, myself. I'll frail her if she don't step lively. Have a nice time in Yadkin, Mister and Missus Broome, and I hope you win somethin'. You got terrible competition, even with that horse and even if he ain't just for looks but can trot."

"Pace," I said. "He's a pacer."

"Ain't a pacer won as long as I can think back," she said firm-spoken. And went out and shut the door, just as firm.

French was sweeping her cloak off. "It is cleaner than I had thought it would be, Tom. But it can stand more cleaning. I'll borrow a pail and some rags from the daughter."

"You still have that notion of this being a tournament?" I said. "With a knight in armour protecting you and bringing you what he wins? And your flyin' jenny standing for the whole world of spears and flags and all that old-time humbug?"

"You know it's not at all humbug, Tom," she said, walking to me and putting her hands on my shoulders. "It must have been like this for them back then, too. No less full of wonder, I'm certain. And no easier." She rose a little on the tips of the ballroom slippers, and kissed me, and I kissed her in solid return. She was roses and gold. I cast a glance down across her hair to the bed. There wasn't time for anything there now, though I had large hopes of it later. I went over to the window; through the wind-ticking upper boughs with some of their leaves clinging and dancing, I could see out and down in front. W. M. was standing just in front of the hitching post where I'd left Grayboy, his skinny elbows spraddled as he held his hands on his hips. As if he was telling Grayboy something important for his own good. I whistled, and when he looked around, I called out, "Be right down," and he nodded and turned all his attention back to Grayboy.

# 30

In and around Dango Falls they always said you never see a bluejay on a Friday. Because the jays go to hell on that day and give the Devil all the latest news.

But going down the stairs now I saw three jays flash by the window-lights of the landings—strange-painted jays with the stained glass from these lights coloring them—so I figured the saying was just a saying. Unless it held only in Alabama and didn't have force in Mississippi.

I got down in the lower hall and noticed a couple of men leaning against the doorjamb leading into the dining room. In there people were already gathering for breakfast. There was considerable cigar smoke going above the cooking-frowst from the kitchen and a hubbub of voices. I could hear one of these men saying, "Charley's got it locked up and nailed down, George. You'd be a fool to put your money anywhere else." I knew he meant Charlemagne, the Standardbred I'd seen coming that glorious proud way in his van into town.

The other man, canting a cigar in his chops, said quick, "I think this Kentucky 'Bred, the one they call Starborn, 's got a fighting chance. And you're too danged quick to discount Bed Forrest."

I imagined the whole town was packed with experts. I went out of the front door and down the steps. But W. M. already had Grayboy off the hitching post and Bell's reins gathered up as well and was leading them, with the merry-go-round traveling behind, up the driveway and under more chinaberry trees and around the house to a back lane. I followed him and caught up. When we got to the lane there were the sheds—the biggest was the one I headed for. They had high doors and looked stout enough to house two horses, a flying jenny, and W. M., all right. This largest one was solid-built so I didn't think any potential horse-reiver could take the hasps off in a hurry. And anyhow, I thought, fitting the lock-key Mama Gatchin had handed me, such a thief would have a hell of a time getting past W. M. Ritter if he happened to be on deck.

There was a pump at this end of the lane. Along the lane I could see more flags whipping in the north-to-south breeze, all colors of flags, and I thought they kind of resembled banners you might see at some old tourney back in the days when knights rode forth. And I could hear melon-sellers hawking their wares, even this early, and ice-ball sellers working even though the sun wasn't yet hot, and I caught a glimpse at the lane-end of a jug and harmonica band marching by playing "Dixie" as they went, the strump of it hitting the ear in a gust on the steady wind. Grayboy was twitching his head toward that music; Bell didn't pay a whole lot of attention. W. M. took Grayboy into the shed, saying as he went, "That's Sutton Road just them three streets over. The town square's on one side; past it's the rent places for the sulkies. Third from the east, like I told you, 's where we git our sulky. Cheaper and they got better ones. And just along the line, you pay your entry-fee. When you pay it they tell you when you can show up on the trying track. I hope it's a little later in the day because Mister Grayboy's been going all night, even if he didn't do no running. I got to get at his feet now, and soothe him down so he feels like sleeping a mite. But we ain't got time to waste."

He already had Grayboy in a stall—the best stall in here, the one beside the window which was taking peach-toned light through its iron bars— and was unsaddling him. He was so small you'd have thought it would have taken him ten minutes even to find out how to reach the buckles, but the way he moved was a marvel of swiftness, and when it came to the bridle he climbed up to a manger-rim and stood there and took the bridle off. I unhitched Bell, and unsaddled him. When we'd hung the tack on pegs I went out and got a couple of buckets of water at the pump, still hearing the jangle and beat of the music—another band had started in now, playing "Garry Owen"—and smelling fried pies which were also no doubt for sale around the town square. I brought the slopping water-buckets back in, and did a swift rubbing job on Bell, but in the next stall, W. M. had finished Grayboy before I was halfway down Bell to the haunches. I started getting out the other gear and food and saddlebags from under the jenny's canvas when I'd finished Bell, and by then W. M. was examining Grayboy's hoofs. He grunted. "Maybe we ain't going to need a smith here in Yadkin till after the first race tomorrow. That there old Gypsy smith knowed what he was doing—for a Gypsy. And the lower road here was easy on Mister Grayboy's feet. You can anyhow run him on the trying track just the way he stands."

"Sure," I said, shouldering the bags and the fiddle. "And maybe we won't even need a new set of plates for the real track. I mean, Grayboy's wonderful, but when I consider what he's up against . . ."

W. M. rolled his eyes around and up to me. Looked at me as if I didn't have ounce one of true sense in my body.

"You just keep talking that half-ass way, Mister Grayboy's going to hear you and mark it in his mind. Believin' in a horse is something the horse knows. Even if you may be jokin', he don't know about jokes. All he knows is you think he's the best on the earth. That news runs right from your fingers on the lines through his back and into his head. I'd think a man rides well as you do would know it by now. If you got to be funnin', do your funnin' outside this here stable shed."

I said, "Sorry." First time I recalled apologizing to a child—and more to the point, a black child—in my whole life to date. But it was partly apologizing to Grayboy too. I scooped up the willow basket with French's things in it and added it to my load. "He's been mine a long time, W. M.," I said. "He was a lot mine even while Daddy was still alive. We've got a kind of understanding going between us. I won't sully it any more by crackin' jokes. You come on up to the back door of Mama Gatchin's when you get through here, and get some breakfast. I'll bring it out to you."

"No," he said. "I don't crave heavy breakfast food. I told you three-four times I eat light. Just like I fed Mister Grayboy light on the road here. All he needs 'fore the trying track is a couple handfuls of oats and a little mash. I'll mix 'em. I'll satisfy my own wants with some of that

Gypsy food. It ain't bad—for Gypsies. I'll feed Mister Grayboy strong tonight, early, so it'll have a chance to sit easy in him by morning tomorrow.''

I swallowed again; he was right, I reckoned, but it didn't keep me from wanting to argue. But I kept all that down and remembered how he'd brought that Bombo along so that even half-dead and owned by a man who didn't even deserve the name, man, the breed-horse had run as if fire was in his vitals and winning in his heart-muscles. I shifted around and got out the shed-lock key. "Here," I said, tossing it to W. M. He grabbed it out of the air without turning away from Grayboy this time. I noted he had some of the Gypsy-salve—I could scent elder-flowers and crabapple from it—down with Grayboy around Grayboy's hoofs in the straw, and was working it into the frog of the off fore. "In case you want to go out later," I said to W. M.

"I'll have to go out. I'll meet you at the rent-stall on Sutton Road, third from the east, you hold that in your mind. I'll not bring Mister Grayboy up to the trying track till we know when it is you're trying. Don't want him to get the eye put on him too much, too quick. That Buck Torbert he already got a gander at him. And right after the trying I'll blanket him and bring him right back here. First, I'll show you the best place to make your bets. Then we'll harness that there stupid bay up to the jenny again and git the jenny going, while I help Miss Chantry so the chirren don't skin her alive by cheatin'.''

I nodded. Which was all I could do. But I couldn't help saying, "Mrs. *Broome.*"

"Don't you bother about that, I'll call her that around other people.''

I left him humming to Grayboy. As if there wasn't anybody else in creation—no bands, no Yadkin Fair going on outside, nothing but W. M. and Grayboy bulking high above him, communing together in the straw.

When I got back upstairs to the room under the eaves and had dumped the saddlebags and the fiddle in the corner beside the bureau—I didn't count saddlebags as horse-tack; any guest in Mama Gatchin's boardinghouse had to have his portmanteau or valise for his goods—and put the willow basket on the bureau-top, and straightened up and looked around, I saw French had already borrowed a water-bucket, a mop, and some cleaning rags, and was making progress in the darkest corner away from the window. She'd borrowed an apron, too—it looked stained like one of Manny Gatchin's—and she was attacking what dirt had the bravery to linger there as if she was a one-woman army cutting a swathe through defeated territory.

The dip and swash of the mop and the slather of it over the flooring mingled with the morning-noise drifting up through these treetops and over the sill. I unbuckled one of the bags—noticing that W. M. had removed the racing harness and thinking he was no doubt going to oil it again as well as bind the tips of the lines as he'd said he would—and got out my razor and ash-soap, and shaved in the wrinkle-glassed mirror. Using the fairly warm water in the basin set on the bureau. When I was through with that, French had the soiled apron off and her hair put up all the way again, and had her hands on her hips regarding what she'd cleaned. "It's better, and it will have to do for now, Tom. I'll get the rest by tomorrow. I declare, what it really needs is a going over with pumice-rock and then a waxing. I cannot stand a dirty sleeping chamber."

"We'll be here just four days," I said. "And it looks grand to me."

"Mister Shangro's horse-cart was just immaculate by any comparison. I imagine—" She gave her forehead hair a push to the rear "—the dust has encroached just terribly back at Chantry, in this time we've been gone . . . and I do hope someone has kept on feeding my Orpingtons and my Dorkings. I sympathize with Mama Gatchin, having to keep up a whole place like this—even if it's just busy for a little part of the year—with no one but her daughter to help. I know the feeling."

I leaned across a corner of the huge bed and took hold of her chin. "Don't take everything on yourself, French," I said. "I'm already saddled with a child who's doing that, I couldn't stand another oration about my sins, or anybody else's, this morning."

She smiled. "All the same, this place hasn't had a good cleansing since John Brown and his rapscallions marched on the ferry. It makes me furious. It's a truly lovely old house." Then she straightened and took my arm, and she looked like the Queen of England about to go down a stairway into a marble ballroom. A ballroom even bigger than the one had been at Fountainwood, and shinier than the one full of easy ghosts at Chantry Hall. While we went downstairs I told her about W. M.'s plans for the day, which didn't include finding a handy church to get married again in, though I didn't say that. I reckoned I'd look around for that on my own after these other rushing affairs got settled.

In the dining room the air was packed with horse-talk and crackling with the voices of men and women eating between blurts of their conversation, so you couldn't hear yourself think when you came in. And the sideboard was crammed with food—pones of hot bread and johnnycake, rashers of bacon, fried squirrel and platters of side-meat, gallons of hot coffee, grits and hot greens and fried turnip and yam. The long table under the chandelier—you couldn't see much of the chandelier for cooking smoke rolling in from the kitchen every time the kitchen door flew open, just a few faded crystals tinkling up there from time to time—was filled with more food. Manny Gatchin was moving in and out like a streak that hadn't ever sat down in one place and assumed girl-form, her eyes frightened in the flashes you could catch of them, her hair flying even more free than her mother's. I pulled out two unoccupied chairs for French and me, having to jostle against a couple of other chairbacks to do it, and as French sat down, there came a light gap in the conversation nearest us. Then the gap spread all the way around the table, to the sideboard, toward which I was marching to fill up a couple of plates.

Everybody was inspecting French as if she'd dropped from another planet and they'd hardly ever clamped their vision onto beauty before. The talk started up again after that, in wedges, but the woman whose chair I'd brushed a little kept eyeing French even while her own talk went on rolling; she had a steamed scarlet face, like a lobster in the pot before the color leaches from it, and a slouch hat on the back of her head. I'd taken my hat off here, but then I wasn't a woman. She was talking fire about the race-committee in Yadkin, saying it was run by fools who didn't have sense enough to raise the entry-fee and keep riffraff out. "Here they come," she said, "all the way from Tennessee and Alabama and Kentucky and Missou' and the swamps of Loo'siana, and the flocks of 'em just draggin' in their three-legged wonders and makin' the winnowin' out harder for the honest contenders. Charge a mint, charge a twenty-dollar goldpiece, is what I say!" She turned to French. "You and your man runnin' a horse, Missus—?"

French nodded, polite and crisp. "Mrs. Broome," she said. "We are entering a horse."

"Where from? What's his line, what stable?"

"I don't believe that concerns you," French said, not loud but clear enough for a lot of people to hear it. "I don't wish to be impolite, but it is up to my husband to speak for our stables, and he is likely to keep such information to himself."

"My!" says the scarlet-faced woman. "Ain't we hoity-toity! From downstate, 'less I miss my hearin', and educated downstate at that! Just like she don't know the war's well over and it's a whole new track for her kind!" She was saying this last speech to her husband, or at any rate to the man I took for that; he wore muttonchop whiskers with a dab of squirrel meat on the right-hand chop, had his head down close to the trough, a spot the size of a teacup going bald in the middle of the crown of his head, and eyes the size of green pinch-grapes, and about the same color. He sat next to her. I was loading two plates, but I kept my eye on French too, and now she was sitting back, addressing herself to the slouch hat.

Her voice like cream and berries, touched with sugar.

"I beg your pardon, Mrs.—"

"Catewell," says the slouch hat. "Missus Fred Catewell."

"And may I ask if *you* have a horse entered or running, Mrs. Catewell?"

"Well—" The lobster cheeks got steamier. "Not in a manner of speakin', we just come here every year and know the ropes inside out, but ever'body knows us, and—"

French was nodding, quiet, and turning away and only looking at the table, and somebody laughed. Just a quick laugh, but enough. Just at that second, Manny Gatchin came skimming in from the kitchen, a platter in each hand, and Mrs. Fred Catewell pushed her slouch hat back and glared at her and yelled as if she was talking to a mule blocking the road, "You, girl!" Manny whirled around, gravy spilling from one of the platters. "Bring another mess of them johnnycakes, can't you see these is about all et? Don't stand there calf-eyed!" Manny set her platters down, and whirled to go, apron strings switching like lean butterflies. Mrs. Fred Catewell said to the whole table and the room at large, "Girl's half-witted—ought to be took away!"

And French said, neat as if she'd dropped my own knife across the smoke and talking, "She is not half-witted. She is doing an intolerable task under unhappy conditions. And, Mrs. Catewell, I will thank you not to raise your voice to her again in my presence."

Fred Catewell was sitting up. He had a roll of flesh at the back of his tight collar. He needed to canter a mile before every breakfast.

In honor of his wife's stare at French, he'd even stopped eating for the nonce.

I was heading back to French, plates heaped high.

Mrs. Catewell said, "Well, excuse me for suckin' breath! The great lady!"

"A lady, to fine it down somewhat," said French. She was gazing up at the chandelier as if musing while she counted what crystals could be seen. "And please do not press me further, Mrs. Catewell, or I shall slap your face. I have never"—she brought her eyes clear to Mrs. Catewell's, and her words were round as turtle-eggs—"never been able to abide trash."

Fred Catewell was standing up. I'd have given him points on girth and general robustness of hock and shoulder, though not on length of bone. He had the stub of a smoking cigar angled in a corner of his plate. Voice nothing to trouble Jenny Lind, though it was high enough. "Did you—did you call my wife trash—Missus Broome?"

I put French's plate in front of her, and mine at my place.

I said, "I think you heard her. Sit down before you get your coat-cuff in the gravy. I don't have a high tolerance for trash myself, female or male."

I didn't look at him, but pulled my own chair out. Manny Gatchin was charging in through the kitchen door again, bearing another platter of johnnycake mixed in with wings of fried chicken. She set it down toward the end of the table and French said, "Thank you very much, Manny," and Manny gave her a flash of her eyes in gratefulness for something she couldn't have heard often, then ran back out of the room. Fred Catewell was sitting down again, and his wife was edging her chair as far away from French's as she could get it, which wasn't far, and all the talk was starting up again around us. I took a forkful of yam. It was succulent; Mama Gatchin set a noble spread. Past the layers of cigar and kitchen-smoke near the windows I could see more jays flashing, and decided they must have enough deviltry right here in Mississippi to attend to, so they could skip going to hell on Fridays. Though I still knew you never saw them around Fridays in Alabama.

# 31

---

After eating—we'd been nearly late so we were the last at the table—we moved on out toward the front gallery into the blowing sunshine. Mr. and Mrs. Fred Catewell were out there, him with his boot-heels on the gallery rail and her in the best rocking chair for seeing anything that went on up and down the street; a couple of the horse-men—or horse-gamblers, which most of them more likely were—tipped their hats to French, and took the turkey-quill toothpicks out of their mouths to wish her a pleasant morning. So I reckoned she'd made a hit with them by putting Mrs. Catewell in her basket.

We sauntered on down the steps and then cut around at the side of the drive toward the sheds. It was a day with no clouds and rounded as a cotton-boll at harvest season; the best sort of weather for good harness racing, aside from the breeze touching through it and lifting the bright silk hem of French's Gypsy gown. And such a breeze could help as well as hinder. I gave French the key to our eave-room, telling her she'd probably be back there before I was, since I intended to wait at the trying track after I'd found out when I'd be up for my time-trial; at our horse-shed the lock was shut and I could just see Grayboy through the iron window-bars; he looked dozeful and quiet, being with W. M. agreed with him, as I had to keep admitting to myself. French and I walked along this lane into the next street, which was alive with people selling everything they could get their hands on to sell, or whomp up out of thin air to exchange for cash. And the banners flapped from the trees and the ropes slung over the street's dust, making a fluttering that caused quick shadows to run around over everyone's bodies, as though there was a clapping of hands all through the air. There were stalls here—just shanty lean-tos put up in haste and to be knocked down in the same haste on the following Monday when all the hullabaloo was over; some of the stalls, manned by farm-people from the countryside round about, were offering Burgoo—bowls of it steaming and hot—for five cents a bowl; yet others had pralines laid out on marble slabs, and there was a bunch of little medicine shows running, some selling elixir bound to cure the most amazing number of diseases, some selling patent whalebone umbrellas that couldn't be struck by lightning, some selling pamphlets of the "Only True History of the War Between the States," with exposés of the seditious truth behind the so-called Union, and blurry photographs of John Wilkes Booth, which they called a martyr—along with stomach-pills which you got free with each copy. There were banjo bands and jug bands and blow-on-grassblade bands, and one old colored man, blind, sitting all by himself with his hat upturned at his shank, playing hymns on a silver cornet whose bell had gone green as spring grasses. We made our way between a stall where hot corn, roasted in the leaf and slathered with butter, was laid out on the counter, and a stall where a man stood letting cottonmouth moccasins shine and wriggle and twine around his bare arms and stare into his eyes—if you gave him a ten-cent piece he would put a snake's head in his mouth—and across to the next street, which abutted the town square where people were promenading. Some were dressed to the nines, walking slow around the bandstand which didn't have any band on it this early in the day, with parasols raised against the sun in the milky hands of the ladies, and their veils lowered against freckles, and the men moving slow in their pinch-toed glossy shoes and brushing cottonwood lint from the shoulders of their arm-binding coats. Others were in general loose clothes, hunters and trappers come here for the fun in their dark battered hats and wool blanket-jackets, most of them already drunk for the day and hollering about it. And children by the score and the shovel-full, and dogs chasing other dogs or their own shadows for the beans of it.

French was looking around. "Right over there in front of the millinery shop," she said with her lips close to my ear. "It's the best place—where the lane crosses and the street divides."

She was settling on a place for her merry-go-round. "Let me go in and speak to the proprietor," she said, and when we'd crowded through people and were over beside the shop, I stood outside and waited while she swept in as if she was going to order six dozen women's hats, with special furbelows. There were a lot of hats in the window, which a good many birds had given their lives to make, all the hats sitting on smooth posts so they resembled headpieces on skinny frail eyeless females. Looking at the moil and swirl of the crowd around here, I could feel the casual meanness below all the frippery, and see why a poor dolt such as Sammy Spelvin the peddler had been thrown out of Yadkin, regular. People can stand any amount of foolishness, but an idiot makes them nervous—maybe because he underscores what they sometimes feel themselves to be but what they'll never admit.

I leaned against the bricks of the shop, turning down a couple of black boys who wished to shine my boots—they were well tallowed—and looking northward to the next street, where the sulky-rent stalls were, and where, across from them, the fence of the trying track stood curving in a dark oval under the already beating sun. This side of the trying track was in shade, and next to it was a long low building with a sign tipped over it, *Harness Entries, Rules Committee*. On beyond the trying track, where a sulky's wheels flashed as its spokes came around into the light and a dark Morgan chested his way along, and people were yelling, was the true track, empty now, its grandstands looming and its mile-oval like a grand eye staring at the sky and waiting. Felt a chill of readiness and hoping climb my arms and legs, and swallowed, and kept looking around for W. M. He wasn't anywhere in sight, as yet. Then French was sailing out of the door of the shop, a small man that looked as if he'd been born in a drygoods drawer behind her, his eyes looking lickerish at her—but stunned by her style as well—and she was introducing us, the man's fingers limp and moist in my hand. "Mr. Anderson, Tom—he has kindly given me permission to set up the carousel at this point. He realizes it will bring many mothers with their children. Do you not, Mr. Anderson?"

"Dear lady, I think they will swarm about, and visit my shop while they wait for their children to ride. I could no more refuse you than I could any other golden business opportunity." He edged to me. "If you are betting, Mister Broome, put it all on Starborn. The dark horse. I have a friend who knows. Charlemagne and General Bed—" He shrugged. "They have had their day. And on Starborn, you would not believe the odds—" He kissed his fingers at the air. "Starborn barely made the time-trials. But that was planned, to keep the odds high, you see. He can take anything, anything, my friend says, and my friend knows."

I thought it was wonderful how people with a tip could hardly ever keep it to themselves. Wondered how many other people he'd whispered this to, and how good Starborn really was. I thanked him; he said he'd see French later that afternoon, and, arm in arm, French and I went on. As we crossed to the next street, well in sight of the trying track now, I heard a booming shout from there, and stood still and jerked my head around; then there under the trying track wire, which I caught just a glimpse of because people were clotting around it like bees around the queen's cell, here came Charlemagne, head up and forelegs flashing in the glimpse, and the sulky behind him moving straight as if it sailed a few inches off-ground; I reckoned he'd not only made the time but bettered it. Hats were tossing in the air. Nearby, the betting stalls had clumps of people around them even thicker than those at the trying track, and men and women were detaching themselves from the rail-crowd and running over to the betting stalls as I watched. I pulled at French's arm, and we went right on to the harness-entries building. A man with hair rucked back from his temples as if a gale had hit him went swooping by us, gurgling in the back of his throat, "Two minutes, half a second, Charley done it, two minutes and half a second, what'll he do *t'morra*?" and rabbit-leaping through the crowd. I thought, two minutes and half a second, on the one mile trying track. Which would be four minutes, one second, on the champion's mile track where you went around twice. My dear Jesus, that was trotting. If the man was right, and I didn't have any reason to think he wasn't.

French could tell what I was thinking, her fingers on my arm dug in a little. Then we were at the stairs leading up to the entries building, and French was detaching her arm from mine and sitting on a bench out here, looking up at me with her slow smile as warm and loving as if it created a cave where only she and I lived, even walling out the noise around us. I patted her head, the hair warm in the sun as if it sent a message right through my fingers into the middle of my being, and went up the stairs. Looked around again when I was at the doorway, and there over cater-cornered from us, hunched on the stoop of one of the sulky-rental stalls, third from the east, was W. M. Could feel him staring at me like a cool piece of ice in the heating morning. He didn't wag a hand to me, just waited there. I went on in.

There was a milling and a crowding going on in here, and a tired man with sleeve-garters wet with his sweat making people stand in line and shove back; I got myself at the end of the line, which didn't make it the end for long, because in back of me a long-faced man surged up in haste, and then others behind him. He had a wen on his nose, which he kept blowing, one nostril at a time, holding the other nostril shut with a finger while he accomplished this tricksy feat. He stopped the blowing and pushed a fingerful of snuff under his lean upper lip. "Bad cold," he honked to me. "Care for some snoose, Johnny?"

Told him no thanks. I took out my father's turnip-watch and opened its case. It was a little past nine. "Oh, we'll make it in time, before ten," says the man with the snuff and the sniffles. "Pretty watch you got there—hunting watch—ain't seen one like it for an age. Be better for me if I didn't make it, but I got the runnin' in my blood. Got a mare's weak in the knees—she ain't stronger this year than she was last—she was scratched at the testing last year. But I keep dreamin' this dream—comes to me regular as Adam's original sin this time of year. In my sleep I can see her comin' up, hear the cheerin'. You hear the news out there? Charley's done it again." He cocked a streaming eye up at the board behind the table where clerks were taking entry-fees and registering the drivers and the horses. "Always just about the last to enter and test, and always about the last to git on board for the heats t'morra and Sunday and Monday. Looks like a three-horse field, to me."

On the board's slate a clerk standing on a stool was chalking *Charlemagne* in careful copper-plate writing.

Above it was written in the same neat hand, *General Bedford Forrest,* and then above that, *Starborn.*

The board didn't give the trial-heat times.

My friend with the catarrh tapped me on the shoulder.

"Charley in two and one half. Best of the bunch. Starborn tested first, yesterday. Two, six—which if you ask me ain't nearly nigh what he can do. General Bed, two, four—he tested yesterday evening, but that wind had come up then and I think it throwed him off on the homestretch. 'Course, you got to consider when they git on the real oval, and go twice around it, there's the stamina comes to the fore. If I was laying money on any but my mare—which I ain't, more fool me—it's costin' me my last ten to git her entered, and I don't have a copper left to lay on any of the others—but *if,* then I'd sink it all on General Bed. I've heard a lot about Starborn, jet black 'Bred from Kaintuck, but he's new to this game and for all they talk about his bein' helt back and barely makin' it to the grandstand track, I don't think he's got the final drive. You driving a 'Bred or somethin' else?"

"Standardbred," I said.

"Trotter, o' course."

"No."

"Oh, Johnny. Might as well save your money like I'd ought to do myself. Ain't it glorious how hope springs eternal, though, as the bard says." He took another lipful of snuff, which I hoped helped cure his ailment, but I didn't want to talk to him—or listen—anymore. I sort of shut my ears to all the chattering around me, and watched a sun-ray falling through a back window onto the rim of the clerks' table; we inched up slow, as if we were waiting like sheep going through a corral to be shorn, or as if we were back in reconstruction and holding our heads high and our bellies in, while the newly appointed northern rascals told us which ones could and couldn't vote.

My turn with one of the clerks came six or seven minutes later; he didn't look up at me, just took my money and folded it in with a wodge of other cash all slammed in a drawer, sweat standing out on his bent brow and easing down to his eardrums, and wrote my name right after I'd told him to add the *e* on the end of the *Broom,* pen scratching away as if his wrist was dead tired, and then out of a corner of his mouth said, "Let's see—four o'clock, thereabout, Mister Broome. At the trying track. Sulky must be in good condition, personal or rented. Horse must not have colic or be underfed or otherwise ineligible, trial judges have the full say-so. Here's your entry slip. If you qualify for the champion track—'' He didn't sound like there was a dim chance in hell of it, ''—you can race in all three two-mile champion heats, t'morra through Monday, champion heats at two sharp each day, good luck, next gentleman please, step up.''

I tucked the slip in my pocket. The clerk still hadn't given me a glance. He didn't look up at my friend with the nose trouble either, though this party gave me a grin and a head-shake which went to say he thought I was just as fated as he was, though just as stubborn. Out in the light again, with the flags dancing through it and French rising from her bench to come and greet me I felt more like myself again, with a name and a man's navel, and a working liver and a beating heart in my chest. And there across at the sulky-renting stall squatted W. M., getting up slow and watching us with his eyelids at half-mast while we came on. He said, "Morning, Miss Chantry—or Mrs. Broome, whichever way you want it. What time?" he said to me.

"About four."

"I'll have him ready at half-past three. Bring him out here just about four. Said I don't want many seein' him till he runs first time, even in a trial. Come on, and leave me do most of the talkin'.''

He had a hand on the rent-stall door. I said, "W. M., I think you ought to have a new shirt and pants. Just some hickory duds, but new. You mind if I—''

He gave me the eye of a frog that had been jostled when it had its attention on nothing but flies.

"You please to save your money. You'll want all you can spare for the betting this evening. Want you to get your bets down just as fast as Mister Grayboy's name starts flowin' around." He looked down at his tatters. "What I wear covers me, and it smells of horse. I ain't going to have time for a long while to break in new clothing. Of any sort.''

In back of us there was a lot of noise from the trying track, but nothing as tumultuous as what had come when Charlemagne finished his trial heat. W. M.'s short nose—there was hardly enough of it to be called a nose, though the nostrils were arched and could express a lot, like some horses—gave a wrinkle. "What them people singin' out for? Ain't seen nothin' they couldn't see better at home. Nothin' yet.'' He held the door open, and we all went in.

# 32

W. M. started talking the second we got in the sulky-rental stall, and damned near didn't stop till we were outside again. The man who was renting the sulkies—a whole line of them, some considerably more gleaming than others, and some made by Forman and Robbins, which were the best kind and known throughout harness racing, took one glance at us—most especially at French, who gave him a friendly nod—and then paid all his attention to W. M., who was saying, "We don't want none of these rust-bearing things you been renting out to them farm-people who come in here and spend their hard-won cash to git a quick run on the trying track and bring it right back. We want your best, for all four days—and we ain't going to lay down twenty dollars for it neither. We aim to win this whole meet, and when we win it in a sulky from your place, you'll share in all the glory. How about that one there?" He waded in through a couple of sulkies and pulled out a beauty; a Forman-Robbins, built like my daddy's watch had been built, and hauled it across the floor, putting himself between the shafts. The spokes rambled along with sun spilling from them and the light whirring of the tires sounded sweet. W. M. went right on, "This one would do, it ain't had the guff and grief them others have, and we're willing to pay you fifteen dollars, cash, for its use. This here's Tom Broome, driving Mister Grayboy—you ain't heard of him yet but this evening about four o'clock you will. Him and his wife here, they are staying at Mama Gatchin's. If you need a deposit he'll give you somethin' within reason, but don't expect a ransom, we ain't the Yankee treasury, our pockets ain't lined with gold."

He kept going in that rolling vein, hauling the sulky back and forth while he talked, and finally the man—who I doubted had ever heard a pint-size child of color speak with such force and not stop for breath—got a few words in edgewise, agreeing to take a ten-dollar deposit along with fifteen dollars advance payment of the rent. The ten to be given back when he'd inspected his sulky on the Monday evening we returned it. I'd have paid more rent for that sulky, and more deposit; it was a point of deep honor with W. M. not to let me do it. The hubs of the sulky glowed like jewels, it didn't even have a wire out of true, and the seat didn't look to have been sat in much except at the factory when it was made. The man made out a paper for me to sign—W. M. kept straight on talking—and took my money as if he had been going to ask for more but would be glad to be shut of W. M.'s voice; it wasn't till we were going out of the door that the man said, "You need any harness?"

W. M. stopped for a gulp of breath then. He observed the harness hanging on pegs along the walls. "That ain't harness I'd fit on a bear if I had a tame bear that could plow," he said. "Let alone put around a horse to pull a sulky even a dozen yards. You keep it for other customers." Head high, nose up, he hauled the sulky out into the day; it balanced well in his hands, though he wasn't much higher than its seat. He kept on pulling it as we went along through the crowd past the entries building, French and I walking at his side. Some folks turned around to give him an extra look as he shouldered along, and some snickered at him. He kept his head up, eyes front. Where this road crossed to the next, he said, "Now you go walk the champion track. All by yourself. Don't waste no time watchin' them nags trying out at the test track yonder—there ain't any profit in it. The trying track's not a patch on the real one, you get the feel of the champion track and notice how it cuts to a special slant in the backstretch. Dirt makes a long hill there like an Indian mound. You can't see it good with the eye—you got to walk it and feel it, the way Mister Grayboy will be feeling it tomorrow. Don't eat you no big noon dinner. You no doubt pigged enough at Mama Gatchin's this mornin'. Miss Chantry—beg your pardon, Mrs. Broome if you like—will go back to Mama Gatchin's and git some rest. Womens needs more rest than mens. We'll see you right here around about four." He turned and went right on, hauling the sulky. French raised her fine eyebrows at me, wanting to laugh but holding it in; I said, "He might be right about walking the champion track. Hell, I'll see you later. It won't take me all that time to walk it, I'll mosey around and find a church where we can get remarried the proper way soon. Don't tangle in any fights with Mrs. Fred Catewell."

"I shan't, Tom, unless she harasses me. And I want to have a chat with Manny Gatchin. There's so much she could do with herself, she's truly a charming girl under all that fright."

She patted my cheek, and went off after W. M. I watched her catch up to him and they went off through the mob, talking quiet together, and I felt that when one wasn't bossing me, the other would be. All the same, through both their special kinds of bossiness was a concern that ran like a river among all of us; I'd always been on my own before and though all this other stuff of being shoved around felt strange, I didn't hate it.

I shouldered around and made my way past the trying track. Where, now, an underbred filly was making the mile-circuit, pulling a potbellied man who kept yelling at her as if she was going to pull his sulky one iota better for his cussing, and where the time-trial judges and timers were leaning on the fence with their watches in their hands as though they were sick of the whole business of testing and couldn't wait for the true racing to begin the next day. The crowd around that test track had dwindled down considerable, too; I didn't linger with them, but made my way across the next street and over to the champion track, where it stood lonesome with the grandstand shadow falling across the dirt clear to the infield fencing. All the whoop-de-do of the town fell away behind me, and I could hear my own footfalls in the ground near the grandstand. There was a row of sheds for the starters, more sheds than would be needed if it was going to be a four-horse field tomorrow—I only trusted to God it wouldn't remain a three-horse field. I knew the racing committee here had set their sights high; the times Charlemagne and Bedford Forrest and this Starborn had made were bound to keep out all but the best. I thought how Grayboy'd never run an important time-heat all by himself before—in any important contest he'd always had something to run against. And I mulled over the point that he did his best—flat-racing or harness—when he was right square behind another horse, not appreciating the taste of any other animal's heel-dust on his lips. I'd learned that mighty well at Pharis.

I vaulted the entrance-gate to the grandstand, where the crowds would start muscling in next day long before the two o'clock race time, and went out onto the track. There's nothing as all by itself as a track with nobody around it—it feels like a deserted battle ground without even Minié balls and spent cartridges around to remind you of what took place. You get a notion of just how long a mile is—it seems to have stretched from what it will be again when the people are whooping it up and the hoofs are sounding, as if the whole length of it was a piece of thread that had wound out a long way off the bobbin. I walked at a good steady pace, feeling the slight bank of the ground under the starting-wire here, and knowing there wouldn't be any groom-starters, but that the head starter would take us back of the wire and make us come up under it level and already breaking into our gaits. I noticed when I was under the cool shadow of the grandstand the way the wind from the north—which might die by morning, but might not—leaned into the channel of the track as if it was blowing down a chute, which might slow a horse by a second. But you could make up the second with the wind behind you on the backstretch. Then I was beyond the shadow, into the first turn, the wind from my right, trying to push me with its airy hands away from the outside rail. I gave my hat a tug, and went on at the same pace, head down. When I got to the backstretch the same breeze, steady as it had been this morning when we'd come off the Gypsy-peddler trail and looked down on Yadkin for the first time, and steady for that matter as it had been since the evening before, was blowing against me from behind, flattening my shirt to my spine. Back in town you didn't note it so much, it just dithered around and snapped the flags, but here it was part of your skin and reaching for your marrow.

Then I felt the dirt tilt, and knew what W. M. had been talking about. They'd graded all this stretch off with care, and it had the firmness that would stay that way unless there was a heavy jouncing rain. Yet the eye couldn't see what the body could feel, that right here—like a long Indian mound for sure—the dirt canted from the outside rail almost like the rim of a bowl, making you lean to the inside enough so, if you didn't know it was coming up, you might well sheer off toward the infield when you were driving. I'd a good notion W. M. had come out here and walked this by himself while French and I were at breakfast and fooling around after it. I looked for prints of his bare feet in the dirt but it was too hard-packed to have taken them. I went on, pacing my own shadow, and went into the far turn, the same wind slipping over the infield fencing and coming against my left side now; then I was coming into the warm sunned stretch again before the clean line of grandstand shadow started, the breeze flattening my hatbrim back as it had when I'd started out. I went along under the wire, finishing, and stood for a second eyeing the whole circuit—silver poplars shining out past the backstretch rail, beeches growing close to the far turn. And the stands so dark up under the roof there could have been a thousand people hiding there, sniggering at me for my foolishness. Except I didn't feel it had been foolish or a waste of breath and time at all. I wondered if the new horse, Starborn, would come to that canted backstretch without his driver knowing about it. General Bedford and Charlemagne knew the course, their drivers had been here before.

I made my way over the slatted entrance-gate again, and back along into the body of town. Noise from Yadkin—a full band pumping away in the town square's bandstand now, I figured they were practicing for tomorrow—came back around my ears in bits and spurts and then as a solid rangle-tangle of many sounds; I could smell people again, and wood and coal smoke, and a thousand different articles cooking. I headed past the trying track, not even giving it a glance now; up ahead where W. M. had said the day before the Church Block was, steeples were rising from the brawny gold and leathery fawn and red of the leaves that brushed their shingles.

# 33

Along the Church Block it was quieter; I had the feeling as I looked back to the stir and whelming of the other streets that Shangro and his people would have done well here this year. But Shangro'd had his mind set on that breeding stallion in Tennessee, and he'd made enough money on the Pharis heats—for all the grief that cost us afterward—to more than balance out any herb-selling loss here. Anyhow, I told myself, Shangro and his people weren't the kind to mix readily with this mob; they had their own proud rites and rules; they stayed above the yammering of the multitude. They were like birds of passage that didn't mingle with other flocks, but kept themselves whole and moved secret through all time.

So thinking, I stopped at the first church in sight. It was built of greenish gray stone with a dappling of shadow across its doorway, and it looked to me forbidding. I'd never been much of a church-joiner, and Daddy hadn't favored it either; Sundays are too free and good to waste on other than training horses. I made out the sign, which said this was a Covenanting church, and walked right along. The next, across the street, was the I-Will-Arise-Second-Coming-Split-Off-Baptist W. M. had remarked on. It had a jollier cast to it, made of split-shake shingles and brown with age, and there were cats sitting fat around its yard, and children amusing themselves with tops and dolls sprawling on the side-steps, and a preacher's house under wistaria vines close by; but this would be Mama Gatchin's place of worship, and I reckoned she took it serious, and wouldn't take gently to learning that French and I'd got married here after we'd told her we were already man and wife. That left the Free-Soul Methodist, which was thin and gaunt with a flowerbed laid out so strict you could have ruled paper by its margins, and another church which was frame-built and sagging a good deal, and stood back under a sprawl of oaks that had been good-sized trees when all this was forest land and belonged to the Indians. I'd have bet those trees had flourished well before Dancing Rabbit ceded his many acres to the white men in Washington. The spire of the church showing above the oaks leaned to the west, and pigeons flew in and out around the bell, making a creak and a whir of wings and calling lazy through the day. I went up its sunken brick walk. Here the preacher's house looked more like a fishing lodge along the big river than any respectable reverend's manse—its eaves hung down like the hair of a woman when she's combing it, and there were traps hung from pegs on the walls under the eaves, and bees had stored honey in the walls and flew in and out of the board-cracks with their heads fierce as black birdshot in the streaks of sun. I called out, "Hoo, anybody home?" and my voice sailed back over a scuppernong arbor at the rear. Then a hound came belling at me—a Plott hound about ten years old, tail up and stiff, ears flapping and flews laid back; I stood still and let him nose me, then fondled his ears when he let me put my hand down. And a voice boomed out from the arbor, "Don't pay no mind to him! C'mon back, stranger!"

The hound padded beside me, sniffing my boots as I walked back there, brushing aside scuppernong vines. In the arbor a big man with a long-tailed baptizing coat whose tails brushed the grapeskin-spilthed ground sat on one of the arbor benches, his clean large bare feet propped on the opposite bench, and his handsome snow-stark beard spread over all his shirt and vest and down to past his belly. He had his head tipped back, and was popping scuppernongs in his mouth, rolling them around and then pushing out the skins with a sound like *thoo*. If he'd have stood up he'd have loomed taller than me by a head, though I'm not modest-sized. But he didn't rise, just stuck out a hand, and when we'd shook, said in a mild voice that could be powerful if he'd let it, "You got the aspect of a man coming for one of three things. You got a girl in trouble and want to do right by her and her poor parents, solidifying the child; or you want to ask me for the loan of my traps because somebody directed you to me; or you've lived a scarlet life and want to get right with the Lord. Or it could be all three. Set down there, have a handful of grapes—they get right at their peak this month, they'll be gone in a week—and inform me of your purpose."

I sat—he pulled his feet back to give me room—and picked a stem of the scuppernongs. I told him my name and went on, "There's no question of a child I know of, but I'm here for the racing only, and I want to get married." He kept regarding me while he chewed and ejected grapeskins, his eyes set in skin that was like beechwood with the burl of the carver's knife all over it. Cool gray eyes with warm-hopping centers. So I went right on and told him I was entering a horse, and a little about French and me, and the fact that we'd traveled for a time with a Gypsy band. Saying nothing at all of the fact that we'd eased out of a tight situation, or much about Lanceton, or anything about Gary Willis, or about our fracas with the Teague crew, or Major Deveraux and his part in our fortunes to date.

Then he said, "Shangro and that bunch, I know him. Heathen, but reputable. Might do you in a horse-deal but wouldn't harm you otherwise. Run across him many times in my travels up and down this countryside. I make a swing every spring and fall—I've done my stint for this autumn— saving souls, washing in the Blood of the Lamb. Carry a bottle of Jordan water to tincture the streams and creeks and rivers with, when I immerse my clients. Mister Broome, I was taken by Yankees at Antietam, and by the second day of my capture I'd converted and baptized half the troop. But you don't have to be converted to be spliced. I've got no hard and fast rules about it. Man sees the native goodness in other men, the evil ingrained along with it, soon or late he's going to swing to God if he's got a grain of sense in his system. I'll marry you and your lady. Do it up fine, with a document to attest to it. I hand-draw the certificates myself. Look here." With the hand that wasn't grape-holding, he reached in a coat-pocket and drew out a couple of scrolls. Handed them to me. "Unbind the ribbon," he said. I did so; they were drawn in blue and pink and posy-yellow inks, with scrolls held by bluebirds in their peaky bills, and with angels flapping their wings around the margins, and cupids hovering close to hand. With places for the names all ready to be filled in, and with this man's name, Apollodorus Miller, Rev., set bold at the bottom.

I wound the ribbon around the scrolls again, and handed them back. He said, "Ap Miller, which most folks call me, will be just fine between us. I don't use the full name save on official documents. Now, you'd ought to know I ain't no regular accredited preacher. I didn't go to any school which taught me how to do it and gave me a diploma. This is a ripe town for churching, which is why I make it my headquarters. During the winter and summers I trap a good deal, and study horseflesh—you're a riding and driving man yourself, and a trader I'd say by the way you talk about the animals—and just at this time of year, I place my bets. This town simmers down to a low boil, soon as the flapdoodle stops, which it'll do come Monday night. Then all them who've been ruttin' around and fillin' their bellies with corn-swill and gettin' steeped in the Devil, come crawlin' to this block and support the churchmen along here—the others who went to the seminaries as well as me—in fair fashion. The Lord has instructed me to take what the sinners offer, and then as I told you, in the spring and the fall to go out and garner in more souls for the golden streets of eternity. I got to tell you somethin' else.'' He patted the hound's head, fingers thoughtful around the plates of bone there, and the hound sat down and sighed. ''I ain't got a name for my church. It ain't any denomination. It's just Miller's church. Built it myself, free-style, with some help from the carpenters in my flock, twenty years ago. My flock fluctuates— sometimes I get a Methodist overflow, sometimes a Baptist, sometimes the Covenanters see fit to give me their trade for a spell. And then there's the hard core of folks, swamp-rats and woods-haunters, most of 'em, that come to me regular. Pay me off in muskrat skins and bear-meat, and whatever else they got. But what I'm gettin' at is, you won't be no more married, if I do it, than you already are under the strange dark rites of Shangro and his Rom. You'll have a document to show for it though, which'll look mighty pretty on the wall of your parlor once you settle down. And I've noticed folks don't ask particular questions when they see such a pretty marriage-paper—they just take it for granted you've done it up in style.''

I lipped a scuppernong, pushed its skin out, swallowed, and said, ''I think it would do well for Francia Chantry and me. I kind of feel what King Shangro already did is firm and solemn. And as long as it's done with a Bible this time, I don't see how it could be more solid. I think she'll feel the same.''

''Good. Then now we got to set a day and time. Today won't do—I got a baptizing at four, and the night's all took up with prayer-meeting— catch as catch can, inspirational and speaking in tongues when the spirit moves us—and tomorrow's full from dawn to sleep-dark. Then there's Sunday, and Lord, Sunday—it's brim-full. But Monday, I'd say, right after the last heat's run and the fuss dies down—say about five in the cool of the evening. You can have the parlor with organ—I play it myself, it's got a few stops busted but in the main it's sufficient—or back here in the arbor, which I favor because it's pretty and wild. Or you can have the hull church, with whatever flowers my flock brings in left over from the Sabbath. There's no organ in the church, I ain't ever had time to move it from the parlor."

I said, "We'll take the arbor."

"All done and set. Five on the Monday. Now let's get down to cases. When I say I'm hip-and-thigh smote with busy-ness, I got to admit part of it's race-business—it ain't all religious. What kind of horse you driving, what time's your trial-running, what's the horse's background, and do you deeply believe you got a chance against Charley and General Bed and this here Kentucky 'Bred, Starborn?"

Well, he touched a nerve and I didn't see what harm there could be in telling him, even though W. M. wouldn't have breathed a word. But I trusted him as I'd trusted Shangro after I'd known him five minutes, and doubted he'd go noise this around to the multitude or even any of what he dubbed his flock. He wouldn't if he was a good gambler, anyhow—and if I was qualified for the race the next day, and if everything went even halfway right—I still had the fingers of my mind crossed on that—he might pick up some money, which I sure wouldn't begrudge him. So I found myself spilling a good deal about Grayboy, and telling him about W. M. as well—and I told him how tickled I was about W. M., but how fretted too, because up to now I'd always done all my own race-grooming, down to the swamping.

Ap Miller drank it all in, eager; he said, "Don't you go against the wishes of that child. He sounds like a child I saw in a back-lot flat-racing down around Pharis late last spring in my travels for the Lord—man he helped out was running a quarter-breed hairy as the sons of Gath, poor old horse with his near eye blinded, but that boy whispered to him and nerved him up and he won more off me than I'd care to drop again. Man ridin' him, his owner, was liquored up and couldn't hardly see, it was the boy did the work. Some people got the knack, and it's a mystery-knack, and he was one."

"That's the very one, it's W. M. Ritter," I told him, leaning forward and getting wound up. And then I told him about Teague's raid after Pharis, and Teague shooting the sorry but wonderful breed and getting his own neck broken. This brought in Deveraux at last, but Ap Miller—Rev.—didn't know him.

"Sounds a haughty man," he said. "Brave, but bravery ain't all the

Lord requires of his servants. There's hundreds of officers in this state and the next, all fumin' at the bit, still, and wishin' they had butternut troops to command. They look back, but their eyes ain't fixed to see forward. God knows I wish we'd won the whole shebang, too, but if the Confederacy rose again it'd kill us all this time, with naught left but our dust to show for it. Just when we're startin' to rise from that dust and be people again. Way you tell it, I'd say this major's got some kind of yen for your lady, this Francia—"

I let that drop, I didn't want to tell him about French traveling under false pretenses or the reason for it. We got back onto the racing then, and just jawed along, and he told me since I was trying out at four this evening, he might well set aside his baptizing obligation for later, and be at the trying track to see me and Grayboy. He mused on, ". . . I've heard of Nickajack, who you say was your daddy's—don't git down to Alabama much, but years back I heard the name. And the sire, Galleon, sticks in my mind as well. You know the men you'll be drivin' against tomorrow, supposing you *do* do well enough to get in the field?"

I told him about catching sight of Buck Torbert.

"Don't let his chunkiness fool you, Mister Broome. He's quick and he's been driving longer than Nebuchadnezzar's beard. And Charley's a nigh perfect animal, not only to look at but to trot. You with a pacer—I'm not saying pacers can't go, but they don't have the reputation for it around this end of the country; they seem to do better in the North. Now, I'll tell you about Budge Fisher—he'll be drivin' General Bedford Forrest. He's a mite older, and slower in his motions than Buck Torbert, and likely— still providing you get to the true track—he'll not pull ahead for the whole first mile. But it's stayin' power his horse has—gallons of it—and he's holdin' that in all the time others are spendin' what their horses have, and then when he cuts loose, well, it's the legions of Caesar comin' over the hill to wipe up the savages. But Rome fell, and I ain't saying you couldn't do it. I *am* going to postpone this four P.M. baptism, I just naturally have to watch you test out. From all you say, maybe I shan't be disappointed."

I greatly hoped he wouldn't be. He went on then, informing me that he didn't know a lot about Starborn's driver, who went by the name of Rankin, but that he'd seen the Starborn trial and felt the black Kentucky horse had been held in for a purpose. He went on some more, with me chiming in from time to time, telling about harness-racing animals he remembered, some of them animals my daddy had known and had talked of often; it was good here in the sun, lacing in through vines and draping the old hound's coat in a net of lacy shadows, and with the scent of the grapes surrounding us like they had already been squeezed into wine. After a time I put my head back against the trellis, crossing my boots, and felt my eyes shut. And some of the tightness go out of me, as if it rambled off toward the spilling sun. Ap Miller went right on speaking, only now and then punctuating his voice by popping a grape in his mouth, he was telling now of a two-week baptizing he'd done down on the big muddy when he'd first started out—"like Saul on the road to Damascus, I was hit by a light which knocked me off my steed, save it was a mule and I rolled all the distance down a bank and into the river where I came right up and started laying hands on the rivermen and their women who were holding a carnal cavorting at that spot. Had to knock heads together, considerably, and fight my way through them while praying, but when I got them on my side both them and their doxies too, carrying clubs and lead-lines for convincers, roved the land snatching evil-doers from the jaws of the pit. I was gifted with strength that has stayed with me from that day to this . . ."

His tone was a bee-buzz now, off in the day. I thought, quiet, how it reminded me a fleck of Sammy Spelvin, except Sammy was just touched and lorn, the Lord never having visited him. I mused how the afflicted and the gifted are a lot alike in general functioning. Was glad Ap Miller was gifted. Then I was off on the champion track again, only now a blue black wind had come up—I was in a sulky behind Grayboy, and the roaring wind had lifted him up and was scudding him along high above the dirt of the track, and in the sulky I was barely hanging onto his lines and soaring behind his streaming tail like a gull, while down below crowds of people yelled that I should get off the track and go to jail in Dango Falls, Alabama, because I had Gary Willis's blood on my hands; the only person on my side was French, who was down below, the Gypsy dress a warm light as she held her hands up to me, her hair a dark cloud of fire, and begged me to come down.

I came awake.

Could tell right off from the way the arbor-shadows slanted that it was later. The Plott-hound was asleep, an ear twitching as it got rid of a gnat. With his large head back against the trellis on the other side of this arbor, Ap Miller was sleeping, his pure white beard spilling down his front and his fingers laced around it as if it was a mighty sheaf of white gold silk that needed guarding. I stood, stretching—hadn't realized how much I needed some sleep—and took out the watch. I'd wound it after breakfast. It was three-ten, and it didn't lie. I shut the case, pressed the spring-butts, and its small gold chimes said three. Ap Miller opened his eyes. He got up, a full head higher than I am, and grinned and creased the sleep-signs out of his eye-corners with his forefingers. "Slept right through noon dinner, Mister Broome. If you want to join me, I can give you collards and hot biscuits, and some bear-meat I've got in the cooling house. But I can tell from your eyes you're set about other pursuits. I'll go around the corner, after supping, and tell my baptism folks they'll have to hold off from grace till suppertime. And I'll be at the rails of the trying track at four. I give you the hull force of the Lord's blessing, as it passes through me and charges the earth with glory."

He clapped me on the back—I wouldn't want to have been sudden-converted by him, it would be a wringing process—and stood watching while I said good-bye and left the arbor and hurried past the sleeping house and the yaw-boarded Miller church and out on the Church Block again. When I came to Sutton Road all the noise of it hit me quick and warming, as if my blood was full of bubbles; and just as I got up to the gate of the trying track, here through the crowd, napped head bobbing like a ball of wool and stick-arms held stiff and hands curling around the lines as if they were riveted to the line-ends—which had been freshly wrapped in waxed thread—came W. M., in the good sulky, with Grayboy pulling it tight and smooth, a whole range of mountains in his glittering and beauty, beside the foothills of horses waiting at the track-side. Heads turned to follow him and W. M., but W. M. wasn't looking at anything but Grayboy. French was walking toward me on the near flank of the sulky. With the least cluck of his tongue and a light line-jerk, W. M. stopped Grayboy. The harness was so shined it made the eyes smart. He said, still looking plumb ahead, "Didn't want to bring him out till three-thirty; I didn't want these folks poking around him. But he told me he'd stand good and wait quiet if I'd let him out of the shed earlier. I believe him. You walk the other track like I said?"

"Sure," I murmured. "It's got a tilt to it all right."

"Didn't I tell you? You ain't been loading your belly down with rich foods?"

"Didn't have but a few grapes." I took French's shoulder, and gave her a brushing smack on the cheek.

W. M. said without turning his attention one hair from Grayboy's crupper, which stood high above him, "I took that gall off his elbow; come away with stump-water, I got the water from back of Mama

Gatchin's in her yard. Seems to me you'd have tended to it long before now.''

He said it as though he'd found and signed the Declaration of Independence after some simple soul who couldn't read had misplaced it. As people started circling closer around us, he kept his eyelids half shut and his face unmoving, as if he was carved of ebony, and the carving was so big it took in the whole sky from horizon to horizon. Exactly that removed, and proud, and still.

# 34

There was an open-ended horse shed alongside the trying track, the only shed they had here to keep the testing horses from the sun, but a pigeon-chested animal was already in it, waiting, a horse that looked to me like a plain American saddle horse, good enough but not created for trotting or pacing with a sulky. W. M. drew Grayboy just a little forward, near the shed; around him people were swarming closer, and when a man in a green coat and a straw skimmer—which had a bite out of its rim—reached a red hand to pat Grayboy on the flank, W. M. said sharp and soft, "He'll take your arm off, you do that. Mean as poison.''

The man jerked his hand back and was quick to inform the persons around him that Grayboy was a killer. So most of them stood back respectfully, waiting for him to kill somebody else. Grayboy must have been wondering, I was thinking, why all these people didn't lay hands on him; he never minded being patted. French had a blanket over one arm; I hung it on the trying track fence for her, and noted that the steady wind was still coming out of the north. The trying track was laid out with the oval paralleling the oval of the champion track; from high above, if you'd been a hen-hawk, you would have seen their fences separated by a wide street and two fields, as though they were big eggs facing the same way in the same nest. I put a foot on the lower rail of the trying track near the gate, and watched as a cloud of dirt-dust signaled that the man who was trying out now was on the backstretch; he went wheeling along there, and rounded the far turn and then came up, slow as clabber clotting, it appeared to me, into the homestretch; he came under the wire, finally, and the time-trial judge nearest me looked at his watch and said, "Three twelve." The driver turned his animal, a light bay gelding, a 'Bred but not anything to write to your Aunt Minnie about in rapt enthusiasm, and came back slow; the man was sweating as much as the horse, and had his head down watching the ground run back between the shafts. A little pink-skinned man in a silk shirt and a chirky driving cap. The trial-judges' helpers opened the gate and the bay 'Bred came out, the driver grunting when they told him the time, and then vanishing with his sulky and horse into the crowd. At my side, French said, "I had a little conversation with Manny Gatchin. Did you know, Tom, she wants to go to Seldin—that's a town downstate on the big river—to school? Her aunt and uncle live there; it's her great wish to get an education while living with them, and then to teach school when she graduates. But Mama Gatchin thinks it's a flighty notion. But Mama Gatchin admitted that if Manny did get a chance to go, she could make out by bringing in somebody to help for toting privileges and board."

She knew how I was feeling. She was talking just as calmly as though my turn for the trial-track wasn't coming up in a few minutes. Hardly anybody had been at the rail to watch the last man finish. I wondered if anybody would remain at the rail to watch Grayboy finish. No matter how irked I might feel from time to time about W. M.'s proprietorship of him, I knew too he was in the best shape he'd ever been. Could tell it every time I took a sidewise glance at him standing quiet, at his speaking eye and his long beautiful neck—a long neck that balanced the rest of him as if all this flesh and blood was also a machine set to do a miracle. For his great size he was the most carefully balanced beast I'd ever seen. I knew if I were just catching sight of him for the first time I'd have sucked in my breath and felt a pang of envy for whoever owned him, a pang that wouldn't ever leave me in my lifetime. I said, "Well, it would be nice to help Manny Gatchin. Though right now all we've got is what I'll wager on Grayboy if he makes this trial. Plus a little I'll save out to pay our board and room and get us back to Lanceton."

At that, French took my hand. She held it tight, and we didn't say anything more while we waited for the horse under the open-ended shed, and his driver, to come out. The trial-judges and their helpers motioned the man to hurry it up, they were impatient and sick of the ragtag and bobtail of track-tryers, and the pigeon-breasted saddle horse hoping to be a fast trotter came out of the shadow, and through the gate and onto the track. The track-gate snapped shut. One of the judges consulted the man's entry-slip, found it in order, and motioned the man—a man with bottom-land-farmer written all over him, from the seams in his cheeks which were still touched with soil even the best soaping couldn't bring out, to the tips of his crabbed fingers holding the line-ends—to go down near the far turn and start back. Which was a good fair start, so he could get up to full gait by the time he was under the wire and they started clocking him. The sulky he sat on didn't appear to me to run quite true, it had a skewed wheel on the right, I thought, but I reckoned it would last the trying mile. The starter hollered to ask if the man was ready, and he called back, hoarse-throated, that he was. And the starter shouted, "Go!" and the horse lunged into the harness, but by the time it came up under the start-wire it wasn't into any pace, or trot, or even a canter—it was just doing a gait that wasn't quite a half-gallop, and that made the sulky rock back and forth as if it was pulling a stone-sled over uneven ground. A slick-moustached man near us, with celluloid collar and stiff-starched cuffs, leaning on the rail the other side of French, laughed soft and shook his head. "Poor bastard," he said.

French said quick, though quiet, "He has paid his entry fee, he is entitled to his try."

The watcher tipped his hat to her. "Sorry for the language, ma'am. I make it a point to be at the rail for all the trials. I did not mean to poke fun at this sorry performance. I was chuckling more in pity than in malice. As an observer of human nature—a journalist, a whilom writer—I find much to be sad about—and much grist for my pen—in exhibitions of this type." He had an accent that wasn't South, but wasn't quite Yankee either. A sort of general word-shaping, which I'd last heard from a trader who'd come down Alabama way with a string of western mustangs. Not one of the mustangs was worth its keep, but they were remarkable vicious and high-strung animals. "My name is Bret Harte," he said. "Again, my apologies for offending you in any manner."

She flashed him a smile, and a nod, and then we just watched the pigeon-breasted wonder carry the bottomland-farmer the rest of the distance around the mile. I noticed in a few side-glances now that W. M. was bringing Grayboy into the tunnellike shed. W. M.'s feet fell quite a distance short of reaching the racks. The people who'd been admiring Grayboy—quite a stir of them by now—stayed outside the shed, not wishing to be confined with a possible murdering horse. W. M. as he disappeared from the sunlight into the shed's shadow had his head so high I feared he might develop a stiff neck and never be able to look earthward again. The Forman-Robbins sulky had such a glow to it I was sure he'd washed it even though it had looked splendid when it had left the rental-stall. I gave French's hand an extra squeeze, then pushed myself away from the rail and went over to the shed. As I ducked into it, it came to me I hadn't yet informed French of the point that we were going to be married again on the next Monday, but I was fairly sure Ap Miller would suit us both. Hadn't yet seen him in the crowd, but I caught sight of the nose-bothered man who'd been behind me in the entry-fee line this morning; he was just drawing up close to the shed, with the mare he'd talked of pulling him in a battered but serviceable sulky; the mare had had her cannons fired, I could see the singe-marks at thirty feet. "Hey, Johnny!" he called to me. He hadn't yet seen Grayboy. "Got your pacing nag all set, hey? Join me in a drink afterward, we'll drown our sorrows!"

I flapped a hand to him and stepped in farther and faced Grayboy. W. M.'s eyes looked larger than usual in this resin- and horse-smelling gloom. He waited till I came up beside him, then handed me the line-ends—he'd bound them as neat as the withes around little baskets—and lifted himself from the seat. I got up on it. Out on the trying track the sun looked brighter from here than it did outside, a million sun-motes falling into the bright air past the track-end of the shed. I could hear the hoofs of the saddle horse pulling the shaking sulky as they came beating, in no regular rhythm, around off the backstretch and onto the far turn.

"No, he ain't got nothing to run against," W. M. said low-voiced, as if he was going straight on with a conversation we'd started a while back, or as if he was reading what I was saying in my head. "But don't let that faze you in any degree. Just let him off the bit early as possible, before the wire, he'll bust ahead then. Bear in your mind he don't have to do no better than two-six—which don't mean you got to hold him in if he's doing better. Against another horse he might shave maybe five seconds off what he does now, but we can't help that—all we got to do is let him go. I told him this is nary to worry about, just a show-off spin. He got it down cold, he wants to move out and show off. Go close to the inside, from the pole on out, but let him see me good when he comes around into the homestretch. Bring him home all the way, let him go damned near the near turn before you bring him back."

I was sitting the sulky seat, feeling the close-bound line-ends. W. M. drifted over under Grayboy's head. I couldn't hear what he was saying then as he stared up, he was talking so easy, but it sounded gladsome and soothing at one and the same time. Grayboy twitched his ears, and more sun-motes drifted down and back over his hide, dancing there in front and above me. Then I could hear the track-gate cracking back, and, leaning, I could see the saddle horse pulling the beaten-down sulky, whose right wheel tilted more than ever, and the man on the sulky set-faced as he brought the horse out. A starting helper was yelling. W. M. stepped away from Grayboy's head. I clucked to him and lifted the lines and dropped them just a shade and he moved on out, the tires of the sulky rolling in a little grit on the shed-floor then hitting the dirt beside the gate as I turned him, and I could feel W. M.—though I didn't move my head—watching us from the shed's cavern.

The trial-judge who took my entry-slip looked at it twice, then back and up to Grayboy; I could smell the sweat-patches of his striped shirt over the oil-and-wood smell of the sulky and Grayboy's own light sweat of glistening readiness. The trial-judge said, "Looks more like it," and folded the entry-slip and put it away. "Damn, I thought we wouldn't get another comer today. If he is a comer." The trial-judge spat and motioned me on. I took Grayboy out to the track. Another judge stood by, cocking his eyes at Grayboy, whistling through his teeth. The starter called, as if he was fed to the chin with calling it, "Take him down to the far turn then bring him back a couple of yards." But he was eyeing Grayboy as the others had. As if maybe the drought of horseflesh had ceased and there was a spate of storm coming. But as if he'd hoped it before only to have his hopefulness dashed. I clucked again, and we started clockwise past the judges and the starter and the timer and their helpers as the track-gate swung shut. From my left eye-tail I could see French back there, and the journalist chap with his elbows on the rail near her, and then a line of other people coming to the railing, and the man with the cold and his leg-burned mare pulling up closer to the shed, his mouth open now but his nose presumably still stopped up. Grayboy's haunches moved as if he was swimming with the breeze that blew along the track at our backs. Then we were at the far turn, lonesome down here by ourselves, and, like the journalist fellow, I had pity in me for anybody who'd come out here without a true horse and on just a trust and a prayer. The breeze started to push against my right cheek and blow my shirt on that flank, and swayed Grayboy's tail a shade to the left, and I kept to the inside rail for a few more steps, then turned him to the left and we made a half-circle, the sulky making no noise under me except for its tires, and I brought him back into the wind; he hoisted his head as if he wanted to whinny, but only snorted. I could see W. M. now, sitting the rail between French and that Harte fellow and the bulk of the crowd. Even from here W. M.'s eyes felt like augers. The starter, standing on the track at the outside rail right under the wire, so its shadow stretched from his toes straight across the track, cupped his lips and his mouth made a dark small hole behind his hands and he called, "Ready?"

"Ready!" My voice didn't sound like mine, it could have been just any voice reaching from space against the breeze.

Grayboy loosed another snort; a black caterpillar hunched its woolly way along the top of the inside railing nearest to me; I could see every hair of it against the sun in this one second.

"Go!"—the voice started far off, but even as it sounded I brought the lines down in a light slap and it was closer, so the last of it seemed drawn out into "oooo," and then all the sound, even of the promenade street and the street of the hawkers behind it, was blocked out by the noise of Grayboy's plates. And ahead, the starter had vaulted back over the rail, out of any danger of interference, but he wouldn't have had to, there was plenty of room, we were skimming along the inside rail. I'd forgotten since the last time I'd been up on a sulky and behind Grayboy what a difference this was from any other kind of racing in the bounden world; my muscles and the tips of my fingers and my bloodstream had kept all the remembrance, though, and for about two seconds as we came up under the start-wire I wanted to yell, but didn't. But the wish was there, as a singer sings for the fun of hearing it even with nobody else around, as Jantil played his Gypsy instrument, and mostly, as Grayboy paced. He had his full gait at least a dozen beats before we hit the start-wire, and even while French and W. M. and then the rest of the crowd along the rail went flashing by, I could feel the pacing move into my ears and flesh as though it rocked and sang in a music I'd been away from far too long.

Oh, a trotter trots, and there's always the breath of a second when the trotter has all his feet off the floor of the world at once, but a pacer flies. His near fore and near back move together, as though he's flinging himself with every ounce of strength he has into the teeth of gravity, and then his off fore and off back are joining in, and it is a flow like an eagle soaring, like a great dance which is performed half the time off the ground, and the double *chug* and rhythm of it make that music and you feel yourself fly harder, quicker, with every double beat. Against the wind we were boring now, it was the only challenger, streaming around us; then we were in the near turn, the sky itself seeming to wheel on a pivot as we made it, the inside rail flickering white and swift as a stark long serpent uncoiling and the breeze pouring from the right again and then, around the turn and into the backstretch, with the wind all at our backs.

I was talking to Grayboy now—whatever W. M. felt about that, I had to—and singing snatches of "Was an old man, had a wooden leg, no tobacca could he borrow, no tobacca could he beg," and laughing at him as he stretched, my voice moving to him on the shunt of the wind, his ears laid back to catch it. The backstretch might have been a road we could go on swallowing for all time, gulping it up. Our shadows in the four o'clock sun went spinning high over the outside rail, all across the track-bed, then they were sliced off as we came around into the far turn, the wind slapping from the left and spreading Grayboy's mane on his right and backward as he soared and stepped, stepped and soared, the inside rail streaming and ribboning by. And into the homestretch, flecks of his sweat blew back against my face, he was breathing like a giant in love with the act of taking breath; his head was up and he was slugging it up and forward with all his weight into the harness, I could feel him seeing W. M. on the rail past the wire. Then the wire was past as if it had never been there to start with, and I was pulling the lines just a touch at first, then stronger, letting him ease down, the pacing flowing slower and slower with each lunge, till we were almost into the near turn again. I brought him down, and checked him, and turned him; and we were moving back, and over the humming of the tires now and his hoof plates spurning the earth slower, I could hear the noises of the town of Yadkin again. But Yadkin wasn't as it had been before for me and for French and for W. M. and for Grayboy. No matter what happened it wouldn't be the same again. The Yadkin Fair and the Yadkin harness racing were, right now, in the living instant, ours.

I licked a dab of dust off my lips, and wiped my face on my sleeve. Through all the clamor and action of the people on the other side of the railing, I saw W. M. sitting like a little dark rock on the rail, hunched. When we came past him he gave one slight smile as he'd done that first time I saw him in a pin-oak tree at the Pharis track when he was about to lave down the quarter-breed named Bombo. Then I was at the gate, and the trial-judge who'd let me on the track and the timer had their heads together, then the judge brought his head up and said, flat and cool but with a heat of wonder behind it, "Two minutes, one second. Quickest next to Charley." He gave me an official slip of paper which he'd signed. The timer reached for my hand, and was pumping it up and down, and across at the entries-building, attracted by the noise, men and women were coming down the steps and running this way. French got caught in their eddy, and was carried along toward the gate, her Gypsy dress swirling like a spring-budding field of laurel in a gale. Behind her and upraised over the bobbing heads of the rest of the crowd showed the lion-head of Ap Miller, Rev., his goose-down-white beard jouncing as he made long strides. Then I could hear what he was singing. Boomed out as if the whole Yadkin Fair band was blasting, and folks faded back for a moment at the sound. He came to the gate alongside French, and laid his heavy, rich-knuckled hands on it, and kept on singing, "On Jordan's stormy banks I stand—and cast a wishful eye—at Caanan's fair and happy land—where my possessions lie!" On the *Caanan* he drew it out as if it was all the rebels trying for Little Round Top through smoke and shell. French leaned over the rail, just looking at me. Then W. M. had worm-and-elbowed his way around many knees and pockets, and stood up lower, also holding to the gate. His tone reached me all right. "Come on out of there now, git over to the betting stalls. As owner you got first rights 'fore the rest of this mess climbs aboard the Jordan train." He had the blanket ready for Grayboy. I took one more brisk breath, savoring just the four o'clock rose-touched evening's moment, hearing the hoof-music and wishing it could have lasted, then the gate was opening and I touched Grayboy forward through it, into the crowd.

# 35

Minutes like that never last; you can roll them over your tongue later, but you don't get back the full savor of them because life just sweeps you along with it; you have to value them for what they were, and be glad they came.

This one was already gone, with French and I and even solid and not-to-be-pushed Ap Miller cresting along with the crowd toward the betting stalls. Back at the outside of the trying-track gate, W. M. had thrown the blanket around Grayboy—Grayboy's head swung around to me, as if he was asking with his inquiring eyes if we couldn't go back to the trying track and take another spin—and climbed onto the sulky-seat. He called out, raising his tone over the jabber and jumble of the crowd, "The stall with the red door!" So that was where I headed, the crowd trailing me and French being steered ahead of me with my hands on her elbows, and Ap Miller right behind us. I caught sight of the man with the leaking nose and the leg-fired mare; he'd driven the mare out of the waiting shed and was craning around to look first at Grayboy, and then over at me as I surged along at the arrowhead of this mob, and right now he and the mare were all by themselves beside the trying track. Up the steps leading to the betting stall with the scarlet-painted door we all swept, and then we were inside, though there was room for only about ten customers in this cubicle. At least twenty-five had sardined themselves in. I picked up French, swinging her by the waist, and set her on the counter in front of me and stood protecting her from being knocked over even that counter in the flurry and crush of the people behind us. And Ap Miller whirled around, shoving away those who were bellying in close, holding his hands out as if he kept off wolves and demons, and shaking his fine old head so his beard made a half-turn to north and south as he spoke. Or as he thundered. I'd have bet when he stood in the pulpit of the Miller Church he made the rafters tremble and the bell-tower quake. The force of his speech sent people falling back from him, so we finally had a slightly cleared space around us here. "Greed!" he roared. "The worship of the golden calf! Are you monkeys from the forests of steaming equatorial Africa that you must make fools of yourselves over a few possible dollars? By the Lord, it sickens me—fair makes my stomach crawl—to see you hasten to lay down your cash before the odds change! A little forbearance here, now—a little human probity—a little gentility in your attitude—step back there, sir, or I'll fling you back—none of you act as though you've ever sat a church-pew or bent your heads before the Lord's wrath!" He'd spread his arms; I stood behind one, French sat with her beautiful legs swinging from the counter behind the other massive arm.

Things were hushing down, a mite. Through the chink-window behind the counter I could see W. M. driving Grayboy away from the trying track, and past the entries-building. He was the head of another streaming crowd—people who wouldn't bet, because they didn't have enough money to, but who just wanted to follow Grayboy as he moved along slow and silver gray and again like a whole mountain-range in this westering sunlight. W. M. resembled a black king's child leaving a coronation ceremony. Behind and around him walked a lashing of other black children, some white children mixed with them as they chattered and followed. And a whole lot of men and women interested only in horse-flesh, watching Grayboy as careful as if he was a fresh comet that had come down out of the blue day to amaze them. The black children were the kind you always see around stables; I reckoned some of them were attached to the stables of Charlemagne and General Bedford and Star-born—little boys who between times of swabbing out and forking hay and walking out and rubbing down would spend their time playing coon can and pitty pat for pennies. The back door of this betting stall opened, and a man wearing a green eyeshade rushed in and said, over the muttering of the crowd in here, "Jed! They got it chalked up—add Grayboy to the champ-track bets!"

Another man, also head-bedecked in a green eyeshade, put his head up from behind the counter, coming up gradual as if he was emerging from some vasty deep, and straightening the tabs of his floral vest. "Grayboy? Who's the owner, Murphy?"

Murphy, whose hair was slicked down with about a gallon of bear-grease or gentian pomade, said, "A certain T. Broome—spelled with an *e* on the tail. Nobody knows a thing about him, or the horse neither. Two minutes and one. Makes it a four-horse champ race, at this late date! Who'd have thought it?" He spread his fingers on the counter beside Jed, two of the fingers adorned with goodsized yellow diamonds or something that sparkled like them. Maybe polished quartz. He looked out around Ap Miller's baptizing-coat-covered back, as if taking a peek at a crowd of tigers. "Je-sus! Wondered why I couldn't get in the front door—thought mebbe you was bein' mobbed by some crusadin' army!"

Ap Miller wheeled himself around, long arms extending behind him to beat the crowd back again if needful, and said in the voice of Moses announcing the arrival of a vision, "Do you intend to open up for business, Martin Murphy and Jedidiah Corum—or do you intend to stand there wambling until *I* prove to you that *I* am a one-man crusadin' army, and usher these folks over to another stall?"

"Oh!" said Jed. "Reverend Miller, I might have knowed you'd have a weather eye out for a new horse on board. If you'll just kindly go right on assisting us in handling this bunch, we'll have 'em step up, one at a time, and place their bets. You can go first, naturally, you bein' just about number one in line, and us always happy to handle the clergy's little flyers into improvin' the breed. Odds will be—" He screwed up his eyes and thought. "No odds, an even bet, on this here, what's the name again?

Grayboy. No odds, another even bet, on Charley, same as it was, and two to one on General Bed, and three to one on the Kentucky flash— Starborn.''

Ap Miller brought his arms forward, and grabbed a tuck in Jed Corum's floral vest, and pulled him halfway up the inside of the counter. "Oh, sly are the connivings of Belial and his sons! You know as well as you know your own name, the owner has first crack! And that odds will *not* be posted or offered until the owner has been allowed to place his bet— which will *not* be at no odds, I do assure you! Now, boys—'' His voice got softer, rounder, almost purring, "You know danged well what the rules are, set down by the race committee year before last. On account of thee's no purse offered here, and we wouldn't have these lovely animals in Yadkin if we didn't give their owners and drivers some little inducement to go to the expense and tribulation of bringin' 'em here in the first place. It'll take me about two minutes to run over to the committee, in my capacity as a man gifted by tongues and secure in the arms of the Lord, and tell 'em what kind of bucket shop you all think you're runnin' here, and shut you down after you've paid off ever' last cent's already been pilin' up in your safe. From Nemo, a peak on Mount Pisgah, will I proclaim your treachery! This is a horse even more unknown than Starborn, comin' right out of the blind blue, and you got to take your chances, time or no time!'' He gave Jed a shake that made the eyeshade jump. "Understood?'' he added in his more dulcet-turning tone. He let go of the vest, and Jed stood back.

"Give it to 'im, Ap!'' called a man in a crushed plug hat just behind the reverend.

"Quiet, you slaverin' sinnin' itcher after wealth and forgetter of your duties to wife and child and hearth,'' said Ap, mildly. To this Martin and Jed he said, "Well?''

Jed glanced at Martin, and Martin glanced at Jed, and Jed plucked his underlip. "All right, Reverend Miller. As you say, it's the ruling; we'll abide by it. Can't blame us gettin' carried away, with all this ruction comin' on us sudden, and bets ain't been rife since yesterday. But where's the owner, and who'll vouch he *is* the owner?''

Ap Miller wheeled to me, and lifted me around as easily as if he was hoisting a long picking-bag of cotton. He placed one hand on my hat's crown. "Mister Tom Broome, a friend of long standing. And Mrs. Broome,'' he said with a good deal of gallantry in it, bowing a little to French, and at the same time tipping me a very quiet wink. "I ain't yet had the pleasure of being introduced to Mrs. Broome, but I've known her husband through several negotiations and can attest to his probity and character throughout Alabama. Mrs. Broome, I am Apollodorus Miller, of the first and only Miller Church, and your husband has set up an important meeting—a meeting whose import is of the first water serene to both of you, and will be all your lives—for Monday at five, when all the heats are run and the town is coming back to nearly normal. Do you take my meaning?''

French was looking at him, amused and even a little delighted, and then back to me, and swinging her legs from the counter. I told her with my eyes that yes, it was true, we were going to be married then. Twice-married, if you wanted to put it that way, but safe then in the eyes of all the nation. She gazed back at Ap Miller, her face like a tea-rose and her smile growing, and said, ''I am charmed, Reverend Miller. I shall be gratified to be part of that meeting.''

''One of the two most important parties in it,'' said Ap; he swung back to Jed and Martin. ''Made up your minds, boys?''

Martin Murphy spraddled his ring-winking fingers on the air. ''Mister Broome,'' he said to me, ''let's get the bad news over. I won't go higher, no matter if Reverend Miller slings me out of this stall straight through the window; we can't afford it. But Jed and me'll give you the same odds Starborn—the dark horse—has got—three to one. And that's bending pretty far for us; it's the difference between two minutes and half a second and two minutes one second. Half a second isn't a damned thing, it don't signify Charley's better'n your—Grayboy. A hair's as good as a furlong when it comes down to the wire, but it's still a hair. Take it, or leave it?''

Jed said, ''And it's a straight two to one to everybody else, and that takes in all three champion heats, right down the line. No money on just tomorrow's heat, or Sunday's, or Monday's—the full bag right now. That's the way we been doin' it for all the other horses, and even if your animal should take two heats and lose the third, and do worse time than the best time of all three, you'd lose your wad. All or nothing, Mister Broome—and Mrs. Broome—three to one for you, and—'' He swallowed. ''—two to one for the rest of these folks. Taking it?''

I said, ''Not unless you give the three-to-one odds on Grayboy to Reverend Miller right along with me.'' I leaned on the counter. ''Seems to me you boys have got this wrapped up, going and coming. I reckon it's in the rules committee's book that you can make the three champion heats a lump, with one horse taking all and the rest going home with nothing but the joy of runnin', but that by itself's a mighty gamble. It sure sweetens the big pot, but it doesn't leave any small ones to spread around. So the least you can do is put Reverend Miller's money right where mine is, in the three-to-one class. If you don't like it, I'll run right along to this committee with my old friend and companion Reverend Miller, and we'll see if we can raise some sand.''

I turned my eyes to Ap Miller. "Providing Reverend Miller wants it that way," I said.

His dark-timbered voice was back. "I do, Mister Broome. I made up my mind about four seconds after I'd seen you move out under the starting wire. Gentlemen!" He was arching above them like the form and face of a prophet leaning from a chariot in a cloud. "What is your story?"

Jed Corum said, "Oh, Cripus, Reverend, you've got no pity on the wicked. We'll do it."

And Martin Murphy shrugged and signaled a yes.

I knew almighty well they thought I was a flash in the powder pan; they were just like every other track-stall gambler I'd ever seen, but with Ap Miller's great help they were giving us the best we'd get at the fair. Ap Miller nudged me—I told myself if I ever went so far as to get baptized with him, to learn to hold my breath, it was a severe nudge—and I got all the money I'd won from the quarter of the Pharis pot, and the picayune amount I'd started out from Dango Falls with, and put them together, which did make a good amount, and kept back only enough to pay Mama Gatchin and buy feed and essentials on the road back to Lanceton, and pushed the rest over to Jed and Martin. They took it and gave me a ticket for it. Then Ap Miller was hoisting his wad from a much-worn poke, the long kind which will hold four plugs of tobacco and a wedge of rind-cheese as well as folding money, and slapping it on the counter. When his bet was laid and he had the proof of it in his hands and the ticket tucked away in the poke, he stood back and returned the poke to one of the bagging pockets of his baptizing coat, beamed at me and at French, and turned to the crowd, which was still milling and had even received some extra members by now. "You had by rights ought to offer us all a bonus, the Broomes and me," he told Jed and Martin. "Look at the trade we are delivering unto you!" Then he faced the crowd and held up his hands. "I forgive you all for your unseemly and unrighteous shoving and slobbering. Kindly allow the lady to march out first, and remove your hats in her presence, or have them removed by me." He steered French out before him, and I went along right after them. In the quick warm evening outside it was good to breathe the smells of dinner already on the breeze, and the heated horse and the dust's pungence, and hear the people back at the Corum-Murphy stall send up a low cheering for Ap Miller, who'd raised the odds on Grayboy their way, while raising his and French's and mine even a notch higher than that.

Miller held me by a shoulder, and French by one of hers. "I am sorely behind in the work for which I am appointed," he announced. "Can't let it shrivel up, the earth in these parts would be a sty packed with Gadarene swine if I evermore laid down on the job. My dear," he said to French, "you are even better'n your man's enthusiasm told me you would be; I compliment him from the heart on his choice. I'll take time off my tribulations with the unregenerate to be at the champion track tomorrow. We go forth to battle together, loins girded and souls washed and willing." He planted a kiss on the top of French's head. Slapped my chest, and stalked off, going as if he bore a lot of poundage on his shoulders but carried it with a handsome flair.

I put my hat on again, pushing it rearward. "He's the man," I said, nodding. "Monday at five. I reckon your brass ring will do well. There's a certificate that goes with the ceremony; you can frame it and hang it back at Chantry Hall."

We took hands and swung our way through the people, and I felt a lot of them remarking about us now. Not so much the looks they gave us—word spreads like wildfire around any track when it's word of a crack performance, and here at Yadkin Fair it went twice as swift—but that these looks said something respectful about Grayboy as well. Daddy would have enjoyed that.

The promenaders were at it, even more thick-massed around the town square, and the band was blatting away, and when we got to the hawkers' street, the sales-stalls had folks lining six-deep around them. My Teague-bullet crease was itching more than it had, so I was glad when we got back to Mama Gatchin's back lane and I could leave French at the shed, beside which W. M. was saddling and hitching Bell to the jenny to take to the Anderson Millinery Shop where he'd help her garner in customers. The marigold leaf poultice makings were in the big saddlebag; I got the room-key back from French. I told them I'd be a minute, and W. M. looked around from where he was buckling the girth of the Spanish saddle, and said, "You get odds?"

"Three to one."

"I've heard worse. Mister Grayboy's plates will do for the running tomorrow. Then when he wins we'll take him to the smith. Only one good smith here in this town, though there's four or five smithies."

I glanced in through the barred shed window at Grayboy; he was chewing corn. Just as if he hadn't given the best solo harness-running of his life up to this time, not long ago. Russet light fell through the bars on his neck and shoulders and barrel, turning part of the slate gray to bronze. If he'd been quite a bit whittled down in size he'd have had the contour of one of those Spanish-Barbary horses I'd always heard about—the golden horses that were lost in ages gone. But he wasn't gold, he was all alive with his muscles lax in the shed's heat and his eye rolling to me in comfort. French was fussing at the flying jenny, fondly, brushing what road-dust had got on it while we were coming here off the flanks of the carved horses, and their color made a rainbow in the lane. In spite of the tickling itch of the Teague remembrance, I felt like bounding, as if I was about ten again and had just got out of the Dango Falls school. I went around Mama Gatchin's house past the chinaberry trees, and in the front door and up the stairs; I was passing through the stained-glass window light of the second landing when Manny Gatchin came down the hall and said, "Mister Broome?" She said it shy and nervous-mouthed, her eyes sizing me up in the strange light. Her apron hadn't improved from breakfast to now. Didn't believe she'd had time to change it, or even take it off.

"Manny?"

"Mister Broome, there's a visitor in your room. I didn't want to let him in at first, but he—he's been powerful about it. I had such a good talk with Mrs. Broome today—she's a gracious lady, she is surely—I wouldn't want to do anything either of you wouldn't like. But this man, he says he knows both of you."

"Say who his name was, Manny?"

"No, but he's somebody important."

Which could cover Sheriff Planteu, I thought, or Doc Mattison, or even Grody Flieshacker, and Howard Markley, and certainly Mayor Marcus Westerfield. Though I didn't think it was any of them.

I told her thanks for her trouble, and went on up the stairs, not bounding this time.

The door to the under-eave room was half ajar, and I saw him reflected in the sun-splintering bureau mirror before he saw me. So I had time to take in a breath. He had his glossy top hat on one knee, and his boots with their equal gloss planted firm on the floor, and his Tattersall vest without a wrinkle in it taut under his box-shouldered riding coat—a gray coat this time—and he was looking out of the window over the enormous four-barreled canopied bed's spread into the treetops, and he could have been the Day of Judgment as summed up by the vanished South. He only moved his head, didn't stir otherwise in the chair, when I stepped in.

"Evening, Major Deveraux," I said.

# 36

The room itself shone and sparkled; I thought French—maybe with Manny's help—must have cleaned it up to suit her feelings about it while I was conferring with Ap Miller. But it was only a boardinghouse room with a steep-pitched ceiling and no doubt, I also thought, appeared to Major Jack Deveraux as the deeps of depravity. For just a hissing in of breath I debated telling Deveraux to get up and go, to leave our home, such as it was. But it would have been just the kind of bravado-brass he expected from me. I recalled French's saying that he placed me in a class with the Teague Yahoos.

So I just said, "Haven't seen you since Wednesday night, Major. And I wasn't in shape to bid you good-bye then."

"No." His voice was as clipped as ever; and no less freezing. His face was a sun-darkened brick. With lines of tiredness around the eye-corners; I reckoned he'd been doing hard and fast traveling lately. "I made sure you were still alive—a nick on the thigh is nothing, Broome. The Gypsies' remedies are excellent."

"You made sure I was alive," I said slow. "Well, that was nice of you. If I'd needed the services of a doctor, would you have got one?"

The creases in his underjaw—very few of them, for a man of his years—didn't even stir.

"I'm not at all certain of that. You did the earth a favor by despatching that scoundrel, Teague—though as a matter of real truth, he did his own despatching, and all you'd done was ride straight into a trap, for which I'd have had your ears if you'd been in my regiment and had lived through it. But as to saving your life—now you ask me—probably no."

I was leaning back against the bureau top. "It's good to have everything out in the open between us," I said. "You hate my very name—it's hard for you to bring yourself to say it, and you've never used my first name since you first clapped eyes on French and me together. Yes, she's Francia. But her name's also Broome. We got married, you know—Major."

"By whom? And where?"

"By Shangro. At Quincyville—or in a patch of trees near a cotton-barn clearing just outside it. And we're being married again—just to cinch it in the eyes of the public, of which you're a member—this coming Monday, after the last champion-track heat."

He didn't blink. Eyes so blue they were like the high noon blue of the sky over a river-landing. Or the clean blue in a new Confederate flag before it had faded out and been tattered. I could have liked him if I'd ever served with him. To different drumbeats, in another time.

"That is not marriage. The Gypsy rites—" He shrugged. "As to your other wedding plans, I propose to stop them. I have done you the honor—which you do not, of course, appreciate, sir—of coming here to speak to you alone. Had Francia been with you, here in your—chamber —" He looked around as if the place was a river dive. "—I would have asked her to leave, while I talked only to you. Not to appeal to your better nature. I don't think you have one. I've dealt with your kind all my life—it is a mistake to treat you as if you were of a superior class. Not to appeal to your sense of fair play, for I know you have none. But to lay out the facts, and to ask you to step aside while I take Francia back with me—to Lanceton."

I could feel red burning on my cheekbones. He was old, even if he was in splendid shape; I thought I could throw him down the stairs without much straining.

But all I said was, "Watch your tongue, Major. Just watch it. I don't come of landed stock—not the way you mean it, though my father ran quite a few acres of good horse-farm, most of his life after Appomattox. He was a cavalry corporal, and a hell of a good one. I dare say he rode better than you—before he got shot up—and he'd have known enough to take your Amber mare and cure her of goin' in a straight line and being hard to turn on a track."

It was a mean thing to say; I knew what he thought of the Amber mare. But I meant it.

I said, "But maybe she does that because she's stiff, like you. Maybe she's got a pattern fixed in her mind, and can't lift herself out of the old ways. Shangro—I value him as much as any friend I'll ever have—told me you were—patrician, all right. And to be trusted. But he also said somethin' that hit home to me. He said you were a man still in battle—on a battlefield that was empty."

I walked over to one of the saddlebags and opened it, my back to him. He could have shot me while I was bending there. But if he had a pistol—dueling or otherwise—I didn't think he'd shoot me while my back was turned. The creaking of my boots on the old floorboards was the only sound in here. The yammering of the streets of Yadkin came floating here through the sun-blazing window. I got out the marigold leaves and some soft thread and came back through splashes of sun and sat on the bed. Which was goose-down, inches deep, under me. I took off my left boot, and started rolling up my trouser leg.

He stirred—the first time he'd made a motion—and said, "You are wanted by my old friend, Will Planteu—who was Captain Planteu, when we served together. But much more than you, he wants Francia. He—and the entire town of Lanceton—needs to know from Francia's lips what has transpired, the exact truth of the Gary Willis death, why Fountainwood was burned, and the whole sordid reason why she ran off, taking with her the carousel which she had formerly sold to Willis and which had been installed at Fountainwood. I know you had a great deal to do with those—reasons. I have been deputized by Will, to bring Francia back with me. And I am authorized by him—in the name of the County of Lanceton, sovereign state of Mississippi—to allow you to go your way, as long as you yield up Francia without force."

I sat back, looking at him across the sun-spears, and felt in my pocket. Got my fingers on the badge Planteu had deputized me with, and stood up and walked across to Deveraux, and held the badge out to him. "Here's another for your deputizing authority," I said. "I haven't worn it since I promised French I'd help her get her flyin' jenny back from Fountain-wood before it burned."

"How did she know it would burn?" He was leaning forward, not taking the badge. "What did you have to do with its firing?"

"Nothing," I said. "And I don't think it could have been prevented. And I'm saying naught more about that. Please to take the badge—it belongs to Sheriff Planteu, in case you don't want two of them."

I wouldn't have told him anything about Jupiter if he'd stood me up against the wall and whipped me. He took the badge in the tips of his fingers, dropped it into a pocket.

His breath sucked in as I went back to the bed again and sat and rolled my trouser-leg higher. I noted the wound's edges had already shut, and it was less bright. I laid the marigold poultice I'd stripped from it aside, and started kneading the leaves for the new one. Wasn't inspecting Deveraux. His breath made another noise, then he said, "Francia only has to tell the truth. It may or may not shed light on who killed her cousin. He was a field unplowed, gone to rot—if I had known, all these years, she was making out by herself at Chantry, and at his mercy, I'd have—" Again, that stitch of breath.

I said, wrapping the crushed leaves around the wound, and reaching for thread, "You'd have shot him. A huge remedy for all things. Doesn't seem to me in your line of thought—your one-track thought, like your lovely mare's—you're so different from Wesley Teague. You're in love with French, that's plain. I reckon you carried the image of her as she was when she was a little girl, all through the war and all these years after. And you now aim to blast through anything in your path, including me. Just to get her. Well, Major, she's not a little girl anymore. She's a full-grown woman, intelligent and glorious—she's pledged herself to me, a couple of times over, and I trust, and hope, that will stand." My touch on the thread wasn't as skilled as Shangro's, or French's, but it was going to hold. "And," I said, pulling a knot, "I think she wants to be free of all the coddling Planteu and Mattison and the rest have treated her to in Lanceton, all these years. She wants to shake free of her past. I'll tell you just a little about the flyin' jenny. She wanted it mainly because Colonel Robert Chantry had told her, in a last letter from the field, to hang onto it no matter what else happened. Then she'd had to sell it—matter of stayin' alive—to her crazy Goddamned cousin to keep on eating, and she made up her mind to get it back after she found him dead in Chantry Hall. That's about as far as I want to go with information, right now. There are a good many other reasons why she made up her mind, a little later, to show the jenny and run it right here in Yadkin durin' this fair, but they've got to do with knights in armor. And even though you think of yourself as a knight, or something similar, you wouldn't understand that." I made the last knot and patted the poultice. Gazed over at him. "Never in the earth would you understand it, even though I heard you say, not so long back, you liked legends."

There was full silence, drenched in sun, between us.

Then he said, almost to himself, "I talked with, or was talked at by—that lackwit and jobbernowl—Sammy Spelvin—"

"Yes," I said. "A creature with no brain to speak of, who got that way in the war. I reckon you dislike him too, because he's dirty and crazed. When the army stacked its arms and went back to a ruined t'morrow, I reckon it didn't faze you. You just returned to Deveraux Farm, and resumed command. You've got courage and fire, but they're all in-turned—twisted the way my father's hand was twisted when the ball hit it. I'm glad he only got a twisted hand."

He was still speaking mostly to himself. "And I had long ago meant to go down Lanceton way, on some cotton-seed oil business—"

"Oh, hell, Major," I said, rolling my trouser-leg down and leaning to grab my left boot. "Wild boars in your path couldn't have kept you from nosing in this business and being a big part of it. You say you want me to stand aside and let French travel back there with you. Right on the eve of the chance I've got to let Grayboy run the best track he's yet hit, for the best wagers. I need French. She's part of my blood now; we're both strong-minded people, but there's something else that keeps bringing us closer together, and I have hope it may develop in the years ahead. But because I respect her—she says I've made her more *herself,* if that means doodly-squat to you—I'll let her speak for herself. You can put it up to her." I stamped into the boot.

Outside, below, somebody was calling. A firm sharp voice. I walked past Deveraux to the window.

W. M. stood down there, hands on hips, yelling up to me.

I whistled to tell him I could see him.

Deveraux could see W. M. from where he sat, not far from the bureau-edge, though W. M. couldn't have glimpsed Deveraux from down there.

W. M. called, "She wants to know if you're coming along to watch us run the jenny first time. It's getting on toward five-thirty if that turnip-watch of yours has stopped and you don't know it. She says if you wish to rest though, not to bother you and let you go right back to nodding. We can handle the jenny very nice by ourselves."

"I know you can," I called down through the brushing boughs around the window. "Keep right up to snuff, W. M. Don't let her take any lead coin. I'll be along a little later."

He gave a quick nod, and ran off.

"Isn't that Willie?" Deveraux said. "That idiot peddler maundered to me about seeing a child with you and Francia, but—I would have given him a job . . ."

"He says you're too high and mighty for him, Major. He's a very choosy child about who he works for, and he's got reason, considering he was with Teague. He's got horse-hands, little as they are, and a horse-brain, and maybe somethin' else I don't have a name for. Well." I looked down at him. "How did you intend to take French back with you?"

"I have a wagon, and a driver. With ample room for the carousel. The wagon is waiting down at the end of this street."

"And if I can ask a little bit more, who told you we were here at Mama Gatchin's?"

"One of the—" His arched nose, not as high-arched as Shangro's but slimmer, with sharp bone in it, made a wrinkle, and his trim moustache lifted in a quirk, then straightened out. "—the denizens of this house. A Mrs. Catewell, I think she said her name was. I started at the end of the street and visited each—domicile. I reached here an hour since. Mrs. Catewell was on the gallery with some of the other—guests. When I inquired of them if they had seen a lady corresponding to Francia and a man who looked like you, she was kind enough to show great interest. She informed me that in her opinion—which I would not ordinarily value, she is a henwife and a slattern—you were a ruffian, and that the horse you were entering was doubtless stolen. Her words for Francia were shocking. It seemed they had had an altercation earlier today." He sat up higher. I saw a pair of gloves in his right-hand coat pocket, peeking out of the flap. These were yellow dogskin, not white. "A boardinghouse!" he shot out. "A boardinghouse, for Francia Chantry! My God, Broome—there are a couple of houses of ill-fame right along this same street! She has already started the process of being dragged down, by you! A gambler and a wandering horse-man, a half-educated ne'er-do-well who presumes, when I make him a fair offer, to tax me with my own code of honorable conduct—stating that, in his opinion, I am to be classed with the dinosaurs for holding to what I have lived by for sixty-two years!" He had stood up; he was just as tall as I am. "Broome, Robert Chantry would have shot you long before this. Had he been alive and here to witness what I have seen—he would not have been forbearing. Nor would he have countenanced your chatter about her becoming herself—whatever that may mean—nor stood, for a moment, your lies and evasions. It would have struck him through the heart to have heard her speak falsely to me, at

Pharis—to deny her heritage. He would have laid it all at your door, as I do. She has a chance for a genteel, infinitely pleasing life—as my wife, as soon as this folderol in Lanceton has died down. As soon as she has redeemed herself—as she will do—by returning with me, and speaking the truth to those who think wonderfully well of her."

I said, "You plan to propose to her first thing, Major?"

I could feel the red coming up in my cheekbones again, and regretted it.

"No sir. I intend to see her through her travail, as any man worth his salt would have done. To insist that she rejoin her heritage and to call upon her own loyalty to all she represents, to make her do so. We are wasting time. You have no notion of what I have just said. I am flinging words on desert soil. Are you ready to let her decide for herself?"

"That's right," I said. "But don't be too sure I don't understand you, in my ne'er-do-well ignorance. I think I do, and I think you're a little touched—not like Sammy Spelvin, maybe, but just as deep. If I was everything you think I am, I'd have hurled you through that window there before you got half done saying what you've said. Sixty-two years and a veteran be damned, I'd have done it. But I'm not like that, and I'll tell you somethin' more—French isn't what you think she is, either. She's not a magnolia, she doesn't bloom quiet and white on a dark green tree and get admired for it, and turn sickly when somebody touches her or bruises her petals. She's not the flower of your old South, which was always sick at its heart—and I say it who'd have fought for it to the end, and been glad to be old enough to perform that duty. If we'd won, Major, there's a lot of folks who think the way I do, and Daddy did—we'd have stopped all slavery and all the saber-shakin', and settled down to being ourselves, and got along with the North, shameful as some of the North was for a time, and built a fruitful life. And in such a life, you'd still have been what you called it—a dinosaur. Now come along, and ask French what you came to ask her. I'll show you where she'll be running the jenny, and leave you to yourselves."

For just one flash, I got the feeling he'd understood me right clear through. At least his eyes got something in them I'd never seen before; a puzzlement, a willingness to be told. Then it was gone, in a snap, and the eyes were fierce as the points of cavalry sabers again, but a lot more blue.

I still wouldn't have minded serving under him, in that gone time, if I'd never known French, and if I'd been a good deal older. He was just right for leading any raid, and he'd have given all he had, and a little he didn't.

I went to the door and opened it wider. He stood for a second, looking at me; his back was straight as if he posed for a Brady picture, with full regalia and plumes.

Then he passed through the doorway, and I went out after him, shutting the door behind me and taking time to lock it and drop the key back in my pocket. On this top landing the stained-glass window lights shed blobs of tender color over his top hat as he put it on again. As we went on down past the other landings I heard on the northing breeze, which seemed a mite stiffer, the reedy, noble notes of the merry-go-round as it started up.

# 37

When we went out through the front hall there were people gathering around near the dining room door again, attracted by the float of cooking odors on the air; Major Deveraux didn't look toward them, or gaze to left or right for that matter, but stalked straight out to the gallery. But I caught sight of Mama Gatchin, flailing in from the kitchen with a side of roast beef fresh from the oven which was so sizable she could barely handle it in the wooden trough-dish; she set it down on the sideboard and waved at me across the dining room and called, "Hear you surprised 'em, Mister Broome! You surprised *me*! Didn't know any pacer in the South had it in him! You get your sleep tonight, now, and shock 'em again tomorrow, and make us all proud!"

I waved back at her in thanks for her good wishes; some of the men and women clumping around the dining room's doorway gazed at me as those people at the trying track had gazed, as if they were summing me up for the first time and trying to get at the mystery of making good time with a horse; Fred Catewell and his high-flush-faced wife—she still had that slouch hat on—didn't look at me at all, but turned away, Mrs. Catewell with a kind of exaggerated flounce. I went out after the major onto the gallery. He was standing at the bottom of the gallery steps; had the dogskin gloves out of his pocket now, and was holding them with his lean right hand and slapping them into his lean left hand. I joined him and we moved along toward the middle of Yadkin, where the sound of the jenny was clearer along the wind. The major's gaze kept cutting straight in front of him as if he was heading for a redoubt where a batch of Yankees waited with cannon, and he was going to storm them all and leave not a body untouched. His boot heels dug into the dirt of the road as if he was propelled by a brush fire. Down the road drawn up under some of the chinaberry trees and the beech that shadowed this street I saw what must have been his traveling wagon—a slick high-boarded beauty with two blood chestnuts in the harness, and the same Irish-faced young man with carroty hair I'd seen walking out the mare Amber, back in Pharis, sitting on the box. There were dust-patches on the wagon but it was a marvel of wagon-making, with the letters *Deveraux Farm* done in glistering gold on the side.

The breeze was stronger, all right—I wondered how heavy it would be now out along the homestretch of the champion track as it whipped in out of the north. Going against such a wind for a couple of hours could founder a horse, though on the track all it could do was slow him until he came to the backstretch, and I mulled over, a little, what the wind at the rear would do when a person hit that canted, Indian-mound part of the backstretch that couldn't be seen with the naked eye. It was fresh enough through this street and the next as we got over to where all the selling stalls were whooping it up; it was turning all the flags and banners endways on their ropes, and blowing scraps of grit along in dust-devils. We came past the town square where the usual promenaders and gawkers were now huddling on benches and in the lee of the bandstand and on the pavilion steps leading up to its wooden octagonal bulk, Major Deveraux gripping his top hat's brim with the same hand he held the gloves in, and new-fallen dry leaves gusting around the toes of his boots. I pulled my own hat down a shade. Then there ahead on the opposite corner was the Anderson Millinery Shop, with the jenny turning in the center of a mob of children pushing in around it, and Mister Anderson, looking happy and delighted as a whole net full of clams, ushering ladies into his store while the music of the jenny—old-time and strange, icy and yet warming to the marrow-bones—whirled up into the evening wind. Through the jumping legs and bobbing shoulders and quick-motioning heads of the children I could see glimpses of the jenny, the eight horses spinning around in their easy pace, flowing by in flashes of blue and black and yellow and purple with spattered pink spots, and gold and cream and green and bronze. And then French, standing beside it, the breeze pushing her Gypsy gown back against her thighs and bosom, her hair blowing in deep red strands and her face lifted and drinking in the late sun and the valorous wind. W. M. was working close to the merry-go-round; I could tell from his stance he was keeping a weather eye on cheaters and possible twice-riders for one price. The bay, Bell, stood in the mouth of the lane next to the shop, eyes gentle and the Spanish saddle burnished from its notable pommel to its high cantle. I stopped walking. Major Deveraux went on a pace, then halted as well.

I said, "I'll be in this tavern." I jerked a thumb toward the tavern on the corner where we stood—it was enjoying a good steady trade, a smell of bitters and gin and bourbon and old natural popskull wafting out to us from its half-open door, and somebody performing on the banjo inside and a babble of horse-argument going on. "Tell French I'll be here. Please to tell her, too, to step over here and give me the news, one way or the other, when you're done talking to her."

That appeared to wrap it up. He gave me not so much as a nod, though I felt he'd tell her; he wasn't ever going to be a man who wouldn't discharge obligations right down to the frog-hair finest. For one more flap of time he stood, hand on his hat brim, assessing me as if there still might be something about me he, from his eminence, could never pigeonhole; then he cut himself around on a boot heel so fast he could have been presenting the bonny blue colors in front of General Beauregard. He crossed the street, not so much elbowing as just pure washing people out of his way, like a steaming ironclad; he marched straight in front of a surrey, which missed running him down by a whisker of his tight moustache, the mare getting pulled back just in time, the driver bawling. But the driver might as well have bawled to a cavalry regiment that had already gone past the *trot* and *canter* and was well into the *charge*. I stayed where I was till I saw that French had seen him, and that she was standing very still—she saw me too, on this corner, and then was looking all the way at the major again—and then I turned and went in through the doorway of the tavern.

The merry-go-round sound died away, and the noise in here overlaid everything with its boozing freedom. I made my way among chairs and tables, past a faro game which had about twenty people in it, and up to the bar, which was as thick with customers as the jenny was outside. Back of the bar above the bottles was a tarnished gold-framed picture of a harness track, but if it was supposed to be the Yadkin champion track the artist had missed by about three furlongs of paint. The animals in it looked more like French's roundabout horses than they did like true beasts, with those spreading forelegs and the back-shooting hocks, save that they didn't have the grace and carving wit that had gone into the jenny's work. The track in the painting was backed up by fluffy trees that looked as though their foliage was cotton wool. And it appeared to be about six miles around. I got myself into a slot between a couple of serious drink-lappers and when the bartender came along to me, I ordered bourbon. He slapped it down with a fat turn of his wrist, took a swig of the short beer he kept under the pump, puffed the head-cream off his dappled moustache, snibbed up the silver dollar I'd laid on the bar-wood, and said, leaning close to me, "You're Broome. Tested the mile in two, one."

"That's true," I said. "But—"

He bellied closer. Back of us the banjo-player strummed with a meaty hand, playing his idea of "Old Cow Died in the Forks of the Branch." The notes came out flawed and got sucked up in the tiers of smoke drifting to the high tin ceiling, which was a kind of poison green. Over that blatting, the bartender said, "I seen you in Corum and Murphy's today. I laid a good pile on you. You going to show them all up tomorrow, Mister Broome?"

"You didn't lay a cent on me, you laid it on my horse," I said. "And kindly don't noise it around, right now—I don't favor drinks at the hands of all these people." I hadn't meant to be short with him; it was only I didn't want to be wonderfully sociable. The time for that isn't ever the night before a true race. The time for it is when the race is laid away and gone and you can discuss it as free as you please, which won't bring back the running any more than a stereopticon machine will bring back the people or the scenes it shows. But is gut-warming.

He said, "The Reverend Ap sure laid it down in there, didn't he? But I didn't mean to bother you. Just want to know if my money's as safe as I got a notion it is."

I said, "Well, I'm pleased you've got it on Grayboy, but I'm not any surer than you are, friend. And I won't be till Monday—then I can give you a report. If you want something safe you're talking to the wrong coon. You'd ought to know a trial heat could be a fluke—and Grayboy might run well tomorrow and then trail the pack Sunday and Monday."

"You're just like Budge Fisher," he said. "Budge was in here today. Sat right about where you are. Man don't talk to answer you, after a while you learn not to address him. All you drivers is a lot alike. Ain't yet seen one you could call full of goose-grease and jollity. Budge says, he says General Bedford's off his stride. Don't know what causes it. I put about as much faith in that statement as I would in another Mississippi Bubble, or cotton futures.''

I wanted to ask him why he talked it up at all, then; but I reckoned he couldn't help it. Most bartenders have large lips, it's a failing that goes with the trade. I was feeling pismires and hookworms moving around in my belly, all I wanted was to sit still and not think. Times when you want that are the times when you start thinking the most. There wasn't a window in here, I couldn't tell whether French and the major were engaged in converstaion or not. Daddy used to say horses were so damned much better—even the selling-platers—than the men who bet on them, there wasn't any comparing the two. Looking around in here—the man on my right talking about how he'd cleared a packet the year before on Charlemagne, the man on my left listening while the man on *his* left spouted about Starborn's reserve speed—the painting of the horses in all their false-limbed striding a kind of insult to any animal alive—I had the feeling Daddy was right with only a few exceptions. One exception would be Ap Miller, and another was and always would be Shangro and all his people. And a tall exception for all his withered size was W. M. I wished I'd just gone back to the shed where Grayboy was and waited outside it in the lane, which I'd have had to do since W. M. had the shed-lock key.

I took a sip. The bourbon was a good four days old, and wasn't going to uncoil me. I should have ordered straight corn, there was usually more purity to it. I thought of the wine French and I had shared on the bank of Toddy Morgan's pond. The bartender was still leaning there, in case I'd let a drop of utter wisdom fall into his reaching ears.

I said, ''You have a back room where I could sit for a little? I'll pay for it.''

I didn't have all that much money left but I needed some silence.

''Sure, Mister Broome,'' he said fairly low—as low as he could above this racket. ''And I want you to know you've made a stir in this town. Wasn't a soul anticipating any more champion track performance in the trials. Just what we needed to boom trade even better than it was last year. Here's your money back—'' He flipped the silver dollar back to me, and I picked it up—I might be needing it soon, for all I knew. ''And the privacy won't run you anything. Set and enjoy yourself.''

He went out through the flap-door at the end of the bar, and I picked up the very fresh bourbon and followed him. He opened a rear door into a six-by-six back room with a candle-stub expired on its own grease on the table, and a single chair, and a couple of mops and brooms looking like

cypress crowns after a gale, and a window through which, if you narrowed your eyes as hard as you could and used your imagination to the
utmost, you could see through the crust and make out something in the
street close by. But I could hear the jenny from here, again. I said, "Much
obliged," and the bartender shut the door. Giving me an owllike look as
he did so, as if he knew I had something up my sleeve in the way of
devious plots for the morrow's running.

I sat and tried the drink again, but it hadn't aged that much further, and I
let it alone after that.

The leaning light tried to fall through the window, just making a
dappled frail square on the flooring.

The shadows of the blowing flags moved across this faint brilliance,
stirring quick. And I could hear the breeze touching a corner of this
building. The jenny's music piped through it as if it stood for all those
things French had spoken of as we came into Yadkin—a carousel, I
thought, a tournament. Music out of a machine that was a glory of skill
and had come from Florence across the water in the easy days of this part
of the land. If it hadn't been for it I wouldn't be sitting here now waiting
for French. I wouldn't have met up with Shangro either, or with W. M. In
its blithesome dancing sound it gathered up all the past and the future as
well, and flung them together in my head—as Jantil's music-making did,
and even, I thought, as the pacing of Grayboy did, when he was going all
out with nothing kept back and his whole great body aimed at something
more than just paring down his time.

Then the door was coming open, letting in all the noise of the tavern,
and W. M.'s head was showing in smoky veils of light. He said, "She
said you'd be here. They showed me where you was. She's waiting just
outside. You please to come right along because I got to git back to the
jenny, it got a full load and I aim to take on a good many more 'fore we
pack up." He came closer, frowning. "That ain't even good liquor. She
told me not to tell you nothin' bothersome, just to come along now. You
ain't a hollow-leg man, like Wesley Teague, are you? It won't do you no
good to drink nothing but the best toddies, and them only when you git all
through with what Mister Grayboy's planning for us these next days."

I said, "You'd tell a banker how to count money, you know that?"

"No. All I know is horse and the riders and drivers for them. Well, she
is waiting, and I got to go."

I got up. Followed him out into the smoke and the blaring. He took one
look up at the painting of the harness track and his eyes got wider—which

they hardly ever did—and he said, "Them animals is never going to finish." Then he was minnowing his way around tables, around the faro game, and outside. He ran on across the street to the turning jenny.

She was standing at the corner of this tavern, the cloak, which she must have carried when she and W. M. had come back from the horse shed against the evening's sharpness, hung around her shoulders, the Gypsy dress gleaming in flashes under its dark folds. She was looking in this direction, as if she hadn't moved her head for some time, or her eyes from the tavern door. Major Deveraux wasn't in sight anywhere. I felt a long, slow leap all through me as though my belly was full of heat and strength after being scooped out like a dugout from a Cajun log. He's gone, I told myself; gone back to Pharis, never to return. In regimental defeat with his head lofty, his standards of conduct or whatever else he wished to call them, still the same, but in defeat for all that. In the pinch of the second I even felt pitying and friendly again toward him, as friendly as I was ever going to get.

Then I was coming up to French, and I could see her eyes up close. She took my hands or I took hers; it was together.

She said, "It's been terrible, Tom. But he's going on. Not to Pharis— he's going back to Lanceton and wait for us. Meeting us—along with all my other friends—at Chantry Hall, on Wednesday night. He says he will have our story then, and if it doesn't suit him, he'll have his way and hound us as long as he lives. He is—I see it clearly now, Tom, through all his honor and his courage which he gave to the cause—a *despicable* man."

She'd had a hard time. Her color was as high as an oak leaf at its peak of turning. I could feel on her finger the small gold-seeming ring that was brass, the ring W. M. had given her. I didn't look down. Went right on looking into her eyes as though we were yet in the stable of Chantry Hall on a Sunday night that felt to be aching ages back, studying the witch-shapes of those eyes in their long brilliance, and their grace like a doe's, and how they went tilting at the corners. Their silver and gray; and the amber, now in the last of the sunfall on this loud street like firefly sparks showing through grasses.

The vein was beating in her throat. I thought of the little fights we'd had, her not wanting to go bare swimming, or being shy-reluctant about it, and then the spats about getting hitched in Gypsy fashion. We'd come far, since.

And even farther in these last minutes.

"He is utterly wrong about you, your spirit is finer than his could ever be. I told him so. I told him we would be married here in Yadkin, that he was not coming between us on that point. I did promise, for both of us, to be at Chantry Hall on the appointed date. I realize you had to let him speak to me alone. It was—more than noble of you, Tom."

"Hell," I said. "I'm about as noble as Adam's off ox. Let's get out of the breeze, it's sharp. Might be bearing rain, and I certainly hope it isn't. You can tell me all about it on the way back to Mama Gatchin's. We'll go across and tell W. M. he can run the jenny by himself till later tonight. I'd say about nine; I favor town children getting to bed on time."

I took her to the street's edge. Was holding her arm as if we were in a cyclone and she was the only creature living to stand up to it with me. She held me the same. The heat and pressing of her breasts through my shirt felt as if it might stay for a long while. We were shutting our eyes against the whirling dust—which didn't reach the merry-go-round across the road in the lee of the millinery shop—and through eye-cracks I saw the machine turning, brisk and lively as it had turned while we were in the clearing outside Quincyville, with the Gypsy children riding. The wind blew her hair up under my hat-brim. I guided her in front of me as we went to cross, as if my whole self went not in my own body but in hers, here in this strip of busy dust, whirling in places as the wind touched it at the heels of her little old, cherished ballroom slippers.

Then along the street before us came lumbering the beautifully made wagon of Major Jack Deveraux, he was up on the box now beside his Irish white-faced carrot-haired helper, the blood chestnuts were pulling well, the whole rig shone. Over the road, the bay horse Bell—or Bellreve, her fancy name for him—nickered to the Deveraux chestnuts, but they didn't answer, and stayed pat as the major's driver swung them past us and onward. Back to Lanceton. He hadn't cast a clear glance at us, though I knew he saw us here. The stout wagon was gone. I took French on across, the leaves hissing around us now and a scent of autumn coming from all the countryside and slicing through the mingled scents of Yadkin Fair.

# 38

Well, all we had to do now was look straight forward at the three days ahead of us. And not to wonder or speculate or get worried and itching about what would happen to us when we got back to Lanceton. It was a relief, like rounding a bad turn in the road or a mud-hole in one of those Alabama back lanes in the rains of November. We stood in the doorway of the Anderson Millinery Shop for a spell, watching the children mount the jenny horses and go soft-spinning around, W. M. allowing them a minute each, no more, which he kept track of by keeping one eye on the Seth Thomas clock hung above the dauncy-feathered hats in the show-window. The music piped steady and the children held to the fine-carved horses as if they were engaged in a real contest, their fingers spread like starfish on the necks of the ramping steeds. The mothers of the children milled through the store, where Mister Anderson and his assistant were doing land-office trade. Some children had had as many as twenty rides. W. M. collected the coins with a sure hand, not allowing any extras even for his best customers. After a time I went over to him and said, "We're going back to Mama's now. I suggest you pack up about nine." Shadows were moving along the street, and down the line at the bandstand some-body had lighted pine-knot torches around the stand, the flames guttering in the wind and the smoke rolling around the bells of the cornets and tubas and trombones and the firelight licking here into W. M.'s cool eyes.

"What you want me to do with all this coin?" he said. He shook his ragged pockets; he jingled like a hundred trace-chains.

"Why, bring it back with you. We'll count it tomorrow."

"All this cash money? Wesley Teague never let me handle no cash. You could use it to make side bets on yourself in the running tomorrow."

"It wouldn't make that big a side bet." I thought how the drivers who had real money and special stables for the animals they drove—Buck Torbert with Charlemagne, and Budge Fisher with General Bedford Forrest, and no doubt the man named Rankin with this Starborn that everybody said could do better than his timing in the trial heat—would no doubt have bets laid down for each champion race of each day. So even if they lost a race and didn't cash in on the payoff for the winning of all three, they'd come out ahead. If I'd wanted to hedge my bets I could have kept back a bigger part of the money from the winning at Pharis and done the same thing, in a more modest way. It wouldn't have seemed fair to Grayboy to do so, though. I could see W. M. was thinking the same thing I was about this.

"I'll come down to the shed and look in about half past nine," I told him.

"You don't need to. Mister Grayboy's got to get his sleep and I wouldn't want you to fuss around him too much."

"W. M.," I said, "I've been fussing around him one way and another most of his life. I'll look in on him. And make sure you remember to feed Bell. He ain't champion stock but we're going to need him to get back to Lanceton."

Over in the doorway of the store French was talking to one of the mothers of a riding child. Beside the woman she looked the way an egret looks alongside a guinea-hen.

W. M. said, "I had the notion when I seen the major bustling in here he was bound and determined to take Miss Chantry back with him. I would miss her. She sits a horse good, and she don't fret too much around me or boss me around." For him it was a large-sized compliment. He wrinkled his nose fast as if he was sorry he'd said such a handsome speech and frowned at a small boy with fat cheeks and eyes like a merry porcupine's who was trying to sneak on and ride around free while standing up. "You there," he said sharp. "You go around one full turn you are going to owe me fifteen cents!" The boy dropped off, and W. M. shook his head. "These is the most cheating chirren I ever have seen. If you got to come bothering around Mister Grayboy, I see you later."

I went over and separated French from the lady she was talking to and we made our way back toward Mama Gatchin's. The music of the jenny fell behind us and blended into the whole of the noises of these streets. The sharpening breeze scuttered leaves around our heads in a gusting rain of them, and I felt the strength and brightness of the whole fall night as if every sound and sight around us was a kind of signal of good luck. When we passed the bandstand the musicians were pumping away at "Over the Water to Charlie," and there was a trick hackney horse stepping bright to it, a black horse with a good arch to his neck and mettlesome feet, going around the stand with its rider wearing a shako and the horse keeping time to the rhythm. There were more people on the streets than you'd find in a year in Dango Falls, people promenading in couples and whole families, and when we'd breasted past the selling stalls over on the next street, with their smells of hush puppies and shoat-hams frying and cider, hard and soft, frothing into tin cups at ten cents the quaff, and passed the snakes writhing in the stall of the cottonmouth moccasin handler, and then came to the old blind-eyed black man still sitting where he'd been that morning with his hat up-ended beside him and his grass-green stubby cornet at his lips, I dropped a dollar in his hat. Daddy would have said that was a sop to fortune, any gambler would know why I did it. We swung into Center Street, the tall boardinghouses warm with lamps and the houses of ill fame—the stars above them looked as if they shone just the same on ill fame and good—looking fairly warm themselves, with a good many customers climbing their shambling steps in this rich dusk. We went along past the blowing chinaberry trees and up the gallery steps and in to Mama Gatchin's. French paused in the hall to smooth down her hair in front of a mirror whose glass wasn't any flatter than the one above the bureau up in our eave-room. Manny stepped out of the dining room for a second, in mid-passage from one duty to another, looking as flustered as when I'd first set eyes on her. "Mister Broome—Mrs. Broome—" She somehow had an expression that was like the old black man's in its blindness, I thought, save that she wasn't naturally blind but just dim-sighted-appearing from having to work herself to the bone each minute of the Yadkin Fair days in this house. "I've saved some supper back for you—it's on the stove. The rest are almost finished eating."

French gave her hair an extra poke, straightened the ribbon in it, and said, "We do thank you, Manny. We are most grateful. If you can find time after dinner, I'd like to talk to you some more—about your plans for going to school over in Seldin. We'll go in the parlor. Come now," she went on as Manny shook her head and said something about the dishes having to be washed up then. "The dishes can wait—I'll talk to your mother and tell her it's all right." Manny said she'd be in the parlor, in such case, and flipped around about her rushing business.

"You planning to take on another project?" I asked French as I took her cloak and hung it with my hat on a rack here in the hall.

"I plan to instill a little gumption in her, Tom. She's extremely intelligent and deserves far better than this. I had a notion of teaching school myself, at one time, and I expect I would have if it hadn't been for Chantry to keep up. Of course Doctor Mattison and Will Planteu and most especially Howard Markley—though you'd think being a teacher himself he might have encouraged me—were all against it. They didn't think it was fitting for Colonel Chantry's daughter."

"No more would the major," I said.

On the way back from the flying jenny she'd told me just the bones of what he'd said to her in their conference. He'd called on every holder of tradition he could think of, it seemed, and for all I know brought in the sacred name of Jefferson Davis to bolster his furied argument. It came to me that I'd never thought when I bedded down for the night in Chantry's stable that I'd end up by shaking the foundations of a strong section of the old Confederacy. She gave me an eye-glint, kissed me on the nose, and smiled. All of Lanceton County seemed a lot farther away than it was out there in the night beyond these lamp-reflecting dark windows. I took her arm again. I could hear the wind sharpening higher, sweeping around the gallery-eaves outside, and smell hickory-wood smoke from a fire in the living room. Hoped to God it wouldn't rain; I'd never before run Grayboy on a wet track. French and I went on into the dining room.

She sailed in princesslike as she'd done in the morning, nodding to a few of these sitting-around-after dining people as she did so, and sat down just where she'd sat before, which was alongside Mrs. Fred Catewell. Mrs. Catewell didn't, in a quick sidelong look I took at her, appear as though she'd had a good day; her slouch hat was squashed more than it had been, and she was tucking into one last bite with her head down like a Berkshire sow nosing after the last of the slops. Her husband Fred gave me the end of his eye and turned away, chewing his after-meal cigar. A man with a silk vest a lot like Jed Corum's at the betting stall caught my arm as I moved along to the sideboard. Over there were the blasted remains of beef and possum and turkey and squirrels and beaten biscuit and hot biscuit, as if a Union troop had struck them all and left the field cleaned of life. The man with the slick vest had a catfish moustache and bagging eyes, but with a sharp shine in them. He said, "Congratulations, Mister Broome. If you need any backing—any side bet cash—please call on me. Pete Tarver's the name, and we're all rooting for you." He said it quiet, under the conversation noise of the rest of the table.

I nodded friendly enough, and went on. It wouldn't do any good to tell him I wasn't going to make any side bets—especially with other people's money—but was going with all the worldly goods I had on Grayboy's back to win the full three races; he wasn't the kind to understand that anymore than Major Deveraux could take in what I'd told him. When I got to the sideboard Manny and Mama Gatchin came through from the kitchen, handing me two plates heaped with samples of the food that they'd kept back from the holocaust of the rest of the boarders, and I carried them back to the table, set one in front of French, and sat down, gazing across to where Mama Gatchin and her daughter had started to carry out the used platters and plates heaped on the sideboard. Mama Gatchin gave me a nice look over her shoulder, and a wink. "A pacer," she called across the table-smoke and chatter. "Never in my days did I think I'd see it. You going to run him with calks?"

All the general conversation died down so people could hear my answer, as if I was the old man of the mountain.

I said, "Not unless it rains."

"Ain't going to rain," said Mama Gatchin, balancing her plates with a hand on top of the stack. "I get the arthuritis when it's even thinkin' about comin' wet. Could rain day after tomorrow, I don't get but a twenty-four-hour warning. But you'll have a clear windy track. You want to watch that Budge Fisher. He'll wait till the backstretch and try to hook you. My husband, bless his mem'ry, got hooked by him once when they were runnin' down at Yazoo City, and was laid up a month. He does it so sly nobody watchin' could tell it wasn't an accident. He's all in all the best driver in the whole lot, though. Got the respect of the Mississippi fraternity. You can bring your little nigra into the kitchen when we've red up, if you want. He can get his victuals there; I noted he wasn't around after breakfast."

She gave a side-shove to Manny to hurry along, and nearly lost her stack of plates. Then she straightened, and so did I a trifle, as Mrs. Fred Catewell sat up with her face putting off rays of heat as if she'd swallowed a hot cannonball, and said in a high splutter, "I'm not staying in a house where they let nigras eat in the kitchen. I don't have to do it, and Fred feels the same way." She was half standing, her sagging blouse curving over the bones on her well-mopped plate. "Fred and I've been comin' here for three years now, we're regular trade, and I'd think you best listen to us if you've a mind to keep the rest of your custom. And that's not all—"

Fred was looking sideward at her as if he feared she might explode in his lap—or maybe as if he might have to clean up the remnants when she did.

"—that ain't the whole of it, Emma Gatchin. I think this whole body of people, God-fearing and true Missi'p'ians all, had ought to know young

Broome, here—'' She said the name somewhat as the major said it, but she lacked his cutting edge even in her rage. ''—is wanted back down around Lanceton, and so,'' she swung on French, who was cutting up a slice of turkey, ''is this highfalutin Miss Priss, who's none other than his kept woman, since they ain't even married. And I had it from the lips of Major Jack Deveraux, of Deveraux Farm, he's a power in Pharis and an honorable adornment to the whole state, his word's as good as money in a vault.''

That old bastard, I thought. He'd called her a henwife and a slattern though, and he was purely right there.

I'd started to get up.

French put her hand on my sleeve. Just light there.

''I see no reason to suffer this stupid abuse while we are at table,'' she said, very quiet. ''Mister Broome and I were married yesterday morning, in Quincyville—as I told Mama Gatchin earlier.'' She held up her hand with the ring on it. In this light dripping easy from the smoked crystals of the chandelier, it had the shine of real gold all right. ''We plan to be married again, simply because we want it done twice—we admire the rituals, and we feel that we should like to celebrate them again with more traditional ceremony. The first wedding was performed by an old friend and a true man of God, but we did not have time to savor it. So at this moment we invite you, each and every one—'' She turned to Mrs. Catewell, ''—with some obvious exceptions—to attend our second wedding, on Monday at five.''

I was sitting again, and Fred Catewell was squirming around in his chair. There was a buzz of talk from the rest of the boarders around this table, and one of the men at the end of the table said, ''I'll be proud to be there, however the champion heats come out. It's pleasant to have a lady in our midst.'' He raised a glass which looked to be brim-full of scuppernong wine. ''To your health, Mrs. Broome—and to your spirit, Lord bless it—and to you, Mister Broome. And though my wad is on Charley, may the best horse win. As for the nigra supping in the kitchen, my God, ladies and gentlemen, I was raised in such a kitchen, and if we don't have room by the wood box for them, then Heaven pity us and all the judgment of mankind be on our heads.''

''Amen,'' said a plump lady sitting across from us. She had the relics of finery around her; her coffee-colored lace dripped around her throat like the bangles of a circus horse that might have come down in the world but still had band-music in its veins.

There was a sort of hushed chorus of cheering around the whole table.

While it was going on, I did stand up. And when the noise died down a hair, I said, "The service'll be at the Ap Miller Church on Church Block. I'm seconding Mrs. Broome's invitation. There won't be any didoes— we're having it in the arbor, outside, if the weather's still good. As for letting W. M. Ritter—that's the black child who's traveling with us—into the kitchen, it's a nice thought but he's already told me he prefers to eat in the shed, where he can keep an eye on my horse. Or our horse, it seems to have turned into his as much as mine in the past few days. Mrs. Catewell—" I faced her. "Might interest you to know my wife and W. M. are running a flyin' jenny down by the Anderson Millinery Shop, too. In case you have something against merry-go-rounds. If you do, or your husband does, I wish you'd either of you speak up right now so I can digest your words of wisdom and chew 'em up with my supper, which is getting cold."

There was a good-sized silence. Then the man Tarver, who'd offered cash in case I needed it for side bets, was leaning around to Fred Catewell and saying, "If you're planning on changing your residence for your stay in Yadkin, Fred, I'd like the fifteen dollars, eighty-four cents you owe me from our last round of cards before you go. I've got your chit, but it don't seem to buy any hog-jowl. And I hear they've got some back rooms real cheap down the street at Miz Farwell's."

I took it Miz Farwell was one of the madams along this block, because everybody laughed a little.

Mrs. Catewell was getting up, then, almost knocking her chair over as she switched off of it, French keeping it from going over; Mrs. Catewell reached to gather in Fred, as if she was roping in a plump calf with one hand while still in transit, and then she was moving fast out of the dining room, Fred following her back-angled hat and the breeze she made in going as close as if he meant to pass her by the time they reached the stairs.

There was a general laughing then, and people were getting up and moving off to the living room—where I reckoned they'd sit tonight since it was too cool on the gallery—and somebody patted me on the back; somebody else said a few neighborly words to French—then they were gone, leaving us to enjoy dinner by ourselves. Mama Gatchin as she pushed out into the kitchen again said, "I told you I don't allow fighting and carryings on in my house, Mister Broome. But there's cases it might be justified. I don't think they'll be botherin' you no more—I got to run upstairs and collect their board and room payment before they try to skip out the side way—but if they should, try to keep from bustin' up the furniture. I got some good pieces left over here from the palmy days, and I wouldn't want to see them broke. I ain't ever favored Apollodorus Miller as a preacher—he gets too downright for me, the I-Will-Arise-Second-Coming and Split-Off Baptist paints a rosier picture of the promised land—but I'll be there. So'll Manny. She tells me you want to talk with her after you've et, Missus Broome. She's got strange ideas of what she wants to do with herself—school-teachin' don't pay any more than bein' her ma's slavey for part of the year and helpin' out down at Thomas's store the rest. But if you advise her she'll listen, and so will I. You've raised the tone of this whole establishment a good notch." She ducked on through the doorway.

The dusty crystals above us tinkled as a good slam of wind hit the side of the house. French laid her left hand on my knee, the hand with the W. M. horse-ring adornment on it, and went on eating with her other hand, enjoying the fine food, and smiling just a shadowed touch to herself. I took a bite, and a sip of water, and said, "They should have sent you and not your father against Grant and Sherman. You'd have talked the North out of the countryside and straight back to Canada. Or to Alaska, with not a shot fired."

"I'm afraid I'd have fired a great many shots if I had been old enough, and a man, Tom," she said.

"Thank God you never were," I told her. "Don't even dream of it, ever."

# 39

I woke up gradually, thinking for a little that French was still in the high-posted bed with me. And reaching for her while my eyes were still shut. Then I opened my eyes. It looked late—the sky was darkening from time to time, sending shadows across the bureau and then clearing and letting the sun show in the whole room. I reached down for the turnip-watch beside the bed, having to angle my arm a long way down to touch it, and fished it up; when I clicked the case open the time was five till ten. I stretched and wiggled my toes, thinking I'd slept like a stone after a lot of love-making; I recalled French and I still doing that when all of the fair noises had died down and it must have been three in the morning and moonlight lay on the window-sash through the broken shadows of the tossing boughs. It seemed to me as it had seemed after that time at Morgan's pond when I'd stolen back to Chantry Hall, that I still wore her around me like a garment. Which nobody could see but was there all the same. But this feeling was even deeper and went down farther into the bone than it had done then. The stiff breeze had kept up all night; it was rushing through the boughs outside and the twigs were changing color from moment to moment as the cloud-scud reflected on them and then gave way to more patches of sunlight.

I sat up, then grasped the sheets and the thick comforter around me as a knock came on the door. Then I said, "Come right on in." Same second, I heard the merry-go-round music in the distance from the center of town. It piped and sang above all the other noises. First-heat day, I thought; I tried to keep any excitement down, tried not to let it run through me like a draught of hot drink. I'd gone back to the shed in the lane the night before at nine-thirty and taken a good look at Grayboy. I'd also made sure W. M. hadn't neglected Bell; he hadn't, though he still treated the bay as if it wasn't worth much more than just getting from one point to another. He'd not exactly been grudging about it when I inspected Grayboy, but he'd not been much more than tolerating about it either. He had also told me again that he didn't need any of Mama Gatchin's kitchen-scraps. He had talked soft: "This here Gypsy fare they loaded us with is still enough for me. I been going around to back doors most of my life. Getting turned away a good many times. I like it not doin' that. Mister Grayboy likes me staying with him as much as I can. Don't linger here now and git Mister Grayboy worked up. I don't want him to even think about the first heat till about one-thirty tomorrow. He got to run it. All you got to do is drive."

While I'd been out there with him—not spending nearly as much time as I'd wished to—French and Manny Gatchin had had their talk about Manny's school-teaching future, in the parlor.

Now the door came open. It was Manny, holding a plate of food. She'd done something better to her hair—I reckoned French had showed her how, or suggested it—and for a wonder she had a fresh apron on. She looked shy as a human hummingbird and about to dart away but braver and more chin-up-seeming as well. "Mister Broome—Mrs. Broome had me put this on the back of the range for you." She set the plate down on the bureau. And took the room key out of her apron pocket and put it down alongside the somewhat chipped but serviceable plate. "Mrs. Broome wanted me to tell you she and W.M. will shut down the jenny at one o'clock and they'll meet you with your horse at the champion track at one-thirty. I do hope you had a good sleep." She was turned away, a little color in her cheeks as if the shyness was about to swarm over her, but putting her message over for all that. She cut an eye to me as I nodded. "The Catewells moved out last night," she said. "I'm very glad about it, and so is my mother. Please have your breakfast while it's still warm from the range."

"Thank you, Manny," I told her. I didn't inquire as to whether or not the Catewells had taken up residence in one of the local whorehouses. She glanced over at the chair where Deveraux must have been sitting and waiting for me when she last saw him.

"I'm so glad everything seems to have worked out for both of you," she said in a quick breath. "I was quite worried about allowing that gentleman into your room—he was as full of himself as an egg is full of meat, Mister Broome, and he did insist. I had little choice. But I felt he boded you no good."

"He didn't," I said. "But that's over now, and whatever he bodes for the future doesn't signify at Yadkin Fair."

"I'm relieved. And I know many will wish you the same, but I'll say it now as I said it to Mrs. Broome—good luck."

"Thanks again, Manny. I do appreciate it."

I thought there would probably be quite a few wishing me luck now—especially those who had money riding on Grayboy—but that her wish did mean more than most others. She went out and shut the door. I got up and, in the swapping back and forth of shadow and sun, relieved myself, and then washed in the basin on its stand, whose water was still middling hot, and then shaved to please even the high shaving standards of W. M. I took off the marigold poultice I'd applied the evening before, saw that the wound was in good shape—wasn't troubling me a tad—and wound it back with the soft thread binding a little tighter. Then I dressed and took the plate of food—there was enough for three people, I only nibbled at it—over to the windowsill where I could look out and down while I tasted it. The town had the feeling of something that had been winding up for a couple of days and was now at one of its peaks of hopefulness and pure racing joy. I thought it was wonderful how not much of this would be reaching Grayboy, back in his shed, and how not even the racket of the middle-of-town streets would do much but make him twitch his ears in his stall. It was when W. M. had harnessed him and put him in the sulky shafts that he would start to move into the challenge of it and toss his head and lay his ears back and pull at the bit. He couldn't yet smell the challenge in his bran-and-straw and warm-horse-scented place. I took one more bite, and, putting the room key in a pocket and carrying the plate, left the room and went downstairs and into the dining room. In the empty dining room I left the plate on the sideboard and then stepped out into the hall, got my hat from the rack—French's cloak was gone from there—and moved on out to the gallery. Wind was pushing against the chinaberry trees lining both sides of the walk, and the sky had that changeable rushing first silver gray then gold look about it, an unsettled morning but still with no rain-smell in it. The pouch-eyed friendly man, Tarver, who'd made me the offer of side bet cash the evening before, raised a hand from where he perched on the end-gallery rail, and I nodded to him good morning, and the four men he had been talking to, and Tarver himself, all watched me as I swung down around the side of Mama Gatchin's house, whose dull chocolate boards caught swashes of sun and shadow in quick changes, toward the lane and the line of sheds. All I could do when I got to our shed was peer in past the iron window bars into Grayboy's stall. He stood there like a lovely monument, half-dozing, but swung his head when I tapped on the pane between the bars, and had that look in his eye which told me he'd have made a stab at lifting my hat off if he'd been able to reach me. If I'd had the shed-lock key I would have gone in for a minute or so, just to let him know—and maybe more, to let myself know—we were still as close as we'd ever been before W. M. had taken over. But, leaning there, I got the notion nothing had changed on that score; and if a horse ever looks amused—sometimes they do, you have to watch them close to see it—he had that warm quiet flickering in his eye now. I turned around and sauntered along the lane toward the teeming streets.

I didn't stop at the Anderson Millinery Shop this time—except to take a look at the crowd of children surrounding it, and riding the jenny, an even bigger crowd than the evening before, and to reflect that if I lost today French and I would still be able to get back to Lanceton in good style, because they were garnering in a lot of coppers with those rides—and to watch French for a minute, as she conferred with W. M. about some point of the jenny's running, his dark-napped head close to her shining hair as she bent talking to him. Over the music and the milling—there were even more mothers spending the time while they waited for their children by examining Anderson's stock; I hoped he had a good supply of those crazy hats—French couldn't have heard me even if I'd roared, and I couldn't get her attention, so I went on by, heading toward Sutton Road. When I got out past the trying track and the entries building and the sulky-rental stalls and the betting stalls—taking just a whiff of time to run up the steps of the entries building, which was shut up now, and to see through the glass, dim in that room on the board's slate hanging in back of the counters, the name *Grayboy* in copper-plate script under the names *Starborn* and *General Bedford Forrest* and *Charlemagne*—I headed across to the champion track. Even this early in the field between here and Sutton Road there were half a hundred rigs of all kinds, buggies to surreys to hackney coaches to farm wagons to buckboards, and I was glad the sun wasn't going to be frizzling today but kept off by that cloud cover because there wasn't much shade for the crowd's horses save around at the backstretch behind the rail where the beeches and the silver-poplars grew. And people were already climbing into the grandstand. The sheds near the gate leading onto the track were genuine waiting sheds, not just an open-ended lean-to like the one at the testing track; on their shake-shingle roofs the sun-and-cloud patterns flew as if a kind of race was already being run there. I got in line at the grandstand gate, fingering the slip the judge had given me after the trial-running the day before, and wondering if I'd need it to get in; but when it came my turn at the gate, the trial-judge and a couple of the timers bade me good morning and waved me through. The trial-judge who'd given me the official slip of paper—he had on a fresh pink-striped shirt today, and didn't look half as sweated up by trial-runners as he had the evening before—nodded to me and said, "Right over there in yonder shed, between Charley and General Bed, Mister Broome. I reckon you'll want to wait around for your boy to bring your horse and sulky up. You're starting second to the pole, Charley's the pole horse, Bed's next after you, then Starborn on the outside." He looked up at the sky. "Ain't a drop of moisture in it, though there might be tonight. Nice dry track. Oh—I know you're with Missus Broome, she's runnin' that roundabout over at Anderson's. She's got a seat in the owner's box up in the stands." He gripped my hand. "Funny to me how you drivers always get here ahead of most ever'body else. Budge and

Buck, they've been here since nine, and Rankin got here half an hour ago. Refreshment cart's out in front of the sheds this side of the rail if you feel peaky or thirsty." I thanked him, but noted he didn't wish me luck. I didn't reckon in his today's job as a judge of the first championship heat he could wish it to any one soul. I walked on through, past the starter and the starter's helper and the timer and his helper, and along to the second shed from this end. Which had the name *Grayboy-T. Broome,* lettered neat and spelled right, on a board above the door. It was a wide shed inside, and high enough to house a brace of elephants, with a couple of buckets of cool water set behind a low fence at its rear, and stalls ready and waiting. When I'd walked past the *Charlemagne-B. Torbert* shed I'd seen a bunch of men inside, playing slap euchre—or it looked like that—on a table in the shed's mouth; they'd just looked at me as I passed, and had nodded at me. One was the round-faced Buck Torbert himself, a silk shirt with bright gold and rose red striping clinging to his round chest and belly and short arms, and a driving cap of red poked to the back of his head; another was the man I took to be Budge Fisher; I reckoned the others were handlers and assistants and well-wishers. Torbert had kept that little pipe in his jaw like a small cannon-barrel.

I was just wondering if he'd have Charlemagne brought from his stable in the same van I'd seen when we first got into Yadkin, right into his shed in grand style, when a shadow fell into Grayboy's shed's doorway, and it was Torbert. "Hey, son," he said in a low friendly voice. A fat man's voice, with a little glue in it. He was just about French's height, if that. Stepped in as I said hello, and shook my hand. His eyes were small and black as peppercorns, sizing me up as in that one glimpse as we first came onto Center Street in Yadkin, he'd sized up Grayboy. "Come to cause us grief and woe, have you?" He laughed. "I never saw a 'Bred quite the size of yours, Broome. Couldn't believe my eyes yesterday mornin'. Fate, us meeting like that, I reckon." He sat down on a box near the cloud-and-shadow striping this shed's entrance. "You care to indulge in a little game of cards to while away the time an hour or so? I ain't bringing Charley on till about half an hour before race time. Me and Budge— Fisher, he's driving Bed Forrest, we're old cronies and enemies—got a game started over next door. We'd like to have you in it. Rankin—Jap Rankin's his name, I hear—he don't want to associate with us. He's either new to the tracks or the meanest rascal I've come across since I started in this profession about a hundred years ago." He had his plump hands—so full of flesh they looked like little sausages, though I knew they could handle a horse better than well—spread on his tight-swelling trouser-knees.

I said, "I'd ordinarily jump at a game of cards, but truth is, I'm as flat in the purse as that track out there." I knew damned well he knew about the canting of the track on the backstretch, and that Budge Fisher did too. But they weren't going to mention it to me, or to this Rankin, before this first champion heat. Saw a small gleam come and go in his bright eyes as I said that about the track, but that was all. "And I don't give I.O.U.'s," I said. "Daddy always taught me to bet with money. And all mine's tied up with Corum and Murphy at the moment."

"So I heard." He wagged his head. "I also heard you haven't got a cent in side bets. Aim to win it all. The confidence of youth." He laughed again, a nice rich sound. "I was like that when I started out. Bet the full stake, throw it all to the wind and trust the wind would bring me home. Speaking of which, if this spanker of a breeze keeps up it'll tear the shirts off our backs in the backstretch and the teeth out of our faces comin' in. Charley don't mind that, 'specially. I run him blinkered on days like this, though. 'Fraid he might get a piece of dirt in his eye and stop to cry it out. Well—even if you don't have the cash to play—and we ain't playin' for stable straws—come on over and join us anyway. Be glad for your company."

I thanked him for the thought, and told him I'd drop over after a time. He got up, and in the shed-door, turned.

"Little chap handlin' and groomin' for you—little nigra lad. What's his name? He was around my stable last year, handy little chap."

"William Makepeace Ritter," I said.

"Mouthful of a name for such a sprite. Tell him if he ever wants to leave you to look me up, I can always use a boy with good hands. Though—" He was staring at me harder now, "though I got the notion, from what I remember, and from seein' you now, he's a lot like you. A loner workin' with a loner. Save that you ain't or don't seem to be a mean loner, like this Rankin. Well, see you soon."

He ducked on out of the shed.

I went over and dragged the box he'd been sitting on to the front of the shed, where I could see the track better, and catch a glimpse to my right of the grandstand. I could feel all the worms and hackles of what was ahead, squirming and rising in me. I put them down in my mind as if I was trying to stuff eels in a box. The Yadkin band was already somewhere in the

stands, warming up. Figured they'd be lip-tuckered and brass-weary by
the time it got to be close on two o'clock. But then I figured, no, they
wouldn't. Everybody in Yadkin appeared to have enough steam to go the
whole day and half the night.

Remembered what Ap Miller had told me about Buck Torbert's skill,
and about Budge Fisher's use of General Bedford's stamina, how he
could save it and then come on like the Roman legions. And what Mama
Gatchin had told me in the dining room last night about Budge Fisher's
hooking her husband at Yazoo City, without one judge being any the
wiser. You have to hook somebody just right or you get tangled in it
yourself, my father had taught me that some time before. It wasn't
something you learned by hearing about it; you learned by solid years of
driving.

Then all at once I heard boot heels chopping the dust on my left, and for
a second they put me in mind of Major Deveraux's striding, and I thought,
Good Christ almighty, has he changed his mind and come back for
French, this time bearing a troop of officers to put me in durance vile
forever?

But it wasn't Deveraux—it was just that the walk was the same; and
something of the manner. This man, wearing a pale blue silk driving cap
and a shirt to match, was dark as an otter or one of Shangro's people, but
with a slim blade of a face above a tiny dab of black beard, and high
cheekbones which gave his whole jaw a spliced-together look. In the
doorway he'd stopped, sudden, and was staring at me. His eyes were as
cool gray as W. M.'s, but much more like the flat of my knifeblade. He
looked me up and down, taking his time. Then said, "Broome?"

I said, "Yes indeed."

He didn't put out a hand, so I didn't; and I didn't get up.

"C. J. Rankin, driving Starborn," he said. "I don't much care for the
other company we're in, Broome. In Kentucky I have been used to better
people. I don't know how you feel about that, but it doesn't matter, does it
sir? I came to ask you if you would care to make a side bet with me—a
substantial wager, anything you care to lay down—on today's heat. I
seem to have used up the resources of the local bettors, who are a piddling
lot."

"Just how high have you gone in these side bets on today's running?" I
said.

"Five thousand. I do say—you don't look like a driver. I mean, your
clothing—"

"I've never noticed that it puts the horse off," I said. "And I don't have anything to bet. I've put it all on the full bag—all three races."

He showed his teeth.

"What supreme arrogance. I can see we have nothing in common, Broome, and it's just as well. It whets my appetite to give you a trouncing. I have already advanced the same warning to the other bump-kins—" He nodded next door to Charlemagne's shed. "They did take my bets, though, which they will soon regret."

He stood about five seconds more.

Then I said, "Good-bye, Rankin."

He whirled and was gone, the same sound of swift purposeful boot heels marching off. As if they flung the dust back at me, though actually he was walking away from the wind this time and back to Starborn's shed. On Wednesday at Pharis, and then somewhat on Wednesday night, and then yesterday for a touch-and-go time, I'd had enough of that kind of attitude to last me a while. I wondered how he was just as a driver, stripped of all the bantam-feathers and feistiness. I had to admit as I wondered that they grew some pretty good ones in Kentucky.

# 40

At about noon by the turnip-watch and the sun, I walked down the line to the refreshment stand which was for the use of the drivers and didn't cost a cent, and got a Country Captain-fried chicken wing and a glass of buttermilk from the shade of its awning. I wasn't in quiet enough stomach condition for all my outside-looking ease to get down more than a bite of the chicken, but the buttermilk was welcome. At the Charlemagne-Buck Torbert shed the cards were still going, save that now, I saw as I drifted over, they'd changed the game from slap euchre to head-to-head poker, and this had narrowed down to a game strictly between Buck Torbert and Budge Fisher. Buck Torbert had his cards held tight to his chest in his round hands and nobody could have read anything of what he held from his snapping black eyes. Or from the puffs of wet-leaf-scented smoke that kept pushing up from his small pipe-bowl regular as the smoke from a packet churning along the big river on a clear day. Budge Fisher watched him across the edges of his own cards, Budge's eyes large and seemingly honest and innocent as a two-year-old child's when the child has been slicked up to look bright for a family reunion. Budge was about twice the size of Buck Torbert, and bigger in the chest and forearms than me, and he wore an old gray silk shirt and a driving cap whose silk had also faded from many washings to a kind of crawdad color. He had a full beard, grizzled, coming down about to his breastbone, and hands that looked stout as a mule-skinner's, even holding the cards as light as he did. Back in the gloom of this Charlemagne shed two or three hostlers and handlers and hangers-on stirred around, and as I watched, hanging on the edges of the group, one of the handlers, a black man moving quiet so as not to disturb Buck's and Budge's concentration, brought over a hot toddy with bourbon and sugar in it and set it down light as a butterfly's kiss on the table at Budge Fisher's elbow. When his shadow fell across the table Budge lifted his eyes and saw me, and laid his cards on the table facedown and got up and stretched out one of his powerful hands to me. "Broome. You came over to join us. That's neighborly. We'll start another open game just as soon as Buck and me get finished with this here hand."

I said, "The way I told Buck, I still haven't any cash to invest in a game of chance today. Any other time I'd be pleased to oblige you."

"Well, just sit down and watch, if you choose. Glad to have you with us." He resumed sitting on his box. You wouldn't have thought from his and Buck's calmness that here at noon with those scudding shadows and those patches of flowing sunlight over the ground, the grandstand was now about half filled and there was already a kind of steady roar like that you'd hear from a bee-tree when the bees were lining home in the gloaming, from every corner of the stands. It was as if Budge Fisher, and Buck Torbert, held a kind of silence between them that shut out all these other sounds and walled them off from any crowd. It was the way Shangro and his son Aldan and his son Pella and his brother Jantil got before a race, and the way the Gypsy women had held themselves miles above the crowd even while they sold their herbs at Pharis. And a little the way Major Deveraux had appeared there at the very first. The black handler brought out a box for me; I perched on its edge.

Buck Torbert stirred his plump shoulders under the gold and rose shirt and slapped down his cards. Facedown as Budge's were. Around the stem of the pipe growing vinelike from his jaw he an rounced for my benefit, "This is the third hand—draw poker. We dealt the first two hands in turn, I won the second hand so I'm dealing the third."

The black handler who'd brought the toddy said, "Mister Torbert and Mister Fisher been playing against each other so many years, sometimes takes a dozen deals before they don't know down to a pip which cards each other man is holdin'." He said it soft to me.

It was amazing to watch. It was cutting-cold as all good cards always are but it had something that went beyond the contest itself, something that through the calling of the cards was an old duel all by itself and made the rest of the hostlers and handlers gather around and hold their breaths and sweat seep out on their brows as they watched. Buck Torbert lost to the high hand and didn't even blink. He stripped off a couple of hundred dollars from the poke in his pocket and pushed the money across as if it didn't mean anything, and it didn't. "Next time," he said quiet. Budge Fisher nodded; it was an old ritual with them and played right down to the knife and always would be. I knew they would drive exactly like that. Budge took up his toddy and put a sip of it through his beard and his innocent, egglike eyes came back to the day and the place and the time; he said, "Well, now, Broome, I see our friend Rankin came to call on you a little while ago. No doubt offered a side bet or two on today's running. Since as you say you are strapped I don't reckon you took him up on it. A pity. Both Buck and me liked the color of his cash if not the manner of his speech." He peered out around the edge of this shed's door. "Him, sitting down there like Stonewall Jackson within stone-throwing distance of Washington. But no true resemblance. I reckon along with trying everybody he comes within spitting range of, that young man tries himself awful high."

"He seems a mite overbred," I said. "You think he got it from his sire, or it was a fault in the dam?"

Budge shook his head. "I am not familiar with his papers, so not knowing, I can't say. But if he was a 'Bred I'd take him out some night and keep speaking to him polite and promising, then shoot him clean when he was looking the other way. I wouldn't want him chewing corn in my stable, he would put the other 'Breds off their feed. He's got a magnificent animal—Buck didn't see him run in the trial, he prides himself in coming in the last day so he missed the testing. But I saw it, and Rankin was holding him in so tight he should have been disqualified." He took another sip of his toddy. "Buck, General Bedford is seedy and poor, off his stride and not at all the creature he was a year ago," he murmured to Torbert. "So I think the least you can do is let me get back more of my losses while we bide our time in these hours before Agincourt."

Buck Torbert said, "I'll let you try, but I shouldn't do it." He slid his jet eyes to me and his plump cheeks wrinkled. "Don't mind Budge, Broome. He talks so mournful he often makes bystanders cry. He's an expert ancient liar. That Agincourt he's talkin' about was a kind of British-French battle I believe took place when he was just a chap, a few million years back. Have a toddy while you watch me try to skin him some more, if you want one." He pushed the cards across to Budge. "I'll even give you the deal this time, you old slew-fingered son of a bitch."

I told the black handler who was looking at me I didn't want a toddy, and sat back and watched the fresh game start up and marveled at how close-matched they were, then after a few minutes I got up and moved out into the hurrying sun and shadow again. I remembered the bartender I'd talked to—or who had mainly yammered to me—the evening before had mentioned how he couldn't seem to get any straight answer to his questions out of Budge Fisher. The only point was, he shouldn't have asked the questions. With the sun hasting along the track now, more cloud-shadows following it, and the band starting up again in the stands but not making much more noise than the whole, collected rise and fall and murmuration of the people in the stands, I could still feel the armour of waiting and quiet around Fisher and Torbert. A tournament, I thought; a carousel as it might have once been called. The flags in the stands were standing straight out on their guy-ropes from the north. With the wind coming from that way as it had done since Thursday evening, along the back trail leading into Yadkin, I couldn't hear any music from the flying jenny. I cast a glance southward past General Bedford Forrest's shed to Starborn's, but there was no whisker of motion from there. If I'd have been C. J. Rankin—which I was sure glad I was not—I wondered what I'd have been thinking in these minutes. I thought if he had one grain of earth-sense under his cocksureness he had better be thinking of those two old men playing another game of dead-set, head-to-head poker back in the Charlemagne shed.

When I went around the flank of Grayboy's shed and leaned there on the back fence which was put up to keep people from sneaking around this way and not going through the grandstand gate, here came the man with the wen on his cold-afflicted nose who had been my companion in the entries-building line the day before. He'd just spied me here and had detached himself from the now lengthy line of grandstand-goers, and he was still chewing snuff, no doubt as a specific against more nose wetness. Only this time he'd put the snuff-pinch in between his lower lip and his teeth, which gave him the look of a very old mule with a drooping lip heading a wagon to a cotton press. He came up to the fence and spread his hands on it and said, "My God, Johnny, that's to say, my God, Mister Broome. If I had a hatful of money I don't care how much, I'd put it all on that there pacer. You have done sold me on pacers, sir. I am going to save up to buy one, I swear I am—after all these years of bein' faithful to my old dream of Beautiful Nell gettin' in the champion heats."

I decided Beautiful Nell must be the cannon-fired mare I'd seen him draw up alongside the trying track shed the day before when I was getting ready to run Grayboy. I said, "How'd she do?"

"She stopped on the backstretch and I didn't have the heart to start her again. Not after watchin' you. I just led her the rest of the way home. Borrowed the price of seein' you run your Grayboy from my landlady this mornin', I'll have to send her the money from home when I git back, but I got a notion it's worth it."

"Well," I said, "if you feel that sure about it I'll just have to stake you to a small bet. Which you can get two to one on if you go with Grayboy at the Corum and Murphy stall, putting it on all three heats."

I got ten dollars out of my pocket, which I could afford at the second just about as much as I could have afforded sitting in on a game with Buck Torbert and Budge Fisher. I'd never done this before in my days but there was a first time for all things on earth, and I still liked the fond way he spoke about his ruined mare and how out of his no doubt puny holdings he'd invited me for a consolation drink the day before, thinking I wouldn't make the time with a pacer. I liked him dreaming he had a horse fast enough to qualify for this track, too.

He took the money fast, then croaked "Thank you," and was off dashing past the people in the grandstand line and threading his way across the field which was now so full of wagons and other conveyances he had to jump clear over a whiffletree in some places. Then I lost sight of him heading for Sutton Road and the betting stalls. I climbed up on the fence and sat there looking away from the track, all the commotion in the grandstand thrumming in my ears and all the center of me trying to get as still as a beetle sunning on a log in the heart of the Lanceton woods. Parting with the ten dollars had been all right though. It was what you could call another sop to fortune.

# 41

Sitting on the fence and letting the warm of the sun and then the sweeping coolth of the clouds run over me, I summed up Budge Fisher and Buck Torbert as men I liked and would have to go on liking even if they beat me by ten lengths each. They would try every trick in the book because they knew every trick. They'd already heard a lot about Grayboy—besides the point that Torbert had taken that one clear look at him the morning before—and honored him, and even though Buck had said that about him being of bigger size than any other 'Bred he'd ever seen, there had been respect in the way he said it too. There are men you favor even though you know they will pull the line tight in any professional dealing—maybe you like them better because you know it; and they were such. It was C. J. Jap Rankin out of sight in the end-shed as if he was sulking in his tent that bothered me most. He acted not quite like Major Deveraux but as if he thought his own breeding qualified him to lord it over every other man, without his ever having done anything to justify such airs. At least the major had fought in a bitter war to prove all the honor he carried with him; no matter how I felt about him, I'd always give him that. I could see how Rankin got the name Jap with those high cheekbones, though I didn't believe Japanese were a harming people. Not taking them one by one.

How long I'd been perched on the fence behind Grayboy's shed I didn't know, but I was getting tired of waiting out here in plain sight. And having to lift my hand from time to time to people in the grandstand-gate crowd who called over to me—some of them were from Mama Gatchin's and some had been in the Jed Corum and Martin Murphy betting stall, but most of them I didn't even know to speak to. Besides, being on plain view here made it look as if I was lapping up their favor, when all the while—as W. M. said—it wasn't me who was running this first heat, it was Grayboy himself. So after a time I dropped off the fence, rubbing my ass where it had got numbed from staying on one rail so long, and went back around to the front of the Grayboy shed again. I decided as I went that I wouldn't go through this waiting again. No matter how much I might want to smell out the shape of the day and the condition of the weather, I would hole up somewhere else until about ten minutes before W. M. brought Grayboy out to the champion track. I wasn't built like Budge and Buck; I couldn't sit in the shade and play hard-fought cards and have a sip of a toddy from time to time and pretend there wasn't anything coming up square ahead of me. I wondered how those knights of old which French talked about had felt while they waited beside the pavilions for the jousting to start. Nobody ever told you about that, and the knights themselves were long dead with their mailed gloves rusting and their ladies part of the high-heaped dust of the centuries. And their horses' bones enriching the roses through the years.

I was just about to visit the gratis refreshment stand for the drivers, again, even though all I could have done was look at the food, I couldn't have taken a bite of it—when I heard a fuss go up down at the south of the shed-guarding fence, and whirled around to look where most of the people in the grandstand line were watching. Four or five of the track-helpers were running down there and starting to lift out a section of the fence that shut off entrance to the track. And across the edge of the field came a van painted a sleek shining blue that caught the sun-dappling between clouds as if it was some kind of blue whale breasting out of the deep; but the name scrolled on the flank of the van in those curling letters like you see over the fronts of fancy bars in big cities wasn't *Starborn,* it was *Rankin.* I wondered how the hell any man with a champion-qualifying horse could put his own name and not the horse's on a van carrying it. Then Rankin was coming around the corner of his shed, sailing along in his own pale blue shirt and blue cap, the wind fluttering the shirt back against him, and he was shouting to the driver of the van—the draught team was as good as any of Shangro's hauling animals, which was about the best there was—to pull in here, though the driver appeared to know his business without any extra orders. I stood at the back corner of my shed and waited while the van swung through the opening; and past the air-slits of the van I caught a view of a black Standardbred, blacker even than you think of midnight, standing with a couple of men inside the van steadying him, and the lights on his coat glistening like anthracite when it is freshly split. I wasn't going to see any of the rest of him right this instant, because the van swung on around the Starborn shed, out of my sight, and in through the doorway of the shed; these sheds were high enough to have taken two vans atop one another. A bunch of wild doves flew close above the shed roofs, carried on the steady wind to the south, their shadows brushing over Rankin who still had his mouth open and was rapping out orders. Then the whole procession was out of sight. Budge Fisher rounded the corner of Grayboy's shed and stood there with the backs of his hands on his hips, his beard lifted and his face still calm as a butter bean. I said, "Who won the hand?"

"Oh, I did. Puts us right even again, more's the pity. We'll have to start all over again tomorrow."

His bland child's eyes might have been surveying the whole day as if there was a special treat in it for him. Maybe a couple of new spinning tops and a hoop. As he pulled a hand around to smooth down his beard I saw that one of its knuckles was flattened as if it had been driven down by a pile-driver long ago. He saw my flick of a glance toward it. "Happened against the inside rail about ten years back," he said. "Couldn't set the bone because the bone was gone. But it doesn't faze me in handling the lines." I thought of how Jap Rankin had mentioned him and Buck Torbert—and me in the same breath—as bumpkins. I knew he'd been driving before I got foaled. And for that matter so had Torbert. He jerked a thumb down the line of sheds, southward, to Rankin's. Down there the track-helpers were leaving the fence-section open, and gathered around it talking among themselves. "Comes in style, doesn't he, Tom?" First time he'd called me anything but Broome; it made me warm even if he was going to be a true track enemy. "But then there's style, and style. Seen an awful lot of women put on high paint and lace and pretend they had it, when all the time they were common beneath as Georgia clay. That's where I come from—Stone Mountain, Georgia. 'Least I got sired there. I go back for the winters—got a house and my stables, and the old woman, near the mountain. Now—" He was gazing past my shoulder at the rim of the field again. "—there's a lady who's got *style,* and no two ways about it." I turned around to follow his sighting. It was French he meant. And now across the field from the east and Sutton Road, with a trail of people following as they'd followed Rankin's van, here was Grayboy. He was chesting patient above the crowd, the glitter of the Forman and Robbins sulky sending off splinters of light rays behind him and his own hide giving back the rolling sunlight as it stabbed and raced, and the little figure of W. M. on the sulky looking as small and black gray as though just something accidental happened to be steering him, but what Budge's eyes were mostly on was French, who was walking at his head, not touching him but pacing herself to him, the Gypsy skirt swinging as she came on, her hair like the time just before sunfall when the earth darkens to a deep ruby glory. I said, "I thought they weren't comin' on till one-thirty," and reached for my turnip. While I got it out and opened the case Budge said, wide-eyed, "It's that now, Tom. You can believe it." All the same I looked at the watch, and he was exactly right. I reckoned all the time he'd been playing cutthroat poker and lying a little, he'd know to a second what time it was. I hadn't even let myself look at Daddy's watch in the past hour and a half. While we stood there and Grayboy and French and W. M. and the train following them came closer, yet another van swung along out of Sutton Road, this one older than Rankin's and not so bright-painted and bedizened, a pair of plain unmatched country work horses doing the hauling, and Budge clapped his hands together soft under the tumult of the grandstand on the air around us. "There's General," he said as if he was sad about it. "Poor old stud, ain't got but four or five races in him yet. I'll put him out to pasture next year or mebbe the year after. Give him his declining years with mares and peace of mind. That's Mrs. Broome, hey, Tom? Well, you're a fortunate man."

Behind him, Buck Torbert who'd just appeared between Charlemagne's shed and Grayboy's here, said, "If there was a purse for falsifyin' facts, you'd be richer than that Yankee Jay Gould. I ain't referring to what Budge said about your wife, Tom. But mark me when I say General Bed's got ten years of hot life in him and in every one of them a trotting style I'd swap for Charley's if I could. As for Mrs. Broome, I don't know what I'd do if I was married to her, no offense meant, Tom. Reckon I'd stay a lot closer to home than I ever have. As it is I got five chaps—four of them girl-chaps—to feed, and a woman devils me from one day to the next till you can hear her outside the North Carolina border which we don't live far from, and four grandchildren, so I just stump along with Charley on account of I own eighty percent of him and might as well get my part of his value." He sucked his pipe, which put up a gentle foul cloud. "Ah," he murmured around its stem, "there he comes now."

Behind the General Bedford Forrest van—which stated *General Bedford Forrest,* in sober dark blue letters on the gray slightly battered side—came the Charlemagne van as I'd seen it first the previous morning. The double team of matched Belgians hauled it with an air, the scarlet and blue striping of it flashed like a parade of Zouaves going by in the early days of the war, and the *Charlemagne* in its sun gold hit the eye like spears.

To Buck Torbert with his round black eyes watching the spectacle and leaping with enjoyment, Budge said, "I was remarkin' about style to Tom a minute ago, Buck. Seems to me yours is a little show-offy, kind of overplayin' your hand. Like some of them gamblers on Beale Street in N' Orleans. Man of your age ought to give some thought to shadin' down his days and getting set for a tasty funeral. Though I reckon they'll put Charley in the ground along about the same day they lay you by."

"You put your dumb big finger on it there," said Buck, serious for a second as he slanted his eyes around at both of us and blinked in his pipe's fumes. "When Charley goes I go. But I don't do no predacious lyin' about it. I'm proud of him and he knows I am, and I blazon it forth for all to see. How'd you ever draw that heart and spade pair of aces all in the same hand?"

Budge shrugged his shoulders. "My natural sober and retirin' nature told me to," he said.

For a second more I stayed back here with them. Then I took just one more breath of a look at the oncoming line of champion track goers, Grayboy closer now and his ears twitching like a cat's when the cat sits in a high place in sunlight and looks down over the world, the mob of folks around him bobbing and pointing, French nearest him with her brightness as sure and proud as his, his sulky inching along and W. M. with the lines stiff as pen-marks drawn horizontal on paper in his dark rocklike hands, and then the General Bedford van rolling, and this time a brief sight of General Bedford Forrest himself, a Standardbred just a shade under Grayboy at the shoulder, I judged, and with his storm-cloud gray nearly the shade of Grayboy's in the rippling of the light and shadow through the vents of his van, and then the circus-shining van of Charlemagne, and his moonlight-on-water hide and the way he arched his neck in there and cropped his teeth and started to sound out, but was checked by one of his van-handlers who put a hand across his muzzle; and after that I said, "Beg your pardon, gentlemen," and went to the back fence here, and vaulted it, and joined French and Grayboy as they drew up alongside, W. M. swinging the sulky in a tight turn which he made without much thought for whatever other bystanders and trailers might get their feet trodden by Grayboy or run over by the sulky-tires, and all of us sweeping on to where the fence-rails lay back and the track-helpers waited for us to drive through. I caught French's hand and she leaned up and we gave each other swift bussings somewhere near our respective noses; behind us Ap

Miller, Rev., his old-time prophet's head nearly up alongside Grayboy's
nigh cheek and his silken beard pushing forward in the drive of the wind at
his back—which also billowed his baptizing coat around him as it billowed French's cloak forward as if she sailed with the wind and the dress
flew out under the drapings of the cloak—called to me in a voice like
mellow thunder, "Dwelling in Beulah Land! Praise God!"

Then we were in between the fence-rails, and curving around past
Rankin's shed, which had its high shed door shut as if it confronted the
track with the tight and sour expression of somebody who said, "Stay
out," and spinning north past Bedford Forrest's shed, and into our own.
Just French and Grayboy and W. M. and me now in this near gloom,
everything and everybody else left outside, all the good-wishing or
anyhow hopeful-betting people and the true friends together left at the
fence. And it was quiet in here save for the wind touching along the high
roof of our shed, and Grayboy was relaxing just a shade as he gazed
around the boskiness, and snorting as W. M. eased him around tight to the
south wall and then brought him up parallel with one of the stalls but
facing out toward the track. He stood all in shadow, harness-buckles
catching shadow-dulled reflections of the light as the sun swept out again
beyond this shed, and French touched my cheek and said, "It was a
terribly long time—it was frightful waiting. But W. M. pointed out that
we ought to keep the carousel running, and that there wasn't anything else
to do with our time till then. Was it bad for you, Tom?"

"Like it must have been before First Manassas," I said.

"Did Manny bring your breakfast, and was there hot water?"

"Yes," I said.

"It sounds so small," she said, "thinking of those things. Like
polishing silver you're going to hide anyway when the Yankees come
through. Mama and I hid the silver, the year I'm remembering. We buried
it, with Jupiter and Luther and Dabney and Mingo watching and helping;
they carried the chest out not far from the cemetery under the cedars. They
didn't know they wouldn't always be with us then."

I said, "Waiting—it made me wonder what the old-time knights did to
while the time away in the real days of yore. In those days you favor."

"I reckon they must have played some sort of quiet games."

"Draw poker, you reckon?" I asked.

"I do most deeply doubt that. But maybe something very like that."

I could hear the General Bedford van stopping to the south of this shed, and then curving into its own shed. And the quiet yelling of Budge Fisher's men, who sounded as if they knew what they were about without his barking out one order at all, while they got ready to unload General Bedford. Grayboy's ears swiveled around, again like a huge cat's, and he shook his harness, making the sulky with W. M. still on it shake a little in sympathy.

Then the Charlemagne van was being tolled along in front of this shed door, blocking off part of the light from the track as it passed, the Welsh pony I'd first seen Torbert on being led behind the van, and this time Grayboy thrust his head out above us and gave a long, sharp greeting. The man leading the pony grinned at us, and Buck Torbert, stumping behind him, touched his cap to French in here, and took his pipe out of his red jaws to call, "Good day, Mrs. Broome!"

French smiled out after him. "That's a most sightly shirt and cap, Tom. You should—"

"No," I said. "It's like W. M. says—it takes too long to break in horse-clothes. I'll stay with what I've got, thank you. I noticed when I put them on this morning they'd been washed."

"I used a tub Mama Gatchin let me have down in the kitchen. I dried them over her stove. I couldn't sleep late." Her color came and went, like the sunlight in all this day, as if she was remembering the pleasuring we'd had during the better part of the night hours. She brushed my hand again with hers. Her head went back. "Well! We took in just lashings more with the carousel this morning, and after the heat W. M. says he'll go right on helping me. I do imagine we'll run it again till about nine this evening. Unless this blow brings rain at last. Reverend Miller came by and took a ride; it took two carousel horses to accommodate him and he had to scrunch himself down so far I thought he'd develop an ague in his spine, at his age, but he insisted—and paid thirty cents for the privilege because of the double load. Not that W. M. would have let him on free in the first place."

"No ma'am," put in W. M. from the sulky-seat. "They ain't good sense to that. You got your living to make like he got his."

W. M.'s feet dangled off the seat, a long way from the racks. He held the lines lower now, nearly slack, and he was gazing out around Grayboy's body to the track. From the stands to the north the band was playing "Magnolias of Memphis," and I'd been right, the band hadn't yet lost its steam but even seemed to have gained more.

In the mouth of the shed against the sun-swash framed there now, one of the track-helpers showed up, blinking in at us with the light in his hair like wheat-furze. "Mister Broome?—Missus Broome?"

He took a step farther in. "We've got your box seat ready, Missus Broome. No ladies down here durin' the running, beg your pardon, ma'am, and I'll be proud to escort you to the box. Mister Broome, your handlers and crew can stay right here if they want to."

"I couldn't *see* from here anyway," French told him. "And I thank you kindly for escorting me to the box." She planted a kiss on my cheekbone, raising herself to do it, a hand light on each of my shoulder blades for the breath. "Conquer, my darling," she said in my left ear. Then she moved away from me, holding her arm out for the track-helper to take it, and not looking back, her ballroom slippers hardly seeming to touch the earth as she went out again into the flailing wind.

The track-handler called back, "Five minutes to the starting lineup, Mister Broome."

I nodded; then he and French were gone.

I looked over at my so-called handlers and crew, W. M. I was standing on Grayboy's off side at his head. W. M. still hunched there on the sulky seat.

He said, "I'll sit right out there on the rail at the homestretch past the wire, way I did on the testing track. Nobody going to see me get up there or put me off. I got a look at that Jap Rankin; he passed along beside the millinery with his bunch last night while I was still runnin' the jenny. Most of them drunked-up and carryin' on and putting up their noses at people and telling Rankin how good he is. Reckon that's the job of some, telling the Man he is good and keeping themselves alive on his money. He'll be the kind carry a heavy whip. Watch out for it. He got a horse good as most I ever see, watch him too. Don't let Charley git ahead of you. You might do it thinking it would whet up Mister Grayboy to catch up and go around, but Mister Grayboy couldn't get around if Charley had got into that much stride. Watch Fisher on the backstretch both times around. He's a hub-hooker and a slammer. He do it neat as sliding a hand under a hen for eggs. When you bring Mister Grayboy around the second time let him get clear sight of me the way you done on the testing track. Bring his head up to do it if you have to."

"That all?" I said.

"All you need. Mister Grayboy got the rest."

He slid off the seat. And stood by. Before I went back to get on the sulky I pulled a cheek strap till Grayboy's head came down and patted his gray velvet nose, soft as a nightmoth, then I let go and went around and got up, and stretched my feet into the racks, and got them solid with the boots there as if they wouldn't ever come out. W. M. watched me as if he wished deep under every one of his thin ribs he could do this part of it too, but gave a short nod as if I'd accomplished it to suit him in spite of that.

# 42

Five minutes after that we were out on the track. We were second in line to move out there, Buck Torbert had Charlemagne already lined up next to the inside rail and down almost to the near turn, sitting his sulky as unconcerned as if he was only thinking about what cards Budge would hold when they next played euchre or faro or keno or any kind of mean poker. All the time I was taking Grayboy down there I studied Charlemagne, standing almost as solid as Buck sat, his beautiful head and eyes up and his mane lying back in the wind that came hooting along and skirling track-dirt in eddies from the north, the music of the pumping band and the noise of the crowd in the stands filling his canting-forward ears as if it might have been just for him. He had on dust-blinkers, cupping a little around his eyes but not harming his sight at all. Grayboy felt as if he wanted to waltz and sidestep just a shade to the music as we spun down, slow, to the position-mark painted in a yellow brush-line on the inside rail down here, and I turned him tight and we drew up alongside Charlemagne and Buck. Grayboy stood higher at the shoulder by inches, as I'd known he would when they came together; he rolled his eyes toward Charley, then back around to the west, where Budge Fisher was coming down the track driving General Bedford Forrest. General Bedford wasn't blinkered, and his sulky wasn't quite as bright and sharp-glinting as Buck's— or my rented one—but there was something about the powerful, quiet surging of his half-gait here to the position-mark that made me sit up higher and hold my boots in the sulky-racks even tighter. Budge turned him, behind us, and came into the slot beside me as neat as if he was bringing a ship to dock. Then the chief judge and two of the track-handlers, up ahead, were raising a fuss and beckoning toward the track, and in the last shed on this side, Rankin's, somebody called back, then the shed door swung out and for the first time all plain and out in the open, I saw Starborn. He came out from under the shed-eave into a streaming of light and shadow as if he was already into a gait, though he was only pulling steady and firm; and I could see that Jap Rankin for all his foolishness had, somewhere, learned to drive, because his hands on the lines were easy and his wrists were quiet, just giving directions with a flick and a touch which Starborn recognized and obeyed as if he was a sparkling black part of Rankin's own body. In his right hand and gathered with the off-side line Rankin carried a whip that looked like a Malacca cane, but heavier; it had his blue colors on it, tied in a ribbon. Starborn came along past Charley, stepping just a fraction high, and behind us I heard the sulky-tires swivel as Starborn turned, then he was bringing up alongside General Bedford and Budge on the outside. I could see from where I sat, looking first to Buck on my left and then to Budge and then to Rankin on my right, that we were well lined up. The wheels of each sulky were so leveled you could have drawn a straight line across them from hub to hub. The starter and his helper, the starter on the inside rail, and his helper on the outside, were squinting down between the spokes, and the starter nodded and stood up and jumped over the inside rail to the near infield and stood there waiting, and beyond Budge Fisher and ahead on my right, Starborn cropped his teeth at General Bed's neck on the off side, and Budge said without turning his head, "Watch your horse, Rankin."

He said it gentle and soft, as if just remarking on the weather through his beard.

Buck Torbert was looking past me over at Rankin, though.

Buck carried a whip, a long thin one for tickling in the stretch; Budge didn't have one.

Rankin's hands moved on the lines; he let Starborn veer a little to the nigh side again, let his head swerve, and this time Starborn nipped General Bedford on the neck. General Bed nickered sharp, and lunged high for a quick breath, without stirring his sulky forward, and Budge brought him down saying, "Sho, sho now, General," and then Budge was turning in the sulky to look at Rankin. I couldn't see his eyes now, they were facing away from me, but I could see Rankin's watching, and Rankin's were that cold knifeblade glint again. As he'd looked when he spoke to me in the doorway of Grayboy's shed. And I heard Budge say, "I wouldn't let him do that once again, you milk-eared shit head."

"Control your horse, Rankin!" snapped the starter from the infield rail.

Around the pipe still clamped in his teeth, but without any smoke from it now, Buck said, "That ain't a good way to cinch your bets, Rankin."

Rankin's cheekbones were bright above his lantern jaw and his face bright down to the roots of his small black beard.

With the same gritting sound, around the pipe, Buck said now, "Or'd you rather be called Jap?"

Rankin said, stiff-voiced, as if holding it all down to a simmer behind a saw-mill engine about to blow up, "I never allow old has-been bastards to call me Jap. My friends call me Jap, and no other."

"You surely must have a passel of friends," Buck said still just as quiet. The wind blowing against us near carried his words away and was lifting the brim of his red cap back against his forehead. "Hardly ever seen a body pass money around as you do. I'm going to be proud to claim some of it, a few minutes from now. So's Budge."

Budge nodded, as if he was a judge in court saying, "Why, yeeees," to a lawyer's suggestion that a felon be locked up for shoat-stealing.

The starter was running down along the infield rail to the starting wire, leaving his helper on the outside to keep the position-line. His hair streamed back in the pouring wind. It was blowing about half again as hard as it had been doing the day before when I'd walked the track. At the grandstand the band had stopped, not resting but waiting for the start. The timers were sitting on the outside rail in front of the horse-sheds and with the wire set square and clean above them across the track. For a second I tried to make out French's Gypsy dress in the owner's box in the stands, but couldn't; it was all a welter of cloud-and-sun down there, but in the same gaze I saw W. M. on the outside rail some distance beyond the start-wire.

When the clouds rushed over, north to south, the stands went dark as if a mammoth blanket had been pulled over the stands and that part of the track, and then the sun came following as if it was running a hard-breathing race itself. The bound ends of the lines felt cool as river-silt to my fingers and palms. The oiled scent of Grayboy's harness and his own excitable, light-sweating scent came back to me on the wind in puffing waves. He tried to shift left, investigating Charley, and I gave the line on his off side a twitch and he brought his head back to center and a fraction higher. Down at the start-wire the starter was leaning out. Then he was calling, "Ready?" Grayboy's tail lifted a little from the wind under his belly, moving lazy as a palm-leaf fan.

The starter's helper took a gulping breath, one last look at the lined-up tires, and yelled into the face of the wind, "Ready!"

For the first time this day the crowd in the stands was all quiet so you could even hear the wind shouldering through silver poplars and the beech beyond the backstretch. The timers were waiting with eyes on the wire and their watches. The starter's voice came leaping back in a burst, "Go!"

We still had to be even as we were now when we came under the start-wire or it would be a false start and they'd send us all back. We were moving out in a clear stream, the tires staying level, Buck on my nigh side starting to lean into it and forward as Charley got the first of the rhythm, and Budge on my off side still sitting foursquare as a courthouse on its foundation but keeping the same line of turning wheels straight, and then beyond him Rankin holding the same line, and Grayboy was already asking to be off the bit, pulling hard, starting to pace, but our wheels were flashing with the others, then here came the wire, the starter and the timers and the judges all brushing by us in the single half a second, and the starter shouting this time, "Go, gentlemen!" and we were off.

Just as the starter yelled—the sound gone in a whisk like buckshot—I let Grayboy half off the bit, and felt him make his first bid, pulling out past General Bedford, who was into his trot, and just a shade ahead of Charley, who was already going in the *chug*-and-*chug* that sounded as if he could keep it up for days and nights, his mane bounding in the same rhythm, his tail standing back and the wind plastering against his chest, and the noise of wheel-tires and harness and hoofs and sulky-strain around us beneath the yelling from the stand. At the same time I saw Rankin on the outside give Starborn a hip-cut with the hard whip, saw the blood slash up from it and Starborn plunge ahead as if he'd truly been dug into with a knife or spooked by a demon, and then I was still moving past General Bed, Budge sitting just as he had from the start, even maybe holding in General Bed more than half, Bed's long body looming on my off side like a gray stone fence a lot higher than my head, his head looming even higher and spume from his lips blowing back and onto his harness and over to mine, and on my nigh side Charley now holding back more than Grayboy was, but on the outside Starborn still keeping as close as he could to the inside while gaining. Then I was past Bed all the way, and even past Charley's head, his dust-blinkers bobbing as if he was a great dark bird wearing spectacles while he flew. And we were on beyond the whole of the grandstand, into the first turn, Starborn with his eye-winking black, trotting as if he didn't have two miles to go, or one, but just a few furlongs, but also as if he could still keep up this speed every beat of the two miles. Rankin was near standing in the racks, and slashing at him again, and he was a length ahead of me, a length and a half in front of General Bed, and about the same spread in front of Charley. I felt Grayboy pull, all at once he was boring, hating the sense and sight and command of any horse in front of him, pulling hard on the bit as if he was trying to break it. I pulled him back, kept him tight and in command and down to what he was doing, while what was making him mad went on happening: Starborn was moving over across the track to the inside, doing it now deep into the near turn, with the sweep of light and shadow gilding and then candle-snuffing the rails curving into the backstretch, and the poplars with their branches already in sight, tossing, and the beech trees farther down standing like dappled women with beautiful arms and the track already beginning to cant and tilt under Grayboy, so all at once the off wheel of the sulky was moving higher than the near. And ahead, now nearly dead-center in front of Grayboy but still moving to the inside rail and going so fast he still wasn't losing much crossing-ground, Starborn kept driving to the inside, and then even quicker than I could think, say, spell it out, or dream it, I knew what was going to happen. Rankin didn't know, hadn't known, about the tilt, and he'd overreached his horse and himself to get to the inside and keep ramming ahead, and now he couldn't stop the drift, the ground was against him and here the wind pushing like giant muscles at his back was against him; he might have fought the gravity but he couldn't have fought the wind and the gravity both. He was a good driver, a sorry man; it wasn't him I was yelling about, hearing my own voice call out as if something burned and rasped in my throat; it was Starborn. I fought the drift of the track myself, this feeling of being on an Indian mound you were tumbling off of and would fall off if you let up the pace, Grayboy coming so close to the inside rail now the near hub of our sulky was turning under the actual rail itself, Charley behind me fighting to keep away from it, and Buck making him do it because he'd known the drift was here to be handled, and General Bed keeping well away from it, nearly in the track's dead center, Budge holding him and steering him with wrists like iron posts, and only a hand's span in front of Grayboy's forehoofs the wheels of Starborn's sulky yawing and then scraping the rail, and then Starborn crashing through the rail and onto the infield, the sulky turned over and Rankin, Jap or C. J. or son of a bitch or whatever, with his boots still in the racks dragging behind it, plowing up furrows in the infield grasses and his whip rising in the air like an arrow turning over and over and his head, the blue cap still on it, hitting a rail post as Starborn went on driving and swerved deeper into the infield. Grayboy went on pacing straight through the splinters of the railing, still so close to the rest of the rail it was as though he'd already gone through it, then I was turning him to the off side, a hair of an inch by a hair of an inch, and General Bedford was in his same position right in the track's middle, and pulling ahead foot by foot, and again on my off side, but a yard closer to me than Bed, Charley had his new positioning set and was coming up on the outside too. They came with me around the far turn that way, and for a blink all of us still driving were looking, just one look, back across the infield, where a bunch of the track-handlers and one of the judges were already running out to catch Starborn and pick up whatever might be left of C. J. Jap Rankin. I hoped they didn't forget his whip. It had seemed such a strong part of his equipment.

All of us, together, took just that one stitch of a look, then we were all bearing into the near turn, the wind slapping against us, and Charley was coming up on my outside faster than Bed, aiming into the homestretch and pulling up stroke by stroke of his lovely hoofs, Buck Torbert standing up just a whit now in the racks, calling to him, reaching to tickle his streaming sweat-patched flanks with that whip, face like it was red earth with a foolish tiny pipe stuck in it. But I couldn't let him get ahead. And I knew Grayboy wouldn't. We were around the near turn, it was a sunned time ahead, the grandstand shadow reaching in the moment halfway across the track, the wire above and ahead gleaming like a twisting silver eel, and I let Grayboy all the way off the bit. Even against the steady sail of the wind I could feel him gather all he had, all of it in the gut and the center and the heart and the massy soul, and feel the lifting, flying of his nigh fore and nigh rear hoofs, then the same beat like a bird's air-rowing wing from his off fore and off rear legs, and we came up on Buck, then on Charley, as we whipped under the wire and past the stands again. The stands' shadow was swallowed by cloud-shadow as we hit it, everything cool as swimming, with the wind trying to dry the sweat on Grayboy and not drying it because he was making more sweat with every lunge, and Charley still bidding, Buck still driving him as if he had never a shallow doubt he could pass me, Budge a shade behind us still, I believed, holding in part of what General Bed had and keeping it for the rest of the last mile. All the way around the turn it was the same, Grayboy keeping in front, with every ounce, and I was yelling now, calling out scraps of songs and fiddle-music and just plain courage and grace to Grayboy. We swept into the backstretch again. Ahead the railing-shards had been cleared from the inside but there hadn't been time to fix the railing, and this time even though I didn't with all my self want to keep as close as I did to the inside, I hung there anyhow, not as close as before but holding my soul's breath even while I kept on singing and chanting and shouting as I felt the track tilt like a harsh wave and the sulky bounce and want to go over on its side, and Grayboy with his shadow whirling beside him like thick mist kept half an inch from any of the rail, and then the poplars and the beeches were past on the off side, beyond the outside rail, signaling the far turn. In the start of the far turn I heard General Bedford, off his own bit, coming up as if he'd just been trotting to a Sunday gathering up to this time, a change in the beat of his hoofs that was like the chugging of a steam-train let out all hell bent for election and running away with its passengers. For just that twinkle of time, hearing it roll on, I thought of the great locomotive engine the South had stolen from an Atlanta railroad shed in the last days of the war, which was also named General, and which had run right through the countryside ahead of the Union troops, even blowing its whistle from time to time, though God knows they couldn't have afforded the loss of power the spare steam cost them. It hadn't done any good but it was a sweet and somehow sensible and heartening act to have accomplished. And it was also a sound like doom at my back, doom in the shape of one of the best Standardbreds the world had ever let come out of a dam, with a child-eyed, tough-skinned, more than able man driving him as no other driver could have. Charley's plate-beats were near enough, but this was an oncoming like an avalanche. I couldn't have spared a look behind. I was standing all the way up in the racks now, and we were flooding, pouring, pounding, savaging and saint-horn-blowing into the homestretch, so I just remembered to keep Grayboy's head a touch high, as W. M. for his own fell purposes had asked me to, and let him go. W. M. had been right as far as W. M.'s thinking went, which was pretty deep. The wire whipped by, silver gold in a flushing touch of the sun this time, then gone past our heads, and behind me I heard Budge Fisher start pulling down General Bed, and Buck gentling Charley down from the peaks where he'd been trotting, and it was one of the most soothing sets of sounds I'd ever expected to hear. I let Grayboy go almost to the first turn, hearing the crowd again now as I hadn't heard people for, it seemed, at least a couple of days of time, and drawing him up by degrees, then turned him and we came back into the grandstand palaver. Budge Fisher came by me, still slowing, going the other way, letting General Bed wind down, his old clam gray shirt soaked over his beefy shoulders, his eyes kind and well-wishing under the brim of his much-laundered cap, and he tipped his cap to me. Nearly alongside him, but a little on the inside, came Buck Torbert, stuffing some shag into the rotten-smelling pipe with one thumb and driving with his left hand as he slowed Charley. He nodded to me. "Tom, you artful young strap," he said, and laughed. Then as I headed on by toward the sheds he said to Budge, "Let's us get these animals walked out and shedded right quick, and get on down to the Moseby betting stall. You didn't tell me what you bet today against that unfortunate bastard creature. I wagered a thousand."

"Couple of thousand," called Budge. "Don't you have any fear, they'll pay off even if he's cold-cocked."

They went on along the track toward the first turn, yammering together like a couple of retired Natchez trappers, the wind blowing their words to me as I went on. People were already trying to jump down from the stands and onto the track, and I didn't want any of them but French and W. M. and Ap Miller to come close, right in the instant, because I was all at once feeling drained to the bone and hungry as a chicken-hawk in the winter, at one and the same time, and the wind felt sudden-cold blowing on the back of my wrung-out shirt; but mainly I was thinking these were the same men I had to beat the next day, and the next. I didn't see how anybody had ever beaten either of them before, though I knew it must have happened. Then we were coming off the track, the track-handlers having a ripe time holding the crowds back from the shed-fences, and the judge was saying, over and over, going hoarse with it as he put his head back and bellowed to the crowd, "Grayboy, four minutes, one second! General Bedford, four minutes, two and a half! Charlemagne, four minutes, three! Starborn, disqualified!" Well, I told myself, W. M. hadn't been proved right yet; Grayboy hadn't shaved five seconds off his qualifying time. But he'd taken off half a second. Shading a hand against one of the spurts of sun in my eyes, I looked off over the infield. C. J. or Jap Rankin was gone now, and some of the track crew were hammering at the railing, getting a new length of rail in place. Down at the Rankin shed I could see Starborn, blanketed, he looked fit enough and I hoped to God the crew and friends of Rankin—whether Rankin was dead or alive—knew what a great horse he was, and that if he got sold it would be to somebody who didn't just know driving, but knew what he drove. When I'd stopped Grayboy at the shed I felt a few bones pop in my spine, as if they were just starting to get back in place after being sprayed over the landscape considerably, and got off the sulky as if I was the age of Mayor Westerfield of Lanceton.

Then French was draping an arm around me, and nuzzling her good-smelling rich hair against my lower cheek, and going with me while I stepped around to Grayboy's head to praise him up, quiet now with no roaring and calling and cheering left in me, and stroked his nose and patted his steaming neck, and looked into his clear, calm-blazing eye. French stayed with me, close as paint, as we stood there, so that Grayboy and French and I might've been made of the single flesh. Grayboy had my hat, all at once, the neatest he'd ever lifted it with his teeth, and I had the notion of letting him keep it, but didn't think it would be good for his digestion. But I took it back soft and thoughtful. W. M. said, at my shoulder, "Let me git him in the shed now, out of this here beating wind. He don't need no more people today, the fewest he see the happier he be. He need me, and Miss Chantry—Mrs. Broome—and you, and maybe that old preaching man knows what he's made of. You drove a pretty fair country race—" He was looking right at me; his skinny Adam's apple moved behind the plum blue and gray neck's skin, and then he said it, "Mister Broome."

Putting just the lightest touch on the Mister.

"Thanks," I said. He knew what I was saying thanks for; it wasn't for telling me I'd done fairly well.

"How's Rankin?" I asked him.

"Bust his head and died. They say he so rich they shipping him back to Kentucky on ice. All the way there, that's a lot of ice."

He started leading Grayboy off toward Grayboy's shed, and Ap Miller had jumped the barrier and was coming in leaps across the shed area to French and me. He got to us and circled us with his arms and lifted us off the ground so for a spell we were smothering under his beard, then let us down but still stood gripping us, and said, "Mrs. Broome, Mister Broome, I'm invitin' myself back to Mama Gatchin's for suppering. That worthy woman—I've been trying to wean her away from the I-Will Baptists and into a more venturesome and philosophical congregation, includin' my swamp rats, these twenty years—that worthy woman didn't get a chance to see this heat, this day. So out of purest Christian charity and because she sets a spanking table, I'm going to give her a masterful description of each furlong of those two miles I just saw.''

He went on talking while we all made our way toward the Grayboy shed.

# 43

Sunday came so fast it might have been the middle of a wave rolling up from the Gulf, one of those tidal waves that wash out all the houses of the people living along the beaches, and leaves them wondering what hit them—even though, the next year, they build their places right back on the soft-powdered sand again. And Sunday had something of the feel of waves to it, as well, with the wind finally bringing rain by the ton, a rain that started late the night before and washed along Center Street and pounded on Mama Gatchin's roof, heavy-sounding up there in the under-eave room, and blew the curtains in over the mammoth four-poster with its mauve canopy and its faded-out red tassels, and licked at the prong of the flame in the coal oil lamp burning low on the bureau. It was a mischievous rain, lying out on the half-gale from the north and making me see in the eye of my mind the condition the track would be in, heavy with mud as a field in river bottomland taken by flood along the Old Man river itself; I didn't sleep as much as I should, though after we'd made good love for those hours, finding many ways to do it, French slept as if she was three years old and anticipated rising to a spring morning at the old Chantry.

The evening before, Ap had come back with us to Mama's, inviting himself in but also being half-invited by Mama—he was a man hard to resist as an ax falling on a chop-log—and when W. M. had rubbed down and cosseted Grayboy and had taken him, all by himself and telling me he knew just what kind of plates Grayboy would need for the next two heats, over to the smith's he favored to be reshod, Ap had started regaling Mama with a recounting of the first heat as if he'd walked every pace of it himself and had memorized it and made it a part of a scripture lesson. But the smell of the rain and the first few warning drops of it were even then on the air, and when I went out to the lane-shed and greeted W. M. and Grayboy and examined the new plates—W. M. had paid for them out of his holdings from the running of the merry-go-round—and helped him, in spite of his not wishing help, to get Grayboy set for the night in the lane-shed stall, it was already too mizzling to even think about taking the jenny back to Anderson's and going on with the running of it till nine o'clock. W. M. said, "Just as well if it rains down t'morra. Keep them people back from tryin' to clutch Mister Grayboy. When we was in the smith's a man tried to tear out a hair of his tail—for a keepsake, I reckon. I told him, he valued his arm, to keep away."

I said, "Happens he's never run on a wet track, or even in a trace of mud."

"You think that's going to stop him? Slow him a couple of seconds, sure. We'll use the toe-calks on the new plates."

I was thinking how, in spite of the warnings I'd had, Budge Fisher hadn't tried any hooking or slamming in the first heat. I didn't believe he'd done that just because he liked me. I knew he'd have hooked his own mother if it had felt advantageous. In the hurly-burly of what had happend on the backstretch he hadn't had the time to try it, at least on the first mile, and during the second he'd not come up close enough to do it. I took it for granted there were quite a few tricks and sleights Buck still had up his own gold and red driving shirt sleeve too. I left W. M. there with Grayboy and walked back from the lane to Center Street, the sky all dark by then, and the hard small drops hitting just a few at a time but stinging and strong as shotpellets, and I went past the stable-drive where Charlemagne was kept when he wasn't running or waiting in the champion track shed or being vanned from one to the other, catching a glimpse of him over the half-door of his stall past the low stone wall there, and then along past General Bedford's ample stabling, and along to the biggest stable on this side of the street, which was Starborn's. The van saying *Rankin* on it stood just as screaming-proud as ever in the yard, but the faces of the helpers sitting around under the magnolia trees wrestling their trunks up through the cobbles of the yard were lorn and sorry. I moved on into the yard, and one of the helpers got up and came over to me while the others watched. I said, "I don't know who to talk to. I didn't like Rankin worth a damn and I got the notion he didn't like me the same, even though we only talked for a few seconds before the heat. But I'd like to tell somebody I'm sorry he's dead.''

"You and Budge and Buck," he said. "They dropped over a while back." He ran his hand back through his stable-smelling hair. "He kind of asked for it. His daddy's Colonel Rankin, Louisville—we're all from there—and from the time he was high as a clevis-bolt, Jap had everything he needed and much he didn't need. If he'd been old enough in sixty-one through sixty-five he'd have torn up the patch as a cavalry officer, but he come along too late. Wasn't ever too much praise for him to swallow, he put me in mind of that Goddamn Yank, what's his name, Custer, ridin' into Little Big Horn thinkin' Jesus Christ was on his side and Injuns wasn't people but spots on a map. We had to put up with it, drink with him and grease him up if we aimed to go on workin', and the totin' privileges was sizable. But the sad part is, he had the makings of a real driver— under it all. Mebbe in time he'd have just got sense knocked into him, a leg broke or his head half knocked off, and that would ha' done it. We was hopin' for that today, but it just didn't come about so." He spat near a drop of rain that had just hit a cobble. "Soon as the undertaker has him iced to go, we got to draw him back to Louisville and greet his pappy with him. Reckon the old man'll not sell the Star—just keep him for a memento and a pet. You can take a look at the Star if you want."

I followed him to Starborn's stall. Stroked Starborn's nose, noted the scraping he'd got going through the rail had been well treated with black salve; he stood quiet while I fondled him, and I hated to think he probably wouldn't run again. The whip-cuts—there were a couple of older ones under them—would heal all right. His hide caught the flickering of a stable lantern and his eyes were near as speaking and bright as Grayboy's, and I wished him well in the earth and a long life in it, in my head. Thanked the helper, and he told me he'd deliver my regrets to the colonel in Kentucky, and said, "Too damn' bad you didn't git a chunk of Jap's cash while he was breezin' it about. But I know how you think about it. Might change the whole three-heat setup for you if you was to change your mind even now."

He did know; only somebody who spent his life with horses and riders and drivers would. I thought to myself how superstitious not cashing in side-bet money would have seemed to most everybody else, but how, deep down, it was a pact I'd made with Grayboy, believing in him enough to know he could win all three heats and not sullying that true feeling. It was a feeling Budge and Buck respected, too, even though they were going to do their damndest to prove it wrong. I said good evening to the helper and went back to Mama's; when I came into the sitting room Ap was just midway in his telling about the day's running, and I sat back next to the fire, a hand in French's, and let him pour it on in Biblical colors. If I'd taken all the drinks offered me the rest of that evening and even after dinner, I'd have had the deliriums for the rest of our stay in Yadkin and maybe never sobered up. But I just took one or two. Between times of listening, and talking a little, I wrangled in my head about having to leave all this come Monday and hit back for Lanceton County again, but it was an obligation, French had pledged it to Major Deveraux. When French and I finally excused ourselves from the boardinghouse crowd and Mama and Manny and Ap, and went into the hall to go upstairs, I noticed that in and around the band of my hat on the rack were still those leaves the old Gypsy lady in Shangro's caravan had woven while our first wedding was going on; like the crowns which French had stowed in the saddlebags, they were dried now but still had a jaunty look, and I thought I'd leave them there for a time, for luck. More superstition, but then, it's a chancy trade. At any rate, I thought, while we climbed past those landings— French moving up ahead of me, me admiring her hips and starting to want her even as we came past the next window light, whose stained glass was so dark against the night outside you could hardly tell it was stained now—anyhow such superstition was better than the kind Gary Willis had carried on at his Fountainwood. I thought of Jupiter with that Arab horse, Robin, and hoped he was sheltered up well against this blow, which I reckoned would be sweeping down all the length of Mississippi into the sea. Up in the low-ceiled hall on our landing, a blast hit the gables close outside and made the lamp-flame joggle in its chimney, and I lifted the lamp higher while French got the room key out of my pocket, feeling her fingers warm there as she groped for it, and a gladness for two people who trusted each other and wanted each other with all the passion and power in them, in the night.

But Sunday with its dark cool rain hit fast, as I've said, like a wave that wouldn't drop us from its clutch for a while, and in its lour and dankness I was close-mouthed all morning, even at breakfast when all the boarders kept asking me how much slower this track would make Grayboy and Charley and Bed—as if I knew—but kept on being civil as I could because they meant well. Pete Tarver, the betting man who'd sided with us the evening before during that Catewell fracas, and his wife, Mae, offered to

give French a ride to the track in a buggy they were going to hire for it, and
Ambrose Farwell, a man who'd also sided with us—it had been him
who'd made that little speech about growing up with nigras in the
house—and his Aunt Darleen—the plump lady partial to coffee-colored
ancient lace—said they'd be sharing the buggy as well, but there was
room for all, and no expense for French involved, and French, who'd I
reckoned always had the trick of accepting a favor with the same kindness
she gave one, it was part of her lady-ness, said she'd join them with
pleasure. So with that settled I said good-bye to French till after the
Sunday heat—there was no question of running the jenny today—and I
bulled my way against the wet back to the lane-shed, finding Grayboy
with the toe-calks already fitted, drowsing and eyeing the raindrops
sluicing down the pane between the bars at the side of his stall, and
Bellreve the bay wriggling his rich coat while W. M. gave him a
currying—he didn't have anything else to do right then or he'd have let
Bell go hang—and the jenny in its side of the shed with the small carved
horses eyeing this day as if it was a hell of a way from Florence, Italy, and
almost as far from a ballroom at Fountainwood, and just as far from the
ballroom of Chantry Hall.

Outside all the church bells, Ap's along with the rest, sounded with a
slight gurgle in their clanging through this sour weather, and through the
window here I saw Mama Gatchin and Manny, holding a bumbershoot
low against spoiling their Sunday bombazine, run down the side yard and
then get into a rig in the lane that some of their friends were driving;
Mama saw me here and yelled as she got a leg up in the rig, "Got to start
my bakin' soon as we git back—but all the services'll be out by half past
one so's the crowds can git to the stands in time for you! Manny and me
wish you the same as yesterday!" I flapped a hand to them and watched
the rig drive off. The lane was full of lakes, and I was thinking about that
tipped-down section of backstretch. For a painful while after that it was a
temptation to tell W. M. to hurry and finish Bell, and get Grayboy
harnessed, so we could make our way to the champion track and size up
ground conditions, but I held in that inclination and just kept my self-to-
self promise made the day before that I wasn't going through that
trackside waiting again. Once had been aplenty and even if I'd had the
wherewithal to sit in with Budge and Buck in Charlemagne's track-shed
and try to bluff their card-sense, I couldn't have stood it again so close to
the wire. It wasn't till one-fifteen by the turnip—which I'd done my living
best not to consult every five minutes, and not succeeded—that I got up

from the pile of hay where for the past hour I'd sat and pretended to rest while W. M. and Grayboy and Bell actually did child- and horse-nap, and woke up W. M. and told him if he wanted to harness now, he could, and please to saddle up Bell as well, and to throw the jenny-canvas over the sulky after he'd blanketed Grayboy and got up, so he wouldn't die of goose-drowning on our way.

He told me he'd swallowed more rain in his life than most children had milk, and kindly not to worry, but that he'd use the canvas anyhow because it would keep most of the sulky dry at least until we got to the track-sheds. When he'd harnessed Grayboy—which he did with such finicking care that I thought for a while I'd waited too long and we'd be late even for the start-positioning at two—I saddled up Bell myself to save time now—he got up on the sulky and drew the jenny canvas around him and the sulky until only his poll and his eyes were showing, and clucked to Grayboy and drove him out, and I followed on Bell, watching the first rain start darkening the pommel of the Spanish saddle, and Grayboy as he shook his head and protested a little about it, and thinking that if ever a knight had a field-boss squire it was me. We went down the lane to the first street over, all its stalls empty with burlap and croker sack coverings blowing against them in the rain's drag, and then came to the town square where the bandstand stood with its roof bouncing back water like the wings of a huge hen with her brood squatted under her, and here the only people promenading were doing it by running from one tree-haven to another or heading fast for doorways with bumbershoots or newspapers held above their heads as they skittered. The hats in Anderson's millinery had the only feathers not sleeked flat in this day. Across Sutton Road, then, where the betting stalls were open but with their proprietors just leaning in their windows and watching us as we passed—and Corum and Murphy no doubt hoping Grayboy might founder at the first turn—and the entries building with its steps running like a river landing's, and the sulky-rental stalls doing no trade either in sulkies or harness but sealed as vaults. Yet when we'd drawn past the testing track and to the field behind the champion track, here were all the buggies and buckboards and wagons and surreys and the waiting animals that had pulled them here, just as many as the day before if not a few extra, and as we slopped and clopped along behind the fencing abutting the track-sheds, Grayboy sensing the champion track close by again and all at once trumpeting through the wall of rain, here came the track-helpers to assist us by pulling the fence-railings wide to let us through. Grayboy sounded again, as if he was throwing down a challenge to the whole evening and all the slashing wetness it could offer, as though he knew something only shared by himself and W. M. and maybe, in a benevolent mood, me. A track-helper squinted up at me on Bell, grinning, waving us along. W. M. drove Grayboy to the north, the stands there black and ringing with the sound of the band playing out its lungs against the horizon. A yell was going up as people leaned from the stands to see us draw past the shed that had been Rankin's, and then the General Bedford shed—but I knew in my bone-centers they'd yelled just as hard for the General and Charley when they showed up. General Bedford's shed door was open, Budge stood in the doorway, touching his cap to me, looking almost jolly and kind as if he was only here for a pleasing ride, raindrops brushing into the grizzle of his beard; behind him in the shed Bed was harnessed and set, his van at one side and the Budge Fisher-General Bedford crew watching us pass with their eyes thoughtful—I took one more look at the rain screening across the track, almost hiding the infield from here, the dirt of the track running with a red gumbo. Then I leaned from Bell and pushed open the shed door and kept riding it back, reining Bell in and pushing, until the door was all the way open and W. M. could bring Grayboy in. He came into the dryness, big even in this high dry space, shaking rain off his mane and with his head up as W. M. turned him and he stood.

W. M. stayed on the sulky-seat, which I reckoned had kept dry for the time being. He shoved the folds of streaming canvas away from his head and bird-scrawny shoulders. I rode Bell over into one of the stalls and got off, and started unsaddling. "All right," I said to W. M. over the echoing space between us in here. "Just sit there till the last second, which I know you'll do anyhow. And tell me what you and Mister Grayboy got planned for the running this time."

# 44

W. M. said, "Keep to the inside. You got the pole start today, all you got to do is hold it. When you bring him in the second time, lift his head again. There ain't nothing to it but that. And today's when Budge Fisher will slam you. Or try to. Keep enough up on him so he never once gets the chance for a real hit." W. M. wasn't moving his eyes from Grayboy's body. A waft of steam was rising from Grayboy's withers and flanks. "You got to know Charley's a good mudder. He don't mind it. Mister Grayboy told me he don't mind the mud himself, even though you say you've never raced him in it. You got to let him off the bit quicker than you done yesterday." There was a pause while I walked over to the sulky. W. M. got down, having to drop quite a few inches to the floor of the shed. Past the doorway the rain lay out on the air as if it was the streaming hair of a woman swimming. Then the track-helper who'd showed up here yesterday evening was standing in the doorway, a blanket drawn over his head and shoulders. "Five minutes, Mister Broome." He saw French wasn't in here with us and didn't have to be escorted to her grandstand owner's box. I nodded, and got up on the sulky. The line-ends were still soft and dry in my hands as I took them up. The track-helper went running off. The tanbark floor of the shed smelled dusty as the inside of a log hollowed out by white ants. Now and then I could hear a gust of music from the band; now it was playing, "Beautiful Dreamer." Which didn't seem just right for the climate, but I didn't reckon anybody had ever put music to "The Wreck of the Hesperus." I took off my hat and shook it, sluicing an arch of drops to the floor of the shed, and pinched its crown and put it back on solid. Then I said to W. M., "If you're going to sit on the outside rail down past the wire again, you better take that canvas with you, otherwise you'll melt right down in the muck." I could just see his eyes from where he stood waiting for me to move out, they were as hooded and still as they'd been when I'd first had him bid for my attention while the Gypsies buried Bombo along the river-path near Pharis. He nodded as though it wasn't important what happened to him, and I flapped the lines and Grayboy pulled on out. The second the sulky tires hit the earth outside the shed-sill, they started to slip a little and Grayboy had to dig his calks in deeper and surge as I yawed him to the north, then we were moving down onto the track and we could have been alone on a back-path the same as we'd been on a gone Sunday night beside a bayou; except this time it wasn't quite as dark around us and I didn't expect to see any faraway lantern bobbing where it hung and leading us on. But the lonesomeness was almost as full and complete, because all I could see was the shapes of the track-handlers and the starter and his helper and I couldn't even make out the forms of the timers and the judge farther along to the north. I could see the white inside rail with its position-mark

looming up all right, staring out under my hat's brim, and hear the
breathing of Grayboy—which was a little disdainful of all this mush and
sea of water and red clay, but had a willing and anticipating sound as
well—and I drove him down and turned him, bringing up the sulky tires,
both settling an inch in the ground, right alongside the faint yellow mark
on the rail. I hadn't sat there more than a breath when here came Budge
Fisher following the bulking shape of General Bedford, who was tossing
his head and blowing like a huge seal, driving along through the mire;
then Budge was behind me, and the General was turning and splashing up
alongside, and it was nice to have company even if the company was
going to give me the worst time it could and knew how to accomplish all
that. Under the brim of his old cap Budge's eyes were half shut and his
knees and thighs looked like carven oak posts with his pants plastered
down on them and his boot-heels steady in the racks and his big chest like
a rum barrel under rainfall. I said through the couple of feet of rain
between us, which was also slicing straight at our horses and reaching
around them to wash our faces, "The General still off-stride?"

Budge said, his face looking very mournful and yet pleased with itself,
"He's poorly. I'd sell him if I wasn't so sentimental about him. I hear you
and Mrs. Broome are having an extra wedding come tomorrow. It's
noised around considerably. Can't for the life of me see why any man
wishes to get married twice, since he's already wedded and knows the
tribulations of it, but all the same I'd appreciate an invitation, and so
would Buck."

"You're invited, Budge," I said. "Win, lose, or draw. And so's
Buck." Neither of our voices made much effect against the pounding
rainfall. There was a slight coldness to the rain as well, falling over the
hides of Grayboy and General Bed and making their harness and the
shafts look like leather and wood that had been sunk in a fathom or so of
river. I could see the grandstand mainly as an extra hulking shape over to
the northwest, and still hear the band, whose fife-section was now playing
the riding-marching part of "The Yellow Rose of Texas," as well as it
could considering most roses would have been mashed down in this
deluge long before now. Budge lifted a hand to squeeze water from his
beard, and I saw the knuckle which he'd said had been squashed against
an inside railing. Then Buck's small round face, pipe angling up from his
mouth, was showing up through the murk, and even though his doughty
red and gold shirt and red hat were already one rain color, he was nodding
to us as though we'd met on the street and had time for a quiet amiable

conversation; as the great body of Charley came pumping through this steady twilight, Buck said out of a corner of his mouth, "Tom, you'll be pleased t' learn I took the old renegade right down the line today, he'll never catch up; king, high, jack and the game." I could hear him laughing as he drove past us and still laughing as Charlemagne blew and snorted and came up on Budge's off side. Across to his sulky Budge said, "Tom's invited us to his second matrimonial venture with the same lady."

"Why, thank you, Tom," said Buck. "I'll put on a funeral suit and be there. Don't recollect ever havin' attended a double knot-tying before, I usually stay a distance from any such affairs. But I'll be happy to sob with the best of 'em."

The insides of my nostrils felt as wet as if I'd been diving and forgetting to hold my breath. I reckoned Grayboy's and General Bed's and Charley's felt likewise. The starter and his helper were moving now, bending through the water to squint at our tire-positioning, and I thought I'd sure as hell detest having to be brought back from even one false start today; the starter's helper had gone over to the outside rail; then the starter was satisfied and was moving along the infield, running down to the start-wire, which could just be seen like a long damp twig stretching across above the track. None of us was talking now; I wasn't lonesome anymore but the other feeling, the one that makes the walls of the belly stiffen up and the liver and lights start to wheel a tad, was coming on, and I sat as quiet as Buck and Budge did, and the starter's voice came thinned by water, "Ready?" And the starter's helper was going along to the north too, his boots spurting in the thick mud. "Ready!" he called as he ran.

And the starter waited till his helper came up alongside, and then, leaning through the rain, yelled, "Go!"

There was a sound like the swash of a paddle wheel starting up, a long heavy curling of water as we all moved out, and on my off side Budge's wheels were level as a plumb line's with mine, the hubs matched in position, the tires with their cresting wave of yellow and dark red mud surging in the same second at the selfsame time, and beyond, on Budge's off side, Buck's sulky was keeping the same distance, Charley breaking much faster than I'd thought he would break in this slew of water and earth, wet platter-shaped gouts of earth sailing on both flanks of his sulky, but Buck was holding Charley back level for the start even though Charley had started the break, and as we came under the wire and the starter yelled, "Go, gentlemen!," Charley's break was full, and he and Buck were already driving ahead past the stands; he'd made his first bid so fast I wouldn't have believed a horse weighing that much could have done it even on a bone-dry day. Right in front of me rain and gusts of wind-driven spume were streaming from Grayboy like waterspouts, the rise and fall of his haunches and the sailing of his pacing just a ghost of sight up there, and as I gave him his full head and felt him begin to drive, and the grandstand went whirling past with a patch of noise loud to the right ear and then tailing away soft as if the whole sound of it had piled up there in one heap for one breath, I felt General Bed break early as well—felt more than saw, as you might see a ship's hull coming up beside you, and I knew they'd both pull ahead, Charley and Bed, and I'd be lucky if I ever got another clear glimpse of them for the whole two miles, if I didn't get more than Grayboy's best pacing now. I knew all this coming into the first turn, which we all fell into as though we were flung down from a height, the streams of water rooster-tailing and spreading over both inside and outside rails as we slewed on the turn; here Charley was almost half a length in front and I was neck-and-neck, hub-and-hub with Budge and General Bed, and Bed's trotting, high-kneed here in the ocean of sliding earth, was just as strong as it had been when there was firm ground under him, he was coming up as sure as he'd done in the homestretch of the second mile on Saturday; I felt myself biting the walls of my cheeks as I shouted something and stood in the racks, seeing from an eye-tail Charley, on the outside, a full length up now, Buck whip-tickling him and yelling, himself, and the giant Charley heading already into the backstretch, where out of the heavens the rain-wind whipped toward our tails, bending us along as if it wanted to help us all alike, no favorites; I brought Grayboy around this turn on the inside again so close to the rail—like yesterday—that I thought, in half a gulp, I'd taken him too far, and as it was I felt the sulky skidding first at the rail, then away from it, then closer in to it again, then wider away from it, shaking me from side to side so if I hadn't been solid on the seat I'd have gone over and been dragged, still holding the lines—Grayboy didn't let up, as we skimmed and wrenched that way half the length of the backstretch, the silver poplars on the outside seeming to reach their boughs and shake them at us as we spun and churned by, then the beeches dark through the sounding rain; and I could feel Grayboy giving more, his head deep into the air as if he drank it for steady sustenance, his breath clean as a bellows in the hands of the Gypsy smith Cando, and we were pulling in front of General Bedford and Budge at last. It was just then that Budge first ticked the off side of my sulky with his near hub, in the swash of eye-shutting rain; as I'd felt him coming up, instead of seeing him, I felt this, and it was as light as a little bell sounding once, a crystal bell icy and cool as the strings of Jantil's instrument, and I knew it would be heavier when it came again. I was high in the racks, almost arching there, and calling to Grayboy and knowing he could hear me, his ears laid back almost flat even as the wind and rain drove him from the rear, and then again the sulky was hit, this time like a gong but with Budge's sulky hub coming free the second after, then we were pulling ahead at last, Charley's heaving and swinging haunches and his trot-driving forearms and knees and his boulder-shining hocks still well ahead. All we had to do now was keep the pace and better it, keep ahead of the General and outdistance Charley. I thought we could hold up in front of Bed, but I didn't know if we could outwear Charley. We were almost around the far turn. The mud had a smell to it as if it was some part of a boiling spring, that sulphurous and rank scent, and I thought of the devil-worship frowst of Gary Willis's Fountainwood ballroom. For a few draughts of time I hadn't been able to see, as a mud-gout plastered itself across my eyes in this wind now from the left in the turn, but in the next second rain had washed that away, and I was keeping my eyes on Charley on my off side and outside; he was holding the line as the major's Amber had held a flat-racing line, I hadn't yet worn him down one inch. So we came on to the stands. We were under the wire with the rain-blast against us and diving past the stands again, the blurt of their noise quicker than just a rattling on the ears, I could hear the squelch and squirt of General Bedford's plates behind me and only a few feet to the outside, but all there was to see again as we rushed the near turn was a dark streaming wave of mud and water and then when it dropped away for a trace, I took one more rabbit-eyed look at the outside, and could see Charley's dust-blinkers—just as good against mud as against dust, but I still wouldn't have used them because I liked Grayboy to have all his sight—bobbing and his head slugging as he kept the same trot; but in the same look, I saw we were gaining on Charley. It wasn't more than the span of a hand at first, then as we bellied and chested and hoof-plated and tire-churned into the backstretch again it was more than that, it was two hands. Behind me Budge Fisher shouted in a gruff boy's voice, as if he was delighted in some game of one-old-cat or duck-on-the-rock, "Take 'im, Tom! The little snipe's goin' to try to fence you!"

If we'd still been in the near turn I wouldn't have heard him; as it was with the wind's help I did, and saw what he meant in another blink. Charley was losing ground, but mainly because Buck was angling him, a gentle chubby hand's twitch at a time, toward the inside; and once he got him there he would have me boxed because Charley could keep up this same gait in the mud all the way home. And though Grayboy might have swung out and passed him even then, mad because of this horse in front of his very eyes and determined to get around him, it would have been too late; we were almost into the far turn now and there wasn't enough race left to pass Charley that way before the wire swam up. At the rate Grayboy was gaining and with what we'd lose by swinging out it would have taken another full mile. So I couldn't let Buck do it. I leaned forward and raised the lines and brought them down sharp, once, twice, I'd never done it before—hadn't needed to—and Grayboy's rising to it came as if he was trying to tear himself out of harness and sulky and all and run free, it was as though he jerked the sulky-wheels above the mud and started straight up in the sky like a cannonball aimed at opposing armies just over the ridge of the day, and then, still holding to the inside of the backstretch, the poplars and the beeches moving by as though they were drawn on the crest of a flood on the outside rail, we were coming up steady and sure, Buck still angling but only touching toward the inside now, ready to sheer off if he had to; then he had to. He couldn't have come farther inside without hitting me, and it wouldn't have been one of those artistic, fiddle-wristing hits Budge could do so well, either; it would have been a wheel-tangle and both of us would have gone over or through the inside rail or both. As we came up on Buck, and he straightened Charley back to his steady line, I saw him gazing straight forward, pop-eyed a little, the mud-flecks black over his forehead and fine shirt and duckbilled cap, his pipe fixed in his lips, and with it just the merest hint of a smile.

We came off the backstretch level as a razor blade, we could have reached through the pounding water and ooze and shaken hands, but into the near turn Grayboy kept up his surging, as if he was already above the mud and winging along at the head of a flock of brant or teal as the master of their V, and as the rail kept whipping by and then made its last curve into homestretch we were a nose in the lead, then a full head, and that was the way we splashed and sang and yelled and, more than anything, paced like fire through the last of the rotten mud under the wire. I'd had Grayboy's head up just as W. M. had desired it, and caught a fleeting glimpse of W. M. on the outside rail, and Buck slowed Charley, easy, and I slowed Grayboy a rod or so beyond him, and then we were both turning, and behind us, Budge was turning the General, whose knees still came up high as though he was parading, a tight turn in the slewing mire, then Buck and Budge and I came back side by side, not looking up into the stands at all as the band oompahed and strained to break a couple of choruses of "Dixie" into the streaming air, and Buck called out, "You *ornery* young strap, you Tom Broome," and Budge said, flat-toned while he wrung his beard out once more, "Told you the General's off. I got to change his feed."

Then W. M. was throwing a blanket, for all the good it would do out here, over Grayboy, and taking him while I got down, and we were curving into the shed where the cutting off of the rain seemed to me as strange as though I'd lived in rain for the past forty days and nights, like old Noah, and the being able to breathe something besides rain seemed a gift straight from the lap of a miracle. And outside the judge was bellowing with his voice still rain-stoppered, "Grayboy, four minutes, three seconds! Charlemagne, four minutes, three and a half; General Bedford, four minutes, six seconds!" He kept repeating this news. For all the point that we'd fatted out yesterday's time by two seconds, it hadn't been a bad go, for the weather. I went to Grayboy and got hold of a strap and pulled his head down and loved him for a little, his wet cheek-hide warm, his eye cheerful and brilliant, and W. M. was already getting him out of harness; then I took off my hat and scaled it across to Bell's stall, where for a wonder it landed upright on a stall-post and twirled around twice before it settled and hung, and did a quick buck-and-wing in my sopped boots, and started peeling off my shirt. W. M. said, "Don't tear up the onion patch, Mister Grayboy'll think you gone out of your head. Good drive, Mister Broome."

I went over half-stripped and took him with one gray black small ear in each hand's cup, and rolled his head back and forth. He didn't look as if he weighed even as much as a puffball, in the instant. He'd kept the jenny canvas around him though, and could have been wetter. I said, "That's twice you've called me Mister. Don't bust your character, I couldn't stand it!" He gave me a mere lip-touching tolerating grin, and moved into seriousness again right off the mark, taking off the harness and getting the shafts out. "We got to walk him out right here, and keep him here till he's heated and dry all through, then warm-blanket him before we take him back to Mama's shed. I got a good thing in mind for his suppertime. Heydy, Miss Chantry—Miz Broome—you see all the running?"

French with the cloak-hood around her head looked about W. M.'s age herself, maybe even a few years younger considering his old-man cast of mind, even if she had once told me she was twenty years old and still an old maid at that telling. She could have been the witch-spirit of the day, making it leap right through the rain with light. She said, "What I could see of it—or anybody could." Then she was against me, rain-speckled cloak's cloth against my wet chest, and behind her was lumbering in Ap Miller, whose baptizing coat I surmised had seen even worse downpours than this; he was bearing a big wooden tub like a vat in his arms, his beard thoughtfully hung on one side of it so it wouldn't drink up all the water that steamed and sloshed in its belly. He even had a couple of lumps of ash-lye soap in one hand. "Borrowed this from a parishioner," he said, spraddling over the tub while he put it down on the tanbark. "Swamper named Gillian—he and his friends use it once a year when they get back from their winter traplines. He don't grudge you using it, he seen you drive yesterday and today. I preached for a dry track today and look what we got—seems if man can never coddle favor with the Almighty if he wants it for personal gain. If this keeps up into tomorrow, though, I'll ask my special angel to intercede. He's Gabriel, and he's done me past favors when I needed 'em. Mister Broome, get right out of them pants and boots and into that tub. Mrs. Broome'll tell you the same. If the water's still sightly, she's welcome to take a soak herself when you're done—I'll turn my back, it's been a good long time since I've looked with lust on female flesh, though if anybody could turn the trick, she might. Lad," he said to W. M., "don't go back out to the pump to fill that bucket, just grab some of this steamin' water if you're going to wash off that marvelous horse." He sighted through his framing hands at Grayboy. "He's a steed of the Apocalypse, returned to earth," he rumbled. "He ain't got the dragony wings and the multifold eyes, but he's got all he needs to prove he sprang from the burnin' heavens."

Grayboy knew he was being praised up; he even looked for a little like the horse of writ the Reverend Ap had mentioned.

# 45

By two o'clock the next evening the champion track was dry as if the rain had never touched it. And had been raked and curried as if the whole mile of it was some kind of horse itself. The wind and the last of the rain had died out during the night, the sun had risen starting to heat the world early. With just a touch of cold through it, so you could feel the winter arriving and hold the whole of this supreme October to you as if it was a pawpaw in the hand, still yellow but going to turn to its full sweetness as soon as the skin blackened. You could have searched through the whole South—I wouldn't know about anything in the North, maybe they had their golden autumn too—and hardly chosen a better Monday to run the last heat in, to be married the second time in, and to start off back for Lanceton County in. Those were the three main events standing just ahead of me and French, but the only one lofty in my mind and spirit at the instant was the first. The night before it had been I who'd slept like a child, as if all thought of the maybes and the ifs and might-haves had dropped away from me like a bothersome extra skin, and I'd shed it and had wakened as if I came fresh from getting born. I'd shed the marigold poultice too, didn't need it anymore. Now I sat on the sulky at the pole position and thought that even if I got whipped today it would all of it have been worth it; worth it to French as well, no matter what kind of puzzlement and tangled spiderweb waited for us back to the south in Lanceton and at Chantry Hall. Sometimes all your past rolls up at once and fixes itself solid in your bubbling veins and beating heart; this was one of those times. I was going to savor it till my wind broke and my hocks went soft and my hoofs grew corns. Grayboy was too; he was standing with hardly a quiver, just ready and itching for the start. The night before French and I had sat up till quite late in the sitting room with Mama Gatchin, Manny and the boarders—we'd made our plans for the return trip, speaking to each other soft under the spate of horse-talk and the snapping of the chimney-fire near us. People moseyed all through Mama Gatchin's tall house that night, drinking everything from good considerate corn to

dandelion and scuppernong wine to mellow juleps, not tearing up anything or engaging in fisticuffs but blithe as chattering starlings, stepping
from parlor to living room to dining room to sitting room and sometimes
clumping on the stairs in their celebration of the last night of Yadkin Fair.
Mama herself had her church-bombazine on and Manny had been
scrubbed up and was wearing a dark blue gown French had bought her and
insisted she take, and one of the lesser bird-adorned hats from the
Anderson millinery which French had also talked Mister Anderson into
letting go cheap in a good cause. French and W. M.—what with his
watchfulness in raking in the coins—had amassed quite a hatful of money
from the merry-go-round; we surmised we had enough to travel with
Manny along back down the side-trail in the direction of Quincyville a
spell, seeing her on her way, so to speak; French had given her some of
the money from the jenny's takings so Manny could cut over from there to
the west, and board the river packet that still ran there down to Seldin,
where she would live with her aunt and uncle and go to school. Mama
Gatchin had asked Ap Miller for the loan of one of his old mules for her to
travel to the packet by and use while she lived in Seldin and attended
school; Ap said he would loan it freely, and that it was a mule well
schooled in piety, which could counsel her in fine style in case she
encountered any of the Devil's minions during her years in Seldin. When
I'd told W. M. that Manny Gatchin, on a mule, would be traveling part
way back with us, he had looked at me for about five ticks of the turnip,
and shaken his head. "Mister Grayboy in company with mules," he'd
said. "The *Memphis Belle* bein' held back by a dugout. The *Robert E.
Lee* poking along beside some river-rat craft." He'd lowered his voice to
a husky whisper. "Don't tell Mister Grayboy about it till after the last
heat's run," he said. "He could git his dander up and go into the sulks."
I'd promised I wouldn't mention it to Grayboy.

The air today was so still, so heated with pleasure, I could hear the
music of the band from the stands as if every brass note trumped up clear
as sun through gin. I'd even been able to hear the jenny's music as it
sounded here for the last time in Yadkin, and had noted when it broke off
and W. M. and French took Bell with the jenny back to the lane-shed and
brought out Grayboy and the sulky. I'd sat up in the eave-room till then,
listening to the whooping and folderol of the selling stalls and the frenzy
of the people here on this final day, and playing my daddy's fiddle as I
listened; I went over every tune I knew, and it was like my elbow was
greased with the mellowlight, and the tunes came out as they'd come

after we'd escaped the attentions of French's friends in the horse-box that morning on the road to Pharis. As if the chanting of the whippoorwills on that road had got into the notes. I had thought Daddy himself might be pleased with the performance, though he was a critical fiddle-man. Then, hearing the jenny music leave off its clean gentle piping, I'd boxed the fiddle and the bow and taken it and the saddlebags downstairs and met French and W. M. in the lane, where together we'd harnessed Grayboy to the sulky and then brought him along to the champion track sheds, French riding Bell and Bell pulling the jenny which had its canvas lashed down over most of our worldly goods including Grayboy's saddle gear, W. M. driving Grayboy, and me walking because I wanted to walk. We'd come so to the track shed, the crowd cheering us as we passed, as of course they'd cheered Charlemagne and General Bedford when they in their vans had showed up, but all the same I thought, I'll recall that cheering a long while, no matter what happens in Lanceton. And now the jenny was with Bell in the track shed, W. M., with his tattered shirt showing his frail plum-colored arms, was hunched down on the rail past the starting wire, French was in the owner's box in the stands—today I could see her there, the Gypsy dress a flare of color even with all the colors around her—and I printed it all on the eye for good remembrance. And in the ear and the recalling bones.

I'm not saying I didn't care if Grayboy won; that was uppermost in me, just as it was in him; but I'd finally reached what Shangro and Aldan, Jantil and Pella and all those other Gypsies could reach; a quiet place as cool-warm as the sunrays themselves, off above the multitude of noise and heat and stir. It felt good being in such a place, the same sort of place Budge and Buck with all their years of driving had learned to sit in and live with even on the edge of a great race. I tasted it, full, even now as Buck who had the next-to-pole position today came out of the Charlemagne track shed and along to where the handlers led him onto the track, Charlemagne looking so fit he might have been a massy peach-pit basket shined by the heel of a hand to his best glossiness, his harness making a soft bright sound through the other noises as he came down along the inside rail and then swung out and passed me and Grayboy, and his eyes—unblinkered today, there wasn't a grain of dust stirring—giving Grayboy a greeting as he rolled by, then the harness jingling as once again he was turned and came up. Buck Torbert was whistling soft and almost not to be heard. One of the few men I'd ever seen who could whistle with a pipe in his teeth; I reckoned he could have done the same with a chew in his mouth. He nodded a good day, I nodded, and he said over the mild blowing of Charley, "I ain't going to insult a friend whose wedding I'm goin' to today, but if you ever want to sell him"—jerking his head, light, to Grayboy—"I'll offer the highest. You know how I'd treat him. I'll better anything anybody else ever offers, by a thousand. Don't tell me he's not for sale, I know that. Just hold it in your mind in all the days to come. I had a fair pacer once, but since then it's been trotting. I've nigh forgotten how a pacer feels on the lines. I'd like to find out again, some year before the boneyard claims me."

He looked forward, then, thoughtful, as if whoever came out on top and whatever the final times were today, he was savoring and summing up the Yadkin champion track as I was. We didn't talk anymore, just sat; until General Bedford came out, and then was drawing toward us. Then he said, "That old bag of guts and bourbon-rotted tripes made his side bets on *me* and *Charley* yesterday. Cleaned up, he wasn't betting against you at all. So I foxed him, I did the same thing today. Bet on him and the General against me, even money. If he should take me, which I immortally doubt, I'll have the deep pleasure of knowin' it's all paid for."

Budge Fisher came rumbling by, touching his cap to me and maybe to Buck, though I knew he'd played skin-hide poker or some other cards with Buck right up until time. His beard had some bear-grease or other oil on it, his eyes looked so quiet and full of goodwill for the whole race of man and horses, you would have trusted him with all your goods and chattels, and his hard monumental belly and the sinews in his wrists under the wristbands of the wan gray shirt looked as if they'd grown from the sulky-seat like a natural tree. Then he was wheeling the General in back of us, and coming up. In the crisp, dried and raked clods of the track the sulky-wheels and General Bed's hoof-plates made a noise like many pecans rustling down in a rainfall. He murmured a few things about General Bed being so off-stride and feed he thought he'd have to take him to a good doctor, but didn't get a rise out of us this time, and then smiled quiet and sat gazing forward as we were, and like us, appeared to be taking the whole day into himself as if he was a sponge that adored it.

Then the starter was leaning, peering, the starter's helper gauging our tires from the other flank, and then the starter was nodding and racing on down under the start-wire, and even through the lines with their ends held quiet in my palms, I could feel the change and flame moving through Grayboy, and knew he was going to give me—and himself—everything he could, on a noble silver platter, barring accidents, and even if the accidents happened, was still going to try to do all that. I looked out all the way past the infield to the inside rail Rankin had gone through, where it was patched up and clean-painted now; the tilt of the track would be something again to reckon with this time, though the gumbo had been so deep there yesterday the cant of the track wouldn't have made much difference. Well, I thought, we all knew about it, so we were starting even again. Down past the wire the starter had already called his *ready* and the helper had answered that we were, and now both starter and starter-helper were stationed, and the "Go!" came just when I'd thought it would, not a paring of a second before or later. So we were moving out, sudden, in a good line, and not breaking fast as we'd all more or less done in the wet, and then holding the same lineup under the wire, with the "Go, gentlemen!" sounding sharp under the crowd's fanning roar, and it was all started. The last of the Yadkin three champion heats, the last of the great Mississippi racing for this year, the only one there'd ever be on this day in this time in this magical evening.

Out from under the shadow of the stands we came into the light, Budge letting the General break now, and then Buck and I doing the same with Grayboy and Charley, so by the time we were into the first turn, with the red clay hardening ahead of us and the horses' three shadows skimming along it as if they were one shadow—or the shadow of three hawks almost melding and one grazing the next as we spun—we were all into full gait, the trotting of Charley and Bedford on the outside a beating music of eight chugging plates, Grayboy's music the plunging, soaring rise and fall that charged back through his body and made the lines sing in tune to it, his great near fore-knee and near hocks moving slick as satin over a rush of floodwater, then the off-knee and off-hocks following and all of it so quick you could only feel it but not count the beats, as if one beat poured into the next so fast there really wasn't that much less than a second of flying clear off the ground. Though if you looked ahead and let yourself be bemused by his motion you could tell there was, that he was even more than a horse, that he was also a bird that flies for the simple creation of it and the boiling joy it brings to the blood. Today when we came into the backstretch we were still even, not a turning spoke's width between us, the three of us moving now onto the tilted ground which had been cleared and pounded but which hadn't had its hill removed, and I felt the change as the near wheel went low, and kept to the railing with the near tire hissing there and cutting a fresh groove in the well-tamped clay, the

off-tire holding well in the surface of the sunned clay, no wind now to
rake us along from the rear but just the horses themselves doing their
damndest and maybe a full ounce more. I was heeling the racks, rising in
them, and so were Budge and Buck, Buck's cap-brim held against his red
forehead like an upstanding sail, Budge's beard pressed against his chest
in a respectable bundle like Spanish moss gathered and pressed, their
sulkies like mine bounding a little on the slightly higher ground, the
shadows of Grayboy and Charley and Bed spreading over the outside
almost to the outside rail, the sulky-shadows looking thinned out and
misted and small behind the great ghosting shadows of our horses themselves, and the sun from the west flashing reflections of wheel-spokes and
harness buckles and shaft bolts into all of our eyes. I was singing snatches
of most of the fiddle tunes I'd played that morning, knowing Grayboy's
ears were catching them. And telling him, between bursts of the singing—I don't sing well, I didn't think any of the Covenanters or the I-Will
Baptists or the Methodists or even Reverend Ap would have wished me in
their choirs—this was the last race here, and to make it good, not for just
me and whoever had bet on him, but for him and for Daddy and the past.
You can summon up a mortal lot of time in brief time, and it seemed to me
as we approached the far turn, I was bringing back into my head and being
all the Dango Falls meadows and the horse-barns I'd grown up with when
Daddy had come home after the war, could smell the Foggy Meadow and
the long grass there, could see Grayboy's Nickajack dam being led out in
the early morning with the shine of her restfulness still upon her, could see
Grayboy himself as a colt-foal, knobby-kneed and even then showing
signs of the height he'd start putting on as he shot up and the grape in his
muscle firmed. I felt as though all that got in what I was yelling as well,
though it was just the same bunch of cussing and craziness Buck and
Budge were crying out to Charley and General. And as we rounded into
the far turn, I knew something more I hadn't known before—as if every
beat of a step Grayboy and I'd ever taken on this track had taught me
more, as if walking it, and then running it twice, had brought more
knowledge that I hadn't even known before was there for the taking—I
knew Grayboy was moving faster than he ever had, and that Charley and
General Bedford were outdoing themselves no matter how well they'd
done in the past.

I think, now, we all knew that by the time we were under the wire again
and running into the stand's shadow.

I think it wasn't any great surprise we'd hoped for, or dreamed of, or refined ourselves to—I think we all understood what was happening, but as if it was a gift and not a trained-for event. As if we'd each man of us found out why this was such a sharp-whetted day, with every slant of its sunlight holding a special meaning, and that even though after the two miles were over and the crush of the crowd started and the yelling swarmed around us, we might lose the whole keenness and grace and joyousness and knife-sharpness of this knowledge, it was all here now among us and shared in full measure by all of our horses. I know I felt the hairs rise along my spine and something come up cool in my throat and my chest open as it had done the first time I'd driven Grayboy in the Foggy Meadow against Sugar Man—it was the same as then, with something else pressed down and running over. Into the near turn we dived, the six of us, horses and men, hub to hub and chest to chest, head to head and mane to mane, and the sun was beating at our backs and we were running together; no horse in front, no shadow changing, as if it would all go on till the last trump had sounded and all the armies of man that had died in any cause, and all the chariots and knights of the past, and all children who'd ever had foolish dreams or nations that had held dreams for a time and lost them through lack of gripping, came rending up from their graves.

So we came into the backstretch again.

So we charged along it, the silver poplars with their falltime-sheared boughs seeming to lean in toward us, the boughs whipping and shaking in our breeze, and the boughs of the beeches with their iron knotted forks trembling stiffer, and the scent of the day harvested and full, a smell coming up from river bottom and side-trail and corn-crib and the whole bobtail and ragtag of the countryside and everyone who'd come to Yadkin Fair from country and city—all of it sweeping in Grayboy's clear-breathing, deep-pumping nostrils, and into Charlemagne's and General Bedford Forrest's and mine and Buck's and Budge's. The breath of this life, and the crest of it. And in it there was French, all of her, and all her past as well as mine, the past that was our single present now, and a small girl who'd loved a carousel and had followed it and got it back from knavery in the teeth of what anybody else thought. For me there was all that too; I couldn't ever start speaking for anybody else.

So we came off the backstretch and into the far turn.

Along the whole sweep of the turn we stayed three abreast, Buck with his whip tickling Charley, but not hard and nearly as if he did it to remind Charley that he was there, that they weren't horse and man but a single flashing, hell-for-leather on-cheering lump, and not to forget it, and Budge humming loud as a hive on a July noon, and I not even yelling now, and the trotting of their horses and the pacing of Grayboy around us in a huge set of flying chimes, and then we were onto the homestretch. The wire ahead. And I heeled the racks again, and called out to Grayboy, not even knowing I was going to till then, the Rebel yell as I'd heard men make it who echoed what they'd done in the Army of Northern Virginia, who had made it then out of scrannel throats and parched and aching and hungry bellies, but who made it, right or wrong, because it was all they had to say.

He rose in the straps and shafts, head up, the extra ounce pulling up from a well deep as the earth under his plates, and then we were just a nose ahead of General Bedford as the wire went whipping back above us, with Charley now another whit, no more, behind Bed.

And we were pulling up, under the thunder of the stands, W. M. watching from where he knelt on the outside rail now, and then getting down and spurting toward us, and hats and scarves and even a jug of corn whirling down out of the stands onto the track, and Grayboy's plates and Bed's, and Charley's all blurring in together in the sound they made as we pulled in, then we tightened into a turn to the off-side, and made it together, and still matched horse for horse, man for man, were riding back to the south. And over the crowd thunder, Buck said, "Ha! I laid a whole wad against me just on *you,* you frightful idgit!" and pounded Budge on a huge shoulder.

Budge patted his lips a little with the back of his knuckle-missing hand, and yawned and beamed up into the sun.

"I bet on myself against you, today," he said easy. "No odds, but a packet. Didn't know if I'd beat Broome, but I felt it was time again for Bed to make a fair showin'. Even if he's feeling his age."

They weren't stopping the crowd now, everybody was rushing at us. Budge whoa-ed General Bedford, and Buck and I hauled in alongside him. A woman with a bundle of soft white feathers—I reckoned an ostrich's—on her hat, was trying to climb in the sulky with me. She carried a bottle of champagne. I waved it away; it foamed and was soaking the ground and a good many other people, all around. I'd never liked it since waiting for Daddy in those whorehouses after Mama had died, those times, when the women rubbed it in my hair, though I vowed to try it again some other time under other conditions. Another woman, weighing a good bit, was trying to kiss me, and two of them were climbing onto Budge and Buck. The Reverend Miller was striding his way through all this, half-carrying French. Through the babble and nudge and shaking and dust and weeping and laughing and shouting around us, Grayboy stood as if pleased but scorning it, then W. M. came worming up from under him, and said to me, sharp enough for me to hear, "I'll take him now. Got to rub him down good and walk him too and give him a good feed before we get set to start for Lanceton with some *mule*. I'll do all that 'fore you gets yourself proper married. Edge out."

I said to him, touching his shoulder, "What else?"

"*Mister,* if you want it. You got the right to be called that this one more time . . . Mister Grayboy done nearly what I said he was going to all along. Oh, reckon you can't hear the judge. Mister Grayboy done the two-mile in three minutes, fifty-nine seconds. Mister General Bedford Forrest in three fifty-nine and a half. Mister Charlemagne in four minutes, cold. Please to git out of the sulky, these people are going to bust it down, we got to pay for it, you know. Even if we did win us a gre't lot over at them no-account betting mens'."

I got out. It was hard, but I made it, in this crush.

Then Ap Miller was here, and W. M. was perched on the sulky and actually moving Grayboy out, calling, "Make way! Make the champion some way!"

And I was trying to duck Ap's whack between the shoulder blades, not able to do it but able to scoop French in with me before he knocked me down in his abounding and teeming joy, so I still had hold of her when we came up from the crowd again.

# 46

I let W. M. take the sulky back to the stall where we'd rented it to start with, after he'd rubbed down Grayboy so hard I feared there might not be any hide left; I felt he'd get back our ten-dollar deposit on the sulky with no argument, and no doubt talk the man out of a little of the fifteen we'd paid for its use, since it would be according to his estimate a famous sulky now, a champion's; and sure enough when he got back he brought fifteen

with him, and by that time Ap Miller was back at the track-shed too, with
the heap of money he'd exchanged for my betting slip at the Corum and
Murphy stall. A lot of people, including the chief track judge and the track
helpers and the starters and timers, were in this shed now, clustering
around the stall where Grayboy stood hot-walked out and rubbed down
and shining like the sun on living granite. Every part of his coat burnished.

Among them was the man with the wen on his nose, still afflicted with
the drips, and he kept moving around among the others and telling how
I'd staked him to a new start in life, though all on earth I'd done was give
him ten dollars for a middling-small bet. He'd paid me back the ten. More
people kept streaming in and out every second. I sat on an upended box,
French standing near me and sometimes touching me on the shoulder;
outside at the shed door there was still a line of people waiting to get in.
My right hand's fingers were tired from shaking hands. I didn't reckon
Grayboy's—and for that matter General Bedford's and Charlemagne's—
records would stand for long in time; I didn't even know how they
compared to any other records in the North or East or West; all I knew was
they were outstanding for Yadkin, and would do me for now. I didn't feel
like any knight of old, or champion myself; it was Grayboy's doing in the
long run, but I was glad he had hoofs instead of hands so I could take the
brunt of all this congratulation and he didn't have to do anything but stand
there. French had draped the wedding crowns we'd been married by
Shangro in, one on each post of his stall-box; they looked like some kind
of crowning laurel wreaths there.

We'd decided we'd all stay right where we were till it was time to go
over to Church Block and get the Miller wedding ceremony over with;
Mama Gatchin and Manny were going to meet us at Ap's. In spite of W.
M. looking like a menacing thundercloud on all his small face here in the
stripes of sun licking into the huge shed, people kept trying to step into the
stall with Grayboy, just to say they'd touched him or had been at his side.
It might have been a general election or a riverside baptizing that was
going on, with a yeasty feeling through it that fitted in nice with the ripe
sun-and-cool of the brilliant day. I'd have liked to stay on at Mama's that
night, but tonight, Tuesday and most of Wednesday weren't any too
lengthy times to get all the distance back down to Lanceton County and
Chantry Hall; we were going to have to make tracks along the side-trail
and down the other roads past Quincyville and Pharis. And already the
light was mellower, with a brandy touch to it; almost the color of the old,

well-stilled bourbon in the glass somebody had shoved into my left hand, and from which I took sips from time to time. It was one hundred percent up on the bar-bourbon I'd tried while waiting for Major Deveraux to have his talk with French. I passed it up to French, and she took a sip; the sun in the liquor under her mouth made her mouth look riper than ever, and sent small flashes of more sun into her eyes. From the Anderson millinery she'd invested in a hat for herself, along with that blue dress she'd got for Manny; she said she had a new gown to be married in, as well, and would change into it at Ap's. She was wearing the new hat, which didn't have a fluff of feather on it, but was just a long sweep of brim coming down over one eye that made her look as though she was shadowed by half an angel's wing, the straw of the hat dark gold and all of it fetching as something you'd dream on an afternoon when you didn't have anything better or worse to do. I decided if in Lanceton County they finally threw us both in jail, she was going in style.

At about half past four Ap Miller hoisted himself up from the platform of the merry-go-round where he'd been sitting on the edge, holding forth on the merits of southern horses and comparing them to steeds mentioned in the Bible and blessed with extra stamina and staying power, and wiggled his long clean bare feet in the tanbark, and said we'd all have to move along now over to Church Block, because Mister and Mrs. Broome—and Manny from Mama Gatchin's—had a journey to go, and the Broomes had to be solid-married first, for the second time because they were so attached to the blessing the ceremony offered. There was a good deal of cheering then, some of it wrapped in various liquor fumes, and I took it Ap had invited all these people here along with those who were already invited, which didn't matter to me—or to French, I thought —but might complicate the rest of the evening for Miller. And by this time we had Bell harnessed back to the jenny, and the canvas drawn over it, and Bell saddled and Grayboy with his own saddle on and the bags and fiddle-box ready to carry, so I mounted him and French got up on Bell, the Spanish saddle almost as elegant as she was, and W. M. got himself set on the jenny, and we rode out of the Grayboy track-shed for the last time, at the head of a train. When we were halfway across the field I looked back in the westering rays of the sun. There were all these folks behind us, some afoot and others horsed and muled or wagoned or whatever, streaming out across the field, waving jugs and bottles and some of the flags that had already been torn down from most of the streets of Yadkin, and behind them was the champion track with longer shadows reaching across it now from the stands; I knew I'd never come to this track again in quite the same way, or know it as I'd known it for four days, and said farewell to it without saying a word aloud, and saw from French's sun-touched face that she was thinking and without words saying the same thing. Then we were moving out of Sutton Road, the betting stalls all shut up now, having paid off for the last time this year, the entries building looking lorn and smaller than it had when I'd first sighted it, the sulky-rental stalls just pieces of wood and slabby roofs in the dark deep sun. Beyond there some old men were sitting on benches beside the promenade not far from the bandstand, talking the old battles and crops and family talk they'd keep up through most of the winter, and one of them waved his stick to us as the horde of us pulled by, then they went back to their chatter. But I noted that as we got over to the selling stalls, which were shutting down for the year as well, we were picking up even more company, both dressed to the teeth and garbed in what they'd always worn on their backs; most of the swipes and helpers and go-alongs from the Charlemagne and General Bedford stables had joined the procession now, and mixed in with them were people from fancier boarding-houses than Mama Gatchin's, and Pete Tarver and his wife Mae from Gatchin's came trotting out of Center Street, in the same buggy they and the man called Ambrose Farwell and his Aunt Darleen had hired the day before to go to the champion track, all of them crowding it, and then Mama came in a rig with a passel of her friends, and cutting in from another street came the man French had chided on Friday for calling one of the testing track tryers a poor bastard, the man named Bret Harte. He walked up alongside us and tipped his hat to French. "I should enjoy joining you at your nuptials," he said, and French said, "You are welcome as flowers in May, sir," and he said, "I made this trip South to seek out material; my western matter is going thin. I have found a rich lode, but I don't know how I can use it. My friend Sam used it so well, and he would accuse me of treading on his territory if I tried. He is preter-naturally jealous as it is. I think I shall go abroad soon, I have been offered a post in Europe. But I merely wished to thank you, sir"—he bowed to me—"for a valiant exhibition of superb harness racing, and you, ma'am"—he bowed up again to French—"for simply being yourself and renewing a tired scrivener's belief in the freshness of all womankind."

"And who is your friend Sam, sir?" asked French as we clopped along. "And why is he jealous?"

"Sam Clemens," said the man Harte. "He resides in Hartford, to the east; our relations have been strained for some time now. I was once his editor, and he has never forgiven me. He has an admirable talent, but I fear he will blow himself up some day in his choler. Which, after all, would leave the field clear for me, would it not? I thank you again for your invitation, ma'am, and if I were in trim I would make it the occasion to compose an epithalamium, or at least a short story. As it is I shall brood on it, and enjoy it. Good day!''

He dropped back with the rest of the mob-procession, and after a while French said over the noise and cheering around and in back of us, ''Sam Clemens. I do verily believe he means Mark Twain.''

''If you can trust anything a writing man says,'' I said. ''Seems a good fellow anyhow, if melancholy.''

Then we were on Church Block, pulling past the Covenanting church and the I-Will-Arise-Second-Coming-Split-Off-Baptist, and the Free Soul Methodist. The church-spire of the Miller edifice was leaning farther west than ever, as if the blow of the day before had knocked the whole affair more skewed on its foundation stones, and pigeons were circling in and out of the bell tower in a frenzy, because there were already what I took to be most of Ap's congregation waiting on the lawn and around the fishing-lodge preacher's house, all talking and cheering at once and hardly giving the pigeons a chance to settle before they got scared again. Back at the scuppernong arbor some of the swamp-rats had decorated it by hanging it with skins of otter and bear and boar and a plenty of squirrels, and there was a trestle table set up alongside the arbor groaning under the wedding liquors and meats. More food than even Mama Gatchin's sideboard and boardinghouse table could hold, which was stretching some. Through the crowding and the whelming as we arrived on the lawn, Ap came shouldering up to us and said to me, ''Who's giving away Mrs. Broome this trip, or is it a point with you, Mister Broome?''

''Nobody gave her away before, she just showed up,'' I said. ''But I reckon I've got just the man for it.'' I turned around to W. M., where he sat high under the flying jenny's pagoda, the rest of it swathed in canvas. ''William Makepeace Ritter,'' I said, ''for once in your life you can be sociable. And I want you to stuff yourself with most of those things to eat over yonder, I'm tired of you looking like you'd just fallen off the back of a wagon with the rest of the chaff. You're the giving away party, and I reckon the best man too. For once in your days, no argument.''

He opened his mouth to bad-mouth me, but then thought better of it and climbed down. Ap said, "I'll tell you what to do, W. M., it ain't complex. And I got an old jacket and some pants I'd say you ought to wear, they belonged to a jockey I saved once, he thought they was too flamboyant for him once he'd sobered up and got his soul in order. You come with me, and you, Mrs. Broome and Mister Broome, you just get on in the house there and clean up and get yourselves set. Same tub of water's all ready on the second floor. Shouldn't of cooled much, my congregation's been keepin' it hot. Here, one of you boys take Mister Broome's saddlebags on up with him, and be a mite careful with 'em, they're the bags of a champion and we all value them highly. Step lively, I don't want this marriage to hold off till after dark, it should be done by the light of day with the heavens arching o'er all." He bowed his enormous head and shoo-ing W. M. ahead of him, went back up the brick walk to the house, and after we'd got Bell and Grayboy tied to the hitching posts out front, French and I followed. In the downstairs rooms of the house there were so many vines at the windows they shut off most of the light, what got in here being green and filtered and tender, and falling over the yellowed keys of an organ and about a hundred mounted deer heads in wide stages of moth-proofing, and there were hunters and trappers and some of their women in here too, galore, and the Plott hound lying under a bench with his eyes red-rimmed and his face philosophic as if he'd seen worse in his time, and could bear more, but didn't enjoy it.

I led French up a wide creaking staircase past a couple of Federal sabers that had been captured long before and jangled from the wall as we brushed them, thinking that if she thought she'd had to cleanse our eave-room at Mama Gatchin's she would have had a year's labor ahead of her in this place, while behind us a swamp-rat with a face like uncured leather heaved our bags on his shoulder, and then he stepped ahead of us and flung open a door to a small room where the wooden water-tub vat Ap had gifted us with after the rain-running heat stood sending up tendrils of steam. He put the bags on the floor, shut the door, and I said, "Here we are. Let's get it over with, even if it's a far way from swimming with Shangro's people."

French nodded, and took off her spang-new hat and threw aside her cloak and started getting out of the Gypsy dress and kicked her frail old slippers aside. I stripped, a little slower than she had, and then we were getting in the tub—which I'd bathed in the day before, though French had declined Ap's kind invitation to use it too—French's skin already turning a milky pink and her breasts glorious with the steam coming up around them, and her hair swept up from her lovely spine's groove with one hand holding it high on her neck while she reached for the soap with the other. We scrubbed each other good and strong, splashing a little like children but not taking time to fool around; looking out past the rich vines at this upper window I saw W. M. moving out in the yard below, dressed now in a bright red jacket which fitted him all right, but belied his scowling face, and a pair of pants that were the velvet kind you might see on wealthy children, but longer, and I watched him as he went down to the hitching posts where Grayboy and Bellreve waited, and where Manny Gatchin, leading the mule Ap had let her take for the journey and her stay in Seldin, was bringing the mule up to a post. The mule wasn't the best creature I'd ever seen, but solid, with the suffering eye of its kind. When Manny had it hitched, W. M. walked all around it, looking from it to Grayboy, and back again, and shaking his head. Down in the yard next to the arbor three banjo-players and a pump-wheeze accordion man had started to join in, and a good many of the crowd was singing along with them. It wasn't a patch on Jantil's playing, but just a bar or two worse than mine, and the tune after a second I recognized as a wedding march. French was smiling at me, and as she got out of the tub I slapped her on her sweet and golden ass, having the thought that there ought to be a better name for such an article when it belonged to a joyful woman. Then we were both rubbing each other down with huck towels, getting ready to show forth in the daylight, to get our frameable hand-drawn certificate, and to head off Chantry-way.

# 47

I don't know how many people were at that wedding. I've sometimes tried to count them later and sum them up in my head. But every time I do it, it just blends into one big brangled stew, with only a face popping up here and there and the noise of it overarching my recollection. The ceremony took place as the arbor-leaves shadowed us while Apollodorus Miller said the words, and as the cooler airs of evening started playing around us, lifting the trim of French's new dress, which was a dark green velvet with a touch of gold at the throat, and as the sky turned easier in its evening shine, and a moon the size of a forty-pound melon dripping with honey around its rind came up and stood behind Ap's silver hair and blazing white beard, and lit up the scuppernongs and spread all over the lawns. At any rate it wasn't a long ceremony itself; when I put the brass horse-ornament on French's finger this time, I felt that I'd liked the Gypsy wedding just as much, even though it sure hadn't had the noise and crowding of this one. W. M. did the services of giving French away to be married, as well as handing me the ring which I recalled had first come out of his own pocket while we were on our way to Yadkin; he spoke what he had to in a clear grudging voice, wanting to get it over with fast. Then it was officially over, and the real celebration had started—as if it hadn't already started clear back at Grayboy's track shed—with people creating as if they'd not get the chance to create again all winter long. Manny Gatchin, who'd served as French's bridesmaid, was crying a little—I reckon you have to cry at those affairs if you happen to be a woman and have any true feeling of wonder—but it didn't half come up to the crying that Mama Gatchin did, which was some kind of record. She said herself she hadn't cried down so since her gone husband had lost his last race and retired from the field. She enjoyed it, it was a kind of salubrious crying— so French pointed out—that lit up her face and made each seam of it shine and renewed her youth.

When the true celebration had swung along another ten minutes more, and French and I and W. M. had sampled the wedding meats enough to take the edges off our appetites, we gathered in Manny to us—Mama Gatchin started up her fountain of joyful tears again at the prospect of seeing her daughter for the last time for a while—and pointed out that we had a good lot of miles to cover between here and the river-landing outside Quincyville, and that Manny's packet according to the latest schedule posted on a tree in the town square left at two the next morning. About that time, Ap Miller's congregation started showering us with gifts, whole sides of venison and mink-pelts and otter furs and a couple of usable if slightly rusty spring-traps, and enough smoked channel cat to last us through a season, and we had to peel back the flying jenny's canvas and stow all that material, along with the fresh new bridle-gear Buck Torbert and Budge Fisher presented us with, and the hand-inked, cupid-studded and angel-winged certificate Ap had prepared for us to prove to anybody we were hitched in perfect tandem. Buck and Budge were wearing checked suits I reckoned they'd brushed out special, though even under those clothes I thought I'd have noted that they were horsemen and wouldn't ever be anything but horsemen, even though they might be strutting now in disguise. About the same time, too, a bunch of the ladies of ill fame from the houses along Center Street—Miz Farwell's, and other of like ilk—came to the fore and offered us their congratulations; they'd been standing staid on the rim of the crowd till now, but pushed forward as we were leaving, and Miz Farwell herself, whose hair was something the color of a hayrick dipped in brass, said, "We're makin' a good-sized contribution to the Miller Church in your name, honey, and I'm God-damned delighted to say Ap's willing to take it." She had a bosom as jouncing as a room full of squirrels, and I thought was well into middle age from assessing her teeth. The Plott hound and a good many of the hounds that trailed the swamp-rats and their women whirled and circled around all of us as if this crisp beautiful autumn night was bringing them special tidings of game on the trails and they were trying to tell everybody about it; and anybody who knows how dignified and self-reserved a good hound usually is could have told it took a lot of human stir and bustle to bring them out of themselves. Then we were set to go, it looked like, and Ap was holding back most of the throng, hugging French and me in one last terrible bear-grip, saying when I tried to pay him for the ceremony and the certificate, "Son, I made enough on *my* Corum and Murphy bets to shore up the whole west wall of the nave, where it's busting its britches, and to stake me and my congregation to a new start in redeeming souls for years to come. I charge you with my final and richest blessing, and take it with you into whatever awaits you in Lanceton County and points south. You too," he told W. M. "And keep them fancy jockey-duds on, they become you." He lifted W. M. onto the jenny and set him down inside the canvas in his riding place. Manny was on the mule, a carpet bag slung by a rope to the mule's neck. I unhitched Grayboy and Bell, and got up on Grayboy, and French mounted Bell with the help of a hand-cup from Budge Fisher. Then we were turning and going out down the Church Block in the star-touched and moon-rising gloaming, people running along behind us for a spell and then dropping off near the I-Will-Arise Baptist, the merry-go-round's wheels humming and its reed pipes catching a drift of the night-breeze and making just a hint of its music under the sounding of our own hoofs. I turned and looked back as I'd done at the champion track, and so did French and Manny and W. M., as we got to the end of the street. Cooking fires were going and pine-knot torches were splashing and the belfry-tower of the Miller Church stood above it all, black on the sky and west-tilting, and the banjo-music was wrangling and the squeeze-box music was puffing, and I thought it might all go on the full night and well into the time of the morning star. French reached up from Bellreve, and touched my hand with Grayboy's reins in it, and said over the dwindling hullabaloo, "The carousel is over. The tournament is done, Tom."

"No," I said. "It won't ever be done, there's too wonderful much of it to remember."

Then we looked ahead, turning off Church Block, and heading along down Center Street—which appeared totally deserted—toward the side trail which slanted up through those armies of pines, the same Gypsy secret trail we'd come in by.

The smell of the pines folded in around us like a green wine to the throat and nostril and tongue as we climbed. The trail was touched with slants of light here and there, enough to make it clear riding for the rest of this night if need be. For all W. M.'s grumbling, Ap's mule with Manny on it was a good traveler, sludging through the dirt of the trail beside us with its sly and patient eyes half shut—I caught a glimpse of it now and then as we came out of shadow—and keeping the same pace we were which would, I trusted, get us to the landing over beyond Quincyville in time for Manny to catch her packet for Seldin. She and French discussed this and that, in low voices, and in little bursts which hardly made much sound over Grayboy's and Bell's and the mule's hoofs and the whispering wheels of the flying jenny. The moon was swimming higher now, bringing out side-trails that branched off from this main one and peaking over the bluffs to the southeast. Now and again we'd come under the lee of a hill farm with its dogs racketing down at us as they scented and then heard us pass, Grayboy shaking his head at such nonsense and foolish tribulation, keeping up the pace which he could hold all night if need be.

We'd been going so for I judged about an hour, once crossing fox-trails which hounds, in the dark-and-light distance, were running, the yap of a foxhorn sounding above and ahead and somebody urging them on in the night. Then we came to a place I recalled from riding in here the other way, though I'd been near asleep then and hoping Yadkin would come to sight too before the morning, and now I was sharp-awake and it all looked different and stranger from this direction. A clump of bois d' arc trees grew from the shoulder of the road to the right, their foliage gone but their grown-together dark trunks appearing in the moon's slant like twisted old ropes, and they cast the only shadows in this yellow-shining place. And I began hearing a noise ahead, not foxhorns and not hounds or men rambling around in the wondrous dark, but a clacking of dry axles and the screaking of a cart that should have been left to the sun and the rains long years before. I checked Grayboy, holding up a hand. Next to me on the off-side French reined in Bell, his deep bay catching the moon's shine like wax poured over his hide, and the mule beyond on the off-side of Bell stopping as well, Manny holding it still. Glancing around, I saw W. M. peering too from his canvas jenny-cave.

We held so, waiting, while the cart-sound filled the air with its caterwauling. Then here into the bright space came the poor nag of Sammy Spelvin's; he hadn't seen us yet, his head was sagging and his black rags were waving against the breeze, and he was singing in a loon's voice, "Poor old Sammy, he's wrenched from town to town—his home's but the moon's home, his luck's done down." The sound was light and faraway as if he was a small boy singing it, cracked, to himself while he sat a fence on a summer day. He didn't see us, it was the nag that did, and it stopped, its bony head shaped like an ironing board and hanging there while it waited for us to move out of the way. Sammy had been holding the nag in the crown of the trail, as he'd done the last time we'd met. With the noise of his cart silent now, he lifted his chin and gazed upon us all with his black eyes widening. His skin was the hue of an old wasp's nest, his lips as gray. Then he laughed high and shrill. "Damned if it ain't the same stallion, and that young chap astride, and the pretty lady with her rosy bay and she's just as rosy herself, and there's a mule and a young lady, and there's the same jimmy-hickle and that pruney child. And I got pots and pans and calico and blue serge and bits of ribbon to sell, and a teapot they throwed at me in Pharis, hardly a nick out of it, and firewood for the chimbley and the Holy Book for all family-readin', bound in mule-hide with copper-rivets—and tonics more'n you could count or relish in a lifetime. I seen the fire-breathin' major from Pharis, some time back, can't recollect the day—I told him what I'd passed and who I'd passed, on Yadkin trail, and he give me a bit of money. Knowin' I'm Sammy Spelvin, lost the mush of his brains at Sharpsburg, flew out through the ear, felt it go and somewhile I can still feel it goin', flyin' with the ball and shot and not to be recovered. And"—his eyes shut and then opened again, like a land-gopher turtle's in slowness—"and I seen the thievin' Gypsies too, goin' the same way you are, they passed me and gi' me a bit of their supper so's I won't starve, though they'll fling me out of

Yadkin again, even though I didn't fret them at all durin' Yadkin Fair, but let 'em alone so's they wouldn't have to look upon me and feel 'emselves shrivel with pity. No man or woman or a'ra child wants Spelvin, 'cause they know it ain't my real name. I lost my names. No soul alive to bring 'em back to me, no matter where I rove.''

He was bringing the red-rusted buffalo rifle with its loose barrel up from under the cart-seat. "Don't set and stare upon me, buy or give, ladies and young gent. I ain't made a sale for a lean time back—I—''

I rode Grayboy up to him. And got out a bill, not a big one, and held it out, and he snatched it like a buzzard plucking warm flesh.

The frost of his beard was earth-caked and crawling, but this time I held back from drawing my hand down Grayboy's hide to get rid of the taint of being so close. I said, gentle, "Sammy, how long back did the Gypsies pass you?''

Back of me, Bell stamped, and the mule shifted. W. M. said clear, "You give him too much again. Silver bit was enough.''

I flagged a hand back at W. M. to shut up.

Sammy scratched his head under the brim of the wool hat.

"Didn't cut a notch in a stick, I never fear me if I don't know what day 'tis. September seventeen, eighteen and sixty-two, 's the only day I recollect full and sure. Time I lost my brains. But I'd put it at a day back—''

"Yesderday?'' I said. "Sunday?''

"Church bells was goin', and it was rainin' fierce while I came on.'' He had scrabbled the bill into his clothes. His hand cupped the air like the leached-out twigs of a cypress. "They don't favor Sammy, even the churchmen, he's too stinking for 'em, too addled. But down farther on this trail, I could hear their mockin' bells. And the rain was heavy, it's raised the big river I hear—''

"Yesterday, Sunday,'' I said. I thanked him and as I pulled Grayboy to the side, and motioned French and Manny to pull off and leave him room to come by, Sammy's jaw dropped again and he only stared, then flapped the worn reins over the nag's hips and clattered and rolled on past. We all sat quiet, hearing him go down the trail and out of sight. He was singing again, the doleful sad tune just a wail over the loud complaint of his cart.

I caught French's eye. She said, "Shangro?''

"I'll watch for a sign,'' I said. Grayboy's and Bell's and the mule's breaths were showing a bit in the air as the night drew on. "He told me how to watch,'' I went on to French, "a while back when we were talkin'.

Before we got married for the first time." She smiled. "He said he might have news of Jupiter—he's had time to get back from Tennessee with that new stallion, by now, and to be somewhere in this Mississippi countryside." I clucked to Grayboy to come up. "I'd like as much news of Jupiter as possible before we come face to face with your friends again," I said, "and the major."

For the first time since we'd left Yadkin I'd felt a goose, or something a lot like it, walk on my grave again. I don't know if they do that for sure anymore than jaybirds visit hell on Fridays in Alabama, but if they don't they should, it feels exactly like a clammy touch. Most of it was from thinking of the major.

We went on up the trail, everybody quieter now as we rode.

I wasn't for stopping at all, since we had to get Manny to her river-landing by two in the morning, and I knew those packets don't wait. Sometimes they're behind time, but with the Old Man running the way he would be with yesterday's half-flood, I thought this would be right on the nose and maybe even ahead of schedule. But even though I kept the pace, setting it for Bell and the mule, I was watching now as I hadn't been before. I couldn't tell if the kind of patteran Shangro had showed me beside that limestone pool would stand up for any length of time; it seemed to me with all the growth that had been laced into by the rain on Sunday, it would have wiped out anything as small as twigs placed a certain way, in a certain manner; all the same I kept my eyes wide, even leaning a bit over Grayboy's neck—which he didn't especially like—and reminding myself of how I'd looked for his prints while borrowing that claybank horse in Lanceton, and how Grody had scoured the ground in the Lanceton woods for the same prints. After a time my eyes got used to the extra strain, the way they will when you let them relax and don't try to squinch them half-shut, and I found myself even able to make out the eyes of possums in the close-by brush, and once a fox—probably one of those the hounds had been belling a while back—looking up at me from under leaves and brush and staying where it was though it knew I'd seen it.

The trail was still wide enough for us all to ride abreast, but I'd pulled ahead; sometimes the low murmur of French and Manny talking about schoolteaching and their own pasts, and such, fell on my ears as the night-breeze made up higher, and sometimes it fell to nothing so there was just the sounding of all our hoofs around me. I'd tried to pay Mama Gatchin more than the twelve dollars for the four days in our under-eave room, but she'd turned it down cold, even though I'd told her it was the best room I'd lived in since leaving home; still, she'd taken the twelve, and when I handed over the room-key and the lane-shed key she'd sobbed even harder and told me she wished she could afford to pay me back what we'd loaned Manny, but that she couldn't just yet. I had the wad of what we'd won, and the big swag of coins from the flying jenny's running, in my poke deep in a pocket; on a trail such as this one, I thought, while keeping an eye out for any sign from Shangro, it would have been simple as still-fishing for any bandits or road-agents to rob us, but I didn't believe the trail was that well known. Grayboy could feel my watchfulness now, and was snorting from time to time as if he wished I'd just fall back into the harness-racing mood and let him and W. M. handle the rest.

But I kept staring down, from side to side, though I wouldn't have had to, as it turned out. For when the patteran showed up, about ten o'clock I judged by the positioning of the moon now over these deep-leaning trees, it was there for any to read who knew what it was. We'd come out in another lake of moonlight, with it picking out the Spanish saddle and Grayboy's gear and Bell's harness and the mule's somber hide—and French's hair, which she'd let stream again under the new hat and down her back and over the cloak's shoulders—and W. M.'s watchful eyes under the jenny's pagoda, as if we were all painted in this light by a traveling limner—when all of a sudden, like a plain greeting, there it was.

Just ahead, the trail slanted up sharp for about a yard before leveling out again, the root of an oak running across it and the ground tamped back in under the root by wind and the sawing away of weather; and to the right of the oak root, tied firm around it, was a forked twig bound with a withe of grass. It angled out a little into the trail. It was bigger than the twig arrangement Shangro'd showed me before; and its downturned end had been snapped sharp to the southwest, like a finger pointing. I halted Grayboy, threw his reins over his head, and got down. Squatting beside the patteran. Then I looked around and up at French on Bell.

I said, "I've got to follow this. I think it's damned important. I'd like to see Jupiter before we get back to Chantry, if it's possible. And it looks like maybe Shangro's making it possible."

She said, "But Tom, we can't leave Manny—"

"No. I don't intend to leave her." I stood up, taking off my hat. "I'll have to go by myself."

From the jenny, W. M. said cold-voiced, "You taking Mister

Grayboy? And junketing off by yourself? And leaving us to git the rest of the way to Miz Broome's house all on our own?"

"That's right," I said. "But you all can take the packet right down southward after you leave Manny off at Seldin, and then cut across to Lanceton from the big river after that."

French nodded, slow. I could see in her eyes the same thing that had been there when she hadn't wanted to say good-bye beside Morgan's pond, in what felt a long span of time ago now. She said, "I don't want us to be parted, Tom. And I might be able to make Jupiter talk, this time, better than you could. Since it's all become so important to us again. But it looks as if this is the design we'll have to follow." Manny murmured something, and French shook her head. "No, I wouldn't dream of allowing a young lady to travel on by herself to the landing. You deserve a send-off for your four years in Seldin, Manny, I have promised you that, and we shall give it to you." She got off Bell, light as though she was all made of feathers, swinging the reins over Bell's head. The new-bought hat slanted over half her face, her right eye blazing from the unshadowed side. She came to me, and stood before me, the dark velvet dress the shading of moss around us jeweled in the moon's touch, all of her so needful and strong there I wished to God Sammy Spelvin, idiot or lost war-casualty, hadn't even reminded me of Shangro and his possible messages.

I felt in my pocket, got out the poke, and tipped most of its contents into her hands. "This is for us, later," I said. "I'm keeping enough to follow on the packet myself. I'll do that if I find myself running late."

She folded the bills and the coins to her, and said, "I'd intended for us to arrive back together at Chantry Hall, as man and wife as we surely are. And to face down whatever accusations Major Deveraux may have brought forth in the meantime, Tom, and to get at the heart of Gary Willis's death once and for all, but together. But since we've found each other, I've discovered a great deal—about myself, as I've told you, besides all I've found out about you. I don't have to act whimsical or put up a snit because you think it's right to leave me now. Once, I reckon, I might have. But those ladies who had to travel their own ways sometimes, while their knights went off about their business—I reckon they felt as I feel now, on my wedding night—"

"—your second wedding night," I said soft, and she did manage a smile.

"—yes, that's so. My second. So I'll act like them, and stop making speeches."

W. M. had got out of his nest in the jenny, and was standing beside us with French's willow basket over one arm.

His scarlet coat, which had been a jockey's, and his velvet pants made him resemble some eldritch creature stepped from the moon itself, not just a black child who knew horses better than most grown men on earth.

He said, mean-sounding, "Miz Broome, you put that money in this basket and I'll keep it back there under wraps. So if we are robbed and gizzle-slitted, since he leaving us like he is, we will still maybe have his and your cash to keep alive on." He glanced to the bushes alongside. "You riding Mister Grayboy into all that thorn and brake?"

I said, "There'll be a path there. Shangro wouldn't tell me wrong."

"Path or no path, you ride him careful. Snakes ain't all bundled up against the cold yet. Bed him down warm at night and if you do any fast going, see he's rubbed down like a doorknob."

French dropped the money into the basket, and W. M. drew a cloth across it, and stalked back to the jenny. Hadn't known he could stalk, it made him appear to be three times as tall as he was. His bare feet left prints in the trail almost as deep as those of our mounts showing behind us. He was back on the jenny then.

I put my poke back in a pocket, and walked over to Manny. She was leaning from the mule, looking worried at all the fuss she thought she was causing us. I said, "This doesn't happen to be your fault. None of it. It's just necessary. I wish you good learning in Seldin, and good teaching later."

Saw she was crying a little. The hat with a few jaunty feather-stubs in it made her look older than the girl I'd seen first in the flustered and streaked apron, and much prettier, and her blue dress was trim and pleasing on her. I had the thought that Mama Gatchin had once looked like this, and I was pleased when Manny bent from the mule to kiss me. "I'll write to you and Mrs. Broome," she said. "I'll write once a week, I promise faithfully."

I told her fine, but she needn't bother that often, and looked back at W. M. He was sitting there with his legs crossed on the canvas, arms folded, gazing over my head at Grayboy.

"You ain't wishing me luck till we meet on Wednesday?" I said.

"I ain't liking none of this. Don't want Miz Broome to slam in facing that old major without you along. And I wasn't studying to take no packet in the first place. First running with a mule, now a packet." He shrugged, still not glancing my way. "And me wearing all this finery, Mister Grayboy ain't going to tell me what he truly wishes again till I get the clothes broke in good. Goddamnit, why you have to go haring off in the night a million miles from nowhere?"

I said, "Good-bye, W. M. Watch the ladies and the jenny for me."

"Good-bye then. And luck—since you dragging it out of me."

Then I went back to French, picked her up a little, holding her near as I could without us actually becoming one whole flesh—cleaving to her, as Ap had said in the ceremony—and when I took my face from hers she was looking at me steady, her eyes calm and as bright as the winking of the brass but gold-glinting ring on her finger.

"Good-bye," she said. Then, very low, "Do you know, I recall having said I love you, Tom. But I do not believe you have ever pledged the same to me."

A man has to say it, I thought. It is always expected, even if it is there in every other way possible known to the wisest human beings in Christendom. A horse knows it just from the way you act with it, but when it comes to womankind a man must say it. I was surprised I'd never said it before.

I said it, quiet and full. And turned and clapped my hat back on, and swung on to Grayboy, and took one more look at all of them in the trail, drowned in the hunter's moon's drenching light, then touched Grayboy and turned him sharp to the southwest. Off the trail. There was a snapping and crackling of bending brush around us for a breath, then solid ground under us, a path twisting through the oaks but wide enough, for all that, for a caravan to have handled, single-file. Holding Grayboy then, over my shoulder I could see French remounting Bellreve, and starting him off along the trail, and the jenny following, and the mule with Manny and her bag going with them. I stayed till they were out of my sight past these branches, then clucked Grayboy ahead again, watching the ground for more of Shangro's greetings and tokens. The saddlebags jounced a little, the fiddle in its case rode right, and Grayboy and I could have been pushed backward into a streaming Sunday night near Chantry. Save that we'd never be by ourselves again, for part of me was still going on down the trail while I went this other direction.

# 48

After an hour of going I could see that in spite of the twists and turns this path took in the deep orange haunted moonlight, we were going about due west. In the hour I found three more patteran signals. Every one of them was fixed so it could have been read in a hurry by anyone following this path and just smart enough in the Gypsy lore to know what it meant. The twig-arrangements could be seen in moonshine and ground light just as well as they could have been made out by the light of the sun. Every one placed where the eye would catch it, note it, and see that the direction hadn't yet changed. The twigs, sycamore for the most part but at one point, oak, were fairly fresh; the grass-withes binding them in position had a sappy feeling to the fingers when I rubbed them between my fingertips. I let Grayboy stop and drink a little at a stream that meandered across the path in one place; around us as his hoofs stopped the noises of the night mingled in owl-whooping and insect-striding, and far off from a rotten log came the rapping of one of those big woodpeckers the blacks call Lord-to-God, seeking for grubs in the cooling, splendid air. We splashed on across the stream.

In the next two hours I found five more patterans, not stopping and dismounting to look at them closer now, but able to read them almost without checking Grayboy's gait. It was about a quarter after one when we came to the valley, with a deep leaf-drift down its shelving rim as if the leaves had gathered here ever since the first Choctaws and Chickasaws looked upon the land; there was a watery smell to the woods all around it, breathing in now all the distance from the Mississippi itself, and mingling with it was the scent of wood fires that had been put out but had smoked not long before, and the smell of horses and leather and herbs that made up the Gypsy camp. Though I couldn't yet see the camp I moved Grayboy down through the leaves, a drift of them rising to his elbows in front and his hocks behind and then almost to his belly, and then we were going on down with the leaves parting and rustling around us, dry on top and dank

368

with ages of leaf-mast below, and coming up nearly to his throat-latch as his head thrust above them. It was like swimming through a sea of fire gold and deep red and dank black hissing water. Then we came out on the floor of the valley, and at its north bend I saw where I'd missed the start of this downgoing trail—but anyone could have seen it anyhow, having come this far with the strong pointing of the patterans—and the caravan carts in a rough circle and the horse-string tied for the night under a clump of gum trees. The purple and the faint gold and the mild blue of the carts showed dull in the moon's probing. There weren't any lights showing from any of the carts. A dog heard Grayboy approaching and barked once, uncertain but nose a-quiver. Then another dog joined in, and both of them were setting up a stir. Then one of the horse-string whinnied, and one of the big draught horses gave an answer which was also a question, and Grayboy as I checked him and sat the saddle, leaning forward and waiting, nickered back, thrusting his head forward and with his muzzle swinging to pick up the scent of these horses better. A light went on in Shangro's cart, the one which he drove and the women traveled in when there was racing and herb-selling in a town, the flame of the lamp behind the cart window-curtains first low and then turned higher, then the lamp itself appeared at the back step of the cart, light downfalling as its door creaked open. In another cart there was another lamp gleaming now. The horse-cart where French and I had traveled loomed big against the drift of stars above this valley, and a horse in it—I reckoned the stallion Shangro had gone up to Tennessee to dicker for—stirred and snorted, making Grayboy lift his head high and swing his attention around that way and give an uneasy snort as if he was recognizing something he might fight for mares if the occasion for doing it came about soon. Then a man was coming toward us where we waited, his lamp lifted high so it spilled yellow back and into his face and eyes as well as his head-cloth, the head-cloth a bright blue like the flickering of a bluejay's wing in the dancing flame-points, and I recognized Pella's high cheekbones and long slits of eyes. Behind him came a bigger man, walking slower, his lamp splashing light over his yellow shirt and upon his ear-hoops and getting lost in the blackness of his moustache. By the time they reached me I'd slid from Grayboy and was holding his reins. Pella clapped me on the shoulder and gave a sleepy smile. He said, "Did you win at Yadkin? Even one of the heats?"

I said, "I won all three. Or Grayboy did."

Pella nodded, slow. "I said I would give a thousand English sovereigns for him once. Not that I will ever have them. But I would still give them if they were mine."

Then Shangro was with us. He handed his lamp to Pella. He looked even bigger than I'd remembered him, and no more surprised than when I'd first showed up in front of his train in the dust of the Lanceton Pike. He took my arm and felt it as though sizing up the bones of a horse. He said, "Mister Broome—hold the lamps higher, Pella—I have been expecting you. And how is Mrs. Broome, that lovely and loving lady? And the little W. M.?"

I said, "They're fine, last I saw them at ten tonight. Or last night." The stars had a getting-ready-for-morning look about them behind Shangro's head. I saw Aldan, coming quick from a cart across the misting grasses, and Jantil behind him; and then Garsina, Pella's wife; her long black hair shook down the back of her shift and drifted with the rise and fall of her walk; in her arms she carried young Tomas, whose eyes were just coming open and who was naked as an eel. Jantil had one of his sons, Jal, with him; the boy squirmed to get down and Jantil set him down lightly. The dogs circled around us, smelling my boots but not going near Grayboy's forehoofs.

Old Cando, the smith, was hobbling toward us, his hands like ginger-roots catching the flow of the lamplight as he came up. He scrubbed sleep from his eyes with the back of a rough hand and put his head close to me and asked a question in the black language. Shangro answered it for him; I reckoned he'd asked how Grayboy had done at Yadkin. For with the answer he grinned, deep, and nodded and spat with satisfaction. I said to Shangro, "Please to tell him his plates lasted all the way to Yadkin and through the trial minute and the first heat." Shangro gave that information to Cando. Cando nodded again, as if he'd known it all the time. He squatted and went moving around Grayboy by degrees, lifting the right fore and then the near fore, and Grayboy lowered his head and looked at him but let him touch him without complaint. Aldan thrust his head closer and said, "We won at Quincyville, and then again at Appleton. It has been a rich season. Flambeaux sprained a hock at Appleton but it is easing out now."

Jantil with his scarlet head-cloth like the heart of a ruby above his arch-nosed high head and his bare chest—he hadn't stopped to put on a shirt—said, "He let Flambeaux break too fast and it hurt him. He is so eager he is still foolish, as he was at Pharis with the Teague breed. But he will learn under good teaching."

Tomas had come awake, Garsina had put him down. He said up to me, "Hola, Mister Broome. I mean—hello. My grandfather let me go along to Quincyville and Appleton both. This winter at the trace he is going to start me racing."

"On a very old horse," said Shangro. "And only if you speak English well at all times. It is late for you to be awake. Get along back to your cart." He gave Tomas a swat on the rear. The boy's jet black eyes were just the shape of Shangro's, as if both of them had come into being generations apart with the exact raking glance. Tomas turned and grabbed Jal's hand and together they twinkle-butted off into the shadows toward the carts. Garsina murmured at Shangro's shoulder, and Shangro said to me, "She wishes to know if Mrs. Broome has the Gypsy dress still, and if she wore it to the racing at Yadkin. And if you were married the second time there. So many questions, we are holding you up, Mister Broome."

I said, "I've got some time, anyhow enough for this. I wish I could spend the night but I have to be at Chantry Hall by Wednesday night." I told him French had worn the beautiful Gypsy gown and prized it highly, and had it with her now as she traveled toward the Quincyville landing. I told him we still had the wedding crowns in our baggage and would keep them always. I told him, shading it a trifle so nobody would feel bad, that the white wedding at Yadkin had been all right in its way but the Gypsy wedding was still the one I'd cherished most and that French felt the same about it. I knew he could see the lacy dried-out chapletlike affair the old lady had woven and stuck in my hat while he had married us, because it was still there. He turned to Garsina and told her all this, in turn, and she held my hands for a moment, murmuring more, and Shangro said, "Her love to Mrs. Broome, she wishes you to carry it to her." I looked at Garsina and nodded up and down, carefully, and shaped my lips hard around, "I will."

Shangro clapped his hands so hard his emerald head-cloth appeared to jump on his brow.

"Back to the carts, now," he said gently. "Mister Broome and I must talk." Aldan walked away, lifting a hand back to me, and Jantil went with him, calling over his shoulder, "We do not know yet if Farella holds a colt—horse or filly. But she is acting so. There is a certain look they get." He called something else, which I thought must mean, Good luck and we hope to see you again. Garsina had gone with him and Jantil. Cando arose from inspecting Grayboy, patted him on a shoulder, and went back along with the others. Shangro fixed one of his yellow shirt's buttons where it hadn't quite fitted the slot over his hard, great old belly as he dressed. He stretched and yawned in the lazy-flickering lamplight. He called back to Pella, "See that my grandson goes to sleep at once. No staying awake and whittling out toy horses by candlelight."

Pella called back in Rom, and called "Good night, Mister Broome," and I wished it to him.

Shangro eyed me and Grayboy beyond me. "I think it is very good you saw the patterans, Tom Broome. Yesterday morning coming back from buying our stallion—he is nothing as fast as your man-horse, but he is capable—we came across another tribe, our friends. The rain was blowing and there was little time to talk. But I asked what was on my mind; for they had come from Lanceton way, they had camped in the woods across Lanceton River. They had seen this Jupiter, the servant of Gary Willis and before that the servant of your wife's mother and father. He is in the burned-out ride leading to the canebrake outside where Fountainwood house stood. He is living back there in a hunting lodge put up once by Colonel Chantry. He does not stay in the lodge daytimes—so when the men from Lanceton, Sheriff Planteu and the rest, come looking for him there is no sign of him—but sleeps there nights. He trusted the Gypsies and traded for some corn meal from them in exchange for quail and venison. He has the Arab horse, Robin, with him. He is afraid to show himself in or near Lanceton because he believes they will clap him in jail for burning down Fountainwood. He is not sorry he did it, he believes, still, that it was laid on him by a greater power to wipe Fountainwood and all it contained from the face of the earth. He asked if my Gypsy compatriots had seen you or Mrs. Broome in their travels, but of course they had not. They told me he acted as though he might like to speak with her, to say more than he has said before. I think this is very sad and I hope you will find him soon. You say you must be back at Chantry Hall by Wednesday night. It is now Tuesday morning, by your so-careful calendars. I do not know if you can ride all the way to Lanceton woods and still arrive at Chantry Hall at your specified time. May I ask why you must be there then?"

I said, "Because French promised it for both of us." I told him about Major Deveraux trailing us—though it was a plain-to-mark trail—to Yadkin, and going all the distance down to Lanceton before that, to get deputized. I told him as little as I could while still relating the facts, but I got the heavy notion he read something of the way Deveraux and I felt about each other now, and he'd already known there was no affection lost between us at Pharis and then again during the Teague fracas. I mentioned Deveraux also having got information about us from poor Sammy Spelvin.

Shangro shook his head, his dark cheeks like bronze stones in the light of the lamp which he'd placed now at our feet, his face a little sorrowful. "I will never understand the Anglo-Saxon race, and its hates and its battles. Had Spelvin—if that is his name, I think he is truthful about losing his mind at Sharpsburg during Antietam—had Spelvin been injured and a Gypsy, we would have taken care of him all of his life. We would have looked upon him not as holy, but as touched by a fate past our grasp. An obligation to be cherished and given warmth and food and our companionship forever. But in your world he is cast adrift and stoned and reviled from town to town—and Major Deveraux! So much passion and so great dedication, yet all of it spent in reliving a shattered cause. But I am holding you."

I said, "I'll ride straight west from here and pick up for Lanceton at the big river. Taking a river packet."

He nodded slow. "Tom Broome, do not thank me. It is very little I have done. Next spring we will start out from the Natchez Trace again as soon as the weather has broken. During the summer and up to the cotton-harvest in September and the corn-harvest in this month we will follow the racing and sell our herbs and now and then, when the time is right, buy or sell a few horses. You walk well, I think your wound has healed—it was a good evening when we met each other, you dropping into the road on that magnificent man-horse before me. What I am saying is, we shall see each other again—you and the proud and bright Mrs. Broome. I told you when we last parted, a Gypsy saying—which is worth no more but no less than the saws of Mister Benjamin Franklin—*Behind bad luck comes good luck.* Our blend of both is what we shall share when we next meet and talk. Good night now, and until we do meet, think of us. As we will of you."

He didn't shake hands this time, as I'd sort of forced him to do after he'd married French and me; I took it this was only something white men did to ease themselves, anyhow, and didn't matter a hang in his estimate. Foursquare as a granddaddy oak himself, he turned and walked away, the lamp scooped up in one wide hand before him, light-circling around him as he covered the ground. The last I saw of him was as he climbed the step back into his cart, then shut the door, and the shine of the lamp through the cart's curtains. I thought of him having come here from England, how

many years back I didn't know; how he had made this country his as his
forebears had made every country—Persia, India, all of them—theirs,
but how instead of building in it, or fighting about it, or in any manner
trying to own it, he and his people had lived in it, knowing that was all it
was here for. Or all any land could be expected to afford. He'd said, that
time before, that he could have wished I'd been a son of his. It would have
been interesting, I thought, and also speculated that toward the last of
Daddy's life, the two of them would have got along like sure finger and
strong thumb. Pinching out all the stupid part of life, war and arms and
bad feeling, between them.

When the lamp in Shangro's cart was blown out, in another few
seconds, I mounted Grayboy again. Turned him due west and we rode up
out of the valley camp. He nickered back over his shoulder as we started
up, then we were in the leaf-drift on the other flank of this valley, and he
was surging up ahead, the leaves flying from us as we came out of them,
and I stopped him on the valley-rim, brushing leaves from my pants and
the saddlebags, and then clucked him straight west again, where the smell
of river-water came drifting across all those miles, the big river sending
this thick river-damp greeting to both of us.

It was near morning by the time we reached the river. The light was
growing behind us on the east, punctured by sounds of roosters scratching
their calls at the false dawn. I was dead for sleep, rolling in the saddle, and
Grayboy though he'd kept his gait through all the hours—as if it was a gait
timed to the wheeling stars—was a little slower now, and shaking his
head and detesting every forward step. Around us up and down this
riverside land small farms were coming awake, their lanterns showing
down through the trees, their dogs starting to stretch and shake out
night-burrowing fleas, their roofs faint in the ground-flush before full
light. We'd found steady paths and a good stretch of road, for a time, and
then more paths and at one place, nothing but overgrown briars, which
we'd had to go around—while I remembered W. M.'s warning about
snakes—before we got back to a crossing again. We'd clumped over low
bridges with the creeks under them still foaming with the spate of the rain
on Sunday, flecks of foam caught in their willow-sprouts and bubbles and
white scum racing past their stones. We'd come to where a battle had been
fought, reaching it about four this morning, you could tell from the
burned-out trees with their stumps still black and slick to the weather in all
these years since then, where the cannon had been brought up and the

charge had gone forward or coiled back on itself. And you could tell even more from the sorry remnants of a cheval-de-frise, pointed stakes facing up from the gloom, meant to catch the charging horse-troops on their chests and make them die screaming as a horse screams under mortal wound. We'd picked our way over and between those stakes, slow, me wishing I had time to root them all out of the holding soil, whether they had been Federal or Reb. We'd come past maples still holding their color this far into the shaft of October, gleaming under the moon's touch like crowns of king's gold. Like everything French had in the back of her mind when she thought of her carousel, conquering, and racing a good horse. And now I checked Grayboy and we both leaned out and down to the river.

It was almost a mile wide here, I judged, putting all other rivers to shame as it always would, and so treacherous in its vastiness no man would ever tame it as you could tame a common passage of water. The smell was fierce and lazy, together, sulphurous and muck-rich and yet fresh—Grayboy was drinking it in as if it had the taste of a race-challenge, his nostrils spreading and stiffened.

"You ain't going to have to swim," I told him. "We'll go along the bank and look for a packet."

I put him down the slope to the path. When we'd picked our way to it, I turned him south. The river was fair-high, the light on it growing and the sound of it just a murmurous friendly spate as we went beside it. Trappers and mudcat-fishers were out along it, ducking through the brush and gazing at us and if they felt strong enough in the earliness, hailing us with their voices thinned by the water-sound as they set out traps and lines. A ragged dock painting itself in the copper-dark water which whispered around its pilings grew up out of the mists and came clearer as the sun struck down this bank. I rode Grayboy out along it, his hoofs ringing hollow, the plates shaking the dock-boards. Out of a box-shed at the dock's end came a stoop-shouldered man hauling up his galluses over his knob shoulders. "Next packet at seven," he said. "Extry for the horse. Ought to charge triple for this 'un."

"Stop at any point nigh Lanceton?"

"Old fishin' camp about even, but you got to get back inland yourself. That'll take you to Lanceton woods. I'd say"—he scratched his weedy poll—"six dollars for you, two for the horse. Ramp'll let down for him, you got to git him on yourself. We ain't got no fixin's anymore, on this line, stevedorin' ain't a steady line of work. Carry a little cotton, upriver, but downriver mostly coal and cattle and mules and odds and ends. Eight dollars, flat.''

I paid him. W. M. would have argued, but I was too tuckered. I got off Grayboy, worked the creases out of my leg-muscles, bought half a loaf of three-day-old bread from the packet-man, and a slab of fresh fried channel-cat, which he furnished the salt for, and fed Grayboy from some of the feed in a saddlebag. Watered him from the spring-pump in the packet-house. And ate the fare, such as it was—all those gifts from Apollodorus Miller's mixed congregation were back tucked away under canvas with W. M. guarding them. Though I reckoned by now French and W. M. were in Lanceton, or near it, and hoped the packet Manny had caught for Seldin, which they'd have ridden with her from upriver as far as she went, had been in better shape than this one that was now whistling for the dock. The packet-man had run up his rag-edged flag. The packet swung in and whistled again. Watching it, I remembered when I'd been very small, when all packets were gaudy as white gold-trimmed birds, flags on their jackstaffs and their chimneys fancy as queen's diadems, paddle wheels going like sweet wet thunder. This one barely let out valve-steam, then swung the rest of the way in, the ramp running down and smashing the dock as if it would bust it the next trip. The captain yelled to the packet-collection man, nodded when the man said Grayboy and I had paid, and I rode Grayboy aboard, he looking around him with a What-have-you-brought-me-to-now? look, and I steering him into a lower deck stall. In the next stalls were mules being shipped downriver, W. M. would have jumped off the packet in disgust. By the time I'd rubbed him down good, both of us were just about asleep. The packet had inched toward midriver, the pilot-captain hollering for bow-port and bow-starboard just the way they'd done in the river-rafting days when the Indians lived here, ''Bow, Injun!'' for one side, and ''Bow, White!'' for the other.

I put my head on a saddlebag, stretching out alongside Grayboy, and fell off to the churning of the wheel.

# 49

We got to the fishing camp on the river side of Lanceton—except it was still about eight hours as a fast crow would fly, and ten hours as a human being and a horse could travel by circling roads, to the Lanceton woods— about three that evening. I'd spent the time, mainly, sleeping, and in the minutes when I woke up wishing the packet could make faster time, though with the high water it wasn't doing bad. And watching the brown water sludge along with the sun streaming on it so strong you could see shoal-riffles half a mile ahead, and then sleeping again. Grayboy improved his condition in about the same way, and we both had a bait of more food in the intervals, me eating what the packet offered—which was plain fare and nothing like what would have been cooked here in its great passenger days—and Grayboy snuffling up more oats and part of a manger of corn one of the roustabouts found for me. So when the packet swung in toward the half-ruined fishing camp dock we were both fit to travel again. The ramp came crashing down and I put Grayboy down it to the dock, hoping the mush-boarded pilings would hold; I walked him, gingersome, along the rickety dock to where tall grass shadowed the camp building, which was parched gray and gradually sinking into the slough beside the river. Behind me the packet puffed black smoke from its stained and tipsy stacks, swinging out again already to the mid-channel, the smoke spreading back along the tawny water like a scarf going filmy and then disappearing as you watched. I lifted Grayboy's head and put him to a long path leading straight east, cross-country to the Lanceton woods.

By dusk we'd come to a tiny crossroads with a tavern that I reckoned had been here since well before Mississippi was a state and in the days of the first touchy trading with the Indians. It had lights in it, so I hitched Grayboy—tight with a special double hitch in case anybody around here might have ideas about walking him off—and when I got in the tavern, I sat near a window so I could see Grayboy in the window-light and keep an eye on the saddlebags and fiddle-case. The man and his wife who ran the tavern were named Mostard, he was Cajun-French and glad to talk to anybody, I didn't see that business was booming, and his wife was a round-faced little coal-eyed woman built in two sections, like ample rubber balls, the upper and the lower all joggling together as she cooked and served in her old pink wraparound. Mostard invited himself to sit with me, admiring Grayboy through the window-pane; I scouring up the red beans and rice and perloo stew fast because I wanted to get on, him remarking on general conditions in his vicinity. When he'd lamented them for a time, he perked up and spread his hands. "M'sieu, a sight, a vision! This morning at maybe ten o'clock, if my timepiece is correct, the lady stopped by. A lady—*la bonne femme*, yes? Me I know a lady when I am lucky enough to encounter one. God, she is beautiful, her. All in green with such a hat, hair burning—" He made his hands describe the hair. "And this you will not believe, a little nigra boy with her, in a red coat—very glum, him, she must speak to him sharply to make him sit with her, he says he would rather wait outside, he does not cotton to white folks' tables, she tells him he had best get accustomed to them for he is going to live in a great hall, Chantry—but the most strange yet, the horse she brought, with a fine saddle, drew behind it—now you will *not* believe—a carousel! I examined it while they were breakfasting, me. I lifted up a flap of the canvas. Marvelous! *Ravissement!* Such delicate work I have never seen, eight or ten little fairy horses."

"You were drunk, René," his round wife said softly. "The brandy tippling so early!"

"Sober, me, woman, hold your tongue. M'sieu, we do not see such travelers or such carousels each day. She inquired the road to Lanceton, the shortest; I directed her down-bayou and along the trace. Logging has made the trace wide, it is safe enough and there are no sloughs."

While I finished up eating I asked him if he had a bait of corn mixed with some hay for my horse, and he sent the tavern boy for them. I had a small brandy while Grayboy fed. It was good to know French and W. M., barring any road-trouble, would be pulling into Lanceton about now on their way to Chantry Hall. Tuesday, a full day early. Their packet had made about the same river-time mine had. I hoped theirs had been in better shape, and that Manny and the mule had dropped off safe at Seldin. I wanted to see French again and get this mystery settled so bad it was all I could do, when I left, to keep from taking the down-bayou trace-road they'd gone by, but instead I kept on eastward, as string-straight as the countryside would let me go. I figured I might reach the woods, with any luck at all, about the same time I'd come onto Shangro's camp the morning before. Was glad French and W. M. and the jenny had lighted up Mostard's day, or maybe even his week. The country I crossed now was hazed with falltime in all its coming night-shadows, what cornfields there were gone patchy with stubble, and from the boughs of gums and oaks and sycamores in farm yards hung the stripped and gutted carcasses of hogs, back legs tied and snouts aiming at the ground as if they were racing for the earth's center in a harvest-slaughtering heat. I passed a wagon full of hunters on a side-road, their wagon-bed loaded with deer and quail and turkey, the mules ambling, and they all stopped their drinking and rife talk long enough to comment on Grayboy and ask me if I'd ever raced him; I said I'd often considered it.

Having had the easy if not comfort-lapped snoozing on the packet, both Grayboy and I were in better fettle than we'd been the night before. It was just quarter-to-one, the moon now even heavier in its swag of orange and fat fieriness than it had been the previous morning, when we came in on the Lanceton woods from the eastern slope. I checked and got off and stretched at the rim of the woods. Most of the lower boughs of the oaks and cottonwoods and gum had lost their leaves, but there were still enough clinging to make the forest a quilting of bronze and scarlet and pale yellow, shifting quiet in the mild edgy breeze. I wound the turnip and put it away again, and reckoned we were just about opposite the burned-out ride where Colonel Chantry had once hunted with his friends and servants and his daughter French, beyond which lay what had been Fountainwood house until the fire. And in which was an old hunting lodge I had to find. I mounted and put Grayboy in and among the trees, thankful for the clear morning and glad as well I didn't have an expert inch-by-inch tracker to contend with.

I thought if I missed the avenue-ride, swerving too far to north or south, I could always find the creek and then double back. But when we got in under the bigger oaks I started to have niggling doubts. A forest—or even any considerable stand of woods—has a way of looking the same from point to point, so that what you've picked out earlier as a landmark may change in some nearly ghosting way or fade away utterly, and then all you have to go by is the sun by day and the stars by night, and on a gray day all you can do is start making casts, in circles first to your right, then to your left, the circles getting bigger as you make them, so that, if you're persistent enough and watchful enough, you may cross the same course you came in by. I kept thinking, though, now with this bright moon moving above as Grayboy and I switched in and around the shapes of trees on the floor of the forest, that I heard the rush and tinkle of the creek. But every time I'd check and listen—Grayboy breathing in scorn now, not liking the checks—there was no creek; only the scent of water somewhere, and night-birds moving through the scurf of dry leaves, and once—with a lurch of my heart and a sidestep from Grayboy—something I took to be a bear, having inspected us and found us not worth attacking with so many grubs and beetles around, crashing off careless through the underbrush. It wasn't for half an hour, or more, of riding mostly due east that I got woods-sense enough to lay the reins down on Grayboy's pommel and give him his head. He hadn't had a drink since the Mostard tavern, and I hoped he'd head for the nearest water which he could smell a hell of a lot clearer than I could.

He tried to look around at me as if I'd gone crazy at last. I slapped him light on the neck to turn his head, and he started on. He shifted as he went in and around the trees—which laid shadows of themselves on other shadows, in a blue-dark heap of blanketing shade that was like riding through a tunnel of midnight with flecks of gold in it—moving more to the south than I had in steering him. Hard as it was to keep my hands off, I let him go. Reins slack, he kept up a nice even gait, and about a quarter-hour later he lifted his head and snorted, a good blast, then picked up the gait. I lifted the reins again, holding them as delicate as if they might break, and then ahead, here was the creek. With its wild mint and wet grassy smell high around us, and Grayboy putting his head down and enjoying himself. While he drank I looked upstream and down.

I couldn't see the lightning-marked silver birch—the one Grody'd thrown his knife at and I'd been fool lucky enough to hit. But it was sixty feet in among the trees on the yonder side of this creek, and anyhow we might have come farther south to the creekside. We'd made enough noise coming here to alert the last woods-rabbit. I was lifting Grayboy's head, he'd had enough, and as water dripped from his lips and he savored its last drops, I heard a soft crackling in the bushes upstream on our side, and then Jupiter stepped out there in a wedge of light, leading the Arab horse Robin.

So quick he could have just grown himself from the shadows, horse and all. And even so quick Grayboy hardly had time to whinny at the Arab. Then Jupiter was coming along toward us, reins bunched in one huge fist, his head cocked and watchful, his eyes white in this flickering light as washed eggshells. He had a fairly new rifle carried in one hand almost as if it was a pistol. His pants cut off just under the knees and frayed to hemp-ends were all he wore, his eye-hollows dark and stained with worry, his head-furze considerably higher than the Arab's ears. And his voice as drum-booming soft as it had been at Fountainwood.

"Mister Broome?"

"Jupiter," I said.

The Arab looked sleek and well fed. Jupiter himself in prime sharpness. I got off Grayboy, holding his reins.

"My, my," Jupiter said. "Me and Robin heard you, Mister Broome, when you comin' in the other flank of these here woods. You ain't no whispering traveler, no sir. Ain't much old Jupe don't hear—since we come to live here, me and Robin, we can make out the very second in time them men start over from the other side the Lanceton River. Can we just talk right here and now, Mister Broome, or you in hurried bother?"

"I came here to see you," I said. "Miss French would have come if she could've. Only she's Mrs. Broome now."

"That so? Well, I am surely delighted on that. You do well up towards Yadkin?"

"Did well," I said. He reached, shifting the rifle under his left arm as if it was a small stick of no consequence, to pat Grayboy's slick-wet muzzle.

"He look bright as a star of hope. How's my Miss French, my Miz Broome?"

"She's just fine, and she's either in Lanceton or back at Chantry Hall by now," I said. "And we're both in a mess of sorriness. Part of it comes from Gary Willis bein' shot about eleven days back, and part of it from you burning up Fountainwood. And part from us going off to Yadkin. She went with me, that's where we were married. We need your help."

He rolled that around his consideration a little while. Robin stretched his neck toward Grayboy, they were almost touching noses.

"Mist' Broome, it's why I been layin' up here, and gittin' out o' sight when the men come, and livin' off the land—it ain't bad livin', but it's lonely in the bones—and almighty scared to set foot back in Lanceton or go nigh it. Why I been huggin' up in that ol' lodge the colonel built them years ago, nights, and scourin' for game and some dry grass fodder and wil' oats for Robin, days. I means the burnin'. I ain't gone say I didn't do it. God, the Lord, laid it on me to. 'Let the palace of the mighty sinner burn,' He tole me. 'Spread coal oil throughout from room to room and do not spare the stables.' If I go back they gone either hang me—I seen men hanged, Mist' Broome—or they gone slam me in jail and pull the floor over me. I couldn't stand it now; I'm too used to bein' free since Mist' Gary Willis got shot. You gone ask me to go back?''

"No," I said. "French is. Both of us are. You saw who killed Willis. That's how you've got to help. You've got to tell Will Planteu and the rest of those people who did it.''

He shook his head. "Miss French—Miz Broome—she asked me that back week ago Monday night at Fountainwood. Couldn't tell her then, 'cause I'm too fond of—nemmine, I ain't gone say the name of the party. Couldn't tell her now, neither. And if I go back and *don't* say the name of the party killed Willis, and *won't* say it, just like I say, they gone hang me, jail me, or maybe jus' burn me up and ash me out. I tell you *how* I seen it done, I ain't say further'n that.''

I let out a breath I'd been holding. "How?''

"You knows how them mirrors in the front hall at Chantry Hall are kind of lined up? They're just the other side of the ballroom, and on the ballroom side. All kind of glancin' into one another. You knows I folla'd Gary Willis all the way from Fountainwood that night when he set out for there, you knows he'd been drinkin' and sat Robin cock-saddle, you knows I tole you I paced him afoot. When he'd been there at Chantry a spell, and Miz Broome—it feel easier I call her Miss French, you mind?—and Miss French had been argufyin' with him, and then had gone out to see about her poultry, and Willis, he was then slumped down in one of them chairs in the vestibule, I slipped in from where I been makin' myself scarce below the front gallery, and went past Willis, he had his eyes shut then, and ducked into the ballroom. But I lef' the door ajar, just a crack so's I could see. Well—pretty soon Miss French she come back, and Willis he comes awake but stays where he is, eyein' her, and she walk past him and put the little bitty pistol—that little hand-pistol Colonel had—''

"Derringer,'' I said.

"Yes sir, she put it in the hidin' place, Willis didn't see her do it, the hidin' place in the stair-post she opens by swingin' that lion-head out. And she let the head swing to. And she go on upstairs. *I* could see all this in the mirrors. And I see another party come in the doorway too. Front door open, and I see this plain. See it in the mirrors, turned backward, but jus' as if I lookin' square at it. Same time, I see Willis lurch and lunge out o' the vestibule chair, and aim himself, all sprawled and kind of swarmin', up the stairs where Miss French's gone out of sight.'' He was looking down at the bright strip of sand under its stones in the creek. "I would have stopped him myself, Mister Broome, it's why I'd folla'd him there. But I didn't have to. I'd swung my head now to see this party—this person I ain't gone say the name of—who was steppin' in the doorway. Now, Willis, he's on about the fourth, fifth step up by this time, and he's chargin' on, but when this party comes in, and sees him, and where he's goin', this party says a word to him—think it was, 'Willis!' or somethin' just that short. And Willis wheels around like a gin-wheel turnin'. And this party has a pistol, and there's a crack of powder and ball, I was lookin' right at Willis then and I seen the ball hit him, the blood come out on his head, and he flings out his arms and slides a little way down the staircase and lays there. Dead. And the party with the pistol walks back out the way he come in, and even while I'm shuttin' the ballroom door—Miss French she saw me then, she'd come to the head of the stairs—and jumpin' out a ballroom window I'd throwed up, and goin' around to the front again and climbin' on Robin, here, and makin' tracks back to Fountainwood—knowin' Willis is dead and what I promised I'd do for the Lord now—even while I'm ridin' off, I can hear this party and the horse the party come there with, goin' away."

I said, very slow, "Jupiter. The derringer *didn't* shoot Willis?"

"How could it? The pistol this party brought along went off. I heard it! Heard the noise!"

"Did you *see* it?"

"No, sir! I was lookin' square at Willis then, seen the ball strike his head and the blood flowerin' out and him go down! But what else could it have been, Mister Broome?"

"Never mind," I said.

I was thinking about French taking the derringer out of the cache again, and finding it had been fired, and putting it back. I was thinking about the derringer coming up missing later, and being found there in the Chantry Hall drive, all cleaned and loaded.

I still felt, bone-deep, that whoever'd taken the derringer away, and cleaned it and reloaded it and put it there to be found, must have been protecting French, and also must be the person who'd shot Willis.

But if this person hadn't killed Willis with the derringer, who'd shot the derringer, and why on earth hadn't it just stayed in its lion-head hiding place unfired?

I said as Jupiter lifted his eyes from the bright-running creek, "Jupiter, do this for Miss French—and for me. I'm goin' on to Lanceton now—I'm

going to tell everything I know to the people there. Miss French has
already told them all she knows, by this time, I reckon. But I'm about to
tell them what you've told me. And when I've done it, I'm going to ask
for their solemn promise not to harm a hair of your head—not to touch you
for burnin' Fountainwood, and not to make you spend even a minute in
jail. I'm going to ask them to do this for you if you'll come forward and
tell them who shot Willis. I know that pains you, but if you *don't* do it,
Miss French will have this hangin' over her head the rest of her days.
Don't you see, that's why you've got to say it? I don't want to hear the
name yet, I want all those friends and worriers about my wife—about
Miss French, to hear it. I don't want you to feel you're betrayin' your
friend—I take it the party who you think shot Willis, and you say you saw
shoot Willis, *is* a friend—''

He nodded, moving the rifle down to his flank.

"—because anybody who did it, should have stepped up by now, and
said so. And it's got to be straightened out, or all her life Miss French'll
somehow be just like you are now—not hidin' up in the woods, but
carryin' a doubt around with her, and with the smirch of the doubt
reflectin' on her as well.''

I didn't think he was going to go on talking then. Thought he was going
to turn around and lead Robin back along the bank and vanish in the
shadows. Which he could have, easy as doing it. Finally he moved his
lips, voice rumbling so soft that under the plash of Grayboy's hoof as he
put one in the creek and then brought it out and back, I could barely hear.

"I'll do it. Only for Miss French, Mister Broome. Only for her. All in
the livin' created world, made from mud in six days, I'd do it for.
But''—his eyes flashed with their whites showing wider—"you got to
give me a sign the promise not to jail or touch me is a true one. I ain't
comin' back with you this mornin', no sir. Tell you what—just out of
Lanceton, 'cross the river from this side, there's a maple big as a cotton
warehouse. Can't miss it. You bring them men along to it about high noon
tomorrow. Goin' to stay faired off, don't have to worry about weather.
And *you* come down through the brush from the maple on the other bank,
the east bank, and give me a sign if everything's set right and if they've all
said they'll keep that promise to me. Hold your hand up high, your eatin'
and harness-bucklin' hand.'' He lifted his right hand. "That'll be my
sign. I'll be watchin' from the west bank. If you don't show up there on
the other side, or if you do show up and don't raise your hand, I'll see it,

but you won't see me. If you raise your hand, I'll come on across the river.''

I waited another gulp.

He was like a woods creature himself, he'd hid up here long enough to get a hermit-look and he'd had plenty of time to brood. But I had to trust him if he trusted me, and I had to make Planteu and the rest trust us both.

I even had to make Major Deveraux trust us all, in the long run.

I said, "All right. High noon tomorrow."

He nodded, and stood tossing the rifle up and down on one palm as if it was a wood-chip and didn't weigh more. "I wouldn't make no trouble with this here rifle, if they tried to shoot at me from across the river. Wouldn't never do that. I ain't never killed a man, it's against God's judgments. But if nobody shows up, or if you show up, Mist' Broome, and don't give a sign, nobody from Lanceton or the countryside ain't never gone see me again. Nobody but my friends the Gypsy folk, when they come through. Rifle come from Fountainwood, I had it strapped to Robin's gear when I left. Got plenty of ball for it, brought that along too. I can live by myself, with the Lord, ever and a day. His bounty will provide. Do say greetings to my little Miss French minute you clap eye on her, now. And I'll be waitin'.''

"So will I," I said.

He turned around, leading Robin away. When he and the Arab went out of sight, just when they dropped back into the brush, I couldn't tell. It was like something floating up from dark water for a hair's split of time, then going down again, covered up, submerged.

I got up on Grayboy, and went on across the creek.

An hour after that we came out of the woods above the Lanceton River, and went on past the fences of Fountainwood, which were just as pearl-white and clean-shadowing in this morning's half-gold light as they'd been when I last looked upon them, but there was a dark ruin back farther above the fences, and Grayboy acted up as we passed what had been the long, sightly house as if a haunt lingered among the smut-ends of timbers and the burned grasses. But I reckon it was just the singed scent, which even after a rain or so would stay. It was a place to stay away from; Grayboy went easier, and so did I, as we turned onto the bridge a few miles further along. It was late, even the trees had that feeling of shutting themselves up—the planks of the bridge boomed like each had been waiting for a disturbance, and was angry about it. For the almighty joy of it, and to bolster my own spirits, I let him out on the rest of the bridge. He loved that. It was as if he had found some grand fresh amusement that answered to a grand need in his own horse-soul, and made every plank thunder. I recalled Jupiter passing us here, and the fire-stain on the sky in the night behind, and as we came off the bridge into the sleepy dust, I pulled Grayboy down and swung out onto Lanceton Pike. French had crossed here for the side-road to the Morgan's pond, on the Monday night.

I set Grayboy to the gait again, toward Lanceton.

We'd not gone two rods before here in the center of the road bulked a gelding; a gelding that wanted currying, a black gelding facing our way, with a carbine sticking up from a saddle-scabbard on it, and on it more solid than anything outside a load of lint could have sat, Grody Flieshacker. His eyes just as small as a boar's at rutting time, and steamy, and his belly lopping over the pommel a mite, and some kind of old hopeful satisfaction in eyes, belly, and hands.

He said, "Hold up, Broome. Been expecting you. Thought you might come in from this side, and I heard you busting across the bridge. Could hear you for five miles. Bring your horse up slow now, and keep your hands where I can see plain. You're under arrest."

# 50

There wasn't a thing to do in the whole misted morning but go along with him. I didn't tell him it fitted in with my plans anyhow, and that I wanted to see Sheriff Will Planteu just as soon as I could. I did feel irked at being under arrest, and wondered if it was true or maybe if Planteu had just told Flieshacker to bring me in, and Flieshacker had taken the rest to his own self-important bosom. For about two minutes we went on alongside the Lanceton River, passing the high broad maple on our left—the one Jupiter had mentioned, which was just a few curves down this road from the point where Grody and I had splashed across to the woods on that first Monday. The maple was so sheltering and many-branched and holding its leaves so well even now in the wet shadows of coming day it was like a torch any man could have seen across the river. The river was about as narrow at the point where the maple faced it across the road, as it was where I'd splashed across on the Alice mare behind Grody. Ahead I could make out the first of the town trees of Lanceton in their back-cropped and lower-growing tidiness.

It was hard keeping Grayboy down to Grody's gelding's dogged gait, even though Grayboy had been going with only a few resting times since three the evening of the day before.

Grody talked first once more this time, I'd been waiting for him to.

"Miss French is out at Chantry Hall."

His voice was round with his own dislike, like the pegged wheel of an ox cart running through wet sand.

"Her name's Mrs. Broome," I said. "Her wedded name, that is."

"So she's said, Broome. Major Jack Deveraux, he's been with her all yester evening. He's an upright and great man. He listened to all Miss French's story, she's told it about a dozen times. He don't believe it any more'n I do or I think Will Planteu does—I ain't speaking for the mayor."

"Then he's still a fool with a one-track mind and not fit to judge anybody's story," I said just above the sounding of our plate-beats. "And it's refreshing to know the mayor's holding his judgment till further developments. He struck me as a man of temperance and smartness when I first saw him while all you seekers and well-wishers were gathered around Chantry Hall's front gallery. While I listened and watched you from the hall out there. Only other time I've come across him—still haven't met him to be introduced to, but I'll be glad when I do so—was when French and I were in the horse-cart with Shangro on a Wednesday morning. Just about a week since. I couldn't see him then, but I liked his conversational style."

When I looked over at Grody—I had to look a little downward as well as sideward—the muscles in his jaws were twitching. He made a motion to the stock of the carbine jutting up from its scabbard. But that was all he made. I'd been shot at by Wesley Teague, twice, the second time hitting home too close for comfort, but Grody wasn't any Teague. He was an upright citizen as sanctimonious and green-envy-tinted as a bowl of molded grits left out on the back stoop. He made my teeth itch at the same time I felt sorry for him. But along with my sorriness was a little more I had to say before I said anything else.

I went on, lifting my voice above the hoofbeats: "All of you keepers of the peace around Lanceton County can draw in your horns now. You can be my friends or not, as you choose—I'd choose it, I like you all right as people—but the days of riding short-herd on French are gone. Whatever fuss the major makes is his to account for. French and I are man and wife, and I think I speak for her when I say we intend to remain so till we're old bones. If you got that plain, I'm damned glad. If you ain't, you'd best understand it soon.''

It wasn't till we were riding past the first of the houses of Lanceton along its middle street—about at the point where I'd borrowed that rocking-gaited claybank horse—that Grody got his double-ax-bitted neck and his voice-box in condition to answer. Then it came out half-choked.

"You was a *deputy*!"

"Sure, and I sent back the badge with Deveraux."

"You was ridin' Alice!"

"She came back to you without the blind staggers, I trust."

"You lived and rode with Gypsies! Makin' Miss French bide with 'em!"

"We even went swimming with them, Grody. I don't know as French would tell you that, but she might if you asked politely."

"You put up in a whorehouse in Yadkin!"

"Three, four doors down from a few whorehouses. It was an old well-run boardin'house. I favored the bed, which was about as capacious as this whole street. So did French—though that's none of your business either, anymore, or even the business of French's godfather, Doc Mattison."

"You're nothin' but a roving by-rider, and you snatched up Miss French and spirited her off and forced her into a life of''—even above our hoofbeats and the jingle and creak of bridle gear and saddle leather it came out as if it plunged through the morning fog and flew—''raw, red sin. Goddamn it, she was the flower of gentility and you've ruined her. She spoke to all of us straight and high-and-mighty, like *we* was partly in the wrong even while she was apologizin'—you've changed her whole bone and breedin'. The major's right.'' He was gulping now, but saying this softer as well. "You done shot Gary Willis in the first place, just walked in there that night and plugged him and started the whole maze. And found out about that there Jupiter goin' to burn Fountainwood from Miss French, and talked her into goin' over there and stealin' back her jenny, knowin' it would be valuable at makin' money in Yadkin. And drug her with you over half Mississippi and even sweet-talked her into marryin' you." He'd drawn up the gelding; it blinked its eyes as if it hadn't heard this much from Grody since he'd last been pushed off in a back-lane ditch when Jupiter came riding by on Robin. "Jail's too soft for you. You're a bastard and a pug-knuckler and the truth's goin' to come out tonight when the major and all of us worm it out, once and for all, out at Chantry Hall."

I had drawn up Grayboy with him. The first light of day was around us, bringing out dark whiskers around Grody's nose. Along here houses and buildings were still wrapped in half darkness but with the blade of daylight showing.

"Yes," I said. "And I heard you telling Will Planteu how you'd suffered in the woods, with me eating all your cherished supplies. And how I was a dangerous knife-fighter and all. But I've been through enough so I'm not even mad at you, Grody. Like the major, all you're doin' is protecting what's never been yours in the first place. And sulling about it because you know in your gizzard it's gone and you'll never have it back the same. Never have it back in the same pigeonhole with the bonny blue flag flyin' over it, and that's what eats into you. I'm sad that it does. Maybe we can be at least nodding neighbors some time—got a notion we will be—but until then, I'm tired and Grayboy needs a stall and I've still got some private talking to do with Will Planteu before I get a few hours' rest."

Up the path behind the hitching posts where we'd stopped was the sheriff's office with its sign in gold framed with black just showing next to the door frame. A damp-boughed ailanthus tree spread above the door with its netting twigs seining the light from a lamp near the office window. I got off Grayboy and stood kneading my thighs for a second before I hitched him. He stood tall above the gelding and breathed a little warm steam out in the hushed morning. I pulled off the saddlebags and got a half-blanket out of the big one and threw it around his withers and haunches over the saddle and the fiddle-case and the rest. Grody got off the gelding and walked around it fast as if I was going to start off down the street seeking for another claybank horse to use in my flight. Then while I stood there, still watching me, he tied the gelding to a post. He went close behind my back as I walked up the path and the low steps to the office door.

"Just push it open," he said at my shoulder. "Sher'f Will might be asleep but he's waitin'. So's Doc and Howard Markley and Phil Adams.

And so's Mayor Westerfield—since you was praisin' him up so much a while back, might interest you to know you'll no doubt cause his death because he's so interested in all the goin's on now, he won't back off no matter what the rest of us keep tellin' him."

I had my hand on the door latch.

"Good," I said. "I mean I'm glad he's here. And where's Major Deveraux?"

"Sleepin' over at the Holly house. It's a hotel don't see his like much no more. He took the whole second floor, he does things in the old style like a gentleman. He's wore out, he's been back and forth between here and Chantry Hall since Miss French come back yester eve. He's got his drivin' man and his blood horses and a mighty wagon with him; he's gone to a power of expense and a mort of strain for his years."

"Which was his idea and his money and his own years to spend," I said. I opened the door.

At the swinging in of the door with its shadow cutting across the lamp's low light, Sheriff Planteu sat up on the scuffed leather sofa where he'd been sprawled out; his leathern vest flapping back from his shad-bellied height as he stood up, and his long eyes getting just a shade wider under the eyebrows as he came toward us. Grody crowded in behind me. "Shut that door," Planteu told him. "Been enough nosing around here all this time, I don't want a passel of old biddies—male and female—to come down on us at this hour. Or any hour." Grody shut it.

Doc Mattison, also sitting, had been sleeping at the other end of the sofa. His hard brown eyes were open now and he was scrooching up. Drawing his campaign hat off the arm of the sofa.

In the center cushions of the sofa, so light he seemed hardly to make a dent in their old leather, was stretched Mayor Marcus Westerfield. He wore a pale gray suit and a yellow cravat that flowed around his small chin like forsythias snugged there in a spring bouquet. He had wheat-straw white eyebrows and a smile on his bird-boned face as he slept. On his forehead but not covering it lay a tall gray hat with a round dome. He stirred as the sheriff spoke, then opened his periwinkle blue eyes. "Mister—Broome?" he said, moving around and getting in position to sit.

"Yes sir," I said. "Mayor Westerfield?"

He was getting up, coming across past the pot-bellied stove and the rolltop desk to the railing with the swing-door in it.

He kept the high-crowned hat in a crook of his elbow, and bowed a trifle. He was no taller than W. M. His voice was like a fife tune played in the distance but with strength behind it as if the fifer knew tunes hardly anybody else alive had ever learned.

"I—am—charmed—to meet the husband—of Francia. She said—you would be with us—and of course—here you are. It will be—such a grand relief—to get to the crux—of all this bother—about poor dead—deluded—Gary Willis. And the burning of—his rather—rococo—home. She has—informed us—that you may—shed additional light—on that—from Jupiter himself—as well information—about who, precisely—did away with him."

I walked in through the railing gate.

Sheriff Planteu was keeping his eyes on Mayor Westerfield as if he'd like to catch him if he fell, or at any rate break the fall with his will. The little man's fingers in mine were light as a sift of wind through lizard-bones. He drew his hand away and said, "A council—of war—is what this—resembles. But—it is—more fruitful—than that—I trust. I remember—many war councils—in the days—behind us—and for all—the sound and fury—they arrived only at—death and desolation. It was—the councils we had—after the war—when we began to reason among ourselves—that brought us back—into the realm—of *Homo* blessed as —*sapiens*. Sit down—Mister Broome. You have—traveled—most of the night?"

I said, "The good part of it."

"Then—you must have a stable—for your—horse; Francia—has told me—about him. About—his feats—at Yadkin Fair. And you must—bring in your baggage—and be—at ease. Please—" He was chirping blithe-faced up to Grody, who hulked at my shoulder, still. "Take Mister Broome's horse—along to Atkins' Livery—and see that he is—cared for—in every way—tell Atkins—it is at the expense—of Lanceton. And bring—Mister Broome's—baggage in here—so he may have—it with him—while he takes over—that sofa—when we are done with our—council. I do not—myself—require much sleep any more—when I—became ninety—I realized—it is never—essential. But I nap—a great deal—in the daytime. Sit down, do—Mister Broome."

Sheriff Planteu nodded to me. I nodded to him, and took one of the straw-seated chairs. Some of the straw was leaking from them, but they were comfortable enough. Next to me on another, Howard Markley was slumped, head down, his white gray beard fanning over the facings of his gray cavalry uniform coat, his forehead furrowed. In another chair in the corner sat little Phil Adams, likewise sleeping.

Doc Mattison was tucking a chew in his mouth. He said, "Good you're back, Tom Broome." His scratching voice clearing as he got the ambeer placed right. He came over and stirred Howard Markley's shoulder, not fierce. "Howard, wake up. Young Broome's back." His moustache worked along with his chewing lips. "He's got news for us, seems."

Howard Markley muttered in his slumber. Grody was opening the door and going out, letting in a gust of freshness before it shut with a rough sound behind him. Doctor Mattison shouldered around to me. Saying soft, "I'd like to break your head for all the Goddamned rushin' around and frettin' you've caused us, Broome. But Miss French—pardon me, Mrs. Broome it is now—had told us how it came about on her part. I believe her. I don't forgive you real sharp but I'd like you to know there ain't bad blood between us."

"Not from me," I said.

He blinked and shook Markley's shoulder-cloth again.

Markley came awake, saying as he saw me, "You are—Thomas Broome?" I said I was, and offered a hand. His hand was more like a farmer's than a schoolteacher's. It had never had a chance to go lax in the palms. His eyes darker blue than the mayor's, more considering blue than the fire of Major Deveraux's. "I taught your wife, sir—before she attended the academy. She was my best student, greatly high-spirited. She is a lovely woman. And I hope and trust you deserve her. I do not hold animosity toward you, but I am deeply hopeful we can solve Gary Willis's murder together." He smiled, wry. "So for one thing, I can stop disrupting the routine of my school. Anxious days, sir."

"And nights," put in Planteu, mostly to me. First he'd talked to me since I'd come in. "Tom Broome, I don't know as I forgive you or not. Personal. Somehow knew in the back of my head, it would be a hard time for us, the mornin' Doc brought you in here and said Mrs. Broome, then French Chantry, was missing. You took good care of Alice. I'd have expected that. But right now when I think—Mrs. French Broome has told us all about it—of you possuming-up there at the hall, spying on us before you and her went off to Yadkin—and when I think of bein' so close to the both of you I could have shoved my hand through that horse-box wall and touched you, out next the county line—well, makes me wish you were kin of mine, so I could tan you legitimate." His light bronze eyes slid to Grody, who was dropping my saddlebags and fiddle-case in the doorway.

Peach-tinted light fell there. Framing Grody, who wouldn't look my way, but was staring only at the sheriff.

"Well, Grody? You goin' to get that horse of his down to Atkins?"

"He ain't—going to jail?" Grody's voice was dry as the iron flakes gathered around the pot-bellied stove's firebox.

"Did you tell him he was?"

Grody's eyes almost shut before he nodded yes. "Told him he was under arrest."

"Well, well." Planteu was soft-purring. "That was tacky of you, Grody. It kind of fits the way you've acted ever since he first showed up. It don't become you as much as it does Jack Deveraux, though—at least he carries it off with an air and a troop-reviewin' eye." His high shoulders straightened. "I told you to meet Broome and tell him we were ready to talk with him here, no matter how late he tolled himself in! Nothin' more, nothin' less!" He made a grab at a fly that had come awake in the first true sun-shafts and was starting to buzz above the rolltop. "Damned flies, I wish to Christ—pardon me, Marcus—we'd get a deep frost and see 'em gone. Go on, Grody." As Grody moved back, Planteu sighted out of the doorway. "Lord, Lord, so that's the Standardbred. All three heats at Yadkin, and me down here poultering around without a copper on him. Grody, treat him even better than you would Alice or your own brute." He was purring once more. "That's a plain order."

Grody shut the door quieter than he had the first time.

Phil Adams, in the straw-bottomed chair next to Howard Markley, had wakened and was shooting his head out a little past Markley's soldierly solid bulk, so he could see me. I raised my eyebrows at him, and he gave me a greeting glance, then drew his nose back.

Planteu hoisted himself on a desk-corner with one hip.

"Our mounts are all around in the town's stables around in back," he said, fishing for a short cigar. He stuck it in his mouth-corner, dry. "I agree with the mayor; I think you'd ought to catch some sleep in a minute or so, after you've told us what you found out about Jupiter. But we're ready to go with you then, or do anything we can to talk to old Jupe. Providin' Shangro—kind of a decent cuss, Shangro, for a Gypsy man, even if I ain't forgetting he helped you and Mrs. French Broome fool me—put you on Jupe's trail, as Mrs. French Broome said you thought he might."

The straw chair creaked under me. I said, "I talked to Jupiter. Just this morning."

Everybody was sitting or standing with gunpowder-scenting attention.

"You found him where we couldn't, I'll give you that," said Planteu. He wetted the cigar-end.

"I started in here intending to tell this just to you, Sheriff Planteu," I said. "And I'd never have found Jupiter if it hadn't been for Shangro in the first place, and even then I wouldn't if Jupiter hadn't trusted both French and me, and as it was, Jupiter found *me*, not the other way around. All I did was crash my way through the woods. But before I tell about that, I see this is a kind of council, as Mayor Westerfield pointed out."

The mayor was smiling from where he'd perched on the rim of the sofa again. He bobbed his head up and down with eagerness. His buttoned boy-small boots hardly touched the floor.

"So I shan't tell it just to you, but to this council," I went on. "It's a promise Jupiter wants you all to make." I drew a breath. Phil Adams had got up and gone out to the kitchen abutting this office; I could hear a coffee pot being sloshed and put on the kitchen stove-hob. Adams paused and gazed in here from the kitchen now. "Before I tell you what it is, I want to know the full size of the council. I mean"—I looked all around, to Planteu, to Doctor Mattison with his eyes hot on me as brown coals, to Mayor Marcus Westerfield, to Howard Markley leaning forward and stroking his sleep-disturbed beard, and to Phil Adams—"I mean, does it take in Major Deveraux?"

It was Planteu who answered, after a glance over at the mayor.

"We're still runnin' our own town, Tom Broome. I respect, admire, and hold strong old friendship for Jack Deveraux. I always will. But he may be kingpin in Pharis and all, and still it don't give his words more weight than any other man's in our estimate. He wants to bushwhack you, I don't need to tell you that—and Grody's on his side there, they're both gun-jumpers in their own set peculiar ways, though as I say, Jack does it with style and Grody just comes out rough as a cob with it. But for this council—and Marcus is right as always, it ain't a council of war, it's aimed at peaceability—what we say and do here and now's among just us. Nobody else—save for the fact that I'll bring Grody in on it after we've decided, because I'm the sheriff and he'll bend my way. But what goes on here's not for Jack Deveraux's ears. Or his butting into."

I said, "Since you deputized him to bring French and me back—"

He flapped a hand. "He volunteered his services, and I wasn't about to refuse 'em. That's over. Mrs. French Broome is back—with her merry-go-round and that peaked little black lad. You're back. That's all that counts. I'm waitin' to hear about Jupiter.''

I thought about Jupiter. Richer sun was falling in through the office windows from the street; it was going to be another fair day as Jupiter had said. Uncommonly fair.

Sheriff Planteu rubbed the back of his tight-corded neck, where wrinkles like the cracks between cobbles showed in a warm circling of sunlight. He got up from the desktop and walked over and held a hand curved around the lamp's chimney in the window, and blew out the lamp.

The smoke from its wick blew over to Doc Mattison, and Doc sneezed. He was sitting watching me now as he'd sat seething inside in Chantry Hall's quiet kitchen while we waited in vain for the sound of Grayboy's hoofbeats and for French to show up, on another morning.

Planteu said, quiet, "We ain't planning on meeting again with Jack till about nine o'clock tonight, out at Chantry, Tom. He's put a bitter case against you. But rampageous as it is, it's all his own case. It ain't ours. All of us here take that into account. So tell us Jupiter's proposition, and what kind of promise he wants from us, and we'll vote on it. And act on it if the vote is aye. Just as we done when we started rebuildin' the town after wartime, just as we'll keep on doin' while we've got our senses and the rivers run.''

# 51

It was half past eleven when the bunch of us, Grody included and quiet as a run-down clock, started out for the pike where it ran out of town along the Lanceton River. They'd all of them there at the sheriff's office voted aye, agreeing to the conditions Jupiter had laid down to me; there hadn't been any real argument. I'd cleaned myself up a little and taken some coffee and bark-back biscuits—reflecting while I ate and drank that Phil Adams might be a capable deputy but wasn't a high-style cook—and then stretched out on the sofa and slept a few hours. When I woke up, Planteu shaking my shoulder, everybody was set to start out but there wasn't a whole lot of talk going on. Just a kind of tightness among everybody, all of us knowing when Jupiter named the person he said he'd seen shoot Willis, it was going to have to be somebody this whole group knew, and likely one of this very outfit.

Grody had brought Grayboy back from Atkins' Livery, and I must say he'd been good about him, I'd not seen Grayboy so shined up since W. M. had last done it in the big track shed beside the champion track at Yadkin. Sheriff Planteu walked around Grayboy, twice, and said, "Well, he is damned near worth all the chasing around. If I owned him I'd just sit a fence and look at him, and get the bloats from purest pride." Then we were all shuffling around in the street in front of the office, Planteu mounting his roan which Grody and Phil had brought around from the stables, Doc Mattison up on Alice—her black socks neat as ever in the sparkling sun—Grody on his gelding again, Phil Adams on his mouse-colored horse, Howard Markley on his farm-broken dapple grey, looking, I judged, about the way he must have appeared when he and Planteu and Doc and Marcus Westerfield had been with the cavalry, only with a dust of age and wear around him now, and his mind set on getting this mystery solved and going back to his schoolroom and students. Looking back along the street as I got up on Grayboy, I could see a good many of the townspeople watching us with curiosity from the town square, the statue rising from it staring our way too, with its blind stone eyes steady and its blanket-roll around its shoulder and its rifle pointing our direction. And I saw Doc's house-office back of its avenue of oaks and his cob grazing there near a stable, and the glint of his buggy's wheels trap, taking the reins without paying attention to them, fixing the hat high on his head, still smiling and as off in the distance as if he was flying far th hair it was a walking garden of curls. The mayor held his hat in his hand and looked down into it, standing beside the cart, as if the lining of the hat intrigued him as a wonder and a mystery past any mystery we were facing, and he stayed there smiling until Planteu reminded him, soft, that we had to be moving to be on time. Then he got into the trap, taking up the reins without paying attention to them, fixing the hat high on his head, still smiling and as off in the distance as if he was flying far above the treetops. We were about ready to get underway, even so, when there was a bustle from in front of a building back along this street and catercornered from the sheriff's office, and here came a top hat I remembered—or one just as haughty—and under it, head up and bones almost showing under the brick-dust cheeks, Major Jack Deveraux, his handsome green riding coat flaring out and his boots sending back reflections of the whole day as if they'd been waxed and boned to the gleam of fresh silver dollars.

Beside me, Sheriff Planteu said, "Oh, hell," low under his breath, and got off the roan. Deveraux was already moving into the street, but Planteu got to him before he'd crossed to us. Deveraux glanced once at me, then his blazing eyes, like the blue around hot shoe-iron in the forge, fixed on Planteu. From where we waited all of us could hear the hard-ridged tone of the major's voice, but only a few words. "Right and privilege . . . must know what is transpiring . . . obligation to tell me . . ."

Grody was gazing with admiration over at the major, the rest of us here were just gazing. Planteu's high shoulders went higher, he was talking sharp now. He finished up in a burst, then the major was swinging on a boot heel and marching off, and Planteu was so mad he lit his slim cigar as he came back across the street beside his roan. I could tell it took a lot of ire to make him do that. He mounted with a solid slap in the roan's saddle, and rapped out, "Let's *go!*"

He rode beside me, the rest stringing out behind us, the pony trap crackling just behind us. A man detached himself from the people watching us, and stumped along up to us, hobbling a mite; I saw it was Ed Travers, who'd glimpsed French on Grayboy on that gone Monday morning. He brushed a hand on Grayboy's flank. "That's the stud horse!" he said, grinning up to me. "And you're the Broome everybody's talkin' about. The one lifted Mort Tyler's claybank! Sher'f, we all got a right to know what's goin' on, if you're goin' to arrest Broome and hold him for trial, we pay taxes and we pay your salary, we've helt off so far formin' a protest committee, but it's our solemn right to know—"

Planteu didn't even slow the roan. He said out of the corner of his lips not holding the cigar, "Get on back to your bench, Ed, and shut up. If you or any of your cronies or the women or the young bloods follow us, I'll fine you for contempt and harassment of an officer of the law in performance of his duty. Worse. I'll tell how you shot your own self in the leg at Boiling Springs, and called it a hero's wound. Tell everybody you see there'll be a general meetin' in my office yard, tonight about eleven, a town meetin' where I'll explain all that's went on, the best I can. We'll put up trestle tables and have a party. Bring your own food, I'll furnish a barrel of liquor. Till then, and about anything else, shut *up.*"

When I glanced back again, Ed Travers had stopped in the street. Gazing after us with his seamed jaws agape.

Planteu let smoke drift around his cheekbones, and said as if to himself, "Highty tighty. Major Deveraux. Town full of prize-ass snoops." We were coming to the first bend out of Lanceton. The pike was packed red clay. The day was one of those you only get a cupful of in a whole fall, not the Indian summer that would come later but the fall in its fullest and sharpest fountaining, as if all the countryside trees out here, in every leaf, were bursting with something brave before their winter drowse. The river bank smell and the smell of the reeds making Grayboy lift his head and want to step out again, as if he was willing to go cross-country clear back to Pharis, Quincyville, Appleton, and Yadkin, and any place in between.

Planteu said, "Jack Deveraux could run me in the army, I was just his captain and anyhow, he was near as good with the troop as Bob Chantry himself. But he ain't runnin' me now, and I just now had to tell him so. Been comin' on for a couple of days, and it's got worse since Mrs. French Broome is back. He's packin' up his wonder-wagon and goin' out there now, to wait for us till tonight. Reckon he'll launch his best guns out at Chantry, and'll still try to talk Mrs. French Broome into cuttin' you off like a chancre. You mind all that?"

"I've minded it sorely," I said, "but it doesn't seem to bother me now. All I want is to get this over with, and settle in."

He ducked his chin. "Yeah . . . speakin' of settlin' in, I don't know if cotton'll ever come back in force, but Chantry land would make a good horse farm. Man like you could use it for a bivouac base, ridin' out whenever he so chose, not feelin' tied down. Tendin' and breedin' horse in the winter, but all spring and summer till the cold hits again, travelin' and racin' and even consortin' with Gypsy bands, whatever he chose. You ain't a planter, you ain't got the nose or hands or eyes for it, but it ain't hard to put in horse-forage which you could do with a middle-buster plow. Be awful good to see that house shinin' again . . . I like a built-up community. Sick of chewin' hind tit and the kind of backbitin' goes on in a place just sits on its butt and blames the North for every windstorm knocks down a pigpen. Hadn't been for Marcus we'd all still be lookin' backward, but we've still got a distance to go . . ."

He looked around at Mayor Westerfield; so did I.

The mayor was asleep while driving, his face raised a little, his old skin clear as lamp-chimney glass, his smile shooting up sunward.

The maple was coming in sight on our right. On this side of it, back near a slat-broken farmhouse with its unpainted boards sleeping behind a broom-swept yard, a dozen or so children were beating a pecan tree with their hands and rocks to make the pecans shower down. One child was shinned up with his knuckley arms and skinned legs twined around a bough. Caught just a flash of them as they yelled and went on beating, but in the flash I thought not one of the children seemed younger than Mayor Westerfield.

The sun was high over the river, we were all drawing up where the maple spread its arms beside the road and over it, its shadows cool under its flaming leaves which looked so bright you felt you could burn yourself by brushing them.

We rode in under the maple, the mayor coming awake just in time to steer his pony this way, then the long grasses, smelling of stem-sap and some of them still holding their green, were rising around, and above us the maple swayed from time to time in the river-wind, leaves floating off and landing on the horses and over our shoulders and adding to the ground drift of them which hissed like half-sleeping snakes as the horses waded through. We dismounted, Doc Mattison going over and giving the mayor a hand out of his trap, Howard Markley groaning and massaging a hip as he got off and pulled the gray's reins over its head, Grody standing with his arms folded stolid as if his world had gone awry but might yet veer back into a time when a man could treat an outlander with the scorn he deserved. Phil Adams squatted back on his boot-heels in the leaves, squinting across the river, dandling leaves through his fingers as he watched over there; Planteu slitted his eyes against sun-dazzle up through the maple crown and said, "Noon, or a fraction after. Go ahead, Tom."

I walked out from under the maple. Back of me Grayboy sounded off a little, blowing and wishing to follow. When I looked back Doc Mattison had a hand on his reins. Doc's eyes were impatient as they'd been when I'd first met him, but with something else in them too. I couldn't read it for fright of any kind, but it might have been puzzlement. Planteu was just gazing at me, his hat-brim low and the cavalry buttons sewn on his vest like time-rubbed small coins. I went on across the pike-road. When I got on the other side, the river's shine was in my eyes, but I went on down through the brush of the bank. And came out on hard-packed mud and sand littered with red and gold smooth stones. Across the river's shallows the light darted in hummingbird spins and jabs, but I could see now. On the other bank there might have been no man treading ever, only the woods rising smoky behind the sand and reeds, the oaks and pines in a rough whaleback that appeared to spread north over the rest of the whole earth. For a couple of bad seconds I wondered what would happen if Jupiter didn't keep his word, if his hermit-shyness had come back and if none of us might ever see him again. The breeze pushing south touched my cheekbones; I'd shaved quick back at Planteu's office-kitchen, hadn't had time to do the task to suit W. M. and his sense of fitness. I thought of Major Deveraux on his way to Chantry Hall right now, and wished I was already out there. Then I whistled in a breath, and raised my right hand as high as it would go.

Across the river a cowbird sailed out of one of the oak-tops near the woods' edge, then another, then Jupiter was coming into sight, leading Robin, the rifle-barrel sending off sun-sparks like heliograph messages from regiment to regiment in the war, both Jupiter and the horse moving down to the water's edge in a steady coming. I kept my hand up till they got to the water and he was mounting, both his and the Arab's skins making diamonds in the dancing light. Then I dropped my arm but stayed where I was. The water was even shallower here than it had been where Grody and I had crossed. There wasn't any noise from in back of me across the road up at the giant maple. Just the splashing of the Arab's plates and its fetlocks out in the river. About twelve feet from this shore Jupiter pulled up the Arab's head and sat there.

I said, "It's all right. They won't harm you."

"I ain't slept well. The Lord God didn't inform me not to tell, Mister Broome, but it's just *me* feelin' bad about it. If it wasn't for Miss French and you I wouldn't be comin' across at all. My, my. Person I got to bother now's always been good to me, how is it I got to repay his goodness with blabbing? But never fear, I'm here and if you say I'll stay free and can help by blabbing, I'll do it."

He brought Robin to this bank. The Arab stretched his neck up to the west, scenting out the other horses across the road. Jupiter got off and led him up the bank, I climbed alongside. His shadow spread over the furzy brush almost as much as Robin's. Even now and knowing it didn't matter, his motions were so quiet you couldn't have heard him rise up through the brush if he'd been doing it by himself. He kept staring across the road, when we reached it, eyes fixed under his ridged forehead. Then we were across the road, into the long grasses, and the leaves were whirling down in another gust of noon wind, and all of the people who'd been waiting on this land-side of the road were watching Jupiter as leaf-shadow played over his shoulder-muscles and prinks of the sun touched his eyes.

I could hear Jupiter's breath going fast under the hard plates of his chest muscles.

Sheriff Planteu said, mild enough, "Jupiter, you're as free as any man will ever be in my county. The fire don't matter. Gary Willis is dead and under the ground. We buried him four days past, his grave's not marked. Wasn't anybody but me and Doc and Grody and Phil at the burying. He didn't have any kin but Mrs. French Broome. Maybe had his money in Yankee banks, but that's up to somebody else to unravel. All we want from you is what you promised Tom, and we'll keep our side of the bargain."

Jupiter lifted a hand the size of a smokehouse ham to rub sweat from a temple. The rifle dangled in his other hand's fingers.

"The Arab's yours, far as I'm concerned," Planteu went on. "Rifle too—I'm just easy somethin' was saved from the burnin'. We all know you as a good worker. If you choose to stay around Lanceton you'll eat and hold up your head with all."

"Now praise God," Jupiter said. He wasn't looking at anybody but Planteu.

All at once I knew he wasn't *carefully* looking at anybody but the sheriff.

As if his eyes were at one end of a tunnel and Will Planteu's at the other.

Then Jupiter shut his own eyes. And he said so low nobody if they hadn't been waiting might have heard it over the wind's skift of the leaves, "The body I seen coming in Chantry Hall door with a pistol in hand and aiming it up at Willis, he was—"

Same second, Doc Mattison was spitting a long stream into the leaves and grasses, and stepping around Planteu between Planteu and Jupiter, Jupiter's Arab backing in a little scare at the sudden movement, and Planteu had shot out a hand and was holding Doc's left arm, and Doc had his nutcracker jaws clamped tight and was shaking his head, then saying, "Lemme go, Will," and trying to get his right hand in his coat pocket.

And Jupiter's eyes were open in wonderment, and Planteu was standing back from Doc. And saying, "I didn't want to hear it from you, Roy, since you've had all the tarnation time there is to say it. You've had from a week ago Monday to now. And I've known it, or guessed it and then hedged my mind off from it, not wanting to even harbor the thought. But it's been mouse-eating at me too long. Hell, Roy, I'm old but I ain't blind. Or dumb in most senses. You're the one of anybody with the most chance to've cleaned up the derringer and reloaded it and left it beside the drive out at Chantry, where Marcus discovered it—and where anybody would have, sooner or later. You're the one who would have known Miss French—Mrs. French Broome—always kept that kitchen door locked, so you wouldn't have ducked out that way after the shooting, knowing you'd have to unlock it and couldn't lock it again from the outside—since the key was kept on the inside—and not wanting it to be found unlocked. And so the one who walked right back out onto the front gallery and got in your buggy and drove off. You knew that house, and know it, the way a leadsman knows the Missi'pp'—yet you let me seek out all the hidey-holes in it, searching for the fool derringer which you'd taken out of the lion-head hole below the newel-post after Miss French Broome had put it back there, after she'd found out it had been fired. I reckon you did that out of protection for her, but there's an element of protection for yourself, which doesn't sit well on my stomach. Since she come back yesterday and told me the whole thing, her complete side of it, chapter and book, I've put the whole body of knowledge together and it fits like breeching on a plow-horse. Hell, Roy. Hell. All you had to do was say it, that first morning when you brought Broome in. Or say it even earlier, say it to Miss French Broome herself. Nobody'd have hung you. The whole county'd been grateful. But now I don't want to hear you say it. I want Jupe to finish. So we'll all know, and hear it plain.'' He swung to Jupiter. ''Jupiter?''

Jupiter's mouth-corners moved, then he said soft as a plum dropping into straw, ''Mist' Doc, you always been fine to me, we always been friends of each other—but Mister Doc, it was you I seen.''

Doc was standing apart from the others, nearest me. He was sweating, but he still didn't look scared, ashamed, or anything but mad enough to spit nails. He had his right hand thrust deep in his old coat's pocket, and he muttered, ''Damn it, it's here somewhere—lining's ripped, and there's enough pills down there to resuscitate a dead battalion.'' He kept screwing his arm and hand deeper. Then he pulled up a stethescope, and yanked it looping around his neck in a rage, and rammed his hand down again. He said, ''Ah,'' and brought up the hand. He opened his palm. It was the derringer, as I'd seen it last in French's hand when we were going into the Chantry stable. Wicked small instrument, catching the leaf-freckling light on its hooked butt.

Planteu's eyes opened the farthest I'd ever seen them go, then went back to their native slits again. "Why, damn your soul, Roy. I've got that locked up—I had that locked up in my safe back at the office, and if you've went and learned the combination and taken to robbing, that's a serious offense. I take it even more serious than your havin' shot Willis, and havin' held back from me all this time and let me and all the others stew. That's the property of the county, it's evidence, and you'd ought to feel real shabby takin' it at this late stage of the game."

"Oh, shee-ut," said Doc, in half a groan. He threw a glance at Mayor Westerfield, who was watching with his bright eyes just visible below the shoulder of Planteu. The mayor had his fine gray dome-crowned hat in his fingers again. "My apologies, Marcus. But anyhow, oh, shee-ut. Take a close look at this derringer, Will." He tossed it across to Planteu, who caught it in a side-hand swoop. "It ain't mine. You're right there. The one you got in your safe is mine—and I wouldn't want to know the combination to any safe, let alone any that's no doubt got as yellowed and seedy a set of papers in it as yours. This one's the one Willis was shot with." He spat over his shoulder, a nice far pitch through the maple's leaves. "Well?" He looked all around. "Didn't any of you all ever hear of two derringers alike before? Bob Chantry and I got 'em same time, same shop in N' Orleans, the week after Sumter was fired on. Thought they might be handy, but they never were. Hair-trigger, and just as likely as not to put the ball through your own self as through an enemy. Forty-one caliber rimfire, like I told you when you asked, after I'd taken the ball from Willis's head. But the one you're holdin' ain't *mine*. It's Bob's. See a little mark down on the butt?"

Planteu was turning the derringer over. Holding it in the sun, eyes even closer to shutting. "R. D. C.," he said.

"Robert Delarre Chantry. If you'll look at the one in your safe, it's got R. M. on it. My mother never gave me a middle name. Just Roy, which has suited me great." Doc breathed in and out fast, and unslung the stethescope and dropped it back in his pocket. "All right. I was out on the pike comin' back from deliverin' an eight-pound, four-ounce son to Widow Planker. She havin' been widowed five years, but still a popular companion of a fall night with passin' teamsters and such. Comin' around front of Chantry Hall, I seen a light in the hall back of the vestibule, door open, and then that horse right there, Willis's pride, tied to the lower front gallery railin's. Seen you too, Jupiter. I pulled up the drive and alongside the bricks so my cob wouldn't make much noise, and left the buggy in the shelter of an oak—it was rainin' like billy-be-damned, you'll all recall—

and started in. Thought for sure Willis was over pestering Miss French again—Miss French Broome, if you like, Tom—and was goin' to kill him if he was. I'd had enough of him in my life, and I wouldn't mind a shred goin' through a trial—be kind of a lark at my age—and I doubt any judge in this county'd convict me for expungin' vermin. About the time I started, Jupiter, here, left the Arab and shot up the gallery steps and went in. As I came farther up the steps I saw him go past Willis, who was slumped over in one of them tapestry-wove old chairs in the vestibule, and seemed to be in a good heavy stupor. But as I came onto the gallery, Willis heaved hisself up and charged for the stairs. Yellin' and carryin' on, his image reflected in them mirrors six ways from Sunday. Seen Jupiter's face at the chink of the ballroom door off the hall. Willis was sayin'—beg pardon, Marcus—he was goin' to breed Miss French whether she liked it or not, hollerin' a mess of tripe about he had the power of darkness in his loins and would raise a race of masters of the world. So drunked-up I doubt he could have raised a finger, let alone his—well, anyhow. I took my derringer—not that one—out of my pocket, where I'd put it about six months before, thinkin' I might drop it off at a gunsmith's some day if I happened to be out on a farm-call in the countryside and found one. Wanted the trigger-action blunted; so I could use it some day. Way them things work is, you cock 'em and the trigger comes out when you do it. Knew it was safe so long as I didn't cock it, but now my mad was up and I had it out and cocked. I looked up"—Doc stared up now into the sun, falling over his grizzled hair and into the hair in his ears—"and says just, 'Willis!' Just that. He whirls around. And I squeezed the trigger."

Came a pause. In it, the horses moving—Grayboy was trying to eat some of the lower-boughed maple leaves, and not getting far—was just about the only noise around. That and the cries of a few kingfishers along the river.

Sheriff Planteu said, flat, "And you shot him. What's more to be said? Whether you shot him with the derringer in my safe, or this one I'm holdin', is what the law calls immaterial."

Doc said, his blood up in the black red veins in his cheeks, "You damned fool! You still don't see! *I* didn't shoot him with either! My derringer, the one you'll see in your foolish safe when you get back, wasn't fired! It misfired; when I pulled the trigger nothin' at all happened! Nothin'll happen now if you go back and get it out and cock it and pull the trigger, even though it's cleaned and loaded and looks lethal!"

He raked hair back off his forehead, pulled his hat down farther to contain it, and said, "Willis come tumblin' down, in good style, dead as mutton but less attractive. I thought I'd killed him. I stalked right out—you're right I didn't go out the kitchen way, but it wasn't on account of any devious plan, I just didn't reckon to stay there long—I'd heard the shot go off, same time I triggered, saw the ball hit Willis, saw him go down. Got back in my buggy and drove right off, and about the same time, heard Jupiter through the rain, heard him raise a ballroom window and then heard him plump down under it, and heard him ridin' the Arab off hell-for-leather. Well. I went on home. Wasn't till I had my nightshirt on I thought to look at my derringer, so I got up and did so. Feelin' quite peart over it's finally havin' done some good for mankind. You can imagine how I felt—no you can't; you got to be my age and think you've rid the country of a stain and done a good night's work, and then find somethin' else done it for you, to get a smatherin' of the feeling—when I found my derringer was still loaded. Aimed it at the floor of my bedroom, pulled the trigger. Floor was still all there. Got out other cartridges for it, took out the old, reloaded with new, aimed it out the window this time, pulled, and just got a click. Tried it a hundred times. Went back to bed, thinkin' hard. Had just fell to a dubious sleep when here came Miss French, knockin' on my door, that brave horse of Broome's standin' by, and her tellin' me to follow her please, that she *thought* Willis might be dead on Chantry staircase. You know most of the rest. *Except*—" He'd stepped through leaves to Planteu. He tapped Planteu's chest as if testing it for rales. "*Except* I'd of told you right off, if I'd done it, and now I thought Miss French had to of done it, standin' behind me from somewheres in the hall. And that notion got firmed up in me deeper and deeper after I'd performed the autopsy and found a rimfire ball in Willis's head. And when we all were rakin' around Chantry Hall on the Tuesday before last, sure, I opened the newel-post hole before you got to it, and took out Bob's derringer, the one you're holdin' now, and seen it had been fired, and smelled it, and it had, and I put it in my pocket and shut the lion-lid, and then when I was gettin' Grody's fouled carbine from his horse down in the drive, I dropped *my* derringer in the leaves for somebody to find. Figurin' it couldn't be told from the one Miss French had, and figurin' it'd at least point a finger in some other direction than her. And I kept shut about all this till right now, knowing it had to come to a head and hopin' she hadn't shot Willis—it'd be all right for a man but unbecomin' her—and then, when she showed up back here from Yadkin, and told us all her tale, I believed her, it'd take a congenital jackanapes not to. And while I'd be just as proud if I'd shot Willis, I'm kind of proud about havin' held my tongue till now—at least it brought Jupe back to the land of the living and people who like him. All I got to say, I'm played out." From the left-hand pocket he fished a buckram flask. "Anybody?"

"Right after you, Roy," said Planteu. He gazed with his eyes like tiny flashes of strong tea while Doc drank. Took the flask when it was handed over. Looked at the derringer he was holding, smelled it thoughtful, slid it in a pocket, and tipped the flask back. He held it to me and I shook my head. Grody nodded and took it. I gathered Mayor Westerfield didn't drink. Wiping his mouth, Planteu said, while he handed the flask along past Howard Markley, who I reckoned also didn't drink, to Phil Adams, who did at least on occasions like this, "Only thing left to say is, somebody had to kill Willis. I'll have to lock to that thought and hold it to my dyin', mystified day."

"No—" It was Mayor Westerfield. I think everybody had forgotten he was standing there right under Planteu's shoulder, until now. He took a step as if he was falling forward, or floating forward, into the leaf-drift. His little hands moving as if to cup and shape the sun-streaks. Jupiter had the flask now but he only held it, didn't drink, his eyes huge on the mayor.

"No—you see, poor Gary Willis—shot himself—he was in Satan's hands—had delivered himself there—in league with whatever powers—he had imagined—and imagination—and acceptance of evil—are as strong—as cannon—or the entire weight of time—in the hands of—the wrong man."

I remembered Shangro telling me of Willis trying to find out about Shangro's knowledge of spells and such, and Shangro's disgust over it.

"War itself—all wars—spring from this—alliance with darkness—no matter how self-justified—the alliance is forever—there—and some-times—the darkness—turns on its—servant—"

Jupiter was moving back, against the trunk of the great tree. "Hoodoo," he said deep in the back of his throat. "Mama Jumbo—"

"—leaving—holocaust—for those who would bring holocaust—" He smiled, bright and quick. "As it has been written of war—the soldier's pole is fall'n—young boys and girls—are level now with men—the odds is gone—and there is nothing left remarkable—beneath the visiting moon—" His smile was even clearer. "And in poor Gary's case—the soldier's pole—fell on *him*—not accidentally—I think—for there is no accident."

Planteu said, "Marcus . . . he couldn't have shot himself. Roy and Jupe both saw him get shot."

"He did it himself," said Marcus Westerfield. "Tonight—at Chantry Hall—I will show you how—but for now—let us only—enjoy the daylight—the one gift—we never appreciate—enough—unless we are children—young children—or men and women—old men and women. Let us go back to Lanceton—and have a little—good food—and company—and then—"

"Suicide?" whispered Planteu. "Suicide, Marcus?"

"No—he did not intend it—nevertheless—it was not an accident. His weakness—was erased—by other powers—but, as I was saying—" He turned, and stumbled a bit on his way to his pony trap, where the pony was investigating some half-dried fiddle fern, and Howard Markley caught him and steadied him as he got back into the cart. He arranged his round-brimmed, round-topped hat on his head with fingers you could almost see through. "As I was—saying—let us now for a while—fleet the time carelessly—as they did in the golden world."

Planteu said, "Come on, Jupe. Bring the Arab."

Jupiter came out from under the tree's darkest shadow.

"I don't want no hoodoo, Mister Sheriff. I had that all them years. Me and Luther, Mingo and Dabney, we all had it—I obeyed God and burned the place, and *he's* dead—I seen him die—I don't want him back."

From the pony cart Mayor Westerfield said, "There was no strange magic—in the manner—of his dying—Jupiter. It is only that—he brought it on—himself—by his paltriness—of playing—at being—a magician. The darkness—swallowed—him. Life—had—enough—of him. Some day—it will have enough—of all his kind."

We were getting on our horses. The voices of the children playing at the pecan tree back along the road came faint here; they were having a good time; laughing a lot.

# 52

The moon was rising over Chantry Hall by the time it came in sight to me and to Jupiter. We were riding ahead of all the other people from Lanceton, where we'd spent more time that afternoon and early evening than I'd wanted to. Though it had all seemed necessary and even important to get as much settled in Lanceton as we could before keeping the nine o'clock appointment called by Major Jack Deveraux. On the clay of the pike Robin's hoofbeats—she had a lovely gait—sounded along with Grayboy's in a long chiming roll of sound, and Jupiter and I got a lot of settling done in the eight miles out to the hall. I'd told him anybody who could keep a horse in the shape he'd kept Robin there in the woods all this time, must be a sound horse-handler; he'd said if he had his druthers he would like to spend the rest of his days doing just that. I'd said the pay wouldn't be much, but that there was plenty of room for good horse-barns if we tore down the old slave cabins and added to the stable. Now we both checked and drew up as the chimneys and roofs of Chantry Hall swam in sight; behind us Sheriff Planteu, Doc, Grody, Howard Markley, Phil Adams, and last but hardly the least for all his tiny size, the mayor in that wickerwork pony trap, were coming around the last pike-bend; they made a tangle of bright noise in the night, nearly as brisk as the passage of Shangro's caravan. While the horses rested, we'd had midday dinner at Doc's; his housekeeper had laid out a good spread for us all, and Doc, over a stirrup-cup at the end of the meal, had showed me a picture of his wife who'd died back in the sixties just at the sag end of the war. In a thumb-rubbed gilt frame, the oval of it like his gone wife's oval face, the hand-tinted face had looked out at me with a touch of brightness still on it. Doc said then, "With her gone, I kind of put everything I had into the town itself. Keepin' people alive, sure, but helpin' the mayor and Will all I could, too. Man does that—turns into a boss mule, when he ain't got other interests." Planteu had brought along the other derringer, Doc's, which he'd had locked in his safe; it wouldn't fire worth a snap, even when we put fresh cartridge in it and aimed out over the japonica bushes under Doc's sitting room windows. The mayor had gone to sleep after the dinner, which he'd eaten about two mouthfuls of. I didn't know quite what he meant about the darkness having swallowed Gary Willis, but it made a tingle of wonder pass up my backbone every time I thought of it, and I reckoned—as I was sure the rest of us did—that he'd bring out the how and the why in his own good time.

Now I leaned up in the saddle to study the lay of the land and let the rest of the crowd come up closer to Jupiter and me. Grayboy was eagering to get there, he shifted with impatience and bobbed his head down to Robin, and Robin's clean small Arab head went bobbing in agreement. Over the clop and creak of the rest of our party coming up, Jupiter said, "Yonder's the cemetery. Where Colonel and Miz M'linda lays."

He pointed with the hand not holding the rifle, up the slope on this side of Chantry, where cedars stood against the yellowing light with their black shapes like shrouds. Fanned out over the glimmer of headstones among the calf-high grasses. From here I could whiff a touch of the sugar-cane mill along the road past the Toddy Morgan farm, and I felt a need for French so strong I could taste it like apples at the root of my tongue, and in the tips of my fingers was a good tingling. I said, "I'll come around that way—want to see if W. M.'s been taking care of Bell the way he should. I'll swing in around the stable. Tell the rest I'll meet them in the hall."

I'd told Jupiter about W. M. Told him W. M. was a smart-mouthed child and he wouldn't have to take any sass from him and to put his foot down if he got it. He'd said he thought he could get along with any child bound up in horses. I wheeled Grayboy off into the edge of the meadow, looking over the oaks and pines and magnolia crowns but still not able to see the lights of the hall, though I knew there'd be lights there. And still not able to see Major Deveraux's high slick wagon, or his blood horses, or any sign of him. He was bothering me, still, at the back of my mind as he'd plagued and unsettled me from the first time I'd seen him gazing at French at Pharis. But right now I wanted to see the cemetery, where French had said she sometimes went to visit. Grayboy went up the slope as if the crisp air was lifting him, as if he floated on it. When we got in among the cedars I dismounted, holding his reins. The headstones were dim with weather, even dimmer in this bough-filtering light, but I could make out the colonel's, and the name *Robert Delarre Chantry,* and the chiseled words about dying valiantly for the Confederacy, and next to it, in clumps of grasses as his was, the stone of *Melinda Armbruster*

*Chantry,* both as quiet and calm and friendly as if they stayed talking to each other about gone times, like two people on a gallery in the evening, with their friends passing by under street lamps. I didn't feel as Deveraux did that they might be rolling in their graves over French and I having got ourselves together. Felt only the quiet here, with a dove *coo-ringing* from a cedar, and farther along, a mockingbird sounding like a dozen other birds but making it evermore blither than they could, his tune icy and liquid and old as the land itself, like Jantil's playing on his Gypsy instrument. I moved along, Grayboy nosing down to the grasses, and got to *Algernon Marsden,* and stood regarding his stone for a second, thinking of him once attacking French—couldn't blame him, I reckoned he had meant it well but been clumsy about it—and then turned and got up on Grayboy again, and rode down through goldenrod and milkweed and past some fallowwater apple trees with the big apples, which turn best in October, lying in the grasses so their shine was only just showing to a seeking eye.

I went around in back of the stable, along the rim of the pike and this back meadow, hearing the horses of the Chantry visitors from Lanceton, and the screel of the mayor's cart, coming up the drive from out in front. From this side of Chantry I could scent the bayou along which Grayboy and I'd first come this way, and Grayboy found it too, snuffling as if he recalled the rain, the lonesomeness, the lost road to Yadkin. Then we were moving behind the compound, and into it, and there was a lantern hanging on a post over the mouth of the stable, shining over Grayboy as I pulled him up and got off. And near here at the stable side the sounds of chickens ruffling in the dark, then from the stable the ring of a plate on its floor. I peered in. Bellreve the bay stood in one of the stalls, his mild saddle horse eye turning as I went in. In another stall stood Amber, Deveraux's wonderful mare; her tight-coupled handsome back sleek in the other lanterns alight in here, her intelligent racer's eye black green and widening as I looked at her. And further along, in two more stalls, were the blood chestnuts of Deveraux. He'd come here in his grandeur this time. The wagon had been brought in back near the tack room. The tack room door was ajar, but its cracked leathers were gone, and hung on pegs was Bell's jenny-hauling harness, and the Spanish saddle was on a rack, and the major's Amber-gear shone with polished leather and there was a smell not just of horse but of fresh hay, alfalfa straw, grain, soap, good iron. I led Grayboy in. Started him over toward a stall, and then W. M. was coming around the flank of the stable and in here like a hound let off a collar. With his red jockey jacket still on, his velvet pants not too dusty and his cool eyes taking in nothing but Grayboy. He said, "Hello," to me, and then was swarming around Grayboy, touching him and stooping to crawl under him, looking at his plates, lifting them, walking around behind him with his eyes closing even farther, coming around under his muzzle, grabbing his reins, leading him to the stall. There wasn't a cobweb in sight in any stall here, or on the roof-beams. I leaned against the Grayboy stall and watched while W. M. jumped on a box to do the unsaddling, while he brought a bucket and sponge and a soft brush and a currycomb. Finally I said, to the whisper of the sponge and to W. M.'s groom-humming—a kind of light soothing music, as he worked—"Man back toward the big river told me you were giving Mrs. Broome some kind of lip. About not wanting to eat at a table with white folks."

He shrugged while he worked. "I don't like to, but she makes me. Making me eat and sleep in the big house now. She's not so bad some ways but she won't let me stay out here where I'd ought to be."

"You'll stay in the house," I said. "Nights and meals, anyhow. And you're going to school. And your name's going to be William Makepeace Ritter Broome."

"No," he said.

"Yes," I said. "School won't take much tuck out of you. And it's a long summer. You're prouder than most white folks—proud even as Mrs. Broome—but it won't cut that any if you learn a few things."

He was frowning like hell now, chewing what there was of his under-lip, leaning to get a dab of sweat with the sponge, looking wild for all the fanciful clothes as if he could just run off into the dark and be part of the swamp.

He said, "I ain't."

I said, loud, "Goddamn it, you are! And don't give me any chuckle-headed proudness anymore; I know it's there, you don't have to prove it to me! I'll have enough on my hands from here on out without worrying about you acting like you were another kind of Deveraux. You're going to be a credit to this farm and most of all, yourself. I've made up my mind. You know me pretty well but you don't yet know when I make up my mind, I stick to what it's made up for."

There was quite a moment, then a flock of them, passing there between us. His little-boned right hand squeezed water from the sponge and he laid the sponge light on Grayboy's neck. Then when he raised his head he was smiling. Not much but about enough, as he'd first looked at me out of that pin-oak tree at Pharis. After still another space the smile faded out, and then he grunted, "Yes. Sir," and went back to working without paying another whit of mind to me or anything but Grayboy. Except in about a minute as he worked over the withers he said, "Deveraux. He was here for night-supper, he was out here last night, his man he's up at the house eatin' his head off now. Brought his own feed for them chestnuts, but what does he think I am, curryin' cart-horses? Told him to have his man do it. Him—major—he just sits and yammers to Mrs. Broome. She listens but she ain't hearing. I don't mind much helpin' her with the housework—she's been movin' through like a mama bear through a beanpatch—but I'll be mortal glad when the major's gone. Keep sayin' you ain't worth spittin' on, or things like that. Keep sayin' you make her throw away all she is, for a hatful of commonness. Keep sayin' you done the murder, no matter what she thinks, and some day if she stay with you, she find it out and weep. Keep sayin'—"

He stopped, sponge in air. Jupiter was coming in the stable doorway. He'd left his rifle at the house, but he was leading Robin. First W. M.'s eyes glittered like a toad's and then they went full open as he clapped them on Robin. A little whistle passed back through his teeth. "Mighty God," he said. "That's a good Arab. That's a horse good as major's Amber here. That's—" Robin's plates sounded on the sill and the flooring. From his height, holding Robin's reins bunched, Jupiter gazed down on W. M. as if he was sighting on him from a polished, haughty cloud. "Young boy," he said. "I'm workin' here. Be here from now on till old Jupe dies. I knowed horse half a hundred years 'fore you was foaled. Mister Broome tells me you workin' here too, he tells me you got a lively eye and a caressin' hand and a bucket of soul. The Lord tells me, now I gaze upon you, you also a whippersnapping imp of Satan, limb of the Devil, and if I am called upon to bring you in shape, I should do so. You look at me now and say we'll git along. I wish you kindly to say it."

W. M. had got off the box, and was standing under Jupiter's shadow. He flicked his eyes from Jupiter's to the Arab's.

As if he and Robin were talking the way he claimed he talked to Grayboy and got himself answered.

Then he straightened his chin and said, "We'll git along, yessir."

"That is just grand and ceremonious," said Jupiter, his drum-voice filling the whole stable-way. "Mind you keep the manners high and your face shied off the pouts. Step over to his nigh side and keep off his right flank. And when you finish up yonder pacing and winning glory, you give me a hand with this Robin.'' W. M. ducked his head, and went back in Grayboy's stall and hopped onto the box, casting an eye from time to time back at Robin, as Jupiter led the Arab past Bell and the chestnuts and Amber and Grayboy and into another stall. Jupiter started unsaddling. And he said, ''Mister Broome, everything going to be calm in this stable. Miss French—Miz Broome—she say I sleep up at the house, that sewin' room down at the back off the kitchen; keep an eye on this here W. M. She'd like to see you, she say, if you're all through here. They all like to see you. They are gathered in the front hall. Place is going to look like it was when Colonel and Miz M'linda was alive in the Lord's beamin' eye, you will see in days to come. Jubilo come to stay now, and it ain't from no North marching through.''

When I went out of the stable door there was just the sound of W. M. working on Grayboy, and Jupiter sleeking Robin and both of them making that high, crooning hum which I'd heard from grooms and swipes and stableboys and horsemen since I could remember hearing anything, and the horses standing in the gentle light with their shadows big on the walls past the walkway.

I walked back through the compound. The mossed ridgepoles of the falling down cookhouse, and cabins, took the red-fox-coated moonlight out here as if they'd already started to slump to dust; I thought I'd be glad when they were vanished. The well-head had most of its magnolia leaves cleared away. I went on around the house, where just a little chopping had been done on the side flagstones, they were still choked with vines and leafage; I got around to the front, looking at the warm lamplight streaming onto the vines here, and noticing as I came up off the old red brick to the gallery steps that the doorknocker had been new-polished, and that the door stood open to the gallery's welcome. A path of moonlight followed me up the steps between the columns like a hound at my boots till I got to the door, then faded into the lampshine beyond. And I went in to see French coming from the hall beside the staircase, from the kitchen, I judged, though I stayed in the vestibule and waited for her to come out, not wanting us to meet in full sight of the others in the hall, for the time being. She was wearing the green dress dabbed with gold, from Yadkin; since the Monday night I'd last seen her I had thought of her through everything else, as if she herself was a lantern hanging in a stable's door at the end of a bitter long rainfall, but for all of thinking of her in this dress, and in the Gypsy gown, and in the dove-gray, and naked as a sword and making love with me, the being here of her beat it by a hundred lengths.

We came together so hard I felt her breath stop, then she was saying quick, breath moist-warm on my earlobe, "Tom, it's certainly time. When the major came back out here today I did worm it out of him that you were safe home—he's mightily put out with Sheriff Will, because Will hasn't let him in on the doings with Jupiter out along the river—Will got me aside and told me what happened there. Oh, and W. M.'s been helping a great deal, but I'm not fixed for guests yet; I reckon I won't be till Christmas." She drew her fingers down my cheekbone. "But they'll have to take us as we are. I thought I'd drape this hall with smilax, starting here in the vestibule, and winding up the stairs, come Christmas—"

I said, holding her so tight she couldn't speak anymore right then, "That's a time ahead. Now we've got to deal with the major. That's his man over there, isn't it?" I let her go, her breath coming back and her breasts moving against my chest as she took in air, her hair, put up high with a ribbon dark green as the dress, flying in little fine beauty-snibs as she turned her head. The Irish-faced man was sitting along the hall, boots crossed; she said, "That's Ryan. Major Deveraux had him come along and drive the wagon. The wagon—just in case I might change my mind or you might be found guilty of murdering Gary, or both. So he could haul my carousel along to Pharis if I went with him. Oh, but the major is indeed a terribly hard-headed gentleman, Tom; he has plagued me since I got back, and I do fear he may expire from not having his own way. He has left the Holly house, though, where he was staying in town. He has told me if you are found absolutely free of stain or guilt in the matter of Willis, he'll go on back to Pharis tonight." She took a small breath. "And of course you *are* free, as I am—Sheriff Will and Roy Mattison told me about it—but they haven't informed the major of it yet, and neither have I."

I sighted past her, at the major. He was sitting bolt upright—an axle-bolt, seasoned with time and with good iron in it to start with—down the hall near the newel-post. His hat was on one knee, his vest was as stretched along his belly as it had been when he greeted me in Mama Gatchin's eave-room in Yadkin, and his dark fierce face was lifted as if he was watching himself and his deportment in one of those time-touched mirrors across the hall. Nearer to us, chairs had been brought up for the mayor, who was chatting kind of benevolently with Phil Adams, who hunker-squatted beside his chair, and for Will Planteu and Doc Mattison, who had their leather-backed hands hooked around their knees and were confabbing as if they hadn't spent a lot of time together these past days and had tons still to say. Grody Flieshacker was watching French and me, his face with an expression like a pothouse politican's hearing the news that an honest man had got in office; he was leaning between mirrors, his arms folded. Howard Markley came out of a side door, from the ball-room, as I watched, brushing road-dust off his cavalry coat and looking along here and spying me and raising a hand. I called a greeting to him, and the rest of the crowd turned, and I walked on in with French. At the end of the old red carpet where it ran on past the staircase, Major Deveraux sat up stiffer, his eyes raking me with the blue that burned and stung, accused and judged, all at one time. There was a load I could have said to him about trying to wear French down these past days, even about coming out here to my wife's home and acting as if his own breeding gave him the right to stable his horses—however good they were—in Chantry Hall stable; there was a cornucopia's plenty.

But I wasn't going to say it. We would play it out on his own dueling grounds, I thought. With his own weapons. French had once called me a gentleman. I didn't know quite what that was, I'd never known, they came in all sizes, colors and grades of stud-book blood, but I felt I was going to make a run for it. French's arm was cool in mine, cool and solid, and I nodded to the major, who didn't even stir a well-clipped moustache hair. And Will Planteu was getting up, unfolding himself, hooking his thumbs in his belt below the flapping leathern vest, and speaking mild enough. "Well, now." He looked all around. "Reckon there's a few things to be said." He eyed Doc. "By Roy, and by me, and then by Marcus."

He launched himself around to Deveraux. Who gave back the look with ten dollars' interest and a gold piece thrown in.

"Most of it for your benefit, Jack," went on Sheriff Planteu. "On account of you've appeared to be the warmest of us all for prosecuting Thomas Broome, or if not prosecuting him then for drummin' him out of Mississippi. I'm not saying there wasn't a time I sided with you. But the time's gone—and this session you've called yourself isn't going to agree with your liver, or your style of ridin' high. When it's all over I hope you'll be the man you were through four years of hot hell and high hopin'. Knowin' Tom Broome is a man good as you are, givin' him that much with a flourish, and maybe even saying so."

He clapped his hands together hard as he faced away from the major. "Folks, let's get it done. Got to be back at the office by eleven, I promised the town a party and a revelation then, and even if it costs the county money, I'm goin' to follow through with it. Roy'll take this hall floor now, and scale down the tale he told us this noon out by the river—scale it down for Jack's benefit. And after that our mayor will tell us how he thinks Gary Willis came to his end on that staircase Sunday night a couple of weeks gone."

"No—" Mayor Westerfield was holding his face up past the shine of the lamp burning at his elbow where he sat with his legs dangling in the soft kid, pearl-buttoned boots over the carpet. He shook his head. "No—I shall not—tell you what I think—Will. I shall tell you—what truly—happened. Not—speculation—you see—but—proof. I believe—the evidence—of things unseen—is amazing—in this world—but here we have—evidence—we shall soon look upon—most plainly."

He sat back, hands laced under his yellow flowing cravat.

Out on the drive past the vestibule's open door the horses and the pony drawn up there were moving quiet in the dark and light of this night. A cool touch of air came in the door and swept along past us and up to the risers of the staircase. I was looking at the staircase now with everybody else—even Deveraux's Irish hired hand, Ryan, staring here from where he sat, with his forehead puckering—and I couldn't have spoken for anybody else but I could feel French's arm tighten in mine, and my own hair rise just a colt's ear upward. There wasn't anything on the stairs but the light touching them lower down, and the shadows crossing them from the balustrade. The lion's head carved into the newel-post caught a waving of lampshine and its old gold eyes and mane appeared to stir. Doc coughed, stowed his latest quid in a much-weighted pocket, and got to his feet as Planteu sat down.

# 53

Doc made his speech short and to the point, more like he'd told Sheriff Planteu about French's being missing and Gary Willis being dead on that first day in Planteu's office, than the way he'd told about the two derringers and about his own derringer misfiring, out beside the river this noon. It was mostly for Major Deveraux's sharp and leaning ears anyhow, since the rest of us here—except for Deveraux and Deveraux's man Ryan—had heard it before. While Doc was speaking, he kept turning around and looking at the lion's head in the newel-post, and at one point, when he was showing how the lion's head swung out when you pressed its eyes, he took his thumb and forefinger and touched the eyes, and the head swung to the side; and from where I was still standing holding French's arm close to mine, I could see the box-square stowage space. About the area of a blacksmith's box where he keeps nails and other needful truck. The cedar lining well joined and tight. The next second, still talking, telling now how he'd taken away the fired derringer and later dropped his own weapon in the front drive on the Tuesday when he and Planteu and Adams had come out to sniff around, Doc leaned back a trifle against the lion-head covering, and it fell to with a tiny click. Then he'd finished, and he stood with his shoulders slumped. And said, scrannel-throated, "So I'd say by tryin' to make affairs better right then, I just made 'em worse. But I was tryin' anyhow."

French left my side, went to him and gave him a dab of a salute on his bronze cheek. "Doctor Mattison. Thank you for trying. But I do assure you if I had shot Gary, I would have told you about it at once."

"I know that. Makes me ashamed to think I suspected you for a time. Misplaced gallantry. Reckon"—he scratched his nose and his eye-corners wrinkled—"you've undergone a lot of that in your life from us, Mrs. French Broome. Reckon we've sheltered you like you protected them damned hens of yours."

She looked at him with kissing-kin eyes. "You sustained my pride, in the main, Doctor Mattison. And I have not yet thanked you for seeing to it that the Dorkings and the Buff Orpingtons were fed while Tom and I were away.''

"Thank Will. He saw to it Phil Adams rode by and fed 'em once a day.''

French turned to Will Planteu. The lamps burning in this hall brought out the cat-sparks in her eyes, the line of her shoulder where it melted bright skin into the neckline of the green velvet dress. I wanted her so much I could have gone over and just quiet and firm, led her up the stairs and started making love to her before we got to any bedroom. But there would be time for that, I thought; there would be all the nights ahead here when I wasn't traveling from one race-meet to another, or seeking out likely horses. But even as she looked at the sheriff, she could feel what I was thinking too, and what she thought lived in the tail of her eye as she glanced at me before switching her gaze full on Planteu. She said, "Sheriff Will, I'll try to make all this up to you some time by doing something—I don't know what, yet. And to you too, Grody," she said, looking along the hall to him where he stood between those mirrors. He gazed down at the carpet, a little flush coming up over his wide jaw and even touching his cheekbones under the pitchball eyes. He gave a nod of understanding. She gazed along at Phil Adams, who was still hunkering beside the mayor's chair. He fingered the brim of his hat which he held before him like a shield he might have to use against getting embarrassed over being thanked, muttered something, and shifted on his heels.

Howard Markley from where he stood with his head that could have been stamped on a coin—the kind of coin that might have been struck if the South had won in the long run—said slow and measured, "I do not deserve any of your thanks, Francia. It is enough to know you are here at the hall once more. I do not always have students of your caliber—or stimulation. Perhaps you and your new husband will send me a few, one day." He cleared his throat. "I agree with Roy that none of us has done much to allow you to live your own life, in the past. We have been overly vigilant. Perhaps if Bob Chantry—and your mother—had not meant so much to us—" He shrugged. "There is a false pride under true pride. The distance between them is dangerous." He was looking past her now, at Major Deveraux. Who sat just as he had at the start of Doc's explanation, his color no different, his boots not having moved the breadth of a plate-nail.

French walked over to the mayor, the dress-skirt whirling in the low draught from the open door, and leaned down and brushed her lips on the top of his silk-haired head, which shone with fuzzy brightness around it from the lampshine at his elbow. He said, "But—though this is pleasant—it is not—necessary—Francia. I merely—came in on this affair— through curiosity—and belated—concern." He started to get out of his chair, and she helped him up. As he'd done under the maple tree, he fell and floated forward—or both—along the carpet to the newel post of the stair. Then he was standing there, so small and frail it was as if he just kept a hold on breathing by the luck of it, yet with his voice so packed with that winter-apple sweetness it spoke of life rich as all harvests. His eyes so much calmer in their blue than the major's, gazed out toward the doorway. Right then Jupiter was coming up the hall from the back way; he showed up behind and at the side of the newel-post like a giant—which he was—looming from the hall's shadows, bearing my saddlebags and the fiddle-case on one shoulder. He stopped and waited with the rest of us while Mayor Westerfield's voice whispered and sang: "There is still— before us—the mystery. Of how—poor benighted—foolish—Gary Willis—met his death. Will—" He was smiling over to the sheriff. "Please—play the part of—Gary Willis. Go out on—to the vestibule— and sit in a chair there—and get up—and simulate drunkenness—reel a little—I am sure you would be a master—of the Thespian art—had your inclinations—taken you in that direction—and go on reeling—in your bibulous loss of control—until you have gone up—four or five steps of this staircase. If you would oblige—Will?"

Sheriff Planteu said, "Oh, hell, Marcus!" Then he lifted his high-planed shoulders and shook his head, moving out down the hall toward the door, then stopping in the vestibule where only a fan of moonlight showed around his boots. He dropped into one of the crown-tapestried ancient chairs, with a clumping sound. He said from out there, "I ain't Junius Brutus Booth, or even Joe Jefferson. But if you want it, Marcus, you'll have it."

I thought he'd have made a pretty fair country actor, at that. When he came into the light he was staggering a good bit, arms swinging; he said half under his breath, "Seen enough one-night lockup drunks to get it down good," and came along the hallway, arms wheeling like boughs in a breeze, and moved past Markley and Grody and Adams and Ryan and Doc and French and me and Deveraux, to the staircase. And when he got to the lower riser, his shadow waggling up the staircase now, he leaned hard on the newel-post. Hitting it with the heel of his right hand where the lion's head held dull sparks. Then his boots were toeing on the risers, he was swaying on up, but I wasn't following him now; I was staring just about where everybody else had turned their attention. Because the lion-head cover of the cache was swinging out, he'd tripped it when he grabbed at it. The cache was open.

And Mayor Westerfield was saying, "Anyone—one does not even—have to be—in a state of—insobriety—anyone—who is even tired—makes that—natural motion—when going up—stairs. Francia—I would say—you have made it—a thousand times. But you are young—and do not require support—or founder in drink—and your fingertips merely—touch the post. I noticed—years ago—when I was visiting here—Bob was starting up—those stairs—he was weary—and leaned hard for a moment—upon the post—and his little secret—was revealed. But then we all—had known about it—it was no true secret—in any event. Not like—his other hiding places—which you discovered, Will—in your search for the derringer. He—Bob—was a boy—in many respects. All honor to—his valiant bones. Now—Will!"

His clear eyes like the light pure blue of an August midday when there isn't even a fishtail cloud around, he was gazing up at Planteu. "Turn around—but turn—in a—*rush.* As if you had been—leaping up those stairs—in headlong pursuit—of Francia—and someone behind you—had said—sharply—"

Doc breathed out, short, quick: "Willis!"

Planteu missed his cue, not having expected Doc to speak now.

I recalled Doc balancing his black bag on the lion's head while we were standing above Willis's body. He hadn't know then that French was going to disappear, bringing more suspicion on herself in his mind. But even at that time, knowing his own derringer had misfired, he must have been thinking she could have shot Willis, and rolling it around in the back of his head. He'd decided either then or later how the newel-post cache must have been the hiding place for the murderer's weapon—Bob Chantry's derringer. He hadn't known French was upstairs at the time of the slaying; he'd seen only Willis swarming up there. And on the road to Lanceton I'd told him she'd had a derringer in her hand.

Thought for another speck of time, how crazy it is that when there's a killing, nobody can ever recall just the exact place everybody was standing, or the fine points of it. Like a race you run over in your remembrance, doing it slow, and you know what *you* did but not just what the other horsemen thought and did. But Westerfield had more up his midget-sized sleeve, he was soaring above all the might-bes, and saying

now: "Call it out—again—Roy. And this time—Will—turn around—
*heavily.*"

Yes, I told myself; it would have been a heavy motion; Willis had
carried a good deal of spare flab.

Doc's eyes slued to Planteu, who'd got himself ready again, facing up
the stairs. And Doc said, this time even sharper: "Willis!"

This trip the sheriff wheeled all the way around, arms flailing out,
thumping his boot-heels on a tread as he did. And at the same time the lion
head swung inward. And just as Planteu made his full half-turn and was
facing us, long legs almost buckling and arms whirling faster as he tried to
keep his balance and then kept it, the lion head over the hiding box fell to
with another soft click.

Teetering on the staircase, Planteu said, "House has settled. Just takes
a good thump to shut that damned thing up." He was coming down the
stairs now. "But—Marcus, that still don't—"

The mayor said, "Oh—but it does—Will. It proves—Bob's hiding
place—was—breached that night. It opened—when Gary Willis—
clutched the post. It shut—when Roy—called his name and Willis
whirled—upon the staircase."

"Still don't prove a pint of mustard-seed. Sorry, Marcus, but—"

Planteu had come back to the foot of the staircase. He pressed the eyes
of the carved lion with the heel of his hand, and it opened. He bent over
and gave a lower tread a thump with the side of his fist, and it shut again.
Clicking lightly both times.

"Proves that much," he said. "But it ain't evidence. Court of law
evidence. Might convince a jury *it* happened, but it ain't going to tell
me—sorry again—who shot the scoundrel."

"I am—coming—to that." The mayor took a slow, float-lurching step
to Planteu. "Roy, let us now—take the derringer—not Roy's—which
you had locked in your safe—but Bob Chantry's old derringer—with his
initials on the butt. You have them both—in your pocket—I asked you to
bring them—from Lanceton. Bob's—derringer—has been fired—we
know that. Please—do not put a cartridge in it—and do not—pull the
hammer—to cock it."

Planteu was reaching in a pocket. His own pistol in its battered holster
on his hip wobbled as he got his lean hand down into the pocket. He
brought up what I took to be the wrong derringer first, Doc's, because
after looking at the butt to see which it was, he dropped it back out of sight
in his pocket, and this time brought up its twin weapon—with a hook-

headed grip like the first. He inspected the initials on this one, holding it crosswise to the lamplight, said curt, "It's Bob's," and eyed it again, and said, "and it ain't cocked, trigger ain't showin'," and handed it along to the mayor. The mayor held it as if he didn't like it anymore than I did. And said, "Francia—"

French moved to him. A head taller, bending to him, the dark red hair and the silver white almost touching as he said, still high and airy, "Francia—please—put this derringer—your father's—in the hiding place just as you did—that night."

French took the derringer, and stepped to the staircase, frowning just a shadow as she thought back. Then she switched it from her right hand to her left, and started up the stairs, pausing on the lowest tread, and pressing the lion's eyes with the finger and thumb of her right hand. And, when the cache opened, she laid the derringer with one quick, neat motion into the box with her left hand, so its barrel was pointing in and up toward the staircase, and both barrel and grip were standing upright, the butt resting in the floor of the box. I was close enough to see it all. And Doc was crowding near to see, and so was Planteu. Howard Markley walked along here and glanced into the box. Then he stood back. French said, "Do you want me to go along upstairs, Mayor Westerfield?"

Before the mayor could answer, Major Deveraux was standing. Like a monarch in the Old Testament reviewing his goats and comely maidens, he stalked over and stooped enough to see the derringer. He carried his top hat in the curve of an arm, white gloves in the same hand. His eyes met Mayor Westerfield's as he raised his head. "I do not consider any of this gallimaufry proof of anything," he announced. He stepped away.

Westerfield gave him a joyous and tolerating look.

"Nor—do I—as yet—Major Deveraux. Please—" He was facing Planteu. "Repeat the process—shut the post—again."

Planteu started for it, but French, still on the stairs, shut it instead. As she'd done on the night we were all thinking about.

There was the click as it fell into place.

The major lifted his hard-haired eyebrows at the mayor.

"Well? And no doubt now you will wish it to be opened again. Children's games, sir. We could be here all night. I want something more tangible. I realize the—hiding place—" He lofted his ridge of a nose, "is fallible. That is, it opens easily when leaned upon, and shuts again when there is a disturbance near it which shakes the spring-mechanism. Yet no one has proved to me that Broome—" Still, he wouldn't say Mister, or

Tom Broome, or Thomas. I could feel his dislike as I'd felt it at Yadkin, only now even closer; but I didn't speak; I was playing with the cards he'd dealt. "—that Broome didn't kill the fellow, in cold blood. Any man capable of running off with Francia, under cover of having been deputized to help find her—"

Jaw-muscles went in and out, in Planteu's cheeks. He was going to say something he might have regretted—Jack Deveraux being an officer he'd respected—when the mayor cut in, soft as milkweed angels if they could speak, "No, Francia—do not—go—upstairs—this time. Just—open the box—again."

On the staircase, French leaned once more to press the wooden blind eyes. The head swung out.

"Will—" the mayor said. "Look—in the box."

Planteu narrowed his eyes down past French's shoulder, to where she was peering. It was French who looked back around at us first. "The hammer is back," she said, clear enough, yet astonished.

Planteu raised his head. "My God, it is."

The major was pushing forward again. He put a boot sole on the lowest stair-riser, and arched himself forward. Staring down.

When he straightened, his face was grayer than it had been, the gray under his riding-and-outdoor color, and he was squaring his shoulders. He gave a slight, polite nod to Mayor Westerfield. "Well done, sir. But I would like an actual demonstration. Of the shot being fired. I realize what you have been getting at. Point one." He might have been laying out a battle plan. "Willis lurched against the newel-post. The head of the post swung out. The base of the post dragged against the hammer of the derringer, cocking it. A hair-trigger, chancy weapon. Now it was ready to fire. Point two. Doctor Mattison—but I know you better as Lieutenant, Roy, just as I know you, Will, as Captain—Lieutenant Mattison called out to Willis. Willis turned clumsily, jolting the stair-treads and the newel-post. This caused the weapon to discharge, killing him. Point three. With the same jolt, the lion's head swung back shut, a fraction of a second after the shot had entered Willis's head."

The major regarded Doc. Doc stared back at him as if it was both a long time since he'd been called Lieutenant, and as if he didn't favor it much anymore. The major said, "So in effect, when you sang out to him—sternly—"

"Oh, real stern," said Doc, with a sigh, and dryly. "I was goin' to kill him, you know, Jack."

Major Deveraux said, "Exactly. The sound of your voice precipitated his death. When you spoke his name you opened his coffin. There was nothing"—he aimed his blazing eyes at Mayor Westerfield—"remotely strange about it. No fate, no Nemesis. With your intuition, Mr. Mayor, and a little common sense, you have merely reconstructed this as any action might be reconstructed away from the field of war."

"No," said Doc, sighing again. "If you're mappin' it out like that, you better add a point four, Jack. Makin' the point that at the selfsame second Bob's derringer went off, I squeezed the trigger on mine. Sounds kind of like fate, to me." He sat down on the lowest stair-tread, his chin in his hands. I figured he wanted a chew again, but wouldn't take another while he was in the house, French not having any garboons around. "Don't believe, honest to heaven, you can lay these things out clean and rapturous, like a battle map. I remember our maps always givin' us a lot of satisfaction, in the old days, but then when you fought the battle it was all mingled and wild, so when you read about it a month later in a dried and yellowin' newspaper, it always seemed like a different smoothed-out tale that'd happened to somebody else. But I can kind of smell out somethin' strange, here. And I know what Marcus means by powers of darkness. Because if this happened like this—and I reckon it did—then Bob Chantry himself shot Gary Willis. From the grave, so to speak."

"He done so, Mist' Doc." It was Jupiter, moving out of the shadows, Grayboy's saddlebags and the fiddle-case still on his shoulder. His voice rattled an oak plank in one of the stair-treads. "And I was back yonder about where that man"—he pointed back to Ryan, the major's driver, sitting on a chair between the lamp-reflecting mirrors—"where he is now, but a little step farther along, in the chink of the ballroom door. Watchin' what went on down here, but not watchin' you, Mister Doc—watchin' Willis, when the gun went off. So I don't even see where the powder-flash come from, 'cept I see there *is* a flash. And I see Willis's head get the ball in it, and the blood, and I see him tumble down, and I see you, Mist' Doc, turn around and walk away."

He raised his arms as if he was giving a kind of benediction. Keeping the bags and the case balanced on his shoulder as if they weighed less to him than the little derringer in its hiding box. And he rolled out in cavern tones, "Old Colonel killed him! Praise the wonderful ways of the Lord, wrapped in His mystery and fightin' Satan by day and night! The Lord come out and helped us cross danger water—my army cross over!"

Major Deveraux said, crisp as a walnut shell cracking, but with his color still ashy in back of the words, "I want a demonstration, as I said. I shall sit here and wait for one."

He stalked back to his chair, and sat.

Mayor Westerfield said, "Provided—we keep it—entirely safe—we can—offer—a demonstration. Though—it may—disturb—the paneling—of your staircase—Francia."

French was at my side again. Holding my right hand, cinch-tight. She said, "A little old splinter won't harm much, Mayor Westerfield." She glanced back at Deveraux, her head high and her nostrils stiff, like a beautiful mare balking. "I'd like *everyone* here to be as certain as possible."

Mayor Westerfield beckoned to Planteu. "Please—Will—load Bob's—derringer—but do not cock it—this time—either. Place it as—it was—in the cache—and shut—the cache. Jupiter—"

Jupiter hulked around toward him. "Fire and sword," he rumbled. "Willis, he put us to the turnin' sword all that time after the war. But a mightier sword come gleamin' from beyond, right to here, and smote him down! And I put his den of iniquity to the fire!" Then a lot milder, he said, "Yes sir?"

"Jupiter," the mayor said, his leaf-thin eyelids fluttering—he was weary but bound to see it all through, I could tell—"Please stand where you are—and—when I tell you to—just heave—one of those saddlebags—they are—yours, Mister Broome? Nothing—that will break—in them?"

"They've gone through rough country," I said. "Take the big one, Jupiter, with the sulky harness in it."

The mayor went on to Jupiter, "Heave it—at the stairs—about—five steps—up. Will—"

But Planteu already had Colonel Chantry's derringer out with its hammer down, and was loading it with a single cartridge from a supply of cartridges in his pocket, and then, easy as touching a brood hen, was putting the derringer back in the open cache just where French had put it, and then shutting the lion-head lid. Then he was pressing the eyes to open it. This time, as it opened, everybody was listening as if to a faraway calling—Howard Markley with his ears close, Grody and Phil Adams drawn in nearby, Jupiter with his breath all held, Doc getting up off the lower step and coming near French and me and almost tiptoeing as he did so, the major's driver, Ryan, tipping the legs of the hall chair forward, and the major himself waiting with a muscle jumping in his cheek.

There came a tiny metal whisper as the hammer of the derringer pulled back inside the box under the drag of the lion's head lid. And a louder but still muted-down click as the lid swung open all the way.

Jupiter bent over and laid my fiddle in its case on the floor, putting the small saddlebag alongside. He straightened, the big bag held between his hands.

The mayor said, eyelids nearly shutting over the flower blue of his eyes, "All right—Jupiter."

Jupiter hoisted the saddlebag over his head, muscles stretching. His shadow and the bag's went sprawling up the staircase as if he was Atlas finally getting rid of an unpleasing world. Same instant, I saw that the major's mouth had fallen open, just a trice, and the lines cut at its corners were heavy as though he wore a snaffle bit.

Then Jupiter threw the saddlebag. It hit with a crushing leathery jouncing boom on the edge of the fifth step up. And so fast you couldn't see it all or ever recount it later to yourself in any military summing up—Doc was plain right about battles versus battle maps—there was a crack like a loud limb snapping and the smell of powder crowding the nostril, and, also in the same less than a second, a blue yellow flare from the corner of the newel-post box. And—still in the same time—the smack of a ball tearing into old dark wood in one of the uppermost risers where they were sheathed by balustrade shadow. And the click of the box-lid shutting again. The lion staring out at us from the post's top as innocent as an old sheep.

Nobody spoke for a brief time.

Till the mayor spread his raccoon-tidy, brittle small hands.

"Selah," he said. "Merely—to say—it is over. All—said—and—done. Whatever powers—poor—miserable—Gary Willis—allied himself—to—recoiled upon him—or encountered—other—higher—powers—at least—that is—and will remain—my feeling." He smiled, bland as sweet butter, at Major Deveraux. "You must allow—a rather—venerable—man—his whims of age—his flights—his fancies."

For just a puff of a meaching second, it seemed to me I could scent that sulphur or brimstone—or both of them—I'd picked up from the air in Fountainwood's ballroom in the night.

But I could have been wrong as wrong.

And here came W. M., making his way from the back hall around the chair the major still occupied. W. M. glanced all around, brisk, and said in a kind of ice-calm, "Somebody please to ask Major Deveraux if he wish his horses for his wagon to be harnessed, and his mare put under saddle. I ready to do it any time, and bring them around to the door. That is, if he is planning to go. Else otherwise, I could wait around all night. Missing the sleep Mrs. French and Mister Broome and Mister Jupiter all wishes me to get. As a growing-up child.''

Jupiter had shouldered the big saddlebag on his way upstairs, and was carting both bags up there. He looked down over the railing. "Child, child," he said, the sound filling the stairwell. "You got so much to learn about livin' on the polite side. So much. But you gone learn it.''

I picked up my fiddle-case, which Jupiter had set down on a chair in the hall. Sheriff Planteu was opening the lion's head and lifting the fired derringer out of the now-not-so-secret box again, and shutting it up—this time I hoped forever. He said to French, "Think I'd like to take custody of this little iron devil, Mrs. French Broome. Along with Doc's, which is probably so plugged up with pocket-lint it never would fire again even if he took it to the best of gunsmiths, the two of 'em'd make a nice set of souvenirs. Unless you still need it to plug hen-slaverin' foxes and skunks with." He bounced it in his hand.

"I think Jupiter can handle that with his rifle," she said. "Please take it, with my compliments, Sheriff Will." She faced Doc and the rest. "I am mortified, gentlemen, that I do not have a collation ready for you, but I have only been back since last evening, as you know—and much of that time has been spent in town, in conversation and in telling of my Tom's adventures at Yadkin—and my own—and in answering many questions. But I do invite you all to drop in just as Daddy used to have you all here in the old days, whenever it moves you to. Chantry Hall's going to be Chantry Hall again—we'll bring in some festive airs. Mister Broome desires this as much as I do, and joins me in thanking you for all your work and trouble and heartache and travail.''

Wondered if she'd been thinking up that speech all along. It would have got her an elocution prize any place in the county, I was certain sure.

I said, "What French says goes for me, gentlemen. Think you already knew that. And it takes in all of you here—" I gazed down-hall at Grody. And around to the major, who still sat; I thought if he'd decided to stay all night, there was probably a room we could put him in, but it appeared as though we might have to carry the chair he sat in too, his features still as carved and unmoving as the chair-back was. "Every one of you.''

Doc said, "Will's havin' a do-all back at the office, you know, to which you're both invited—right, Will?—and we got to get Marcus home, he'd dead on his feet. Even if he claims he don't sleep much of a night.'' He had the mayor by one shoulder, Planteu by the other.

French said, ''Thank you so much, all of you, but we'll stay here for now. My carousel's back in the ballroom—where it started from some time back—and I do want to see if it's still working well after that journey from Yadkin, and on the packet, and across to Lanceton. And—'' She gave me an eye-tail look, and flushed to a faint rose.

''And there's other considerations,'' said Doc, bringing up a plug from a low-hanging pocket but not putting it in his jaws yet, since he wasn't yet outdoors. ''I can barely remember 'em, been so long I've widowered and batched it—but I look upon 'em with a mellow eye.''

Howard Markley said, hovering close to the vestibule, ''Your carousel is most magnificent, Francia. I was surveying it a while ago, in there in the moonlight. I had not seen it to truly inspect it since an evening long ago, when Bob and M'linda and most of the horse troop were here—you, Will, you, Roy—you''—he gestured to the major—''Jack. So far in the past, and so many ties still holding us to that desperate enterprise. Four years of it against a quarter of a million Union troops. But we have lost the dangerous false pride now, in Lanceton—or at least we are losing it. We have the older pride, pride in one another. And perhaps we may some time have''—he scraped a hand along his sightly beard—''pride in all men. It may even come to that, if we are fortunate. I don't know, for sure. It has to be taught.''

Then he was waving and going onto the gallery and down the gallery steps. Grody and Phil Adams were already down in the drive, mounting up. Doc and Planteu led the mayor down between them, treating him like rare glass and fragile spring buds. He lifted a little hand back to us, then he was out of sight below the gallery as we stood watching, then Doc was helping him into the pony cart. The pony came awake with a snuffle of its lips, and Mayor Westerfield took the reins, loose, and looked up at the moon through the oaks, keeping his head back so, moon-appreciating, as everybody from the Lanceton guardian-flock moved on out, in procession down the drive to the leaning iron gateway.

French and I went back to the major.

W. M. was still standing there beside him. Neither looking at each other.

Jupiter came down the stairs, not making much noise when he trod the risers, as he hadn't in the fern and brake of the Lanceton woods, or at Fountainwood.

The major's man Ryan was still sitting patient-bodied in this hall. While we all kept on eyeing the major, he got out of the chair. "Yes," he said, shaking his head, as though he'd just heard W. M. for the first time, as if it had just reached his eardrums. He drew himself up higher, haughtier, the daze he'd been in falling away. "Yes, bring the horses around. And my mare. Ryan—" Ryan got to his feet; he still appeared joggled by the demonstration with the derringer, the freckles over his forehead and cheeks now fading as blood came back under his skin. "Ryan," the major said, "help the boy fetch my wagon." The major swung to French. Past her I could see his poker-straight back in its handsome green coat showing in a mirror. "I shall be on my way, now, and not see you again. I did my best. I wash my hands of you, Francia." He was pulling on his gloves. "Say my obligances to Captain Planteu— Lieutenant Mattison—Sergeant-Major Markley." He didn't even mention Grody, or Phil Adams; I reckoned they hadn't been in his personal part of the war. "And to Westerfield. Strange man. An amazing eye for detail, but not a sound man in essence. Fanciful, I'm afraid. If I believed in the supernatural, I would be more impressed. I don't, and I am not." He made his way along the red old carpet and through the vestibule, heels echoing through it, then he was on the gallery, standing out there alongside a column, looking just as upright as it did, only he wasn't about seventy feet high.

He might stay there and die of his own stiff-neckedness, I thought, unless his mare and horses and wagon came around soon.

W. M. was scudding out the back hall again, I heard the kitchen door open and slam as he made his way to the stable. Jupiter said behind me, "I will see he delivers them horses right, in style, not putting his mouth on white folks. Not putting his mouth on any folks." He was talking about W. M., and he followed W. M. along, padding out and down the rear hallway. Ryan moved along after him, and again in a hall mirror, I saw the Irish driver cast a last wary glance at the newel-post as he passed it.

I handed my fiddle in its case to French. "Think I'll keep that in the ballroom," I said. "On the stand where the fiddlers used to play. Maybe some day I'll join them, if we have some fiddlers in here. Be nice, for Christmas—or any time." She took the boxwood case in her hands, and leaned over it as she held it, and we touched lips. "I'll be back in, shortly," I said. The lamp-flames were flickering in her eyes. "Like to hear your jenny before we go up to bed. See it and hear it again, it's just as good as fiddle music itself." She smiled that old, sudden yet slow way, brightness growing around her as if it came from the center of her, spreading gold over her whole face. "Right this instant I'll take a turn in the night," I said. "Somebody's got to see him off."

She looked out toward the major. He had his top hat on now, but hadn't changed position aside from that. The noise of the Lanceton people and their mounts and pony was fading away past the trees. French left me and went along to the ballroom door, pausing in it to give me the same look, which there should have been some special word for—warm as nooning but even deeper—then she went in the ballroom, and I walked out to the gallery with the major.

# 54

Already I could hear the good tough hoofs of the Amber mare coming on the stable road from where it hooked around and joined the Lanceton Pike. And the heavier plunge of the blood chestnuts along with the rumble of the major's polished wagon, following the mare. While the major and I stood there, side by side but unspeaking—as if he hadn't even heard me come out on the gallery, or even seen me from a corner of his eye—the mare came in sight. W. M. was leading her, bringing her up out at the leaning iron gateway at the end of the drive. Jupiter was up on the major's wagon's box, beside Ryan who was driving the chestnuts. I figured Jupiter had put a few fleas in W. M.'s ear about courtesy to his elders— even if W. M. might not ever consider them his betters—because W. M. didn't yip out to the major now, or call sharp for him to come and get on his mare and be off, but just stood down there at the drive's end, the reins in his fist, his scarlet jockey-coat catching the puddling light through the oaks. And Ryan brought up the chestnuts in back of Amber, and beside me, the major took a step down from the gallery. I said, "Major Deveraux."

At first I could tell he felt like just going on down the steps, not acknowledging that I'd made even a peep. But finally he halted his motion, and turned and stared up at me. Just waiting. It struck me we were like two hunting dogs, each honoring the other's point, only he appeared a lot more as if he might break off point first. I said, low, "I won't wish you Godspeed. I reckon you wouldn't accept it from me. Maybe I even know, a little, how you feel. But aside from that, I'd like you to know it was a pleasure running against you, that day at Pharis. I never had a better flat race. That's all I wanted to say."

He didn't nod. Stood there, the light coming down between the moon-splashed columns striking his eyes which were unforgiving as caged-up lightning. Then he said, short-clipped, "Broome. Would you care for another race? No wagers. Simply your horse against my mare?" He faced away from me. Gazing out past the pike and over to the southeast where the fallow field stretched to the hummock with marsh-reeds and grasses beyond it, all of it lorn but golden under the bathing moon. "From the large oak across the pike," he said very quiet. He had his hands behind his back, one gloved hand tight-holding the other. "To that rise of ground where Chantry starts, and back to the oak. One time."

The ground out there would be dry now. Over the neglected cotton rows—or what had once been cotton rows—it wouldn't be bad going. Grayboy had rested a good deal today. He would be as fresh as Amber in any case. I said, "I'm willing."

He went on down the gallery steps. I followed. We walked together along the drive to where Amber and the chestnuts and his wagon waited. W. M. was gazing straight ahead as he'd sat in the crowds at Yadkin when he was sitting on the sulky and scorning everything but Grayboy at the end of the harness lines. But Jupiter gave me a curious look as he got down from the wagon-box. W. M. handed over Amber's reins to Deveraux. The major said, "Here, Willie," and from his vest pocket took a short bit ten-cent piece and flipped it to W. M. W. M. caught it with a downturn of his hand, and turned his hand over and stared at the coin. Jupiter cleared his throat like chains rattling, and W. M.—who I knew had been about to toss the coin back at the major—just slid the coin into a pocket. But he did say, "My name is William Makepeace Ritter Broome."

The major swung up on Amber. She stood gold and russet and faint yellow in the patching of shadow, and I felt about her as I had first sighting her at Pharis. There wasn't a hair of her that wasn't bred as a good breeder dreams of breeding, without over-fining, just with the best of many bloods coming out in the whole line and the eye and the willing grace. I said to W. M., "Please go saddle Grayboy. Major Deveraux and I are takin' one turn across the meadow and back."

W. M. didn't bat a deep eyelid. He cut back along the drive to go through the house and out the back and reach the stable faster. His feet on the drive spurted around the flagstones and grasses. Ryan was blinking from his driving box at the major, and the major said, "Pull the wagon off to the side of the pike, Ryan, and wait. We shall not be long." I thought of him leveling that dueling pistol at Teague, and how he'd no doubt saved my life even if it wasn't my special life he'd been concerned with. Jupiter said to me, deep as bear fur at my side, "You wish me to help W. M., Mister Broome?"

"Not right now," I said, so just he could hear it. "Just keep him from sayin' one word to the major."

"Yessir." Jupiter stood back, aiming his sight up through the leaves moving dry and red above us, and sang "Cross over, cross over danger water, oh, cross over to Jordan." The blood chestnuts, with Ryan clucking to them and them pulling the wagon off into the shallow ditch beside the pike, seemed to appreciate the low-voiced singing; they looked around with molten easy eyes, and stamped in the ditch-grass and dust, lazily, and the wagon-traces chimed.

On the wagon-box, Ryan sat hunched, and after a time he started whistling a quick jig between his teeth. I put him down for a good groom, and supposed his days with the major were solid enough, if he saluted and jumped quick when summoned. The singing and the whistling didn't mingle badly; the mare Amber took a flowing step across the pike, the major hardly seeming to guide her, and flame-forks of the moon's touch licked along her hide as if she was created of river water and fire. Then from the house came a little piping sound, through a ballroom window, and both Jupiter and Ryan stopped their quiet singing and whistling, and we all listened. The old-time carousel music floated out from Chantry Hall into this dark, and I remembered it as I'd first heard it, with Shangro's tribe's children leaning from the little horses to grasp air with their hands as they circled around, or clutching the bright-colored horses, and the reedlike fluting speaking of a time long before ours, as it would speak of a time long after. The major's head was in shadow, I couldn't see his face, only his hands firm on Amber's reins. The white gloves as if they were extra skin, not hampering his touch.

Then through the jenny's music here came Grayboy's plate-beats, I could tell even before he came in sight around the pike that W. M. was riding, not leading him; he looked mammoth of a sudden, as he came in sight, as if a horse had been called up out of the past by the jenny's music. A charger, I thought, coming up to the lists. Which was French's fancifulness coming up in my mind. But he was just Grayboy as I'd known him since he was hardly out of the birth-sac, as I'd known him since Daddy had cut the sac open with the very knife I carried now, and let the air in so the colt-foal could breathe his first air. I didn't know what W. M. had been telling him in that language they were supposed to have between them, but if it was anything it had to be good news. Because Grayboy was set for a run, and he snorted as W. M. checked him and then dropped from his neck like a short waterfall smoothing down, and he gazed at me with that half-joke in his eyes I'd seen there sometimes before a good run, and W. M. held him as I swung up, then let go of the reins as I gathered them in.

Ryan stayed where he was, minding the chestnuts, while the major turned Amber onto the pasturage. The oak the major had mentioned stood by itself almost directly across from the iron, leaning gate. Amber's plates touching the earth of the pasture, which smelled of good loam for a long time unused for growing, made crisp little hollows and cups as she walked. W. M. and Jupiter followed me as I brought Grayboy up beside Amber in the thick shadow of the oak. But they stopped outside the shadow, and then both were climbing onto a half-ruined fence-rail that stuck up beside this field-pasture. They sat without a murmur, looking for these seconds almost alike, even though one was lean and small and the other huge as a half-mountain, their sameness being in their eyes and the way they waited, as if they were up beside me on Grayboy. The jenny music traveled out here, floating and crystal and blithe. Amber and Grayboy flicked half glances one to the other in the fall-pungent shadow. They were just about level. No groom-starters, this time. Deveraux said, "Can you see my hand?"

His right hand, it was, the glove stark as snow in a streak of the light.

I said, "I can."

"When I drop it, then."

I didn't answer. I watched his hand.

He brought it down in a chopping motion, as if starting a charge and leading it. Amber broke so fast she was out into the light before Grayboy and I had cleared the last leaf-shadow. Then Grayboy was gathering up his gait, sailing and free. I let him off the bit fast, feeling his need, and Amber was up on us by two lengths still, the dust of the field-pasture with its ancient tares and sere cotton stalks that had dried out again for three days since Sunday's all-over-Mississippi rain, flying up to us, a stalk-husk hitting my face and stinging, and Grayboy's rhythm-beat sounding faster and harder as the clods spun behind us in turn, and the hummock that gave onto the swamp across the field, moving up to us as if we stayed in one place and it ran toward us in great dark surges. Amber's fine tail was streaming, her body flashing as if she was made, now, not of just water and fire but something even more part of the earth and the long time men had been loving and honoring horses on the earth, maybe just sheer courage, the kind that sits in the middle of the bones and will never quit. The major riding with all he had, green coat laid back like a sail, body as much Amber's as his own, and then we were pulling up, nearly beside him, the rise of ground ahead that was our turning point plain now in the flooding light, its shadow lying beside it in a pool of deepest blackness. This was where the major would lose ground, I thought; Amber in her straight line stubbornness, her only flaw, would be slow to answer and Grayboy could pull ahead when we came out of the turn. And then if I lost ground again, which I knew I would, for she was faster than Grayboy on the straight when we just ran side by side all out and hell for leather—then I could swing Grayboy in behind her, get him mad enough to pass her in one of those raging surges, and come in ahead at the oak. It was the only chance we had to come in ahead, it was what we'd done at Pharis. The major was already turning, we were into it a spasm of a breath behind him, Amber's haunches flattened out and her hocks bulging as he brought her around, then I was wheeling Grayboy—not checking as I'd done in the test-race with Aldan, but curving him in a short, deep-yawing cut that plowed up dry ground and into the mud below, and we were coming out, Amber already in the full light again, a length back of us but with her head nosing up alongside even as we started back to the oak. In the distance past the flying dust and rubble around Grayboy's head and mine, the air whipping by as if it was all cold as it would turn in January, I saw W. M. and Jupiter, stone-still at the fence. And Amber came up. Faster than Grayboy, a better animal on the flat, running so well I would have liked to be with Jupiter and W. M. only watching her, the smell of her hot as if her blood ran wet along with her sweat, her nose level with Grayboy's; then she was ahead, and we were just a quarter of the field along to the oak, and it was time to bring Grayboy in directly behind her. To give him what he would answer to, a challenge that brought out his last drop of willingness, that made him rage and would bring him up in thunder around her to the finish.

I started to swing him in, to pull him to the right; then let my hands go half slack on the reins. As if a bird had lit on my fingers, pecking them back where they'd been. Amber's shadow spun and leaped ahead. I didn't have to even start checking Grayboy, Amber would win now all on her own, and so I just rode Grayboy in, Amber a full clean length ahead on our right, the major starting to check when he was forty yards from the oak, but keeping his lead as, now, I started pulling up too. And then I was bringing Grayboy all the way in, Amber breathing light, and quick, Grayboy breathing deep and savage, and blowing, and the night outside the tree coming back with its sounds clear over the creak of our saddles and the breathing of our mounts. Deveraux dismounted, and led Amber out of the tree-shadow. I got off Grayboy, taking his reins over his head.

Jupiter was marching toward us, to take Grayboy. Ryan came running up from the wagon across the road. W. M. was sitting on the fence as if he hadn't, couldn't have, moved anything but his eyes for a long time. Jupiter led Grayboy around the oak's spraddling roots and then across the pike. I followed close, and beside Grayboy's head, I reached for a cheek-strap, and pulled his head down while Jupiter halted, and looked at Grayboy's eye, also close. It was merry and quiet; like a pool where lights come and go and butterflies dawdle near on a good day. I patted his muzzle, velvet-soft and damp, ducked out before he got my hat which he was cropping his teeth to do, and let him go on with Jupiter along the pike and around to the stable road. Ryan had taken Amber, he had a blanket from the wagon ready for her, her head was a quiet princess's, her eye black green and mild. Deveraux was standing beside me again, then. Watching Amber, not me, not anything else. He called, cool-voiced, "Walk her a little, Ryan. When she is cooled out, tie her to the wagon. I'll not ride her tonight, she deserves coddling. And mind you pace the chestnuts slowly when we go."

I'd been right about Ryan's job. He did salute. Or it could have been just a touching of his forelock.

I could hear the jenny's music whirling again. It was softer now; as if the boiler-fire was slumping to ash, the platform turning slower.

When I looked back at the gray white, time-eaten fence-rail, W. M. was gone.

I went on across the pike-road. Ryan was unsaddling Amber, the mare standing easy, and then he was throwing the blanket over her and she was moving behind him with a fine unbothered walk, up and down in the square-cut high shade of the wagon. The major came on across the road. Its dust didn't seem to remove or cover any of the shine on his boots. His neck-cloth and gloves shone like the feathers of an egret at dawn's edge.

He kept on watching Amber as she moved up and down in those passages back and forth beside the tall wagon, then he looked at me over his shoulder. "An excellent run, Broome."

"Good," I said. "I enjoyed it too."

I went on up the drive toward the front gallery.

Then W. M. was standing in front of me, on the gallery floor, watching me arrive. I mounted the steps, until I was level with him, our eyes meeting square on.

He said, "All you had to do. Just bring Mister Grayboy in tight behind the mare. Then you knew what he'd do. You let him get beat."

I didn't reckon I had to answer that.

"He is all right, he don't even seem to mind. He told me he is all right. I'm goin' back there and bed him down for the night now, Mister Jupiter, he said how I could, but I already talked to Mister Grayboy some. He is all right. But that ain't it, I want to know why. I just got to know."

Stayed where I was, looking in his eyes. Dark and hooded as stones under sheathing dusty leaves.

"You goin' to tell me?"

"No," I said. "You've got to learn for yourself. Any man or horse has to get beat some time. So some other man or horse can win a little. But you can't just hear it, you've got to learn it. You come right back to the house with Jupe when you're through back there. Good night."

I went up the rest of the way onto the gallery. There was just one lamp in the hall past the vestibule now, wick turned low for the night. The flying jenny's music was softer and almost stumbling; now and then it would pick up, then it would sink to feather-brushing quiet. W. M. came in and past me, shutting the front door as he came in, walking around me small and straight without looking back, then he was through the back hall and kitchen, and the kitchen door shut after him as he went out toward the compound and the stable, but with no slamming. I opened the hall door to the dining room, and looked in at the old coffered ceiling, striped with light coming past the tall windows to turn its paneling tawny as milk full of clotting cream. Shut the door, and went along to where the music came in zephyrs and murmurs from the ballroom.

The ballroom was empty save for the jenny, the platform-balcony with its uprights loose and leaning inward, but they could be straightened, and the light was streaming in past vines at the panes, touching my fiddle in the case set up on the platform where French had put it. The jenny turning slowly, the waft of smoke from its boiler-stove moving out of the open

He kept on watching Amber as she moved up and down in those passages back and forth beside the tall wagon, then he looked at me over his shoulder. "An excellent run, Broome."

"Good," I said. "I enjoyed it too."

I went on up the drive toward the front gallery.

Then W. M. was standing in front of me, on the gallery floor, watching me arrive. I mounted the steps, until I was level with him, our eyes meeting square on.

He said, "All you had to do. Just bring Mister Grayboy in tight behind the mare. Then you knew what he'd do. You let him get beat."

I didn't reckon I had to answer that.

"He is all right, he don't even seem to mind. He told me he is all right. I'm goin' back there and bed him down for the night now, Mister Jupiter, he said how I could, but I already talked to Mister Grayboy some. He is all right. But that ain't it, I want to know why. I just got to know."

Stayed where I was, looking in his eyes. Dark and hooded as stones under sheathing dusty leaves.

"You goin' to tell me?"

"No," I said. "You've got to learn for yourself. Any man or horse has to get beat some time. So some other man or horse can win a little. But you can't just hear it, you've got to learn it. You come right back to the house with Jupe when you're through back there. Good night."

I went up the rest of the way onto the gallery. There was just one lamp in the hall past the vestibule now, wick turned low for the night. The flying jenny's music was softer and almost stumbling; now and then it would pick up, then it would sink to feather-brushing quiet. W. M. came in and past me, shutting the front door as he came in, walking around me small and straight without looking back, then he was through the back hall and kitchen, and the kitchen door shut after him as he went out toward the compound and the stable, but with no slamming. I opened the hall door to the dining room, and looked in at the old coffered ceiling, striped with light coming past the tall windows to turn its paneling tawny as milk full of clotting cream. Shut the door, and went along to where the music came in zephyrs and murmurs from the ballroom.

The ballroom was empty save for the jenny, the platform-balcony with its uprights loose and leaning inward, but they could be straightened, and the light was streaming in past vines at the panes, touching my fiddle in the case set up on the platform where French had put it. The jenny turning slowly, the waft of smoke from its boiler-stove moving out of the open back where they'd been. Amber's shadow spun and leaped ahead. I didn't have to even start checking Grayboy, Amber would win now all on her own, and so I just rode Grayboy in, Amber a full clean length ahead on our right, the major starting to check when he was forty yards from the oak, but keeping his lead as, now, I started pulling up too. And then I was bringing Grayboy all the way in, Amber breathing light, and quick, Grayboy breathing deep and savage, and blowing, and the night outside the tree coming back with its sounds clear over the creak of our saddles and the breathing of our mounts. Deveraux dismounted, and led Amber out of the tree-shadow. I got off Grayboy, taking his reins over his head.

Jupiter was marching toward us, to take Grayboy. Ryan came running up from the wagon across the road. W. M. was sitting on the fence as if he hadn't, couldn't have, moved anything but his eyes for a long time. Jupiter led Grayboy around the oak's spraddling roots and then across the pike. I followed close, and beside Grayboy's head, I reached for a cheek-strap, and pulled his head down while Jupiter halted, and looked at Grayboy's eye, also close. It was merry and quiet; like a pool where lights come and go and butterflies dawdle near on a good day. I patted his muzzle, velvet-soft and damp, ducked out before he got my hat which he was cropping his teeth to do, and let him go on with Jupiter along the pike and around to the stable road. Ryan had taken Amber, he had a blanket from the wagon ready for her, her head was a quiet princess's, her eye black green and mild. Deveraux was standing beside me again, then. Watching Amber, not me, not anything else. He called, cool-voiced, "Walk her a little, Ryan. When she is cooled out, tie her to the wagon. I'll not ride her tonight, she deserves coddling. And mind you pace the chestnuts slowly when we go."

I'd been right about Ryan's job. He did salute. Or it could have been just a touching of his forelock.

I could hear the jenny's music whirling again. It was softer now; as if the boiler-fire was slumping to ash, the platform turning slower.

When I looked back at the gray white, time-eaten fence-rail, W. M. was gone.

I went on across the pike-road. Ryan was unsaddling Amber, the mare standing easy, and then he was throwing the blanket over her and she was moving behind him with a fine unbothered walk, up and down in the square-cut high shade of the wagon. The major came on across the road. Its dust didn't seem to remove or cover any of the shine on his boots. His neck-cloth and gloves shone like the feathers of an egret at dawn's edge.

window beside it, the jenny horses shadowing the floor as they circled by, the gold and the dark purple with blush-pink and the cream and gilt one and the forest green and the burnished bronze and the sky blue and the jet black one and hearth-fire flame-yellow one, each moving into its flicker of moonlight, and out again. A board creaked as I walked to the jenny and threw the lever to stop it. The curtain-shaped wood-frill under the pagoda stopped turning, the platform was still, the carved horses waited. I'd been thinking of Colonel Robert Chantry, his liking for hiding places. Took my knife out, holding it by the cool blade, and with the handle tapped the little horses, soft enough upon their bellies. I moved around the carousel, doing it. Colonel Chantry had written to French and her mother just before his death on the field of battle, cautioning them, not once but twice in the same letter—so French had told me—never to let the jenny go. Well, French hadn't, in the long run.

It wasn't till I got to the gold-bullion-bar colored horse that the wood rang hollow. Like tunking a load of watermelons, and all at once you know which one to eat.

I felt up and down the smooth-worn, clever carving of this creature. Putting my knife away, leaning and moving my fingers around the hollows and swellings of the sleek wood.

And it wasn't till I'd turned the ears of the dark gold horse all the way around, so they slanted back sharp as if he was hearing some echo of a hoofbeat—maybe in Florence—behind him, that his head swung out, with a sighing creak and the scent of much-seasoned, long-traveled, gently musty wood rising from the dark space under the head. I reached down and in.

In this tender light the money didn't even look like true money as I brought up a handful.

But it had been true money once.

Nothing was ever any prettier than Confederate bills, I thought. Printed in the time of Judah P. Benjamin, and surely worth a little today, if just for the comeliness of the paper.

The bills fluttered back into their secret cave in the jenny-horse's belly. I swung the head back, twisted the ears around to their natural places. It was an artful piece of work. I decided I'd show French, and tell her, some time soon. Not tonight, for too much had already happened tonight. And I had other, more rewarding plans for a good part of the night ahead.

Then I was shutting the ballroom door, the mirrors along the hall reflecting the motion, and going along the hall. Out past the front door I could hear no horses from the pike-road now, the pike would have swallowed up Deveraux, he would be heading for Pharis. I doubted he would brag much about beating the stallion that won at Yadkin. It wasn't for any other human he'd won. Just him, and Amber.

The back door opened, out at the kitchen, then shut, and I heard its key turn. And Jupiter's bass voice and W. M.'s sharp cold child-voice, both of them arguing a little as they went along to their rooms near there, and then no voices but a mockingbird tuning his notes beside the cemetery.

I started up the staircase. Then French was standing up there waiting for me. In a shift I reckoned had come out of one of her mama's cherished trunks. Or it could have been a night-dress, I didn't know much about such fripperies. Save that it was thin silk which didn't appear it would be too difficult to handle, whether you took it off over her head, or just let it stay on and folded it back. And her hair was out of its binding ribbon, falling in paths of brightness like many torches around her shoulders. Made me think of a harvest filling a mow with light-shot beauty at the end of a long, good journey. She yawned, but not a yawn of sleepiness, only one of waiting with a tide of excitement running. She said, "Well, Tom." Raised the lamp she was carrying up higher. "I heard all the to-do out across the field. I saw you all going across the old meadow. You were running against Major Deveraux, weren't you?"

"Like a gentleman, quiet and calm."

"Who won, my love?"

I took her by a warm shoulder and brought her close. "We did," I said.